Jennings, J

NEXT TO VALOUR

THE MACMILLAN COMPANY
NEW YORK · BOSTON · CHICAGO
DALLAS · ATLANTA · SAN FRANCISCO

MACMILLAN AND CO., LIMITED
LONDON · BOMBAY · CALCUTTA
MADRAS · MELBOURNE

THE MACMILLAN COMPANY
OF CANADA, LIMITED
TORONTO

NEXT TO VALOUR

A NOVEL

by JOHN Edward JENNINGS

NEW YORK

THE MACMILLAN COMPANY

1939

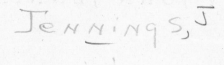

TO DAD

Whose constant faith, encouragement, and support were so largely responsible for this book

6077

¶ "Next to valour, the best qualities in a military man are
vigilance and caution."

BRIGADIER GENERAL JAMES WOLFE
*in an order issued to the
troops before Quebec, 1759*

CONTENTS

CONTENTS

NEXT TO VALOUR

❡ A letter to the Right Honourable Sir William Pitt, Earl of Chatham, Lord Privy Seal, &c, &c. Dated at Portsmouth, in the Province of New Hampshire, August 8, 1766.

Sir,

Your Lordship has had the great goodness to suggest, in view of my poor services during the late hostilities with the French and Indians, both in the York Province and at Quebec, that were I to set forth my claim, formally as the law demands, your Lordship would be pleased to expend every effort toward the restoration to myself and to my family of our ancestral lands at Kintulloch, near the Spittal of Glenshee, in Perthshire, Scotland, and of the title which accompanies them.

The delay with which your Lordship's letter is being answered, let me hasten to say, is in no way due to lack of appreciation of your Lordship's generosity in offering to aid me with the claim; but rather to the difficulty with which I have come to my decision in the matter. This difficulty I am sure your Lordship will appreciate the more when you learn the result of that decision. In short, after much hesitation, I have at long last made up my mind to relinquish all claim, both to the estates and to the title. And though, perhaps, I should feel some sorrow at thus forfeiting all chance of ever again returning to the home of my fathers, yet I cannot truthfully say that it is with regret that I must refuse the honour you do me.

As your Lordship is aware, the title never rested in my father, Alan Ferguson; but would come to me through my uncle, Sir John Ferguson, Bart, and his son, Sir Hubert, who was the last of his line. What your Lordship cannot realize is that neither the baronetcy nor the lands themselves can bring me aught but sorrow; for the title serves only to remind me of black treachery, while the Hall of Kintulloch, where I spent only the earliest years of my childhood, could recall to me but the tragedy of my father's death.

But there is another, and more valid, reason for refusing your Lordship's generous offer. Following my father's fall on the field of Culloden, my mother, as had been agreed between them before he left, packed up our few remaining belongings and, together with my sisters and myself, removed to the colonies. It was there, in the town of Suncook, on the banks of the Merrimack, in the Province of New Hampshire, that I grew up and made my home.

The twenty years which I have spent in this new land have accustomed me to a way of life totally different from that of Scotland. My recollections of Kintulloch are of the faintest. Were I to return at this late date, it would be as a stranger to a strange land, rather than as a home-coming. Here, on the other hand, in a new country, where new traditions are in the making, I have fought and striven to build up a new home, a new estate, a new name, for those who will come after me. The services for which your Lordship has so graciously commended me, I must confess it, were given not so much from loyalty to the crown, but rather that that home and that name might be forever safe from the hideous cruelty of a barbaric invader.

That, in itself, must make plain to your Lordship my feeling in the matter. But that you may understand the more readily my reasoning, I attach hereto an account of those years, both here and at Kintulloch, which should be ample to explain my reluctance to return.

Lest it should seem to your Lordship that I have been somewhat too wordy in this, my explanation, I hasten to add that what is hereinafter set down was done, not only for your Lordship's benefit, but also that those who are to follow me, my sons and my sons' sons, may read and understand why it is that they are but plain Fergusons, of Portsmouth and the Upper Cohos, in the Province of New Hampshire, and not the Lairds of Kintulloch, in the valley of Glenshee, Perthshire, Scotland.

With my most humble thanks for your Lordship's most gracious offer, and with the hope that your Lordship will find no occasion for offence at my refusal, I am, Sir,

Your Lordship's Most Humble & Ob^t Servt

JAMES FERGUSON

(Late Captain in Major Rogers' Rangers)

The 8th August 1766

WAR CLOUDS GATHER

¶ 1 Since it has always seemed to me logical that the proper place for a tale to begin is at the beginning, let me state, once and for all, that I was born at the Hall of Kintulloch, which stands near the village of Persie, not far from the Spittal of Glenshee, in Atholl, county of Perthshire, Scotland, on the 7th day of August in the year 1730.

My father was the son of Sir David Ferguson, Bart.; one of twins, and to the best of my memory as fine a man as ever walked this earth. My mother, before her marriage to my father, was Sheila Ross, of the Galloway Rosses, a sept of the great clan of that name.

Our branch of the Ferguson family came not originally from Atholl, but rather sprang from the Fergusons of Balquhidder through Donald Ferguson of that branch, who inherited Kintulloch from Angus Ferguson, a distant cousin who had died without issue. Donald, in his turn, passed the estates on, as the least desirable and most newly acquired portion of his holdings, to his second son Adam, from whom our line sprang. Now, it may be that all this seems unimportant. Yet it must be told, for, as will presently be seen, this question of inheritance bore strongly in shaping the course of future events. Adam had two sons, through the elder of whom our line descended. The younger, Dougald Ferguson, being left to his own devices, as so many second sons are, made his way to Edinburgh, where he was apprenticed to the Drummonds; and after serving that house for a number of years, he finally established the well known house of Ferguson & Co., Bankers. It was his grandson, Sir Archibald Ferguson, who was raised to the baronetage in recognition of his services to the crown during the rebellion of 1715.

Sir Archibald, however, died without issue, a striking example of the way in which divine power guides our ends, for by that fact both the business and the title passed to my grandfather, Sir David, as the nearest male relative. As has already been pointed out, Sir David sired twins. He was an exceedingly fair-minded man, and until the time of Sir Archibald's death he had lived in a state of considerable perplexity as to the manner in which he should divide his estates equally between his two sons; for Kintulloch, though ample for the support of one family, would scarcely bear division. Consequently the inheritance from Sir Archibald must have seemed to him in the nature of a gift from heaven. On his deathbed he called his sons to him and gave them their choice; the business and the accompanying title, or Kintulloch and the estates.

Now although, as I have said, my father and my uncle were twins, none could have guessed it to look at them, for no two men were ever less alike. My uncle, a tall dark-skinned man, thin almost to the point of emaciation, and with a sour, sober-faced look about him, habitually dressed himself in black and spoke seldom save when he was spoken to. My father, on the other hand, was a lithe handsome man, with fine brown eyes, a ready smile, and always a gay word for the lasses. Nor was this difference to be found alone in their appearance. Rather it extended even to their very likes and dislikes; for my father, though he seemed a gay blade, loved the open and all that went with it. He was seldom met with out of doors but he had a fowling piece or a fishing rod in his hands, or a fine horse between his knees; while my uncle cared naught for such rustic pursuits, preferring the smoke and bustle of the cities, and having time only for moneybags and what might contribute to them.

Thus it was but natural that, when it came to choosing, my uncle, who was the elder by a matter of a few minutes and so was entitled to first choice, should select Edinburgh and the title. And, though he never said it to me, I make no doubt but that it was a pleasing choice to my father as well, for he loved the peace and solitude of our high, wind-swept hills and heather-choked glens, so that I daresay he would not have traded Kintulloch for all the gold in all the banks in Scotland.

Of those early years of my life there is little enough to tell. They passed all too swiftly in a jumble of childish joys and sorrows that seemed of greatest consequence at the time, but since have all but faded from the memory. There were long days and hours spent in dull study with my sisters in a great gloomy room in the west wing of the Hall. There were other bright days; days devoted to pursuit of the wary trout in the tumbling Shee Water or the near-by Ardle or one of the many tiny burns that rushed joyously down from the mountain slopes that hemmed us in all about. Not too infrequently my father allowed me to accompany him: on hunting excursions to Glas Maol and Glen Beg, or perhaps to the rugged slopes of Mel Choire Bui or Ben-y-Gloe, away to the north and west, or salmon fishing as far afield as the river Tummel or the Dee, which I mind I thought was a mighty stream in those days. But of events of importance there were none, so that I will pass those years over swiftly and come at once to that gloomy day in August, not long after my fifteenth birthday, in the year 1745. Gloomy I call it, and gloomy it was; not because of the weather— for today I cannot, for my life, remember whether it were bright or dull—but rather because on that day befell an occurrence which was destined to change the lives of most of us, and to bring sorrow to us all.

Of the particular events of that day I can recall but little until the dinner hour. My uncle had come down from Edinburgh, paying us one of his infrequent visits, impelled, no doubt, by the persistent, though as yet unconfirmed, rumour that Prince Charles Edward had landed at some point among the Western Isles and had already raised his standard in the north. He had arrived a day or two before, bringing with him his one son, my cousin, Hubert —a slender, somewhat sullen-faced youth, though undeniably handsome in his dark way, with the mincing manners and flamboyant dress of a London fop—who, although he was but four years my senior, looked at me down his long nose, and gave himself such airs that I heartily disliked him from the start.

This was Hubert's first visit to Kintulloch and our first meeting. It was but natural that the task of entertaining him should fall to me, and I attacked the problem eagerly and at once; for company, especially that of other boys, was rare. But my eagerness to please was soon dashed to disappointment by the discovery that nothing I could show him could elicit more than the scornful superiority reserved by big boys for little boys' pleasures. In childish desperation I brought forth my dearest treasures, my darkest secrets, and laid them at his feet. Nothing moved him. Even the great trout in the pool by the bend above the ford; even my own secret cave, securely hidden, high on the flank of Mel

Uan, towering behind the Hall, left him cold. This was more than I could bear. In disgust I gave him into the care of my two elder sisters, whose company, I must confess, he appeared to find more pleasing than my own, and retired, sulking, to my room, so that the remainder of his visit, up to that fateful evening, lies in my memory as a session of blank, dreary boredom.

My father—it can do no harm to tell it now—was an ardent Jacobite. My uncle—and here again the twins ran true to their pattern of dissimilarity—was, if anything, a Whig. Still—he was a cautious man. His fortune came before all other considerations, and must be protected at all costs. An uprising indicated the imminent possibility of a change in the reigning House; and any change spelled disaster for those who chose the wrong side. Whichever way the cat might jump, someone was certain to be scratched. A family conference must have seemed to him to be in order.

It was but natural in these circumstances that conversation that night should turn upon the subject of the rebellion, a topic to which we children lent eager ears; for the romantic figure of young Prince Charlie had caught at our imagination, and my sisters and myself, at least, had been taught from babyhood to look upon James Stuart as our rightful sovereign, and upon the House of Hanover as that of a usurper. It was my uncle who did most of the talking.

"In my opinion," said he with an air of finality, as though that were to settle the matter once and for all, "the talk is all pother and poppycock, with no more to it than a puff of smoke. When the truth is out I'll warrant we'll find there's nothing to the rumour at all."

My father cocked one eyebrow up and looked at him.

"Aye?" he said.

"Aye!" my uncle replied, with an impatient gesture. " 'Tis clear enough, if ye will but see it. Your Bonnie Prince Charlie will hardly dare to land without an army to back him up."

He leaned back with an air of triumph. My father laughed.

" 'Tis logic," he admitted, "but that does not prove it so."

It was at this moment that I noticed Andrew MacNiel, who was serving at the great door, come in quietly and speak softly to Old Dougal Forbes, who had been steward in the house since the days of my grandfather, and was hence considered rather one of the family than a servant. Old Dougal rose at once, excusing himself, and followed Andrew from the hall. Intent as they were upon the discussion, I believe that no one but myself noticed the incident; and even I forgot it a moment later when I turned back to hear Hubert speaking.

"It would seem likely," he was saying, "that the Prince would be consistent in his attempts. After his failure to land last year with an army of fifteen thousand, is it probable that he would try again this year and alone?"

Had the words come from my uncle, I doubt if I could have found an answer. But Hubert had addressed my father, and in a patronizing tone that aroused my anger and goaded me to retort.

"Aye!" I cried. "It is probable. For where fifteen thousand men might fail, one man might succeed. The Prince knows there's fifteen thousand true Hielan'men ready and willing to lay down their lives for him. What need has he for an army of Frenchmen then, eh?"

My father laughed again.

"Out of the mouths of babes, John," he said to my uncle. "The lad may have hit upon the right answer!"

Hubert and my uncle glowered at me, and the latter was about to make some reply, when a commotion at the end of the hall interrupted him and drew all eyes in that direction. Old Dougal entered, and close at his heels strode a stranger: a stranger who, once they were fairly within the hall, shouldered his way past the steward, and strode with a jingle of spurs towards the long table.

He was a short man, this stranger, scarcely more than a head taller than myself, and I was considered to be small for my age. Yet he bore himself with an air of dignity that was almost defiant. His slight figure seemed hardly stronger than a girl's, yet he must have been wiry withal, for he bore the evidence in his face and on his clothes of many a weary mile. The high splatterdashes which encased his legs, and the skirts of his sober black coat, were stained and smeared with mud. The lace ruffles at cuffs and jabot were wilted and grimy.

He stopped just within the ring of light, and bowed low, first to my mother, with a flourish that included all the rest of us, and then to my father. When he straightened there was a smile on his lips and a twinkle in his eye, in spite of his evident fatigue, so that you liked him at once. When he spoke it was in a deep resonant voice, surprising in one of such slight stature, and very pleasant to hear.

"Your pardon, sir," he said, "for this intrusion, but the news I bear is not such as can wait. Have I the honour of addressing Alan Ferguson?"

My father nodded gravely.

"I am he," he replied.

The stranger bowed again in acknowledgement, making a very elegant leg.

"James Johnstone, of Edinburgh," he announced himself. "Your servant, sir."

My father accepted the introduction with a bow.

"You do me rare honour, Mr. Johnstone," he said. "You bring news, no doubt, of the Right Cause?"

Johnstone nodded, his face grave and serious again.

"I do that," he replied, "and since it is of the gravest importance, I will ask to speak with you alone, sir."

He looked about at us hesitantly, ending with my uncle, where his gaze lingered questioningly. My father made an impatient gesture.

"You need have no fear, sir," he reassured him. "We are all of the family here."

Johnstone smiled once more.

"A thousand pardons," he said. "You will understand my apparent overcarefulness when I tell you that the Prince has landed."

My mother said "Oh!" in a voice that was scarcely audible. But the rest of us had begun already to pour forth a stream of questions, each striving to be heard above the others, so that whatever else she might have said was drowned in the babble, until father thumped the table with his fist and bade us be quiet.

"Can you not see," he roared, "the gentleman is fatigued?"

He turned to Johnstone.

"You'll sup and stay the night with us?" he asked.

" 'Twould give me great pleasure," the latter replied, "but I may not. I must be in Perth tomorrow night."

But my father would take no refusal.

"You canna reach Perth the night," he said, "though you may do it easily by day. Come, both yourself and your beast will fare the better for a night's rest, and I give you my word I'll see you upon the road before the dawn."

Seeing his protests overridden, Johnstone yielded with good grace to my father's insistence.

"As you will," he said, and with a bow to my mother accepted the chair which Dougal had placed for him at my father's right hand.

Since it is now a matter of history, there is no need here to go into the details of his story. Needless to say we listened, scarce daring to breathe, as he told how Charles Edward had landed at Moidart, two weeks since, with but seven followers and a slim purse; how MacDonald of Clanranald, with his kinsman, Mac-Donald of Kinloch-Moidart, had first declared their willingness to aid him; and how Cameron of Lochiel had followed closely in their footsteps. He went on then to tell of others: MacDonald of Glencoe, Stuart of Appin, Glengarry the Younger, who had flocked to his banner. Already, he told us, first blood had been drawn at Spean Bridge, where MacDonald of Keppoch, en route to join the Prince with his followers, had fallen in with two companies of regular troops on the march from Fort Augustus to Fort William, and all but annihilated them.

As it fell from his lips it was a tale to stir the blood and set the pulses racing. We heard him through without interruption, save at that point at which he spoke of the Prince's slender resources. Here my uncle snorted audibly, and seemed about to speak; but my father silenced him with a look that penetrated even his obtuse mind, and he subsided without comment.

When it was at last finished my mother arose.

"Though it be wrong to say it," she said sorrowfully, "I canna help wishing that your fine Prince had stayed where he was in France, where there was sma' harm he could do."

We all looked at her in surprise, and my father reached out and took her hand in his.

"Na, na, Sheila," he protested. "You'll not be meaning that."

"Aye," she insisted, "but I do mean it: for though I'm as good a Jacobite as you, Alan Ferguson, his coming means war; and war means death, and I'm afraid of it."

She looked at each of us in turn, but no one spoke. At last she shrugged.

"Aweel," she sighed. " 'Tis time the children were in bed."

She nodded to Johnstone.

"You'll excuse us, I hope," she said.

He was on his feet in an instant, bending low over her hand.

"It grieves me to be the bearer of sad news, ma'am," he said. "I hope you'll not think the less of me for it."

"No, lad," she replied, "there's no blame to you."

We said our good nights regretfully, and I fear with bad grace, for we had had high hopes that this night would be one in which the ordinary rules were suspended. Indeed it was doubly bitter for me, for as I followed my sisters from the room I noticed that Hubert had hitched his chair closer to the end of the table and was, for the time being at least, allowed to listen with a knowing air to the discussion which was already under way. In my room upstairs I could hear the rumble of voices below, long after my mother had blown out my light. At last I must have dozed off, for all of a sudden I found myself riding my father's little chestnut mare close behind the Prince at the head of the army, while at my side rode James Johnstone, who looked at me and winked out of a merry grey eye.

When I awoke it was broad daylight, and the sun was streaming in my window. As I rose, I wondered if there were anything of prophecy in the dream. But it seemed there was not, for it was many a long day before I was once again destined to encounter the Chevalier de Johnstone; and then it was to be under circumstances far different from any I might ever have conceived.

I will not dwell upon the week that followed. I remember it as one of the sorriest of my youth. To begin with, it must needs be decided who was to go and who should stay at home. Naturally it was a foregone conclusion that such a strong Jacobite as my father would go. It was agreed before Johnstone rode away that he would raise a troop of horse and join the Prince at the earliest possible moment.

My uncle's position was not quite so plain. His every instinct was to guard his moneybags, and in order to do this he was placed in something of a dilemma. If he supported the House of Hanover, and Stuart won, his property would be confiscated; likewise, if he supported Stuart, and Hanover won, he would lose all. And the thought that he must make a choice was almost more than he could bear. In the end, however, it was decided that he should remain in Edinburgh, ostensibly supporting the House of Hanover, while Hubert, his son, would ride forth, a cornet in my father's troop, and do battle for the Stuart Cause. Thus, no matter which side won, they could not lose. To me at the time, I must say, this smelled something like treachery, but I was later to discover that it was a practice so general as to be almost customary.

When I learned that my cousin was to ride in my father's troop my envy knew no bounds. I begged and pleaded with my father to take me too, but all to no avail. Someone, he said, must stay at home to look after my mother and the girls; and since I was the youngest I must be that one. Not all my tears and entreaties would alter him in this. Nor did the knowledge of this decision serve to lessen Hubert's air of insufferable superiority. Indeed he swaggered and sneered and lorded it over me in such a haughtily patronizing manner that I was more than once tempted to kick him soundly on the backside, big as he was.

Throughout the week there went on the most tremendous bustle of preparation. There was gear to be repaired and put in order, and all the womenfolk were kept busy sewing and stitching and polishing. There was the troop to be raised, and on this my father rode about the countryside, day after day, from long before dawn till long after nightfall. In addition to this the family affairs must needs be put to rights in the event of calamity, so that there was an almost constant coming and going of advocates and their clerks from Blairgowrie. Indeed, everything seemed to me to be in such a welter of confusion that I sometimes wondered when my father might find time to go to the wars.

But at last the day came. Spalding of Dunkeld, a neighbour, came clattering into the courtyard at the head of a troop of forty men. As he caught sight of my father, he gave a bellow that made the windows of the Hall rattle.

"Ho, Alan, mon!" he roared. "Mount an' ride! Mount an' ride! Johnny Cope has marched from Stirling, and the Prince is on his way to meet him. We've nae time to lose if we're to be in the fichtin'."

My father nodded and signalled MacNiel to bring his horse. My mother and my sisters came down from the terrace, and he kissed them each in turn, tenderly, before he swung into the saddle. Hubert rode over from the far side of the court, and leaned down from his saddle to plant a kiss square on the upturned mouth of my sister Edith, much to my disgust, and her evident pleasure. Then all at once the troops were up and in the saddle and filing out of the courtyard at a trot, sending up blinding clouds of stifling dust, and with the thunder of horses' hooves all but drowning out the wild skirling of the pipes.

I felt a hand upon my shoulder, and turned to see my father leaning down to me from his saddle.

"Mind the girls, Jamie," he said, "and God bless ye!"

And before I could answer he was gone, with a wave of his hand, out the wide gate in a swirl of dust.

My mother and my sisters and I stood on the terrace and waved as long as we could see him. And all the while I kept thinking what a fine thing it must be to be a soldier and go riding off to war!

THE 'FORTY-FIVE

¶ 1 The story of the 'Forty-Five has been told and retold too often to need repetition here. Numberless accounts have already recorded the marches and countermarches, the battles and skirmishes, the blunders, the intrigues, and the remarkable fortunes, both good and bad, of that extraordinary campaign. So that I hope I may be excused if I refrain from dwelling upon it, and confine myself simply to such incidents as bore directly upon the lives of my family and myself.

Needless to say, we followed the movements of the Jacobite army with breathless interest. Sir John Cope's blundering flight to Inverness amazed us. The march on Edinburgh thrilled us. Preston-Pans filled us with delight. We watched the advance into the Midlands with anxiety, and were dismayed at word of the retreat from Derby. The fall of Carlisle was a blow to our hopes, plunging us into the blackest despair, from which we were but momentarily raised by the news of the Battle of Falkirk. The retreat of the Prince's army to the north again filled us with grave doubt. We knew not whether to applaud these tactics or condemn them, for, though the end seemed almost inevitable, yet, while the army retained the field, there was always some hope.

Several times my father wrote at length. Upon joining the army at Corryarrack he was graciously received by the Prince himself, commissioned a major, and attached with his command to the Atholl Regiment. Later, at Preston-Pans, where he and his men fought on foot with the left wing, he so distinguished himself that he was promoted to colonel and given command of one of the few regiments of horse in the Prince's service.

The capture of Edinburgh, however, swelled the ranks of the army, and led to a feeling of strength and confidence not warranted by the facts. Certain of the Prince's advisers urged him to the invasion of England, a plan which my father, among others, opposed strenuously, for he believed, with Lord George Murray, that their forces were insufficient for the project, and that the conquest of Scotland was far from complete. This attitude placed him in none too good a light with the Prince, whose mind was being slowly poisoned against the able Lord George by the jealousy of his Irish friends, and though he retained his commission, he was from that day looked upon with ill concealed suspicion.

Our little valley saw few of the outward and visible signs of the war. Indeed, had it not been for my father's letters, which brought the scenes of army life into our drawing room, we should have found it hard to believe that such a state of affairs existed. Only a dearth of familiar faces among the young men of the region, or the occasional appearance of a wounded warrior, usually a native of the hills about Braemar, taking advantage of the short cut past the Spittal of Glenshee to reach his home, bore witness to the fact.

But all this changed gradually. More and more frequently the red coats of King George's troops began to appear in the valley, and finally an event occurred which brought the war to our very doorstep.

Following the Battle of Falkirk the Prince marched with his army to Crieff. There it split into two divisions, one of which, composed chiefly of western Highlanders, followed the Prince by the mountain road to Inverness, while the other, made up of the Lowland troops and the cavalry, was led by Lord George Murray through Montrose and Aberdeen. At the same time a small party, chiefly members of the Clans Farquharson, MacPherson, and Robertson, inhabitants of the upper Dee valley and the regions about Braemar, availed themselves of the opportunity afforded them by the short route through Glenshee to visit their families en route to Inverness. They passed by Kintulloch in the early morning hotly pursued by a company of grenadiers, marching so rapidly that we were hardly aware of their presence in the valley before they were gone again out of sight in the direction of the pass.

At the head of the pass the Highlanders turned at bay, and there followed a short, sharp skirmish in which the clansmen came off with a slight upper hand. That is to say, they were able to continue their march towards Braemar unmolested, while the redcoats beat a none too orderly retreat by the way they had come.

Now it happened that Kintulloch was the first house in the line of their route, and almost before we were aware of their presence in the neighbourhood we were routed out by the thundering of musket butts upon our front door.

I confess I thought they had come to burn the house about our ears, and perhaps they would have done so, my father's connection with the other side being perfectly well known to them; but it seemed that at the moment they had another and greater need for us. Their commander, a young lieutenant whose name I cannot now recall, had been most grievously wounded in the fight above and was in grave need of care. The boyish ensign, to whom the leadership of the party had fallen begged—nay, commanded— my mother to take him in and care for him. Needless to say my mother, who was a soft-hearted creature, would not have let a dog lie dying on her doorstep. She took the man in, over Dougal's bitter protest, and sent posthaste to fetch old Dr. Balfour to tend him. The young ensign was most pathetically grateful for this and, after assigning one of his men, a corporal, to act as guard and orderly to the wounded officer, stammered out his thanks and marched away without permitting his men to inflict any damage whatever upon the neighbourhood.

It must be admitted that this event did nothing to enhance our popularity with our neighbours. The good folk of our valley shook their heads in wonder and looked at us askance to think that we would stoop so low as to shelter one of the hated lobsterbacks. Only old Dr. Balfour had the good sense to see that, quite aside from the question of humanity, there was naught else we could do. Had we refused, I doubt not the redcoats would have burned us out lock, stock, and barrel.

Actually, however, as it proved, the presence of the two Englishmen in the house was a blessing in disguise. Because the wounded officer's presence there was known to all the military in the district, patrols gave us a wide berth, and by the same token foraging parties treated us with far greater consideration than was their custom. Three times in as many weeks the redoubtable corporal drove off small wandering parties of desperate deserters, banded together for banditry and pillage, who hoped to find the Hall emptied of its menfolk, and easy pickings.

2

These were dreary days to me, for since the first appearance of the redcoats my mother had forbidden my going beyond sight of the house, so that most of my favourite pastimes were barred. Even the cave on the mountain side above was out of bounds.

As the days wore on, however, and February turned into March, it became evident that the majority of the soldiers were not disposed to harm us. My mother's vigilance relaxed somewhat, and I began once more to wander the wooded hillsides in search of game, and to wet my lines in the tumbling rivers and splashing burns of the neighbourhood.

It was early in March that I set out, one wet misty morning, to try my luck in the Shee Water. Starting in front of the Hall, I fished downstream slowly, casting carefully among the riffles at the head of the pools, where I knew the greatest trout to be at that time. I was intent upon the task, for the fishing was good, and I had gone something under a mile, taking five or six good trout in the way, when suddenly I was startled to hear someone call.

"Hist! Jamie!"

At first I could not locate the source of the sound but stood in midstream looking stupidly about, as one does sometimes, feeling foolish to be seen and yet not to see. But presently a movement among the thick bushes that crowned the overhanging bank drew my eye to a gaunt, pale face peering down at me. I did not recognize the man at once, so drawn and wan was he. Then all at once I saw with a shock of surprise that it was Tom Ogilvie of Glenisla, a distant neighbour, who like my father had ridden forth at the head of a troop to join the Prince. My astonishment was doubled by the knowledge that, scarce a fortnight since, Major Ogilvie had come home to Glenisla with a hole big enough to stuff your fist into torn in his side by a musket ball. By all reports he should be at home in bed with friends to wait upon him, not here in the heather, hiding away like any wild thing that is hunted.

I dropped my rod at once and scrambled up the steep embankment.

"Major Ogilvie!" I cried. "In God's name, sir, what do ye here?"

He placed his finger on his lips and pointed up the slope behind him.

"Hist, Jamie lad," he whispered hoarsely. "They're after me, and I fear I'm finished. I can run nae farther."

The mist of the morning had lifted somewhat with the rising sun, until it no more than covered the highest points along the ridge. Now following the direction of his pointing finger I could see, high up on the slopes of Mount Blair above us, a dozen or more little groups of red dots moving slowly here and there, combing the mountain side thoroughly, working their way down little by little into the valley. As I watched, more groups came into sight to north and south, searching carefully. I judged there must be a hundred or more men in the chase; and covering the ground as thoroughly as they were, it could be only a matter of time before they came up with him.

"Well," I said, "you canna be staying here, that's plain, for they'll find you surely!"

He shook his head ruefully and grimaced.

"Aye, Jamie," he replied, "I ken that well enough. But ye see, lad, I canna walk."

And with that he hitched himself about and shoved his right foot forward. He had slashed away the laces of his Highland brogue, and I could see that the ankle was swollen and misshapen beyond all reason. With an exclamation I dropped to my knees beside it and touched it gingerly.

"Is it broken?" I asked him.

"As to that," he replied, "I could no just say, lad, but I dinna think so. I fell running in the dark frae the redcoats on yon mountain in the night. It doubled under me like a bit straw. When I got me up again it wouldna take my weight."

"And you walked to here?" I cried in amazement.

"Na, na," he told me dourly, "I creepit on my hands and knees."

I made no reply to this, but fell to pondering what I might do to help him; for here was a dear friend of my father's—indeed, an old friend of my own, for I had known him all my life—and it was plain that I could not leave him there. Yet neither could I take him to the Hall. The presence alone of the corporal and the lieutenant prevented that. And the stables were no more likely to be safe, for there was no question but all our buildings would be thoroughly searched.

It was then that I bethought me of my cave upon the hill behind the house. If I could but get him so far unseen I might in some way be able to draw off the redcoats long enough for him to make his escape.

"Can ye stand, sir?" I asked him.

He looked at me inquiringly.

"Aye," he said, "I can do that."

I explained to him the situation which made the Hall unsafe for him, and told him of the cave. He eyed the opposite slope speculatively.

"Ye think they'll not be finding yon cave?" he asked.

" 'Twill be my business to see that they don't," I replied.

He looked at me sharply, and then out across the valley again.

"Aweel," he said, " 'tis worth a try."

He scrambled to his feet then, and stood supporting himself upon a near-by sapling, and resting his injured foot gingerly upon the ground.

"Now, Jamie," he said, "if ye'll loan me your twa guid legs for the one of my ain we'll have a try for it."

I took his arm across my shoulders, taking the weight of his right side upon my back, and in this way, like a three-legged man with two bodies, we made our way up the valley, keeping close in under the river bank, where we were sheltered from the eyes of the soldiers above, until we reached a point well above the Hall. There we crossed over the stream and got onto the wooded ridge that ran down from the top of Mel Uan to the road. By keeping to the shelter of the woods we worked our way along the ridge, around behind the house, until we came at last to the pathway leading to the cave, and a moment later slipped into its welcome shelter.

Since it was evident that he was in some pain from his hurts, I tried during the journey to keep his mind from them with a steady flow of talk. It was then that he told me what had happened. Somehow word of his presence had reached the ears of the British at Aberdeen, where General Hawley was in command of active operations. Hawley had every reason to dislike Major Ogilvie, for at Falkirk the latter had aided materially in producing the rout which brought such black disgrace upon that general's name. Moreover, throughout the march to Aberdeen Major Ogilvie and his raiders had harried the flank of the general's army, bringing him near to apoplexy. And Hawley was not one to be lenient. Already he had hung several prisoners in chains as "examples to the countryside," refusing the honours of war, and terming them rebels and traitors.

Two days since, a bouman* of Airlie had come running in the dusk of the evening to warn the major that the redcoats were coming. Indeed Ogilvie had had but time to leap from his bed and dress and run out the back door even as they were pounding upon the front. At that he had had no time to get a horse from the stables, for they had seen him as he left the house and fired upon him, driving him before them up into the forest of Alyth and on to the hills beyond. For two nights and a day he had ducked and dodged upon the mountain side, until on the second night, he had seen an opportunity to cross over the ridge to the Glenshee side by slipping through their lines. But luck was strong against him. There had been but a feeble moon that night, but it had been sufficient to reveal him to the watchful redcoats. There had been some shouting and much shooting, and the chase was on again. In the rocks and the brush and the darkness he had managed to give them the slip temporarily. But then had come the crowning disaster of the wrenched ankle, and despair. The sight of me fishing down the river had rekindled a hope that had long since died.

All this he confided to me as we struggled wearily and with frequent rests up along the ridge. Toward the end he fell silent, holding his upper lip grimly between his teeth. I could see that it was only by the strength of his will that he managed to keep going at all. Indeed, what with his weight upon my shoulders, I was glad enough to see the cave myself.

I helped him through the narrow opening that gave access to it, and, bidding him lie down upon the pile of furze and bracken I had gathered together in one corner, I went outside to mark the progress of the pursuit. It pleased me to see that they were moving slowly, only two of the small groups having reached the river while the others were scattered halfway up the mountain. It was evident that those who had reached the river were waiting for the rest to come up before venturing across. With luck I should have time to carry out the rest of my scheme. When I went back into the cave I found the major already sleeping soundly in the

* Tenant.

corner; and there I left him, confident that he would not awake before I returned.

I lost no time getting down to the Hall. Once there I realized that, if my plan was to work, I must take Dougal or my mother or both into my confidence, for there was the question of certain supplies which would not be available to me otherwise. Accordingly, I went at once to Dougal's little counting room, where I had the good fortune to find them both together, poring over accounts.

Breathlessly I blurted out my story and told what was in my mind. Dougal was inclined to oppose my plan, saying that it would be better for him to go in my stead. For once, however, my mother upheld me. This, she pointed out, would require some one who was both small and fast. If it were necessary for Dougal to take to the heather, she said, the redcoats would overtake him before he could run fifty yards.

With so much settled we scattered then to our several tasks: my mother to find arms and clothing; Dougal to gather food and money; and I to saddle my own little brown mare against a journey. As luck would have it the wounded lieutenant sat huddled in blankets upon the front terrace, watching the progress of the redcoats across the river with curious eyes, while the corporal, who the night before had somewhat overindulged his fondness for our good Scots usquebaugh, lay still snoring it off on his bed above stairs. By the time I had the nag saddled and ready my mother came out to the stable with shoes, shirt, breeks and a greatcoat, a pistol with powder and ball and an old claymore of my grandfather's. Dougal appeared with a packet of food and a heavy purse. These I made secure on the saddle, and after bidding them good-bye slipped out the back door, leading my beast, and made my way cautiously through the woods and bushes to the cave—arriving there not a moment too soon, I could see, for already the first of the redcoats were across the river below.

I was not surprised to find that Major Ogilvie had not stirred from the position in which I had left him. When I shook him lightly by the shoulder to waken him, he started up in sleepy confusion, his right hand flying to the dirk in his belt. But when he saw who it was he apologized, in some alarm until I assured him that, for the present at least, there was nothing to fear. I gave him the packet of food and a flask of brandy then, for I

judged it to be his greatest need, and he fell upon them raven-
ously, like one who had all but forgotten what it was to eat—
which indeed must well-nigh have been the case. I told him of
the purse and weapons I had brought him. And when I spoke
of the horse, tied in the birch thicket above, he whooped as gleefully as any schoolboy, embraced me with tears in his eyes, and
declared that in all the Highlands there was none he loved so well
as Jamie Ferguson. But presently he fell sober again, and I could
see that he was weighing his chances of slipping, once again,
through the line which the redcoats were drawing ever closer
about him, even with all this aid. At that I bade him rest easy
and have no fear, for I had a plan whereby all would go well;
so that he fell again to eating. And as he ate I talked.

The soldiers, I told him, were already across the river, and
were spread out along the valley, systematically beginning the
thorough search of Mel Uan's slopes. Unless something diverted
them from that search, in an hour or two at the most they must
discover the pathway to the cave. After that it would be too late
to escape. Even then, I said, it was doubtful if he could ride away
in safety, for the British were spread out along the mountain side,
and anything so large as a horse and rider would be quickly seen
by them.

To this he made no answer, merely gnawing upon a ham bone
and waiting for me to unfold my plan. But when I suggested that
he give me the tattered shirt and tartan that he wore, he stared
at me in surprise.

"And what's that for?" he demanded.

"Why, 'tis plain enough, sir," I replied. "These soldiers drove
you from your home. They saw you then. They've seen you since.
Now if they see a man, dressed as you were dressed, jouking*
in amang the heather, him they will surely chase, thinking him
to be yourself."

He laughed, and then grew solemn-faced again.

"Ye're owersma' for the part," he said doubtfully.

"Aye," I said, agreeing, "if they see me too close. But from a
distance they'll no can tell, and I've no intention to get within
range o' their guns."

He did not answer at once, but looked at me for a moment in
silence, then shook his head.

* Ducking.

"Na, na, Jamie," he said, "I canna let ye do it. There's danger in't."

I laughed at that.

"Hoot-toot, man," I told him, "there's little danger in it for me. I know the hills too well. I'll lose them when I'm ready. In the meantime, think o' your ain danger, and you'll see it's little enough I do."

He smiled at that and clapped me on the back.

"Ye're a braw lad, Jamie," he laughed, "and I'll hinder ye nae mair."

With that he stripped off the garments I had demanded, replacing them with the others I had brought from my father's wardrobe, while I, by means of a tuck here and a tie there, managed to drape his torn rags about me so that they did not appear so very much too large. After that I took him to the entrance of the cavern and pointed out the clump of birches where the horse was tied.

I warned him then to lie close inside the entry, where he could watch all that passed below without himself being seen. If my ruse succeeded and the line swung after me, then he must return to the bed of bracken, and there rest himself till dark, by which time I should have the troops drawn well to southward. If I failed, he must take to horse as quickly as he might, and trust to the animal's speed to carry him to safety. When I had finished he gripped my shoulder affectionately.

"God bless ye, lad!" he said.

A moment later I was slipping through the thin woods, angling down from the mouth of the cavern and southward, to keep the ridge above me on the right.

Down below, midway between myself and the road, I could make out a group of four redcoats, beating slowly up the hillside. I could even hear their shouts, faintly distant, as they kept touch with similar parties to right and left. As soon as I judged myself to be a safe distance from the cave I stopped on the edge of a clump of heather to survey the situation.

From this point I could overlook the entire valley to northward, as far as the point where the massive shoulder of Mel Uan jutted out to meet the river. All around the basin thus formed the entire mountain side lay exposed. But southward the view was cut off by a bare, humpy hogback that ranged downward from the main ridge beyond the patch of heather in which I had taken refuge. Thus, although I was familiar enough with the lie of the land, I could only guess at the position of the troops beyond. However, judging from what I could see in the valley, I felt safe enough in assuming that those who were out of my sight would only carry out the same tactics on a diminishing scale.

The little group of soldiers I had already noticed were out of sight now among the trees. But by searching carefully I could pick out, here and there at intervals along the slope, an occasional flash of scarlet as the redcoats worked their way upwards through the woods. At a point almost directly below my hiding place the line seemed to have reached its highest point. From there, in either direction, small parties like the one I had already seen moved at a distance of fifty yards or more apart up the slope, each group a little farther down the mountain than the last, so that the whole line stretched in a huge crescent, with its point on the line of the road, its centre at the high point below me, and its lower end tapering off to southward, to disappear from sight behind the humpy ridge which blocked off the view in that direction. On the road a platoon of soldiers moved northward; and even as I watched, another group, just a speck at that distance, separated from it and turned up the mountain.

I turned from this survey to draw a mental picture of what lay beyond the lumpy ridge; the direction I must take if my plan were to be successful. First came the patch of heather in which I lay, perhaps seventy yards in width. Beyond that was the bare hogback. And on the far side of that, in turn, I knew was a shallow gully, some three hundred yards across and thickly wooded. After that came a second patch of heather, in the midst of which was an immense boulder. It was here, I decided, that I must show myself; for if I climbed upon the rock I could not miss being seen from below; and I knew that from its elevated summit I should be able to judge if the northern end of the line turned at the alarm to join the chase.

With this in mind I crept cautiously through the heather to the edge of the open ground. From here to the woods beyond the ridge, a distance of some hundred yards or so, there was not a vestige of cover. The sharp slope of the hogback lay bare and open to the winds that swept up from the glen; and to reach the boulder in the heather, as I had planned, I must cross this space unseen. I had no choice, for I could not go around it. There was nothing for me to do but run for it.

Gathering my legs beneath me, I looked carefully to see if there were any soldiers in sight below. On my side of the ridge, at least, the coast was clear. What lay beyond, I could not tell; but it was a risk I must run. And run I did, for somehow the thought of showing myself in the open, a clear target for those long muskets that glinted so ominously in the hands of the red-coats, did not seem so romantic to me now. I desired to postpone the moment as long as possible. But there was no turning back. Half scrambling, half galloping, tripping and stumbling over my floundering feet, I won safely to the height of the ridge. And there I stopped abruptly, for not two hundred yards below me, following the fringe of the woods upward, was a party of red-coats.

Even as I saw them they saw me, and one of them shouted and flung his musket to his shoulder. I saw the puff of smoke that blossomed at its muzzle and heard the angry whine of its bullet, ricochetting from a stone below me, long before the sound of the report carried to my ears. For an instant my heart seemed to stop its beating. I stood rooted to the spot, paralysed by surprise and fear, unable to move, perfectly outlined against the sky for every soldier on the mountain to see.

That they were as surprised as I was, there can be no doubt. For the space of perhaps ten seconds there was no sound, nor did any one of us move. Then from the side of the ridge I had just left a musket banged, and another followed it; but the shots went wide.

Down below me the other redcoats, who had not fired at once, brought up their pieces. The movement frightened me into action, and I raced for the woods, thanking my stars that the range was so great. Even at that, one of the bullets striking at my feet flung dust and gravel in my face, and another buzzed by me close enough for me to feel the wind of its passage. In the next instant I was safe within the cover of the trees.

But I did not stop there. My plan had succeeded with a venge-ance as thorough as it was unexpected. I knew without looking that every soldier in the neighbourhood would be running toward the sound of that firing. And those redcoats who had seen me first were much too close for comfort. I longed for distance between us. It was not Tom Ogilvie I was running now to save, but myself.

The next hour was one which I shall not soon forget. I ran at first like a frightened rabbit, darting from cover to cover in an erratic course, but bearing always southward, away from the cave; not from any thoughtful purpose, but rather because I was forced that way.

I had miscalculated the position of the southward line grossly. It was much higher on the mountain side than I had thought possible; so that I was hard pressed from this quarter as well as from behind, and while the detachment of redcoats that had first seen me rushed to enter the woods at my heels, the rest of the line surged upward to intercept me. In my headlong flight I could not consider the effectiveness of my cover from so many angles at once; so that at one instant I would be in full view of those behind me, and hidden from those upon my flank, while at the next the pursuers on my heels would lose sight of me, to have their cries of triumph taken up by those below.

Although I have likened myself to a frightened rabbit, I take no shame in saying that no rabbit was ever so afraid as I. For this was not the orderly luring away of the redcoats that I had planned. Such a hullabaloo of shouting and cheering and hallooing rose from the soldiers as must have carried, it seemed to me, well-nigh to Blairgowrie. And the whanging and banging of muskets which rose from the mountain must have made it seem as if a major battle were being fought there. But the thing that made my blood run cold and lent wings to my faltering feet was the buzz and whine and rattle of balls in the brush around me. The range was great and, scurrying as I was, I must have made a difficult mark, so that many shots must have gone far wide; but for all that they were all too close for me.

No doubt this was very fine, taken in terms of my little scheme. It was probably far more effective than if it had fallen out as I had planned it. But I did not have time to care for that. Nor did I stop to see how it was working out. I ran as I have never run before or since, with my heart pounding in my ears and my breath coming in great short gasps and the mountain side dancing before me in my dizziness. I felt as if my lungs must burst; yet I knew that if I hesitated for but an instant they would surely overtake me.

Little by little they forced me up onto the ridge; and there, where the going was easier, I managed to distance them a little. Taking advantage of a brushy gully and a low ridge, I was able to give the impression of heading back down into the valley, the while I doubled back instead and regained the summit of the ridge. Here I flung myself down beneath a clump of heather, to catch my breath and watch the baffled redcoats search the gully from end to end.

From this vantage point I could see back along the valley, over the top of the bare hogback, to the Hall and beyond. The platoon which had been bearing northward along the road had turned now, and was far south of the house and hurrying. The whole line beyond the hogback seemed to have doubled in upon itself and was moving in my direction; and as I caught my breath and my heart gradually ceased its pounding, my fear wore off. I smiled inwardly, knowing that, accident or no, my plan was working.

Down along the ridge to south of me, well out of musket range, yet visible to all the country round, a bare-topped nubble thrust up through the heather. Let me once win to that unseen, I could play the game as I had planned it. The redcoats below were still beating through the gully in search of me. Other parties were scattered on the slope. Carefully I marked down each one. Then, bending double to avoid detection, I scuttled through the brush, like a wary partridge, zigzagging from clump of heather to stand of birch and back again, until at last I came to the hillock, and started up. I was near the top before anything happened. Then far behind me a faint shout went up; a musket popped and then another. I knew I had been seen.

I halted at the top of the rise for a minute and stood watching while the redcoats piled up out of the gully and took up the chase once more. Then I dropped on down the other side and dodged away among the woods to westward, toward Strath Ardle and Kirkmichael.

For the next few hours I ran and dodged and hid among the heather, bobbing up at intervals, only to drop from view again and reappear a thousand yards away. I had the advantage now with distance. It was a game I had played a hundred times before. And always I led the soldiers south and westward away from Glenshee and the man they sought to capture.

Afternoon came and went. A light drizzle set in, making it difficult for me to stay in sight of my pursuers. I came out on the Ardle road below Kirkmichael, and turned southward toward Blairgowrie, making sure first that the move was seen. Let them think that they had tired me, I thought. Let them believe that they had forced me to take to the road for the easier going. I would lead them south past the Bridge of Cally, and then again I would take to the heather and lose them once and for all.

I trotted doggedly, holding a steady pace. Behind me when I looked I could see that detachments had taken to the heights on either side of the glen. I knew that the main body held to the road—that they thought they had me—and I laughed. Yet I was puzzled that they did not close in more rapidly. Could it be that I had worn them down? After all, these men had been working in the heather for two days and two nights with hardly a break. The thought of it reminded me of my own weariness.

Down past the Bridge of Cally I led them, where the Shee Water bubbles down from the north to join the Ardle and form the Ericht. On my left rose the hills of Alyth, beyond which lay Glenisla. It would be fun, I thought, to lead these soldiers back whence they had come. I made up my mind that after the next turning of the road I would strike off in that direction. Darkness was not far off, and I was doubtful of my ability to stay in sight of my pursuers. Yet it was worth a try.

I jogged down a long straightaway at the end of which the road swung sharply to the right. As I came to the bend in the road the first of the pursuit came into sight above me, and I decided that if I were to strike off to the east it must be done soon. Not far below I could see where a footpath crossed a field to the river's edge and climbed the bank on the farther side. It was an opportunity not to be ignored. Another hundred yards along the road should bring me to the corner of the field, and from there I could strike across to the ford. I hesitated a moment to make certain that the soldiers were still coming behind me. Then I turned and trotted on around the bend, to run full into the arms of a half a dozen redcoats!

For the second time that day surprise robbed me of the power of motion. Nor could I think of words to say. A burly corporal, evidently the commander of the detachment, took my arm in a grip like iron.

" 'Oity-toity, 'oity-toity!" he demanded. "Wot's orl this bloomin' 'urry?"

I made feeble motions with my lips, but no sound came forth.

"Well, nah," said he after a moment, " 'ave yer swallowed yer tongue?"

The sound of running feet came from the road above. The corporal snapped an order, and his squad spread out across the road, their muskets ready. Still gripping my arm, the corporal turned.

" 'Alt!" he thundered. " 'Oo goes, in the King's nyme?"

The steps ground to an abrupt halt, hesitated a moment, and then came on again slowly. The first of my pursuers appeared in the dusk at the bend above. At sight of us in the road below they stopped short in a confused huddle. More steps ground on gravel in the background, and more figures loomed in the dusk. Presently one detached itself from the rest and strode toward us.

"What's all this?" the man demanded in gruff, authoritative tones. "What troops are those?"

My captor responded in a tone of respect.

"Corporal 'Apgood, sir," he said, "commanding the advanced guard, Major Wolfe's brigade, Barrel's regiment. Would this be Captain Ball, sir?"

The other snarled angrily.

"Aye, Captain Ball," he replied.

He came on through the gloom past our front rank to where the corporal stood holding me by the arm. He was a stoutish man, not above middle height and with a very red complexion. Just now he was breathing heavily, and looked near to apoplexy. I was somewhat behind Corporal Hapgood's huge bulk, and it was evident that he did not at first see me.

"Major Wolfe's brigade, eh?" he growled. "Sent out to hurry us up, no doubt. You stopped that man who came down the road just now, I hope, corporal. I want that man. That's Major Ogilvie. The same who gave us so much trouble on the road from Stirling."

Corporal Hapgood looked astonished.

"Major Ogilvie?" he blurted. "Ow, no, sir! Ah've seen Major Ogilvie, sir. This couldn't be 'im, sir."

Captain Ball sputtered.

"You fool!" he shouted. "You've let him pass? You had him in your hands—Ogilvie of Glenisla, the man I've been chasing for two whole days and nights—and you let him pass!"

He raised his arms above his head and shook his fists at the lowering sky in impotent fury. The corporal stood impassive before the blast, awaiting a chance to speak.

"Beggin' the captain's pardon, sir," he said woodenly, at length, "there hynt anybody pahssed 'ere. A lad came dahn not 'arf a bit ago, sir. Hi 'ave 'im 'ere. But if the captain'll pardon me syin' it, sir, as shouldn't, hif it's this wot you've been chysin' for Myjor Ogilvie, sir, you've been gulled, sir, that's orl!"

With that he thrust me forward roughly, so that I was brought suddenly face to face with the captain. He looked at me a moment blankly.

"God's blood!" he swore. "What's this?"

Corporal Hapgood allowed no flicker of expression to cross his face, but I thought I detected a gleam in his eye, as though he were thoroughly enjoying the officer's discomfiture.

"There's no other livin' soul come down this road the last two hours past, sir," he said.

Captain Ball reached out and grasped me by the shirt front, yanking me forward roughly. He thrust his face close to mine for a moment, staring at me fiercely, as if by so doing he could change my very features to those of the man he sought; after which he let me go with such suddenness that I staggered and should have fallen had not the corporal reached out and caught my arm once more. The captain's face was a study in frustration and bewildered rage.

"Is it this we've run our hearts out for all day?" he grated. "God's wounds, but I'd have sworn 'twas that rebel hound we were chasing!"

Corporal Hapgood ventured no reply. The captain seemed on the point of bursting with his rage. Behind him I could see his soldiers dropping beside the road in postures of fatigue.

None of us had heard the other troops coming up from below, but suddenly they were there in the road behind us. An officer thrust through the little group that surrounded us. I was surprised at his youth, for though he wore the uniform of a major he could not have been much more than out of his teens. His figure was slight, almost girlish. And his face was more so. His nose was sharply pointed and almost ridiculously long, like a sparrow's beak, over a small mouth and a slightly receding chin. Even in that poor light I perceived that he wore his own hair, rather than a wig, and that this was of a reddish cast, unpowdered, and caught simply in a club at the back of his neck. He strolled among us unaffectedly, his hands clasped behind his back, his short stick caught beneath his arm; yet withal his youth he carried himself with an air of authority.

"Ah, Captain Ball!" he said, in a pleasant though somewhat high-pitched voice. And at the sound of it I saw the troopers in the background stir and look up interestedly. "Your servant, upon my honour. This is fortunate indeed, to come upon you so readily. What seems to be the trouble?"

"Trouble?" sputtered the captain. "'Od's my life, Major! Trouble enough! That scoundrel Ogilvie's given us the slip and sent this damned young whippersnapper in his place to lead us, God knows how far, off the track!"

The major looked at me out of large, somewhat popping, and, I thought, faintly amused eyes.

"Did he so?" he said. "Now that's unfortunate!"

Captain Ball choked.

"Unfortunate?" he fumed. "Aye, unfortunate indeed! But now, sir, with your aid I'll catch him handily!"

I could not resist the opportunity to taunt him.

"Ye'll find him unco hard to catch," I cried, "for I misdoubt he's well awa to Inverness the now."

Captain Ball whirled on me and struck me hard across the face with the flat of his hand, so that my senses whirled with the sting of it and I could feel the hot blood spurt from my nose. Though I kicked out with my feet at his shins, I could not reach him; but in the next instant I had the satisfaction of seeing the major's stick thwack across the captain's cheek, and of seeing him fall back a pace, clapping a hand to the white welt that it left behind. The major's eyes popped more furiously than ever, and a spot of red glowed on either cheek.

"Would you strike a child, sirrah?" he demanded.

Captain Ball was white with anger. An expectant hush settled around us. In the dusk I could see the soldiers staring, rigid, incredulous.

"You struck me, sirrah!" cried the captain in a choked voice, "By God's flesh, I'll have satisfaction for that, Major Wolfe!"

Wolfe bowed stiffly.

"That you will, sir, and gladly," he replied, "when we return to Aberdeen. In the meantime, I'll remind you that we are here on duty. You will march your men down into yonder field, where we will bivouac the night."

Captain Ball was sulky.

"And what of Ogilvie?" he asked surlily.

"You heard the lad," Wolfe told him. "And without that I would venture to remind you that even soldiers must rest. Look to your men, sir. They are played out. Would you drive them further?"

The captain chose to disregard the reasoning.

"You'd take the brat's word for it?" he sneered.

" 'The brat's word' is but common sense, if you will but look at it," said Wolfe. "D'ye think as smart a fox as Ogilvie will wait about for you to return?"

"My orders were not to return with you," Ball replied sourly, "but to find the rebel dog and bring him in."

Wolfe shook his head impatiently.

"I care not what your orders were," he snapped. "D'ye think I do not carry fresher ones? My instructions are to find you and assist you, if that is possible; and if it is not, which is clearly the case, to bring you back to Aberdeen, for the Duke is anxious to be off. D'ye think I shall follow your instructions or my own?"

But Captain Ball was still not satisfied.

"But—" he began.

Major Wolfe lost all patience.

"Goddamme, sir!" he swore. "Did you hear my orders? Then see that they are obeyed at once, or I'll give you your satisfaction now for the mutinous dog you are!"

With that he turned to Corporal Hapgood, who had not released his hold upon me.

"Let go the boy," he said. And to me, "Stay close by me, lad."

And he turned away upon his heel and strode down into the meadow that lay between the river and the road.

I followed at his heels, stanching as best I could the flow of blood from my nose, and presently the troops came down and took up their positions along the river bank, where they kindled their fires and set their kettles on to boil.

The major kept me close by him while he inspected the camp; and when at length the rations were ready and served, insisted upon sharing his with me. Never did food taste so good, for all it was but bread and cheese and tea (which was a new beverage to me, its cost being prohibitive in the Highlands) with a dash of rum in it.

Captain Ball sat across the crackling fire from us, eating his meal in sulky silence, with no words for anyone. The major seemed to have forgotten his anger of the moment before and chatted with me amiably, speaking to me as though I were his equal in age and rank, and drawing from me little by little the whole story of the day's happenings. It was then that I confided in him my wish to be a soldier, and I was pleased and flattered that he did not laugh as did others, but nodded gravely and understandingly. Presently he stretched out his legs toward the fireside and set down his cup.

"You're at home in these hills," he said. "I doubt you'll find any difficulty getting home tonight."

I did not reply at once. Indeed, I could not, for I had not dared to think what was to be my lot. At the very least I had thought that they would carry me to Aberdeen. But if I was voiceless, such was not the case with Captain Ball. He thumped his cup down upon the ground beside him and leapt to his feet.

"Goddamme, sir!" he exclaimed. "You'll not be letting the fellow go?"

Major Wolfe looked up at him coldly.

"I'll remind you, sir," he replied, "that we do not make war on children."

"But, damme, sir," the captain sputtered, "the brat's my prisoner. I'll not permit it!"

I could see the major's cheeks glow in the firelight.

"You forget, sirrah, that you are no longer in command here," he said. "Moreover, I would advise you to consider how it might appear if it became known that you had spent the entire day chasing a child through the heather, as must surely be the case if we take him in."

Captain Ball's jaw dropped, and he sat down heavily, his florid face stupidly vacant. Here was evidently a consideration which had not previously struck him. For my part, however, I was stung; for thrice over the major had spoken of me as a child; and much as I admired him as a soldier, yet I was angry. I could feel the hot Scots blood rising within me.

"Sir," I said, "three times tonight ye have called me a child, which I am not, but a man grown; for I am sixteen years of age and old enough to be in the fighting, which I make no doubt I will be within the year, for my father is Alan Ferguson, of whom, no doubt, you've heard."

At that the captain looked up.

"You hear?" he said triumphantly. "Surely you'll not be turning him loose in the face of that?"

Wolfe stared across the fire without expression.

"I have not changed my mind," he said.

Ball sneered.

"And what will the general say to that?" he asked.

"That will be for him to say," said Wolfe.

He turned to me.

"You have not answered my question," he said.

I was angry with myself for having spoken so foolishly. And because I was angry I was graceless.

"Oh, aye," I told him, "I can find my way."

He gave me a hard look and scrambled to his feet.

"Good," he said. "I'll see you to the road."

And with that he turned away and strode off through the camp, while I trotted at his heels like any puppy in the steps of his master.

We went out past the pickets and across the meadow without a word being spoken. But when we climbed up to the road he turned to me.

"You have said that you would be a soldier," he said.

"Aye, sir," I told him, " 'tis what I wish."

"Then," said he, "you have much to learn."

I did not reply, but waited for him to continue, which he did presently.

"In the first place," he said, "you must learn to be watchful; for had you been more so you would not have been so easily taken on the road."

I nodded.

"And secondly," he continued, "you must learn caution; for down yonder by the fire your tongue played you into the hands of the enemy."

I hung my head, ashamed of my quick temper.

"I'm sorry," I said contritely, "if aught I said should make trouble for ye."

He clapped me on the shoulder and started walking slowly with me up the road.

" 'Tis nothing that need worry you," he replied. "Captain Ball is not well liked at headquarters."

We walked a moment in silence.

"My father," he continued presently, "is a soldier, as are all the rest of my people. We have an axiom among us which runs, 'Next to valour, the best qualities in a military man are vigilance and caution.' You'll do well to remember that."

"Aye, sir," I said, "I'll mind it. And thank you."

He stopped and held out his hand.

"Well then," he said, "you'll be a good soldier, lad, for there's few enough who do. I'll say good night, and good luck. Perhaps we'll meet again."

And with that he turned and strode away down the road, leaving me standing there in the darkness with his words ringing in my ears, little dreaming what a prophecy lay in them.

TRAGEDY AND FLIGHT

¶1 It was this episode, I believe, which finally determined my mother to withdraw to the city. Before my father's departure it had been agreed upon between them, if for any reason it should appear unsafe to remain longer at the Hall, to adopt this course. Now it seemed that time had come.

As a matter of fact the decision was mainly the result of an accumulation of alarms. Of late, conditions in the valley had gone steadily worse. More and more frequently the redcoats appeared at our door. The roving bands of lawless deserters grew bolder with each passing day. Searchers were more insolent, foragers more exacting, until there was scarce a beast or a sack of grain left in all the country between Blairgowrie and the Spittal of Glenshee.

It was true that the presence of our two involuntary guests protected us to a certain extent from these molestations. But the lieutenant was by now vastly improved. He had already sent word to Aberdeen of his fitness to travel, and lived in daily expectation of the orders which would invalid him home to England. Once this slender prop was gone we should find ourselves at the mercy of all who might come our way. It was a difficult decision to make, for my mother was deeply attached to Kintulloch. Indeed we all were. Naturally she was reluctant to come to it, so that she hesitated, putting it off from day to day, until my adventure on the mountain with the redcoats broke down her resistance and convinced her at last that it was no longer possible to remain.

It was only then that I learned that our destination was not to be Edinburgh, as I had supposed, but Glasgow, which, it seemed to me, was somewhat out of the way for father to meet us. I protested on this score. But my mother replied to this that, as Glasgow had been my father's choice, thither we would go, whether I liked it or no. And so it was to Glasgow that we went.

Our host, in the city, Mr. Abernethy, was a widower, a gentleman in his late fifties with ruddy cheeks and a mild blue eye, which glowed with pleasure at our arrival. He was an old friend of my father's, the pair of them having for some years previous been associated together in mysterious business dealings which I strongly suspect had to do with the procurement of arms and supplies for the honest party* in the years just prior to the rebellion. However that may have been, there was no doubt that he was genuinely glad to receive us; and in the days that followed I was forced to the conclusion that a kinder man had never lived, a judgement I have never found the least occasion to alter. The first few weeks of our stay with him, at least, were pleasant and passed all too swiftly. If the last half of our visit remained in our minds as a period of horror and suspense, it was not the fault of our good host, who did all in his power to relieve our minds, but rather the fault of the times and our own imaginations, which would not give us rest.

It was toward the end of March when we arrived in Glasgow. And it was more than a fortnight from that day before ever we heard from my father. The army, he told us, lay at Inverness watching and waiting for the enemy's next move. The English, under the Duke of Cumberland, remained at Aberdeen. Their departure from that place, however, was expected momentarily, and when it came, he assured us, the Prince would move forward to battle.

Almost on the heels of this letter came the word that the Duke had marched northward at the head of his army. A few days later we heard that he had crossed the Spey unmolested and was marching on Inverness. A day or so later they were at Nairn. And then all news suddenly ceased.

There followed, then, a period of intense excitement and suspense, not only within our small circle, but throughout the city. Whig sentiment prevailed in Glasgow, but there was no dearth of staunch Jacobites as well. Both sides felt that a crisis was at hand. Defeat spelled disaster for either side. A decisive victory for the Prince would rally his wavering forces, enabling him to

* Jacobites.

carry on the fight, besides bringing recognition and aid from France. Victory for the Duke meant the end of the rising, for the Prince was at the end of his resources. Men met in the streets with anxious faces and questioned one another eagerly for the least scrap of recent news. At the coffee house the young bloods made huge wagers on the outcome. Days slipped by into a week; and still there was no word.

Then, at last, one evening almost four weeks after our arrival, our host came home from his place of business in the Trongate, and for the first time since I had first seen him he looked a weary, sick old man. My mother gave one look at his grey face, and her hand flew to her throat.

"You have news, Mr. Abernethy!" she cried. "Tell us! What is it you've heard?"

He looked at her and shook his head.

"It is the end," he said bitterly.

And then he went on to tell us of the terrible disaster that had come upon our army at Culloden Moor. How the two forces had faced each other across open ground, ill suited to the Highland tactics. How the Prince's right wing had charged gallantly, while the left had refused their orders. How the British had fought off that first fierce charge and broken the Highland ranks by a flanking movement. And how at last the Prince and his supporters had turned about and fled in panic from the field. He gave us the bare details and no more, for that was all that he or anyone else yet knew. That night we went to bed wondering how fared the father that we loved. Had he won free? Or had he fallen? Beside this the fact that a cause was lost was nothing.

That was all we knew of what had happened for the next day or two. Then little by little reports began to come in driblets; reports not only detailing the battle, which was bad enough, but, what was worse, telling the horrors that followed.

To us, of course, those days were like some awful nightmare. The horror of the stories seared our very souls. Daily we hoped and prayed for some news from my father. But each day passed without a word. It was possible that he had escaped, with the thousands of others who had escaped. But it was possible also that he had fallen—that he had been wounded—that he had been one of those unfortunates who had been tossed in a heap to be shot to pieces with a six-pounder.

Naturally enough we none of us mentioned these thoughts to one another, yet we could not but think them. Hour after hour, day after day, we came and went in silence, not daring to voice our fears. My sisters never laughed in those days. I believe my mother aged more in two short weeks than she had done in all her life before. For my own part, what can I say? I went about with a heart like lead and my head in a daze, so that I hardly knew when I was spoken to. Until at last I took to going down to the Broomielaw, with its ships and its sailors and all its rush of life, just so that I should not have to think about the thing I could not keep out of my mind.

On one of these occasions I received a rather considerable shock. It was one of those dull, grizzly days, so common in Glasgow, when the fog swirls dismally through the streets and folk who have no cause to go out are glad enough to stay at home by the fire. For my part I preferred the moist impersonality of the fog that cloaked the city to the almost tangible sense of impending disaster that pervaded the Abernethy household, and I had gone out to wander along the Clydeside where business went on as usual despite the weather. There I picked my way among the scattered drays, piled high with boxes and bales, being soothed in some way by the rush and clamour and hustle all about me without in any sense heeding it.

How long I wandered thus along the quay, I do not know. But suddenly I realized with a start that it was growing late and I had best be on my way home if I wished to find my way there before dark. In pursuance of this thought I was turning away, when a movement in the fog on the waterside caught my eye, and I stopped to look.

As I watched, a ship materialized, ghosting through the gloom; a brig, evidently from some berth farther upstream, slipping down seaward not more than a few yards offshore. Even as I stood there for a moment she came more plainly into sight. I could make out her spars and rigging and see the canvas hanging limp in the light air. On her deck, barefoot foreign-looking sailors moved silently about their tasks. Her bluff bows turned aside the fog in a little eddy to either hand as a ship's cutwater cleaves the sea.

I watched her slip by like some grey ghost, and for the second time was about to turn away when I spied a white face peering from one of her stern ports. There was something about the face that made me look again, something furtive and shifty—fearful yet at the same time almost triumphant. I looked, and as I looked a breath of wind blew the fog momentarily aside so that I had a clear view of the man who stood peering out at the green-grey of the river. For a moment I thought my eyes were deceiving me— then I knew it must be so. Dirty, unshaven though it was, there could be no mistaking that face. Those black eyes, the waving hair, the long aristocratic nose and the cynical mouth could belong to but one person. I gasped. I shouted.

"Hubert! Hugh! Hubert!"

His eyes swung to meet mine, and for an instant I read in them stark terror, which in turn gave way to bitter hatred that was frightening in its intensity. Only for the briefest moment did our eyes meet across that narrow stretch of water. Then, before I could cry out again, the face was gone and the blank port slammed down in its stead. I knew he had seen me and had known me, for I had seen recognition in his eyes before he turned away. But I could not understand the obvious fear I had seen in his look.

I stood, stricken to lifelessness, staring after him, and as I stared the fog rolled in once more, giving me only the briefest glimpse of the vessel's high poop as she drifted by. In that instant, before she was swallowed in the whirling, grey-brown mist, I made out the high gilt letters across her stern, "João Fernhão-Lisboa."

I made no mention of this incident to anyone, for there was something vaguely disturbing about it that I could not put my finger on, and I could not see that any good purpose would be served in its telling. Nevertheless the memory of that ghostly, frightened face, staring at me through the fog, remained with me sharply for many a long day.

It was four or five days after this that the news for which we were all waiting arrived. It was raining out, I mind, and I, neither caring to remain in idleness at home, nor being able to walk abroad in the sodden streets, had accompanied our host to his office. Mr. Abernethy and his chief clerk had gone out about midafternoon to the Broomielaw to overlook a cargo of tobacco that had but just arrived, consigned to his house, from Virginia. They left me with the inner office to myself, to pass the time as I chose, telling me that they would be back within the hour. Business was slack, and in the outer office there was but one clerk, so that to all intents and purposes I was alone.

The hour was nearly up, I remember, and I was intent upon a bill of goods which our good merchant had suggested that I might total up for him, when I heard the front door open and the drone of voices coming from the outer office. Busy as I was, and believing it to be my friend and his clerk returning, I paid no attention. But, when a moment later the door to the inner office opened, I dropped my pen and sprang to my feet with an exclamation of amazement; for instead of Mr. Abernethy and his employee, who should appear upon the threshold but Old Dougal, whom we had left behind to look after things at Kintulloch, and close behind him no other than Tom Ogilvie.

"Dougal!" I cried. "What brings you here, man?"

Before the words had passed my lips I knew well enough what had brought them, and the look that passed between them confirmed the thought.

"Is it father?" I asked.

Dougal came to me and set a hand upon my shoulder.

"Ye must no tak it too hard, lad," he said.

"He's—" I could not bring myself to say it.

Dougal nodded. Tom Ogilvie cleared his throat gruffly.

"It grieves me sair to tell ye, Jamie," he said, "Yer father is dead."

I sank dully into the chair from which I had but just risen. This was that for which I had been waiting. Now it seemed to me as though I had known all along that it must be so. I wanted to cry out against it, but I could not find my voice. I could have wept, but the tears would not come. Three times I tried to speak, but no words came. Then on the fourth effort I found a word my tongue would speak.

"How—" I began, and even in my own ears my voice was harsh and bitter and rasping.

A quick look passed between the two men.

"He died a brave man, lad," said Ogilvie. But he did not look at me.

"How?" I rasped again.

Again the two men looked at each other, and it almost seemed that Ogilvie was pleading something with Dougal. In that moment I was suddenly afraid.

"Let me know the truth," I said harshly.

It was Dougal who spoke.

"The lad should know," he said.

Ogilvie nodded, and wet his lips.

"He was never a coward, lad," he said.

I made a gesture of impatience. Nevertheless I felt as though a weight had been lifted from my mind.

"Tell me," I said.

"Ye know the way it went," said Ogilvie. "How the Prince thought to catch the redcoats unaware; how we charged and were outflanked, and how they finally broke us?"

I nodded.

"Go on," I told him.

"Then there's no need to gie ye details," he said. "Yer father's troop, and mine, were in the centre of that charge. We were dismounted, for the Prince wanted his full weight of infantry to smash their lines. But when they took us in the flank with the six-pounders it broke our force. 'Twas there I saw yer father fall. I went to him and lifted him and saw that he lived."

"He lived?" I cried.

"Aye," he said grimly, "he lived."

"What did ye then?" I asked.

"I saw yer cousin," he said, "and he was running. I called, but he paid me no heed. Then I ran and caught him by the arm. E'en then he would have torn free and gone on, but I beat him with my sword, and presently he came back wi' me.

"Between us, we raised yer father and carried him back, and when the army broke and fled we carried him off until we found a bit stable amang th' heather in a gully, such as our people use sometimes for the sheep. There we laid him down and rested, for we could go no farther. And there others came to join us, until there were fifteen or more of us."

"Get on with it," I interrupted him.

"Aye," he said. "They were all of them wounded, in one way or another, some badly, others no so bad. Yer cousin and mysel' were all the whole ones among us.

"We stayed the night in yon stable, for there were scarce any that were fit to move. In the night I slipped out to make a bit scout, and the things I saw would turn yer guts. The bloody lobsterbacks were out with orders to murder, and all they put their hands on, be they whole or wounded, they slew!"

"The butchers!" I swore through clenched teeth.

"Aye, butcher's the word," he said, "though it libels a decent trade! I went back and told what I had seen, and all the next day we lay close hidden, without food or water, waiting for the night. We knew we must make shift to leave as soon as we might, for though the bit stable was well hid, 'twas but a matter of time before the redcoats found it.

"When night fell it was decided yer cousin and I, being the only whole ones, should go out and scout the land and mark down a way out of the country. We drew lots to see which way we'd go, and it fell to me to go west towards Kingussie and Fort Augustus, the whiles your cousin was to go south and east towards Grantown and Nairn. We were to return not later than midnight, for we would need the rest o' the night to be awa' in."

"Did you find a way?" I asked.

He nodded.

"I did," he replied, "a way as good as any, though I've no means of knowing what yer cousin found, for I never saw him more!"

"The coward!" I cried. "He ran away."

"I didnae say that," he said. "Ye see, lad, when I returned it was to find yon stable in flames, and all those wounded inside it."

"No!" I cried out, horror-struck. "They would not! They could not!"

Ogilvie looked grim.

"They not only would and could," he growled. "They did. An' in the bargain they lay waiting outside, and any man that showed himself to come out was shot down in cold blood!"

I buried my face in my hands.

"Ah, Christ!" I groaned. "That God could let such swine exist!"

He nodded bitterly. A thought struck me.

"Hubert!" I exclaimed. "You don't think he—"

"I wouldnae say that of any man unless I knew it to be so," said Ogilvie. "Pairhaps he was inside."

"He was not," I said. "I saw him, not six days since."

I told them then how I had seen Hubert's face on board the Portuguese brig. Tom Ogilvie shrugged.

"Belike," he said, "he came as I did—too late to do aught but lie close in the heather and watch."

I nodded and fell silent then, brooding upon the horror of the thing. I found it hard to believe it could have happened. I knew Tom Ogilvie would never bear such a tale unless it were true. Yet I was prepared to clutch at any straw that offered.

"You think he could not have escaped?" I asked.

Ogilvie shook his head.

"Yer father?" he said, "No, lad."

"But mightn't he have just stepped outside before the English came?" I persisted.

Ogilvie shot a pleading look at Dougal, but the latter shook his head firmly.

"Tell him," he said.

Tom Ogilvie nodded resignedly, and turned back to me.

"Nay, lad," he said, "he might not. Ye see it was a bit o' grape that did for him—"

"But I don't see—" I began.

"I dare say ye don't," he replied, "but I'm telling ye. Ye see, lad, when we pickit him up, yer father's back was broke. He couldnae walk!"

2

Need I tell of the awful agony of grief with which I heard him? Must I describe the numbness that came over me as I sat stunned beneath this crushing proof that gave the deathblow to all our hopes? I cried out once in horror that it could not be, and after that my throat went dry and hard and painful, so that I could not speak a word. All inside I felt pressed down as by some dead, dull leaden weight. I made no effort now to restrain the tears that sprang into my eyes.

Mr. Abernethy, coming in at that moment, heard the news from Dougal's lips with a drawn face. When it was finished he turned to me kindly.

"Your mother must be told this, lad," he said.

I stared at him dully, only half comprehending, so that he repeated. I nodded.

"Aye," I replied slowly, "there is no need to keep it from her longer."

We went out in a body then to Mr. Abernethy's house, and as soon as my mother saw who my companions were she knew that the long awaited news had arrived. She must have guessed also, from our faces, something of its nature. I for one could not speak. Nor was Old Dougal in a better case. Tom Ogilvie hung back as if reluctant to repeat his ordeal of the office, so that the painful duty fell to Mr. Abernethy. He went toward her with outstretched hands.

"My dear," he said, "I need not tell ye of the pain it gives me to be the bearer of such news."

She stood before him bravely, her head held high.

"He is dead?" she asked.

Mr. Abernethy nodded. It was plain that she maintained her composure only by a great effort.

"Tell me," she begged, hesitantly, "how—how did he die?"

A hush fell upon the room. Mr. Abernethy hesitated, and Tom Ogilvie spoke quickly before the old gentleman could reply.

"He died, ma'am," he said, "like a good soldier and a fine, brave gentleman, quickly and easily on the field of battle!"

My mother gave a little gasping cry and sank to her knees, her hands clasped before her.

"Ah! Praise God for that!" she cried. "It is something to know that he was not tortured, at least!"

Poignant as it was, the death of my father, beyond the actual fact of its occurrence, did not vastly affect our immediate future. The course which we followed thereafter was the same which in all likelihood, in view of the complete collapse of the Stuart cause, we would have followed anyway. Hence any recitation of the events of the days immediately following that tragic announcement would only renew old sorrows without serving any good purpose; and I pass over that mournful period and come at once to other events which bear importantly upon our story.

After her first outburst of passionate grief my mother took to her bed, where she remained for almost three weeks in a state of dull despair, evidently not caring greatly whether she lived or died. But presently she rallied somewhat, and called me to her side.

My father, she told me, had at the outbreak of hostilities very wisely taken steps to provide for his family in the event of just such a disaster as had befallen. Knowing that if the Cause he had chosen to follow should meet with defeat, he himself would be attainted and all his property forfeit to the crown, he had undertaken to convert as much of his possessions as he could into ready money. This he did very shrewdly, selling everything that he possibly could, so that although Kintulloch and the Hall were lost to us, we thought, beyond all hope of recall, still we were by no means destitute. Indeed, as a result of his careful manipulations, we found ourselves possessed of a modest fortune which, with proper care and good management, would provide for us all a comfortable place in the world.

We should, however, because of our known Jacobite connections be forced to leave Scotland, and for this contingency my father had also provided a plan. Then, as always before, France was the haven for all disgruntled followers of the House of Stuart. It was near. It was comparatively easy to reach. And it was hostile to the House of Hanover. It was a logical refuge, but not one that appealed to my father who considered all Frenchmen to be foppish braggarts and popish knaves. Although he was willing and ready to fight and die for his rightful sovereign, my father had never felt constrained to adopt the religious views of the Stuarts, so that we had all been brought up as good Presbyterians. Hence it was almost necessary that we look elsewhere for a safe retreat.

Now, my mother had an older brother, one David Ross, who upon the outbreak of the rising of the 'Fifteen had foreseen its inevitable conclusion, and desiring to be identified with neither side, had removed to Londonderry in the North of Ireland, where he married and settled for a time. After a matter of four years or so, however, he became dissatisfied with his lot there, and as a number of his Scotch-Irish friends and relatives were about to embark for the American colonies, he made up his mind to join them with his family and seek his fortune in the New World. They landed at Boston in the Massachusetts Province, where they at once applied to the Governor for a grant of lands. This was refused them, the Governor and Council maintaining that Irishmen, for such they were considered from the fact of their having resided for a period in Ireland, were not a desirable addition to the community. Undaunted by this rebuff, they applied to one

Colonel Wheelwright, who was said to have title to certain lands in the Province of New Hampshire which certain of his ancestors had purchased from the Indians. Here they were more favourably received, and were permitted to purchase a tract of land known as Nutfield, which name they promptly changed to Londonderry; and there they settled despite the protests of some of their neighbours who eyed them askance. A year or two later their town was officially incorporated and recognized by the Provincial Assembly, and from that day their affairs prospered.

The affairs of this uncle, whom I had never seen, also prospered, it seems, along with the rest. In the Indian troubles of 1725 he served with distinction in the company of the well remembered Captain Lovewell, and was present at the memorable fight in which that worthy was killed. In recognition of his services on that occasion, he, with several other survivors of the battle, received a grant of wilderness land on the Merrimack River known as Suncook (a name which many years later was changed to Pembroke). Thither he removed with his family and settled once and for all. And from here he wrote to my mother at rare intervals, long letters filled with glowing accounts of the new country in which he had chosen to cast his lot.

All this might well have meant nothing to me had not my father decided that here was an ideal haven of refuge in case of defeat. Before he had left for the war he had worked out with my mother a plan which each was to follow in case of just such a disaster as had occurred. My mother, it was determined, should wait a reasonable time for him to join us, or until she had received news of him. If possible he was to come to us in Glasgow. Otherwise he would try to make his escape from the country as best he could, trusting in his luck to be able to join us as soon as possible in the colonies, whither my mother was to repair with us when it became evident that we could wait no longer. In case of his death, of course, she was free to alter the plan in any way that seemed to her fit.

"I see no reason," she said, "to change that plan. Scotland, in view of our known political attachments, will be a hard place for us. It may well be even downright dangerous for you, Jamie."

She paused, but I did not reply.

"For my own part," she continued, "I confess that after this I cannot feel much sorrow at leaving!"

Her lip quivered, just for an instant, and I took her hands in mine and pressed them, so that she knew I understood.

"We'll go," I said. "We'll go and get a new start. Everything will be new."

She patted my hand gently and smiled a little.

"Everything will be new, lad, except Dougal," she said, and turned to the old man who stood near the door. "You'll come with us, Dougal man, won't you? You know we couldna get along without you."

The old steward came forward with tears in his eyes and threw himself to his knees beside her.

"That I will, ma'am," he cried, "and God bless ye for saying it! Ye know there's naught for me here now!"

At that I turned and fled from the room, daring not to stay for fear the good old fellow's obvious emotion should also reduce me to tears, in which case we should have presented a sorry spectacle, for neither he nor my mother made any effort to restrain them, but wept openly in concert.

If our plan were to be acted upon it must be at once. Bills of attainder had already been passed against all who had been active in the rebellion. The Duke of Cumberland at the head of his army was scouring the Highlands, shooting down every man who dared to wear the tartan or carry a dirk, burning and pillaging indiscriminately on every hand. Daily it grew more difficult for fugitives to escape the country. Ships outbound were carefully scrutinized. The patrols along the coast were doubled, and the garrisons in all important seaport towns increased.

Indeed it might well have been impossible had it not been for our good friend Mr. Abernethy, who once again brought his wisdom and experience to our assistance and placed the entire facilities of his office at our disposal. He it was who found the snow * *Badger* outbound within the fortnight for Boston. It was he who made the necessary arrangements for our passage with her master, one Amos Henbury, a colonial inclined to looked upon us with some suspicion until he learned that my mother had a brother in the Hampshire Province whom she was going to visit, whereupon he unbent sufficiently to confide in her that he had feared lest we

* "A two-masted vessel closely resembling a brigantine"—Funk & Wagnalls New Standard Dictionary.

should prove to be "a passel of Jacobite fugitives, a-fleein' from their just deserts," in which case he should have refused to carry us as he was "afeared for the good name of his ship."

Under my mother's maiden name it proved simple enough for Mr. Abernethy to procure for us all the papers and passports which were needed to enable us to leave the city, and at the appointed hour we went aboard with all our boxes and baggage, our party consisting, besides my mother, my sisters and myself, of Dougal and Anna Bailie, my mother's waiting woman, a gaunt, dried-up spinster of some forty summers, who when she heard our plans had begged my mother on her knees not to leave her behind.

At dawn of the following morning our old friend and host came down to bid us Godspeed, lingering until the whistle of the bos'n's pipe gave warning that all visitors must go ashore or be carried to sea, at which he descended to the quay where he stood waving his handkerchief while the longshoremen cast off our hawser and we slipped out into the stream.

· 4 ·

AN INNOCENT ABROAD

{[1 It was on July 16, 1746—just eight weeks and four days after our departure from Glasgow—that we dropped anchor in Boston harbour. If I say that we were amazed to find the provincial seaport so large a town I shall not be putting it too strongly, for somehow we had always thought of it as a mere outpost of civilization. That evening, however, as our little vessel swung at anchor in the harbour, Captain Henbury told us that it was even more extensive than it appeared from the waterfront, and that it contained in the neighbourhood of four thousand houses and had a population of more than twelve thousand souls; we should not, he said, find it greatly different from towns of a like size which we knew at home. And indeed when we went on shore the next morning we found that beyond the fact that wood predominated in the construction of the houses, with only here and there an occasional brick building, he was not far wrong.

Along the waterfront, at the long wharf where we landed, lay the same ships (except that they bore different names painted across their stern boards) that I had seen lying in along the Broomielaw in Glasgow. The streets were well paved with cobbles, and though they were mighty irregular many were wider than was the custom at home. Shops were just as well stocked and as numerous as on the Trongate or the High. Mercers and milliners, tailors and haberdashers, jewellers, saddlers, cobblers, apothecaries, victuallers, chandlers, taverns, all did a thriving trade. Indeed, many of the taverns bore the same familiar signs: "The Beehive," "The Bible and Key," "The Jolly Sailors," "The Ship in Distress." The Exchange had its coffee house, the meeting place, as at home, of a crowd of dandified young macaronis. Men and women in the streets dressed no differently from similar crowds in any English or Scottish city. Only one group excited unusual curiosity. These were young men, generally seen in groups

49

of three or four, who swaggered and roistered about the streets in a rowdy manner. They wore their own hair, caught in a club at the back of their necks under large black hats which they cocked at a jaunty angle. Their jackets were short, their breeches tight; often they were stockingless. So similarly were they dressed that, save that their colours did not match, they might almost be thought to be in uniform. Indeed I learned later that these were members, volunteers gathered from all parts of the provinces, of the great expedition projected against Canada, who were at that time encamped outside the city awaiting the arrival of the fleet which was to join them.

Even these, however, would not have appeared at all unusual but for their numbers and their boisterous ways. For the rest of the people they might have been lifted bodily from any street in London or Glasgow or Edinburgh. Much to my great chagrin, we did not see so much as one red Indian in all the time that we were there. In fact, the closest we came to such a sight was the young blackamoor in livery who served the inn at which we stayed. My sisters were delighted to find everything so modern and up to date, while I was doubly disappointed, for somehow I had expected to see a small stockaded town, huddled on the water's edge in the midst of dark, forbidding forests which echoed the hideous yells of bloodthirsty savages, and all this was far too tame and ordinary for my young tastes.

At Captain Henbury's suggestion, we made at once for the Brackett Tavern, at the sign of the O. Cromwell's Head, in School Street, which he recommended as being the best which the city afforded and the one most frequented by the gentry. Here we found everything to our liking and engaged suitable accommodations for an indefinite stay.

As my mother was most anxious to meet her brother as quickly as possible, her first act was to sit down and write him a letter. This done she sent for our host and inquired by what means it might be despatched. He was most sanguine at first, saying that if the address did not lie on the route of a postrider we should find no difficulty in hiring someone to make the journey for the purpose. When, however, he learned that it was directed to Suncook in the Hampshire Province, he looked grave and said that that was another matter. He expressed doubt that we should find a carrier, without giving his reasons therefor, but withdrew promising to do everything in his power.

It being then somewhat after noon, and the blackamoor having informed us that dinner was ready upon the board, we went below stairs to the dining room where, as was customary, the guests of the house who did not care to pay an extra charge for the privilege of being served in their chambers, dined at a common table.

Since it was midsummer and visitors to the town were few, aside from the army, the table was not crowded. Those officers who lodged at the tavern either were on duty at the camp or took their meals elsewhere, so that we had but three companions. Of these, two were quiet young gentlemen of the Connecticut Province, travellers to the metropolis on business, while the third was a short, stout, rather pompous little man in an old-fashioned full-bottomed wig and a plum-coloured coat with huge brass buttons, who made my mother a very elegant leg and announced himself "Phinehas Drew, a lawyer, of Portsmouth, ma'am, your servant."

We had scant opportunity to gain acquaintance with the two young commercial travellers, for they ate rapidly in diffident silence and promptly excused themselves when they were finished. The lawyer, however, was the personification of officious affability. He leaned over backwards, as the saying is, in his efforts to be polite, and at the same time questioned my mother so shrewdly as to our voyage and all our affairs that she found herself telling him more than she intended to divulge. There was no harm done, however, since she merely said that she had lost her husband in the war, without mentioning the circumstances, and added that we had come to the colonies to find her brother, who had settled in the Hampshire Province.

At this bit of information he threw up his hands and behind iron-rimmed spectacles ludicrously rolled his eyes toward the ceiling.

"Oh, la, ma'am!" he exclaimed. "Now there's a coincidence for you. My own dear wife was carried off only last winter by a throat distemper—a very common disorder in these parts, ma'am. You must guard against it, both as to yourself and these dear, sweet little children here. But, Lud now, you'll think I talk like an old woman, indeed you will! She was carried off, I say—it is my dear, departed wife I speak of, ma'am—by a throat distemper last winter, leaving me with the guardianship of my only daughter, a lovely creature! A lovely creature, if I do say so myself. You must meet her, ma'am. She is visiting at present with friends in town—the Boylstons, ma'am, a prominent family, a very prominent family indeed! What did you say your brother's name was, ma'am?"

"David Ross," said my mother, smiling. "He lives in Suncook."

"Oh, David Ross?" he said. "Hum—David Ross? Oh, yes! Oh, yes, yes, yes, indeed! David Ross! Of Suncook, I believe you said? I've heard of him. 'Pon my soul I believe I have! He was one of Lovewell's men, was he not? Serjeant Ross—isn't that the man? He was at Pigwacket Pond, I believe, in '25. One of the survivors, to be sure. A remarkable battle that, ma'am. A remarkable battle! You've heard the story? Of course you have, if your brother was in it. We taught the red savages a thing or two then, I'll tell you! We gave them a lesson in bloodletting! But it appears they've forgotten it. Now we'll have it to do all over again. Why, only last month they killed four men and carried off another in a raid at Rochester, and I've no doubt we'll hear more of them presently. Does your brother know of your arrival, madam?"

My mother replied that she had been unable to give warning of our approach as we ourselves had come as rapidly as a letter would. She added, however, that she had written him that very morning and was now in a quandary as to how she was going to have it delivered.

He looked at her with pursed lips and bobbed his head soberly.

"Gadso, ma'am," said he, "I should think you might have some difficulty on that score. You see, ma'am, there is no regular post in that direction, and since the outbreak of the war with France the Indians who inhabit the woods lying between our colonies and Canada have been exceedingly troublesome—'pon my soul they have! The consequence is that it is difficult to find anyone who is willing to venture into those frontier settlements for fear of losing his hair."

At that he drew a circle around the top of his head with his forefinger and laughed uproariously; but presently he grew sober again, and continued.

"However, ma'am, on my way down here from Portsmouth I had the honour to ride from Newburyport in the company of a young man who comes from the region of Suncook; a dashing young man, ma'am, a very dashing young man, of the name of

Rogers. Robert Rogers, ma'am. His father settled in Starkstown Grant not far from Suncook a few years ago. Young Rogers in ordinary times styles himself an Indian trader. That is what he styles himself, ma'am, but I"—here he lowered his voice confidentially—"just between us, ma'am, would say that he traded more with the French than with the Indians, and not through the customhouse, either, you may be sure! At any rate, upon my soul, he seems to have a most extraordinary knowledge of their country and their cities for a young man who spends most of his time among the Indians, ma'am. Just at present, it would seem from his conversation he is engaged in the business of—ah—um—shall we say—um—ha, ha—yes, yes, yes, by all means let us say 'Indian trading'!"

And here he slapped the table and went off again into another immoderate fit of laughter, while the rest of us sat and looked at one another in blank astonishment, completely ignorant of the point of this latest joke. Though I was to learn later that by "Indian trading" he meant the procuring of Indian scalps for the bounty the Province offered on them. When he had recovered himself somewhat he wiped his lips with his napkin and went on.

"I daresay, ma'am, you'll think me a gossipy old woman, prying into affairs that are none of my own. But what I was about to say, ma'am, was that I believe this young man will be returning to his home in Starkstown within a day or so; and if you should wish it, ma'am, I believe I might prevail upon him to carry your message to your brother for you. As God's my life, I believe I might!"

"Indeed, sir," said my mother in some confusion, "but this is too kind of you. I hardly know what I should say."

He made a grandiloquent gesture and cut her short.

"Say no more, ma'am," he insisted. "It is always my greatest pleasure to serve beauty in distress." And here he made an elegant low bow. "The thing's as good as done. Upon my word, I'll search him out this very evening at his tavern. You may count upon it, ma'am. He will carry your letter for you or be answerable to me!"

During the afternoon my mother and my sisters and myself strolled out to see the sights of the town. We were properly impressed by the new town market, a modern brick structure of two storeys with a gallery running completely around it, and were pleased with the pleasant aspect of the town common. The most substantial houses of the town were built upon what was called Beacon Hill, and for all they were mostly of wood, many of these were pleasant-appearing and with a distinct air of prosperity and wealth. Here and there we saw a house of brick, and these, of course, we found more admirable since they were what we were used to at home. We were told by a passer-by who overheard our exclamations that almost all of these mansions were built of brick imported at enormous cost from England, the local brick being considered unfit for the purpose, though he added (somewhat sneeringly, I thought) that many houses in the York Province were built of it.

During this ramble I could not help but notice some differences between the dress of the young men of the town and my own, that which I wore being not only old and somewhat out of fashion, but also considerably younger than my years and my present station warranted. It was the fashion here, it seemed, for the younger boys to emulate their elder brothers in matters of dress, even to hanger and snuffbox; and I saw many a lad of thirteen in powdered periwig and buckramed waistcoat. If I were to appear my age, I decided, I must above all dress the part.

I pointed this out to my mother, and she agreed with me that it would be well to follow the fashion. Accordingly upon our return to the tavern I inquired of our host, Mr. Brackett, the name of a good tailor, and upon receipt of this information, promptly repaired thither where I ordered for myself four new coats, one of mulberry and another of pea-green velvet, the former to be trimmed in gold and the latter in silver lace, and the other two of a dark blue stuff, more modest for street wear, with large gold buttons. Besides these I ordered a half-dozen pairs of breeches, one each of green and mulberry velvet to match the coats, and the rest of white cloth; also a waistcoat of gold brocade and another of silver, and two more of blue satin trimmed in gold to wear with the street coats. I had already purchased stockings of white silk and a dozen or more ruffled shirts of excellent quality in Glasgow, and as the suits which I had but just then purchased were ready made up, to wear with a few small alterations, I was able to put on one of them then and there, leaving orders for the rest to be delivered at the tavern on the following day. This piece of business attended to, I went at once to a hatter's and there provided myself with a new hat tastefully trimmed in gold lace; and thus, resplendent, I reappeared at our apartments to bedazzle my mother and sisters and strut with all the airs I could command until suppertime.

It was after that meal was finished and we had withdrawn to our rooms, that Lawyer Drew waited upon my mother and said that he was about to go in search of Mr. Rogers at his tavern. He asked if I would care to accompany him and, perhaps, see that the letter was delivered to him that evening—which, he pointed out, would save my mother the trouble of an interview with him later. My mother did not at first greet this idea with the enthusiasm which I thought it deserved; but I remonstrated with her, on the ground that if I were to be the man of the family it was time I took up a man's pursuits: a theory with which our new-found friend agreed so heartily that at last she relented and gave her consent. Whereupon I ran to get my new hat and joined the gentleman below.

As we went out onto the street he surveyed me, I thought, not a little critically, and asked me where was my hanger. When I told him that I had never in my life owned a sword, much less worn one, he threw up his hands in surprise.

"God's my life, sir!" cried he. "Why, no young gentleman of fashion would be seen upon the streets without one here!"

Whereupon, in spite of my protests, he insisted upon taking me into a shop displaying the sign of the crown and razor, and buying me one then and there; and a very handsome one it was, too, with its silver hilt and its chased blade. I would have wished to pay him for it, but he would not hear of it, and pressed it upon me as a gift. As I did not wish to offend him I yielded as gracefully as I could, and buckled it about my waist with the remark that I should not know how to use it if it were necessary. He replied that that was a matter easily remedied, and promised to give me in the morning the name of a good master who would be able to teach me in a few lessons the rudimentary principles of the fence.

With this matter attended to we set out at once in search of Lawyer Drew's young friend. We had not gone far when it became apparent that our barrister was not at all certain as to just where to look for Mr. Rogers. He might be, it seemed, at this tavern or that, so that before long our search degenerated into a sort of round of the taprooms of the city. We visited the King's Head, the Hat, the Jolly Tar, the Key and Anchor, and the Good

Woman Tavern (which last bore as its sign the figure of a woman
without a head!), ending up finally at the Green Dragon in Corn
Court. At each of these places my elderly friend insisted that I
join him in a glass of punch, although I told him that I had never
before drunk anything stronger than beer in my life. He would
not take no for an answer. At first he scoffed and said that he had
never before encountered a Scotchman who would not drink, and
when I persisted he took offence and grew huffy, whereupon I
again thought it best to humour him and joined him in his
pleasure, though I insisted, at the beginning at any rate, that my
portions be made small.

In spite of my protests I was flattered that he should treat me
so much as his equal in years, and in consequence, as may well be
imagined, we were in a merry mood when at length we left the
Green Dragon and came to the sign of the Bunch of Grapes in
King Street which he told me was one of the most popular meeting places in town.

We had no sooner entered the taproom of this tavern than
Lawyer Drew let out a whoop and cried:

"Hi, Rob Rogers! I had begun to fear you had gone back
already to the tall pines and your Indian friends."

At the sound of his voice a young man who was seated at a table
in the corner with three others, evidently members of the Quebec
expedition, turned to look at us, then rose and came toward us.
I was startled by his appearance, for though to judge by his features he could not be many years my senior, he stood well over
six feet tall and at least three feet across the shoulders. He had an
enormously long and rather flat nose, a small petulant mouth, and
heavy eyebrows over eyes of a neutral shade. His face was heavily
tanned from the summer sun, but most remarkable of all was his
dress. He wore on his head a hat made of some close-growing,
smooth, brown fur, which I later came to recognize as that of a
beaver. His short jacket was of smooth pliable leather, fringed
with short lengths of the same material, as were also his breeches,
which reached, tight-fitting, all the way to his ankles, to disappear
inside a pair of supple leather slippers which appeared to be sole-
less. I came later to know this dress as that which was fairly conventional among woodsmen; but at the time it was exceeding
strange to me, and I must have stared at it somewhat rudely.

Lawyer Drew introduced me to this gentleman as the man for

whom we had been searching all evening. I acknowledged the introduction and held out my hand to him, but he did not take it at once.

"I am not sure, sir," said he, "whether this is a pleasure or not." And turning to the lawyer, he added: "God's blood, Mr. Drew, has your friend never seen a man before? What is it makes him stare so?"

I apologized in some confusion, whereupon he, rather grudgingly, shook hands and invited us to his table, where he presented us to the other three young men, who he told us were William Stark, of Londonderry, and Jeremy Sullivan and Stephen Sparhawk, both of Portsmouth.

These introductions accomplished, Rogers called for another bowl of punch, in which he pledged the King's health; after which Lawyer Drew proceeded to draw him into conversation. From this it appeared that Stark frequently joined Rogers on his trading expeditions, and the other two young men occasionally shared their adventures in this line. Hearing of the projected expedition to Quebec, Stark, Sparhawk, and Sullivan had hastened to join, in the hope of excitement and adventure. Rogers, however, preferred to remain alone in the woods, where he said he found a profitable business in hunting down hostile Indians, for whose scalps the government was at that time offering the sum of two hundred and fifty pounds each, new tenor. He told us, somewhat naïvely, I thought, that rather than jeopardize his relations with the Indians of his own province he had journeyed to the north and east along the borders of the Maine grants, among the bloodthirsty Amariscoggins, whence he had but lately returned with a round dozen of scalps on which he claimed the reward. Asked if he had collected his money, he admitted that he had been able only to take a part of it, but said that he had left the scalps as evidence and was confident of receiving his pay in full when next the assembly should convene.

Lawyer Drew then asked him if he intended to visit his home before returning to the woods, to which he answered in the affirmative. Thereupon the lawyer explained our case to him, and asked him if he would be so kind as to carry our letter. To this I must needs add my own voice, by which it will be seen that I had not yet any great experience of men.

"Aye, Mr. Rogers," said I, "and you need have no fear about

the pay, for I guarantee it will be sufficient to reward you for your trouble."

At this he looked at me rather dourly, and said:

"Look ye, Mr. Whatever-your-name-may-be, I am no postboy to be sent hither and yon with messages and billets-doux, by anyone who sees fit to hire me. If I may do a service for a man I like, I will do it gladly, and accept no pay for it. But if I do not like a man all the gold in the colonies cannot make me run his errands for him."

I was nettled, and I showed it. I was never one to keep silent when I felt myself affronted, and on this occasion no doubt the liquor which I had drunk did not make me less belligerent. Because I was angry I spoke in the broad Scotch which has ever been my habit in times of stress.

"Aye, Mr. Rogers," said I, "for I'll do ye the civility to remember your name. I'll no be hidin' my opinion o' ye and your trade, which is simply that ye're no better than a cutthroat—tradin' upon the blood o' your fellow humans. If it were I that was askin' ye there'd be nae matter o' bones about it a'. I'd carry yon message mysel' an' be dommed to ye. But 'tis for a lady I'm askin' it, my mother, sir; and for her sake if I've said aught tae offend ye I'll tak it back, whether I like it or no!"

The three young soldiers roared heartily at this, while Lawyer Drew looked highly alarmed. But Rogers, far from being offended, banged upon the table with his noggin and joined in the laughter.

"By the blood of Christ!" he bellowed. "Here's a young fire-eater. I'll take the message and gladly, sir, and here's my hand to it!"

And indeed he insisted upon my handing over the letter then and there; nor would he consider the least recompense for his trouble, which I afterwards discovered was not inconsiderable.

With everything so happily arranged, I perceived what was expected of me and called for another bowl of punch, whereupon Lawyer Drew proposed as a first toast my mother and her ever-lasting success in the new land. This was followed by toasts to the King, to the success of the coming expedition, to my sisters individually, to Lawyer Drew's daughter, and finally to the old New Hampshire Province, after which, about midnight, we took our departure, staggered out into the street, and—somewhat groggily, it is to be feared—made our way homeward and to bed.

When I arose the next morning my head felt as though my brains were being drawn slowly out through the top of my skull, and my mouth was as if stuffed with wool. My mother laughed shortly when I spoke of it, and said that if I expected to indulge in men's pleasures I must learn to accept the discomforts which they produced. She added that she supposed a few such experiences were necessary before I could be expected to learn moderation. I said that I could not in honour refuse a toast without offering an insult to the man who had proposed it, to which she replied that I learned rapidly and that it would be much better if men were less touchy upon what they considered their honour. By which I saw that she was none too pleased though she could not complain too strongly, for we had accomplished our object and despatched the letter. However, by noon she had recovered her usual good nature and thanked Lawyer Drew graciously for the service he had done us.

"Bless you, ma'am!" said that worthy gentleman pompously. "But 'twas a pleasure, indeed it was! You must believe it, ma'am! Indeed my greatest regret is that I shall not have more time to serve you. My business here is nearly finished, and I must return presently to Portsmouth."

My mother smiled.

"Indeed?" she said. "Perhaps we will see you there. It was in Portsmouth I asked my brother to meet us."

Lawyer Drew puffed and sputtered in evident surprise and pleasure.

"Do you say so?" he cried. "Upon my soul! Upon my soul! Life seems to be made up of coincidences these days. I believe you'll conceive a fondness for Portsmouth, ma'am. If I do say so myself it is far more attractive and every bit as lively as Boston, if it is not so large. When do you go, ma'am?"

My mother replied that she had not settled that point in her mind as yet, but that she intended to leave Boston as soon as she could find the best means of making the journey and make the necessary arrangements.

"Gadso, ma'am!" the little lawyer exclaimed in evident pleasure. "Why, then I can be of further service to you! You must permit me to make the arrangements. I should like nothing better, upon my word!"

When my mother protested that this was too great an imposition upon his good nature, he cut her short impatiently.

"Not another word, ma'am!" said he. "Not another word! I should have to make arrangements for myself and daughter—why should I not do the same for you? Indeed we can arrange to travel in company, which I assure you will prove a great economy for both of us."

He paused and hrumphed importantly behind his hand.

"You see, ma'am," he continued, "ordinarily the bulk of the travel between this city and Portsmouth is by sea; but just at present, owing to those infernal scoundrels of Frenchmen—saving your presence, ma'am,—whose privateers have been lurking off our coasts, and even venturing into the very mouths of our harbours, cautious persons have chosen to move by land, which puts up the price of coach hire—there is no regular stage, ma'am—and sometimes makes it difficult to procure the kind of conveyance desired. Upon my soul I can't see why Governor Shirley should exert himself so to go and attack the French in Canada when he might better put the money he wastes in such tomfoolery into protecting our own coasts from such scoundrely pirates! And as for our own Governor Wentworth in the Hampshire Province, why, everyone knows Benning Wentworth's nothing but Shirley's creature. As God's my life, ma'am, do you know 'tis even said that Governor Shirley has agreed to appoint Benning Wentworth as Governor of Louisbourg so that he may flee thither to escape his creditors when they grow too importunate—which I assure you will be soon, ma'am. My word, it will!"

He paused for breath, and my mother took advantage of the moment to say a word.

"Is there no regular conveyance between here and Portsmouth then?" she asked.

"Eh?" He started. "My most humble apologies, madam! I grow indignant whenever I think on it! You were saying? Oh, yes, about conveyances! Of course! of course! Upon my soul! No, there is no regular conveyance, unless you would call the line of freight carts such. They make the journey twice each week and sometimes carry passengers at a price." He stopped and chuckled, then added pompously: "But of course, ma'am, no person in our station would patronize such a carriage. No, indeed not! May I suggest, ma'am, that you send your baggage and servants by that route, while we follow in more comfort in a hackney coach, the expense of which we may share in proportion to the size of our several parties?"

He seemed so pathetically anxious and willing to serve us and took such evident pleasure in his ability to do so, that my mother had not the heart to deny him. Indeed his proposal seemed so fair to all concerned, at the same time having the great advantage of relieving us of the trouble of making our own arrangements, that it seemed wise to accept.

He expressed his pleasure at our acceptance with a low bow, and suggested that we take a coach of four places and a horse saddled a-pillion. He confessed himself to be no great shakes as a rider and proposed to join my mother in the coach, while the three girls took turns at riding the pillion behind me. This being agreed to, he took his departure with a profound obeisance to my mother, promising at the same time to make the necessary arrangements that very afternoon for us to leave in the following week.

On the following day we sent off Dougal and Anna together with the bulk of our baggage in the regular freight cart, with instructions to go directly to Mr. Stavers' tavern at the sign of the Earl of Halifax, which was recommended to us as the best in Portsmouth, and there take rooms and await our arrival. Thereafter we had little to do but see the sights of the town and wait until Mr. Drew should be free to join us in our journey. On Sunday we heard a sermon preached upon the common by the well known George Whitefield, who had come to Boston to give his blessing to the Canada expedition as he had the year before to the Louisbourg jaunt. It was a powerful sermon, and was attended by a crowd of some three or four thousand persons; but I confess I had not much interest in it, having been out the previous evening with my friends Stark and Sparhawk, who had heard rumours that the expedition would probably be postponed for that year because of the nonarrival of the fleet from England and hence must find solace for their sorrows in the flowing bowl.

Much of my time during that week was spent at the rooms of one Mr. Brooks; for Lawyer Drew had remembered his promise to send me to someone who could instruct me in the principles of swordsmanship, and, true to his word, had introduced me to that gentleman. Mr. Brooks, it seemed, had at one time been a captain in His Majesty's forces; but, having gotten into some difficulties over cards, he had withdrawn from his regiment under a cloud and retired to Boston, where he made a precarious living by imparting his skill with the foils to the young of that city.

I was not entirely ignorant of the proper use of the short-sword, as my father had on some various occasions undertaken to give me some instruction in it. Hence I was able to make some fair degree of progress in my instructor's eyes as well as pick up the first principles of the more refined art of the fence, which, though I anticipated no immediate situation in which I should need it, still I felt it might be useful to know. Consequently, during the week that we stayed there, I went every afternoon to Mr. Brooks', sometimes staying until well after dark perfecting by practice some fine point of technique.

Wednesday noon our friend Lawyer Drew met us at the table with a lugubrious countenance. From his appearance I expected to hear at least that he would be unable to accompany us upon the journey. In this, however, I was mistaken, for it seemed that the cause of his disquietude was simply that his daughter, who he had hoped would be able to join us at that time, had sent word that, owing to a tea party which her young friends were giving in the afternoon, she would be unable to come to him before evening. In consequence of this, to his great distress, we should not have the pleasure of making her acquaintance before the hour of our setting out in the morning. It was evident that he had set his heart upon this meeting, and so was greatly disappointed. My mother soothed his ruffled feelings as best she could by saying that Mistress Dorcas (for that was the young lady's name) must do as her hosts wished so long as she remained their guest, and that we should all have ample time to know one another on the journey, which, it seemed, must occupy two full days. For my part, I must confess, it did not seem a matter of great importance, since, man though I considered myself already, I had not developed any great interest in petticoats.

I went that afternoon, as usual, to Mr. Brooks', and since it was the last instruction I should receive at his hands I stayed even later than was my wont, gaining a few last pointers in the art of cut and thrust. As a result I was obliged to make my way homeward in the darkness from his house, which stood, somewhat isolated, on the shores of the Back Bay, on the neck of land which separates the town of Boston from that district known as Roxbury.

As was my custom I made my way to the long street which skirts the Common, and turned up it toward the centre of town, striding along briskly with my hand upon the hilt of my hanger, feeling very warlike as a result of my lessons, and half hoping for an opportunity to put in practice the intricate strokes and manœuvres which I had just learned. Halfway past the Common stood a small tavern known as the Crown and Bees, which was a favourite roistering place among the soldiery of the expedition, some numbers of whom were encamped not far off. At all hours of the day or night a group of half-tipsy volunteers would be found sitting upon the bench outside the tavern door smoking and drinking and arguing and frightening innocent passers-by with their horrible oaths.

Now as I came in sight of the place I could see, by the lanthorn that hung outside, that on this particular evening there were but three roisterers at the door, though these seemed more than usually drunk. Save for these three and myself the street seemed deserted, a fact which I did not notice particularly, since this was a lonely section of the town, until two other figures appeared from a street which came in at an angle from the left to join the Common road at a point almost opposite the tavern door. The appearance of these figures put a new colour to the picture, for one was that of a young woman, wrapped and hooded in a voluminous cloak, while the other was that of a lackey who lighted her way with a lanthorn.

At the sight of the three bullies by the tavern door the woman hesitated and looked around; but, as I was still some fifty yards down the street in complete darkness, it was evident that she did not see me. Nor could I see her face, for though she stood between me and the tavern light the distance was too great for me to make out her features in the shadow of her hood. After a moment's pause she evidently made up her mind that there was nothing for her to do but put on a bold front, and thereupon she straightened a little, threw up her head, and at a fast walk continued her way past the tavern door.

As she came abreast of them one of the volunteers, a great burly fellow in a ragged jacket, lurched to his feet and barred her way.

" 'Od's blood, Jonas," he hiccuped, "here's an answer to thy prayers, man! As fine a wench as ever lay abed! Come, lass, give us a kiss!"

He reached out his arm to grasp her by the shoulder, but she eluded him swiftly and with her open palm dealt him such a blow in the face as sent him staggering back against the tavern wall. In the next instant she was flying up the street as fast as her feet would carry her.

The man's two companions cackled alcoholically and slapped each other's backs.

"Ooh, Lige!" howled the one who was evidently known as Jonas. "Thee picked a tartar that time, mun!"

But Lige was not so easily to be put off. The slap had evidently roused him to an angry pitch.

"By God's wounds," he swore, "no wench can treat Lige Hawkins so! I'll show the bitch her place."

And with that he started after her, his two companions stumbling along behind him, whooping and laughing in drunken joy, anxious to see the fun to follow.

The whole thing had happened so swiftly that I had not had time to move from the spot to which I stood rooted. I have said that I had not as yet developed an interest in petticoats, and indeed that was true enough. But my father had taught me that no true man would ever stand by to see a woman wronged, however unfortunate her station, and this, it seemed to me, was just such a situation as he had described. At the first sign of trouble the lackey had turned and taken to his heels in cowardly fashion, and if I did not interfere the woman, whoever she might be, must fend for herself. Moreover, was I not an accomplished swordsman? And was this not a perfect opportunity to display my prowess? I hesitated not one second longer, but set out after them as quick as I could gallop, tugging at my hanger all the way.

When I came up with them the young woman was struggling in her tormenter's arms, while his two companions were capering about them in drunken glee. Without a moment's hesitation, and with a recklessness which I would probably not have exhibited in later years, I flung myself upon them, making a swift though ineffectual pass at Jonas with the flat of my sword and following it up with a vicious jab at the tight seat of Lige's breeches, at the same time crying out with all the force of my lungs:

"Leave be, ye dog! Leave be, or by the blood of Christ I'll slit your gullet to gie ye a taste o' your ain blood!"

At the prick of my sword upon his rump Lige released the girl with a howl of surprise, and turned upon me with an oath in which I thought I detected fear mingled with rage. But when he saw himself confronted by one he evidently considered a mere stripling he howled with laughter and reaching out caught the young lady by the wrist.

"Oho, ho ho!" he bellowed. "Run along, sonny, lad, run along home and play. Leave a man's business for men to do!"

And with that he burst again into laughter. But I stood fast and faced him resolutely.

"Nay!" I said firmly. "I'll no be going until ye turn the lady loose!"

At which he cursed me foully for a meddling brat and made as if to strike me with his free hand.

Seeing that there was nothing else for it, I made a lunge at him and pinked him in the throat with the point of my hanger, whereat he clapped both hands to the wound and fell to the ground howling bloody murder, evidently believing that he had received his death wound. At that both of his companions, who had stood watching in drunken stupidity, turned and took to their heels, crying that murder had been done, and calling for the watch. Emboldened by this easy victory I strode over to the fellow Lige, who still lay grovelling in the dust, and kicked him soundly, bidding him get up and be off before I slit his throat for fair. He, finding himself still able to feel the sting of a boot, made up his mind that he was not yet dead; but, fearing that he might be if he stayed longer, he ceased his howling and, gathering his feet under him, made off after his companions as fast as his legs would carry him. And with that I turned to the young woman whom I had rescued so spectacularly and, making what I meant to be an elegant leg, said that I hoped she had not been harmed.

Now, it has been said, and with some truth, that we spend many an hour secretly anticipating a situation in which, when it comes to us, we behave in a manner exactly opposite to the way in which we had thought we would. Here, surely, was such a situation. Most boys and, I think, all little girls, dream of just such an occurrence with themselves in the role of rescued or rescuer. They rehearse the pretty speeches they will make to one another, and how they will vow eternal love and live happily ever after. Yet here I was in just such a position. I, by the help of my trusty blade, had put a foul fiend to flight.. I had rescued a lovely maiden in distress, for her hood had fallen back and there could be no doubt, under the soft light of the pale moon, that she was lovely beyond description. Yet there I stood awkwardly, first on one foot and then on the other, as self-conscious as any bumpkin, knowing neither what to say nor what to do.

Nor was she in a better case. She was a dark-haired girl of about my own age, with great dark eyes and delicate colouring, heightened now by the blushes that suffused her face and neck. She knew no more than I what to say in such a moment, but her eyes sparkled and her lips smiled and her breast heaved with excitement, so that my heart swelled within me and I knew that I could never again say that I had no interest in petticoats! But presently her eyes dropped before my gaze, and I, because I was embarrassed and because I had always despised girls and found I could not despise this one too, kicked at a stick that lay in the pathway beneath my feet and turned rudely away to wipe the tip of my sword upon the grass.

Now whether it was my movement that broke the spell, or whether she had already made up her mind to speak, I know not. But this I know, that when I turned away she came after me and touched my sleeve.

"I must thank you," she said, and her voice was sweet, "for what you did. It was brave of you to stand against all those men for the sake of a girl you did not know. They might have done you some harm."

At this I was even more embarrassed, and moreover I was torn by conflicting emotions which I knew not how to define. I sheathed my hanger and replied somewhat rudely that it was nothing, and that girls were helpless creatures, and that it was often the task of men to see that they did not come to harm. She tossed her head at that and seemed about to make some reply, but evidently changed her mind, for she dropped me a curtsy, saying that she thanked me anyway, and thereupon turned on her heel and walked away.

This behaviour on her part filled me with unaccountable dismay, and I ran after her, calling out to her to wait; at which she stopped and waited for me to come up with her and then asked, with a disarming smile, "Why?"

"Why?" I said, more flustered than ever. "Why—because if those toughs come back again they may give you some trouble."

"And you want to be near to prove me helpless again?" she added.

Her tone piqued me and I grew haughty.

"Madam—" I began.

But she came close to me and laid her hand gently upon my arm.

"Forgive me," she said. "You know I am grateful."

And at the look that she gave me I found myself sunk again in the deepest confusion, so that I knew not what to answer beyond mumbling that I was happy to be able to serve her; and presently—I know not how it happened—I found myself walking toward the town with her hanging closely upon my arm.

We walked for the most part in silence, since I knew not what to say to her but went along tongue-tied, furtively studying her profile by the light of the moon, so that before we had reached the end of the Common I had come to the conclusion that most girls were ugly but that this one was the lone exception, and that she was beautiful beyond words. As each step brought us nearer to the end of our walk I finally screwed up enough courage to ask her where she was going, and if I might have the privilege of escorting her thither, since her former escort had left her so precipitately. To which she replied that she was going to the O. Cromwell's Head, where she was to meet her father and would be glad of my protection thus far.

This intelligence so surprised me that I could think of nothing more to say; nor was I able even then to make a guess as to her identity, so that we came in silence to the inn, where I held the door for her and followed her within.

Lawyer Drew was standing by the great fireplace talking to two other gentlemen when we entered, but upon our appearance he turned with an exclamation and came toward us. My young companion, at the sight of him, ran to him and threw her arms about his neck. He kissed her fondly, and then held her at arms' length.

"My dear," he said, "'tis late for you to be upon the streets, upon my soul! I hope you were not unaccompanied?"

"Oh, Daddy!" she said breathlessly. "I would have come earlier but Mr. Boylston had to use the chair, and they could not find Robert, and when Edwin came in he was tipsy and had to be sent to bed. So I just made up my mind I would come alone then and did, with but a lackey to light the way."

"Gadso!" the lawyer exclaimed pompously, "I never heard of such a thing. Why, why, why—"

But she shut him off before he could continue.

"And, Daddy," she went on excitedly, "some toughs tried to make up to me on the common, and this young gentleman came along and drove them away with his sword! Wasn't it lucky, Daddy, that he happened along just at that time?"

Now for the first time Lawyer Drew saw me standing in the background, my jaw hanging down in sheer surprise.

"Upon my soul!" he exclaimed in evident amazement. And then he began to laugh. "You young dog!" he said, digging me playfully in the ribs. "So you've stolen a march on me, have you? Upon my soul, it was a good thing I bought that hanger for you! As God's my life it was, now, wasn't it?"

He saw then by his daughter's expression that it was all a surprise to her too.

"What?" he demanded. "D'ye mean to say you two young people have not told each other who you are? 'Od's death! Why, this is the best joke I've seen in years—upon my soul it is! Come, come, we must remedy that, 'Od's my life! Jamie, this is my daughter Dorcas. Dorcas, James Ferguson, the young man who rides with us tomorrow for Portsmouth!"

2

We were up early the next morning and ready for the road; but early as we were we found Lawyer Drew before us, and the coach and saddle nag which he had ordered for us, ready at the door. I was conscious of a sinking sensation at the absence of the fair mistress Dorcas, and for a moment I found myself wondering if it had been decided that she would not accompany us: a thought which for some reason plunged me in the blackest gloom.

I was presently relieved, however, and it seemed as though the sun were breaking through the clouds, when she appeared at the breakfast table, dressed in a riding costume of some heavy grey stuff, which in spite of its bulk and ruffles could not conceal the trim lines of her tiny figure. By the light of day, I thought she was even lovelier than she had been by moonlight, for now I could appreciate her daintiness and see the true perfection of her colour.

She acknowledged her introduction to my mother and my two sisters with a pretty curtsy, and gave me her hand with a gentle pressure of the fingers and a little smile of greeting, which seemed to me to convey a world of tenderness. I saw then that her eyes were of the deepest blue—rather like the blue of the sea, I thought at first, and then at once rejected the idea as silly, for that was but a poor dull colour by the side of this. I clung to her hand for some seconds, ecstatically returning her gaze, my mind lifted up to the heavens in sheer bliss, until all at once I heard my younger sister titter slightly, whereat I released her fingers and looked away in some confusion to see both Alice and my elder sister Edith, and indeed even my mother, regarding me with sly expressions of amusement which brought the blood rushing to my face and plunged me in the deepest mortification.

I had dared to hope that I might have the fair Dorcas as a passenger upon the pillion; but with breakfast over, it soon appeared that I was doomed to disappointment. My sisters had evidently been putting their heads together, and had made up their minds to torment me, for no sooner was the question of places mentioned than they both insisted that Dorcas accept their comfortable seat in the coach, while they took turns at the pillion. Since Dorcas quite evidently could not ignore such courtesy, it fell out that I rode first with Alice, as far as Medford, where we stopped at the Fountain Inn for small beer and refreshment, and then with Edith until noon. Nor could I at the time have told aught of the way we went (which was through Charlestown, and Cambridge to Medford and thence to Danvers), of the road we travelled (which was excellent), or of the country through which we passed (which was lovely). So occupied was I with my new-found love, and so enraged was I at my sisters for plaguing me about it, that I saw nothing, heard nothing, and said nothing until the noon halt, when Edith and Alice, wearying of their game, changed their tactics and grew sweet and considerate.

We stopped at midday at a tavern not far outside the town of Danvers—about halfway as I understood it to Ipswich—where we were to spend the night. I was determined to give my sisters no opportunity to repeat their tactics of the morning; and with that in mind, as soon as we were ready to resume our journey, I spoke up bravely and suggested that Miss Dorcas might be pleased to accept the pillion and ride with me; which to my great delight she agreed upon readily. A few moments later we set out upon the road without so much as waiting for the others to embark in the coach.

Now indeed the sun shone brightly and the day was fine. The birds sang sweetly in the trees, and I remarked upon the beauty of the countryside, which grew wilder as we continued upon our way; upon the different kinds of trees, many of which were strange to me; and upon the excellence of the road, which was as fine as ever. But even now all was not as I had hoped it would be, for while before I had ridden silent in anger, appeasing my chagrin with thoughts of all the pretty things I would say to my fair companion when the opportunity came, now that I had that chance I could think of none of those things, and I still rode silent, as tongue-tied with pleased embarrassment as any bumpkin in the presence of his maid.

Nor did she prompt me. Instead she rather heightened my confusion by ignoring the grip, provided upon the pillion, and steadied herself in her seat by slipping her arm about my waist.

We rode thus in silence, broken only by an occasional dropped remark, for more than an hour and a half. And as I did not now hold in my nag we were far ahead of the lumbering coach, which must of necessity move slowly, when all at once she straightened abruptly and removed her arm from about my waist.

We were riding then into a little hollow, down the centre of which flowed a tiny stream flanked on either hand by lush meadows and shaded at intervals by tall drooping elms. Not a soul was in sight, and her move startled me, for I could see no reason for it.

"Why did you do that?" I asked.

She did not reply at once, but after a moment's hesitation slipped her arm back again around my waist and, laying her head close against the back of my shoulder, so that I could feel her breath gently upon my neck in a way that sent a little thrill of pleasure chasing down my spine, said, "I was afraid you were angry with me, you did not speak for so long."

"Angry!" I exclaimed with a laugh. "Indeed, how could I be angry with you?"

"But you were so stiff and silent," she said.

Now that the spell was broken I found my tongue suddenly turned loose and wagging at both its ends.

"I was angry with myself," I replied, "for that I am so stupid. This morning I thought of things I would say to you when I could, but now I can't seem to remember them."

I stopped, embarrassed.

"What kind of things?" she asked, sweetly prodding.

"Oh, la, all kinds of things!" I replied, confused, and then went on quickly. "I was angry with my sisters too for the way they acted this morning. They knew I wanted to ride with you, and they did it out of spite and to tease me."

"But you mustn't be angry with them!" she exclaimed. "I don't think they meant any such thing! I think they are both sweet and nice—and so fond of you!"

I said that only she would say such things; that other girls were not as nice as she in such respects. All the girls I ever knew, I told her, made mean remarks about one another behind their backs.

"Oh, hush, now!" she said. "You're just trying to be sweet and flatter me!"

"I am not!" I protested vehemently. "I mean it: every word! And besides I was angry with them. I did want to ride with you."

And to this she replied in the same low, caressing tone, "And I wanted to ride with you, too, Jamie!"

At that moment we were riding across the rough wooden bridge spanning the little brook that ran down through the meadows. She finished speaking as the horse stepped from the rumbling planks, and no sooner had she done so than the nag, suddenly and without the least warning, doubled in the middle, went across the roadway in a tremendous leap, lashing out viciously with his heels, so that I was nearly unseated. I heard Dorcas give a little scream, felt her arm slip from about my waist, and the nag danced sideways up the road a few steps. As the beast felt himself lightened of her weight upon the pillion, he stopped as unaccountably as he had begun and stood docile while I flung myself from the saddle.

Dorcas was lying in a crumpled heap in the roadway. I dropped the reins in the dust, and running to her knelt by her side and raised her head in my arms. Her eyes were closed, and her face was very still. For a moment I could not tell if she was breathing, and I was suddenly in a panic lest she were badly injured and dying—or perhaps even dead already.

I said, "Dorcas! Dorcas, are you hurt?" But she showed no sign of having heard me. I looked about me wildly. Here was an emergency I had never thought to foresee, and I had no idea what to do. I listened, hoping desperately that the coach was nearer than I had at first thought; that someone would happen along to tell me what should be done. But the only sounds that broke the summer stillness were the chuckling ripple of the little brook as it boiled across the stones of its bed, and the buzz of locusts in the near-by field.

Close by the roadway, on the bank of the stream, stood a great elm. In its shade the grass looked soft and cool and green, a far safer and more comfortable place to lie than the hard, dusty road-way. If I laid her there first, I thought, then I might be able to think what to do next. I had some vague idea of getting water from the stream to bathe her face and wrists, but it seemed to me the first thing to be done was to move her from the highway.

Ordinarily this would have presented something of a problem, for though she was not large—indeed I rather think she was some-what smaller and more finely made than average—neither was I; and I firmly believe there was not a stone's difference in our weights. It is strange, however, what hidden springs of strength desperation can discover in us. I slid my right arm beneath her shoulders and my left under the crook of her knees and struggled to my feet. This in itself would have been difficult enough, as you who have tried to raise the limp, dead weight of an unconscious person in your arms will understand, even though that person may have been somewhat lighter than yourselves. But there was an added factor of embarrassment which almost brought us to disaster.

When I had knelt beside her in the road, she had lain on her left side, facing me, so that I could not see that in her fall the skirt of her costume had been caught up well above the knee. So it was that when I slipped my left arm underneath her knees it went, all without my knowledge, beneath her skirt; and when I closed my hand against her thigh, as was necessary to lift her, instead of meeting the coarse grey stuff of her habit, what was my confusion to find my sweating palm resting against soft, bare skin, warm with life and smooth as satin, in the midst of dainty under-things!

The shock and surprise of this was such that I very nearly let her fall again; and had I not been certain that she was entirely unconscious I could almost have sworn that I felt her stir slightly beneath my touch. I could feel the blood mounting to my face, and in spite of my surprise I was conscious of a thrill of pleasure and excitement, so that my breath came quickly even before I started to carry her toward the roadside.

This I accomplished very clumsily, as may be imagined, twice stumbling over sticks that lay in the way, and once very nearly upsetting us both into the brook when I stepped upon her long skirts which dragged about my feet. Despite that, however, I was distinctly sensible of reluctance when I came to the shelter of the great elm and I had no longer any excuse for holding her in my arms. I set her down somewhat unwillingly upon the soft green-sward, and wondered what I should do next. I did not want to leave her, even to go to the brook, a distance of some ten feet. I had a dim recollection of hearing somewhere that when a lady fainted the proper procedure was to loosen her bodice; but this I could not have brought myself to do, even had I known how, for some-how there seemed something profane in the very thought. The fact that my hand had touched the soft, warm flesh of her thigh was accidental, no matter how deliciously pleasant it had been, and therefore not to be thought of in the same light. But the idea of my making even the first motions of disrobing her person, no matter how unimportant, was to me utterly impossible. And so, quite instinctively, and because I could think of nothing better, I kissed her; first upon the forehead, then her cheek, and then upon her lips, at the same time saying her name over and over as if the very sound of my voice would bring her back to life.

Imagine my astonishment, then, when at the touch of my lips to hers her eyelids fluttered, and I found myself gazing into the liquid depths of her great blue eyes!

I started back, blushing furiously. But her arms, soft and white, slid about my neck and clung there, so that, though I struggled against them for an instant, I could not tear myself away. Then all at once a feeling of recklessness surged from the very centre of my being. I felt suddenly weak as water. The delicious scent of her rose in my nostrils, and made me pleasantly giddy. I flung all sense of caution to the winds and strained her to me, showering her face, her neck, her lips with kisses which I could not control.

For a moment she returned my passion, clinging to me ardently. Then presently her grip upon my neck relaxed, and she lay back limply in my arms regarding me with a provocative smile.

"Ah, Jamie," she sighed, "but you do kiss magnificently!"

I leapt to my feet, my face hot and flaming.

"Dorcas!" I cried. "Miss Drew—forgive me! I—"

She cut me short with a little trill of laughter.

"Why, Jamie!" she said, reproachfully. "I am not angry!"

And at that I was on my knees beside her again, clutching both her hands in mine.

"You're wonderful!" I said breathlessly.

She sat up then and laid a finger upon my lips.

"Hush!" she said. "Silly!" And fell to straightening her dishevelment, covering an ankle which, all undiscovered by me, had lain clearly exposed. I remembered myself suddenly.

"Are you all right?" I asked her.

She felt herself gingerly and nodded.

"I think so," she replied. "Oh, Jamie, why did you clap your spurs to the beast so suddenly?"

"I?" I said, startled. "I never! I swear to you I never touched him!"

She leaned over, laying her hand upon my shoulder, and brushed her lips to mine.

"Sweet!" she murmured. "Forgive me for believing it. It must have been some insect that stung him."

Her words reminded me of the nag, and I looked around for him wildly. It was as well I did, for the beast, relieved of our weight and given his head to do as he pleased, had wandered off down the road in search of a succulent blade of grass. With a word of apology I leaped to my feet and dashed off in pursuit of him. He did not relish the idea of being taken again; but after a moment of dodging about I managed to catch him by the reins, after which he came along, docilely enough, to the bridge rail where I tied him.

I noticed then, just behind the pillion upon his rump, an infinitesimal spot of blood, and called out this discovery to Dorcas where she sat beneath the tree. For a moment I almost thought she looked surprised; then she smiled and replied:

"It must have been a deerfly. They do bite mightily and often draw blood."

That was a fact to which I was later able to testify; but at the moment I had but a slight interest in it. I returned to her side, and dropping to my knees held out my arms to her; but now she would not come into them. Instead she stroked my cheek gently with her fingertips.

"Jamie," she said, "I've lost my brooch that I wore here." She laid her hand upon her breast. "I think it must have come unfastened when I fell. Will you find it for me?"

Eager to do anything that might please her, I ran at once to the road, and after a short search found the pin lying open at almost the very spot where she had lain. I brought it to her, and she jumped to her feet and thanked me sweetly while she replaced it in her bodice. The pin had belonged to her mother, she told me, and she would not want to lose it. With that she kissed me quickly once again and danced lightly, with me at her heels like a devoted puppy, to where the horse stood tied.

"We must ride on," she said, "before the others come."

Indeed at that very moment the rumble of wheels upon the hillside above warned us that the coach was approaching.

I swung up into the saddle and gave her a hand to the pillion and, after making sure that this time she had a good grip of my waist with both her arms, clapped the spurs to the nag and galloped away.

3

I have never ceased to wonder at the amazing effect which so frequently results from the mere acquaintance of a man with a woman. To me, at any rate, in this particular instance, it was nothing short of incomprehensible. In one moment I was a normal, healthy lad, with a lively interest in all that went on around me. No one ever had occasion to doubt my sanity. In the next, and all because a pretty wench had smiled on me and kissed me, I was as daft as a moonstruck calf. I became inattentive, so that people had to speak to me twice or even three times before I realized I was being addressed. I grew absent-minded and forgetful. I no longer took notice of my surroundings, but sat for hours in a sort of daze, dreaming of my beloved, and laying fantastic plans for our future.

Consequently if I saw but little of Portsmouth at that time it is not to be wondered at. When I walked abroad in its pleasant, tree-lined avenues, past substantial dignified homes, I may have looked at them but I did not see them. If Governor Wentworth came riding by in his magnificent chariot, complete with liveried coach-man and outriders, I did not bow respectfully and raise my hat, as did others, but merely stared rudely though blindly, my mind a thousand miles away. If I met any of the town's worthy citizens—the Sparhawks, the Langdons, the Atkinsons, the Odiornes, the Jaffreys, the Warners, the Meserves—indeed, if I met anyone, I did not remember it two minutes after the introduction.

It was not until I came to Portsmouth to live, many years later, that I really saw the place. Not until then could I appreciate the beauty of its setting, with the wooded, rolling hills all around it dotted with snug farmsteads, and the deep sparkling Piscataqua widening below it to form the harbour, teeming with maritime life. Then I came to know its busy shipyards and hear the in-cessant pounding of the shipbuilders' hammers; then I could see the gaiety of its social life—a life which in the grace and fulsome-ness of its manners in its own way, due no doubt to the miniature court with which Benning Wentworth has surrounded his office of Governor and Surveyor General of His Majesty's Woods, sur-passes even that of Boston.

But at that point, on that, my first visit to our provincial me-tropolis, I was suffering all the sweet and violent pangs of ado-lescent love; even to loss of appetite, a thing which never happened to me before or since, for I have always been noted as an able trencherman. The consequence was that I stored away but a few memories of what I saw.

In spite of all this I did not see as much of my beloved Dorcas as I should have liked. During the three days that we waited in Portsmouth for word from my uncle, I found it suddenly became difficult to get in touch with her. On the day following our ar-rival, I restrained myself as long as seemed proper and then went at once from the tavern at which we lodged to her house, where I bade the glum-faced waiting woman who met me at the door carry my name to her mistress. What was my disappointment and chagrin to find that she was already gone out, and was not expected back before late that afternoon. Not one whit rebuffed, I scribbled my name in my notebook, together with a note to the effect that

I would call again that evening, and, tearing out the leaf, folded and addressed it and handed it to the servant with dire warnings and admonishments not to forget to deliver it at once as soon as my fair lady came in.

When I repaired thither again in the dark of the evening, I was utterly dashed to discover that she had again gone out, this time to attend a ball which was being given by the Warners in honour of their daughter's birthday. And, what was the worst blow of all, she had not even left me a note of condolence and explanation; not a single word to excuse her extraordinary cruelty!

Naturally I was furious. I accused the servant of failing to deliver my message, but this she denied stoutly. It was then that I learned the name of my rival; and if ever I hated a man from the moment I heard his name it was this same George Stapleton. Yet I was later to discover that he was not so black as my imagination had painted him. Indeed in time he was to prove a true friend.

Since there was nothing else to do I returned to the tavern, where I consoled myself with a solitary bowl of punch, and presently retired to bed where I tossed restlessly the night through, plunged in the deepest gloom.

On the next afternoon I was reluctant to submit myself to the same humiliation, and in consequence I wasted much of it in the taproom, unable to make up my mind to go. When at last I could stand it no longer and flung out of doors with the determination to seek her out and fling myself at her feet, one of the first sights to meet my eyes was Dorcas, resplendent in a gown of blue silk with a cloak to match, seated in a passing chaise at the side of one of the most bepowdered and belaced young prigs it has ever been my misfortune to behold.

On this occasion she either did not see me or did not recognize me, for when I swept off my hat ironically and made a low, derisive bow, she rode by without the least change of expression. To say that I was enraged at such treatment would be to put it mildly. I swore then and there that it would be many a day before I would put myself out for her again, and went back bitterly to nurse my grudge in the taproom.

That evening, however, when Lawyer Drew, who had been most assiduous in his attentions, came to pay his respects to my mother, he drew me aside and chided me gently for that I had not come to call. His sweet child, he said, was hurt that I had not appeared to see her, and anxious lest for some reason I was angry with her. To this I replied somewhat cynically that it was she who appeared to be angry with me to judge from her behaviour, and went on to describe all that had taken place since our arrival. But he only laughed at me for my fears.

"Look ye, Jamie," said he. "Upon my soul, you must not blame the girl if she but keeps an appointment to a ball she made long before ever she met you, as God's my life! Indeed, you may not! By your own confession, my lad, 'twas past midafternoon when you started off to see her yesterday. 'Od's blood and wounds! It's not to be wondered at, then, that she gave you up at last and took the air with young Stapleton. Igod, my dear young sir! you must not forget, 'Faint heart' and so forth." Here he dug me in the ribs and tipped me a prodigious wink. "She has a fondness for you, Jamie, upon my soul. And if she is my daughter, God bless me, and I shouldn't say it, there an't many to compare with her."

Overjoyed by his reassurance I begged him to bear my compliments to Mistress Dorcas and inform her that I would wait upon her the following afternoon with a chaise of my own hiring, and hoped that she would honour me with her presence for a drive. At that he laughed heartily and clapped me on the back, promising to do as I asked, whereupon I called for a bowl and we pledged the ladies' healths in punch.

As soon after noon, therefore, as propriety would admit I appeared the next day at my beloved's door dressed in my best mulberry coat and breeches, and was delighted to find her awaiting me eagerly. As I whirled our carriage away proudly through the town I accused her of cruelty in her treatment of me. But this she denied, arguing with such sweetness that I readily forgave her, especially when she sat close against me, squeezing my arm in both her hands and looking up at me out of her great blue eyes pleadingly.

It was a still hot day, and at her suggestion I had turned our nag's head out along the river road, with the hope that among the hills above the town we might find such breeze as might be blowing. But no breath of wind came to stir away the heavy air. Dust rose from our beast's hooves. In a field beside the road the locusts buzzed monotonously. Down by the river somewhere a white-throated sparrow whistled the call that I later came to know as the loneliest sound of the woods. "Oh, Sam, Sam, Peabody, Pea-body, Peabody, Peabody!" We knew then that we were at last alone.

We came after a time to an open wood of tall pines, set on the hillside sloping down to the blue water of the river beneath, and here we got down and tied the horse to a sapling and sat, side by side, upon the soft pine needles under the tree where we talked the soft foolishness of love and laid plans for the future without a thought for circumstances. When at last we arose happily yet reluctantly and brushed each other off and strolled with arms entwined about each other's waist to the chaise it was approaching twilight, and the sun had dropped behind the hill on which we stood.

I left Dorcas at her door with a promise to return again on the next day, and perhaps even sooner. But in that I was anticipating.

I returned horse and chaise to the stables from which I had hired them, and thereafter, with a lightened heart and a song on my lips, made my way to the tavern, where I bounded lightly up the narrow stairs and burst cheerfully into our apartment. But once over the threshold and into the room I came to an abrupt stop and looked about the room in surprise.

It was evident that I had arrived at a crucial moment. My mother was there, of course, as were my two sisters. And over by the window, looking glumly out into the street, his ruddy face, usually so cheerful, now as long and solemn and sour as ever a face could be, stood Lawyer Drew. But it was another occupant of the room, that caught and held my eye. This was a man standing with his feet spread wide, his back to the black hole of the fireplace in which no coals now glowed. He was a thick-set man, just above middle height, and was, I judged, in his late fifties. He was dressed in a sober blue coat with pewter buttons and breeches of the same soft yellow leather, somewhat resembling doeskin, that the woodsman Rogers had worn. In this case, however, they were the conventional knee length, and the rest of his leg was encased in white thread stockings, while on his feet he wore solid, heavy shoes, much like our Highland brogues, with great solid silver buckles. His face was ruddy, and heavily weathered, and as I stood there in the doorway he looked at me appraisingly with a pair of steady cold grey eyes set beneath shaggy brows. Even before my mother spoke I knew that this could be no other than her brother, my uncle, David Ross.

"So," he said, when the introductions had been made, "this is Jamie!"

And he looked me up and down so critically that I suddenly became acutely aware of my own foppish splendour which was in sharp contrast with his own rugged plainness. I could feel the hot blood mounting to my face.

"Ye're a bit of a dandy, aren't ye, lad?" he said.

I felt impelled to defend myself.

"'Tis naught but what the boys in Boston are wearing," I said sulkily.

He eyed me shrewdly.

"Aye?" he growled. "The lads in Boston? The fops in Boston, I'd say."

He must have seen my feelings were hurt then, for he brightened up and clapped me on the shoulder and laughed.

"Never ye mind, lad," he said, "we'll get ye some honest rags in Exeter. Ye'll have scant use for these in Suncook."

He turned to my mother.

"It's settled then," he said. "Ye'll be ready in the morning?"

I was aghast.

"In the morning?" I echoed, breaking in upon them. "You don't mean we must leave tomorrow?"

My uncle turned and eyed me with evident disapproval.

"Aye," he said, "that's what I mean."

I looked at my mother miserably. If this were true I saw all the fine plans and dreams that Dorcas and I had laid out that afternoon crumbling in ruins about my ears. She must have guessed something of what was going on in my mind, for she came to my side and put her arm about my shoulders.

"Uncle David came down," she said, "to try and persuade us that we must not go to Suncook. He says there is constant danger there of an attack by the red savages, but I would not listen. By his own admission it is in those frontier settlements that a family such as ours, a family seeking a chance to begin again, will have its greatest opportunity for success. I insisted, and he finally agreed. So, Jamie, you must blame me if we must leave."

I made one last desperate effort. I had expected that sooner or later we must leave, but this seemed cruelly sudden and unnecessary.

"But tomorrow!" I protested. "Why tomorrow?"

My uncle swung on me with a grim smile.

"Tomorrow, my lad," said he, "because tomorrow a militia company sets out from Exeter for Pennycook, and in these times travellers on the road are grateful for the company of the military!"

I saw at once that it would do no good to argue. Indeed I was conscious of a thrill of anticipation at the prospect of this final move. But at the same time I was plunged in the deepest gloom at the thought of leaving Dorcas.

I lost no time in carrying the news to her. She greeted me at the door with an expression of surprise and led me to the drawing room. But when I told her what had happened I could see that she was as ill pleased as I.

"And you let them do this," she said scornfully, "without one word of protest?"

I looked at her helplessly.

"What could I do?" I asked.

"If I were a man—" she began.

I cut her short.

"If you were a man," I said tartly, "you would do just as I have done! There is nothing to this that we did not expect, only that it has come sooner than we thought."

"I believe you are glad," she cried, twisting her handkerchief between her fingers in agitation.

I took her in my arms tenderly.

"You know that's not true," I told her. "Else would I come to you like this? If ye will wait for me, Dorcas, I'll come back to ye, and after that we'll never twine!" *

She lay silent in my embrace for a moment, thinking.

"It is not fair you should ask me to wait for ever," she said at length.

"I did not ask that," I replied. "I only want you to give me a chance. If you loved me you'd promise me that!"

"Don't you think I love you, Jamie?" she asked.

* Part.

I remembered the sweet pressure of her lips on mine—the soft urgency of her arms about my neck, and nodded.

"Aye," I said. "May God forgive ye if ye do not!"

"Then do you need more than that?" she demanded. "Isn't my love promise enough?"

I kissed her then, passionately. She led me toward the door.

"You must go now," she said, letting me out. "Daddy will be home soon, and he would be angry to find you had stayed late!"

I clung to her desperately then, for I knew that it would be long ere I would see her again.

"Remember, Jamie," she whispered, "as long as I love you, I will wait for you, and you must have no doubt of that!"

Her tone rather than what she said convinced me of her sincerity. Indeed, I hardly heard the words, for I was trying to swallow a lump in my throat as big as an apple. For a brief moment she clung to me, pressing herself against me so that I could feel the softness of her breasts and the firm warmth of her body. Then, with a sound that I took for a half-stifled sob, she broke from me.

"Good-bye, Jamie," she whispered, and in the next moment she was gone and in her stead I faced the heavy door with its plain brass knocker.

¶ 1 It was late on the fourth day following our departure from Portsmouth when we came at last to Suncook. Gloomy as I was at leaving my new-found love so soon after making her acquaintance, I was not, perhaps so sharp an observer of the countryside as I ought to have been. Yet there were some features of it I could not help noticing.

All the way our route had lain through a country of low rolling hills, thick-wooded, so that the narrow cartway which was our highroad seemed to wind its way through a never ending tunnel of green, giving us only occasional glimpses, where it dipped down over the brow of a hill or skirted the shore of some solitary pond, of mile after mile of unbroken forest. In the beginning there had been frequent little settlements and prosperous-seeming farms, their compact fields and pastures partitioned from one another and from the encroaching woods by low walls of broken stone. But beyond Kingston the settlements grew more and more scattered, and the prosperous farms with their neat framed buildings gave way to an occasional isolated log hut of one or two rooms, chinked with mud and moss and thatched with bark; sometimes with an acre or two of good cleared land round about, but more often than not with blackened stumps peeping through the waving corn, attesting the laborious effort with which each tiny patch must have been wrested from the surrounding forest. During the first half of the journey our passage along the road was a matter for scant attention from those who dwelt beside the way. But once the more thickly settled regions lay behind us I noticed that men stopped their work in the fields and came down to the fences, while women came to the doorways of the cabins, to watch us pass in a sort of dour, stony silence that was almost hostile. I noticed, too, that wherever men worked out of doors they had always a musket within easy reach of their hands.

Between Kingston and Exeter we fell in with Captain Ladd and his company of Exeter militia, en route to Rumford to assist in the defence of the northern settlements against the mischiefs of the Indians, lately reported in the neighbourhood of Canterbury and Contoocook. The captain himself was a stoutish man of a cheerful, ruddy countenance and a mild blue eye. To all appearances he was almost too easy-going—too good-natured a man—to make a soldier. Yet he had a warlike reputation and was said to be inhumanly ferocious in battle. It was whispered that after Captain Phinehas Stevens, of Number Four, there was not a man from Wiscasset, on the coast, to Fort Massachusetts in the west that the savages feared more and would go farther to avoid meeting than Daniel Ladd.

His men, however, were with a few exceptions raw, gangling farmers' lads with no concept of war's deadly earnestness. They took the whole thing as a great lark, singing and shouting to one another on the road, marching in no kind of order whatever, and falling out whenever it suited their whim to pick berries, to shoot at hawks or squirrels, to relieve themselves, or even just to rest a few moments by the roadside.

Their company slowed our progress considerably, but, as my uncle had prophesied, we were thankful for it in the end. At Chester, the only sizable settlement between Kingston and Suncook, we found the people agog over the report, just brought in by a local scout, of a band of Indians which had passed northward through the eastern section of the township not longer ago than that very morning.

The information set my heart to thumping with excitement, for I must confess one of my chiefest disappointments lay in the fact that since our landing not one red Indian had we seen. On the outward voyage my callow imagination had pictured them lurking behind every bush and stone. Yet in the near three weeks since our arrival in Boston, and in a hundred miles of travel through the country, I had seen nothing more savage than Governor Wentworth's two blackamoors riding resplendent in plum-coloured liveries behind His Excellency's carriage.

However, it seemed I was once again to be doomed to disappointment. I had not reckoned with the red men's distaste for the company of whites in force. It was soon apparent that they had no intention of being seen if they could help it. Captain Ladd took up a prompt pursuit with thirty men, while we were left to pursue our journey along the road, by now become monotonous in its sameness, with the rest of the company under the command of his lieutenant, Jonathan Bradley, a stocky, flint-faced man, whose sole claim to distinction lay in a habit of prefacing his every command with some pious utterance delivered in a nasal twang.

At first the supposed proximity of the enemy had a somewhat chastening effect upon the spirits of our escort. They marched for a time in accordance with the directions of the drill manual, as interpreted by Lieutenant Bradley, talked in whispers, and broke ranks only at regular halts. As the day wore on, however, and it became more and more evident that the enemy had left for other parts, their exuberance returned, and at sundown, when we took our leave of them at a place they called "Isle Hook's Pond," they were once again behaving with all their former riotousness, to the despair of the lieutenant, who, while his men made camp in a bedlam of whoops and shouts, sat disconsolate upon a rock and called upon the Almighty to look down and witness the tribulations of an officer of Colony Militia on active duty.

As my uncle's house lay but a few short miles farther along the road, we did not stop with them, but pushed on in the hope of arriving shortly after nightfall. Nor would my uncle accept the lieutenant's offer of a detachment to guard us safely upon our way. Had the savages remained in the neighbourhood, he pointed out, we should have heard from them or from Captain Ladd ere now, and it was best that Bradley should not divide his force.

We went on from there, around one hill and up another, and came out at last on a cleared slope with a broad, shallow valley spread out below, through which flowed a swift little river. My uncle halted the cart and pointed.

"Yon's the Suncook," he said. "The settlement lies beyond."

We followed the sweep of his arm with an interest far beyond that which the casual beauty of the scene warranted, for, after all, this was to be our new home. On our right the forest trees crowded along the edge of the hill, coming to an abrupt halt at its very rim as though they had been suddenly cut off there and pushed back by the stone wall that separated them from the cleared land below. All around the bowl of the valley, to east and north, the effect of conflict between field and forest continued strong, until in the distance, a mile or more away, the cleared ground ended and the trees broke through with a rush that carried to the very river's edge. To westward, on our left, the aspect was different. Here a shoulder of upland jutted out, narrowing the valley, and though the stone fence carried on across the hill it did not crowd the forest back nor hold it in check, but let it spill over, so that a little scattering of hardwoods ran down along the ridge. Through the trees we could catch a brief glimpse of another river, the broad Merrimack, rolling down out of the north, catching now the last blood-red rays of the vanishing sun which still tinted the western sky. Directly before us the green fields, dark in the twilight, sloped down gently, to rise again abruptly on the other side to a shallow plain, which climbed gradually to a height, then dropped from view beyond. Even as we watched in the gathering dusk the first lights twinkled on, here and there across the plain, indicating where stood the beginnings of Suncook Village. My uncle spoke sharply to the oxen, and pricked them with the goad. The ponderous beasts started forward gingerly, breaking their descent of the hill with clumsy jerks of their great knock-knees against the pull of the grade.

The highway dipped down into the hollow and crossed the river at a ford, though my uncle told us there was a bridge farther downstream—used mostly in times of high water, the way by the ford being more direct. Once across the stream it climbed to the plain and ran straight across and a little down to Meetinghouse Brook, whence it climbed easily into the Soucook Hills, skirted the valley of Soucook Brook for a short distance, then dropped down sharply and crossed that meandering little stream on a plank bridge, there passing out of the limits of Suncook Town and into those of Rumford.

I was surprised to see, as we crossed the long stretch of the plain, how the village spread out. Indeed it seemed to me that it could hardly be called a village at all, so scattered were its houses along the four good miles between the Suncook and the Soucook. Some huddled close along the road. Others lay back aloofly in the midst of fields. Some were close together, within shouting range of one another. But most of them lay far apart, separated in some cases by as much as a half a mile. There was no store, no public house. In fact the only public place seemed to be the big framed meetinghouse, standing hard by a little brook that ran down across the plain to the Merrimack.

It occurred to me to wonder how such a place could be defended in case of attack, and even as I had the thought I had my answer, for my uncle pointed with his goad to a building that loomed in the darkness close beside the road.

"Aaron Whittemore's garrison," he said.

I looked, and even in that murky light could see that the house in question was a large, stoutly timbered structure; and that two sides and the rear were enclosed in a sort of stockade of logs at two corners of which loomed squat towers.

"Garrison?" I asked, for I could see no evidence of soldiers anywhere about.

"We call them that." He nodded.

He went on to explain then the system by which these frontier towns guarded themselves against destruction. In Suncook, he said, there were six of these garrisons, each capable of accommodating a certain number of families, and each fortified against attack. In such times as these, when none knew where the enemy might strike next, members of the colony militia were lodged at each garrison. Guards were maintained continually in the lookout towers, and regular patrols combed the surrounding forest. Thus, as soon as the presence of an enemy in the neighbourhood became known, it was reported at once to the nearest garrison, the alarm sounded, and at that signal each single family withdrew to its appointed stockade and there stood ready for a siege. The house thus abandoned might be burned to the ground, the farmer's crops destroyed, his stock killed, and his lands laid waste. But if he heeded the alarm his own life and those of his family would be safe, and it was this which was important.

My uncle's house, as it turned out, was one of the six garrisons. It occupied a knoll at the extreme north end of the settlement, overlooking the point where the road dipped suddenly to the Soucook bridge, and, because of its strategic position guarding the northern approaches to the town, was considered to be of sufficient importance to have double the customary quota; six instead of three militiamen, to assist in its defence. All around its stockade for a distance of some hundred yards or more the ground lay cleared. Not a stick nor a stone nor a solitary bush was left to provide shelter for any skulking enemy, so that although the full darkness of the night had fallen, yet, as we approached, we could see its dark bulk looming against the sky above us. And presently, as we drew closer, we could make out the bright streaks of cheerful light that gleamed out through the chinks in the shutters.

The creak of our cart must have carried before us, for as we turned off the highroad and started on the short ascent to the door, a challenge rang out from above.

"Who's yon?"

My uncle chuckled.

"They keep good watch," he said. Then, raising up his voice: "Ho, Donald! Have ye killed the fatted calf against your father's coming?"

"Hallo, father," came the reply, and now I could make out the dim bulk of the speaker's figure in the tower. "We've saved the calf for a better use. Have ye come alone?"

"I have not," said my uncle. "I've your aunt beside me, and forty starving cousins at my back. So pass the word to the kitchen, or I doubt not we'll be put to it to save the oxen."

The sound of laughter floated down to us through the dark; a happy laugh, full of good humour, so that even before I saw him I knew I should like my cousin Donald.

"Aye?" he called. "Well, ye'll find us short o' veal, I misdoubt, but ye may find a bit o' venison or some cold pork or maybe a brace o' birds below. I'll pass the word."

We could hear the bang of the trap behind him, and the scuttle of feet upon the tower steps; and presently the great front door swung back, throwing a patch of yellow light on the ground before it, and a crowd of figures burst out to greet us with yells of welcome and delight.

It was pleasant to step in through that doorway, out of the blackness of the night, which was already growing chill, to the bright cheerful glow of the great log fire and the light of tall homemade candles, gleaming mellowly upon the wide yellow planks of hand-hewn pine in which this central room of my uncle's house was finished. Scarcely had we set foot within the door when a small, ruddy-cheeked woman, with greying hair and cap askew, scarce taller than she was around, came flying from a passageway to smother us with overwhelming greetings. There was no mistaking that this was my aunt Katherine. Nor was there any doubting the sincerity of her welcome. At first she tried to embrace us all at once, though she had never before seen any of us. Then she must needs kiss us each one separately. After this she embraced my mother with genuine affection, and the two women sobbed on each other's shoulders in mingled joy and sympathy, until my uncle gruffly reminded her that we had come a long day's journey and should be glad of some supper.

Thereupon she clapped her hands to her head, declaring that she would soon be losing it, what with the excitement and all, and turning she scampered for the kitchen, calling loudly on the way for the girls to come and help.

Over her shoulder for a brief instant as she plunged into the passage, I caught a glimpse of a thin little face; a freckled, sunburnt face, with wide cheekbones, a slash of a mouth and a sharp turned-up nose, topped by a crop of sandy reddish hair cut close all around. It was a face that might have belonged either to a girl or to a boy; but without seeing the body to which it was attached there was no way of knowing, and this was hidden in the shadows of the passage, while the face itself seemed to float in midair, peering out through the gloom with a pair of remarkably bright and curious eyes.

I do not think I was a particularly sensitive lad; yet when I suddenly realized that I was the object of that steady, curious stare I was conscious of a flush of embarrassment. But for all that I was able to return the look with one which I considered to be equally insolent and properly defiant. At the same time I vowed to myself that so soon as I was free to learn the identity of my rude observer, and lay my hands upon him, I should certainly give him a lesson in proper manners. Something of my thoughts may have shown in my face, for of a sudden the freckled nose wrinkled, the wide lips parted in a grimace, and a sharp red tongue darted out at me. In the next instant my aunt had swept whoever it was before her, down the passage, leaving me staring after them in mingled surprise at that parting gesture, amusement at the childishness of it, and mounting annoyance at its rudeness.

There was scant time for speculation concerning it, however, for my uncle had begun to present the other members of the family; no simple matter, for the brood was numerous. First came Donald, whom we had discovered in the tower. He was the eldest, a young man of twenty-four, tall and fair, with his father's grey eyes and jutting jaw. After him came Anne and Mary, both remarkably pretty young women, followed by Davie, a sandy-haired, freckle-faced lad of my own age. Doris came next, a stocky, placid girl a year or two younger; then Rob, twelve, and finally Sheila, aged nine, the baby of the family, who already gave evidence of following in her mother's footsteps, for she was round and ruddy as an apple.

Nor was this the end. In addition there was Donald's wife Abigail, a sweet-faced girl with great brown eyes, comely still despite the fact that she was far gone with child. Also there were three of the militiamen attached to the garrison, at the moment off duty. Of these last, Caleb Crowe and Asa Hatch, lanky, gangling men, with little to distinguish them, bobbed their heads to my mother and the girls with awkward politeness, and attempted to hide their confusion by burying their noses in their noggins of small beer. Shem Sanborn, however, was of different stuff. A great hairy man, with small black eyes set too close together in his face, and a little mouth, whose meanness was not entirely hidden beneath the heavy beard he wore, he spat loudly into the fire, and grumbled a surly "Good evenin'." Whether it was the man's manner, or the way he looked at my sisters, or whether it was purely a matter of instinct on my part, I know not; whatever the cause, this I do know, that I loathed him from the very first. And that is important, for had I never met this Shem Sanborn, or had I, perhaps, liked him (though I cannot imagine such a thing), much of what follows in these pages might never have been written.

Perhaps my uncle scented some of the trouble that was to spring from this simple meeting, for he turned to the militiaman.

"The south tower's without a watch, Sanborn," he said. "Ye'd best take it."

At that the fellow sprang to his feet.

"Now by God!" he swore. "When's a man to have a bit of rest here, eh, by God?"

"When the King sees fit to make his peace with the French, lad," said my uncle, "then ye'll have rest, and more of it than's good for ye. Now get ye up there."

"Well, by—" Sanborn began. But something in my uncle's face stopped him, and he gathered up his musket, grumbling, and went out, slamming the door behind him.

Scarcely had he gone when my aunt reappeared, bearing aloft two huge platters, piled high with steaming vegetables, that gave off an aroma which drove the incident from our minds and set our mouths to watering. Close at her heels, staggering beneath the weight of an enormous deep-dish venison pie, trotted the face in the passage, complete now with arms, legs, and a body. In the light one could tell—though not without difficulty, for she wore breeches and a boy's shirt, open at the throat—that here was no lad but a girl of eleven or, possibly twelve years. As she set the steaming pie upon the long table, my uncle grasped her playfully by the arm and swung her about to face us.

"And this," he said laughingly, "is the final member of our family: Mistress Purity Stiles, who lives with us and is one of us while her father goes to the wars."

"Mistress Stiles" stood awkwardly embarrassed, glancing wildly about as if in search of some avenue of escape. She curtsied shyly to my mother and my sisters when they greeted her. But when I ventured to make a polite leg at her, she gave me one frightened glance and, turning, fled for the passageway.

"La, David," said my aunt, reprovingly, "ye know the child is easily frightened." She raised her voice. "Come, Purity, lass, there's none will hurt ye."

But Purity had taken refuge in the shadows, and did not propose to come out. My aunt shrugged and smiled an apologetic little smile as she herded us all towards the table.

"Why, the child is like a wild thing of the woods," said my mother, as we took our places.

My aunt nodded at her.

"'Tis exactly what she is, my dear," she replied. "Her mother died when she was born, and her father, who is an Indian trader, kept her with him in the woods until David convinced him 'twas no way to raise a girl. When he went away to Louisbourg last year he left her with us for good keeping, and this year he's joined up for Quebec."

"Aye," growled Uncle David, though the twinkle of his eye belied the gruffness of his tone, "and belike next year 'twill be for something new, so long he is not burdened by the child!"

The conversation swung then to the expedition and its prospects, and to the news of Boston and Portsmouth, while my uncle served us all with heaping portions of delicious food. I for one needed no second invitation to eat, but fell to at once and in silence; for we had eaten but lightly on the road, and I was near famished. In fact so occupied was I with my trenchering that I left conversation to the others, and even neglected to keep my ears open. Yet once when I looked up for a moment it was to meet the wide eyes of Purity Stiles, fixed upon me curiously from the gloomy shelter of the passage, and suddenly I was most unaccountably covered with confusion and embarrassment, so that I looked quickly back at my plate and did not again raise my eyes from it until the meal was finished.

2

I call to mind the weather plainly enough that first Sunday after our arrival, for it came off cold in the night, as our weather so often does early in August, breaking the long, hot, sultry spell that had lasted since our landing, and the day dawned clear and cool with a northerly set to the light wind that is refreshing even to remember. At breakfast Uncle David asked my mother if she had objections to attending service at the Established Church.

She looked at him reproachfully, and replied that she was a good Presbyterian.

"Aye," said he dryly, "I had it in mind ye were. And so are we all, but we attend the English service all the same."

My mother sniffed.

"The more shame to ye, David," she said. "Have ye none of the courage of your convictions?"

He chuckled.

"Courage enough," he replied, "but not much money! You see, lass, we're a poor lot who cannae afford to pay the taxes for the Established Kirk and still support a minister o' our own. We've petitioned for exemption, but there'll be naught come o' that until there's more o' us comes proprietors."

" 'Twould do you no harm to stay away," my mother retorted mighty high and haughty.

"Nay, lass!" said my uncle. " 'Tis a fine of ten shilling for each who stays from worship the Sabbath: a law of the Province!"

He looked at each of us in turn.

"Is't worth forty shilling a week to assert yersel's?" he asked.

"Ah, well," sighed my mother, acknowledging defeat, "at least 'twill do us no harm if we bear in mind the true Kirk."

Uncle David nodded.

"Aye," he said, "and 'twill do ye no harm to be seen about, either."

The matter rested there for the moment, and presently when the big bell in the meetinghouse began its tolling, we scattered to our various quarters to dress for the occasion. When we came down, I in my blue coat with the gold buttons, for I felt that the plum coat was a bit grand for the surroundings, cousin Donald had the cart ready hitched, and my uncle was busy giving his final orders to the three militiamen who were to remain behind on guard. Shem Sanborn, evidently, was to accompany us, as was his particular crony, Joseph Merrill, a lanky, sheep-faced man who seemed not to know the use of soap and even now had a week's growth of whisker across his cadaverous jaw. These two men lounged at the stockade gate, talking in low tones, spitting tobacco juice at the gatepost and shooting occasional sour glances at my uncle, but for whom, I suspect, they might have found means of avoiding attendance. When I appeared in the doorway, however, Sanborn brightened and nudged his companion.

"Ain't he the young buck though?" he said loud enough for all to hear.

Merrill spat sourly, eyeing my plain stock.

"Where'd ye leave yer ruffles, m'lord?" he said in a high mincing falsetto, which he evidently considered very funny, for they both roared with laughter.

I waited until they had caught their breath before I replied.

"The same place, I doubt not," I replied, "where you left your soap and razor."

He fingered his stubbly chin then, and squinted at me with watery eyes.

"Arr!" he said at length. "Listen to his imperdence. A whuppin's wot he needs, that's wot!"

He reached out a grimy paw to grasp me by the collar.

But I was in no mood to have his dirty hands upon me. I aimed a hard kick at his shins, landing with a crack that could be heard across the yard. Merrill gave a howl of agony, clapped hands to his injured leg, and hopped about on one foot, grimacing in pain. Sanborn made a grab for me, but I eluded his grip and ducked behind the cart, where I placed my thumb to my nose and waggled my fingers at him.

For an instant I thought he might follow me, and half hoped that he would, for I was confident of my ability to outrun the pair of them. Instead he hesitated and glanced at my uncle, who was trying hard to look severe, though not quite succeeding. The other men had burst out laughing. Sanborn glared from me to them and back again, and I could see that he was in a rage at being made a laughingstock. Then abruptly he turned away, taking Merrill by the elbow.

"Ah, th' hell!" he said. "Come on!"

And without further words they went off down the road.

The girls came down presently and climbed into the cart, and a moment or two later my mother and my aunt Kate appeared, adjusting bonnet ribbons and chattering away. Uncle David helped them up and clambered in beside them, chirping at the team. Donald had already ridden on ahead, with Nabby apillion despite her condition, and Davie and Rob and I trudged along behind the cart afoot.

We reached the bottom of the hill and turned left onto the high-road just as another cavalcade came plodding up the hill from the bridge. My uncle pulled up the team and waited until they had come up with us. Then began another round of introductions. These, it turned out, were Amos Rush and Jonathan Stinson, Rumford men both, from just across the Soucook Brook, with their families. Close neighbours and close friends apparently, they were distinct opposites. Stinson, who was driving their cart, was a long, sad-eyed individual, looking as solemn as a judge advocate, while Rush, who sat behind him, was stocky, with a great round face which was always beaming, giving him the appearance of being fatter than he was. For once two men seemed to have married women who were not their opposites, for Mrs. Stinson was a great strapping woman with a sallow complexion and a drawn-down mouth, which gave her a look of constant disapproval. Mrs. Rush was a buxom, cheerful, grey-haired dame, who nodded brightly as a bird at my uncle's introduction. It was Mrs. Stinson, however, who monopolized the conversation, giving her friend and neighbour no chance to speak.

"Mrs. Ferguson?" she said, in a whiny, nasal voice. "Well, I declare! You ain't a mite like I pictured you. Not a mite. I don't know as I could say rightly now just what it was I did think you'd be like, but whatever it was you ain't it. Katie tells me you've lost your husband. Well, now, ain't that too bad? I allus say we all got to go some time but we hate to see the time come! Now you take me, fer instunce. I know John here'll go afore me, an' I dread the day. There ain't a thing in the world the matter with him. Healthy as the day we was married, he is, an' me, I'm always ailin'. If it ain't one thing it's another. You know how 'tis. But I allus say he'll go afore me 'cause that's the way it is in this world. Ain't that what I allus say, John?"

"Eeyah!" said Jonathan, sombrely agreeable, and winked at my uncle.

All the while she was speaking my cousins were not neglecting us. I saw Edith flush and lower her eyes shyly as Anne presented the handsome Moses Rush, who bowed mighty nicely and fetched a flashing smile. The three Stinson girls, buck-toothed wenches, with wide grey eyes and tawny hair, simpered and giggled when I made a leg at them. But their brother Daniel, a towheaded lad my own age and not much larger, was unimpressed. He stood in the road behind the cart and glowered.

"Banty!" he said when Davie introduced me.

"What?" I said, taken aback.

"Banty," he repeated. "That's what you are, a little bitty banty."

"You're not so big yourself," I retorted, stung, and at the same time amused.

He came closer, looking fiercer than ever.

"Say that again!" he said, truculently.

"You're not so big," I said.

He hit me a crack on the nose that sat me down in the dust of the road and made bright-coloured lights flash and dance before my eyes. For an instant I was dazed, but only for an instant. In the next second I was on my feet, standing toe to toe with him, giving as good as I took, both of us oblivious to the girls' squeals of alarm, and our elders' commands to stop it.

It was Davie who dragged him off, while Moses Rush held me securely by the collar and kept me back.

"Jamie!" my mother scolded. "Aren't you ashamed!"

"Tut! Twas Dan'l sta'ted it," said Mrs. Stinson, looking at me with something like approval stamped upon her stony features. "Ain't he the little catamount though! Fit just like a reg'lar wildcat, I declare. Now Dan'l 'll have someone his own size can peg him down a notch or two and not allus be havin' to tackle them bigger lads. You better hang together, you two."

She jogged her husband in the ribs with a bony elbow.

"Come on, John," she said, "we best be gettin' on or we'll be late and the Reverend Whittemore'll be shuttin' the doors."

We met other families on the road, all on their way to the meeting, though none of them were so interesting as these two. The Richard Eastmans, John MacNeill and his wife, Thomas McConnell, all alone since his wife was expecting and could not come, Ephraim Blunt, with two grown sons, Moses Tyler, Joseph Baker, John Fife, Joseph Brown, all overtook us or we overtook them, and fell in line, until we made a very respectable-sized column along the roadway. All the way Daniel Stinson trudged along beside me, glum and morose, saying nothing, but eyeing me covertly when he thought I was not looking. We were approaching the Meetinghouse Brook before he spoke.

"Banty!" he said then.

"Aye?" I said as sourly as I could, for I was amused but could not allow this to go indefinitely. "Banty yourself!"

His sombre face split into a sheepish grin.

"Maw's right," he said, "us runts should stick together."

I gave him my hand on that.

"But I'll fight ye again some time for the fun of't," he added.

I laughed.

"Maybe," I said.

"I'd rather fight 'n most anything I know," he said. "If I wa'n't so, some o' these big lads'd be takin' advantage o' my size to have me fetchin' an' carryin' fer 'em."

I nodded. I knew how he felt, for I had had the same thoughts myself, though I had never put them into words. His attitude was simply that of a little man in a big man's world.

We were near the meetinghouse by now, and his elbow jogged my ribs again. He jerked his head toward a black-browed, loutish-seeming young lad who was that moment about to enter.

"Ben Holt," he said, "the young un. He's mean. He'll pick on ye if he thinks he kin, but he ain't no in'ards. Le' me know if he tries anythin'. Me an' you between us can take him down a peg."

Ben Holt glanced in our direction, but catching our eyes fixed upon him, looked uncomfortable and ducked inside. I suspected that he had already tasted more than enough of Daniel Stinson's wrath. We moved up to the door. Stinson nudged me once more.

"Tell ye what," he said. "Let's lay for Ben Holt after meetin'."

"Ye'll do nothin' o' the sort, my young bucko," said his mother, who had swept up behind him at that moment and overheard him. "Don't ye go teachin' this young lad any o' your tricks!"

And with that she swept us before her into the church.

I slipped into a seat between young Stinson and my cousin Davie, on a backless bench near the end of the room. Presently an enormous, towering old man, with a great red face and a shock of white hair, rose from a seat beneath the pulpit, looked at an enormous silver watch, and then came heavily down the aisle toward the door. Stinson poked me sharply.

"That's the Reverend Whittemore," he whispered.

The white-haired man saw him whispering, and gave us both a look that set me to quaking in my seat. I believe I held my breath as he passed. Presently I could hear the doors being shut, then some commotion, and the sound of voices raised in protest. A voice I knew could belong to no one there unless it was the Reverend Whittemore began booming, filling the great high raftered room with noise, drowning out all other sounds.

"No, ye can't come in," he bellowed. "If ye can't git to the Lord's house on time, the Lord don't want ye in!"

The doors slammed, making the building shake, and I could hear the bolts slide home. A moment later he came back up the aisle, walking heavily, breathing loudly through his nose. Without a backward glance he mounted the dais at the far end of the room and began his services in a droning monotone that had me nodding sleepily before he had spoken two sentences.

I fear I did not pay very strict attention to the service. Only one sentence of all that came before the Reverend Whittemore

mounted to the pulpit to deliver his sermon sticks in my mind:
"And we give thanks unto Thee, O Lord, for that Thou hast seen
fit to send victory upon the arms of Our Most Royal and Gracious
Master, enabling them to turn back the rebel forces of the base
pretender on the field at Culloden Moor."

I wanted to raise my head then and shout that I for one was not
going to give thanks for that, and perhaps I might have done so,
had not my cousin at that moment thumped his knee sharply
against mine while my uncle gave me a short, quick glance of
warning, so that the moment had passed and it was too late before I could act.

But presently, when the Reverend Whittemore had finished
with his prayers and his thanksgivings and had climbed to the
pulpit to deliver his sermon, I found myself watching him and
listening attentively for what he might say.

He took his time, wiping his hands upon an enormous white
handkerchief, opening his Bible on the rail before him, and consulting some notes. For a moment he stood looking down into our
upturned faces. Then he cleared his throat.

"My text for today," he boomed, and paused impressively, "is
from the fourth verse of the eighth chapter of the Book of Hosea:
'They have set up kings, but not by me: they have made princes,
and I knew it not.'"

I think I knew then what he would say, and I braced myself,
trying to get a grip upon my feelings, so that I would not cry out
in protest. But as luck had it no one of us ever heard that sermon.

In the instant when he paused, gathering his breath for the onslaught, there came a little gust of wind outside, making the leaves
in the great maples rattle. Then for the briefest second all was
still. But brief as it was, in that instant there came, clearly, distinctly, a distant pop like the sound of a cork in a bottle.

I looked around, wondering if anyone else had heard. Over by
the far side of the room Joseph Merrill had also caught it, for
now he was standing up, craning his head foolishly towards the
window. The Reverend Whittemore looked at him in surprise.

"Sit down!" he bellowed.

Joseph Merrill sat, but he also spoke.

"I heerd shootin'," he announced.

I could feel the rustle of apprehension that passed over the
congregation as they turned to look fearfully at one another.

"Quiet!" bellowed the old man in the pulpit, and there fell a silence so thick and heavy that I thought it must shut out all sound. Outside a cicada buzzed, and the sound seemed as loud as the whine of a sawmill. The Reverend Whittemore looked impatient. The buzzing stopped. And then the sound came again; a series of pops this time, scattered, irregular, and very far away. Everyone heard it.

Several of the men started to rise.

"Sit down!" roared the Reverend Whittemore.

They sank back. The old preacher turned toward the altar.

"The Grace of Our Lord Jesus Christ, the Love of God, and the Fellowship of the Holy Ghost be with us all evermore, Amen," he said all in a breath, and turned holding up his hands. "You all know what's to do," he shouted. "That shootin's a long ways off yet. Rumford by the sound of it. You'll have time to git to your homes and git things together. Then git to your garrisons as quick as you can. We'll be all right if you all keep steady heads. Git now!"

3

There was no gathering about outside the meetinghouse; no stopping to talk or conjecture as to the source of the shots. People moved off, grim, silent, following the quickest way home. By the time we reached the turn in the road the Rushes and the Stinsons were already far across the bridge, and were toiling up the far side of the gully to the plain beyond. Nor were they sparing the whip.

Where the road forked Uncle David ordered the women out of the cart and turned back, taking my aunt with him, to help Thomas McConnell, who anticipated some trouble with his wife. The rest of us climbed up to the fort on foot.

Above us, in the watchtower, the alarm bell, which had been tolling dolefully since we left the meetinghouse, stopped, leaving our ears ringing in the sudden silence. Somewhere in the woods a squirrel was chattering fiercely. Below us we could hear the low steady chuckle of the brook as it rippled across a sand bar. Across the Soucook hollow the tall elms drooped, still and graceful in the warm sunlight. In the field in the bottom little haycocks stood in rows ready for gathering. In the midst of such calm serenity it seemed to me absurd to think of danger. Yet others did not share my sense of security, as was evidenced by the bells on the other garrisons to southward, which were still tolling, as though everyone in the settlement did not know all about it by now. I wondered if the alarm would go on from here as it had come, to Isle a Huckset, to Derryfield, and then on to Dunstable perhaps, or even Haverhill. In an instant's flight of foolish fancy I had visions of each succeeding village and garrison taking up the alarm from the one next north and passing it on farther south, until places hundreds of miles removed from the original danger stood warned and waiting. It even occurred to me that the shots might have been the work of some Sabbath breaker bagging a brace of partridge for his Sunday supper. But since there was no one to whom I could confide these thoughts, I kept them to myself.

There were accommodations for six families at my uncle's garrison. First of these to arrive was Ephraim Blunt, with his two sons and their wives, who had less distance to travel than the others. Their cart was piled high with household goods and personal belongings, and their three cows plodded along before them, patiently ignoring the yapping of the dog at their heels as if they were already tired of the whole affair. Old Ephraim and Joseph, the eldest son, took the cart inside the enclosure, while Ezra, the younger, drove the cattle to the pen, which stood at a little distance from the log stockade, though close enough to be protected by fire from it. Inside the yard the women, who already looked worn out and sorry for themselves though neither of them could have been more than twenty-five, took what they needed from the cart, which was then wheeled back out of the way, and carried it into the tiny cabin which had been assigned to them, and which they must share with another family so long as they were there.

The McConnells came next, Thomas looking pale and anxious upon the driver's seat, while his wife, a pretty young thing, her face twisted now in agony, lay in the bottom of the cart with her head upon my aunt's lap, and Mrs. Mann, a tiny, sharp-featured woman, as twittery as a sparrow, who had been attending her while the others were at meeting, walked beside. Uncle David brought up the rear, his own cart piled high with their possessions, while their only cow tugged recalcitrantly at his tail-board.

They carried Mrs. McConnell gingerly into the big house, while my aunt went away fussing to see that hot water and blankets and warm flannel were ready, for it seemed the child might be expected any minute. Presently my uncle reappeared, swearing that babies had a way of appearing at the God-damnedest times, and bundled Davie off on the horse to Benjamin Holt's garrison to fetch old Dr. Webster, who should be there by now.

There followed an interval of waiting while the other families—the Fifes, the Manns, the Rushes and the Stinsons—arrived in the order named. Davie came back presently with Dr. Webster, who plunged at once into the house. Thomas McConnell watched him with anxious eyes. Once we heard another spattering of shots, off to northward but closer now and unmistakable. After that everything was quiet save for the moaning of the woman in the house. The men sat around and smoked, or stood talking in little groups, waiting.

At length my uncle came out again carrying a musket. He stopped and said something to Thomas McConnell and clapped him on the shoulder. McConnell grinned wanly and looked sheepish. My uncle laughed and came over to where I was standing with Davie and Daniel Stinson.

"Can ye shoot?" he asked shortly.

"Aye," I replied, not without pride for it was a thing my father had insisted upon, that I be able to hit a shilling at seventy paces ere ever he would take me hunting in the hills with him behind Kintulloch.

"Aye," he said, slowly, "I had it in mind your father would have taught ye that."

He handed me the gun.

"It is yours," he said. "Look after it."

He turned before I could thank him, and looked at the others.

"Line up," he said.

We were twenty-one, including the five militiamen—the sixth, I had not yet seen. Uncle David looked us over carefully, checking in his mind to see that all were there.

"Where's Toby?" he said at length.

"He went over toward Plausawa's hill," said one of the militiamen, Timothy Stevens by name.

"All right," Uncle David replied. "You, Stevens, go up through the pasture. He'll come down that way. When you find him tell him to scout up around Rumford way and find out what's happened."

Stevens turned with a short nod and headed for the gate.

"And tell him to be careful," my uncle called after him.

The militiamen waved his hand and was gone. Uncle David turned back to us.

"That's all, I guess," he said. "Just be ready for what comes. Hatch, you take the west lookout, and hold it until I relieve ye. Keep your eyes skinned. Davie, take the east." He looked at me. "Jamie, go along with your cousin. The sooner ye see what it's all about, the better for ye."

There followed what seemed an interminable period of waiting. In the east tower Davie and I at first kept a strict watch together. But as the afternoon wore on we took turns. About two o'clock my uncle came and called me down for dinner. As soon as I had finished I returned to the lookout and took Davie's place while he ate. But this was our only break. About three, Timothy Stevens came in, sweating but cheerful. Uncle David met him at the gate.

"Did ye find him?" he asked.

Stevens nodded.

"Aye," he replied.

My uncle looked relieved.

"Did he know anything?" he asked.

Stevens shook his head. Uncle David shrugged.

"We'll have to wait then," he said. "Toby'll come in as soon as he finds out what's up."

The men, who had gathered about, returned to their seats listlessly. The inaction was beginning to bore them.

Towards four the woman in the house screamed once in pain, and then fell silent. Everyone, even the watchers in the towers, looked towards the house uneasily. Young McConnell was white as a ghost. Presently the back door opened and my aunt looked out. She beckoned to McConnell, who went over and listened intently while she said something. As she spoke the look of worry faded from his face, and a broad grin took its place.

"It's a boy!" he shouted. "Hey! It's a boy!"

Some of the men whooped. All of them crowded around to pound the father on the back. Uncle David disappeared inside the house, to reappear a moment later with cups and a jug. He distributed the cups and began pouring from the jug. As fast as the men received their cupfuls they drank to McConnell, to the baby, to Mrs. McConnell. The black-bearded Sanborn wiped his lips, having finished his off at a draft, and eyed the bottle.

"Hell," he said, "is that all? If I was you, McConnell, I'd feel downright insulted."

"We'll have to take it easy now," said my uncle, not looking at Sanborn, but rather as if explaining to McConnell; "but once this thing's over we'll do it right!"

"Whee!" shouted someone in the back of the crowd. "Double celebration! Ye sure it ain't twins, McConnell?"

Everybody laughed. My aunt appeared at the door again and beckoned McConnell inside. Uncle David, having served everyone, put the bottles away, and presently everything was quiet once more. We heard no further shooting to the north.

It was after sundown when my cousin Donald came up into the tower to relieve us. We went down into the great common room and stood before the log fire, which felt comfortable upon the seats of our britches, for the evening had begun to grow chill. Supper came on the table hot and steaming, making us all sleepy. Afterwards, while we lounged about the fire, I was overwhelmed with a sense of security. All this precaution now seemed to me senseless and stupid. How much better if all these people had been let to stay at home instead of upsetting their lives this way! Mrs. McConnell might have lost her baby, what with the moving and the excitement and all. It was the first time I had been so close to the miracle of birth; but thinking the matter over soberly it seemed to me that peace and quiet would be what a woman would need at such a time, not a lot of worry about Indians and being carried about in rough riding carts. That seemed sensible to me. Here they'd run all that risk and nothing had happened. Nothing was going to happen either. That was what I believed. I began to think of bed, but before I could bring myself to get up from my comfortable bench Ezra Blunt thrust his head in the door. His face was white, and his eyes were big with excitement. He looked at Uncle David.

"They sent me in to tell ye," he said. "They're burnin' over west."

There was a rush for the door, but I was among the first out.

It was long since dark, and the glow from the fires was plain enough, lighting up the whole sky to south and west. In two places the flames showed red and angry over the tops of the trees. From where we stood it seemed to me that the fires were just across the river, but my cousin Davie said they must be at least five miles away, there being nothing in between to burn.

"Who is it, would ye say?" said John Fife.

"I'd say Rogers's," replied my uncle slowly, "and either Page's or Putney's. I can't say for sure which."

There was a moment's silence.

"Do ye think some o' us maybe ought to go over?" said Jonathan Stinson presently.

My uncle shook his head.

"Don't be foolish, John," he said. "What good could we do now?"

No one spoke then for a long time, but all remained watching until the flames had died away, leaving only an angry glow in the sky. To me the effect was startling. Only a moment before everything had seemed so absurdly safe and secure. Alarms seemed foolish, almost craven. It had been hard to believe that that quiet countryside at which I had stared so hard all afternoon could hold anything more dangerous than a milk adder or perhaps a nest of hornets. But now all that was changed. Here was evidence which I could not ignore: something that I could see; something tangible, unlike those shots of the morning which had seemed distant and detached and hardly worth bothering about. Here was proof of danger, dark, furtive, slipping silently along beneath that green cover, which until this moment had seemed so kindly; watching with cruel dark eyes one's every movement; awaiting with malevolent patience the brief moment when one's guard was down to strike. Now the woods and the night seemed not so friendly, but suddenly became evil and full of menace. The croaking of a frog in the marsh below the bridge, the sad hooting of an owl in the eastern hills, seemed all at once heavy with warning.

At last my uncle turned away frowning.

"Where in hell is Toby?" I heard him mutter.

Davie and I crouched shivering in the darkness a moment longer, watching. Then quietly we slipped off to bed.

I do not know what the hour was when I woke and heard him stirring about.

"What is it?" I whispered.

"Nothing," he replied. "Go back to sleep. I have to go back on watch."

But I was wide awake by now. I knew it would be hours before I could sleep again. I sat up.

"I'll go with ye," I said.

"Suit yourself," he grumbled sleepily, then added more cordially: "Wrap yourself well. 'Tis cold up there at this hour."

I dressed quickly by the light of the guttering candle and followed him out and down the stairs. Outside, the night was chill. Overhead, the stars glittered against a black sky. A thin sickle of a moon had risen in the east, and by its feeble light the barn, the house, the cabins loomed darkly enormous against the deeper shadow of the stockade. Our feet crunched upon the gravel of the yard. Overhead a window squeaked and a white blur appeared.

"Who's yon?" said my uncle's voice. "Davie?"

"Aye, pa," said my companion.

"Is Toby come in yet?" asked my uncle.

"Not yet," said Davie.

My uncle muttered something beneath his breath.

"See I'm called when he comes," he said, and drew back his head.

We crossed the yard and climbed the steps into the east tower. The night seemed quieter now. Even the nocturnal prowlers in the forest seemed to have crept away into their dens to sleep. To westward, where the fires had been, there was not even a glow. We sat still for a long time in the darkness. Then away off somewhere, so far that it was hard to tell from what direction the sound came, some beast called, an eerie, crying call, not unlike the single hoot of an owl save that it had a wailing quality and a rising note at the end.

I shivered and nudged my companion.

"What's that?" I whispered.

"Bear hollerin'," he replied shortly.

Once again the cry came down to us through the darkness. After that the silence closed in about us more solidly than ever. I must have dozed off presently, for all at once I felt someone shaking me, and opened my eyes to a world turned blue-grey with the coming dawn. I looked up to find Davie leaning over me, blinking sleepily.

"I can't hardly keep my eyes open," he said. "I'm goin' down and brew up a cup o' tea. Hold on here while I'm gone, will ye?"

I nodded and picked up my gun. Davie lifted the trap and started down. On the top step he paused and swept his arm toward the dark line of the woods.

"Watch there," he said. "If anythin' stirs call me."

In the next moment he was gone. I stepped to the breast-high rail of logs and leaned upon it, staring toward the woods. Little by little the blueness of the air gave way to the grey of the morning. I was still sleepy and found it hard to keep my eyes open. I shook my head sharply, and then tried sweeping my eyes along the line of the woods, starting with the stone wall in the bottom of the gully, climbing to a point behind the cattle pen, then circling around to the top of the hill beyond. Three times I did this, and then suddenly my heart gave a wild thump and almost stopped beating. At a point almost directly behind the cattle pen I thought I saw a willow bush shake violently.

I stood stock-still, rooted to the spot, and stared. The bush shook again, even more violently this time, and then suddenly, almost as though coming out of the thin air, a man appeared standing beside the bush, staring hard toward the fort.

I caught my breath sharply. This was no such painted, be-feathered savage as I had imagined. He was not even stalwart. His body, naked to the waist, was short and thick, with a definite bulge in the belly. His greasy black hair hung straight upon his shoulders. His face, the colour of well tanned leather, though creased and wrinkled, was ageless. He might have been any age between forty and a hundred. He looked harmless, but in his left hand he carried an old-fashioned long-barreled musket, and there was a knife at his belt. I knew that I was looking at my first Indian.

After a long look at the fort he edged out into the clearing, coming straight toward me, as if he had not seen me. I raised my gun, looking at him across the sights, wondering what it was like to kill a man. It came to me suddenly that I *was* going to kill a man. The thought made me feel a little sick in the pit of my stomach, and my hand shook. He was coming toward me at a dogtrot, without hesitation. It did not seem right to shoot him down without warning. Yet if I did not act quickly it might be too late. Behind me I heard the steps creak. I got him in the notch of my sight and curled my finger about the trigger. But I could not shoot without giving him some chance.

"Stop!" I called.

He came on as if he had not heard me.

"Go back," I shouted. "Go back or I shoot!"

He stopped at that and looked up, standing stock-still; I saw that he had been smiling, but now the smile froze into a look of complete bafflement. For a long instant we stood thus facing each other. Then there came the sound of a step behind me, and a hand reached out, pushing my gun aside.

"All right, Toby," said my uncle's voice. "Come on in."

4

My uncle stood holding the musket which he had taken from me and looking down at me sternly, almost accusingly, while I stared back at him with mingled feelings of amazement at his sudden appearance and relief that I had not been compelled to shoot. At the same time his look made me feel somehow guilty, as though I had been in some way lax or failing in my duty. It was he who spoke first.

"Would ye shoot down the only scout I can rely upon?" he asked.

"I saw only that he was an Indian," I replied—somewhat sulkily, I fear, for I felt that it was unfair of them to set me up to watch and then condemn me for doing it well.

My uncle made a gesture of impatience.

"Is he painted for the warpath?" he demanded.

I hung my head at that, for now that it was over it seemed to me that this was a thing I should have known. I remembered that the fact that he was neither bedaubed nor befeathered had struck me as strange at first. Yet, after all, how was I to know that my uncle had any dealings save hostile ones with Indians? From all the talk I had heard since our landing I had been led to the belief that there was no good Indian save a dead one. Seeing me so ashamed, my uncle's stern look softened, and he laid a hand upon my shoulder.

"Nay, lad," he said, "ye've no call to feel so downcast. I mind now ye'd no way of knowing the look o' a hostile buck. Why did ye not call Davie?"

"There was no time," I replied. "He came from out the brush yon and came straight towards me. I had in mind it was some trick."

He gave my shoulder a gentle shake.

"Aye, lad," he said, "ye've kept a good watch, and the fault is mine for not tellin' ye what to expect. But 'twas a lucky day for all of us I couldna sleep!"

I heard my cousin's foot upon the tower steps, and at the same time heard the creak of the great gate as it swung open to admit the Indian.

"Come below," my uncle was saying, "and meet the man ye might have shot."

I hung back then, ashamed to face him. But my uncle laughed.

"Nay, lad," he said, "come along. He'll not hold it against ye."

We met him in the open yard below, and I saw that he was chuckling, so that his ponderous belly shook with his mirth and his little black eyes were almost lost behind the wrinkles of his fat cheeks.

"How!" he said as we came up.

"How!" replied my uncle, and shook hands solemnly.

He reached around behind me and pushed me forward.

"I'll acquaint ye with my nephew, Toby," he said. "He's new come from Scotland, and did not know ye for a friend."

The Indian thrust out his hand.

"How!" he said again.

I shook hands and returned his greeting. At the same time I noticed that he gave off a peculiar sickish smell that was not entirely that of drying sweat and grease. He looked from me to my uncle.

"White boy make good scout," he said. "Him see quick before Toby leave bush."

He chuckled, and his big belly jiggled above his belt.

"Him say, 'Stop.' Toby think him play big joke. Him say, 'Stop,' one time again. Toby look see him take one step more him dead Injun. Toby stop!"

The words bubbled out, mingling with the laughter until they became laughter in themselves. It was plain to see he bore no grudge. Uncle David slapped his thigh and chuckled. I grinned sheepishly.

"Him make good scout," Toby continued. "Must learn first not shoot good dog for bad wolf."

He looked at me, this time with definite approval written upon his jovial countenance, and laughed again.

"You go Rumford?" my uncle asked.

The Indian's face sobered instantly.

"Go Rumford," he said.

"What did you find out?" In his excitement Uncle David forgot to mimic his broken English.

Toby held up his hands and counted his fingers.

"One, two, three, four, five, six, seven, eight, nine, ten. Ten times fingers on Toby's hands Injuns come from Saint Francis. Lie outside Rumford meetinghouse. Girl look see-um window, give alarm. White men chase away."

He waved an arm towards the west.

"We saw fires last night across the river," said my uncle. "What was that?"

"One Putney, one Rogers," Toby held up two fingers. "Injuns burn house, cut trees, kill cows. Toby warn. All go safe away Lovejoy garrison, Rumford."

My uncle looked relieved.

"They got away, eh?" he said. "Good work!"

Toby beamed.

"Where did they go?" my uncle asked.

Toby looked serious again and waved his arm in an arc.

"Make circle," he replied. "Toby think come back. Hide near Rumford. Not know. One scout find Toby track, make run like hell!"

He wiped his brow eloquently in a white man's gesture. Uncle David smiled.

"Did they come this way at all?"

The Indian shook his head.

"Not come," he replied. "No Injun cross river. Only Toby."

"But you think they've swung back towards Rumford?" asked my uncle.

Toby nodded.

"Do they know that at Rumford?" my uncle demanded.

Toby shrugged and shook his head.

"Not know," he said.

"Go up then and warn them quickly," said my uncle.

Toby looked sullen. He pointed at me.

"White boy go," he said. "Toby tired. Rumford men not like Toby."

My uncle laughed.

"Ye mean they'll not trust ye near the rum," he replied. "Get ye along now. The lad would only lose his way."

The old Indian shrugged. He looked at me.

"Soon you me go scout," he said. "Bimeby you good scout. Then Toby get rest."

With that he turned, trailing his long musket, shouldered his way out through the gate, and was gone.

5

It was two days before Toby returned to garrison to report that the raiders had drawn off and taken the trail to Canada. During those two days men went warily, keeping an eye cocked over their shoulder, and such outside work as was done was done in groups. No man set his foot beyond the stockade alone. Even old Ephraim Blunt, who complained continually of his "misery"—which was in truth naught but a slight dyspepsia and a sour stomach—and kept his long-suffering daughters-in-law a-waiting upon him day and night, would not stir from the garrison, though he said it was all blasted nonsense and tarnation foolishness to keep people cooped up so. After Toby brought in his report, however, the families moved out quickly to their own homes, and the routine of life was picked up where it had been allowed to drop.

In the weeks that followed I had ample opportunity to observe the life of the community; more than ample, perhaps, for it was plain from the start that every man must do his share. More than ample, I say, not because I was not willing to do my full share of the work, but rather because that share at once presented a difficulty which to me seemed well-nigh insurmountable.

From the very outset it was evident that to make a success of this new life a man must be above all things a farmer. All about me this was plain. Except for the saw and grist mills on the Suncook in the South End there was no other activity in the town. Even the Reverend Aaron Whittemore was more farmer than minister. On every hand men were mowing and gathering the hay, tending crops, clearing fields, doing all the thousand and one tasks there are to be done about the farm. And I had neither the right dexterity for the work, nor sufficient strength of back to blunder along until I had gained it. I was not tall enough to pitch the hay upon the cart; and if they set me upon the cart itself I loaded it so clumsily that it slipped off upon the other side as fast as I took it up. If they set me to hoeing corn or potatoes I was like to do more injury to the plants themselves than to the weeds. If there were logs to be hauled or a field to clear, I had not sufficient strength to lend a hand with the heavy timber, wiry though I was. I was not even handy with a hammer and nails.

This deficiency on my part was as noticeable to others as to myself. Although I did my best, it was not a thing I could help, and I came in for something more than my share of gibes at my clumsiness and my small size. On this latter count, however, I stood ready, with the whole-hearted support of little Dan Stinson, to stand up to all comers, until at last I had sufficiently demonstrated my touchiness on the subject, when my companions of the field took shame to themselves and began to encourage what they were pleased to call my cockiness and to applaud my spirit.

Exceptions to this were Sanborn and Merrill, who seemed to have conceived as great a dislike for me as I had for them. They with the child Purity, who for some reason from that very first night of our meeting seemed set upon tormenting me and annoying me in a hundred little ways, combined to mar what might otherwise have become a most pleasant existence.

If I was a failure at the business of life, however, in those first days at Suncook, I came off not so badly at sports. In the "wrastling," which was perhaps the favourite, I could not, of course, compete, my size having me at a disadvantage. Thanks to my father's careful tutelage, on the other hand, I was able to hold my own with the best of them in shooting at marks. And as I had the small man's gift of speed, it took not many days to establish the fact that there was not a man or boy in the town I could not beat in a foot race over any distance they cared to name. Indeed there was only one person in the entire region who could outrun me, and that was a girl. Purity Stiles could always show me her heels whenever she wished; and since she so wished upon every possible occasion this may have accounted for no small part of my annoyance with her. Indeed this small wench, with her myriad little pestiferous tricks, her saucy grimacing, and her dartings in and out and round about, soon became like a veritable burr in my smallclothes and would give me no peace.

We had been in Suncook close on three weeks when one evening my uncle David drew me to one side in the chimney corner and beckoned to my mother to join us.

"Well now, Jamie lad," he said, with a twinkle in his grey eye, when at length she had come over to a place beside us, "and how do ye like the life o' a farmer?"

"Why," I stammered, flushing, for I did not like to admit to failure, "I like it fine, Uncle David, only there's that about it I can't quite get the hang o' things."

He smiled a little.

"Aye," he said dryly, "I'd noticed something o' the sort."

He sat for a moment with his stocky legs stretched out to the fire, the blue smoke from his pipe curling up lazily into the wide chimney above our heads.

"Have ye seen Toby of late, lad?" he said finally.

"Eh? No," I said, startled by what I considered a long jump from what he had set out to speak about.

He was not long in showing my error.

"The Indian took a liking to ye, Jamie," he said. "He thought ye'd the makings o' a woodsman, or he'd 'a' paid ye scant heed."

He paused. I waited for him to go on.

"Now I've kept a careful eye on ye these last few days," he continued at length. "I see ye've a sharp eye in your head. Ye're quick upon your feet, and quiet too. Ye'd have that from your father, who taught ye the art o' stalkin' i' the Hielan's, I've no doubt. On top o' all that ye're a first-class shot. I'm inclined to agree wi' Toby that ye'd do a good turn o' scoutin' in the woods. Would ye like to try your hand at it for a change?"

I sat up with a jerk at what he said, for no sooner were the words out of his mouth than I knew it was the very thing I had been hoping for. But my mother spoke before I could answer.

"Ah, shame, Davie!" she cried. "Do ye mean ye'd let the lad go out with the woods full of red savages?"

"Bless ye, Sheila," Uncle David replied, "there'd be no danger so long as he went with Toby. The old man's the best scout in the province, and he'd watch the lad like a hen partridge watches her brood. Ye've naught to fear."

"No!" said my mother sharply.

My uncle saw the disappointment on my face and smiled.

"Well, look ye, lass," he said, leaning forward and tapping her knee with the stem of his pipe to emphasize his words. "Ye made your mind ye'd live in Suncook, did ye not?"

My mother nodded.

"Aye then," said he, "ye'll have to take the bitter with the sweet. Is the lad cut out for a farmer, think ye?"

She looked at me dubiously. My uncle leapt into the breach.

"No," he said, "any fool who's watched him these three weeks gone can see that. He's not the build nor the spirit for it. He's not the patience to sit by and watch the seeds send up their slow shoots. He must be out and doing. He must be going."

He watched her nod, and sat back with an air of triumph.

"Well then," he cried, "since ye see the truth o' that, how's the lad to earn his bread in Suncook?"

My mother looked down at her hands in her lap and twisted her handkerchief.

"I don't know, Davie." Her voice sounded a shade desperate. "I don't know. I've thought and thought on it these last three weeks, and wondered if I did the right thing to come."

He nodded soberly.

"Aye," he said, "and well ye might. But put it from your thoughts, for I've the answer here." He tapped his forehead with his pipestem. "And I'll tell it to ye when the time comes. But first the lad must learn his way in the woods, for the man who's not to be a farmer here must at least be a woodsman."

My mother hesitated. He saw it and went on hurriedly.

"And that's not all," he said. "In October the militia's time is up, and those that live away—Sanborn and Merrill and Hatch and Crowe—will be going home. We'll need all the scouts we can spare then until snow flies. And Jamie's one we can spare for the duty."

My mother looked at her hands again.

"And ye think there'd be no danger, Davie?" she asked.

He shrugged.

"I'll not deceive ye, lass," he said. "There's danger in't. But no more than we all run in this very house."

She looked resigned.

"Well, then," she said, "if ye think it best, Davie."

He chuckled and turned to me.

"And what think ye, Jamie?" he demanded.

"Oh, aye, Uncle David," I said eagerly, for indeed I was excited at the prospect, and curious as well. "But what is't you've in mind for me?"

"Na, na, lad," he laughed. "We'll take one thing at a time."

Nor could I get anything more from him that night.

I felt then as I still feel that that night's conversation marked the real beginning of the new life for me. What we should have done had the thought behind it been impracticable, I cannot say. I doubt if I could have become a farmer. And what else there was for me to do, I know not. Certain I am of one thing, and that is that, but for that night's work, much of what is here related might never have happened as it did.

Fortunately I was not entirely without grounding in the fundamentals of woods lore. My father had insisted that I learn to shoot. Later, when I had accompanied him into the hills, he had shown me some of the tricks and intricacies of stalking and tracking. My eye was sharp. I was possessed of a good sense of direction, which, when all is said and done, is in the end no more than a sharp knack for observation. My hearing was good. I knew how to listen for those sounds of the woods that are important: the snapping of a twig, the rustle of a leaf, the thump of a wild thing's foot upon the ground. And by the same token I was able to exclude from my consciousness the chuckling of a distant brook, the flutter of a leaf in the breeze, the soughing of the trees in the wind—noises that are constant, even though unimportant and sometimes distracting, even in the most silent of forests. Besides this, I was able to move silently in almost any cover, and my small size enabled me to remain hidden where many another man must have shown himself.

Indeed, on that first morning when we trotted out from the fort for the day's scouting, I felt confident of my own ability to compete with Toby, at least without discredit, on his own grounds. To be sure, these rolling, wooded hills and valleys were not like our own rocky, heather-clad Highlands. In the first place they were much more densely timbered, so that much of the time we jogged along in the forest shadow. Nor were they so towering.

Far away, to northward, on a clear day, one could see from the lookout towers the dim blue outlines of many great peaks, such as might put even the lofty Ben Nevis himself to shame. But near at hand the hills were all low and rounded and with a sameness that was confusing to a newcomer. But in spite of this I did not feel myself to be at any disadvantage at first. As we trotted away along the path that led off north and east, skirting the rim of the Soucook valley, I even began to have a twinge of pity for the old fellow for having been coupled with such a spry, young, active lad as myself, who was like to walk off fast enough with whatever glory there might be in this business.

We had not gone an hour from the fort, however, when I was forced to recognize my mistake. I was in the presence of a master woodsman, beside whom my own efforts to swing along easily, quietly, swiftly, were as the wobbly antics of a stumbling calf. He jogged along smoothly at an effortless trot, seemingly reckless of where he placed his feet, and yet so quietly that even I, close as I was behind him, could scarce hear the soft pad of his moccasins as they touched the ground.

Three times in that hour he stopped to point out to me places where some small forest animal had crossed our path, though try as I might I could see no sign of their passing. Once he pointed out the spot where a rabbit had sat for a moment beneath a bush. Again he showed me the light footprints of a fox in a damp spot in the path—stalking a partridge, he told me. And sure enough, in a short distance along the way we came upon a handful of scattered feathers where the beast had struck. A little later he stopped and grasped my arm, pointing silently. It was a full minute before, following his pointing finger with my eyes, I was able to make out, standing on the edge of a thicket upon a little ridge, not far away, a magnificent buck watching us with steady curiosity. Farther along he stopped again to listen to the distant angry chatter of a red squirrel. A bear, he told me after a moment, was in the neighbourhood, and master squirrel was fearful lest his winter's store of nuts be discovered and raided.

Seeing the incredulity in my eyes, he bade me follow him. We went across the shoulder of a hill, moving silently from tree to tree, and came out above a little hollow in which was a scattering of oaks and beeches. Toby pointed triumphantly, and there below me, as he had foretold, was old bruin rooting and snuffling in a rotten log, while from the comparative safety of a tall oak the squirrel scolded furiously, all oblivious of our presence in the neighbourhood. There and then I made up my mind to cast aside all of my former pretensions and sit myself down at the feet of the master.

My education went along swiftly from that point, for I was quick to learn, taking a real interest in the things I saw. I soon learned to identify the various animals of the forest: the wolf, the wildcat, the bear, the catamount, the deer, the fox, the mink, the beaver and the otter, the weasel and the rabbit, the racoon and the hedgehog, so many of which were new to me. I learned to know the tracks of one from another, and where to look for them. Painstakingly, and with infinite patience, Toby taught me their various calls and made me imitate them again and again until he felt that I knew them thoroughly. He introduced me to the three watchdogs of the woods—the squirrel, the jay, and the crow—and taught me to heed their warnings. He said that if one listened closely enough to their jabberings and scoldings one could identify the danger that had set them off. Indeed he proved his point time and again, though I was never able to tell more from their racket than that something had disturbed them. He concentrated mostly upon hunting, saying that the man who could successfully hunt wild beasts would have no trouble tracking men. He taught me to know where a deer had lain and where he had browsed, and what he was feeding on, and whether he was running or walking and why. He taught me to watch where the bears had rooted about in rotten logs and stumps and where they had trampled the berry bushes and broken down the young wild cherry trees or raided a bee tree for its honey. He taught me to call the sharp-eyed fox and the overcurious wildcat to my gun by imitating the plaintive squeak of a rabbit in distress. He taught me what to look for, and how to go silently through the fallen leaves so that my prey would not be disturbed.

Nor were hunting and its allied arts all I learned. He taught me to identify the various woods which made up the forest: the oak, the beech, the maple, the white and yellow birches, the cherry, the hornbeam, the basswood, the alder, the butternut, the poplar, the ashes, the sumac, the willow, the fir, the spruce, the hemlock, the pine, the cedar, the tamarack, and others. He taught me to make a fire when the woods were dripping, to choose a camp site, dry in wet weather yet not without water, to make a bed of balsam boughs as comfortable and feathery as one of down, to handle a bark canoe in swift water and slow. Indeed, in time, it was he who taught me nearly all I know of woodcraft.

But it was not all learning on my part. I too could do some teaching: little things which tickled the old man's fancy. One day when we had tried for hours unsuccessfully to lure fat trout to our lines with fat wriggling worms, I tied a few small feathers and a bit of bright flannel to a hook and showed him how they might be taken on the surface. Later, when the leaves had gone and one could see to do it, I showed him how to bring down a whirring grouse upon the wing, though this last was scarcely necessary here for I found the birds so tame and chuckleheaded that it was possible to slip up upon them and knock them out of trees with sticks.

September had gone and most of October, before there occurred anything to break the even routine of the life into which we had settled. Five days each week I accompanied old Toby upon a swing to north or east or west. Sometimes we went as far afield as Epsom or Canterbury or even Hopkinton. But nothing ever seemed to come of it, though we were always on the alert for any sign of a hostile party in the neighbourhood; and in the end our excursions would generally break off into hunting or fishing trips which were much more fun.

Then suddenly, one gloomy dripping afternoon, we came upon the thing for which we had been watching all these weeks; the fresh print of a moccasined foot in the wet sand of the trail.

It was a miserable, rainy day, one of four all in a heap, with a dank east wind and frequent showers to keep us soaked to the skin. We had no thoughts of hunting that day. All we hoped to do was to keep the canvas covers tight across the priming of our guns, against the weather, and to complete our circuit as soon as might be so that we might return again to the welcome warmth of my uncle's hearth.

We left the fort in the morning, striking eastward to the Suncook and thence north some distance, to swing slowly in a great circle back to westward and across the Soucook Brook. It was past midafternoon, and we had come down out of the Broken Ground onto the Rumford Plain and were jogging across it at a steady gait with home almost in sight and the thought of the cheerful fire already warming our chilled bones, when suddenly Toby stopped with a guttural grunt and stood pointing to the ground before him with the muzzle of his musket. I pushed up close behind him and looked. There in the sand was the human print, as plain as the words upon this page.

I need hardly describe the excitement that gripped me at this discovery, nor the twinge of apprehension that accompanied it.

Toby seemed completely unconcerned. He squatted down in the path and studied the track carefully for several minutes. Then, rising, he signalled me to stay where I was and struck off the path to the left and began running in short circles like a quartering dog, searching the ground thoroughly for further signs.

Presently he stopped and beckoned me to him. Coming up, I saw that he had found several more tracks, bearing away in a general easterly course. He nodded vigorously without words, and then to my intense amazement struck directly away from them, going back into the Broken Ground, whence we had just come. I followed him without protest, for by this time I had learned that he had excellent reasons for anything he did.

We trotted in silence for some minutes, then turned sharply to the right and dropped down to cross the brook. Once across we turned right again, and bearing a little away from the brook towards the high ground, jogged south. Presently Toby stopped again, straightened, and gave a little grunt of satisfaction.

"Him cross brook down there," he said, pointing. "Not come back."

I looked but could see no sign that could tell him so much. Seeing my perplexity, he grinned and showed me where several blades of grass had been trodden down, and again where some wet leaves had been kicked over.

"You come," he said, and turning, led the way along the trail.

Presently we came to a small swamp which the track skirted to north and east. Here we stopped again and Toby came close, pointing to a hill that rose sharp upon the far side of the swamp. He held up three fingers.

"One, two, three Injun come Plausawa Hill," he whispered. "Plausawa Injun live on hill one time. Not bad, not good. Have bad friend. When war come he go. Now maybe come back again. No good!"

He grinned and looked at my gun.

"You ready?" he asked. "Maybe some shoot."

I nodded, tingling with excitement at the prospect, not willing to admit even to myself that I felt at all frightened.

He grunted his satisfaction and led the way, striking away from the trail of the three Indians and skirting the swamp to south and west.

Once around the swamp we climbed swiftly, skirting the southern slope of the hill to a cleft near the summit. We went through this and came out upon the far side. Here Toby stopped again, drew the cover from his gun and examined the priming. I followed his example. He leaned over to whisper in my ear.

"Plausawa camp near here," he said. "You come me."

I followed him then, treading close at his heels, trying hard to make no sound. Luck was with us, for the wet leaves did not crackle beneath our stealthy feet.

The Indian camp was well hidden. I doubt if any but an Indian could have found it. It consisted of a single small open-front bark shelter, backed against the hill in a tiny clearing in the midst of a thicket of tall firs. In front of the shelter was a tiny fire of dry hardwood twigs, as near smokeless as a fire can be; and about the fire sat huddled three Indians, one short and stocky, with a broad, stupid, good-natured face, the next two about the same build, of medium height with broad shoulders and slim waists, one with a look of stolid sullenness about him and the other with a face in which I believe was concentrated all the cruelty and meanness and evilness of a hundred generations. Their three muskets leaned aginst a tree on the far side of the clearing.

We had crept almost within hearing distance of their low voices, when Toby sprawled down behind a fallen spruce and beckoned me to him.

As I crept in beside him, he drew up his long musket and sighted carefully. Realizing what it was he meant to do then, I stopped him.

"You cannot," I said. "Not in cold blood."

He looked surprised and would have shaken me off, but I insisted.

"Bad Injun," he said. "Sabatis and Christo no good."

"None the less," I replied, "they must have their chance."

He gave me a peculiar look.

"You lie close," he whispered, placing his lips close to my ear, so that I was near overpowered with the stench of him. "Look good. If Injun make bad move you shoot."

I nodded, looking toward the camp, and stretched out behind the brush on my stomach. I pulled up my gun and thrust it through between the dead branches, lining up the nearest Indian, he of the evil face, across my sights. It occurred to me to ask Toby what he meant to do. But when I turned around he had vanished as completely as if the earth had swallowed him.

There was nothing for me to do but wait, and I waited for what seemed an interminable time. Once I had the panicky thought that the old man might have abandoned me; but I put it from me immediately, there being nothing else to do, and concentrated on trying to hear what it was the Indians were saying. But this I could not do. Now and again a word would drift to me, but it was in a language I could not understand. I gave it up presently, and was at once seized with an almost uncontrollable desire to scratch my back, though I knew the noise I must make in doing so would surely betray my hiding place. The itching grew stronger and stronger, until I all but cried out with it. Then suddenly, so suddenly that even I who had been half watching for something of the kind, was startled to see Toby appear suddenly upon the far side of the clearing, standing between the Indians and their guns.

"How!" he said.

The Indians looked up, the sudden surprise of his greeting robbing them for the moment of the power of speech. Before they could recover he spoke again.

"Toby not alone," he said.

They looked about them then at the sides of the clearing, nervously, apprehensively. I lay as still as death, scarce daring to breathe for fear some telltale movement would betray me. But Toby was speaking again, and their attention swung back to him.

"Why you come here?" he demanded.

He looked from one to another. It was the stocky, broad-faced one who answered.

"Plausawa afraid white man come kill," he said. "Plausawa go way long time live with friends. Now Plausawa come back for things."

Toby looked at the other two.

"Sabatis and Christo come help Plausawa carry all things?" he said.

The evil-faced one, whom I took to be Sabatis, nodded to three small packs that lay ready, unopened, before the shelter. Toby gave them a quick glance, then looked back at Plausawa.

"You go way Saint Francis?" he asked.

Plausawa did not answer. Toby grinned flatly.

"Good," he said. "Toby help. Toby carry guns."

He backed toward the guns and kicked them over and knelt beside them. Christo stirred slightly, and Toby swung the muzzle of his gun in his direction.

"Remember Toby not alone," he said.

It was plain that they knew not whether to believe him or no, but none of them cared to risk the proof. Fumbling Toby passed a thong through the trigger guards of the three guns, knotted it in a loop and passed it over his shoulder. He stood up.

"You take packs," he said.

He stood back and watched them pick up their bundles in sullen silence. Then he placed his fingers to his lips and whistled sharply. I knew it could only be a signal to me. I stood up.

"You come in," he called.

I came on into the clearing, and saw with amusement Sabatis' look of disgust at the way in which the old man had tricked them. Toby made them stand for a moment with their faces to the wall of the shelter, their hands behind their heads, while I moved along behind them, relieving them of knives and tomahawks. When this was done it was plain that they were disarmed, for in the leather leggings and breech clouts that each of them wore there was no hiding place for other weapons. Toby then jerked his head, indicating the path by which they had come. A moment later we were trotting in single file down the mountain side toward the west, Toby and I bringing up in the rear.

We went along behind them, escorting them on the first leg of their northward journey, across the brook and over the Rumford Plain, until we came to the Merrimack a little above the settlement at the Sugar Bowl. Here Toby stopped and pointed north along the river.

"You go," he said.

They hesitated an instant, as if uncertain whether to obey. Then Sabatis looked briefly at the smoke from the houses close at hand rising above the trees and turned away abruptly. The others followed one by one.

We stood and watched them as long as they were in sight. Once they turned and looked back at us, stolidly, hatefully. Then they turned again and were swallowed up in the gathering dusk.

When they had disappeared Toby sat down on a rock and carefully drew the charges from their guns. After that he took up a stone and smashed their locks, and finally, as if to make assurance doubly sure, he hurled each weapon as far as he was able into the river.

As we jogged homeward along the river road the old man looked sober and disturbed; but only once did he speak.

"No good!" he said then. "No good. Better we kill quick. Make trouble now."

And he shook his head, muttering over and over again to himself, "No good, no good."

6

Toward the end of October the four militiamen who were not natives of the settlement—Sanborn and Merrill and Hatch and Crowe—returned to their homes, the time for which they had contracted to serve having come to a close on the twentieth of the month. Unfortunately for us all, however, this did not occur before high words passed between Sanborn and myself over the way in which I had allowed the three Indians to escape whole-skinned.

I was not the first to have trouble with the man. Naturally lazy, he had grown sick of his job before he had been in the fort two weeks and began heartily to wish himself elsewhere. He began to grumble over the accommodations, which indeed were better than he would have enjoyed at home. He complained of the food, though I have yet to see how that might have been improved upon. He took to interpreting his duties as a militiaman in the most literal fashion. He would willingly stand guard in the pasture while the maids were milking, for he said that this was one of the things he had contracted with the Province to do—though secretly I believe it was because he had an eye for the girls. But he would not patrol the woods in the vicinity of a working party, saying that this was work for the local scouts. He was extremely fond of liquor and took to drinking in great quantities, and at all times, so that it was difficult to know when he was like to be sober. The worst of this was that drink had not the jollying effect on him that it has on some. On the contrary it made him meaner and more belligerent and more difficult to deal with. By the end of August he had become so bad that my uncle had to threaten him with a touch of the cat: a move which only drove him to be more secretive in his tippling. He shirked his duty whenever possible and loafed about the place, eyeing the girls with the greatest of insolence. In the end it became so bad that the women were afraid to be left alone in the fort with him. Indeed there were none who trusted him and few who got along with him save his friend Merrill, who toadied to him in sickening fashion.

All of this was bad enough, though, as I have since discovered, rather to be expected, for it has always been my experience with militia and the lax discipline that obtains among them that there are always some who are so inclined. But the most difficult of all to put up with was the man's boasting. A blowhard by nature, he bragged endlessly of his own prowess and constantly criticized the way in which the defence was handled, leaving no room for doubt as to how he would do it. The worst of this was that his talk was not without foundation; for the constant watching and waiting was irksome in the extreme, and whatever one might think of the man he was at least no coward. Indeed it was well known that once in Bakerstown, where he lived, he had single-handed attacked and put to flight a band of seven hostile Indians who had come upon him while he was hunting in the woods. Instead of giving him an understanding of the problem to be faced in the protection of the settlement, however, this only served to make him the more arrogant and critical. Most of us looked forward with pleasure to the twentieth of October as the day on which we should at last be shut of him.

Notwithstanding his anxiety to be off, when that day finally arrived he astounded us all by refusing flatly to leave. The Province, he maintained, owed him four months' pay as a militiaman, and he would not stir until he had received it. In vain my uncle argued with him, telling him that the money would be sent to him at his home or any other place he would be pleased to designate. He would not go. Merrill, of course, followed his hero's lead and also refused to leave. The others, Hatch and Crowe, being slow-witted fellows, were bewildered by the turn of affairs and hung on in indecision, uncertain what to do, so that we were burdened by the support of them at a time when they should have all been gone.

To make matters worse Sanborn and Merrill steadfastly refused to continue their duties, their time being up. Somewhere they laid hold of a cask of rum, and with this between them they loafed about the enclosure day and night, tippling constantly and making complete nuisances of themselves.

It was three days after their scheduled departure that my encounter with the three Indians on Plausawa Hill took place. When we reported the occurrence that night to my uncle he shook his head and agreed with Toby that it undoubtedly meant trouble, for he had no doubt but that Sabatis and Christo at least would attempt to retaliate. On the other hand he agreed with me that there was little else we could have done. To shoot them down without warning and in cold blood was out of the question, and we had no facilities at Suncook for prisoners. Moreover the Indians had not been painted for the warpath, though there could be no doubt that they meant to work such mischief as they might before returning to Saint Francis. All in all it had been a sort of stalemate, and we had followed the best course possible in the circumstances.

The next day came off clear and cold after the rain; and as it was Davie's day to accompany Toby it was, strictly speaking, my day off. Not wanting to remain idle, however, I volunteered to help guard the working party, which was that day engaged in clearing away some woods on a lot near the river. When they finished, late in the afternoon, I left the rest to hunt back along the south bank of Soucook Brook. I came in about dusk with a brace of fat partridges which it was my intention to drop at the kitchen in passing.

As I crossed the enclosure I could see three or four of the men lolling about before one of the cabins, smoking and talking in low tones. I had my hand on the kitchen latch and was about to open the door when someone grasped my arm and jerked me about. It was the man Sanborn, and the aura of rum was thick about him. Even in the half-light I could see that he was drunk and was in an ugly mood.

"Ha!" he snarled. "Here's a white-livered lad turns Injuns loose upon the country to scalp honest men!"

"What would ye have me do?" I demanded, trying to free myself from his grip.

"I know what I'd 'a' done," he growled, thrusting his bleary face into mine and blowing his stinking breath at me so that I was nigh overpowered. "I'd 'a' made good Injuns of 'em 's quick 's pull a trigger. That's what I'd 'a' done!"

"Aye," I said, and sharply too for I had no patience with either him or his talk, "and without a whisper of warning, I doubt not. 'Twould be like you, Mr. Sanborn, to take that way. But for me I've a mind to shoot down no man without he knows at least that he's in danger!"

And with that I gave my arm an angry wrench in a last effort to get free.

Now it so happened that he held me by the gun arm, so that when I twisted, it raised my rifle. It may have been that he thought I meant to shoot him then. He was fuddled enough for such thoughts. But, whatever it was came into his mind, I never knew the gist of it, for he acted too quickly for me.

Shifting his grip to his other hand, he knocked my gun flying with a blow. I saw his great knob of a fist coming, and I tried to dodge it; but he held me so that I scarce could move, and he caught me on the side of the jaw, just beneath the ear. I felt myself spinning through the air to crash against the side of the house. A great stab of light went flashing before my eyes, and then I went down all in a heap.

When I opened my eyes, all wet and dripping a few moments later, Old Dougal stood by with an empty bucket, and cousin Donald was bending over me. A little knot of men had gathered about Sanborn and backed him off against the wall, and he was standing wobbly before my uncle, who, white-faced with anger, was speaking to him rapidly through grim, tight lips. What it was he was saying, I could not hear, for my head was still ringing from the force of the blow; but it was plain that it was not pleasant from the expression of sullen hate upon Sanborn's face. It was also equally obvious that it was popular with the men, for they grouped about them nodding vigorously and eyeing Sanborn with open hostility. Indeed Timothy Stevens was poking the muzzle of his rifle into his stomach in no friendly manner, and looked only too eager to pull the trigger. I have a faint recollection of

Merrill hovering somewhere in the background looking white and not a little frightened.

Cousin Donald helped me to my feet and took me in the house. When I came down to supper some time later the two men, Merrill and Sanborn, were sitting together in a far corner of the chimney, arguing angrily in lowered tones over their small beer; and when I rose in the morning they were both gone. It would have been well for me if I had been able to say that, at least as far as I was concerned, this was the last of them. As luck would have it, however, I was not destined to be so fortunate.

After the flight—for such it almost appeared to be—of our guards, those of us who remained found our work cut out for us. Toby and Timothy Stevens were all that were left to us of the militia. Daniel Stinson and Moses Rush were called into the fort and pressed into service as scouts. But even at that there was plenty of work for us all. On days when we were not out with Toby in the woods we took turns standing guard over the work parties or patrolling the neighbouring forest. At night we divided the tower watches among us, and since there were but eight of us, with two to be on guard at all times, there was always someone who was cheated of his rest.

For all we were busy, however, I did not forget that my uncle had said he had something in mind for us, and naturally I was curious about it. Day and night, whenever I had the opportunity, I plagued him about it, begging him to give me even a hint. But always he shook his head, and sometimes he put me off with more impatience than was his wont. I guessed he was worried lest the Indians attack us in our weakened state, and in the end it proved that this was so.

But no suspense can last for ever. For all his apprehension the Indians did not come near us that fall; and when one considers it coldly, in the light of reason, it would have been surprising indeed if they had. It was a long journey to Saint Francis, almost to the Saint Lawrence, and for Sabatis, Christo, and Plausawa to have made it, unarmed as they were, in time to return with a war party bent on revenge, would have been a remarkable feat. Still my uncle was plainly nervous. Day in and day out he gave the impression of waiting; waiting either for the attack or for something else. And one day in mid-November something else happened that ended all fear of attack for the moment.

It was my turn to go out with Toby, and we slipped out about dawn, crossing the Merrimack at the falls, a little to the south of Rumford, intending to make a wide circle to westward into Starkstown, swinging back to the river at Isle a Huckset, below Suncook. The night had been cold, the ground was frozen hard as a stone, and there had been a heavy frost. The day gave every promise, when we left the fort, of being clear and sharp; but we had not reached the river before a bitter wind came up out of the northeast, whistling and rattling in the bare branches of the trees. Overhead the sky began to grow hazy, and the temperature of the air dropped steadily.

At noon we viewed the ruins of the Rogers homestead, and a little later ate our midday meal beside a little pond. We had seen no sign of an enemy aside from the charred remains of the house above us. Nor did the animals of the forest seem on the move. Not once throughout the morning had I seen a sign of deer feeding; nor had I even seen where they had moved from one spot to another. It was unusual in this country, usually so overrun with game. I thought it sufficiently remarkable to speak of it to my companion.

Toby grinned. He looked up at the sky. It was by now completely overcast by dull, low-hanging, slate-coloured clouds that spread in tumbling waves from one side of the horizon to the other. He sniffed the wind, which had swung about to the east.

"Snow comin'," he said. "Big storm. Deer stay hide till go by."

It seemed to me early for anything like that, yet I reminded myself I knew nothing of this country's weather. It might very likely be so.

Toby's prophecy proved correct. When we had finished our meal we turned toward home, travelling steadily at a good pace. It was midafternoon, and we were yet a mile and a half from the river, when the first great flakes began to drive against our faces. The wind died entirely, and the snow began to come down faster. By the time we reached the river the ground was already white and the snow was falling so thickly that we could not see across.

It was dark when we reached the fort. My uncle met us with a cheery hail, and the weight of years seemed to have fallen from his shoulders.

"Good snow, hey, Toby?" he said as we swung in through the stockade gate.

The old man nodded solemnly.

"Good snow," he replied.

"We'll have a foot and a half by morning at this rate," said my uncle, eyeing the whitened ground before the fort. There must have been two inches of it even then.

Toby lifted his face to the light wind and watched the snow swirling about the corner of the stockade.

"More snow come," he said. "Now just begin. Tomorrow morning have plenty."

He held his hand halfway up his thigh to indicate the probable depth of the snow in the morning.

"Maybe him come more snow tomorrow," he added. "No can tell."

My uncle laughed gaily as he herded us inside the house.

"Let it snow for a week," he boomed. "We can't have too much for me! As long as the snow lies between here and Canada I'll sleep easy o' nights."

His humour was contagious, and we were a merry crew that night. When supper was finished he reached over and laid his hand upon my mother's arm, nodding at the same time toward the chimney corner.

"A word with ye, lass," he said.

He caught my eye fixed eagerly upon him, and he laughed.

"Aye," he said, "an' ye too, Jamie, for 'tis business o' your own I'll be speaking of."

I lost no time in accepting his invitation, for as I have said I was eager to learn what he had in mind. When we had settled ourselves in the corner and he had his long pipe going well, he leaned over and tapped my mother on the knee.

"Now, lass," said he. "Ye've told me ye were worried as to what's to do here, an' I've taken the liberty o' doin' a bit o' yer thinkin' for ye."

My mother nodded, but he did not wait for a reply.

"There's a need here, in the North End," he went on, "that I've been a-watchin' grow for a long time. 'Tis a thing I'd have done long since myself; but ye know, lass, we're a poor lot, and to tell ye true I'd not the money that it needed."

He paused a moment and looked from me to my mother and back again. Neither of us said anything.

"But now," he continued, with just a touch of embarrassment, "ye've come with a little money in yer jeans and an eye out for work the lad can do. Perhaps ye an' me can work together for the thing ye want an' the thing we need."

I could tell by the thickening of his brogue, a sure sign with him, that he was growing excited as he warmed to the subject. But my mother was as yet unmoved.

"Aye, Davie?" she said. "An' what is it you've in mind?"

"A sawmill!" he replied, slapping his knee with his open palm, and sat back to see the effect upon her.

If he expected to surprise her he had certainly succeeded.

"A—a sawmill!" she gasped. "But, Davie! How—what—"

He leaned forward, chuckling, and tapped her knee with his pipe.

"Aye," he said, "a sawmill! Ye've a hundred questions ye want to ask, but I'll save ye trouble an' answer some o' them now, if ye'll listen."

He paused. My mother nodded.

"In the first place," he said, "ye'll tell me there's one sawmill in the town already. Aye. John Cochran's in the South End. But John can't take care o' all the demand as it is. As a result there's those are using logs in the north'd use sawn timbers if they could get them."

Mother nodded again.

"Second," he went on, "ye're wonderin' how Jamie could buck the heavy timbers about. But there'd be no need o' that. The lads and myself would take care o' that end. I wanted Jamie to learn the woods, so 'twill be his task to go out and spot the timber we must cut. That and the handling o' the business end, with Old Dougal yon to help him, will be his share. The town will grant ye some o' the land ye need and the rights to the power; an' what other land we need, we'll buy. We'll do the thing together. What do ye say?"

"But, Davie," my mother protested feebly, "granting there's a demand for timber now, is there enough demand to keep it going?"

"Na, na, lass," said my uncle, smiling, " 'tis a good point. But ye need not worry about the mill. 'Twill continue to show ye a profit, though it may not be large after the first couple o' years. But the splitting o' sticks is not all I have in my mind. There's a demand for lumber for the building o' ships on the coast from Portsmouth all the way to Boston. 'Tis an undeveloped thing as yet, but 'twill grow. By the time the lad's of age 'twill be a business like to make his fortune."

He paused.

"Aye," he went on before either of us could speak, "an' 'tis not all I'd thought of. There's the matter of masting for the Royal Navy—cutting out the great pine sticks and floating them down for mast in His Majesty's ships. 'Tis a game that's lined many a pocket ere now, and not all may do it; only those who hold the Royal warrant to cut the King's Woods."

"But could we get the warrant?" said my mother a little doubtfully.

He laughed and winked.

"Aye," said he, "it might be done with the proper sort of persuasion."

"Now, David Ross," said my mother, "ye know I'll have naught to do with bribery of public officials."

He chuckled.

"Nay, lass," he said, "ye're wrong to call it bribery. Why, Benning Wentworth himself paid two thousand pound for the post of Surveyor o' the King's Woods. 'Tis only business if he seeks to get it back!"

But my mother still looked prim.

"Come, lass," he said, "the masting's a thing to be decided upon later. 'Tis the other that's important. What say ye?"

He swung to me.

"Aye, and ye too, Jamie," he added. "Let's hear your own mind on't."

If there was the least doubt in my mother's mind, there was none in mine. Indeed, even had I not been enthusiastic in its favour, I could see that it was no choice at all that he was offering us. I had already proven that I should never be a farmer, and if I were not to follow my uncle's suggestion, what was there left for me to do? It was either that or return to Boston, where perhaps something in the way of a clerkship might have been found for me; and the life of the city seemed to me dull by comparison with what my uncle offered. I had no hesitation in speaking my mind. My uncle beamed.

"There, lass, ye see?" he said. "The lad's an eye for an opportunity. Follow his lead and ye'll not go wrong."

My mother looked at me. Perhaps it was the eagerness in my face, perhaps it was just that she looked to me for confirmation of her own thoughts; but, whatever it was that moved her, I know that in that instant when our eyes met she made up her mind. She turned.

"All right," she said, "and here's my hand on't, Davie."

They shook hands across my lap, and my uncle clapped me on the shoulder.

" 'Tis a decision ye'll ne'er regret," he said. "Ye'll see."

He leaned forward and began to speak rapidly, seriously, punctuating his sentences with short jabs of his pipestem.

"Now, look ye, to begin with we'll have to get the water and milling rights o' Soucook Brook. 'Tis for the proprietors to grant them—propose them myself at the next meeting. In return . . . have to mill town lumber at . . . price they set . . . one day a week for ten years . . . lumber . . . we get off ourselves . . . sell at our own price."

As his voice rumbled on I found myself growing more and more sleepy. The heat of the fire, the long hard day I had put in, and now this droning conversational monotone, all combined to send me off. More than once I caught myself nodding, and presently all I heard was occasional words: "Prices . . . markets . . . board feet . . . stumpage . . . woods crews . . . free timber . . . King's Woods . . ." At last even he noticed it. He laughed.

"But see, now," he chuckled, "I've talked the lad to sleep."

He clapped me on the shoulder and shook me awake.

"Come, lad," he said, "ye've had a long day o't. Get ye away to bed. We'll have time a plenty to speak o' this again."

And so I rose and stumbled across the room to the kitchen passage, whence the stairs led up to the room I shared with my cousins Davie and Rob. But though I was tired and had fallen asleep in the midst of the talk, still it was as if a great weight of uncertainty had been lifted from my shoulders by the decision, so that I was ready to be gay and happy, to dance and laugh and sing, had I not still been half asleep. Indeed, even so, when I met the waif Purity in the passage, I did not properly resent her sharp remarks upon my dishevelled appearance, my cap being set askew upon my head and my coat pulled awry by the position to which I had slumped in the chimney corner. Instead I laughed and chucked her lightly beneath the chin, then clapped my arm about her waist and bussed her soundly upon both cheeks, much to her amazement and indignation. For once as I stumbled up the stairs she stood silent, staring, without words to express herself.

· 6 ·

WHICH TREATS OF A PASSAGE OF YEARS AT SUNCOOK

⟨ 1 When I arose the next morning the ground lay hidden under a knee-deep blanket of snow. All that day it continued to fall steadily, in ghostly silence, sifting down out of leaden skies, with scarce a breath of wind to carry it, piling up in the corners of the stockade and on the roofs of the cabins, where it melted slowly and ran down, decorating the eaves with long rows of hanging icicles.

There were some pessimists who said that it came too early and could not last. But no one paid them any heed. And indeed they proved false prophets, for though we had a warm spell almost immediately afterwards, that in turn was followed by a storm of blizzard proportions that raged for four solid days and nights, banking the snow up level with the windows, and heaping it in immense drifts in the lee of the hills. After that there could be but small cause for worry, for Canada and Saint Francis were cut off and as far removed from us as if they had been in another world.

But the coming of the snow did not mean idleness. I for one found that much of what I had learned during the summer and fall I must now learn over again. I found that the animals we hunted did not keep to the same ground nor follow the same runs that they had before the snow came. Trees looked different now that their leaves were gone and the ground covered, and I had to learn to identify them by their bark. I went out frequently with Toby on his trap line, so that by the time spring came I knew how to rig a snare or set a deadfall to take anything from a rabbit to a bear. I learned to trap beaver beneath the ice, to search out the sheltered spots on south-sloping hills where the deer yarded for the winter, and there set my traps for the wary bobcat and the gaunt grey wolf, on which last the Province paid an excellent bounty. I learned to watch for blowholes in the snow in the shelter of overturned trees and rocks, which might indicate where a bear had lain out for his winter's sleep. But first of all I must learn to use and make the great, cumbersome webbed snowshoes, without which any kind of travel in the deep snow was impossible.

Nor was this all we had to occupy our time. True to my uncle's predictions, the proprietors were anxious to see us settled in the town. For a matter of twenty pounds old tenor they granted us a hundred-acre lot in the northwest section, bordered by Soucook Brook and the Merrimack, the lower half of which was comprised of meadow land in the river bottom, while the upper portion was wooded hillside with a magnificent view: to northward over the expanse of the Rumford plain, and to southward over the broad valley and river bottom of the Merrimack itself. It was on this hilltop that we determined to build our new home.

In addition to this the proprietors agreed, for a further consideration of twenty pounds, to grant us a mill site on the Soucook, close to the highroad where it crossed into the town of Rumford, together with a four-hundred-acre wood lot, to begin above my uncle's property on Soucook Brook and to extend well up above the northern slope of Plausawa Hill. In return for this we must agree to build and equip the mill, and in addition to set aside one day each week in which we would saw free of charge, for the next ten years, any lumber which any resident of the town might haul to us for his own cutting.

Once this was settled, the work began in earnest. Ground had to be cleared for both the house and the mill, and lumber chosen for the construction of each. Construction itself could not begin until the snow was gone and the frost out of the ground. But the timber could and should be selected, cut, and hauled to the site while conditions were favourable. It was on this task that I accompanied my uncle every day to the wood lot, where we marked trees for cutting, choosing stout oak for flooring and heavy timbers, resilient spruce for rafters and studding, great pines for boarding and for the panelling of the rooms in the house (despite the fact that these were marked as the King's Trees, and their cutting prohibited), and cedar for clapboards and shingles.

In this way I had my first schooling in what was later to become my work. I learned then how to estimate the approximate number of feet in a stand of timber, to know which trees would saw well into straight-grained, knot-free boards, and which woods were good for what purpose.

Towards the middle of December cousin Abigail took to her bed and there produced for Donald a ten-pound boy—an event of course which gave the signal for a round of celebration and merry-making. Uncle David turned positively silly over this, his first grandchild. Aunt Kate and my mother wept tears of joy and gratification in copious quantities, wrapped in each other's arms. Donald sat bursting with fatherly pride over a can of ale in the chimney corner and drank solemnly with each neighbour who came to wish them joy and congratulate them, while Nabby, bundled in warm blankets, held her place proudly beside him and fondled the youngster in her lap. Old Toby created a stir by appearing with a pair of tiny boots which he had made himself of the soft white winter fur of the weasel.

The sight of so much domestic happiness and felicity evidently produced a feeling of sentimental envy in more than one breast, for I noticed that the two sad-faced Blunt women were diffident and eyed Nabby rather wistfully. And once, much to their confusion, when I was going to the kitchen to replenish the great pitcher of ale, I came upon my sister Edith and young Moses Rush embracing fondly in the passageway. The only person in the house whose temper did not seem in any way improved by the event was young Mistress Purity, for she rated me soundly for a clumsy clod when I collided with her, quite by accident, in the dim light at the foot of the stair.

In the midst of the revelry we had our first visitor from the outside since our arrival. This proved to be none other than the great-nosed Rob Rogers, the same who had carried my mother's letter from Boston to my uncle, and whose father's house in Starkstown had been razed by the Indians. He was journeying through to Rumford, and he brought with him the first news we had heard of the world beyond Suncook.

The Quebec expedition, it appeared, had come to naught when the worthy burghers of Boston and Portsmouth had been frightened out of their wits by the news of a great French fleet hovering off the coast. They could not, they said, allow the troops to go and leave them defenceless in the face of such a threat, and indeed it is doubtful if the expedition would have taken place even so, for the promised transports and reinforcements of regular troops from England had never arrived. Fortunately the elements had taken a hand on the side of the English and sent a storm to scatter the Monsieur's fleet beyond hope of reorganization that year. In consequence the troops of the various provinces, which had been gathered at Boston, were being sent to their homes, the New Hampshire regiments having already been marched, by way of Dover and Rochester, to camp at the foot of Great Winnepiseogee Pond where Governor Wentworth had some holdings for whose safety he was evidently anxious.

Rogers told us further that it was rumoured that the Hampshire troops had been ordered thither for the purpose of marching later to destroy the Indian village of Saint Francis. Hearing this, my uncle shook his head soberly. How, he demanded to know, could an army be expected to march three hundred miles through deep snow in a trackless wilderness in the dead of winter and return? The problem of supply alone would be insurmountable. And he added that, although the object of the expedition itself was worthy beyond doubt, the idea of effecting it at this time of the year was utterly ridiculous and sounded to him like one of Governor Shirley's crack-brained schemes.

As it later proved, the idea was indeed that of the worthy Governor of the Bay Province; and like so many of that gentleman's grandiose plans it came to naught. In the meantime the troops were held throughout the winter in their wintery camp, spending their time in idleness. Many of the men sickened from exposure and died. Many, having nothing else to do, wasted their time in drinking, gambling, and fishing through the ice; while others, weary of the inactivity and stupidity of the life, simply deserted.

We heard plenty of talk of this in the next few weeks in Suncook, but it was turning into February before we came across a definite example. My uncle and I had been out in the wood lot all day combing the hillside for a stand of white ash suitable for use as window and door frames in the house. We had been singularly unsuccessful in the search, and towards evening had worked well around onto the north side of Plausawa Hill. I was about to suggest we give it up for the day, when my uncle uttered an exclamation and, gripping my arm with his left hand, pointed down the hill with his right.

Looking in the direction he indicated, I saw that we had come out at a point somewhat above the Indian, Plausawa's, hollow, and from the clump of spruce in which stood his camp there now rose, clear and sharp in the crisp, cold air, a thin streak of blue smoke.

There could be no mistaking the location. It was plain that someone was occupying the camp. I wondered if the Indians had returned. My heart thumped, and I looked at my uncle inquiringly. Evidently enough he too was worried. He cautioned me to silence and led the way down the hill.

As quietly as possible, we circled around the camp and moved up through the thick cover of spruce and balsam. As we came close to the little clearing in the centre my uncle parted the branches before him slightly, so that we could look through and see without ourselves being seen. There, sure enough, was the bark shelter, just as I had seen it last, save for the snow piled deep around it. And there was the fire whose smoke we had seen, and squatting beside it on his heels, his back to us, roasting a partridge on a stick over the coals was a man.

Even though we could not see his face it was plain that here was no Indian. He was clad in the conventional buckskin shirt and leggings, and on his head he wore a great bushy cap of coonskin which hid his neck; but the hands that turned the spit were white. Apparently some sixth sense warned him that he was being watched, for suddenly he looked back over his shoulder, turning his face in our direction; and at once I had the feeling that somewhere, recently, I had seen his face before. There was an elusive familiarity in the dark eyes set deep under shaggy brows, in the long straight nose, the wide jaws and generous mouth with its humorous quirk at the corners.

But I had no chance to voice my surprise or ask questions. Before I could speak, my uncle stepped forward into the clearing with an exclamation of welcome, not unmingled with reproach.

"God's my life!" he said, the strongest oath I ever heard him utter, " 'tis Jed Stiles! What brings ye here, man, and for why do ye not come to the house instead o' skulkin' out here on the hillside like a man a-hiding?"

The other stuck the end of the ramrod on which the bird was spitted into the snow so that it was hung over the fire just out of reach of the flames, and stood up facing us, I thought, somewhat sheepishly.

"Ah," he said, " 'tis you, Mr. Ross! I'd a mind someone was a-watchin'."

He came forward and held out his hand, stepping up out of the low pit in which the fire was sunk. I saw then that he was very tall, towering head and shoulders over my uncle, and thin in proportion to his height.

They shook hands.

"We saw your smoke," said my uncle, "and looked into it."

He caught the man's glance fixed curiously upon me.

"I'll acquaint ye with my nephew," he said. "Jamie, 'tis Purity's father."

He had no need to explain the fact, for I had realized it the moment he spoke. The child was the feminine miniature of the man. We shook hands cordially.

" 'Tis the lad helped old Toby clear the camp for me," Stiles said, nodding toward the shelter.

It was my uncle's turn to be surprised again.

"And how did ye know that?" he demanded.

Stiles grinned slowly.

"The news travels," he replied. "With Sanborn and Merrill telling it all about the country 'twould be a wonder if I hadn't heard."

My uncle looked grim.

"No doubt they've a deal to say on't," he said.

"Aye," said Stiles, "no doubt they have, but I've my own mind as to the how of it."

He grinned dryly and spat.

My uncle looked at him sharply.

"Ye've not said what brings ye here, Jed," he reminded.

The other looked sheepish and kicked at a crust of snow with the toe of his moccasin.

" 'Twas a matter of disagreement," he said, " 'twixt me and the colonel. I'd a mind to leave, for I told him I'd 'listed to serve against Quebec. But he said I must stay my time. I'd no stomach to stay in camp all winter, a-drilling on the ice, so I came away."

My uncle looked at him severely.

"Aye!" he said. "And now ye know ye're liable to the cat for desertion if they take ye?"

Stiles laughed heartily.

"Faith!" he roared. "Then they must needs flog half the army when they catch 'em. I'm not the first to leave."

My uncle shrugged and shook his head hopelessly.

"Aye, Jed," he said, "I mind ye were never a man to sit still for long."

He turned and looked at the shelter.

"Well," he went on, half musingly, "ye've no need to stay here. Ye'd be like to die o' the cold, and good hands are too few in Suncook for that. Kick out yon fire, and come along."

The winter dragged on slowly. Cousin Donald, in charge of the woods crews, saw to it that the timber we had marked was cut, peeled, and skidded out to be piled close by the clearing that had been made at the mill site. Twice Uncle David took the oxen, with Jonathan Stinson handling the other team, to Haverhill, whence they returned laden with machinery for the mill; and once they went north to the quarries in Rumford, where they found great millstones ready-cut for them.

Jed Stiles spent the winter in the fort, helping with the logging, and Robert Rogers, who was staying in Rumford with his people, was a constant visitor. These two soon struck up an acquaintance that presently grew into something like friendship. Although Stiles must have been close to twenty years Rogers' senior they would sit for hours toasting their boots before the great fire in the long evenings, each nursing a noggin of flip or toddy, trading stories of camp and forest that kept us all on edge with excitement or howling with laughter and went far to keeping us all hearty and cheerful in one another's company despite the dreariness of the season.

Toward the end of March the ice went out with a rush, and the snow began to melt rapidly. Slowly the frost came out of the ground and it became possible to get on with the building. Work on the mill must be completed before anything could be done on the house, if only for the reason that my mother had said that if live she must in a wooden house, it must be of sawn timbers throughout with none of your rough logs to be found in it anywhere. If he laughed at this feminine conceit, at least my uncle respected it, and work on the mill went forward swiftly. Foundations were laid, and then the timbers and floor. A temporary wheel and a wooden flume, leading from the brook above, were built, to serve until the coming of low water in August when a dam and permanent wheel could be installed.

By the middle of May my uncle announced that work had progressed sufficiently on the mill to hold a raising. This was a new word to me, though from the excitement his remark created I judged it to be something extremely pleasant. The girls clapped their hands and giggled with delight. Donald and Davie and Rob greeted the announcement with whoops of joy; Jed Stiles slapped his thigh and laughed with great gusto and told my uncle to see to it he had rum and cider a plenty. Over in the chimney corner Toby's beady black eyes glistened in the firelight, and he grinned and licked his lips and rubbed his stomach in anticipation. Later when I questioned Davie about it I learned that a raising was an affair at which the entire neighbourhood turned out to assist in the building and completion of a house or other structure, and that such occasions were always the signal for much merrymaking. I remarked that the raising would be like to last a week or more, since so little of the actual building, beyond the foundations, was as yet complete. But there I showed my ignorance of raisings.

The next Sunday at meeting the Reverend Whittemore announced in booming tones from the pulpit: "Next Friday—May the 17th—there will be a raising held at the site of the new Ferguson mill on Soucook Brook, starting at six in the morning. Refreshments will be served, and in the evening there will be supper for all comers."

If I expected a show of excitement at this I was doomed to disappointment, for not a face in the congregation changed its expression. I began to fear for the success of the venture, but when the meeting was over and the people had streamed outside, Deacon Whittemore's sermon was forgotten, and all conversation hinged upon the raising.

In the week that followed we boys were kept busy hunting. Monday and Tuesday venison was in demand, and our orders were to search out young bucks and does, whose meat would be sweet and tender, and to let the old ones go. Davie, Dan Stinson, and myself each accounted for two. Donald brought in three, and Toby produced five. This was considered enough, and after that we were set to chasing pigeons, partridges, rabbits, squirrels, and any other small game that would make a tantalizing pie. Squash and pumpkins, turnips and potatoes, were brought up from the cellar. Crocks of green beans, salted away the previous summer, were produced; and the girls went daily into the meadows with pails and paring knives, in search of tender young dandelion greens which were just beginning to show. The older women kept to the kitchen, up to the elbows in flour and dough, baking and making pies and cakes and bread and biscuit against the great day.

Friday came bright and clear, with a red sun climbing up over the rim of the hills to draw the mist thick and white from the river and the marsh. By five o'clock we were all of us down at the mill site, though for company we had none but the birds and two kegs of rum and two barrels of cider. By half past the hour I began to have my doubts, and by a quarter to six I had become downright pessimistic: certain that our raising had been forgotten. But no sooner had I made up my mind to the fact than the first cart appeared on the roadway. It was James Moore and his family, whose garrison stood between my uncle's and Deacon Whittemore's. With his two sons he climbed down and came towards us. The women stayed in the cart and went on to the fort, where they fell to and helped in the kitchen.

By quarter past six nearly thirty carts had arrived, and more than fifty men were at work, some squaring timbers, others fitting joints, still others boring holes or shaping pegs, for we had no nails heavy enough for timbers. By seven, more than a score of others had arrived, including some from as far away as Epsom and Rumford. Among these last were Robert Rogers and his younger brother Richard, a lad about my own age though, like his brother, large and on the blustering side. Indeed had he not lacked his brother's huge nose I should have been hard put to it to know the difference between them. They brought with them two young men who had been trapping on the river to northward, and who had stopped off to visit the Rogerses on their way home to Londonderry. These were that same William Stark whom I had met in Boston with Rogers, and his brother John, a hawk-nosed, droop-mouthed, saturnine youth, tall and wiry, some two years my elder: a lad with a dry sort of humour, to whom I did not at once take greatly, but who in later years was to prove a friend indeed.

If I had had doubts as to the possibility of completing the mill in a day, these fourscore men soon showed me my mistake. They worked as busily as a hill of ants: hauling, rolling, squaring, fitting, hoisting, boring, pegging—all interspersed with frequent trips to the liquor barrels, so that during the day the rum kegs had to be replenished three times and the cider barrels twice. By noon the open framework of the mill was in place. By midafternoon the machinery had been installed and the roof timbers were on. By evening the logs were piled on the skids ready for feeding to the rollers, the saw was spinning, and the roof shingled with hand-riven shakes. A crew was already sliding the carriage back and forth, preparatory to sawing the first log, and already the wrestling and foot races that marked the climax of the day's fun were getting under way.

I was tired then, for I had done my share. I wandered up by the cider barrels to quench a thirst that had been growing steadily. By the rum kegs I could see Toby and Jed Stiles, apparently unwilling to leave lest the rum be gone when they returned. The Indian was sitting on the ground laughing foolishly at nothing, his fat belly shaking up and down with the motion of his laughter. Stiles was teetering back and forth, heel and toe, waving a brimming mug of potent rum, and tunelessly singing "Old Benning Wentworth." At sight of me dipping my cup into the cider he loosed a dismal howl, and lurched toward me.

"Shbellywash, m'lad!" he hiccuped. "Godshblood, shbellywash I shay! Shnot fit for feedin' hogsh! 'Ere!"

He knocked the cup from my hand and thrust his own at me.

"Thash mansh drink," he roared. He leaned down and picked up my cup, filling it at the rum barrel. "Thish 'casion f'r mansh drinksh. Thish pro'er shcasion. Thish grea' gra' glorioush 'casion! Fergshul—Fergshik—Fergshon mill finish. Aw done. Grea' folksh, Fergshers. Heresh to mill!"

And with that he raised the cup to his lips, draining it at a single gulp. As the fiery liquor burned his gullet he screwed up his face wryly, then lifted his head to the sunset and gave tongue to a long sorrowful wolf's howl, "Whooeee! Whooeee! 'Ray f'r mill!" And he pitched over on his back upon a pile of brush, where he lay sprawled out flat, his mouth wide open, dead to the world.

Then I became aware of someone beside me and, looking down,

saw the child Purity. She was looking up at me with pleading in her eyes and humility on her lips.

"We must get him to bed," she said, "help me—please!"

I glanced toward the mill. The men were swarming out on the logs, searching a good stick. I wanted to be present when that first log was run through, but I could not resist the pleading of her look. I nodded and set down my cup.

It was not easy to get him up the hill between us, for he was tall, and for all he was thin he was not light. But we managed somehow, coming at last into the fort by the main gate. As we passed inside I heard the big log thud down onto the carriage below and the great cheer that accompanied it. Inside the enclosure we met my aunt. She looked at us with amusement.

"So soon?" she said. "Ha! That's not like Jed. He must be aging! Take him in the barn, lad. Ye'll find straw ready spread out there. Get him a blanket, lass. Ye know where they're kept. He'll be all right in the morning."

Somehow I dragged him to the barn while Purity ran for the blanket. We laid him out upon the straw and covered him gently. For a brief instant as we did so our hands met; and feeling in a sentimental mood, what with the completion of the mill at last and the scent of spring upon the night air, I squeezed her fingers gently. To my amazement she wrenched her hand away and stood up, her eyes blazing.

"You did this!" she said furiously. "You with your fine airs and manners! I'd think you'd be ashamed!"

I looked at her completely befuddled by this sharp attack.

"But I'd naught to do with it," I retorted stumblingly.

"You can say that," she demanded, "when with my own eyes I saw you drinking with him? I hate you!"

And with that she turned and fled through the gloom. I moved to follow her, to catch her, for I wanted to explain. It seemed to me it was ungrateful in her to accuse me thus unjustly, and after I had helped her get him up the hill. The thought that she could be so blind angered me. I would make her see that she had been wrong.

But at that moment came the high whirring screech of the saw upon wood. The sound brought me up short. They were cutting the first log. I hesitated, then told myself it did not matter what she thought, and headed toward the mill and ran.

2

Our little community recovered slowly from the celebration of the mill's completion. Having come, long since, to the conclusion that these were a staid people, it amazed me not a little to see the way in which they let down the bars upon occasion; though young Rob Rogers dug me in the ribs with a knowing leer and hiccuped that I had seen nothing yet to compare with the fun of a husking bee. For all that there was many a splitting head and fuzzy tongue along the Suncook road the next morning, and work upon the house, which was our next step, went but slowly. On Sunday the Reverend Whittemore spoke highly of the service which the new mill must render the community, though he deplored mightily and in no uncertain terms the "ungodly behaviour" which such occasional celebrations always seemed to call forth.

Sunday night it rained, drenching everything thoroughly. But by daybreak, when my uncle routed us from our beds to start work upon the foundations of the house, the skies had cleared, and the rosy glow in the east gave promise of a hot still day. At the gate we found Jonathan and Daniel Stinson and the Rushes, father and son, awaiting us. Here Uncle David divided our party, sending Donald and Toby, Amos Rush and Jonathan Stinson to the mill to start work on the lumber, and taking Davie, Timothy Stevens, Moses Rush, Dan Stinson, and myself to help in setting the foundations about the cellar hole, which was already dug, and in placing the heavy sills upon which the framework of the house was to be built.

At the fork of the road, near James Moore's garrison we fell in with two men and a boy, William Carr and Robert Buntin, both of Buckstreet on the upper Suncook, and Buntin's son, a thin, sallow lad of ten, as shifty-eyed as his father. They were bound, so they told us, across the river to work on Nathaniel Whitehead's lot, which he was preparing for spring planting; and as our ways were the same they walked with us as far as the building site. When he heard where they were bound my uncle shook his head and pursed his lips.

" 'Twould be well," he said, "if Nathan'l 'd leave his planting there for later, when we've the men to spare for guards. Both Ladd and Eastman have reported Indians in the neighbourhood of Rumford and Canterbury, and I doubt not they'll be paying us a visit ere long."

But William Carr, who was on the stout side and jolly, laughed.

"God's blood, cap'n," he chuckled, "if ye wait upon the Hampshire assembly for militia ye'll be like to wait all summer!"

My uncle scowled and nodded.

"Aye," he said, " 'tis plain enough that they've no love for us; but since they fought to have us in their bounds, and 'tis the King's decision so, 'tis only right they grant us the protection that we need."

At the moment his speech bewildered me, for I could not understand what he meant. But later I was to learn what lay behind it. Rumford and Suncook had been granted by the Massachusetts Province and settled by their people at a time when the territory was in dispute between the two colonies. Notwithstanding the King's decision had placed the region within the jurisdiction of Governor Wentworth, nevertheless the assembly still continued to feel some jealousy in the matter, considering the inhabitants of the two towns as usurpers and interferers in the claims of New Hampshire, and lavished their care upon their own towns of Rochester and Canterbury, both New-Hampshire-granted, at the expense of Rumford and Suncook. Indeed they refused pointblank to maintain the forts along the Connecticut, although all the territory to the York border had been ceded to them.

"If 'twas me had the doing of it," said Buntin, "I'd waste no time in petitions to Benning Wentworth, for he'll squeeze a penny till the King's head sweats blood. For action I'd go straight to Boston."

He spat sourly.

"Aye," was Carr's laughing echo, "yon Shirley's a pompous fool, but he hates the French and the Injuns worse. They say 'tis because he married a Frenchwoman and knows their nature he's so strong agin 'em. But I mind you'd get action there. They say now he's set a garrison, on Fort Dummer, which the Hampshire people refused, and another at Number Four."

My uncle smiled wryly.

"Ye come late with the suggestion, boys," he said, "for 'tis a thing we've already tried. Governor Shirley wrote we must depend upon our own assembly for aid."

Buntin cursed and spat, and Carr rolled his eyes and drew down the corners of his mouth ludicrously.

"God's life, now!" he ejaculated. "Think o' that! 'Tis well we've good men like yourself, cap'n, in charge. I'll warrant we'd show the savages a fight if they brought their ugly faces hereabouts!"

But my uncle was not cheered. He looked worried, and glanced at the boy.

"Ye'll leave the lad with us, anyway," he said, half inquiringly. "'Tis scarce wise to expose him to the danger even if you've a mind to it yourself."

It was plain that it was the wrong attitude to take with the elder Buntin, for he shied away from the suggestion like a skittish colt.

"I mind the lad'll look after himself," he said sourly. "Or if he can't I'll use a birch to teach him how."

The way the youngster cringed at its mention showed that he was no stranger to the rod. I felt sorry for him despite his stupid vacuousness. But my uncle flared up.

"You're a fool, Buntin," he declared. "Ye've no right to risk the lad's life if ye are his father."

Buntin flushed angrily and spat again.

"Fool or no, David Ross," he said, "I have the handling o' my own affairs, and I'll thank ye to keep your long Scotch nose out o' them."

My uncle shrugged at that and turned away.

"'Tis on your own head," he said. "Ye cannot say I did not warn ye if aught goes amiss."

He gave them not another glance then, but fell to rolling rocks into the cellar hole for the retaining wall. The two men and the lad turned away without further talk and went down over the hill toward the river.

It was weary work, moving the great stones into position in the rock wall with only the help of bar and lever, and for the most we worked in silence. The sun must have been an hour high when at last my uncle stood back and eyed what we had accomplished.

"'Fore God, lad," he said to me, "'tis well your mother did not insist upon a stone house such as she'd have at home, else 'twould never be done."

He mopped his forehead and picked up the jug he had brought with him from the fort. He shook it beside his ear, and finding it empty, held it out to me.

"Ye know the spring," he said. "Be a good lad and fill it up."

I was glad of the chance to do something useful, for I was but a poor hand with the heavy stones, and I could not but feel that my efforts there were more of a hindrance than a help. I took the jug and ran.

The spring lay on the flank of the hill near the ridge and somewhat above the house, so that there could be a constant flow of water through the kitchen. From there one could look out across the valley, over the meadows that lay close along the river to the low hills beyond. North to the bend above Soucook mouth and south almost to Isle a Huckset, the broad river gleamed and sparkled in the morning sun. There was green among the elms and willows on the river bank; and on the hillside, here and there, a basswood or a hornbeam or an early maple made a splash of colour among the still bare black branches of birch and beech. Off downstream, near the mouth of the Suncook, John Cochran's apple orchard in full bloom stood up in brilliant contrast, pink and white against the fresh green of the new valley grass.

I drew the cork from the jug and plunged it in the clear cold water. Water sucked down into the neck, and bubbles plopped and gurgled on the surface. I glanced out across the river to where I could see the figures of Carr and Buntin at work in Nathaniel Whitehead's field. Even at that distance Carr was distinguishable by his white shirt. The Buntin boy was nowhere to be seen. I thought he must be cutting a fish pole, or perhaps even fishing in the river. Idly I searched the brush beyond the field for a sight of him. Something moving in the bushes caught my eye, and I began to congratulate myself on being able to see so small a lad at such a distance in such thick cover; but in the next instant my heart seemed to skip a beat, and I rose to my feet, the jug forgotten and a cry of warning on my lips. For the figure had moved from one bush to another, and as it crossed the open space between I saw that this was no lad but a grown man; a man naked to the waist and with a coppery skin. As he moved in the open I could see the streaks of yellow paint across his chest, and when he turned his face in my direction I could see that that too was daubed, although at the distance I could make out neither his features nor the weapons he carried.

What followed seemed to come with a slowness and deliberation that was the more agonizing because I could not help but must look on, frozen to inaction. I could see more of the savages now, and thought there must be twenty of them, and perhaps more. I feared to shoot a warning signal, for I knew that at the first shot both Buntin and Carr would be dead men. I shouted at the top of my lungs, though I doubted if my voice would carry to them.

Yet some whisper of it must have reached their ears, for I saw them stop work and look up. It was at this instant that the Indians chose to attack. They burst from the brush along the fence rail and ran toward the two men. Though I knew they were yelling savagely, yet no sound of it reached me, and they seemed to move in utter silence like a picture that has come to life. I saw Buntin throw down his hoe and go down on his knees, holding his arms above his head, as if pleading for mercy. Carr turned and ran toward the river. At once several of the Indians stopped and stood still. I could see the sun flash upon the barrels of their muskets as they levelled them. White smoke mushroomed out from their muzzles in silence, and it was a long instant before the crackling reports came across the river to my ears. Carr stumbled and fell face down in the fresh-ploughed ground. Several of the bucks raced toward him and clustered over him. There was confusion, some pushing and jostling, then a tall brave stood back and waved his arm aloft in triumph. Even so far away I could see the fresh blood that stained his hand and arm to the elbow.

But something else was happening as well. Taking advantage of the flurry over Carr, Buntin had seized his opportunity and fled. Already he was halfway to the river, bending low and jigging erratically from side to side. Apparently the Indians did not at first notice his flight, being busy with the scalping of Carr, though they must have noticed before I did, for it was the sound of a shot that drew my attention from the ring about Carr's body. A dozen or more of the savages ran to cut him off, while the others, who had not fired on Carr, threw up their weapons. But Buntin already had too good a start. Their shots went wild, and by the time the pursuit reached the river bank, he was already slipping and stumbling over the slippery rocks towards deep water and safety. One or two of the Indians, their guns still charged, fired as they came up to the bank, but by the splash of the balls their shots went wide. Two bucks appeared on the bank holding the struggling Buntin boy between them. They did not seem inclined to hurt him, but stood on the bank apparently shouting something at the fleeing father. But Buntin did not hesitate in his flight. One savage ran down to the stream behind him, coming to a halt perhaps fifty feet from where the head of the swimming Buntin bobbed upon the current. He drew back his arm, and I could see the sunlight flicker upon the hatchet in his hand.

The chase had brought them nearer, and though the range was still too far to hope for much, a shot might have some effect. I threw up my rifle and, taking quick aim, fired. I had the satisfaction of seeing the ball strike the water directly in front of the Indian, startling him so that he flung himself sideways and fell full length into the river, to the evident amusement of his companions, while the tomahawk curved harmlessly high in the air and fell with a splash in deep water. A moment later Buntin scrambled up upon the near bank and found safety in the willows.

He had scarce disappeared among the bushes when the signal gun at James Moore's banged its warning, and the bell in the meetinghouse began to toll. The whole affair had not taken as much as the time it takes to tell it, and the sound of the bell startled me to action. I fled along the pathway to the clearing where the others were at work, leaving the jug still gurgling in the spring.

I found them ready and waiting only my return before deciding upon their course of action. Breathlessly I blurted out what I had seen to my uncle. He heard me out without a word. When I had finished he sent Davie at once to warn the others at the mill, and taking me by the arm and beckoning the rest to follow, set out at a trot towards the river.

As we jogged he questioned me.

"Could ye guess their numbers, lad?" he said.

I made hasty calculations and replied that as far as I was able to see there must have been nigh twoscore, though there may have been others remaining hidden from me in the brush. He shook his head soberly at that, though he showed no sign of turning back. In my excitement it did not then occur to me as anything out of the ordinary that with but three lads to support him he should run directly in the face of such odds.

At the foot of the hill, where the Soucook wound out into the flat of the river bottom, we met Buntin. He was stumbling in blind panic toward us, his normally sallow face now a pasty yellow, his small shifty eyes wide with fear and horror. And who could blame him? It had been a near thing. He would have passed us unseeing, but my uncle grasped him by the arm and shook him roughly.

"How many, man?" he demanded breathlessly. "And have they yet crossed the river?"

Buntin merely stared at him stupidly as if he had not heard, and indeed I believe he had not, for my uncle repeated his question thrice before he at last shook his head dully and said never a word.

My uncle thrust him from him with impatience and something of disgust in his look.

"Get ye to James Moore's," he said, "and gather your wits the while. Ye'll have need of them again before this day is done. Me and the lads 'll hold them while we may, though I'll not say 'twill be for long. So have them hurry the folk inside!"

He sent the man along his way with a slight shove and, turning, beckoned us to follow.

Now, indeed, I began to see the danger of our position; for it seemed to me scarce possible that some of the savages had not already come across the stream in pursuit, and I judged our chances slim to say the least if we were to encounter them upon the open field. But it was to appear my uncle knew them better than I. Our way lay along the bank of the brook, keeping to the cover of the alders. And when we reached the brush of the riverside it was plain he had not misjudged them. Those who had begun the attack had stopped upon the other side, waiting for the rest of their party to come up before venturing across. My uncle, when he saw it, smiled grimly for the first time since the alarm had sounded.

"Your shot has served us well, lad," he said to me. "It has made them overwary, and they'll not think of crossing until they have held a council to weigh the risk."

He placed us in position then along the river bank, with the deep mouth of the brook upon our right flank and the river in front, taking advantage of such cover as was offered. Me he stationed behind the protecting roots of a great elm whose foundations had been undermined by the force of the spring freshet and whose top now lay projecting out into the water. Here he bade me lay my shot pouch and powder horn before me, where they would be available for quick reloading, and await his signal before firing.

Now, at close range—for the river at this point was a scant fifty yards across—I had opportunity to study the enemy for the first time; and truly they presented a sight that might well strike terror into braver hearts than mine. From the shelter of my log I could make out the rings of ochre and vermilion with which they had encircled their eyes, and the streaks they had daubed across their cheeks and upon their foreheads. Many were painted across their chests and bellies, and I noticed that with some of these the stripes ran round and round, while in others they were diagonal or even vertical; and I guessed that these variations in marking must have some tribal significance which I could not even imagine. Whatever they may have meant, the daubings together with their shaven polls and naturally fierce countenance made of them a sight more hideous than I had ever believed possible, even in my wildest nightmares.

As I watched I could see that the number I had at first estimated was now nearly doubled, and that more were constantly coming in from the hill beyond. As far as I could see there was not a white among them, though of this I could not be certain, for I remembered having heard that on occasion some of the more woodwise Frenchmen were in the habit of accompanying such expeditions in the guise of savages.

Minutes passed as we lay waiting for their first move, and all the while they appeared to do nothing but loll about in arrogant confidence of their safety under our very noses. It is true some of their chief men gathered in a little knot to one side, but most of them lay about, loafing upon the bank. Some, wearied apparently with inactivity, came down to the river's edge where they used the smooth surface of the water as a glass and looked to their daubs and decorations, of which they seemed inordinately proud and childish. But beyond this it was near half an hour before they made a move in our direction.

All this time we could hear the bells tolling and clanging upon the hill behind us, and scarce had we gained our position by the river when the double shot that warned of urgent danger sounded from James Moore's fort, to be taken up and repeated by garrisons up and down the length of town. In my mind's eye I could picture the scene upon the plateau, the families feverishly loading their carts, whipping up their beasts to get more quickly in to shelter, running their cattle to save what they might. At this urgent signal, I knew, those not already upon the road would leave their belongings, stopping only long enough to gather up the barest necessities and bar their doors and windows before fleeing to safety. I wondered if the savages would choose to fight, or whether they would be content to burn and run.

A movement on the far bank caught my eye and brought me back to my surroundings with a jerk. The Indians had evidently decided to risk a crossing, and a dozen or more of them were already down the bank and wading out into the stream, holding their weapons high to keep them dry. Others, less impatient to be at us, were dragging up logs and driftwood, making a raft for the purpose, so that it seemed, at least to begin with, we need not have the whole party with which to deal. Nevertheless, small as it was, the advanced party outnumbered us by three to one, and it seemed to me high time we did something about it. I dragged my rifle forward to be ready and glanced at my uncle, but he, catching my glance, shook his head warningly.

I suppose it could not actually have been more than a matter of seconds, though it seemed an interminable period that I lay there, trembling between excitement and fear, awaiting my uncle's signal, while over my sights I watched the red enemy approach step by step along the stony bar that shoaled out gradually from the far side towards the deep water upon our own. Strangely enough, as my body tensed and my finger tightened about the trigger I felt none of that horror of what I was about to do that had so assailed me as I had levelled my gun upon the Indian Toby. Nor did I feel any of those scruples that had forced me to withhold my fire at the camp on Plausawa Hill. There were men before me, framed in the sights, coming towards me step by step, all unaware that each passing instant brought them nearer death. Yet not for an instant did I feel compunction. On the contrary I was anxious, eager, so that I must needs hold myself in check lest I open fire too soon.

And yet, when the matter is considered for a moment, the answer is simple enough and none so strange. The truth of it was I had seen these men stand deliberate and shoot down a harmless, happy man in cold blood, and then quarrel among themselves for the possession of his dripping scalp; I had seen them drag the young Buntin boy struggling up the bank—though what they had since done with him I could not tell, as he was nowhere to be seen—and I had seen them drive the father into the river and follow him as far as they might, intent upon their savage game. I could not look upon them as men, but only as savage dangerous beasts who would do the same for me if they were to have the chance, and who must be shot down at sight and killed whenever there was an opportunity presented.

All the time I was thinking thus, they were advancing deeper into the river, until at last they stood waist-deep and seemed about to plunge in and start swimming.

It was at this instant that I caught my uncle's eye and saw his head nod.

I needed no second invitation, but steadied my aim upon one tall buck who came in directly opposite to me, his eyes encircled with yellow daubs and a crimson streak running from ear to ear across his face like a bloody gash. He had a crude design that might have been the head of some forest beast in red and yellow upon his chest, and it was upon this that I drew my bead. For the briefest instant I held my fire. Then my finger tightened upon the trigger, the gun flashed and kicked, and I had the satisfaction of seeing my man take one or two stumbling, hesitant steps, his face a study in amazement and unbelief, and fall forward slowly, almost ridiculously, into the water.

At the same instant I became aware of my companions' guns crashing on either hand. Three of the enemy fell at that first volley; and of those that were left, half of the original party stood hesitant and bewildered in the open stream, not knowing which way to turn; two fled for the farther shore, while one flung himself into the rapid stream and swam strongly directly towards us.

As I reloaded feverishly and with trembling hands I wondered who among us had missed. Then it occurred to me that two of us must have picked the same man, for the range was such that a miss was hardly possible. On the far side of the river the Indians had begun to shoot in our direction. I could hear the balls clipping through the brush above my head, and one bullet that buried itself in the log before me sent me ducking for cover. I heard my companions fire again, and lifted my head to look. Four men still stood in midstream. One of those who had been there now lay face down, writhing in the water, his hands clapped together across his stomach. One of the others was fleeing towards the farther shore, while of the brave who had started towards us a spreading stain upon the surface of the water told the story.

I took quick aim and fired upon the Indian already in flight, and was conscious of a peculiar satisfaction when I saw him leap in the air and clap his hand to his side.

"To teach ye how it feels," I growled beneath my breath.

A hand upon my shoulder brought my attention round to our own side of the river. It was my uncle shaking me.

"Come along out o't, lad," he said, placing his lips close to my ear and shouting to make himself heard above the rattle of musketry upon the far side. " 'Twill soon be too hot for us."

Twigs and bits of bark rained down upon us like a shower as we backed off and worked away into the brook bottom, and the air was full of buzzing and whining lead. Once something plucked at my sleeve and I looked around to see who could be a-jerking at me; but there was naught there but a jagged tear in my coat.

For all that, though, we drew off unharmed, and a moment later were beyond range of their fire and running back the way we had come.

3

We might have spared our haste, it seemed, for our savages showed no great eagerness to follow. Upon our arrival at the fort we found our people all within, some with, but most without their effects. My uncle lost no time in assigning us to our places so that if they chose to come against us they would not catch us napping. But, though we waited for them in constant readiness until the sun was well down beyond the river, they did not again come within range of our guns. Apparently the damage already inflicted upon them; the loss of five of their number at the hands of so small a band, had taught them respect for our marksmanship, and they had no stomach for further contact with greater numbers protected by the stout walls of the garrison house.

We had ample evidence of their presence in the neighbour-hood, however, for toward midmorning we could see them at the mill below, just beyond gunshot. It was not at first apparent what they were up to, though it was simple enough to guess, and pres-ently a flicker of flame and a thread of smoke confirmed the sus-picion that they would try to burn the building.

It was an agonizing experience to lie there in full view of their action yet powerless to lift a finger in defence of what was ours. Good fortune was with us, however, for much of the timber in the building was still green, and it was thoroughly drenched with the torrential rains of the night before, so that after several fruitless attempts they gave it up and moved away in search of more dam-ageable property.

From the mill they went up the hill to Ephraim Blunt's. But this, though distant, was still within range of our fire, and we dropped lead so close about them that they quickly drew off and cast about for a less troublesome section. Later, the sun being a little past noon, we saw smoke rising to the south, and feared lest they had succeeded in firing one of the houses. To our relief, how-ever, we learned the next day that what we had feared was a house was only a hay shed belonging to Caleb Lovejoy; and this they had succeeded in firing only because it lay beyond reach of fire from Aaron Whittemore's garrison. During the afternoon they broke into and plundered a number of houses in the south end, though they accomplished no further damage. Late in the day, when we had begun to suppose that they had drawn off entirely, we were brought again to the alert by the rattle of shots at some little dis-tance. This we discovered presently was a direct result of that same false sense of security. Benjamin Holt, it appeared, had not had time to bring in several of his cows and two of his horses. Toward evening, believing the Indians to have gone away, he took four men and went up into his pasture to look after them. His mistake was evident when a small band of the enemy saw him at a distance and betrayed their presence by opening fire too soon. Holt and his companions returned the shots, though at the range and in the failing light it was impossible to tell what effect they had, and withdrew in safety to the shelter of the fort. It was not till two days later that they found both horses and all but one of the cows lying slaughtered near the top of the pasture. The remaining cow they found near three months later in the woods near Chester, whither she had wandered. The find was worthless, however, as by then the animal was so wild that she would suffer no one to approach, and so she was reluctantly slaughtered for her beef.

Following this visitation it was some days before our people would venture forth again. When no attack came the next morning Toby and I were despatched from my uncle's fort, while others were sent out from the other garrisons, to scout and find out if possible what position the enemy had taken or if they had drawn off entirely. Towards midday came Captain Ebenezer Eastman of Rumford with a half a dozen men to inquire the cause of the shooting which had been heard the day before. These joined us in the search; but though we covered the ground thoroughly we could find no trace of the enemy lurking in the neighbourhood, and to judge from all the signs they had withdrawn in the night in the direction of Rochester.

All our assurances, however, were of small avail. This was the first time Suncook had been visited in such force, and the people were thoroughly frightened. It was old Ephraim Blunt, I believe, who first remarked that the savages had seemed suspiciously familiar with the lay of the ground.

" 'Twas Plausawa, and maybe Sabatis or Christo, led them, like enough," he said, and cast a sour glance at me.

I was quick enough to feel the slur he cast upon me, but though the hot blood mounted into my face I held my tongue, for I could not help but feel that there was some justice in the accusation. If I had not let those precious three go their way it is likely the raid would never have occurred.

The idea stirred up no little comment and controversy in the compound, however, and as days went by it spread about the town. Looking back upon it now, I realize that by far the greater part of my new friends and neighbours understood and sympathized with my position and the action I had taken. But there was a little knot of others who held that I should have been guided by

Toby and shot the trio out of hand. These succeeded in stirring up such a storm of dispute that in the end the proprietors saw fit to call a meeting of the heads of garrison and call myself and Toby up before them. Deacon Whittemore, who despite his position as cleric was of the opposition, was their spokesman; and so fierce did he appear, with his great red face and shock of snowy hair and his down-drawn, disapproving mouth, that I must confess my knees shook beneath me as I stood up to face him and hear his questions.

"James Ferguson," he rumbled, "it has been brought to the attention of this committee that in September last ye did, in company with the Indian Toby, while out upon a scout in the interests of this community, come upon the three Indians Plausawa, Sabatis, and Christo encamped upon the northeast part of Plausawa Hill, so called, and that at that time, though ye might have settled them out of hand, ye let them go in safety to be a plague and a curse upon the Province."

And with that he read me a lengthy lecture upon the grave reprehensibility of my conduct and demanded to know what I had to say for myself.

All the while he was speaking I had felt my indignation growing, until I forgot to be frightened longer and wished only a chance to protest against his accusation.

"Would you have me murder them in cold blood?" I demanded hotly when he had done. "I am not one to be shooting men without warning. If that is what you wish from your scouts you'd best find another man for your work, for 'tis not a thing that I'll be doing."

"Ye were none so slow at the shooting the other day, by all accounts," he replied. "Will ye tell me there was warning given then?"

" 'Twas not the same thing," I retorted. "You forget, sir, that there I had seen murder done upon an innocent and helpless man, and moreover in this case the Indians were armed and painted for war. As to the matter of warning, in a sense they were warned, for 'twas I who fired upon them ere ever Buntin had crossed the river."

This seemed to discomfit him somewhat, but he stuck to his guns.

"Better had ye killed the three upon the hill and had less thought for ethics," he grumbled. "Then there may have been no need for William Carr to die."

" 'Tis not so I read the teachings of Our Lord," I said angrily.

He rose to his feet choking in rage.

"This is blasphemy!" he cried.

" 'Tis no blasphemy intended, Mr. Whittemore," I replied, not too cool, "unless it be against yourself! Have you thought that had I murdered the three last autumn their friends in Saint Francis might have seen fit to exact a worse revenge?"

He looked at me with hate in his eye and his heart so full of anger that for a moment he could not speak.

"Is it so," he said at last, "that ye were taught to address your betters? 'Tis such impudence as I have never seen, upon my soul!"

"I will admit you my elder, Mr. Whittemore," I retorted, stung, "but never my better!"

And at that I heard a titter from the rest of the committee which heartened me mightily, though I had known before that Aaron Whittemore was none too popular with many of our people.

"As for impudence," I continued, "you asked for my defence, and I gave it you in plain words."

I might have said more had I not at that moment caught my uncle's eye and seen him give an almost imperceptible shake of his head. Instead I clapped my teeth upon my tongue, bowed shortly, and turning on my heel strode from the room, which was perhaps as well, for from that day on I heard no more of the matter.

Such was the first and only raid on Suncook in King George's War, and its upshot. Yet even so disastrous an occurrence could not be said to have been without its brighter side, for it did bring the attention of the Assembly to our plight and induce them to station a detachment of militia upon us until October. It also brought to Ebenezer Eastman a warrant to organize a strong company of scouts for the further protection of Rumford and our own town. Among those who joined Captain Eastman and served throughout the summer were Rob Rogers and Jed Stiles and, I also heard, the infamous Shem Sanborn and his shadow Joseph Merrill. Whether it was these precautions or no, I cannot say, but certain it is the Indians did not appear again within our borders, their nearest approach being at Epsom in the latter part of August, whence they carried off a woman prisoner, who, by all accounts, was only too pleased to be freed from the ungentle attentions of her bullying husband.

The respite thus offered enabled us to return to work on the house with renewed vigour, though scarcely with speed. The work went slowly for a number of reasons, chief among them being that my uncle and others who might have helped otherwise had their own duties to attend to—ploughing, planting, haying, and harvesting—so that they were able to lend a hand only at odd intervals.

Another, and perhaps even more potent, factor in the delay was my mother's insistence upon the kind of house it should be. This, she insisted, was like to be her last home. Here she would spend the rest of her days, and she would brook no makeshift to serve until a better was built. Chimneys, she stipulated, must be of brick rather than the customary stone. The windows must have real glass in them, and the plans which she drew were a shade more elaborate than was customary in that place at that time. If live in a house of wood she must, let it at least be a well built house, she said, with the best woods in it, with joints snugly fitted and tightly joined, and things as near as might be to what she was used to having at home.

She cared not, she said, for the usual type of dwelling then in vogue, with a great chimney running up through the centre and the rooms all built about it. Rather, she planned for a house in the shape of a T, with a chimney at either end of the main house and a third in the ell, to serve the kitchen, a feature in itself unusual in the region. It was to rise a storey and a half from the ground, with a cellar beneath the main house. In the fore part were to be the common room, with a great fireplace at one end, and a parlour-chamber, also with a great fireplace, for ceremonial occasions and the entertainment of important guests. Above stairs in this part were to be four chambers, each with a fireplace, for the family, while the ell housed the kitchen and two chambers for Dougal and my mother's waiting woman, who still clung to us. In addition, attached to the ell was a woodshed and buttery, and beyond this was a small barn, only large enough to fill our needs. Unusual as the house was, both in design and in the construction, when finished the feature which called forth the most envy and comment in the neighbourhood was not the glass in the windows, nor the brick chimneys, nor the wide-panelled, comfortable common room, but rather the kitchen chimney, which was made extra wide and deep to accommodate the roomy cooking fireplace, with its iron lug pole—the first in the settlement, though there was said to be another at Rumford—brought all the way, as had been both glass and bricks, from Haverhill and Portsmouth. Also calculated to make the neighbouring housewives green with envy were the ovens, built in upon either side of the fireplace, so that when it came to do her weekly baking it was not necessary for my mother to go outside the house, a bitter task during the long winter months when the snow and wind whistled in the housewife's ears as often as not while she tended to her baking in the yard oven.

It would be of but small advantage, not to mention something tedious and overlong, to tell in detail of everything that occurred from the moment of our arrival. Many things were of immediate, though passing, interest. Our house was finished and we moved in, bag and baggage. My sister married Moses Rush. James Rogers, the father of Rob, was shot in the woods by a hunter who, seeing him approach clad in a fur coat, mistook him for a bear. The boundary dispute with Bow, whose proprietors held a grant from the Hampshire Assembly to much of the property already held in Rumford and Suncook under grants from the General Court of Massachusetts, dragged on over almost the entire period between 1746 and the beginning of the Seven Years' War. These grants were both made before the boundary dispute between the two Provinces was settled, though it was under the Bay Province charters that the greatest steps toward settlement had been taken, and now the Bow proprietors hoped to oust these original settlers from their lands and claim the fruits of their labours for themselves. Such an unjust claim could not have been supported for an instant had it not been for the interprovincial jealousy that still persisted and the political intrigue that sprang therefrom. In the end the matter was settled in the only way that justice would permit; but this came only after years of higgling and lawing, so that many of the original claimants had grown disgusted and moved away.

Absorbing as these matters were at the time, they had but a

slight bearing upon the matter of my own story. Consequently I hope I may be forgiven if I seem to pass over them but lightly to dwell at greater length upon what were to me affairs of far greater importance.

Toward the middle of November my sister and Moses Rush were married, their betrothal having been announced formally from the pulpit, as was the custom, by the Reverend Whittemore in October. After the ceremony they moved into the small house that Moses had built with the help of the neighbours upon a lot in Rumford directly across the Soucook Brook from the mill.

Edith was scarcely gone from the house when my mother declared that here was a state of affairs that would never do. She was, she said, accustomed to two girls in the house, and she was too old now to change her habits. Moreover, she added, she could scarcely keep the kitchen with less. And with that she put on her bonnet and hurried away to my uncle's house, whence she returned looking wise and very secretive.

For all her mystery, however, I was not surprised the next day to find the child Purity, for whom she had formed a great attachment, moved in upon us bag and baggage. The truth of the matter, I firmly believe, was that she had planned the whole affair long since, but fearing lest I might prove obstinate she took this means of forestalling me, a move that was wholly unnecessary for, though I had at first felt some annoyance at the child's sauciness, I had soon learned that her bark was worse than her bite, and that her heart was not nearly so hard as she chose to make it seem. Indeed, although we bickered often in the year since our arrival in Suncook, it was a friendly bickering, not devoid of understanding, and I had grown to have something of the affection for the child that I would have for a younger sister.

Jed Stiles, when the matter could be broached to him, approved heartily. In fact, if the truth were known, I believe he was secretly immensely relieved, for he was not one to enjoy responsibility, and the arrangement left him free to enjoy life as it came. He agreed to allow my mother full charge of the child's upbringing and education, while on her side she promised that she would have every advantage, just as though she were her own daughter.

During the winter that followed Stiles was a constant visitor in the house, where he frequently repaid us on the long evenings with rambling swashbuckling tales of his doings upon the Louisbourg expedition, or in Boston with the Quebec troops, or with the Indians and French before the war; tales which more often than not presented him in a light which could scarce be strictly considered as either moral or honest, though indeed if only half the yarns he told were true he must needs have been possessed of superhuman powers to have figured in them.

If at first I looked at him somewhat askance, believing him but a sorry rogue, I was soon to change my view, for to his friends, no matter what face he might present to the world at large, he was loyal beyond reckoning and generous to a fault.

Another frequent visitor was the Indian Toby, who formed a strong attachment for Stiles, so that these two were seldom seen apart. Toby would come and sit by our fire, nursing his pot of flip and filling the common room with the greasy Indian stench of him, chuckling, till his belly wobbled, over Stiles' stories and saying never a word for himself though his little black eyes missed never a thing that happened in the room. At last when Stiles would stand up and announce that it was time to be going, Toby would toss off the rest of his drink, for he never left anything in the can, and trot away at his heels like a faithful dog.

4

All through the winter Stiles and Toby hunted and trapped and fished through the ice together, and not infrequently, when business would allow, I went with them. Thus little by little we were thrown more and more in company, until at last I came to be included naturally in their plans and there was scarce a thing they did but they consulted with me about it first.

So it came about that, when in March they proposed to journey up the river upon a trapping expedition, they took it as a matter of course that I would go with them. At first I was reluctant to consider it, my Scots conscience bidding me remain at home to look after the womenfolk. But sober second thought told me that my only use at home was to eat my mother's cooking. There was little I could do at the mill, having attended my task of timber cruising earlier in the winter. I was curious concerning the rugged mountain country to the north, as well as to the more northerly settlements, and this seemed my opportunity to see them. When my uncle suggested that I might, with profit, look into the timber prospects to the northward my mind was made up for me. I agreed, and one cold morning about the middle of the month, long before the coming dawn had begun to spread its thin grey light across the Rumford Plain, we set out.

Our way lay up the Merrimack, through Rumford and Canterbury and past Bakerstown, the last a sorry sight bearing all too plainly upon its handful of scattered cabins the marks of savage warfare. Of a score of cabins less than half remained standing, and but four or five of these were still occupied. At the forks, where the river comes in from Great Winnepiseogee Pond, we took the left, continuing up the Pemigewasset another ten leagues to the mouth of the Asquamchumauke,* which is lately more often called the Baker, from the captain who on its lower intervals slew the Indian Waternummus.

This was the route most often followed by the raiding bands from Saint Francis in periodic forays along the Merrimack and to eastward. It was their habit, so Toby told me, to come in one large band up the Saint Francis River to Lake Memphremagog, thence by a series of ponds and carries to the Connecticut, which they descended to the Lower Cohos. Here they would separate, some going on down the Connecticut to the settlements about Number Four and Fort Dummer, a fact which explained the Massachusetts Province's willingness to maintain those two posts. The others would cross, by another long portage to the Asquamchumauke and down to the Pemigewasset. Here again, if they were in force, they would divide, one party descending to the Merrimack, while the rest proceeded through a series of ponds and lakes to Great Winnepiseogee and from thence to the more easterly settlements at Rochester and along the coast.

But it was in the country itself that I was most interested. As we pushed northward from Bakerstown the hills rose more steeply on either side, their rugged, rolling flanks blanketed mile after mile with unbroken forest; tall pines, straight sturdy spruces, and massive oaks and maples; trees that had never heard the ring of the woodsman's axe. In places they crowded down to the river's edge, offering a tempting prospect to one who viewed them, as did I, with a professional eye. Now and again the hills drew back on either hand from the river, taking the forest with them and leaving wide elm-lined stretches of open intervale in the river

* Present site of Plymouth, N. H.

bottom; lands cleared by Nature, ready for plough and shovel, waiting only the coming of peace and the settler's cart to blossom forth.

It is in the midst of one of the widest of these intervales that the Asquamchumauke comes rolling down in leisurely fashion out of the west to add its bright clear waters to those of the Pemigewasset. Here on the narrow spit of land formed by the junction we camped for a day; and when I climbed the steep heights about whose base the combined rivers swept I could look away northward, up the Pemigewasset valley to where the forest-clad hills gave way to ridge upon ridge of snow-clad mountains: mountains whose rugged outlines dwarfed even the massive proportions of Lochnagar and Ben-y-Gloe that I had until now thought of as the highest mountains in the world.

I should have liked to push on northwards to explore the deep valleys close underneath them, and perhaps to climb a little upon their slopes; for their peaks, thrust up so clear and sharp against the cold hard blue of the wintry sky, seemed almost like a challenge to me. But when I spoke of it to Stiles he chuckled and shook his head. There were falls, he said, in the river, some short distance up, that would bar our way and make further passage that way difficult if not even dangerous. Toby seconded him so eagerly and at such length that I was convinced that the falls, if they even existed, had little or nothing to do with their opposition. What their objection was, I could not imagine; but it was plain that they were set against it, and in the end I withdrew the suggestion and let them have their way, though my determination to make the journey some day, if I must do it alone, was no whit lessened.

On the next day we set out once more, following up the Asquamchumauke which meandered down slowly with many bends and turnings through a broad elm-spotted intervale. At something above two leagues from its mouth we came to a place where a sizable brook tumbled in out of the north. Here we turned away from the river and, climbing perhaps two leagues more, came at last to a pond, about half a mile in breadth, set in a deep hollow in the midst of high wooded mountains. I thought Toby looked somewhat uneasy at the hills, but Stiles dropped his pack and sat himself down upon it.

" 'Tis a good place," said he. "We'll make our camp."

He was right enough in saying that it was a good place. The pond itself and the two brooks that fed it were the home of many beaver, mink, and otter. Foxes ran upon the high slopes; and, early though it was for them, I came several times, near the top of the mountain, on signs of bear. Three ponds, still farther to the north and west, emptied into the one upon which we camped, and these too proved well stocked. Working one day through a notch to eastward, beyond the head of our lake, I came upon another brook. Following it down I came to still another pond. Here again were signs of beaver and of otter, and never a trace to show that man had ever set foot here before. A second eastward exploration carried me over the mountain that loomed upon the east shore of our pond and down upon the other side into a broad swampy basin with a long narrow pond fed by half a dozen tiny streams. Once again, everywhere I looked were signs of game, dams thrown up in swampy spots, trails and paths beaten in and out in every direction.

In the six weeks we stayed in camp here we took almost more furs than we could find means to carry; beaver, muskrat, fox, otter, mink and marten. Nor were we embarrassed for want of meat. Deer and partridge were plentiful and without fear, and the lake itself abounded both in trout and in the great grey char which Stiles called "Togue" and Toby spoke of as "Touladi."*

It was a time that I enjoyed beyond the telling. To me there was a peace and joy in the forest such as I found nowhere else, while to be able to go out into the woods with nothing but a gun and a bag of bullets and wring a living from them gave me a sense of satisfaction not equalled in the sharpest deals of trade. Here time seemed actually to stand still, and the only care there was in the world was for the next meal and shelter against the rain. At night the soughing of the wind in the pines lulled me to sleep, and in the morning the scolding of a squirrel or the song of an early robin awoke me. I should have liked to stay indefinitely, but even the best of things must end.

Each day that we lingered brought spring a little nearer to the mountains. The snow melted, and the ice disappeared. The alders and moose maples burst into bud. Each day some new bird appeared, working northward on his annual journey, and each day my companions grew more restive.

* Lake trout.

I knew the reason well enough. Each day we stayed brought danger closer. Soon the raiding bands from the Saint Lawrence would be starting southward, and then woe to any isolated parties who might lie in their path. Stiles took to counting over our catch, estimating the profits, and Toby spent much of his time lying out along the river below, watching constantly for signs of the enemy passing downward.

How long this might have continued I cannot say. I know that I for one was starting at shadows; and Toby, though he concealed it with all the stoicism of his race, I felt sure was fretting to be off. Stiles, I believe, would have been willing but for one old grey fox who had, time and again, eluded our most carefully laid traps, and whom Jed considered it almost a point of honour to catch before we left.

One evening, however, we came into camp to find Toby already there before us. I saw that he had baled up the furs we had already taken in neat bundles, and packed up all but the most necessary articles of equipment. He looked up at us inscrutably as we swung in off the trail.

"You ketchum fox?" he asked.

Jed flung down the three red fox pelts he had taken from the traps on the hillside and kicked at a bale of furs, cursing.

" 'Tis the very devil himself," he said, "that grey one. He goes from trap to trap along the line, springs them, and steals the bait!"

The Indian shrugged.

"Mebbe nex' year," he said. "We go now."

Stiles swung around on him.

"Do ye say so?" he demanded. "They've come then?"

Toby nodded.

"How many?" said Stiles. "Or did ye see?"

The Indian appeared to think for a moment.

"Mebbe twelve—fifteen Injun go down river by canoe," he said at length. "No good!"

"The devil ye say!" Stiles exclaimed. "Would they be towards Rochester, d'ye think, or Rumford?"

Toby shrugged.

"How can say?" he replied.

Now indeed it seemed to me the fat was in the fire, for with the savages between us and home, how were we to pass them unseen?

The others seemed to consider this fact also. It was Stiles who spoke at last.

" 'Tis for Rumford, most like," he said. "We can take the chance and go by Winnepiseogee with a carry at the far end into the Suncook, or for Rochester, whichever we've a mind to; or we can cross up and take the Connecticut for Deerfield."

But the old Indian shook his head at this.

"No good," he said. "Injun on Asquamchumauke, more Injun on Connecticut."

A crafty look came into Stiles' eyes.

"Aye," he said, " 'tis a risk any way at all. But lookee, there's another way still, a way 'twill pay as well to take. Who gives the best price for furs, d'ye think?"

The Indian shrugged.

"Ketchum good price Albany," he said.

Stiles laughed.

"Right!" he cried. " 'Tis the Dutchmen have the longest heads and the best prices."

"Here!" I cried, alarmed. "You'll not be thinking of going to Albany!"

"Why not?" said Stiles.

"Why," I cried, "if the distance alone means naught to you, think! 'Tis the enemy's own country we must go through. If we've a dozen or so of the savages between us and home, how many d'ye think will lie 'twixt us and Albany?"

He chuckled.

"Aye, lad," he said, "but think o' this: the savages below are on the watch for parties such as ours—but would they think to look for us in their own territory?"

Toby grinned.

"Plenty rum Albany," he said, and rubbed his belly in anticipation.

"Aye," said Stiles, "and more money to buy it with."

"What will it profit you," I demanded, "to get more for your furs if you squander it in rum?"

"At least 'twill buy more rum," replied Stiles sharply.

At that I fell silent, for I saw that it was of little use to argue, and presently Stiles spoke again.

"Ye're not afeared, lad?" he said.

"Aye," I replied, thinking how William Carr looked as he fell among the fresh-turned furrows. "I am afeared—as much one way as t'other."

Stiles nodded.

"And so am I," he said. "But I'm more afeared o' the handful that lies below us than of all there may be 'twixt here and Albany."

He was silent for a moment, then added: "You may take my word on't, lad, 'tis the best way."

I looked at Toby. He nodded. I shrugged.

"Well," I said, "you know best between you, but I'm thinking 'twill be many a day before we see Suncook again, and I'm wondering what they'll be thinking of us the whiles."

Stiles chuckled again.

"But ye'll agree," said he, " 'tis better to come home late than not at all!"

And there the matter rested.

We were away the next morning with the dawn, and by sunup were come to the river. There we loaded the canoes and began our cautious upstream journey.

Our way lay up the winding river to the carrying place, and thence across into the valley of the Connecticut. Here we turned north again for a short distance to the mouth of another river, flowing in from the west, and here we struck out across the Hampshire Grants,* following the stream through two or three small ponds and several carries, into another larger stream flowing westward, which Toby said was the Winooski. This we followed down, with many portages, for it was a small stream and in places rocky, until at last we came out at its mouth in Lake Champlain.

All this way, for it had taken us the better part of a fortnight to come so far, fortune had smiled upon us. Not once in all that time had we sighted a hostile party, though twice we had come upon recent signs of large bands in the vicinity. But it was at the lake that it became most evident that we would have to go carefully, for there were boats passing to and fro upon it in a steady stream, battoes and canoes, and even a schooner or two, laden with furs and supplies from or for the settlement and fort at Crown Point.

* Vermont.

From there on we travelled at night, lying out in the bushes by day, well hidden and watching all that passed us on the lake. In the second night, slipping along in the shadows of the east shore we passed the settlement at Crown Point and made out the black bulk of the fort against the night sky where it stood upon the point guarding the narrows of the lake. So close did we have to pass beneath its walls that I could hear the faint scrape of the sentry's boots as he made his rounds above. Three times after that, while we were yet upon the lake, were we forced to land to avoid meeting with hostile parties, and once in the daytime a fleet of fifty canoes passed within forty yards of our hiding place, so close that I could have tossed a pebble among them, had I been so minded. The Indians were whooping and yelling triumphantly, and I noticed a dozen or more Frenchmen among them. These last I was startled to see were painted like their red allies, and at their belts I could make out the fresh scalps, the blood upon them as yet scarce dried.

I paid but slight attention to the country, for I was in haste to get through, yet what little I did see was destined to be of well nigh immeasurable advantage in later years, though I little realized it then. Each day I lay in fear of discovery, and each night I laboured to gain as much distance as I might. One night we were held up, unable to move at all for head winds, and in that night I felt I knew the depths of despair, for I had visions of being marooned there unable to move either forward or back, until in the end we needs must die of starvation if we were not discovered. But the next night was dark and still, and we took advantage of our good fortune to reach the head of the lake and Wood Creek.

Our luck held despite my gloomy fears. The following night we crossed the carrying place, perhaps the most dangerous stretch of the entire journey, without seeing so much as a sign of an enemy. The next day brought us to the first settlements along the upper Hudson, and we rested in a settler's cabin and slept in a bed and ate from a table for the first time in nigh three months.

The next morning our host, a stolid, square-bottomed Dutchman, gave us hints and directions as to our route, and by nightfall, by dint of hard paddling and at the risk of a ducking where we should have carried, we raised the roofs and spires of Albany, and that night slept in a small ordinary near the riverfront.

We had no trouble disposing of our furs the next day, for with the French and Indians out there were but few who would risk capture for a trapline in these parts. Nor did I feel that this was anything but sensible on their part what with Crown Point so near and the French so active.

For their part the traders called us brave fellows, and made much of us, keeping our cups full and each insisting upon his turn to treat, though I more than half suspected the method that lay behind their hospitality and spilled as many of my drinks as I might beneath the table. It was as well I did, for in the end my companions were completely fuddled, and had I been in like condition we would have been diddled of our furs for fair. As it was I merely pretended drunkenness and played them one against another until at length they forgot about me in their rivalry and took to outbidding one another, so that in the end I think they paid us rather more than the top price for them, and Klaus, the paunchy Dutchman with whom I had finally dealt, paid me out of hand with a sober face, and left immediately afterwards.

The others, I doubt not, would have stayed to help us drink away some of our profits. Indeed I believe they expected something of the sort, for they looked not a little put out when I bid them a very good afternoon, and gathering up my unsteady companions made the best way I could back to our tavern. There I tumbled Stiles and Toby upon their beds, where they promptly fell to snoring, while I sat down to think what to do.

Now this was no mean problem, for we had taken near twice for our furs what we would have received for them in Boston, partly because of the scarcity of the article here, and partly through my luck in trading, and there I sat with something under a thousand pounds, old tenor, in my pocket and two drunken companions on my hands. It was a long way home, and I knew that already our people must be fearing lest we were lost. If I divided the money now, with my friends in their present condition, I had no doubt they would spend it there. Nor would I be able to move them on the road until they had. What was I to do?

Then all at once I had an idea that seemed to me little short of brilliant. I would get them home with their money intact, and perhaps give them a lesson in the bargain.

Making sure that they slept soundly I crept from the room and went downstairs and went in search of the innkeeper's daughter, a buxom lass with a roguish eye and a fancy for her own face.

I found her in the taproom keeping the bar while her father attended some business in the town, and after a word or two of flattery that put her in a friendly mood, I broached the subject that was on my mind.

"Look ye, lass," I said, "have you any old jugs and bottles lying about?"

She was curious at once, as I had thought she might be, but I satisfied her by saying only that I meant to play a trick on my friends, whereat she fell into the spirit of the thing and found me a dozen or so of assorted sizes. These I took up to our room and hid carefully.

Next I went out and found a horse dealer with a nag for sale that looked capable of withstanding the journey we were about to make. His price was, of course, out of all bounds at first, but after some haggling I beat him down to what I thought was reasonable and we closed the deal. I took the animal back to our inn and stabled him, after which I went to a nearby store and bought a loaf of hard bread, a bit of cheese and a bottle of sour wine.

It was well after dark when I returned to our room with these last. My companions were still snoring lustily, and though I lit a candle I let them sleep. Slipping downstairs I got a bottle of rum and several cups. Back again in the room I spilled rum about and scattered bottles here and there in confusion. The cups I set upon the table and poured in rum in varying amounts, merely wetting the bottoms of some, and filling others near half full. I placed a pair of dice upon the table, and brought out a pack of greasy cards, which we had kept in camp to amuse ourselves in the evening, and scattered them willy-nilly about the room, so that before I was done the place appeared as though the great grandfather of all brawls had taken place there.

By this time it was approaching midnight and my companions were beginning to show signs of waking. I decided that it was time. I shook Toby until he rolled over and opened his eyes upon the scene in wonder. Stiles was harder to rouse, but in the end he sat up on the bed and swung his feet to the floor, after which he sat moaning slightly and holding his head in both his hands.

I pushed some of the debris on the table out of the way and broke the bread into three pieces. I sat down.

"Supper?" I said.

"Whut?" said Stiles.

"Supper," I repeated.

He looked up and gazed around the room blankly.

"Have some supper?" I said.

He stood up and came over to the table, wobbling a little.

At sight of the bread and cheese he stopped short. He looked around him, and for the first time seemed to see the disorder of the room.

"God's blood!" he said, "what happened?"

"Don't you remember?" I asked innocently.

He shook his head.

"Perhaps Toby can tell you," I said munching a crust of bread.

He looked at Toby who only gazed back at him blankly and groaned.

Stiles sat down heavily in the chair opposite me and picked up a bit of the hard cheese and a crust, staring at them dully.

"But why this?" he said.

"Why not," I replied, "when we can afford no other."

"Did ye not sell the furs?" he asked.

"Aye," I replied.

"But the money," said he.

"The money's gone," I said.

"What?" he shouted, bouncing up out of his seat.

Toby sat up sharply and looked at us stupidly.

" 'Tis gone," I said, struggling to keep from laughing at the picture of dismay they presented, "four hundred pounds you and your gaming friends went through. Look at the bottles. Three days now you've done naught but drink and play. And now your money's gone, where are these friends o' yours?"

They looked at one another aghast, and I could see they had taken the bait, hook and all.

"Man," cried Stiles, "for why did ye let us? Why did ye not stop us?"

"Was there ever a time," I said, "drunk or sober when you listened to my counsel?"

He stumbled over to the bed and sat down heavily, his head in his hands.

"I promised the lass a dress with the money," he said half in a whisper.

I was near to telling him the truth of it then, but I knew it would be fatal if I did so. I hardened my heart.

" 'Twas luck I put by some of my own," I said, "or we'd be put to it to get home."

He leapt to his feet at that.

"The dogs!" he cried angrily, "to take such an advantage of a man. Come, show me the men and I'll twist their necks for every penny they've had of us!"

"And find a rope about our necks," I replied dryly. "These Yorkers have scant love for us, you'll mind. 'Twould be a pleasure to them to hang us all for robbery."

He opened his mouth to say more, but I cut him short.

"You've done badly enough till now," I said coldly as I could. "If you'll but leave things to me now I'll see you home, and we'll say no more of what you borrowed of me and lost."

He sat down then, all contrition.

"As ye say, lad," he said. "What will ye be doing?"

"I've arranged for a horse," I said. "We'll leave with the dawn."

They looked at one another then, and shrugged. I offered them some bread and cheese, but they would have none of it. Neither, to my great amusement, would they drink. And presently they stretched out again and fell asleep. I made a show of cleaning up the debris, after which I blew out the light and lay down.

In the morning, before the dawn, we took our departure. I was relieved to see that we were too early for the buxom wench who had found me the bottles, for I feared lest she might ask me embarrassing questions which would throw the fat in the fire. As luck would have it, however, we were away before she was down, though, glancing over my shoulder as we clattered down the cobbled street, I thought I caught a glimpse of her face at an upstairs window. By sunup we were well upon the road.

Our way lay through Kinderhook Mills and Sheffield to Springfield, thence to Worcester from where we cut overland to Haverhill and from thence, by the highroad to Suncook. We used the ride and tie system, whereby one man rides ahead, dismounts and, tying the horses for the others, proceeds on foot. The last man then, coming up, mounts and rides on past the others some distance and the performance is repeated. Thus each had a turn at riding, and by this means we made excellent time, reaching Haverhill within the fortnight. There I sold the horse, to my great satisfaction at a handsome profit. We made the rest of the journey on foot.

It was not until the last night before we reached home that I confided in my companions and told them the trick I had played upon them. At first they were inclined to be angry, and for a moment I feared I had done wrong. But when I brought out their shares—three hundred twenty-seven pounds, eighteen shillings, and sevenpence halfpenny each, for I had kept meticulous count of it—they were overjoyed and forgave me readily. Not in their wildest dreams had they anticipated more than half as much.

Early in the next afternoon we arrived home in the midst of great excitement, for we had all been given up for lost and prayers said for the peace of our souls. My mother embraced me with tears in her eyes, and even little Purity threw her arms about my neck and kissed me and had nothing but nice words to say. As for my companions they were only too pleased to be back again with pockets intact, and not a word was said of our Albany adventure, save that we had been there. When we sat down to table that night I think there was not a one of us but did so with a heart full of thanks.

5

The summer of 1748 proved an eventful one. In June came rumours of the end of the war abroad, confirmed the following month in the report of the Treaty of Aix-la-Chapelle. This, however, did not mean peace for us. Through the summer the Indians continued their raids, striking now for the most part at the outlying posts: Fort Dummer, Number Four, and the Ashuelots. In August their chief men were prevailed upon to meet in conference with our Governors, Wentworth and Shirley, at Falmouth on the coast, to discuss a truce. Their agreement was announced in a proclamation by Governor Wentworth in September.

The relief which this announcement occasioned may well be imagined, particularly in those more northerly settlements which during the past four years had lain in constant danger of attack. There, a great burden seemed lifted from men's shoulders. Many who had moved the bulk of their belongings into the garrisons for safe keeping, now moved them back and reopened their houses. At Bakerstown settlers who had been driven back to the security of the larger established towns returned to rebuild their razed cabins and clear again their neglected lands, and the town was re-named, Stevenstown. In the garrisons military stores were checked over and stowed away in lofts. For the first time in five long years the women could go into the pastures for the cattle unguarded, and men left their rifles at home when they went to work in the fields. No longer was it necessary to work in groups. A man could do his own ploughing and planting when he had a mind to, and bring his hay when it was ready without fear of molestation. To be sure there were still a few scattered bands, out since early sum-mer, who either had not heard of the proclamation or pretended ignorance of it. These attacked in one or two places, notably at Number Four and along the Connecticut, but were driven off, and by October the war was ended.

At the first whisper of peace my uncle stirred himself upon a scheme to expand our business. He had been much interested in my report on the timberlands of the upper Merrimack and Pemi-gewasset rivers, and expressed pleasure that I had learned my job so well. Only that spring a King's ship had been laid down in Nathaniel Meserve's yard in Portsmouth, while at Newburyport and elsewhere upon the coast new shipyards were building. The prospects of peace and free movement once more upon the sea had wrought a boom in shipping circles, and yards were working day and night to meet the demand for ships. This demand, my uncle pointed out, must, of itself, create another for lumber: oak and spruce and pine for timbers, masts, and planking; ironwood and maple for braces and belaying pins. To the northward of Stevenstown, in the ungranted lands, was timber for the taking. All that was needed was capital to hire a crew and an agreement with the yards to buy. Having the one, we might the more easily obtain the other. It was my uncle's proposal that he go to Ports-mouth and Newbury, there to arrange contracts with the various yard owners to supply their needs. As an afterthought he also de-cided to wait upon Governor Wentworth, in the latter's capacity as Surveyor General of the King's Woods, to obtain from him, if possible, a warrant to cut the King's trees for the Royal Navy.

It was when he announced this last that I got out pen and ink and sat down to write a letter to Dorcas Drew; a letter, some may say, that was long overdue. But here let me hasten to explain, lest I be counted remiss, that conditions were not then what they are today. Now, with weekly postriders to carry the mails, a man may send a letter from Rumford to Portsmouth in two days and at a cost of a shilling or less. But then there was no regular post. Whoever would send a letter, no matter where, must first find a traveller willing to carry it, or send his own messenger, and often as not this was a costly matter involving sometimes as much as twenty shillings.

This being so, it is nothing wonderful that I had not heard from her nor she from me. But though it was now two years and more since I had seen her last, I had not forgotten. It may be that the first sharp edge of my passion had worn off. Perhaps I did not think of her as often or as much as I once had done. I no longer tossed for hours on my bed, unable to sleep for seeing her face before my eyes and hearing her voice in my ears. The memory of her lips on mine no longer seemed real. And yet her image was always before me, less as a tangible person than as an ideal to be sought after and attained. I had given my word and received hers in return. And as I knew my own good faith, so was I confident in hers.

But the writing of that letter brought everything back to me sharp and clear. The soft touch of her fingers upon my cheek, the music of her voice, the gentle pressure of her body as I held her in my arms, the sweet fragrance of her hair upon my shoulder; all these swirled in upon my thoughts as I sat twisting my uncle's great quill pen in my fingers and wondering what I should say, so that my love which had lain so quiet all these months rose up again and was alive and filled me near to bursting.

In that letter I wrote of what I had done and of what I hoped to do, of what I had thought and seen and heard and felt since the day I had left her. I spoke often of my love and renewed my promise to come for her some day when the time was right. I opened my heart and let her see all that was in it. Taken all in all, it was a very callow letter; a very youthful letter, and one that was not a little vain. Yet into it I poured all my hopes and most of my fears, and when I sealed it up and gave it into my uncle's hands for delivery it was with a feeling of now or never, all or nothing, as if my very world depended upon its safe arrival in her hands.

This was in October, when the hills were turning flaming red and gleaming gold and bright burnished orange, when the days were growing shorter, so that we had need to light the candles be-

fore the sun was scarce six hours past the noon, and when the bite
of frost was in the air and ice was like to be in the buckets of a
morning. Soon the hills would be stark and grey with the bare
branches of the gaunt hardwoods their only cover, and the snow
would lie deep in the hollows and in the lee of the crested hills.
If my uncle succeeded in getting the contracts he sought, we
should need to have the trees marked down for the cutting so that
the work could begin at once upon his return. And as this was
my duty I turned to it with relief for an occupation that would
keep me busy the while he was gone.

I had already, during the summer, marked out the cutting to
be done upon our own lot for the mill. There remained the lots
to be cut against the contracts, and for these I had my uncle's instructions: so much of pine, except the white above twenty-four
inches in diameter at the butt, which was reserved by law to His
Majesty, so much of oak and maple, so much of spruce, so much
of hornbeam, or as it is called "ironwood"; and mark out a stand
or two of good white pine, clear and free of knots and of a good
height, against the possibility that he might return with the Royal
warrant in his pocket.

For this there was no doubt, and it was obvious that he so intended, that I must go north along the river, above the limits of
the granted townships, where the timber stood free and unencum-
bered and ready for the cutting. And since everything was thus
plain as he had intended, I lost no time, but on the day following
his departure set out upon my own journey, travelling by canoe
as was best in those regions, and taking with me for companions
only the Indian Toby and Dan Stinson.

We pushed upstream rapidly, but it was not until we passed
the mouth of the Winnepiseogee that we found timber upon ungranted lands. Even here it was not strictly speaking free timber,
for some years before a grant had been made of the land on the
right bank. But the grantees had done nothing with their land,
and I risked censure, marking out tentatively a stand of white
pine, mostly small timber suitable for planking, but with a scattering of tall sticks, much in demand for masts.

For the better part of a month we travelled the river, up and
down, between the mouth of the Winnepiseogee and the Baker,
exploring tributaries and cruising the hillsides. Maple was easy to
find, as was hornbeam. Pine was plentiful enough, though for

spruce we had to go back upon the high hills to westward of the river, and oak we found to be scattering. We did our work, however, and I flatter myself that it was done well, before, toward mid-November, we turned our faces homeward not a day too soon; for already there was a shelf of ice jutting out from either shore, and rocks in midstream had grown fangs of white to rip the heart of any canoe that might come within their reach.

I found my uncle home before me, elated and at the same time somewhat crestfallen, for though he had secured excellent contracts to supply yards at Portsmouth, Newburyport, and Ipswich, he had failed altogether to gain the Royal Warrant. This was only what I had foreseen; for it seemed to me that if Benning Wentworth had paid two thousand pounds, as it was said he had, for the Surveyorship, he was hardly like to hand out warrants to all who came begging, and my uncle had neither the money to make his application interesting nor anyone to sponsor him.

It appeared, however, that we should have all we could do to fill the contracts he had gained, and I counted us lucky in that. For the rest, I listened in ill concealed impatience until I could ask news of Dorcas. Had she sent no reply to my letter?

I had to ask twice before he finally heard me. Then he broke off his talk of trees and grants and warrants and contracts, and looked at me sharply.

"Aye," he said, "I delivered the letter to the door myself."

"Did you give it to Mistress Drew herself?" I asked.

"Na, na, lad," he replied, "the serving wench said Mistress Drew was not at home, so I gave her the letter with word to pass it on."

"And did you not return for an answer?" I persisted.

"Aye," he said dryly, "I did that, an't appears to me yon Dorcas is a flighty wench, for the lass said she was out again an' had left no answer."

I must have shown my disappointment in my face, for he took a softer turn then and laid his hand upon my shoulder.

"Na, na, lad," he said, "don't take it to heart. 'Tis like the serving wench lost it and durst not tell me, for she seemed a lying slut. I would ha' gone again and paid my respects to the lass herself; but my time was short, and I was away for Newburyport the morning."

And with that he clapped me on the shoulder and bade me

sleep on it, while I for my part dragged away to bed, trying to swallow my chagrin, and seizing upon the faint hope his words held out that somehow the letter had miscarried.

This was a serious blow to my self-esteem, for though I clutched at straws in an endeavour to convince myself that somewhere something had gone wrong, I could not help but recognize how great were the odds against it. And if the letter had not been lost, if it had found its way into her hands, why had she not answered it? For two years I had heard no word from her, yet I had not been disturbed. Now because a letter went unanswered I was plunged, heels over head, in fear and desperation and worry. Had she forgotten the words we had said at parting? Was she angry that I had not written sooner? Had she found another more attractive to her tastes? These and other questions kept running through my mind so that I knew no rest. I ran the whole gamut of a lover's emotions from apprehension, first, lest something was amiss, to anger, last, that she could have thought to treat me so. In the end it came time to go out with the woods crews, and the work which this involved drew my thoughts to other channels, so that after a time the sharp edge of my disappointment became dulled and I all but forgot the matter.

Throughout the winter we kept four crews in the woods above Stevenstown, cutting, peeling, hauling, and yarding, until by the beginning of February the greater part of the contract lumber lay piled in readiness upon the river bank, awaiting only the spring thaw to be rolled in and floated down. My own duties had been comparatively light, nature not having designed me for work with cant hook or ox team, and I had been given an axe and placed in command of one of the felling crews.

My men were good workers all, and I flatter myself that I had a way with them that enabled me to get the best from them, with the result that we were finished a good week in advance of the other crews; and by the end of January I was free to do as I pleased. Accordingly when, in mid-February, Toby and Jed Stiles with Richard Rogers and William Stark proposed a second trapping expedition to the north they found me ready and willing to start at once.

[1 It would be but repetition of what I have already told, to describe that expedition and all the others that followed it. During the next two years the annual trapping trip became something in the nature of an institution. Sometimes we were accompanied by the Rogers brothers, sometimes by the Starks, or others, but always the nucleus was the original trio: Jed Stiles, Toby, and myself. It was not until the spring of 1751, however, that an event occurred which was destined to have far-reaching results.

In that year our party was a large one. Besides the original three, both the Rogers brothers, William Stark, Daniel Stinson, and Moses Rush had come with us. We had pushed on farther than usual, camping on the great oxbow at the Lower Cohos on the Connecticut. There we had met and camped for several days with a party which had come up from Number Four with the intent to survey a route by which a road might be laid down to open up that fertile region. While we were there several parties of Indians came by, going down the river to trade at the forts, and I noticed that though we made them welcome enough they received our greetings with a coldness that was little short of downright hostility. Even Toby took notice of it, and made his usual comment, reserved for things he liked not the look of.

"No good!" he said, and shook his head ominously.

Perhaps it was because we were trapping a new country with which none of us were too familiar; perhaps it was because the spring came early; but whatever the reason trapping was poor that year, and it had scarce turned the middle of April when at last we packed up our traps and blankets and set our faces for home.

We packed over the long carry to the Asquamchumauke and floated down into the Pemigewasset without mishap, travelling fast with few carries, for the water was high.

180

A little below Stevenstown there is a great bend in the river, where the deep water swirls against the east bank and a wide sand bar juts out from the west. Here the road to the north settlements runs close to the river, and there is a path that runs down from it through the tall elms and the alders to the water. The sand bar makes a convenient landing spot, and one much favoured by the Indians who come down to trade, and it is not unusual to find them there with white traders who have come down along the path from the road to meet them.

It was about midafternoon when we reached this point in our downstream journey. I was holding the bow paddle in Jed Stiles' canoe, and as we swept around the great bend before coming to the bar we were perhaps three hundred yards ahead of the rest.

As we cleared the bank and came in sight of the long sand spit I saw that there was a canoe drawn up upon the shore, and a little distance from it two Indians and two white men stood in converse with something, I could not at that distance make out what, held between them. My own inclination would have been to sweep on past, for it was not unusual since the peace to see Indians upon the river, and whatever their business there I felt it was none of ours. Stiles, however, must have seen something suspicious about their attitude, for no sooner had he caught sight of them than he swung the head of the canoe inshore and steered directly towards them. For their part they had seen us as soon as we had seen them, and as we approached they stood stolidly waiting, with an air that even from so great a distance was unmistakably hostile. As we drew closer, so that I could see their faces, I was surprised to see that the Indians were my old acquaintances, Sabatis and Christo, while the white men with whom they were speaking were those precious scoundrels, Shem Sanborn and Joseph Merrill. The object that they held between them, I saw, was a gallon jug of a kind most frequently used for rum.

Stiles swung the canoe close inshore and held it in shallow water with his paddle while he nodded pleasantly. I saw no answering smile upon the faces of the men on the bank, and I noticed that the two Indians fixed their eyes upon me, darkly, and fingered the locks upon their muskets in an unpleasant way.

" 'Lo, Shem. 'Lo, Joe," said Stiles amiably enough. "What ye got there, rum?"

"What if it is?" growled Sanborn after a surly pause. "Whut's it to ye?"

Stiles clucked derisively and wagged his head.

"Don't ye know there's a law agin trading liquor with an Injun?" he said.

"I ain't needin' yore advice," Sanborn retorted sourly. "I kin do my tradin'."

Jed nodded and spat over the side into the swirling water.

"Mostly," he said, "I guess you kin. But them two are bad medicine. Them and rum don't mix."

I heard the chunk of paddles as the other canoes came down behind us. Sanborn sneered.

"Ye're gettin' mighty high an' righteous, Stiles," he said. "Since when have ye been so partic'lar?"

I felt Stiles shrug in the back of the canoe.

"I've got a pretty good acquaintance," he said, "with most of the Injuns 'twixt here and the River. I ain't been trading with 'em for twenty year for naught. There's some I'd trust with liquor, an' others I wouldn't, an' them's the last two'd ever get a drink off me. You mark my words, Sanborn, them an' liquor's poison. You give 'em that much rum to once an' there'll be murder done afore it's night."

I heard Rob Rogers call, and knew the last canoe had come up.

"What's up?" he said.

Sanborn looked away at him.

"I was doin' a little tradin' here," he said, "an' here's Stiles gone pious on me."

In another canoe I heard Toby belch and spit.

"No good!" he said.

Sanborn whirled on him.

"You keep out o' this," he snarled, "or by God I'll see the colour o' your guts."

All this while I had been fidgeting with impatience, for the sun was sinking lower, and I had hoped to be at home that night. It was plain that Sanborn, even now, was none too sober, and it seemed the thing might soon become a brawl if something were not done quickly. Sanborn was still holding the jug before him, not twenty paces from where I sat. All was clear behind it, and it occurred to me that here was the key to the situation in my hands.

Sanborn was still cursing Toby when I raised my gun, and such was the pitch to which tempers had risen, that no one noticed. I took careful aim at the jug and fired.

I think it was a full minute before anyone realized just what had happened. The two Indians stood, with muskets half raised, staring at me in blank astonishment. Merrill backed off along the sand, step by step, face white and eyes bulging, as if he feared the gun might next be turned on him. As for Sanborn he only stood with drooping jaw, looking bewildered upon the finger ring and jug neck that was all that remained in his hand of a gallon of rum. For a moment he was speechless with rage and amazement, then the colour ebbed back into his face and he burst out swearing.

"By God!" he cried. "By God now!"

Sabatis and Christo moved a step apart and started to raise their guns. There was murder written plain upon their faces.

"Easy," came a voice I recognized as Rob Rogers'. "Easy now. Just put those guns down!"

I saw the Indians hesitate an instant. Then slowly they obeyed.

I looked around and saw that both Rob and Richard Rogers had their flintlocks up and cocked, as did Will Stark and Moses Rush. Toby was edging his canoe in toward shore. The two Indians, hate and uncertainty in their eyes, stepped back a pace and waited. Toby's canoe grated upon the sand, and the old Indian stepped ashore. He looked at Rogers, half questioningly. Rob nodded.

"Draw the charges," he said.

Toby picked up the guns and fired them into the river. Sanborn took an angry step forward, but Rogers' musket swung to cover him.

"Stay where you are," he said, and his voice was hard and sharp. "Put the guns in the canoe, Toby."

Toby obeyed and stood back. Rogers looked at Sabatis and Christo.

"You two," he said. "Quick now—get on with it."

For just the briefest instant they seemed uncertain. Then without a word they moved down and stepped into their canoe. They shoved off and rode in the stream. They swung in a wide arc and headed upstream, their canoe passing close to ours as they bent to the paddles. I could feel their eyes on me, burning with hate.

As they passed close I saw Sabatis draw back his lips in a snarl. "White boy not come on river," he rasped harshly. "Some day Sabatis kill!"

They swung away across the current, and Will Stark and Moses Rush swung their canoes to cover them as they went. Rogers turned back toward shore.

"That's all, Sanborn," he said. "Go home now. Ye'll find the price of your jug and liquor at Osgood's tavern in Rumford when ye call."

For an instant the men stood balanced, hesitant, and in that moment I thought he meant to attack us, single-handed though he was. Then he gave me one glance so charged with venom that I shuddered in my seat, and, turning, stalked away across the sand to the pathway where Merrill had already disappeared among the brush.

We waited until they were out of sight, then pulled out once more into the stream and turned away, drifting down the current in silence. For full a mile we paddled on in silence. Then Stiles spoke.

"A neat shot, lad," he said. "I could not ask for better. But ye've made a bitter enemy this day."

I nodded, for I knew it was true. Yet I believe there was not one of us who could foresee the evil that was born of that shot, and that one day was to touch us all.

2

For us, in Suncook, the summer passed quietly enough, though in July upon the Connecticut occurred the first of the long series of incidents which here preceded the outbreak of hostilities with the Indians of Saint Francis; and which in the end were to plunge New England into the last French war long before her more southerly neighbours had awakened to the danger that threatened. There, at Number Four, a deputation of Indians from Canada appeared to protest the proposed settlement of the Lower Cohos, claiming that for unnumbered years these meadows had been a favourite hunting ground of their people, and that if the English continued their northward progress it would not be long ere the Indians were crowded from the land entirely.

For my part I was not unsympathetic with the red men, for

indeed it seemed true enough that as they drew back the whites pressed forward seizing upon the land and cutting the forests so quickly that in time there would be no further place for them to go. Our own operations in lumber upon the upper Merrimack were a fair enough example, though for these I could feel no remorse. Had we not done the cutting someone else would. Certainly Benning Wentworth was not deterred by their mere complaint, for he made several new grants upon the Merrimack, about the mouth of the Winnepiseogee—the old ones, before mentioned, having by this time lapsed—retaining as was his custom a lot of 500 acres for himself in each grant. Nor was that all. He openly encouraged the continuance of the plan to settle the Cohos meadows, and in his official capacity appointed surveyors to forward the scheme.

While all this was going on I could not help but remember the ill concealed hostility of those Indians we had met there during our trapping expedition the year before, and wondered if the course was the wiser one to pursue. Likewise, I sometimes thought of the Indians Sabatis and Christo, and of my encounter with them and Sanborn, wondering what might be the outcome of that meeting, or if ever it was to have any. But as the months passed and nothing happened I forgot about it, and indeed I believe that by the time we met again on a blustery February night in Osgood's tavern in Rumford, before starting up the river once more, there was scarce a one of us who recalled the incident.

James Osgood's long low taproom was smoke-filled and crowded when Dan Stinson and I pushed open the door and stepped in out of the wild night, shaking the light snow out of our clothes and stamping to warm our half-frozen feet. There had been a town meeting that night in the meetinghouse, which, following the custom, was drafty and unheated; and it seemed to me as I came into the room that half the town had stood in the cold as long as they might, and then adjourned to the tavern for the external comfort of Osgood's cheery fire and the internal solace of his rum.

We had left Suncook early, yet it was late when we arrived, for the wind blew a bitter gale from the north, piling up deep drifts of light, feathery snow in the hollows across the track, and setting it to dancing in the air upon the flats, so that although there was no snow actually falling it might as well have been a blizzard for the effect. Toby and Stiles had already come on ahead, and with Will Stark and his dour younger brother John, were awaiting us at a table near the fire. At our entrance Jed arose from his chair and bellowed at us, beckoning across the intervening heads to make sure we saw them. We shed our heavy outer garments and joined them. As we threaded our way through the close-packed room toward them, Stiles seized a pair of mugs and dipped them into a steaming bowl before him, raising them above his head for us to see.

"Here's a cup will warm your in'ards," he called, "and take the sting out o' your toes!"

I took the steaming mug and sipped gingerly, for it was flip; and to my way of thinking all flip is bitter enough to gall the most leathern stomach, with Jed Stiles' flip far and away the worst. As I sipped I looked at him inquiringly over the rim of the mug.

"Here's Will and young John," he said, "come to go with us. And here's a note left last week by Rob Rogers to say he'll not be able to come with us this year as he's got some business to attend to"—he stopped and looked across his shoulder at the crowded room adding in a loud voice—"in Albany."

I looked at the note and saw that it was much as Jed had said, except that it made no mention of Albany, but rather spoke of going northward on business, which would only mean to Canada, a fact which explained Stiles' loud insistence upon the former, for honest men were supposed not to have dealings with the French. As I read, Stiles wagged his head in mock solemnity. It was plain to see that he had already imbibed freely of the steaming bowl.

"Mortal bad doin's," he said, lowering his voice and looking as pious as a preacher. "I don't hold with it myself!"

I burst out laughing at that, for it was common knowledge that he was better known in Quebec than in Portsmouth, and that scarce a summer passed but he visited Saint Francis and Lorette and even Caunawaugha to trade and drink with the Indians with whom he was on good terms.

It was not until then I noticed that there was a fifth member of the party, who had stayed somewhat in the background but now came forward into the light. I recognized at once young

Amos Eastman, and though I did not know him well, I had some acquaintance with his father, the captain, and judged the family to be well liked and respected in Rumford. I greeted him cordially, and we shook hands.

"Stiles tells me ye'll be trapping northward o' the Baker," he said, giving the stream its English name. "Will ye have room for another in your party?"

"Why," I cried, "come along and welcome. There's fur enough for all."

There was a slight commotion at a table on the other side of the fire, and I turned in time to see a tall man turning away and catch a glimpse of furtive shifty eyes.

"Here," I said, turning back to Stiles. "That was Joe Merrill. D'ye suppose he heard us?"

"What if he did?" Stiles demanded.

But this I could not tell him. For my life I could not have said why it was, but some furtive eagerness in the man's glance, something in his evident haste to be quit of our presence, left me with an uneasy sense of premonition.

"I don't like it," I said.

Stiles laughed.

"Ye'll be suspecting your shadow o' following ye next," he said.

He took the mug from my hand and refilled it, thrusting it at me.

"Here," he laughed. " 'Tis calming to the spirits!"

I sat down then and we put our heads together, drawing our plans for the morrow's journey. When I looked up half an hour later and glanced about I saw that Merrill was nowhere in the room. Idly I noted the fact, and after that gave it no further thought.

The wind died away in the night, leaving the dawn clear and still and so cold that despite the fire in the Osgood kitchen ice froze in the buckets on the shelf. We were up and away before the first silver sliver of light had streaked the ragged hilltops across the river. As Stiles had already pointed out, the day being a Saturday, we must be well beyond the farthest settlement at Stevenstown by night, else the next day cool our heels in camp, for there was a ten-shilling fine for travelling on the Sabbath.

But for all our haste we made slow time. The wind of the night before had laid bare great patches of glassy crust on which our snowshoes skated and slipped, while in between were waist-deep drifts of fluffy snow, so that we could not take them off. Towards midmorning, however, the sun came out and softened the crust so that the going was easier, and by nightfall we had reached our objective, the mouth of the Winnepiseogee, and there made camp.

Three days more of travel brought us at last to our pond in the shadow of the mountain. There in the first day we made our permanent camp, and that night divided the territory into equal parts, drawing lots for the sections. During the week that followed we ran our trap lines carefully, so as not to interfere with one another's territory, and settled into the routine of camp life.

For all our care, however, the furs did not come in as we had expected. Jed Stiles swore that someone else had been before us and already trapped out the district. This I took the liberty to doubt, for I had already observed an orderly nature at work and evolved my own theory; namely, that at regular intervals of something like five years there were seasons of relative scarcity and abundance of game, and that between these seasons the game was either on the increase or on the decrease. This year I judged to be the second in the downward trend, and the old Indian Toby bore me out, though the others laughed at my expoundings. I had never given a thought to the causes of this cycle, though I had observed its workings. It was Toby who gave me the reason for it. It depended, he said, upon the scarcity or abundance of small game—mice, chipmunks, squirrels, rabbits, partridge, and such. In the years, he said, when these were plenty predatory beasts, such as wolves, catamounts, wolverenes, foxes, owls, hawks and eagles, were attracted to the region. For a time they preyed upon these small beasts until they had become scarce. When this happened they would turn to other species, beaver and racoon, and even to deer. At the end of the period the region would be stripped nearly bare, and such game as remained become wary and difficult to catch. When this state of affairs was reached the predators themselves began to starve or migrate to more attractive fields, and the small game had opportunity to revive.

Whatever the cause, whether a natural cycle or other trappers, one thing was certain, and that was that game was scarce. In the six weeks that followed our arrival I took scarce half as many furs in my traps as I had taken in the like period on our first visit to the place; and of these the greatest number were cat and fox with some wolverene, though these were ferocious and difficult to take. Next to these were racoon and otter, with mink and then beaver, which had once been most abundant, last upon the list. Wolves were plentiful, and more than one night they kept us awake with their howling. We killed several of them, but these, too, were wary and hard to catch. Their pelts had but slight value, and it was often difficult to collect the bounty which the Province offered for them, so that we wasted little time hunting them.

My section was one of the poorest of the division we had made, being a piece lying south of the pond along the brook and west across the summit of a high wooded mountain to the river and as far beyond as I cared to go. My luck being what it was, about the third week of our stay I took to exploring across the mountain and beyond the river, partly from curiosity, partly in hope of finding a region beyond in which game might still be more abundant. On these occasions I would go out along one line of traps, swing away and poke about for a few hours, and then swing back upon another line and so into camp.

It was this that I was intending to do one day when I started out over the north line which stretched along the mountain side almost to the summit. Some days before, I had gone over to the river, and, following it down upon the west bank, had stumbled upon a fair-sized stream flowing into it from the dark hills beyond. It was dark water, which seemed to me to indicate alders higher up, and probably beaver, and today I meant to find out.

I climbed to the ridge, taking a pair of foxes from my traps on the way, and resetting the two that had been sprung and robbed by wolverene. From the ridge I turned south, heading towards a small hollow that I knew would bring me out almost directly opposite the mouth of my new-found stream; but when I reached the gully I stopped short in surprise, for there, plain in the snow before me, were fresh tracks where someone had passed before me not above an hour since.

The tracks came up from the pond side of the mountain, leading away from our camp and heading in the general direction of the river. At first I was inclined to think it might be Toby, on the lookout for me, for he alone of us all used the bear-paw type of snowshoe which had made this track, the rest of us preferring the more wieldy beaver-tail shoe. But then I remembered that the Indian had gone that morning around to the northeast with Will Stark and Dan Stinson to look at a pond they had found there. Moreover it seemed to me that these shoes were somewhat bigger than the ones Toby used, being about the same breadth but somewhat longer.

It was this last discovery that aroused my curiosity, for it was possible that Toby had changed his mind. But if he had not made these tracks—and the track itself seemed to indicate that he had not—then who had made them? I cached my pelts beneath a near-by fir, and thus lightened took up the trail, determined to find out; for it struck me as odd that a stranger should be in the neighbourhood and not show himself at our camp.

For a time the tracks clung to the hollow, going at a leisurely pace as though their maker had no fear of being seen. Then presently they swung a little northward and slabbed the hillside, bearing all the while in the general direction of the river. From this I gathered that the valley was his first objective, and since he had borne away to the north I assumed that when the river was reached he would more likely turn up than down. Bearing this in mind I climbed higher up the hillside and crossing a knoll dropped on the other side into the river valley. With a little care I found a wild meadow that lay upon either side of the stream, and dropped down towards it from the ridge. I crossed no tracks as I approached, and when I came out upon the steep bank above the open space that marked the former river bed, I could see that the clean snow there was still unbroken.

From the contour of the land below me, and the direction which the tracks had taken when I had last seen them, I judged that unless the person who had made them became aware that he was followed, he would strike the river some distance below and strike upward, passing through the meadow either on this side or on the other. On the other hand, if he became aware of my presence and wished to avoid a meeting, he would in all probability avoid the open ground and make a wide detour. He might even double back and come upon my track. This would place me in a predicament, for then I should become the game and he the stalker.

The likelihood of his discovering my presence on his trail I judged to be remote, however; and I decided to give him an hour, in which to reach this point. Then, if he had not shown himself, I would decide what was next to be done.

Scouting around a little, I located a convenient clump of brush upon the hillside near the lower end of the meadow, from which I had a good view of both banks of the river; and there I lay down in the snow and waited.

I had not long to wait, it seemed, for scarce had I settled myself to watch when there was a movement in the brush at the foot of the meadow, and an instant later a figure pushed out into the clear. It was a stocky figure, clad in tattered buckskins and carrying a long musket in the crook of the arm. An Indian plainly; but though there was something familiar about the man I could not identify him, for he wore a huge coonskin cap that came down about his ears and stuck out above his features so that from my elevated position I could not see them.

Evidently he had not seen me, for he plodded steadily across the open, glancing neither to the right nor to the left. I followed him with my eyes, not daring to move lest I show myself, yet consumed with curiosity, for though I could not recognize him there was something sinister about him that kept plaguing me in my mind.

All the way across the meadow he kept his head down, and I thought I must let him go without ever discovering who he was. But there I was wrong, for at the far side he stopped and looked back, raising his eyes to the hillside, searching it with some care. In that moment I knew I had been right not to show myself, and I lay close in my hiding place, scarce daring to breathe lest the movement of my sides reveal me, for I recognized the Indian Christo.

For the merest instant his eyes rested upon my clump of brush, and in that instant I thought he must have seen me. But evidently he did not, for after a minute's hesitation he turned again and, plunging into the bushes, was lost to sight.

For full half an hour after he had disappeared I lay where I was, certain that he would not hesitate to shoot if, looking back again, he saw me. Then, reassured at last, I crept down from my cover and set out upon my back track, my mind full of conjecture as to what he did there.

I followed the back trail swiftly enough, even taking several short cuts, for I had learned what I had set out to find. At the fir in the hollow I picked up my two pelts, thereafter taking up his back trail with more care.

It led me down the mountain side towards the camp, following about a hundred yards above my own middle trap line, so that had I not just happened to stumble upon the track that day I might never have done so, though I visited the line daily. About a quarter of a mile from camp it turned sharply south, and for a moment I lost it, for where he crossed my own path he had taken pains to hide his own, a circumstance which added fuel to my suspicion that he was up to mischief.

By making a wide circle I picked up his track again on the far side of my own and followed it down to the brook below the pond. There another track came up to join it; a track this time made by a beaver-tail shoe. Here the snow was trampled underfoot, and there were marks upon a fallen log where the two had sat and talked for some time. Then the beaver-tail tracks led off again, down the brook, while the Indian's crossed and came down from a bluff that overlooked the lower end of the pond and our camp.

Until they reached the shoulder of the bluff the tracks were plain enough, but beyond that point it was evident that he had been at some pains to obliterate them by dragging brush across them. Indeed, had I not known they were there I might have crossed them a dozen times without being once aware of them. As it was, however, I managed with some difficulty to follow them to a point a little above our camp, and there I discovered evidence that he must have lain for a night at least observing us and all we did. Looking down, I found that I could see all that went on below. Stiles and Toby were lounging in the open-front shelter before the fire. Will Stark was taking his turn at cooking supper. John Stark and Amos Eastman were at the pond shore, cleaning some trout they had taken through the ice. Moses Eastman was nowhere to be seen, and I assumed that he had not yet come in, as he had set out on a long swing to northward that morning. Faintly the acrid smell of wood smoke came up to me, mingled with the odour of frying bacon, reminding me that I had not eaten since morning. There was nothing else that I could discover at the moment. I shouldered my pelts once more and scrambled down the hillside through the brush to camp.

It was not until after supper, when the pans were cleaned

and the fire built up and sending off a shower of sparks and we were all sitting around enjoying its warmth before taking to our blankets, that I loosed my bombshell and told them what I had that day seen. Stiles and the elder Stark, I could see, were plainly concerned, and Toby looked glum and shook his head. But John Stark and Amos Eastman and Dan Stinson only laughed and said I was starting at shadows.

"Why," cried Amos, "what if he did lie and watch? Most like he only sought a chance to steal some furs, and when he saw how poor the catch was he thought 'twas not worth the risk. 'Tis peace now 'twixt here and Saint Francis. He would not dare aught else."

But I could not bring myself to believe him.

"If 'twas only furs he was after," I replied, "then why did he so avoid my trap line? For he never once went near it. And how do you account for the other that he met upon the brook?"

"I'll warrant ye 'twill have a simple answer when we know," said Stinson.

But Toby shook his head.

"No good," he said. "Christo bad Injun. No good thing he do!"

I took Toby down the next day and showed him the track by the brook and the trail across the hollow, and though he said no word at all I could see that he was badly troubled. That night in camp he spoke but once.

"Toby think white man come brook meet Christo," he said, and looked at me. "No good!"

But when I asked him to identify the man he only shrugged and said he could not tell.

Stiles and Will Stark were inclined to agree with him, that these skulkers meant no good, and though I could not see what harm they might do for all their snooping and spying, I could not help but agree. John Stark had learned to respect his brother's judgement in such matters, and in the end he came over to our view, making it five to two, for Eastman and Dan Stinson steadfastly refused to take the matter seriously. When morning came, however, despite their opposition and grumbling, we broke our camp and moved it down the brook and across the river to what Toby considered a safer spot, and from that day one of us always stood guard.

But in time our precautions came to seem useless and silly,

much to Eastman's and Stinson's glee, for a week went by, and then another and another, and we were not bothered. Nor did Christo and his mysterious friend return. In the end, as these things go, the episode was forgotten, our vigilance relaxed, and life in camp went on serenely as before.

3

As the spring came on and the ice left the river and the snow began to melt upon the hillsides I began to grow restless. Our take in furs had been only fair. Every day from some high point along the ridge, or from the summit of the mountain itself I had opportunity to turn my eyes towards the mountains that rose in tumbling confusion all about the horizon from west to north and east, and never once did I look upon the view but I felt the stirring of curiosity, urging me to go and see what lay beyond.

I had ample time to think upon it, for my traps occupied but little of my attention; and in my spare moments I took to nosing about among the hills and sketching rough maps of the country round, so that in time I came to know it as well as any in our party. Once I followed north along the mountain ridge that lay to westward of our pond, towards a massy mountain bulk Toby called Mooselauke, whose northern and western slopes, he said, had in days gone by been a favourite hunting place for the great northern moose and caribou—even then becoming scarce in our neighbourhood. On clear days I could see the bare, treeless summit of this great hill, white and gleaming with its cap of snow, promising a wide view round about; and it was in my mind as I went towards it that I might there learn something more of what lay beyond. But I never came to the top. My ridgeway began to descend after a distance, and led me into a deep, narrow gully through which brawled a good stream of clear white water which I gathered was the upper Asquamchumauke. This I followed high up the mountain side until I came to a deep ravine with a precipitous head wall, still waist-deep and more in snow. Here I could look up to the bare ground above the last scattering fringe of dwarfed and twisted spruces, and see here and there the rocks and heathery growth pushing through the whiteness of the snow, reminding me for all the world of our own Scottish Highlands in winter. But though I could see the top I could not reach it, for there was not much of daylight left to me; so after looking upon it with a sense of nostalgia that was near to overpowering I turned my back and came away, following down the brook until it became a river, and then on down through miles of twisting and turning to our camp, where I arrived after midnight to find my companions certain that I had lost myself and firing off their guns at intervals to guide me on my way home.

But this was a mere whetting to my appetite. What I had seen was but an indication of what to expect, and in the evenings in camp I plagued my companions to know still more about it. In this Eastman and Dan Stinson were no help at all, for they seemed to be lacking in curiosity entirely, and had not seen so much of the country as had I. The brothers Stark were scarce better; though the younger, John, shared my inquisitiveness he had had no opportunity to indulge it. Toby refused to drop more than a word here and there, for it was his contention that the higher summits were the home of evil spirits, and that on Agiochook,* the highest of all, away to the northeast, dwelt the mighty Thunder God whose wrath it was death to encounter. I reflected that for one who professed Christianity the old Indian clung mighty tenaciously to his old beliefs.

It was Stiles who gave me such information as I could gather. For years he had roamed these forests, in peace and war, trading when he could, making friends among the Indians of the north, and in war hunting their scalps to eastward, a proceeding which seemed little to affect his prestige, for by their simple philosophy an enemy in war might easily be a friend in peace. He it was who told me of the forests of the Androscoggin and the north country; of the pleasant mountain valleys closer at hand; of the fertile sunny meadows of the Cohos above the Ammonoosuc. But though he told me everything he could think of I would not give him rest, constantly plaguing him for more, until at length, one evening after supper, when I was more than usually persistent, he flung up upon his elbow from his bed and spat loudly.

"Now, by God's blood!" he swore. "If ye've such a monstrous curiosity for it, why do ye not go and see the country?"

"I would," I replied, "for God knows there's naught to keep me here. But who would show me the way?"

"Who was it showed me first?" he retorted.

* Mt. Washington.

His tone stung me, and I got to my feet angrily.

"Belike," I said, "you'll tell me 'twas no one. Well, what you've done once I can do again. Tomorrow I'll be off on my own, and I'll see the country for myself."

"Now, lad," said he, very conciliatory, for I think he feared what my mother might say should he allow me to get beyond his ken, "there is no need for hurry. I'll confess it to ye 'twas Abner Love first showed me beyond the hills, and who it was showed him I could not say. If ye'll but wait a day for me to collect my traps I'll take ye along and show ye what I know, for there'll be no peace for me until I do!"

But we did not go the next day or the next. I believe old Toby would rather have lost both hands than go into those mountains, but then neither did he care to see Stiles going off without him. He tried to dissuade us from the project, but Jed, having got the idea firmly in his mind that I would give him no rest unless he went, was determined not to be put off. In the end Toby reluctantly made up his mind to go along. Having done so much, I tried to persuade some of the others to join us; but they were there to trap, and they had no intention of abandoning that purpose, however poor the results might be.

Ever since the first warm days, when the sap began to stir in the trees, Toby had been working with the help of one or another of us at building of canoes. One, a large one capable of carrying four with all our furs, he had already completed. The other, a smaller craft, was better than half done, and we decided to abandon the first plan of going on foot, and await its final completion. As Jed Stiles pointed out, it made for more comfortable travelling most of the way, and being lightly made of bark would not hinder us much upon the carries.

The task, although both Stiles and myself took turns at helping, took Toby the better part of a week to finish, and sometimes I even thought he was deliberately soldiering to delay the evil day of departure. In the meantime I gathered in such of our traps as remained out and baled up our furs, which the others promised to carry out for us in the event they left before we returned, for we were not certain that we would come by this route. We agreed in any event to meet on the fifteenth of May at Osgood's tavern in Rumford.

By the end of the week all was in readiness, the canoe completed and tried and our scanty belongings (for we were travelling as light as we might) packed and stowed. I remember it was a grey, drizzly morning when at last we slid the canoe into the water and stepped in from the shingle. The others came down, Will Stark and Amos Eastman cracking jokes about our journey, telling us to keep clear of Quebec and mind our step with the French girls, while John and Dan Stinson remained silent. We had a pull at the rum bottle all around, and then they crowded about us, slapping our backs as we climbed in, and wishing us a good trip, while overhead the grey skies threatened and the bushes along the bank dripped rain into the leaden swirling water of the river beneath. With a last good-bye we pushed off and swung into midstream, floating down. When I last looked back the others had gone up the path to camp; but Dan Stinson still stood on the shingle, smiling and waving to us. I remember it because it was so different from the circumstances in which I next saw the place. Yet how were we to guess the things that were to happen while we were gone? I waved back to him. Then the current swept us on around a bend and shut him from our view with a finality I did not then realize. I turned and bent to my paddle once more.

Our way lay down the river to its mouth at the Pemigewasset. There we turned northward and camped about a league upstream at the foot of a rocky gorge through which the water foamed and boomed across falls to a long deep pool where the salmon lay like great logs along the bottom. That evening we enjoyed some of the best fishing I have ever known, and the next morning carried around the falls to the still water above.

All that day and the next we poled upstream through thick-wooded country, with here and there a wild meadow dotted with elms, until on the evening of the third day we came to a deep basin, set in the midst of high forest-clad mountains, where the river split in three parts, to west and north and east.

To me it seemed a gloomy place, all shut in with the dark green hills, and the craggy peaks frowning down into it from the north. I thought I could well understand the Indians' superstition concerning the region. But to Stiles, who had always branched off to westward well below, and who consequently had never laid eyes upon the spot before, it was a little paradise.

There is no accounting for tastes. For myself I prefer a high spot, from which I can look down upon the country round. If there are to be high mountains, I say, let them be at a distance so that their harsher outlines are softened and their frowning flanks do not dominate my every waking thought. But this was not Stiles's way. I think the high green wall on every hand gave him a sense of security, as if this were his world where none might enter but he knew of it. A little below the forks on the east bank was a natural meadow, high enough above the stream itself to be safe from floods, and small enough to be easily worked by one man. Everywhere else was the tall dark forest, mile upon mile of spruce and fir, with a scattering of hardwood in the valley itself. There was plenty of evidence of game, though even there it appeared to me that the wild life was not what it should be. So enamoured of the place was Stiles that we spent three days poking and exploring its every nook and corner; and in the end when we left he declared that this was his choice, and that when it came time for him to stop his roaming and settle down this would be the spot.

Fortunately, however, he had no intention of settling himself to the quiet life for some time to come, and after a few days' rest we set out again, following this time up the east branch of the river. It soon became evident that the canoe would be of little use to us here, for though the stream was large it was strewn with boulders and flowed in one long roaring rapid, mile after mile, only stopping for an occasional pool, so that its navigation, even in our light craft, was out of the question. Accordingly, after a conference on the matter, we decided to cache the canoe and proceed on foot. We could always, Stiles pointed out, if need be build another, though it seemed to me that Toby showed but scant enthusiasm for this. That evening we stowed the canoe on poles between two tall spruces, a little way back from the river, and the next morning pushed on afoot.

We stuck to the north bank of the brawling stream, always with tall mountains rising on either hand, and camped that night where a sizable brook came down from the north behind the craggy peaks that shut us in on that side. Fishing for our supper in both the main stream and the tributary, we found both abounding in small trout, so that we did not want for meat. Nor did we lack for company, for when we awoke in the morning and rubbed

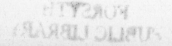

the frost from our eyes, it was to find an old she bear and two small cubs watching us curiously from the farthest bank. When she saw that we were awake and watching her she showed her teeth in an ugly coughing snarl, whereupon Toby laughed almost for the first time since we left our camp upon the lower river, and threw water upon her. At that, instead of carrying out her original threat, she proved herself the merest bluff, calling her cubs to her with a series of grunts and growls, and with an air of injured dignity that was laughable to behold lumbered off into the woods with the young ones at her heels, leaving us to our own devices.

We pushed on that day to the place where the river forks once more, there taking the northern fork, and working up higher into the hills. Here we encountered not a little difficulty, for though, it being well on into April, the snow had long since disappeared from the warm banks of the river below, in these dark mountain gullies it still lay deep and wet across our path. We spent a bitter night in a deep notch between two high-flung mountain shoulders, beside a tiny frozen pond scarce a hundred yards across, and the next day pressed on down the little stream that was its outlet until we came to its mouth in a good-sized river flowing through a warm wide valley in which the sun shone and the birds sang and the trees were bursting into bud.

If spring had touched the air, however, the waters of the stream had heard naught of it, for they were bitterly chill, and since they flowed waist-deep and more full twenty yards across, we turned our faces upstream in search of a better place to cross. A walk of four miles or so brought us above a tumbling fall to a broad intervale, the whole eastern side of which was shut in behind a range of great dark mountains, mightier than anything I had as yet seen, and dominated in the middle by one great snow-capped peak that towered majestically above the surrounding hills, and made them puny by comparison.

Here the river flowed more slowly, and at one of its bends we were able to fell a tall pine across, so that we might walk from one bank to the other dry-shod. Now again it seemed we were on familiar ground, for Stiles had been here before in company with Robert Rogers, and he told me the river was the Ammonoosuc, while the mountain was Agiochook itself, the most feared of all among the Indians, on whose summit, by their legend, dwelt the

Thunder God, and in the dark gullies of whose flanks were hordes of evil spirits held by him in readiness to wreak his vengeance upon any who ventured too near his home or in any other way displeased him.

We passed a miserable night that night, for Toby was in a blue funk at being forced to sleep in such a spot, and could do naught to help us with the camp. To cap it all, as if in answer to his fears, about midnight it came on to snow and blow, which toward morning turned to an icy driving rain, which soaked us to the bone and laid our fire dead in its ashes.

We made a meagre breakfast of cold jerked venison and pushed on, eager to be away from such an accursed spot, our route taking us directly over the summit of a low mountain to westward of the intervale. It was a route, incidentally, which well repaid us for the climb, for though the great peaks to eastward were hidden beneath a lowering blanket of clouds, the southern line of mountains through which we had come stood out sharp and clear and we were able to trace something of our progress thereby. I noticed in looking back that we had made a long detour to eastward when there seemed a more direct way, and indeed a more pronounced pass through the mountains under the foot of the sharp rocky peaks that dominated the three forks. Indeed, studying the lie of the land from this point, it seemed to me that that pass must lead directly into the valley of the middle fork. But when I asked my companions about it, Stiles said frankly that he did not know, and Toby only rolled his eyes so that I could see plainly he was horrified of the place.

The rest of our northward journey was uneventful. From the mountain we dropped down into the valley of still another river that flowed northward through somewhat less rugged country, and on the third day thereafter we came out upon the broad meadows of the Upper Cohos.*

If the little basin at the three forks of the Pemigewasset had captured Jed Stiles's imagination, the broad flats of the Upper Cohos took mine by storm. Here the hills had been pushed back on either hand, forming the broadest natural meadows I had yet seen, rivalling even those of the lower Merrimack. Through the midst of this fertile plain the broad Connecticut wound in great

* Present Lancaster.

twisting curves. The little river that we had followed down from the mountains, clear as the air we breathed, tumbled between two pine-clad hills upon the southeast corner, turned sharply to the west, and, ceasing its brawling, wound in miniature imitation of the broader stream into which it presently poured its waters. Where the rivers joined, the meadows were near two miles across; and though they narrowed north and south, for miles they lay athwart the river, so that nowhere did the hills come closer than a half a mile. Behind the meadows were dense forests of pine, and back of them again gentle lifting hills, covered clear to their rounded summits with heavy hardwood. Deer browsed in the meadows, and partridges drummed up on the hillsides. If one climbed the southern tier of hills, one could gaze northward across the valley to tumbled forest lands beyond and southward to the mountains, near enough to be picturesque and yet far enough to be no longer forbidding. It was a pleasant country, ready-made and waiting only the coming of man to be fruitful, comfortable, livable.

For more than two weeks we rested at the intervales, hunting, fishing, exploring every hill and corner. Immediately upon our arrival Toby set to work upon a new canoe, for he said it tired his legs to walk too much. In this Stiles and I took turns at helping; but the making of a bark canoe is a task that calls for much skill and, since I had had little experience at it, there was little that I could do beyond helping to gather the bark and the wood that went into the ribs and gunwales. Consequently I spent the greater part of my time poking off into far corners of the region, exploring it thoroughly, for I had already made up my mind that when the time for settlement in this region came I should have a hand in it.

I went up and down the river, northward as far as the mouth of the Upper Ammonoosuc, south to the stream since known as John's River. Eastward I went as far as the foot of the high mountains; but to westward across the river I did not explore at all, for this was a country of wooded hills, and seemed from a distance not greatly different from what we had come through on our way thither.

Stiles also shared my enthusiasm for the place, for the river was full of fish, and if there was any scarcity of game we could not notice it. Toby alone seemed restless and apprehensive, as if this were an evil spot. For a long time he would say nothing in explanation, but at last, one evening, Stiles badgered him so that he was at last goaded into speaking his mind.

"This place no good for English," he said. "This place Tom Titigaw's hunting ground. Tom Titigaw hate English. He catch here—no good!"

He shook his head with violent solemnity.

"Who's Tom Titigaw?" I asked, for I had never heard the name before.

"A bad one, lad," said Stiles. "He was chief of the Anasaguntic-cooks east o' here a piece. He's always hated the English, and moved his people to St. Francis a few years ago to get quit of 'em. If there's any dirty work brewing in Canada any time, ye may be sure Titigaw's finger's in't, for the older chiefs have no hold over him. Sabatis and Christo are of his lot, an' I doubt not Plausawa's joined with 'em, for he always was a mild sheep to follow where he was led."

The splash of a great salmon leaping in the darkness on the river below the camp drew our attention at that moment, and when conversation was resumed it followed different lines. But if the subject was not mentioned again, I think it rode in the back of all our minds, casting a gloom upon our spirits and filling us with a sense of apprehension, so that Toby worked double shifts to finish the canoe, and Stiles gave up his hunting and fishing to help. For my part I had seen much of the region already, and had formed my own opinion of it; yet even I did not care to stray far from camp.

Three days more sufficed to finish the canoe, and at last on the twenty-eighth day of April we were ready for the return. I had accomplished my purpose, which had been to visit the Upper Cohos and see something of the mountain country en route. There was nothing left but to turn our faces homeward, and so about midmorning on that fateful day we piled our scanty belongings in the canoe and turned downstream, little dreaming what at that very instant was taking place at our old camp far to southward on the Asquamchumauke.

The day was clear and warm, with the touch of summer that sometimes comes in May; and with the wind and current at our backs to sweep us along, we made excellent time, down through the winding meadows below the Cohos to the narrow place where the hills run together and the still, calm waters give way to mile upon mile of foaming, tumbling rapids through which we shot with breath-taking speed that left me at once awed and exhilarated.

Thanks to the swift rapids in the middle stretch and the fair wind farther down to help us over the long stretches of still water, we covered an immense distance that day, getting well below the mouth of the Passumpsic and camping for the night at the mouth of a small brook which tumbled down from the west not many leagues above the great Oxbow at the Lower Cohos.

The brook came down directly out of the hills onto the plain, where it meandered in wide curves to the river, which it joined at an angle forming a narrow spit of brush-covered land between it and the river. Its mouth was overhung with alders, and I think we might have passed it by; but Toby had been watching for it and swung our bows in through the tangled mass into a tiny bay with a sandy shingle along one side. Although I did not at the time realize it, I came later to see that we could not have been more securely hidden had we sought the spot.

We were tired from our long run, as was but natural, and as the evening was warm for the time of year, we made our camp in the simplest possible manner, kindling only the tiniest of cooking fires upon the shingle and spreading our blankets upon the higher ground of the spit, from which, as we lay, we could see both the brook on the one hand and the river on the other. Immediately after supper we rolled up in our blankets underneath the overhanging bushes, and I for one was asleep almost before my head had touched the ground.

I do not know to this day the exact hour when I awoke, but it must have been some time after midnight, for the great white moon which had been rising when we lay down was now well over in the west, and our little cooking fire was long since dead in its ashes. I lay still for some minutes, on the borderland between sleeping and waking, half wondering that I should start thus out of a sound sleep, without the least notion of what might have aroused me. I was about to roll over and doze off again when a sound from downriver brought me up upon my elbow twisting my head in an attempt to pierce the shadows farther down.

For several minutes all was still, until I almost thought it must have been my imagination. Then all at once I heard again, more clearly this time, the steady rhythmic chunk of paddles in the river.

I rose then on all fours and craned my neck in an effort to see whence the sound came; but a sharp hill looming above the river threw that portion of the stream in shadow, and though the sound came steadily nearer I could see nothing in the darkness. I held my position, however, waiting, and presently I made out two dark blots upon the water. I watched them, fascinated by their stealthy approach, and after a minute or two they began to take form beneath my eyes, changing from mere formless blobs of darker black against the blackness of the river to two large canoes with a smaller one between them. As they came nearer I could make out the shadowy outlines of the men in them, and saw that each of the large canoes held six paddlers, and the smaller one but two, though who they were, or what they were, I could not see. When they approached the strip of moonlit water I could catch the faint gleam of reflected light as their paddles rose and dipped in steady rhythm.

What prompted me to call out to them, I cannot to this day tell. I had no apprehension, yet the very fact that they travelled thus stealthily at night should have warned me that they were up to no good. But even as I opened my mouth I felt Toby's hand upon my arm and heard his hissing whisper in my ear.

"Quiet! Lie down!"

I choked off the hail that had been at the very tip of my tongue, and sank down looking curiously at the old Indian, for it was the first inkling I had that he was awake. He was paying me not the slightest heed, but lay flat upon his belly, his eyes straining towards the river, his whole body rigid with a tenseness I had never before seen him display. I was amazed, for I could not imagine that any danger threatened. I wondered what Stiles would make of it, and turned my head cautiously towards him, to find that he too had come awake and was staring intently out at the river.

All this had taken much less time than it takes to tell, and all the while it was happening the steady chunk of paddles had grown clearer and louder with the swift approach of the craft. Presently we could hear the ripple of water at their bows and hear the grunts of the paddlers as they bent to the work. Then all at once the leading canoe came out of the shadow and into the broad bend of white moonlight almost directly opposite where we lay. It was then, with a gasp, that I saw the wisdom of Toby's quiet warning, for in that cold light the paddlers were plain to be seen. These were no friendly red men returning from peaceful trading mission upon the lower river. Indians they were, but what Indians! For they were stripped to the waist and their heads were shaven save for a single scalp lock along the top of the crown; and even in the moonlight I could make out the hideous daubings that were traced across their faces and bodies. The truth burst upon me in a flash of horror. This was a war party returning from a raid!

The fact was plain enough to see, and yet it seemed impossible. When we had left we had been at peace. True there had been no love lost between the Indians of the north and our own people, but there had been no hint of war. Was it possible that in our absence war had broken out?

The question raced through my mind, fair screaming for an answer. Yet I knew that the least movement on my part might betray our presence and mean death. I clung to the earth, scarce daring to breathe lest the sound of it carry out upon the river. In the tension of the moment it seemed an interminable time before all three canoes drew even with us. It was plain to see that all of them were heavily laden, and once the stern man in the small canoe lifted his paddle and poked at something in the bottom of his boat and laughed. But his companion spoke sharply to him, and he returned to the task of paddling with a sullen air.

It seemed to take hours for them to pass, but in the end they did, disappearing around a bend high up the river, far beyond earshot. Not until then did we dare to speak or even move. As the last canoe rounded the bend I heard Stiles stir uneasily beside me.

"Ye saw them, Toby," he whispered hoarsely. "What did ye make o't?"

The old Indian was silent for so long that at first I believed he had not heard. Then, with an apparent effort, he wrenched his gaze from the spot where the canoes had disappeared upstream and turned to Stiles.

"Tom Titigaw!" was all he said.

4

It was some minutes before we dared to move, for even though the canoes had gone we did not know but that there might be more to come. Nor did we speak, for each was busy with his own thoughts. Their stealthy passage in the night, the fact that they were painted for war, their coming in such force—all these indicated that they had been raiding. But even had they washed the paint from their bodies and travelled by daylight, the very fact that they were led by Titigaw was sufficient to prove their evil intent.

It was a full half-hour before Toby finally roused himself.

"No more come," he grunted. "We go."

The words were as music to my ears: I longed to put as much distance as possible between myself and the savages, for the memory of their cruel faces, made a hundred times more hideous by their streaks and daubings, clung in my mind, and I knew that there would be no more sleep for me that night.

We made hasty packs of our belongings and launched the canoe. Ten minutes later we were slipping down the river on the gentle current.

We kept to the west bank, hugging the shadow wherever possible lest we meet another party upon the river. But no more came, and for all our caution we made swift time; coming by daybreak into the upper reaches of the Lower Cohos.

Midmorning brought us to the carrying place, and here we paused for a quick breakfast. There were marks upon the bank of the enemy's passage, and Toby, studying them, announced solemnly that sixteen people had passed this way, evidently coming across the carry from the Asquamchumauke. I remembered that there had been but fourteen of the Indians and remarked upon it. Toby shrugged.

"Take two prisoner," he said.

The discovery filled us with apprehension for our friends, for though it was probable that they had already gone, it was also possible that they had not, and in that case it was likely that they had been the victims of the raid. As we hurried across the long carry my mind was filled with misgivings. I remembered the stealthy visit of the savage Christo, and wondered if this could have had any connection with it. If our camp had been their objective, why were there only two prisoners? Who were they? And where were the other two? Had they escaped or had they been killed? By my companions' solemn faces and the haste with which we travelled I knew that the same thoughts were running through their heads.

We were a weary trio when at last, with the approach of darkness, we came out upon the upper waters of the Asquamchumauke. There again we had need for caution, for it was still possible that there were other parties below us. The river was narrow, and if we should meet them there was no hope that we could pass unseen in the darkness. Nor would it serve any practical purpose to continue by night. Accordingly we moved a little upstream, covering our tracks as best we might, and made our camp where we could overlook the landing place without ourselves being seen.

There followed a restless night, during which one of us stood constantly on guard. But we might have spared ourselves the trouble in the end, for though we watched carefully for any passing enemy, none came. In the morning we embarked once more and headed southward.

Here, however, we could not make the speed of the day before, for the upper waters of the Asquamchumauke are swift and shallow and it was necessary to proceed with caution lest we damage the canoe. It was in consequence of this enforced caution that we did not reach the site of our camp on the river until the following morning.

As we pulled up upon the shingle, however, I think we all shared the same anxiety for the fate of our companions. I know that I for one felt a sudden reluctance to climb the bank to the grounds above for fear of what I might find.

It was Stiles who was first up. His shout brought Toby and myself on the run, and my relief at finding the place abandoned and apparently undisturbed beyond a slight trampling of the surrounding bushes brought a cry of gladness from my lips.

Toby, however, was not so easily satisfied. He turned away abruptly and made a complete circuit of the outskirts of the camp, after which he returned to the cleared circle and made a thorough search of the ground, even scattering the cold grey ashes in the fireplace and examining the charred ends of the sticks that still lay there. Stiles and I watched him with interest but without interruption, for it was plain that he knew what he was about. Presently he stopped his nosing and sat down upon the bed of balsam tips that still lay spread a few feet from the fire.

"Injuns come here," he announced.

Stiles nodded.

"I figgered as much," he said. "This ground's too trampled and mucked up for four men. What d'ye think happened, Toby? Did Titigaw catch 'em here, or had they left?"

The old Indian shrugged.

"No can tell," he said, and looked around. "If Titigaw catch um here, no fight anyway."

"Why then," I cried, "it's all right. Titigaw had two prisoners. It's plain that if they came here they found them gone, for there were four here, and the other two would scarce have escaped without a fight."

But Stiles and Toby did not share my optimism. I saw them look solemnly at each other. Stiles shook his head.

"It might be so, lad," he said. "But can we be sure on't? Maybe the savages came on them away from camp."

My heart sank again within me, for I could not but see the possibility of what he said.

We began a search then, a search that scoured the environs of the camp to the river's edge and up and down the bank for a quarter of a mile in either direction. Toby spent a long time examining the marks upon the shingle, but there the sand was so tracked and trampled that it was impossible to make head or tail of the signs. The result was that by noon we had discovered exactly nothing that would give us a clue as to the fate of our companions.

We ate a hurried noonday meal in silence, and afterwards crossed to the far bank, landing and leaving the canoe above the mouth of the brook. From there we followed up the north bank of the little stream as far as our old camp site at the pond. But here again we found nothing, and my spirits, dashed by my companions' persistent gloom, began to rise. When we came at length to Rumford, I assured myself we should find all four safe and sound awaiting us at Osgood's tavern.

We crossed the pond's outlet at its head and, following down the south bank perhaps half a mile, we came upon a thing that dealt my hopes a staggering blow, for there we found signs that a large party had lain in the brush. That they were Indians there was little doubt, for the stones of the brook were here and there smeared with paint where they had crouched and touched up their daubings while they waited for someone or something. But worst of all was a broken trap which had evidently been cast aside carelessly and which Toby salvaged from the brush. I recognized it at once as one of Will Stark's.

We travelled from there on in grim silence, following a pathway trodden down by the Indians before us on their way to the river. It brought us out upon a low bluff, where the river swept against the near bank. On our right was the mouth of the brook, while to the left was thick brush, slightly trampled, a still back eddy, and beyond that more brush, low by the river, and then another sandy bar. Directly in front of us lay the river, clear to view for several hundred yards to a bend below and another above. On the far bank lay the shingle below the camp which we had always used as a landing place.

Here the trail seemed to end. The indications were that one or two of the Indians had thrust their way through the brush below towards the sand bar, but the rest had embarked directly from the bank, for there were scrapings there and footprints that led down to the water's edge.

My companions looked relieved.

" 'Twould seem perhaps ye were right, lad," said Stiles. "They must have gone before the devils came."

My heart gave a great bound at that, but Toby still seemed a little dubious.

"No can tell," he said. "In Rumford we know."

"Aye," said Stiles. "Yon's the answer. We'll have our answer tomorrow in Rumford. Wait here, lad, while Toby and me fetch the canoe."

They turned away to cross to the north bank of the brook where we had left the boat.

"I'll go down to the sand bar," I called after them. " 'Tis a better place to land."

As they disappeared from sight I plunged into the brush on my left and worked around the river bank to the still backwater. This I skirted for some distance down, hoping to find its end around a corner, but when I had turned the bend I saw that it continued for another quarter-mile before ending in a rank marsh. To circle it would take too long, and the alternative was a wetting. I retraced my steps to the river and pushed my way down through the thick willows that lined the bank, intending to wade across the end of the backwater, which I could see was not deep, to the bar beyond.

It was thick going, however, and I had some difficulty in making my way. I had to keep my head down and my face covered with my arm as I pushed through, for the tangled bushes were like so many spears striking for my eyes. Consequently I could not always see where I was placing my feet, but had to feel my way as best I could.

I reached the bottom of the embankment, and felt my way forward gingerly towards the water. One step, then two steps, with creepers and brush clinging to my leggings. Then on the third step I felt the cool water close about my ankle. I thrust my head clear of the brush and stepped out briskly, hoping by hurry to avoid some of the wetting. But my haste was my undoing. My toe hooked on something that felt like a small stump, and in the next instant I was floundering headlong in the shallow muddy water.

I rose cursing, for there is nothing to my mind clammier than wet buckskins, and, in annoyance, turned to see what it was that had so set me by the heels. As I did so the words died upon my lips, for there, sticking out through the shallow water under the low bushes was a moccasined foot.

For an instant I stood rooted in horror, for it was plain to see that whoever owned that foot was dead. I opened my mouth but for a moment could make no sound. Then, as life came suddenly back to me, I shouted at the top of my voice and set to work feverishly to pull the bushes aside.

It was not easy, for the branches were thick as my arm and springy, but my horror lent me strength and presently I had uncovered the body. It lay face down, rigid in the shallow water, the arms stretched stiffly above the head, hiding the face. Even through the brush I could see that the scalp had been ripped away, leaving a gaping wound, white at the edges where the water had lain on it, and with the black blood clotted upon the bone of the skull. In the middle of the back was a clean bullet hole.

I knew, even though I could not see the face, that this must be one of my friends, for it was no Indian, and I shrank from the touch of him. Yet I felt I must know for certain. I summoned all my courage, and conquering my horror for an instant, reached down quickly and grasped the leg that had tripped me, pulling the body out from beneath the bushes. Once in the clear it was easy to turn him over. I took one swift glance at that ghastly face, the cheek muscles flabby and relaxed where the split scalp had ceased to hold them up, and the horror-stricken eyes already staring through a whitish film from lying in the water, and turning, stumbled for the sand bar, where I was promptly and violently ill, for I knew that face. The dead man was my own friend Dan Stinson!

· 8 ·

GOOD FRIENDS AND BAD ACQUAINTANCES

❲ 1 My companions must have had the canoe in the water when I shouted, for I had scarce reached the sand bar when they came driving up.

"What is't, lad?" said Stiles. "Have ye found something?"

I had no voice to answer, but could only nod and point where Stinson's body lay half hidden beneath the overhanging brush. They turned the canoe about, and following the direction of my finger slipped into the backwater.

It was Toby, sharper-eyed than any white man, who first saw the body. I heard him grunt and saw him point with his paddle. I heard Stiles draw in his breath sharply.

"Christ!" he said. " 'Tis little Danny Stinson!"

I will not dwell upon the events that immediately followed, for even today I cannot think of then without dread. It was my first actual contact with death, and its memory sticks in my mind as the horror of a nightmare clings through the day.

We gathered up the body and carried it up on shore, where we stretched it out upon a blanket before deciding what should be done. By this time I had taken a grip upon my reaction and could consider things in a more sensible light. This man had been my good friend, and I felt it was my duty to see the right thing done. I even thought perhaps we should carry him back to his father's house.

But when I spoke of this to Stiles, he shook his head.

" 'Tis better," he said, "if we just dig a decent grave and bury him here."

"But his people will want to see him," I protested.

Stiles cast a sidelong glance at the still figure stretched upon the blanket.

"D'ye think so?" he said. "If 'twere me, I'd say 'twas kinder if they didn't see him. 'Tis not a pretty sight, lad; not one I'd care to carry about of one I loved."

I could not help but shudder, for what he said was true enough.

"Besides," he added quickly, seeing me hesitate, "these three days in the water have softened him. He'll look far worse before we reach Suncook."

So occupied were we with the discussion, that we did not notice the approach of another canoe until a hail from the river brought us about, startled. I recognized at once the other canoe which Toby had built, though it took me a moment more to identify the people in it. Will Stark occupied the bow, looking haggard and worn out. Behind him was Phinehas Virgin, a Rumford man whom I knew but slightly, and in the stern were Moses and Joseph Eastman, father and brother respectively to Amos. It was plain that they had come up from Rumford without a rest, for they were all drawn and weary-looking.

We faced about, waiting in silence until their keel grated upon the sand before us. Will Stark was the first ashore. He stepped out heavily and gave one glance at the blanket and then turned and pulled the canoe up. The others climbed out stiffly and crowded over to look at the body. Stark turned to us.

"Did you find any sign of John or Amos?" he asked.

"They're safe enough," said Stiles, "though maybe none so comfortable."

He told then of how, on the Connecticut, we had been awakened in the night by the sound of paddles; of how we had slipped away down the river in the darkness, and found the tracks of sixteen people at the carry when but fourteen of the savages had gone up.

"Had 'em tied in the bottom o' the canoe, most like," said Virgin. "They ain't like to carry 'em so far if they meant to do 'em harm. Like as not they figger they'll fetch a good price in Canada in spite o' the peace, an' I ain't a mite o' doubt but what they will."

Stiles nodded his solemn agreement and looked curiously at Will.

"What happened here?" he asked.

Stark shrugged.

"We'd have done well to leave the traps," he said. "Monday, Amos found sign they'd been about, up by the pond. He told me that night. Tuesday I sent John out to bring in the traps. When he didn't come back we thought might be he'd got twisted, so we shot off our guns to give him the direction back to camp. When he still didn't come in I began to think maybe the savages had come on him, and we'd best be getting out before they come on us."

"What about John?" said Stiles, and there was a tinge of reproof in his tone.

"God a'mighty!" Will replied. "I hadn't any fear for him. I figgered if they'd took him there wasn't nothing we could do, an' if they hadn't he'd take care o' himself. We waited all night an' he didn't come, so just afore daybreak I sent off Amos to scout along the bank, while Dan an' me brought down the canoe."

He paused a minute then and shook his head, as if wishing he had done differently.

"I guess maybe Amos got careless, or something," he went on, "for first I knew there was a holler from the bank, and I looked up and there was John standing up a-shoutin' to me. I could see one o' them painted devils behind him a-talkin' their lingo fast and angry. I never could understand 'em, but John, he could speak it good. Anyways, I guess the Injun was a-tellin' him to call us in. But John, he hollered there was fourteen on 'em an' to get away quick."

"What'd ye do then?" Stiles asked.

"What'd I do?" said Will in a surprised tone. "Why, hell! I paddled. Out o' the side o' my eye I could see them Injuns jump up all along the shore. I saw John grab for all the guns he could reach. There was a lot o' shootin'; an' I guess John spoiled it for some o' them. Just the same there was others shot straight enough. One o' them went clean through my paddle, an' another took poor Dan'l right in the back. He never let a sound out o' him. First I knew of it he kind o' jerked forward an' then slumped over an' slid out o' the boat. I had to rare back real hard to keep the whole business from going over with him. I made a grab for him as I went by, but I could see 'twas no use. He was dead afore he hit the water. Then the Injuns shot some more, and John hollered to paddle quick 'cause all their guns was empty, and I did. Last I see when I looked back, just afore I rounded the bend, three or four of the Injuns was wadin' out to grab hold o' Dan'l. I turned and paddled quick, for I knew they'd get me too if I didn't look sharp!"

Moses Eastman, who had paid but slight attention to the story, turned away from the still body on the blanket, and interrupted.

"It's gettin' on to night," he said. "We'd best get this done with. I don't guess any o' us care much for campin' right here."

I noticed then, with a start, that the sun was low on the western hills, and for the first time since noon I became again aware of the passage of time.

The party from Rumford had come well equipped with shovels, having been warned already of what they might expect, a fact which facilitated matters exceedingly. We chose a location high upon the bank, at the foot of a great elm above the reach of floods, and there dug the grave, each one taking a turn at the task so that it was soon done. When it was ready we rolled Dan's body in a blanket and lowered it gently in, while Mr. Eastman, who was an elder of the church, said a solemn prayer for the rest of his soul.

All the while that this was happening I moved and acted mechanically. Even my responses were automatic. My mind was with the dead. I found it hard to realize that this was the end of Danny Stinson. Small he had been and unprepossessing, but I knew him for a true friend. In spite of his quick temper and brittle sensibilities there had been a solidity and genuineness about him, so that one always knew that no matter what the test he would always remain loyal and true. And now all this was gone. I could scarce bring myself to think it possible.

When the business of the burial was finished, and the last shovelful of earth had been tossed in place, I went up on the hill and found a flat stone. This with the help of Toby and Will Stark I carried down and placed at the head of the grave between the gnarled roots of the great elm. On it I scratched with the point of my knife:

H.I. D. STINSON
b. 1731   d. 1752
R.I.P.

We camped that night at the mouth of the river, on the intervales where it joined the Pemigewasset. There was not one of us who was not too weary to sit up late, and I know that even had we been inclined to loll about the evening fire, I for one had no wish to discuss the raid.

If we did not talk, however, we had ample time for thought. I

remembered again the mysterious visit of the Indian Christo, and
our fears at the time. Was it not possible, I asked myself, that the
Indians had purposely delayed until the road should be open and
more easily travelled to make their attack? Might not this raid
have been Christo's work? I did not remember having seen him in
either of the canoes that had gone up-river that night we lay upon
the Connecticut, but it could be that I had not recognized him in
full war paint.

That evening after supper I spoke my mind, giving my reasons
for believing as I did. Moses Eastman heard me out in silence and
then shook his head.

"Ye say the Indian, Christo, lay upon the hill and spied upon ye
in your camp?" he said, when I had done.

I nodded.

"And slipped away after covering his tracks?" he persisted.

"He met somebody by the brook first," I said.

"Ye've no idea who that might be?" he said.

I shook my head. That had been an aspect of the visit I had
never understood.

"After that," Mr. Eastman went on, "ye moved your camp.
Could he have known that?"

"No," I said, "but you forget, sir, that John Stark first came
upon signs of the savages at the pond, where no doubt they first
came looking for us."

He shook his head.

"Aye," he said, " 'tis suspicious enough appearing, I'll grant.
But ye see, lad, there's one hitch. Both Sabatis and Christo have
been this six days past in Canterbury at the house of Josiah Miles.
They came about a week ago with furs to trade, and have stayed
on with their money making themselves very disagreeable with
their rum, I hear, though poor Josiah durst not drive them out
lest they revenge themselves upon him!"

"Why," I cried, " 'tis plain enough then, 'twas Christo set them
down upon us, else why is he here now? 'Tis full a month too
early for the trade, as you know well. No doubt he led them down
and showed them the place, and then went on to Canterbury to
divert suspicion from himself. 'Twould be a favour to the world if
we were to arrest them and make them stand their trial."

" 'Twould be a greater favour to shoot them out of hand,'
growled Stiles.

" 'Twould seem ye've more than mere suspicion to prove your point," the elder Eastman agreed; "but ye've naught would stand in court. There is nothing we can do about it."

"Are we to sit still," I cried, "while they murder our friends and carry off captives from under our very noses?"

"What would ye do?" he demanded. "There is not evidence to hang the scoundrels. Even if there were 'twould not be done for fear lest it might stir the savages to war."

I laughed bitterly.

"War!" I cried scornfully. "Is this peace? Then let us have war until all the Frenchmen and their devil's allies are driven into the sea. We will have no real peace until 'tis done!"

And with that I snatched up my blanket and stalked away to the shelter where we had spread our bed of balsam tips. There I lay down and thought angry thoughts of the cowardice of my people, until after a little I remembered what war had meant to this country: scalped women, and slaughtered babies, and men going down to their work in gangs like prisoners, scarce daring to set foot outside the house alone and never sleeping without a gun close to the hand. I remembered how little protection the provincial government had been able to give, and how ineffectual that protection had been when it came. I remembered how the British had returned Louisbourg to the French after the colonists had taken it from them, and how all the gains of the last war had been swept away by the stroke of a pen. I began to see Eastman's view that anything was preferable to war when the war could not be carried with a strong hand into the enemy's country, and I cursed a king so rotten that he would not protect his own nor hold his gains when he had got them. It seemed another score I had against the House of Hanover. And it was on this bitter, helpless note that I finally fell asleep.

2

I passed a restless night, for I was troubled with dreams. For the most part they were of the usual stuff of dreams, light and illusive, forgotten before one is well awake. But there was one which kept recurring, and each time at the end I awoke in a cold sweat and filled with horror. In it I found myself following snowshoe tracks through a long valley which I knew not. Far ahead loomed great snowy peaks, in the midst of which I recognized the mighty Agio-chook, and the tracks I followed seemed to make directly towards them. I was in a breathless hurry, for it seemed imperative that I catch up with the man ahead, though for what reason I could not tell. Every now and again I would catch sight of him—a great hulk of a man clad in thick bearskins, lumbering along at a leisurely pace. But, though each time I saw him I ran with all my might to overtake him, I could gain no ground on him and my feet moved with painful slowness. Nor did he once look back, so that I never saw his face. This continued for what seemed hours, and always we went towards the mountains which never seemed to come any closer. At last he dipped down over the crest of a hill, and then I ran with all my might, for I was filled with dread lest I lose him. When I came to the crest I found myself looking down on a broad lake, frozen and covered with snow. Along the shore of the lake I saw a crowd of people, but the man in the bearskins was nowhere to be seen. I followed his tracks straight down to the lake, and found myself suddenly surrounded by people I knew. My mother was there and Purity Stiles, and Moses Eastman, and Will Stark, and Phinehas Virgin, and Robert Rogers, and a slight man with a long nose and reddish hair in an officer's coat who seemed vaguely familiar and who kept repeating, "Remember, next to valour, vigilance and then caution." I asked all those people if they had seen the man in the bearskins and whither he had gone, but though the tracks went straight through their midst they all shook their heads and denied that they had seen anyone such as I described. They tried to hold me back, but I fought with them and said I must catch him, and presently I broke away and hurried off. Before me stretched the white expanse of the lake, mile upon mile, with the great mountains looming still and cold beyond. The tracks went straight out across the ice, but nowhere was there a sign of the man. I hurried on, and presently made out a black dot in the snow ahead, and I broke into a run. But as I approached I saw that this was not the man I was following, but another, a small man dressed in buckskins and stretched grotesquely in the snow. When I came up I saw that it was a dead man, and that he lay face downward, his arms stretched above his head, his hands clutching at the loose snow. I knelt beside him and turned him over and saw again the dead white-filmed eyes of Dan Stinson staring at me. I rose to go on along the track, but the dead hand moved and clutched my leg; and at that I would break out into a panic and kick and scream and fight to break that deathly grip. Then I would awake to find one of my companions shaking me and telling me for God's sake to be quiet and quit threshing.

When the dawn finally came I felt limp and washed out, as though I had not slept for weeks, and I saw that Stiles, too, was hollow-eyed and weary. We were a silent crew that paddled down the river that day, but as the sun came up and warmed me I felt better and somehow comforted just to be alive. Throughout the day, however, the memory of that dream kept running through my head, and for some reason, which I cannot even now explain, I connected it with those other tracks I had discovered near our camp at the pond; the tracks of the man Christo had met, but whose maker I did not know. Somehow I felt that if I could once discover who had made those tracks I should know the answer to the whole affair. But when I spoke of this to Stiles he only shrugged and spat.

We did not hurry but took our time, stopping for our noonday meal on a narrow bar behind which was a sunny meadow. When we had eaten we all stretched out in the warm sun upon the fresh sweet-smelling grass of the meadow, meaning only to doze for a moment, though I for one fell promptly into a deep dreamless sleep.

When I awoke with a start it was to find the air grown suddenly cold with the chill of a spring evening and to see the sun already sinking beyond the western hills. I woke my companions and we launched the canoes once more, paddling swiftly now, for we meant to stop that night in Rumford.

It was after dark when we came to the landing place at Eastman's ferry in the north end, and there was no one there but Benjamin Fifield, whom Mr. Eastman had left in charge in his absence. There we left the canoe, and while the Eastmans went to their home, which was not far distant, the rest of us crossed the flats in the darkness and climbed the hill to the town, making our way directly to Osgood's tavern, where we planned to stop the night.

There were perhaps a dozen people in the long low-ceilinged taproom when we stepped in through the door which opened directly upon the street; but the light was low, and there was a haze of tobacco smoke which prevented my recognizing any of them at once. Other eyes were sharper than mine, however, for I had scarce time to turn around to greet Jim Osgood when there was a crash of an overturning chair and a gasp from the corner by the fireplace. Attracted by the commotion I turned my head to look and saw the man Joseph Merrill standing beside the table, gripping it hard with both his hands, his jaw hanging slack, his popping eyes more protruding than ever, his gaze fixed upon me as if he were seeing a ghost. Behind him, still seated, I could see Shem Sanborn glaring at me with hatred and baffled anger in his eyes.

For an instant our eyes met, and in that instant I found the answer to all my pondering. I remembered how eager and excited Merrill had seemed that night in this very room at the outset of our journey; how he had risen and scurried out. I knew, as surely as if I had accompanied him, that he had gone straight to Sanborn with the news of our destination. I remembered Sanborn's curses on the day more than a year since when I had spoiled his trade with the two renegade Indians. I remembered the trail in the snow beside the brook, and called myself a fool for not having seen it sooner. As certainly as I was standing there I felt that either Merrill or Sanborn had met the Indian Christo there that day and set him to watch upon us; indeed, had probably managed the entire business.

I felt my cheeks grow hot as the blood mounted in them, and for an instant my anger blinded me. I turned and strode across the room towards them, and as I did so I saw Sanborn rise and stand truculently waiting. Merrill sidled around the table as if trying to hide behind the larger man, his furtive eyes darting from side to side, seeking an avenue of escape. If ever I saw guilt written bold upon a man's face I saw it then.

It was instinct, I suppose, that made me choose Merrill, for I recognized in him the weaker of the two, the one more likely to confess. I ignored Sanborn and placed myself directly before the other.

"Do ye see a ghost, Merrill?" I said, scarce able to bring the words out—for my anger was near to choking me. "You thought you'd done with me, didn't you, damn you? But you haven't, d'you see? You haven't. There's an innocent lad lies yonder in the mountains, and his blood's on your head!"

I could see his teeth fair rattling in his head in fear, and he scarce could speak.

"I God, Mr. Ferguson, sir," he babbled, " 'fore Jesus, I don't know what ye mean!"

But his eyes gave the lie to his words. He knew as well as I. I was never known for my patience. It might be better for me if I had a more abundant fund of that virtue. But human beings have their faults, and this is one of mine. Had I been able to restrain myself I might have been able to wring the truth from him then and there, but the sight of those furtive, hateful eyes, the man's abject terror, his cowardly babbling, were more than I could bear.

"Ah, God," I cried, "that I should waste my breath on such a lily-livered rat as you!"

And I struck him with all my might upon the point of his chin.

I had the satisfaction of hearing his teeth click together and of seeing him stagger back against the wall, for light as I was I was strong, and I had struck with all the force at my command.

But even as I did so I heard a shout from across the room and half turned, just in time to see the terrific blow that Sanborn had launched at me. There was no time to duck. I did the next best thing, and flung up my shoulder barely in time to divert the blow, which was a blessing, for had it landed square as it was aimed I doubt not it would have taken my head from my shoulders. As it was it glanced across the top of my head and the ceiling seemed to open and burst in a thousand varicoloured lights. I spun across the room, caromed into a table, cartwheeled over it and landed in a tangled mess of chairs and crockery upon the far side of the room.

For a long moment I lay there, my head clanging and ringing like the clatter of a thousand anvils, and every bone in my body seemed torn from its socket. Then I shook my head and got groggily to my feet.

The room was in a turmoil. My friends had not stood to see me knocked about, and in the centre I could see Sanborn exchanging blows with Stiles and another whose back was towards me, but who had something mightily familiar about him. Will Stark was hanging onto Merrill across a table and the latter was trying to get away, while Toby danced about the pair, first on one foot and then on the other, shrieking and yelling with delight. Over near the bar I could see that several innocent bystanders had gotten embroiled in the affair and fists were flying indiscriminately, while poor Osgood behind the bar was pounding with a bung starter and crying at the top of his voice, "Gentlemen, gentlemen!"—much like crying to the wind for all the good it did.

But I was in no mood, nor indeed any condition, to be a patient observer. My head was sore and my spirits ruffled. I thirsted for revenge, and the wish was father to the deed. I thrust swiftly between Stiles and my new-found friend, whom I now recognized as Rob Rogers, and lowering my head launched myself fists flying and feet pumping at Sanborn's midriff.

I felt my head strike his middle like a battering ram, and heard him grunt. I felt my fists strike and was conscious with a thrill of savage delight that he cringed slightly beneath them. Then it seemed as if all the mountains in the Province had chosen that moment to fall upon me. Something battered me in the ribs. An elbow jabbed me heavily just below the eye and turned me sideways, a great fist landed square upon my nose, and once again I felt myself spinning in light air to land with a thud in the corner.

I lay there shaking my head to clear it, and heard Osgood's bung starter thudding on the bar.

"Gentlemen!" our host was shouting. "In God's name, gentlemen!"

Then all at once the street door burst open, and I felt a draft of cold night air run across the floor.

Someone shouted, "The bailie!" and the fighting ceased as abruptly as it began.

I opened my eyes and stared at the doorway, first in chagrin to be so caught brawling by the law, and then in amazement, for the figure that stood framed there was not that of old Captain Ebenezer Eastman, the local guardian of the peace, but rather that of a young woman; a tall young woman of the most breathless beauty, who stood surveying the scene at her feet with a faint grimace of disgust. This in itself was startling enough. The very fact of a pretty girl arriving in Rumford at such an hour was surprising enough. That she should burst in upon a tavern brawl at just that instant was astounding. But that it should be this girl, of all the girls it might have been, was nothing short of a miracle; for though it was six years since I had seen her I was not like even in such a time to forget her. The girl in the doorway was Dorcas Drew!

3

Despite the years that had passed since we met, I knew I could not be mistaken, for except that she had grown taller and more lovely with maturity she had not changed greatly. She stood framed in the low doorway with the velvet blackness of the night behind offering a perfect setting for her beauty, and the smoky light of the room before softening the severity of her dress, a travelling habit of some heavy grey stuff; so that for the merest instant, while she remained motionless surveying the scene before her, she seemed rather to be a delicate painting by a master's hand than a person of flesh and blood. Then there came a movement in the darkness behind her and she stepped to one side to admit Osgood's black Veranus, laden with baggage, followed closely by the familiar, pompous little figure of her father, Lawyer Drew himself—a little fatter now, a trifle aged, and with his bulbous blue-veined nose bright and shining, attesting a somewhat too meticulous devotion to the flowing bowl, but aside from that unchanged from the day I had first laid eyes upon him at the O. Cromwell's Head in Boston.

It was the movement that awakened me from the startled trance into which her sudden appearance had thrown me. I forgot where I was and scrambled to my feet, advancing across the room with outstretched hands.

"Dorcas!" I cried. And when she looked at me distantly, with the air of puzzled indifference, I added, "Dorcas, d'ye not know me? 'Tis Jamie!"

I saw slow recognition come into her eyes, replacing the puzzlement, but there was no gladness there, only a distant coldness. I was suddenly aware of the trickle of blood that ran down from my nose across my chin, and of my left eye which was already growing puffy and doubtless blue.

"What's this?" puffed Lawyer Drew, bustling forward full of self-importance. "What's all this? On my soul!"

He stopped short, and I saw him thrust his head forward and peer at me from beneath his bushy eyebrows.

"Why!" he cried suddenly. "God bless me, 'tis young What-d'ye-call-him!"

I bowed with as much dignity as I could summon in the circumstances.

"Ferguson is the name, sir," I said.

"Ferguson," he repeated after me, "Ferguson, yes, yes, yes, of course! God's my life, but this is remarkable, remarkable indeed! You remember the lad, lass?"

She looked at him, I thought, a little wearily, and then flicked me with a scornful glance.

"I remember Mr. Ferguson, father," she said, and despite the disdain with which she spoke I could not but thrill at the richness of her voice; "but I had scarce thought to meet him again in the midst of a low tavern brawl."

A hot retort sprang to my lips, for my temper, never too good, was strained; but she gave me no chance to speak. Her eyes swept the room, and I saw her glance rest a moment upon Rogers, who was still holding Sanborn by the scruff of the neck and one arm, and upon Will Stark, who sat upon the man Merrill.

"Considering the company he keeps, however," she said contemptuously, "I am not at all surprised."

Rogers's petulant mouth twitched into a sardonic grin, and he inclined his head with exaggerated courtesy but said nothing. I heard Will Stark chuckle sourly. Their restraint served to check my own hot temper. I turned to Lawyer Drew.

"Mistress Drew," I said, bowing, "does us an injustice. She does not understand that what she has just witnessed was something more than a mere brawl. Murder has been done no great distance from here: a murder instigated and abetted by two persons in the room. What she took for a low tavern brawl was in reality an effort to prevent the guilty ones from escaping their just punishment."

Lawyer Drew looked startled, but Dorcas merely seemed impatient.

"God bless my soul!" exclaimed the old man. "Murder, d'ye say? As God's my life, this is serious indeed. I must hear more of it."

But here Dorcas interrupted him.

"Father," she said imperiously. "I grow wearied of this. If you care to listen you may do so; but first I should like to see my room, for it has been a long day."

He clapped his hand to his forehead, a gesture which knocked his big wig slightly askew.

"Bless me!" he said. "The excitement is too much for me! Of course, my dear, of course!"

He turned to me.

"You'll excuse me?" he said. "I'll not be long."

They turned away towards the stairway, and for the first time I noticed that Mistress Osgood stood waiting there, a candle in her hand, to light them to their rooms.

Dorcas did not give me another glance, but swept away up the stair, angry indifference in every line of her back. Nor did I feel that I could blame her greatly, for I must have presented a sorry spectacle. But if she was indifferent I was not, for the sight of her had stirred something within me, bringing back all my old feeling for her, in spite of her shabby treatment of me, and I fear I stood like any bumpkin at the foot of the stair, gawping after her until they turned the corner above and disappeared from view.

It was the thump of Osgood's bung starter on the bar that brought me back to the present.

"By God!" he swore. "Ye start a brawl that does more damage than I'll be like to make up in a month o' trade if it doesn't get me closed by the selectmen, and to cap it off ye frighten my guests with talk o' murder! If 'tis a joke, I call it a mighty poor one!"

His voice reminded me of the matter in hand, and I turned to him.

"I'll settle with ye for the damage, Mr. Osgood," I said. "I'd no mind to cause ye trouble, but looked only to see justice done."

He looked across the bar at Sanborn standing sullen between Rogers and Stiles, and at Merrill, still pinned flat upon his back by Will Stark, his face pasty and his eyes rolling in fear.

"Let that man up," he said. "If ye've a charge to make against these two I'll call the bailie and have them held for the sheriff. If ye've not, then let them go, for ye cannot hold them here."

He spoke with the finality of a man who wished to wash his hands of the entire matter, so I spoke up and told him the entire story from the very beginning, pointing to Sanborn's hatred of me for motivation of his scheme, dwelling on such points as Merrill's eagerness at overhearing our conversation, the tracks in the snow, the presence of the Indian Christo, who I also had good reason to feel was no friend to me. As I talked the whole devilish plot fell into line so neatly and so evidently that whatever slight doubts I may have entertained vanished entirely; and I could tell, by their growls and the black looks they cast upon the pair, that my listen-

ers were also convinced, though Jim Osgood pursed his lips and
shook his head and shot sharp glances from me to Sanborn and
Merrill and back.

In the midst of the telling I heard steps upon the stair, and a
moment later Lawyer Drew came to stand beside me before the
bar, silent for once, and listening gravely to what I had to say.

When I had done I saw Osgood shake his head, and he and the
lawyer exchanged glances.

" 'Twon't do," said Osgood. "Ye've naught to hold 'em on."

The words emboldened Merrill, who until now had been whim-
pering like a whipped cur.

"No, by Jesus Christ!" he shouted. "I ain't done nothin'. I
didn't hear nothin' that night, I ain't seen Sanborn sence Christmas, only tonight, an' I ain't ben up-river in more'n three year.
By God, I can prove it! You ain't goin' to tie nothin' like that onto
me, you dirty little—"

Sanborn stepped an inch forward swiftly and, reaching out,
smacked his friend sharply across the face with his open hand.
Merrill broke off short and cringed back against Will Stark.

"Hey!" he whined. "What th' hell? Ain't I—"

"Shut up," snarled Sanborn. "Ain't you got the brains God give
a mudworm? Keep your big mouth shut!"

Osgood and the lawyer looked significantly at each other again.

"It seems to me," I said, " 'tis plain enough!"

Osgood shrugged.

"Oh, aye," he said, " 'tis plain enough for any but a court o'
law."

I had no experience with courts and evidence, and this seemed
like quibbling on the matter to me.

"But what more could ye want?" I demanded, hotly.

Lawyer Drew laid a hand upon my sleeve.

"Tell me, lad," he said, and suddenly he seemed to have shed
all his vagueness of manner and become quick and shrewd, "tell
me, did ye see the man who met the Indian Christo, or was it just
the tracks?"

" 'Twas but the tracks I saw," I replied, "but 'tis a simple
enough matter to reckon the obvious."

He smiled slightly.

"But the law can be concerned only with what can be proved,"
he said.

"Are not the circumstances proof enough?" I demanded with impatience.

He shook his head.

"You did not see the man," he said. "The circumstances might indicate that 'twas he, and yet it might have been another. You cannot prove beyond a doubt that it was he, and the courts cannot be cognizant of any but facts borne out by evidence."

I could see what he meant, I could not prove which of them it was. It might even have been Sabatis or Plausawa, for I suddenly remembered these last might be involved. For all that, however, I did not see how such a minor point could affect the whole. I said as much.

"When you saw the Indians pass up-river," continued the old lawyer, "did you see Sabatis or Christo among them?"

I shook my head.

"Mr. Eastman tells me they've been in Canterbury these six days past," I replied.

"Ye see," said he, "even the savages have covered their tracks. You've not a shred of evidence for a court, lad. You'd best turn them loose."

"D'ye mean," I cried, "that the law will protect these rascals, though honest men know them for what they are?"

The old man nodded.

"Until ye've proof of what ye know," he replied.

There was a mutter from the little crowd.

"By God," I heard Rob Rogers exclaim, "we ought to tar and feather 'em anyway!"

"Let them go," I said wearily, sick with disgust. "The law will hang them in the end!"

Osgood bustled around the bar and seized the two men each by an arm.

"Aye, let 'em go," he said, hastily leading them toward the door. "We've had enough of brawling here for one night."

He thrust them out into the night.

"And don't come back!" he shouted after them, though this seemed to me scarcely necessary. I knew it would be some time before any of us saw Sanborn or Merrill again.

As the door thumped shut behind them I turned away with weary disgust, for it seemed to me that in some way I was to blame for the business. If I had not gone out of my way to make an enemy of the man Sanborn (for I judged Merrill to be incapable of any vengeful action on his own initiative), none of this would have happened. I was thinking then of young Stinson, but Lawyer Drew, seeing my expression, must have put the wrong interpretation on my thoughts. He clapped me upon the arm.

"Come," he said, dropping once more into his old manner. "God bless my soul! They've got away. But don't ye grieve. It's not the first time, nor the last, a rogue's escaped unhung!"

He paused a moment and appeared to think, then added, "No, as God's my life, nor are all prisoners rascals!"

I looked at him surprised, for I did not see what he was driving at.

"And what d'ye mean by that, sir?" I demanded.

He looked at me peculiarly.

"Now, by Heaven," he said, "I knew ye were innocent o' the law, but I had not thought ye quite so naïf!"

I must have looked my bewilderment at that, for he took my arm and drew me away to the end of the bar.

"Look ye, lad," he said. "God bless me, 'twas well for you those two were as ignorant of their rights as yourself, else by this they might have had ye behind the bars for libel. Ye'd no case against them, and ye said some hard words upon their characters."

I looked at him aghast, for artless though I might have been I was not so innocent I did not know the severity of the accusation. I was ignorant of the law in this Province, but I had heard of men at home transported on such charges.

"But I could have proved it," I protested.

He wagged his head.

"God's blood!" he swore, "he prattles still of proof! Ye'd have proved naught without more evidence than ye have, Od's my life! Take the advice of an old man, lad, and let the matter drop."

I was willing enough for that, for I was sick to death of the whole affair, and there seemed little sense in wrangling about it. I steered him across the room to the table at which my companions had gathered. Stark and Rogers he, of course, knew already. To the others he bowed with pompous dignity and said that he considered their acquaintance an honour, shaking hands all around. I left him there to further the friendship, for I saw that he needed no assistance from me, and went to wash the bloodstains from my face and clothing.

It was Osgood himself who brought me the bucket of water. As I sloshed it into the basin I nodded across my shoulder.

"What brings the Drews to Rumford?" I asked.

He cast a wary glance into the room behind him.

" 'Tis something in the matter o' the Bow controversy," he replied in a hushed voice. " 'Tis said old Benning Wentworth sent him, and that he brings the power, if not the title, o' the King's Attorney. 'Twill be well to warn the lads to keep a guard upon their tongues and talk o' other things than politics."

He winked, and I nodded, for I knew that the Governor and his friends were shy of criticism and were like to be heavy-handed in their dealings with it; not but what there was plenty of it.

When I returned to the table Lawyer Drew greeted me effusively, and I saw that he had already partaken liberally of the toddy bowl.

"God bless my soul, lad," he said, "ye're a new man. Here, let's have a look at ye. How are ye, and how's that charming mother? There's a woman in a thousand, I'll be bound!"

I said that my mother did nicely. He looked at me again.

"And yourself, lad?" he demanded. "Od's my life, I believe the life agrees with ye. Do ye find it hard going in the back country?"

"On the contrary," I replied; and because I thought I detected a slight hint of derision in his tone I told him of our lumber operations and their success.

As I spoke his face sobered and his eyebrows went up in surprise.

"Why, then," he said, when I had done, " 'tis you that's Ferguson, o' Ferguson & Ross."

I nodded.

"God bless my soul!" was all he could say.

He appeared to think for a moment.

"I've heard o' ye," he said at length. "An' who hasn't upon the coast? Ye've the reputation for picking honest lumber and giving fair measure on your price. Ye've made a good thing o't then?"

He cocked an eye up at me where I sat upon the table before him. I admitted that we had, not without some pride, for we had done well, and I was in a fair way to take a moderate fortune from the work.

"Well, well!" he exclaimed, thoughtfully. "Upon my soul!"

He drained his tall glass at a draft and thumped it upon the table.

"I'm glad to hear it, lad," he said. "As God's my life, 'tis good news."

He got a little unsteadily to his feet.

"It's been a long day, gentlemen," he said. "We came from Chester since midmorning, and, upon my soul, I find I'm not so young as I once was. It wearied me. If you'll excuse me, I think I'll retire."

I stood up to shake hands with him.

"I hope you'll present my apologies to Mistress Dorcas, sir," I said.

He cocked an eye at me quickly.

"She's wearied, too, lad," he replied, smiling. " 'Tis not to be wondered at she's tempery. But she'll have forgotten all about it by the morning. I'll warrant that upon my soul!"

He laughed heartily, as if he'd made a great joke, and bade us all good night once more.

I watched him make his way unsteadily to the stair, but my thoughts had gone ahead of him to the girl above, and my heart thumped in my breast. The sight of her had roused all my old feeling for her, and though in the excitement of the moment I had not the time to dwell upon it her disdain had cut me to the quick. I had not recognized my despair until the father's words had given me hope. Did he really believe that she would forgive me? Behind me I heard Rogers chuckle.

"Pompous as a hedgehog," I heard him say, "and just about as shrewd, they say."

Will Stark laughed.

"Aye," he said, "and the girl! There's a luscious piece, I'll warrant!"

I whirled upon him.

"Keep your filthy tongue from her," I cried furiously.

They looked at me in amazement.

"Why, what's it to you?" he demanded.

"Only that I mean to make her my wife," I retorted.

I saw Stark and Rogers exchange a rapid glance. Jed Stiles's jaw dropped; the laughter left his face, and a peculiar expression came into his eyes. Then Stark laughed.

"D'ye think she'll have ye?" he demanded.

"I have her word for it," I said stiffly.

"God's life!" swore Rogers, and there was a note of admiration in his voice. "Our gamecock's full of surprises tonight!"

Toby grunted, and looked at me impassively with beady eyes.

"Why, God's blood, man," cried Stark, "d'ye know the gossip o' Portsmouth?"

"Gossip!" I cried angrily. "What's gossip but the lies of idle women? I want none of it!"

But there was no stopping him.

"Why, man," he roared, " 'tis common knowledge that she—"

I seized my glass and dashed its contents in his face. He jumped to his feet, his chair clattering over behind him.

"Now, by God," he shouted, "I'll have satisfaction for that!"

"You shall," I said, coldly, "whenever you are ready."

He stood looking at me for a moment, and as he looked I saw the fury die out of his eyes. He shook his head.

"No," he said, finally. " 'T'will not be said I fought a friend in such a business."

He held out his hand.

"Shall we forget it?" he asked.

But I was too angry to take his hand. I could only glare at him. He shrugged and turned on his heel.

"Good night," he said.

As he stalked from the room I turned to Rogers.

"Have ye aught to say of this?" I demanded.

His heavy booming laugh filled the room.

"Not I, fire-eater," he said.

Then he too got up and laid a hand upon my shoulder.

"Ye'll do well to think carefully," he said, and gave me a playful punch. In the next moment he was gone.

I sat down then and swore lightly, filling my glass and Stiles's and Toby's.

"Come," I said, "at least we three can drink to Mistress Drew!"

But Stiles did not respond. He looked soberly at his glass a moment, and then shook his head and dumped it back into the bowl.

" 'Tis late," he said, getting heavily to his feet. "I'm off to bed. Come, Toby."

He clapped the old Indian on the shoulder and dragged him from the table. I sat staring after him in amazement, for it was the first time I had ever seen him refuse a drink. Then, with a gesture of defiance, I raised my own glass.

"To hell with them," I muttered.

I raised my eyes to the ceiling.

"My love," I said, and drained the glass at a single gulp.

4

I must have been well-nigh exhausted, though in the excitement I had not realized it, for I was asleep almost before I could reach my chamber and undress. It was midmorning when I awoke, and every bone in my body seemed stiff and sore from the buffeting I had taken the night before. There was a lump on my head like the half of an egg, where I had twice bumped it against the wall. My back and side were black and blue from tumbling across the chairs and tables. My nose was swollen out of all proportion to its normal size, and my left eye was puffed and blackened so that I could scarcely see with it.

I had no thought for aches and pains, however, as I rose and dressed. My head was full of Dorcas and what she might be thinking of me at the moment; for in my vanity it never occurred to me that she might not be thinking of me at all. I wondered if she had meant the harsh things she had said to me in the evening, or if perhaps she had relented a little and softened towards me somewhat. It was true her father had sought to reassure me, but anxiety made me doubtful whether or no he could tell. It was the sort of thing a man might do without thought. Moreover, I asked myself, what man could predict the caprice of a woman's mind? When I looked at the stained and tattered condition of my buckskins, for I had no other clothing with me, and viewed my battered face and tangled hair in the glass, my spirits sank to a lower pitch than ever, for who, I thought, could ever become sentimental over such a ragged, uncouth figure as I cut?

I must have spent nigh on an hour removing stains from my clothing and combing the knots from my hair. In the end I was not satisfied, but there was nothing more that I could do. I went out and down the stair.

When I came into the taproom there was no one there, but from the private dining room that opened to one side came the low murmur of voices, topped presently by Lawyer Drew's booming laugh. It seemed to me an opportunity, too good to miss, to learn once and for all my standing. I squared my shoulders, and after an instant's hesitation crossed the room and tapped upon the door frame.

The door stood open, and looking through into the room I could see the small table set for two, upon it the remains of breakfast. Dorcas sat just out of sight, but Lawyer Drew himself was plainly visible, his back towards me, a mug of steaming tea laced with rum in his hand. At my knock he slewed about in his chair.

"Why, bless me," he cried, " 'tis the lad himself! Come in, sir. Come in, and join us."

I entered with a pounding heart and bent low over Dorcas' hand. It was too soon to tell what her attitude might be, but as I mumbled my apologies for my appearance, explaining that I had but just returned from a long stay in the north woods, it seemed to me that she smiled not unkindly.

"Oh, your poor eye!" she exclaimed, giving me no chance to finish my explanation. "Does it hurt very much?"

My heart bounced within me. This was more in keeping with my hopes. I thought she would scarcely be so solicitous were she still in the mood of the night before.

Something of my pleasure must have shown in my face, for Lawyer Drew laughed and wagged a finger at me.

"Have ye breakfasted, lad?" he asked.

I said that I had not, and he rang a bell. Presently Jim Osgood's wench appeared and took my order for eggs and ale and a slice of fresh-killed ham. When she had gone Lawyer Drew began to question me afresh about life in Suncook and about our business: How did we live? How did we conduct our business? How much did we make in a year? Did business improve? Was competition keen? Had we done any masting? Had we considered any speculation in land?

I would much rather have preferred to talk to Dorcas. There were a thousand questions I wanted to ask her. But it was plain that I was not to have that opportunity for the present at least, so I made myself as agreeable as possible to her father and answered all his questions civilly and to the best of my ability. He seemed pleased with my answers, and pleased, too, to hear again that we had done so well. Every now and again Dorcas would interrupt with a question concerning myself or my mother and sisters—polite inconsequential little questions that signified nothing; yet my heart leapt within me at her voice, and I was flattered by her interest. It showed, I told myself, that she bore me no ill will. And so long as that was so there was yet hope for me.

But when the girl brought my breakfast, steaming on a tray, Lawyer Drew pulled an immense chronometer from the depths of his flowered waistcoat and examined it with a start.

"Od's blood!" he swore. "I'd no thought 'twas so late. Come, lass, we're appointed to pay our respects to the Reverend Walker this very minute."

He stood up.

"You'll pardon us, I hope," he said to me, "and take dinner with us tonight?"

I stood up in confusion, for I suddenly remembered that my duty lay elsewhere. Word must be carried without delay to the Stinsons of the fate of their son, and my own family must be assured as to my safety. My every inclination was to stay, but even as I hesitated I felt shame that I should even think of delay.

"I fear that it is impossible, sir," I said, and looked longingly at Dorcas. "I should like nothing better, but I must get on."

I explained my reasons and thought, with joy, that I detected a flicker of disappointment in Dorcas' eyes. Lawyer Drew looked solemn.

"By all means, my boy," he said. "We must not neglect the dead, upon my soul!"

"We shall miss you," said Dorcas, and my heart thumped wildly at her words. "I had hoped we might have more chance to talk."

She gave me a warm pressure of her fingers as I bent over her hand.

"Why," I cried, in my recklessness at the thought of parting throwing all reticence to the winds, " 'tis what I hoped for, too, and we shall have it! Suncook's none so far away."

I turned to her father, as a thought struck me.

"Why, look ye, sir," I said, "your way must lie through Suncook on your return. Will ye not plan to stop with me a week or so then?"

He looked quickly at Dorcas, and I saw her nod slightly.

"Od's my life," he said, " 'twill be a great honour indeed!"

"Then I may expect you?" I cried, scarce daring to believe it true.

He nodded.

"In a fortnight's time," he replied. "Upon my soul, I shall look forward to it! I have thought often of your mother, lad, and wished I might renew our acquaintance, as God's my life!"

I saw them to the door, my heart singing within me, and watched them as they went away along the path towards Timothy Walker's house. Before they turned the corner I saw Dorcas turn and wave a hand to me, and I waved back. When they were gone I returned to my breakfast, which I ate, scarce tasting anything that passed my lips. It had gone cold in the waiting, but that was a matter of but small importance to me then.

I had scarce finished eating when I heard the outer door to the taproom open and a voice called my name. Steps moved across the outer room. I went and stuck my head through the door in time to see Will Stark's back as he turned onto the stair.

"Looking for me?" I said.

He turned and caught sight of me.

"Hullo," he said. "As a matter of fact, I was."

He came across the room to me, holding out his hand. I took it a little sheepishly, for I could not but feel that in our quarrel of the night before he had in the end acted rather handsomely, leaving me ashamed of my burst of temper.

"No hard feelings?" he said.

"None," I replied.

"Let's forget it," he laughed. "I guess I had it coming. I wouldn't hear that talk of anyone I liked."

I made no reply to that, and he looked at me sharply.

"You've known her long?" he asked.

"Long enough," I replied shortly, for I thought if we were to forget it the matter was best dropped there.

He shrugged.

"Well, 'tis no affair of mine," he said. "I wish ye joy of it."

I thanked him, and asked where the others might be.

"At the landing," he replied. "We thought to let ye sleep a bit, but now 'tis time to be away."

I bade him wait while I gathered together my few belongings which I had brought up with me, and paid my score. Presently we were off down the road towards the landing.

Only once during that walk did we break the silence. Then it was I who spoke.

"I've been thinking of John," I said.

I looked at him and he nodded.

"I think he's safe enough," I went on. "He was all right when they reached the Connecticut, and I think they'd hardly carry him so far if they meant him harm. Probably they'll carry him to Quebec and try to sell him to the French. We'll hear presently he's being held for ransom."

"Like enough," he replied.

"Well, then," I cried, quickly, hurrying lest he cut me off, "look here. I was responsible for all this. But for me it would never have happened. If there's aught I can do to help bring him back, you'll let me know?"

He made no answer then, but merely nodded and gripped my arm in friendly fashion, giving it a small shake. It was a small thing, but I felt the better for it.

There is little enough to tell of that day's journey homeward. Stiles was glum and uncommunicative, and Toby, never garrulous at best, was more silent than ever. Rogers came along to help Stark at the carry around Isle a Huckset falls, but they, too, seemed wrapped in their own thoughts, so that there was no sound to break the stillness of the day save the chunk of our paddles in the water or the chatter of redwing blackbirds upon the bank and the mutter of the river at the rapids halfway down.

For my own part I was not sorry for the silence. I rode with mixed emotions. One part of me was gay and happy at my encounter with Dorcas and the thought of seeing her again, which kept me singing to myself all the way. But the other part of me was gloomy at the sorrow I must presently release with the sad news I bore, and not a little shamefaced at the thought that I could find any joy in the world at such a moment.

We ran the falls at Bow Bend and Garvin's, not being in a mood to carry, and so gained time to reach the mouth of the Soucook Brook by early afternoon. As we approached the brook the other canoe slipped up alongside. Rogers looked at me and grinned.

"You're a handsome sight for your mother to see," he said. "Next time pick on a man your size."

"Like yourself?" I asked.

He shook his great head, laughing.

"Not me!" he replied, hastily. "When I fight I want a man knows when he's whipped!"

"Come up to the house," I said, "and stay the night. 'Twill be dark before you reach Derryfield."

Rogers looked at Stark, but the latter shook his head.

"Thanks," he said, "but not now."

I did not press the invitation, for I saw that Stark was anxious to reach home with his own news. The canoes drifted apart. Rogers waved his paddle, and they swung on down the stream. Toby turned our bows into the backwater at the mouth of the brook and a moment later we stepped out upon the bank.

The first person I saw as I entered the house was Purity. She was watering some plants by the window as I came through the door, but at my step she turned. For a brief instant she stood and stared at me. Then she gave a little cry and the watering can crashed to the floor.

"Jamie!" she cried. "Good Lord ha' mercy, is't really you?"

I thought she was going to faint, and rushed to catch her. She clung to me, sobbing incoherently, and I led her gently but somewhat bewilderedly to the window seat where I sat her down. As I did so I heard a step in the kitchen passage, and turned to see my mother in the doorway. At sight of me she turned white, and in the next instant she too was sobbing in my arms.

Not until I had quieted them somewhat did I get an explanation. Then it came out by degrees, first from one and then the other.

"We heard you'd been set upon by Indians," said Purity in a muffled voice.

My mother gulped down another sob.

"We thought ye dead or carried off," she added.

I wondered how they could have heard. Then all at once it occurred to me that of course the word had been sent down by Stark upon his escape. I thought myself stupid not to have thought of it before. All the countryside must have some sort of distorted version of the affair by now. I wondered if the Stinsons knew.

It was Purity who answered the thought as if I had spoken it.

"They told us Danny Stinson and John Stark were killed," she said, "but no one seemed to know about you."

"John was captured," I said. "Only Dan'l was killed. Your father and I were not there."

I went on then to explain what had happened, telling of our departure from the camp; how we had sighted the returning party upon the Connecticut, and how I had stumbled upon poor Stinson's body.

"Poor lad!" said my mother then.

She looked up at me, seeming to see my battered features for the first time.

"Land sakes, lad!" she exclaimed. "What's happened to your face?"

I grinned sheepishly.

"There was a fight at Osgood's last night," I said.

She sniffed.

"A low brawl," she said, "and at such a time!"

" 'Twas no common brawl," I replied, and told what it had been about. As I spoke I could see the indignation mounting in my mother's eye.

"Why did ye not tar and feather 'em on the spot?" she demanded when I had done.

" 'Twas against Lawyer Drew's counsel," I replied. "I was for seeing them arrested, but he said we'd not the evidence."

"Ah, the old goat!" she exclaimed. " 'Tis like a lawyer to be always thinking o' the law and never a mind to justice!"

I had no answer to that. She cocked a sharp eye at me.

"Was the girl with him?" she asked.

I nodded—eagerly, I imagine, for she shot a quick glance at Purity and looked wise.

"She was," I said, "and I've asked them to stop here for a visit on their way home. You'll be nice to them, won't you, mother?"

She looked put out at that.

"Have ye ever known me to be aught else to company?" she demanded sharply.

"No, but—" I said, confused.

It was Purity who came to my rescue. She rose and put her hand on my sleeve.

"Is she pretty, Jamie?" she asked.

"Indeed she is," I replied, thinking now I was in for it, for I believed she would tease me about it. "She's beautiful! Wait till you see."

I was wrong, it seemed, to think she meant to plague me; for instead she gave my arm a little squeeze with her fingers and seemed to hesitate.

"I'm sure she must be!" she said at last in a voice scarce louder than a whisper.

I looked up surprised, but she had already turned away with a peculiar expression, and in another instant she was gone from the room. I looked at my mother, who was staring at me with a faintly quizzical expression.

"What the devil ails the girl?" I demanded.

She stood up and gave me a look of exasperation.

"Oh, don't be such a ninny!" she exclaimed impatiently, and swept from the room, leaving me staring after her, scratching my head and wondering at the ways of women.

5

The week that followed my return to Suncook seemed the longest I had ever known. Each day brought me nearer to my beloved Dorcas, and that thought alone was enough to make each day interminable and each night endless. Every morning I was up with the dawn. By nine I had finished the chores that were mine to do when I was at home, and by noon the time lay heavy on my hands. Fishing was some help as it kept my mind occupied for the moment, and I turned to this in the afternoons. But the fish bit too well, and by the end of the third day my mother begged me almost tearfully to have done lest we all begin to grow fins and scales. Already, she said, I had brought in enough salmon to supply two families for the rest of the summer, and there was no room in the spring box for butter and milk as I had filled it to overflowing with trout. This protest, instead of deterring me, gave me another idea, and with Toby's help I built a long smokehouse of bark and fell to smoking my catch—not that I was ever overfond of smoked fish, but at least it was something with which to fill my time.

It was not all so simple, however. There was one duty to which I must attend, and which I could not postpone much as I should have liked to. This was the call upon the Stinsons. It was something of a relief to know that news had gone before me, though I felt a miserable coward to admit as much even to myself. But, even though they had already heard the worst, he had gone out with me and I felt it my duty to call upon them and tell them what I knew so that they might have the straight of it. It was this that sent me to their door the first evening following my arrival at home.

I found their little house heavy with gloom. Jonathan himself opened the door to me, his long face longer than ever now. Nor was there any twinkle in his dull eyes.

"Come in, lad," he said when he saw who it was.

He stood to one side, and I went past him into the one big room that served as both living room and kitchen and bedroom for the elder Stinsons. I was relieved to see that the girls had already crawled up to bed in the loft above. The smaller my audience, I felt, the easier it would be to speak. Mrs. Stinson sat in a straight-backed chair beside the fire, rocking gently back and forth. As I entered she turned a tear-stained face to me and looked at me dully with reddened eyes. I saw that she was already far gone with another child.

Jonathan closed the door and came in behind me, dragging a chair.

"Sit down, lad," he said.

But I shook my head. It seemed almost indecent that I should intrude upon their grief. I wished only to tell my story as quickly and as gently as I might, and go.

"I'll not stop long, sir," I replied. "I only came because I thought you'd want to know the rights of it. I don't want to intrude."

Mrs. Stinson, usually so garrulous, only stared at me. But Jonathan nodded.

" 'Tis no intrusion," he said. "We've wondered what happened. All we heard was that the Injuns came and Danny was shot."

"He was murdered," I said, "in black treachery and cold blood!"

I went on then to tell the story from the beginning, for what I hoped was the last time, for I was growing heartily sick of it and wanted no better than to be shut of the whole business. They listened patiently to the end, and when I had finished there was a moment's silence. It was Jonathan who spoke first.

"Why did you not take him with you to the Cohos?" he said.

By his tone it was more an entreaty than a demand.

I shook my head.

"Had I known what was to happen," I replied, "I would have insisted that we all go. But none of us suspected the danger."

He nodded, but something in the telling of the story had fired a spark in his wife's breast. She glared at me now, and stood up.

"You killed him," she screamed. "You killed him and buried him where we'll never find him! And now ye've come to mock us with your sanctimonious airs!"

I stared at her, horror-struck. I had always thought of her as calm and phlegmatic, a solid, courageous person to depend upon in times of stress. The sight of her going all to pieces now was unnerving. I shook my head.

"Don't say that!" I begged.

But there was no stopping her now.

"You did!" she screamed. "You might as well have fired the shot! Oh, go away! Get out! Get out! Get out!"

And as she screamed she came towards me, trembling with the fury of her hysteria.

Her husband grasped her by the arm.

"Now, Nanny," he said soothingly, "easy, lass."

At the same time he jerked his head towards the door. I took the hint and fled, but not before I saw her break from his grasp and start again in my direction. He ran after her and threw his arms about her, struggling to hold her back. As I went out the door I saw her suddenly stop trying to get away. All the fight went out of her and left her limp and sobbing. I shut the door gently behind me and walked out onto the road.

The night air felt cool and good upon my head, and I found that I was trembling like a leaf and sweating profusely. I sat down upon a stone and mopped my forehead. Presently the Stinsons' door opened and I saw Jonathan's figure outlined in the square of yellow light. He stepped out, shutting the door quietly behind him and came towards me.

"She's wrought up, lad," he said as he came up. "She doesn't know what she's saying."

I nodded.

"Sometimes I feel that way myself," I said. "Except for me Dan'l 'd be here now."

He put a kindly hand upon my shoulder.

"No, lad," he said gently. "Ye could not tell how 'twould happen. 'Twas God's will that it should be Dan'l and not yourself or any of the others with ye. I know ye did the best ye could, and so will she when she comes to think on't. There's no blame to ye, and I'd not want ye to think there was."

I gripped his arm in silence, for I found I could not speak. He hesitated a moment before he spoke again.

"Make me one promise, lad," he said, at last.

I nodded.

"Ye'll show me where ye buried him?" he begged.

I gave him my hand on that.

"Whenever you wish," I said. "We gave him a decent burial."

"God bless ye, lad," he said huskily, and turned away.

I watched him go back to the house slowly and saw him lift the latch and enter. After that I turned and set my face homeward in the darkness.

As may be imagined, this occurrence did nothing to soften my disposition. Rather it served to heighten the tension of the period. I could not help but brood upon it, and the more I thought about it the more glum and moody I became, until by the end of the week I was as taut and drawn as a bowstring.

Nor was I the only one out of sorts. In that fortnight I think all of us deviated somewhat from the normal. Jed Stiles remained morose and gloomy and hardly drank at all. My younger sister Alice turned sharp as a snapping turtle, and scarce spoke to me except to nag. My cousins seemed bewildered but disapproving, as though they suspected I had done some awful thing, but knew not what. My mother seemed preoccupied and scarce spoke to me all week.

But strangest of all was the child Purity. Almost from the very first day I met her she had plagued me without mercy, ragging me for my small size or my hot temper or my clumsiness in the farmyard. Never had she given me a moment's peace when she might be teasing me, until I had discovered that she was as touchy as I, after which we had many a battle royal of words between us with neither one of us ever giving or taking quarter.

Now, however, all that was changed. She became silent and sensitive, and my slightest gibe would draw tears to her eyes, so that after a few sorry attempts to rally her I drew off and let her alone. Nor did she plague me. Rather she grew sweet and gentle, and whenever she spoke she did it softly. Sometimes in the evening, when the supper things had been cleared from the table, I would look up to find her looking at me with a strange expression upon her face; and when she saw that I had noticed she would look away quickly and presently leave the room. It worried me, for despite our bickering I was fond of the child, and it was not at all like her to behave so. I spent long hours alone wondering what it might be that had wrought such a change, or if nothing could serve to set her back into her old ways, which I liked much better than this mooning about. At last it occurred to me that she must be passing through one of those mysterious stages that bring young girls to womanhood. I had seen my sisters grow moody and irritable. Perhaps the effect in this case was just the opposite. I preferred that thought to the alternative: that perhaps she imagined herself in love with me. That, I thought, would be awkward at this moment. But there was nothing to be done about it. Girls, I told myself, were like that; and I felt certain that presently it would pass, and she would be herself once more —the good companion of other years. On that note I forgot about it, confident that in the end all would turn out right.

The awaited day came at last and found me in a dither of expectancy. I was up with the sun, puttering about the house, getting underfoot, starting at every sound from without, and rushing to the door to see if it could be our guests arriving. Even at that, however, I was not on hand to greet them, for about midafternoon Moses Rush came across the brook to report his cow Betsy missing and asked that I go with him to help find her. After some little search we found where she had broken down the brush fence with which he had surrounded his pasture, and headed out across the Rumford Plain. It was nearly dark when at last we found her far up in the Broken Ground to eastward of the plain, bawling loudly to be milked. We led her home as fast as might be, but even so it was long past suppertime when at last I came home.

I saw the chair,* its black varnish gleaming dully in the thin moonlight, and heard the horse stamping in the barn as I passed through the yard, and so knew that I had missed their arrival even before I lifted the latch and entered the long common room. I

* Chaise. At this time the French name for a two-wheeled carriage was generally translated "chair." It was not until after the Revolution that "shay" became accepted as the more elegant word.

had a moment's qualm lest, lacking my presence, they had been greeted without all due cordiality, but I might have known better. Whatever my mother may have thought, she was never one to smother hospitality.

Lawyer Drew was standing by the great fireplace, a steaming mug of flip in his hand, a pipe between his teeth, in deep converse with Jed Stiles, who seemed to have brightened somewhat, and Old Dougal. On the seat by the window Dorcas sat between Alice and Edith, who had come over to help my mother during the visit, and it seemed to me plain that she was charming them with her sweet graciousness and had quite won them over. From the kitchen came the rattle of pots and pans, indicating that supper was still to come. The child Purity was nowhere to be seen, and I gathered that she was in the kitchen with my mother.

Lawyer Drew swung round as I opened the door, and beamed upon me.

"Ah, Jamie," he said, "we thought ye lost, upon my soul!"

"I'm sorry, sir," I said. "I meant to be on hand to greet you, but my sister's cow upset my plans. I hope you've made yourselves at home?"

He chuckled.

"Your good mother has made us most heartily welcome," he replied.

It was at this moment that my mother looked in through the kitchen door.

"Land sakes, Jamie," she said, "we thought ye'd never come. Supper's been waiting this past half-hour. Did ye find the cow now?"

"We found her," I replied, tossing my hat in the corner. "Moses'll be along as soon as he's done the milking."

"High time too," she grumbled. "The meat will be overdone as 'tis!"

And with that she withdrew once more and scurried back to her cooking. I could tell by the way she fussed she had taken pains with the supper. I crossed the room to where Dorcas sat, and bent low over her hand. My sisters rose and, excusing themselves, went out to help my mother.

I was glad of the chance to talk with Dorcas, though as I slipped onto the settle beside her I found my heart was thumping so that

I scarce could speak. She had changed from her stiff grey travelling habit to a dainty gown of plain white silk that set off her dark beauty admirably. Her eyes were bright and sparkling, and our country air had whipped the roses into her cheeks. I thought I had never seen her look so radiant, and—rather clumsily, I fear—I said as much. She cast down her eyes demurely and flushed at that, but I could see that she was pleased.

"La, Jamie!" she said. "You flatter me. 'Tis but an old gown, scarce fit to wear in public any more."

I made so bold as to disagree.

"I care not for its age," I said. "I think it is a lovely thing, and one that suits you perfectly!"

I saw her glance go about the room.

"What do you think of it?" I asked.

She turned to me full of enthusiasm.

"Why, Jamie," she cried, " 'tis a palace! I love it! Why did you not tell me what 'twas like?"

"I wanted to surprise you," I replied, pleased that she should think so highly of our home. "I only wish I had been here when you came."

She was sympathetic.

"I missed you," she confessed. "But never mind, you've come back now, and 'twas all it needed."

I thrilled to her words, but could think of no suitable reply. She saw my confusion and chattered on.

"Was it hard to find the cow?" she asked.

I described the afternoon, and tried to give her some idea of where we had been. When I told how far away the beast had wandered she threw up her hands.

"Gracious!" she cried. "So far away! But you must be tired and thirsty. Let me fetch you some flip."

"No, no!" I protested. "I can get it."

But she had already leapt to her feet and was on her way to the kitchen. I remembered my duties as host and joined the others. As I crossed the room Lawyer Drew turned to me.

"Have you heard?" he asked. "Your red friends have folded their tents and stolen away in the night."

I looked at him blankly, for I could not think what he was talking about.

Old Dougal gave a wry chuckle.

" 'Stolen' is the word," he said, "for they carried two blacka-moors as well!"

It was Stiles who came to my rescue.

" 'Tis the Injuns Sabatis and Christo," he said. "They slipped away from Canterbury three nights since, carrying with them Jose Miles's nigger Tom and Squire Lindsey's Peer."

"No!" I exclaimed. "D'ye suppose Sanborn or Merrill warned them?"

Drew shrugged.

"Like as not, upon my soul," he replied. "But, God's my life, the theft of the two niggers has set the town by the ears!"

"Aye," I said bitterly, " 'twill cause more stir belike than Dan Stinson's death and the capture of Stark and Eastman!"

The lawyer smiled deprecatingly.

"If ye go beyond the limits of settlement," he said, "ye must look for some danger; and the place ye were in, I understand, has been the Indians' hunting grounds for a long time."

"Is't what they're saying in Rumford?" I cried. "Why, God's blood, 'tis no wonder the Indians feel they may do as they please when our own stand is so spineless!"

He shook his head.

"But this last business," he went on, ignoring my interruption, "is beyond endurance, upon my soul! To think they would have the impudence to come right in among us and lift our property from under our very noses! Why, it's past bearing!"

I might have had more to say on the subject, for it seemed to me a matter for indignation that a murder should be looked upon so complacently, while the mere theft of two black men—one of whom I later learned escaped before the Connecticut was reached and returned home to his master—should be made so much of. At this moment, however, Dorcas reappeared with a steaming mug of flip for me. I turned my attention to her, and in no time at all had completely forgotten her father's piece of news, though I was to remember it again at a later date.

Supper that night was a merry business, for Lawyer Drew, warmed by the flip and heartened by the sight of food, was at his jovial best, and though he said but little of importance he managed to keep us all in a happy mood. For my part, I should have been happy simply to be in Dorcas' presence, even had the others been as glum as parsons. But the others' merriment added to my own enjoyment, so that it seemed to me I was never so happy before. I listened to her every word, and told long tales of all I had done since we had parted last, paying little heed to any of the others or to what they might be saying or doing.

We lingered long over the meal, and afterwards we sat talking far into the night. The others spoke of politics, of Benning Wentworth and his wife, of the possibility of war in the near future, and of other questions that were discussed whenever men met in these times. But Dorcas and I heard none of it, for she was telling of her life in Portsmouth, and how dull it was, while I told of my life in the woods and how I loved it. It was past midnight when at last we began to make our several ways to bed. It was not until then that I noticed that the child Purity had slipped away some time since. I thought I remembered her sitting quietly at table, eating little and saying nothing at all; and it struck me suddenly, with something of a pang, that no one had presented her to Dorcas. We had all been much too occupied, each one assuming that another had attended to it. I felt sorry, for, as I have said, I was fond of the child, in a brotherly way, and I did not wish to see her slighted. I made up my mind to rectify the oversight at the earliest possible opportunity; and in the next moment forgot about it, for my lady was bidding me good night and there was no room in my thoughts then for any but her.

The week that followed was one of completest bliss for me, though looking back upon it now I doubt not that others found me trying, to say the least. When I was with Dorcas, which was as often as I could manage, I was witty, brilliant, a very devil of a fellow. But when she was not there I grew gloomy and morose, silent and preoccupied, so that those who spoke to me must needs repeat themselves before I could fetch my mind to concentrate upon their words. In plain language I was heels over head in love. At one and the same time I was miserable and enraptured; miserable lest by some word or deed or look I might offend her, and enraptured in the attention she showed me and by the very thought that she felt me worthy of her time.

In that week I spent every hour, every minute possible, in her company. There were walks and picnics in the woods and meadows. We spent hours lolling in the warm sunlight upon the river bank, or drifting in the canoe. One day we went far up Soucook Brook and cooked our lunch upon Plausawa Hill, where I showed her where we had come upon the three Indians, years before, and told her how we had driven them off. On another I poled the canoe far up the river and shot down through the rapids, much to her vast excitement and delight, for it was the first time she had felt the thrill of the white water. Out of my knowledge of woods lore I taught her to know the songs of the birds: the plaintive call of the white-throated sparrow, the whistle of the phoebe, the trill of the wood thrush, and the chuckle of the robin. I taught her to imitate the cavernous *thunk-clunk* of the bittern and the weird cry of the loon. When we walked out in the evening by moonlight, whispering and holding hands, I identified for her the sounds of the night: the shivery wail of a wandering bear, the shrill yapping of a fox upon the hill, the solemn hooting of an owl, or the ghostly call of the whippoorwill.

I should have been increasingly happy just to be with her, but instead I grew daily more miserable and morose, for each passing day brought us closer to the end of her visit; and though each day I made up my mind to speak, still when the moment came I found myself tongue-tied by the fear that she might laugh at me, and so could not bring myself to say the words that were struggling to get out.

The day came at last, however, when Lawyer Drew announced with a great show of regret and many profound bows that they could rest no longer. They had, he said, greatly enjoyed this all too brief interval of peace and quiet before returning to the rush and bustle of the town. But, alas, all good things must end, and matters of business made his presence in Portsmouth imperative. On the morrow they must leave, he told us; and here he glanced quickly at me.

I protested, of course, but it was to no avail. The old man had made up his mind, and nothing could shake him. In the end it was settled. They would leave after breakfast, about nine in the morning; and if the weather favoured them and Lawyer Drew's little brown mare ran well they would be in Kingston by night.

This announcement came at the noonday meal, and for the rest of that afternoon I went wrapped in the gloom of despair. I thought how long had been our last parting, and the fear that this might be my last opportunity gave me a sort of coward's courage that would have driven me to speak had she given me the least encouragement. Now, however, she seemed to avoid me. I wanted her to come and walk beside the brook with me, but she protested she was too tired. I offered to take her in the canoe, but she said she had her packing to be done. In the end I flung away in a pique, leaving her to her packing, and went to lie beside the river in the meadow and sulk till evening.

At supper, however, she seemed herself once more, and as soon after the dishes had been cleared away and the others settled themselves before the fire, I drew her to the window settle and pointed to the great lopsided moon riding high in the heavens.

"Aren't we to have one more walk together before you leave?" I begged.

She nodded readily, and ran to fetch a cape. A few moments later we were wandering hand in hand along the hillside pathway that led down into the meadows beside the river, where the moonlight lay white upon the blackness of the water and the soft breeze sighed in the alders.

Now indeed I grew desperate, knowing that this was my last chance. And in my desperation I stammered and stuttered and hemmed and hawed and stopped and started again, until at last she took both my hands in hers and turned to face me in the moonlight.

"Why, Jamie!" said she. "I do believe you're going to miss me!"

"Miss you!" I cried. "Oh, my dear, there'll be no living for me when you are gone!"

And with the words all my reserve was suddenly swept aside, and all the things I had so long been trying to say burst forth in a perfect torrent. I laid my heart bare at her feet to do with as she pleased.

How long we sat beside the river in the chill moonlight, my arm about her waist and her head upon my shoulder, talking and planning against the future, I know not, but it was nearing midnight when we returned to the house.

We found all the others retired long since, but her father still stood before the fireplace, slowly sipping an evening noggin of flip before retiring. As we entered he cleared his throat severely and looked at a huge chronometer. I imagined that he was about to chide us upon the length of our stay, and I determined to forestall him. With Dorcas' hand in mine I felt very bold indeed, though at another time I might have been diffident and somewhat nervous. Now I bowed to him with great ceremony.

"Sir," I said, with as much dignity as I could summon, "it may seem something sudden to you, but our time has been short and we have had need to make the best of it, lest after tomorrow we might never see one another again. We have talked things over, and agreed, Mr. Drew. Sir, I have the honour to request your daughter's hand, and your blessing on our marriage."

He puffed out his cheeks and pretended to look surprised, though I knew well enough he had been half expecting it from the very day of their arrival.

"God bless my soul, lad!" he exclaimed. "This is indeed a surprise. Hrumph! hrumph! God's my life!"

He turned to his daughter.

"And you, lass," he said, "are you agreed to this?"

Dorcas looked at me shyly and nodded.

"Yes, father," she said simply.

He frowned importantly.

"You love him, think you?" he persisted.

"Yes, father," she repeated, "I do."

"Ha!" said he. "Hrumph, hrumph! Damme! Then let it be so, by all means, and an old father's blessing on ye both, God bless me!"

He pulled an immense kerchief from his pocket and blew his nose lustily.

"God bless me," he said in a voice that was all choked up with emotion, though to be sure I later found he felt nothing but relief to see his daughter married at last. "It is hard to think of parting with my little lass after all these years—and I as much a mother as a father to her. When is't to be—or have ye thought o' that?"

"The sooner the better, sir," I replied.

"Nay, nay, lad," he chuckled, winking and jabbing me in the ribs, with a look in his eye that made me blush to think that Dorcas could see it, "ye must not be too impatient. Ye must give her time to prepare for it. There's dainties to buy and such what not as ye'll never imagine."

"Why, sir," I stammered, for he had confused me now, "I—

we thought a matter of six weeks might be decent—say the end
of June."

"Oh, aye," he said, "well, and that's better."

He turned about to Dorcas.

"Now then, lass," he said, "kiss your gallant and run along to
your bed, for I've that to discuss with him is not for your ears."

She turned to me dutifully, but I cared not to say our good
night there. I took her arm and lighted her to her chamber, where
in the doorway she embraced me fondly. After she had gone within
and closed her door, I stood a moment in the darkness of the
hall, still feeling the thrill of her arms about my neck and the
warmth of her lips on mine.

When I had stilled the thumping of my heart somewhat and
felt a little more composed, I went downstairs once more, to find
the lawyer had dipped himself a second noggin of flip from the
bowl upon the table and set out one for me.

"I'm a poor man, lad," he said by way of greeting, when I had
rejoined him. "Ye understand that. 'Twill be little enough I can
offer as a dowry for the lass."

He looked at me anxiously as he said it, as if he feared I might
be inclined to change my mind for that. I was indignant at the
thought.

" 'Tis the girl herself I love," I said stiffly, "not what she has
or has not!"

He looked considerably relieved.

"Of course, of course!" he said, placatingly, and pushed a noggin into my hands. "Shall we drink to it?" he asked.

For nearly an hour, we sat and talked, setting the place and
date of the wedding, while he made great inroads upon the flip
bowl. At last I got to my feet.

"Well, sir," I said, "hadn't we best be turning in? You've a long
day before you."

"Ah, hrumph!" he said. "There's just one other thing I'd like
to speak to you about, lad."

I could not think of anything we had not covered, but I thought
best to humour him.

"What is that, sir?" I said.

"Well, hrumph!" said he, making a show of confusion. "You
see, lad, I'm—ah—a bit financially embarrassed at the moment.

God bless me! Ran short of funds, so to speak, in Rumford, and —ah, hrumph!—I thought maybe—that is, I hoped perhaps— hrumph—you might—well, you see!—a couple of pounds, if you could spare it. 'Twould see us through to Portsmouth. A loan, ye know. After all, it's all in the family now—heh, heh, what? God bless my soul!"

I will say he had the grace to pretend embarrassment. It was not until later that I learned that the borrowing habit was strong in him. Needless to say, however, I took it then in perfect good faith.

"Why, of course, sir," I replied, "anything you like! I'll see to it in the morning, first thing."

He heaved himself to his feet then and stood weaving somewhat unsteadily, for the flip was not without its effect.

"You're a good lad, Jamie," he said. "I can see you'll be a comfort to me in my old age. As God's my life, 'twill go to make up for the son I never had."

I steered him gently though firmly towards his chamber, steadying him with the one hand while I held the taper in the other, for I saw that unless I got him into his bed the flip he had guzzled would have him blubbering on my hands ere long. Above stairs I deposited him upon his bed, and after helping him off with his boots bade him a very good night.

When I went down again to bar the doors and put out the lights, I noticed a gleam of light still shone beneath my mother's door. I attended my duties first, and then went and tapped softly. Her drowsy voice bade me enter.

I found her propped up among her pillows, reading by the light of two candles, a favourite habit of hers since my father's death, though one that always seemed to me somewhat wasteful of good tallow. She looked at me over the iron rims of her spectacles.

"A fine hour to be coming in!" she grumbled.

But I paid her little heed on that score, for I knew that she had long since ceased to worry over my comings and goings, and that now she was merely offering a sop to her own pride.

"Mother," I said, "I've just asked Mistress Drew to marry me!"

She turned a page of her book, scarce giving me a glance.

"Well, and did ye now?" she replied. "And what did the lass say to that?"

"She agreed to it," I said.

She lowered her book at that and looked at me with a glimmer of interest.

"O, aye?" said she. "And when's it to be, or did ye go so far?"

"The end of next month," I told her shortly, for I thought she had received the news with neither enthusiasm nor the proper gravity.

She set her book aside, then, and gave me a long look over her glasses.

"But what do ye know of the lass, Jamie?" she said finally. " 'Tis scarce two weeks since you met her again."

"I know enough," I said stiffly, "to be sure I love her, and she loves me, and it seems to me there's no more to be said than that."

She did not answer at once, but sat looking at me a little sadly, I thought.

"Are ye sure, Jamie, 'tis what ye want?" she asked finally.

I nodded.

There was another silence, during which she dropped her eyes and studied her hands lying folded on the counterpane before her. At last she sighed.

"Well, lad," she said, "ye're a man grown. Ye'll be twenty-two come August next, and ye've your own life to live. I'll not pretend 'tis what I would ha' liked. Between us, I hoped ye'd choose another. But if ye've made up yer mind to it and are sure 'tis the girl ye want, I'll not be the one to stand in your way. Rather, I'll say take her, lad, and God bless ye both!"

She took my face in both her hands then and kissed me gently. Not until then did I see that her eyes were full of tears.

I was up with the dawn, hoping perhaps that Dorcas might be up and about early. But though I whistled and sang as I sponged down the little mare, so her coat glistened in the sunlight, and polished up the chair, it was breakfast time before she appeared, clad again in the heavy travelling habit of grey stuff.

Edith and Moses were there, as well as my uncle and all his family, who had come up to speed the parting guests, so that we made a respectable party at table, and it was here that my mother chose to announce our betrothal.

There was a moment of silence. I saw my sister Alice thump her spoon upon the table and open her mouth to say something, but at that instant her eye caught my mother's, and she closed it again without uttering a sound. At the end of the table my uncle leapt to his feet, holding his can of ale aloft.

"We'll drink to a happy couple," he said.

The spell was broken. The party stood and clinked their ale cans, while Dorcas and I looked fondly into each other's eyes.

I blessed my uncle for coming, for it was his merriment and good spirits that kept the party alive. My sisters sat silent, almost gloomy, and I thought my mother gave poor Lawyer Drew short answers to his rambling questions.

But breakfast was over at last, and our guests' baggage all carried out and strapped on board the chair. The little mare stood patiently between the shafts, ready and waiting for the long day's drive. As he left the house, I managed to draw Lawyer Drew aside and gladden his spirits with a five-pound loan. When we stood beside the chair and hands had been shaken all around, he turned to Dorcas.

"Come, lass," he said, "say your good-byes. We must be on our way."

She blushed prettily and cast her eyes down upon the ground, and I think she would have been content to simply murmur good-bye, but I would have none of that. I caught her hand and drew her to me in a fond embrace, though she would not bend her head to me, and I had to stand on tiptoe to kiss her. I heard my sister Alice titter at that behind me, but I paid her no heed beyond making a mental reservation to speak my mind to her as soon as Dorcas had gone.

I handed Dorcas up as elegantly as my height would permit and, after kissing her hand tenderly, stepped back. Lawyer Drew chirped to the mare and flicked her with his whip. In the next moment they were off down the road in a swirl of dust.

The others waved and went about their business, one by one. But I stood waving and staring after them as long as I could catch a glimpse of them. At last, however, the road dipped around the hill, and they disappeared from sight.

I turned then and started for the house, but suddenly remembered that I had neglected to clean out the little mare's stall and turned away to the barn. I was too moody with the departure of my beloved to whistle, and cutting across the grass as I did my footsteps were muffled, so that I came to the barn door in silence.

As I stepped inside someone jumped up from the feed box hastily.

For an instant I was blinded by the gloom, having come in straight from the bright sun, and I could not see who it was. But in the next moment I saw that it was the child Purity, and as my eyes grew accustomed to the dim light I saw that her shoulders were shaking.

Gently I turned her around to face the light, and saw that her cheeks were streaked with tears, and that she clutched a tear-soaked handkerchief in her hand.

"Why, child!" I cried, bewildered. "What is it? What ails you?"

But I might have saved my breath, for she stamped her foot and cast me a scornful look.

"Oh, la!" she cried. " 'Tis nothing you would understand, Mr. Ferguson!"

And with that she fled up the pathway towards the house, leaving me staring after her and scratching my head in perplexity and annoyance at the perversity and stubbornness of some females.

❨ 1 We were married in Portsmouth, on the last day of June, 1752, at Queen's Chapel, the Reverend Arthur Browne officiating; for Dorcas, following the fashion of the Province, was of the Established Church.

Despite my father-in-law's protestations of extreme poverty I noticed that he spared no expense. Indeed I was somewhat embarrassed at the lavishness with which the church was decorated and the board spread at the reception, for it seemed to me these things were somewhat beyond our station, and I cared not for vulgar display. There were flowers for the church and candles for the altar, while afterwards at the house the board fair groaned beneath the weight of food and drink. There were turkey and partridge and pigeons and venison for meat, and all manner of fruits and vegetables besides. There was punch for the guests, concocted of white sugar and lemons and limes, brought up from Boston at a cost of three shillings fourpence halfpenny a dozen, and sack posset for the bridal party.

For my own part I could have done with less of show, and should have preferred a small gathering of a few good friends who knew us well, rather than a churchful of comparative strangers, whispering and giggling behind their fans or casting shrewd glances at the bridesmaids' gowns. Even the Governor, Benning Wentworth himself, looked in upon us, his pendulous belly bulging beneath a flowered waistcoat, though he knew me not from Adam, and had scarce more than a nodding acquaintance with the bride or her father. But it was plain that all the pomp and ceremony was as pleasing as incense and fine perfume to Dorcas, so I suffered it with a good grace, and consoled myself with the thought that it happened but once in a man's lifetime if he was lucky.

Before the ceremony I found a true friend in George Stapleton;

the same on whom I had looked with such green eyes of jealousy so many years before. He had grown tall and stalwart, and for all he was one of the most reckless, swashbuckling dandies of the town, he had about him an engaging air of frankness and sincerity that won me to him at once. It was he who warned me that Warren Ames and certain others of the "Louisbourg Boys"—an organization modelled along the lines of London's famous Hell Fire Club, and of which, incidentally, Stapleton himself was a member—planned to raid the wedding procession, kidnap the bride, and hold her for a ransom of two kegs of rum wherewith to drink our health.

I had no objection to their drinking our health as often as they wished. Neither did I think their price too high for the ransom of my bride. Such wild, high-handed raids I knew were quite customary on these occasions. Nevertheless, I was determined, if possible, to prevent any such disruption of our party, and in the end I flatter myself I turned the trick rather neatly.

Before setting out for the church I gathered my groomsmen about me, together with several others of my friends who, I felt, would fit into the scheme of things, and unfolded to them my plan. It met with the hearty approval of all concerned, and I rode off to the church feeling somewhat easier in my mind.

When the ceremony was finished and we came out again into the late afternoon sunlight I saw that Stephen Sparhawk had done his work, for the macaroni whom Ames had set to watch and report our departure from the chapel was nowhere to be seen. If Sparhawk had followed his instructions the pair of them should even then be taking a pot of ale in the tavern on the corner, where the watcher could hear the grating of our wheels as we departed, and run to warn his comrades that the procession was under way.

As our chariot pulled up with drawn blinds, Dorcas and I stepped aside to let six of the most massive members of our party jam themselves within. Rob Rogers and his brother Richard, Will Stark and Peter Davis and Homer Odiorne and George Stapleton all squeezed inside, and the chariot whirled away in advance of the procession, while Dorcas and I followed by a roundabout route in a hackney coach.

We missed the fun, of course, for we were nigh home by then, but I heard of it later. It was said that when Warren Ames and his fellows seized the horses' bridles and wrenched open the chariot door, to find, instead of a dainty lady and a half-portion of furious husband, a half-dozen of the Province's most truculent blades, their demoralization was already half complete. And before the bailie and his men could come puffing up, in response to the shrieks and screams of the wedding party and the thuds and whoops of joy emitted by the erstwhile victims, now become the attackers, the rout was accomplished, the procession had moved on, and more than one of Ames's party were left upon the field to nurse a split lip or a broken head.

The wedding feast was a sumptuous affair, and one I thought would never end. From six in the evening until almost ten o'clock we sat before the groaning board, receiving congratulations and felicitations until I felt my arm must come off with the next handshake and my head burst with the next cup of sack.

At last, however, the supper came to an end and the room was cleared for dancing. I wondered how long this was to last, but it seemed, as far at least as bride and groom were concerned, it was to be but a brief interlude. Promptly at eleven the brides-maids whisked Dorcas upstairs to the bridal chamber, while at the same time my groomsmen carried me off to another room, where they arrayed me in a brocaded nightdress, and afterwards led me to my bride.

When we were at last safely tucked in bed together there was more sack posset to be drunk and toasts to be made, before the hilarious crowd could be induced to leave us alone. When at length the last of them waggled his head about the sill at me and gently closed the door, I was prompt to jump up and turn the key in the lock behind him. It was evidently an awaited move, how-ever, for at the sound of the grating key a burst of hilarious laugh-ter went up from the hall outside, leaving me standing behind the tight-closed door, barefoot in my silly splendour and blushing furiously in confusion.

Nor did this end their pranks. Scarce had I returned to my bride when I heard the rattle of a ladder upon the window sill. Running thither and thrusting out my head I saw that Warren Ames had by no means forgone his avowed intention. Indeed, I believe they would have kidnapped us from our very bed had I not bellowed for my friends at the top of my lungs. As it was, Ames was almost at the window ledge, and there were others on

the rungs behind him, when my groomsmen, headed by George
Stapleton and Robert Rogers, burst around the corner and top-
pled them from it. For a time, thereafter, there arose the sound
of thuds and friendly curses, mingled with not a little good-
natured ribaldry. But presently my friends drove the invaders
off, and we were left in peace at last.

On the following day we embarked in a sloop for Boston, where
we spent a quiet but idyllic week, after which we returned to
Portsmouth for an extended visit before going on home to Suncook.

It was during this visit that George Stapleton introduced me
at a meeting of the Louisbourg Boys at Stavers' Tavern. Originally this organization had been composed exclusively of ex-
members of the Louisbourg Expedition, their object being the
enlivening of town life by all manner of pranks. Of late, however, the original members had begun to grow staid and stolid,
and many of them had dropped out. In order to maintain its
standard the club had been forced to extend its membership to
include the younger blades of the town now coming to the fore.
Among these last were the Sparhawks, the two younger Odiornes,
Warren Ames, Stapleton, Davis, not to mention others. And as
I came well recommended by all of these, the meeting accepted
me with open arms and voted unanimously to make me an hon-
orary member, so long as I should remain a resident of the
Province, and a member in full standing whenever I moved to
Portsmouth, the which they all held was bound to happen sooner
or later, though of this I had my own opinion which I kept to
myself.

Such membership, ordinarily, was not to be had without an
initiation, usually consisting of the perpetration by the novitiate
of some prank or practical joke, in the London manner, which
must pass the approval of the high council; and for the purposes
of which he might call upon the members and resources of the
club for assistance. The rules, however, were not always rigidly
adhered to, and in my case the initiation was waived, the method
by which I had managed to foil Warren Ames at my wedding
being held to be sufficient evidence of the nimbleness of my wits
in such matters. I could not but think that this was fortunate for

me, for without the pressure of necessity, such as I had had upon that occasion, I much doubt if I could have produced a prank of sufficient daring to pass the scrutiny of the council.

Pleasant as all this was for me, it would have taken far more, I think, to make me an enthusiastic devotee of the town. When I was not drinking or playing at cards in the taproom at Stavers' with these new-found friends, there was little else for me to do. I cared little for the round of teas and parties that made such a part of Dorcas' life, nor could I interest myself in the petty politics of local affairs. It was not long before I found myself longing for the open fields and forest, the still lakes and rugged mountains of the upper Province. As a country boy born and bred it was but natural that after the first few days of growing acquainted I should turn my steps out into the fields beyond the town in search of something that would be familiar to me. At first Dorcas would accompany me on these rambles; but it was plain that she did not enjoy it, and before many days she found it kept her too much from social activities and after one or two more attempts dropped it entirely, leaving me to enjoy my afternoons alone as best I might.

I could not find it in my heart to blame her for this, however. Indeed, my own enthusiasm soon dwindled, and had it not been for the exercise it afforded me I think I too would have given up. For this was not the country I was used to. The farmers were a dour and suspicious lot, who looked upon a man crossing their fields as a trespasser and were like as not to set the dogs upon him. The woods round about were but poor scrawny second growth, for the most part, the only decent stand of stout timber being across the river behind Kittery; and even there it was so cut up and chopped into as to be but a sad mockery of what it once had been. I soon found that the salt marshes along the bay bred mosquitoes much larger and more ferocious than any that ever came from a fresh-water bog, and on the infrequent occasions when I wandered to the ocean side the mournful booming of the surf and the hollow gurgle of the sea among the rocks soon so depressed me that I fled as fast as my legs would take me to the cheerful warmth and conviviality of Stavers' taproom, there to raise my spirits once again in a bowl of punch or a tankard of ale.

All this, however, I am inclined to think, might not have been so bad, once I grew accustomed to the change. But there was a side of Portsmouth life into which I was never able to fall, and in which, though I learned to harden myself to it, I feel to this day the veriest country bumpkin. This was the social whirl of balls and routs and teas and levees, which gave the town its reputation as a social capital which bid fair to rival even Boston itself.

Now that I look back upon it, I feel sure that this antipathy on my part was not due to any sense of inferiority. For I could then, and I flatter myself I still can, tread a measure with the best of them. Neither was it from any lack of sociability, for I have always been a ready mixer. Rather I think it was due to a certain coolness which seemed to follow us as we entered a drawing room, and of which I am certain Dorcas was as well aware as myself.

From the very first it was evident to me that the society of the town was ruled by a comparatively small clique, headed by the Governor and his lady and the Reverend and Mrs. Browne, and composed for the most part of Warners, Meserves, Langdons, Odiornes, Atkinsons, Jafferys, Sparhawks, and others, all following the leader in matters of acceptance, and scorning those upon whom the bigwigs frowned. Only the most élite were bidden to the Wentworth mansion. Those slightly less élite might occasionally be seen in the homes of the others. But for the rest of the world—they might be recognized upon the street or in the tavern, one might nod to them in church, one might even speak to them of a Sunday afternoon on Buck Street, but beyond that intercourse must not go.

From the day of our return from Boston it was plain that we fell somewhere between the two. Invitations we had in plenty, but they were from the lesser lights of society. I might play at cards in the tavern with the men, whom I found likable enough, but it was the ladies who ruled the drawing rooms, and there we were never bidden.

For my own part I cared little enough for that; but it irked Dorcas, and in consequence irritated me. It irritated me, too, the more because I could see no reason for it. At first I thought it might be due to my having come to Portsmouth from the upper colony; but on second thought I discarded this as foolish: my background was as good as most, and this was well enough known, for a man's past is not easily hidden in a town as small as Portsmouth, unless he sets himself to it.

It was not a circumstance over which to lose much sleep, however, and I think I should scarce have noticed it but for the fact that it fretted Dorcas. As a new-fledged husband, how was I to sit by and see my bride eating her heart out over something that might be helped? I made up my mind to do what I could about it, and so set to cultivate Nathaniel Meserve, the shipwright, whose yards we had supplied with lumber steadily from the very start of our operations.

This was not difficult, for he was frequently to be found at Stavers' having a tankard of ale in the late afternoon, and I made it a custom to drop in about the time I might expect to find him there. As he seemed to have but little interest beyond his ships and the lumber that went into them, I had no trouble in maintaining a conversation that was congenial to him, and it was not long before we had struck up a firm friendship. Indeed, before the week was out I began to feel somewhat ashamed of my motives, for I had conceived a genuine liking for the tall, dour old gentleman—I always thought of him as old, though he could not have been much past middle age—and had it been possible I would have let the matter drop.

This was not to be, however, it seemed, for on his side he had also taken a liking to me. He had had dealings with us, as I have already mentioned, and the fact that he had found we gave honest measure and handled none but the best was in itself my recommendation to him. He was a man who had somewhat more independence of spirit than had most of the other social leaders of the town, and he was one who would not hesitate to take under his wing anyone he liked. The result was that within a week he had bidden me to a tea at which the Governor was expected to attend; and he made it a point to insist that I bring my wife.

When I broke the news to Dorcas that evening she could scarce believe her ears, and I had no little difficulty in convincing her that the invitation was genuine. Once that was accomplished, however, she could scarce bide the day. For my own part, now that I had what I had set out for I began to have my doubts. I wondered if perhaps we were not laying ourselves open to a certain snub.

This feeling was not lightened when the day finally arrived. And when we were announced in the Meserve drawing room by a footman resplendent in livery I could not swear that it was not my imagination that caused the brief silence or brought several of the ladies' heads together with sidelong glances.

But there was no mistaking the colonel's welcome. He came across the room from the great fireplace, where he had been in converse with the Governor, and greeted us with outstretched hands. Thereafter he carried us over and presented us first to his lady and then to Benning Wentworth himself.

His Excellency bowed as low as his great paunch would permit to Dorcas, and shook his great periwig at me.

"They tell me, Mr. Ferguson," said he, "that you have visited the Upper Cohos, and are acquainted with the valleys of the Ammonoosuc and the Connecticut."

"That I have, sir," I replied, eagerly, for there was no subject upon which I could converse with him with greater enthusiasm.

He became interested at once, and while the colonel and his lady moved away with Dorcas, he smothered me with questions about the north country. Was it habitable? Would it lend itself to colonization? How was it best approached? Could a road be built thither? Did I think it advisable to build a fort there? Or would this be likely to bring a protest from the French? Indeed, so engrossed did he become in the matter that for three solid hours he plied me with his queries, ceasing then only when his lady plucked him by the sleeve and insisted that it was time to be going. Even then he went only after bidding me wait upon him on the morrow, and extending an invitation to a levee to be held some three days hence.

On our way home that evening Dorcas was jubilant.

"Oh, Jamie!" she cried. "It has made us! The Governor was never so attentive to anyone before! What did you talk to him about? They'll never dare ignore us after this!"

As it turned out, she was right, for the next day brought us a basketful of invitations from those who would follow the Wentworths' favour. From that day on, routs, balls, and levees became a nightly occurrence, while persons who had hitherto no more than nodded stiffly to us on the street now bowed low before us and cultivated our acquaintance. I found it all a stiff business, full of frills and formalities, without the lightening influence of wit or good humour, and boring in the extreme. But I kept pace with it as best I could, for it pleased me to see Dorcas happy, and there was no doubt but she was that.

It was September before we finally returned home to Suncook. Even then it was only because I insisted. Dorcas wanted to stay for the Governor's Ball, which was to be held on the first of October. But my affairs were such that I did not feel it possible to stay longer. My friendship with Colonel Meserve had resulted in more and larger orders for lumber, which would call for more extended operations during the following winter; and so far as I knew even our standing orders had not been marked out on the stump as yet. I should have to hurry if I were to do a year's timber cruising before the snow flew, and it was this thought that made me put my foot down. We had our first quarrel over it.

We left in the grey of a cold dawn, driving the new chair that I had purchased, with all our trunks strapped on behind, and Dorcas furious because I hoped to make the journey in a single day and so considered it necessary to leave at such an hour. As we pushed farther into the country my spirits rose little by little until I could scarce refrain from bursting into song. Indeed, had Dorcas not sat so glum beside me I believe I might have whooped from sheer joy. Her mood, however, seemed to grow more despondent with each turn of the wheels, and all my efforts to cheer her up were of no avail.

We ate a quick noonday meal by the shores of Massabesic Pond and pushed on again. During the afternoon Dorcas dozed, with her head upon my shoulder, but I could not see that it improved her humour. When we arrived, shortly after ten, she swept away to bed with scarce a civil good night to anyone, though after our long ride this was scarcely remarkable, for she must have been well-nigh exhausted.

To me it was a relief to be shut at last of the tosh and pother of Portsmouth life and to be back once more among homely, natural folk who were not for ever bowing and scraping, and who cared not if one's clothes were not always of the latest cut.

For Dorcas, however, I fear it was rather dull. To begin with she missed the gaiety of life in Portsmouth, as was natural enough, for it was what she had been raised to, and there is no denying that life in Suncook was like to be something on the quiet side.

Neither could she accustom herself to the country routine. Breakfast with the dawn, midday dinner, and an early supper seemed to her almost barbarous, and hers was not a nature that adjusted itself easily to change. I believe she would have helped about the house, had she but known how. But the truth was that, having been waited upon hand and foot all her life, she knew not where to start. She could not tell the difference 'twixt flax and wool until they were made into cloth, and as for the churn, it was a complete mystery to her. I really believe that, until she saw it made, she believed that cheese and butter grew in the garden or perhaps were mined from the earth—if, indeed, she had ever given it any thought. Cooking was a complete mystery to her, and, though in time she learned to turn out an excellent fudge, she never did learn to roast meat without burning it to a crisp or to cook vegetables until they were done. As for the cows, she was actually frightened of them, and would no more think of trying to milk one than she would consider taking a snake into her bed.

Under these circumstances the task of adjustment to a new life was difficult enough; but she herself made it doubly so. Raised as she had been, with servants constantly at her beck and call, hers was an imperious nature, and at times I think she was apt to speak more sharply than she intended. Twice in our first day at home I had to reprimand her, gently at first and then more sharply, for the tone with which she addressed old Anna and little Purity. They were not, I found it necessary to point out, mere servants. Dougal and Anna by the length of their service with us and their devotion, and Purity by virtual adoption, had become in reality a part of the family, and I found it necessary to insist that they be treated as such. I might have saved my breath for the wind, however, for she could never bring herself to that viewpoint, and as long as they remained with us she maintained her attitude of hauteur towards them.

It was only natural that this trait should cause her to be misunderstood. I will say that Anna and Purity bore with her gently and kindly—rather, I think, for my sake than from love of her. My younger sister Alice disliked her cordially, and made scarce an effort to be civil to her. Indeed, I think that aside from myself, her only friend in Suncook was my mother.

Perhaps it was because of me. Perhaps it was because she was genuinely sorry for her. But whatever the reason my mother did make some effort to understand her, and for this Dorcas was almost pathetically grateful. My mother was an avid card player, despite her Calvinist principles; though since we had left Scotland she had had scant opportunity to play. Dorcas had learned to play a fair hand of whist or piquet at the tables in Portsmouth, and as the latter was my mother's favourite, their evening game soon became an established custom; as soon as the dishes were cleared from the table, off they would go into the chimney corner with a board between them on their knees and fall to counting out the cards.

I should have preferred to stay at home under these circumstances, but there was far too much to be done to admit of that. The year's entire crop of timber had yet to be picked and marked out ready for the cutting crews, and it would not be long before the snow flew. I spent three days seeing that Dorcas was comfortably settled, and on the morning of the fourth set out upriver in company with my cousin Davie, who had filled out into as fine and strapping a young man as any who had ever swung a paddle.

It was fortunate that I had a reasonably definite idea of where to go, for I had made a mental note of several excellent stands the year before. We went up the river to the mouth of the Winnepiseogee and there turned northeastward, following that stream up through Winnisquam into Great Winnepiseogee Pond, marking timber all the way. We paddled the length of the big lake to the Indian carry through two small lakes into another large one, which the Indians called Asquam. Here we found more fine timber and marked it. Afterwards we went on down through the great pond into another smaller one that lay below, and so on down the river that was the outlet into the Pemigewasset some three leagues or so below the mouth of the Asquamchumauke.

All this was not done in the short time it takes to tell it. By the time we struck the river again we had been gone ten weeks from home—not that the distance was so great, but we had our work to do and it was that which took the time. Even so, we had hurried over the last three days, all the time we were upon the lower Asquam, for the weather, which until then had been balmy, had turned suddenly chill and sharp, and we knew that Indian summer was at an end and we might look for snow any day. Indeed, Davie swore that he could smell it coming; and though I laughed at him I knew what he meant, for there was a sharpness to the air and a bite to the wind such as only comes before a snowstorm.

We camped at the mouth of the Asquam that night, and awoke in the morning to a dull leaden sky out of which there dusted occasional solitary flakes, whirling on the bitter wind that howled down out of the north. It was biting cold, and we hovered over the campfire long after we should have been on our way. When at last we drowned the fire and stowed our duffel in the canoe it was past nine o'clock.

We were ready to leave when I suddenly remembered I had left my knife sticking in a log beside the fire. Davie climbed into the canoe and took his place in the stern, holding the bow on the sand spit, while I climbed back up the bank to get it. I had just pulled it from the log when I heard his exclamation.

"What is it?" I called.

"Someone's coming," he replied.

I slid down the bank rapidly, for since the occurrence of the last spring we all had gone warily in fear of Indians.

He was pointing up-river, and following the direction of his finger I saw a canoe with a single figure in the stern.

We waited, for it was plain enough that here was no Indian. Indeed, though it was too far away for me make out yet who he was, there was something familiar both in the figure and in the canoe. He came on rapidly, however, for he had both wind and current at his back, and he was paddling strongly.

"Why, hell!" said Davie, presently. "It's Jed!"

He was right enough. Even before I recognized the man I spotted that canoe for the same one we had left hidden at the three forks of the Pemigewasset. I was surprised, for Stiles and Toby had gone away more than a month before our wedding, no one seemed to know just where, and no word had been heard from them since.

We shoved our canoe out into the river, and lay drifting with the wind and current until he caught up with us. He greeted us cheerfully and drove his canoe in close to ours. I was pleased to see that he seemed to have recovered from his fit of sulks. He laid his paddle across the gunwales and rested on it, giving me a grin.

"All hitched good an' proper?" he said.

"All hitched," I replied.

"Hell!" he said, and spat over the side. "I thought maybe you'd show better sense when it come right down to it."

I laughed.

"Where'n hell you been?" said Davie. "Where's Toby?"

Stiles jerked his head.

"Up-river," he said. He looked at me. "Remember that place I liked up at the forks?" he asked.

I nodded.

"Well," he said, "we been up there all summer. I built me a cabin, and Toby built him one. We cleared a patch and set out some corn and potatoes and suchlike. And, mister, I want to tell you it's as snug a spot as a man could wish for. Toby's up there now. I just come down for some supplies. Then I'm goin' back and spend the winter."

"You're gettin' old, Jed," said Davie.

Stiles laughed as he dug his paddle in the dark water.

"Eeyah!" he said. "Guess maybe I am, settlin' down and all. I'll have to pick me out a nice girl next an' get married."

He looked at me and chuckled.

"Mister," he said, "you don't know what you're in for!"

He spoke in jest, but the words were prophetic.

I did not go out that winter with the woods crews. During the preceding year my uncle had experimented, on a small scale, with masting. As we lacked a warrant to cut the King's trees, we could not, of course, take the great white pines which were the cream of the crop, and in consequence, being unsure of our market, had to go warily that first year. As it proved, however, there was a good demand for stout spruce sticks, as well as for the various other species of pine, and the venture proved so successful that my uncle decided we must organize a mast crew—swampers, choppers, peelers, tailsmen—and construct a mast yard.

It was to this task that I was assigned; and since it was deemed best to have the yard as far downstream as possible, in order to shorten the long river journey and lessen the danger of breaking the great sticks in the falls, I was able to spend much time at home, walking daily to and from the yard which was situated at the foot of Garvin's falls, a mile or two above the mouth of Soucook Brook.

It must not be imagined, however, that because of this I was idle. On the contrary, masting is a trade that involves no little hazard, and the responsibility of the mast-master is not one to be taken lightly. To begin with, trees are picked for size: thickness at the butt, slight taper, and length. Besides this they must be straight-grained and as knot-free as may be. The expense of yarding alone is enormous, involving as it does the hire of twenty to thirty men and anywhere from thirty to sixty oxen; and to cap it all the sticks must be safely run in the spring through all the hazards of the river, falls, rocks and rapids, to the market. Many a master, operating on scanty capital, had been ruined by the loss of a single stick upon the jagged fangs of Amoskeag.

I found it interesting work, however. The first choice of sticks fell upon me, and proved a test of my knowledge. When the timber was selected the crews were sent out. Swampers cleared the ground for the tree's fall and prepared a cradle of brush to receive it. Choppers then felled it, peelers removed the bark, and the teamsters hitched their oxen to the log and hauled it as gently as might be to the yard. But it was the tailsmen, it seemed to me, who had the most arduous and yet the most amusing task of all. It was their duty, once the teams were hitched, to walk beside the hindmost yoke, and when the tongue of the sled, on which the great stick was loaded, in crossing a hollow or topping a slight rise, would rise so high as to lift the beasts into the air, they would seize their tails and pull them outward to prevent their being injured by the tongue in its descent.

It was work which called for plenty of snow, and we were at first hampered by an almost complete lack of that article. In spite of the early promise there was scarce more than a light powdering of the ground until the first of December, and after that, although it snowed heavily several times before Christmas, each time it came off warm after the fall, turning the snow to slush and setting us all to snuffling with colds. By New Year's there was no more than six inches; hardly enough to cover the tops of the stones along the woods road that led from the yard up into the cutting. It was past the middle of January before the skies opened and let down the feathery blanket. By the end of the week the snow lay deep across the entire countryside, piling high up under the eaves of the houses and lying waist-deep in the woods beneath the trees.

Even though we could do no cutting and hauling, we were not without work. There was the yard to be cleared, the timber itself to mark, and wood roads to be laid down. We managed to keep ourselves busy enough with these duties to remain within the bounds of respectability. Nevertheless, we chafed under the delay, and when at last the snow did fly it came so late that we had to work at double pressure, in order that our crop of logs might be yarded by the river's edge, ready for rolling, when the ice broke up and the spring flood came to carry them down to the sea. This added burden of extra work might, at another time, have chafed my spirit. As it was, however, in the closing days of the old year and the opening days of the new, there fell upon us a blow, so shocking in its suddenness and so terrible in its consequences, that the extra labour came to me as a relief from a burden of sorrow that I fear I might otherwise have found impossible to bear.

I have never heard the weather blamed by professional men for the various epidemics of throat distemper with which New England has been visited so frequently of late. Indeed, it seems to me that but little is known either as to the cause of the sickness or as to its cure. Many doctors have placed its seat in the belly, although its very name indicates that part which it affects the most. These men have seen fit to blame it upon a species of food poisoning, which seems to strike the country, up and down and round about, quite simultaneously. Their treatment differs little from that of most other ailments, be it a bullet in the chest, a broken leg, or the black plague itself. A little bloodletting, a few herbs and purgatives, and if the patient be strong enough he may survive.

Now I could never pretend to any knowledge of medicine, yet it seems to me that one thing about this scourge is too obvious to be ignored or set down to mere coincidence. The winter of 1735, in which this dread disease—which strikes so boldly at either the very young or the very old, leaving those in between, whose strength might the better enable them to withstand it, first appeared—was a mild one, or so I have been told. In that year thousands—more than had ever fallen victim to the knife and tomahawk of the red savages of the north—were laid away in their graves. In 1741 it struck again, and again in '45, and in '49, and all of these were mild years, in which there was more rain than snow, though to be sure, not since its first appearance had it reached such terrifying proportions.

When all is said and done, however, it appears that the cause was but a matter of small importance. The main thing is that the pestilence appeared again during that winter of 1752–53 in the Hampshire Province, raising its head first in Exeter and then in Kingston a few days later, and within the month spreading far and wide to Rumford, to Rochester, to Portsmouth and Souhegan, and Epsom, and Upper and Lower Ashuelot, and Contoocook and Hopkinton. We even heard of a case reported from Number Four. All around us it struck, yet seemed to pass us by. It came up the river from Haverhill to Londonderry to Chester, and when we thought surely we must be next, it skipped over our heads and appeared at Starkstown and Bow.

At first we watched its spread with dread, for we had our share of children and oldsters, and it seemed impossible that it should pass us by. But as the days lengthened into a week, and the week became a month, and still no single case appeared among us, even the best of us could not but feel that Providence had singled us out for its mercy and with but a little more luck we might escape unscathed.

It was thus matters stood at Christmas time. On the Sunday before, the Reverend Whittemore recommended to us that we give thanks for our continued deliverance, yet I think there were but few of us who were in a holiday mood. Nearly all had friends elsewhere, either stricken or already dead of the disease, and the very thought of it cast an air of gloom upon our tiny community.

As if this were not enough, I had troubles of my own to add to it, quite aside from the worries and delays of the business. Since the middle of November the breach between my sister and Dorcas had been growing, until Alice could scarce be persuaded to stay in the same room with my wife, and indeed, when my mother was not present, she more than once jumped up and swept out when Dorcas came in. Alice could be sharp-tongued when she had a mind to it, which was often enough. And Dorcas was not one to sit down under a gibe or to turn the other cheek to any wrong, real or fancied.

Of late, however, Dorcas had been growing silent and moody. When she was not playing piquet or cribbage with my mother, she would sit alone by the fire, with scarce a word for anyone beyond a complaint as to the cold or to some other minor trouble. When we went to our bed at night she would lie stiff and silent, brooding upon something, though I could not get her to tell me what it was that troubled her. She was near six months gone with child at the time, and I laid it mostly to this. Nevertheless I worried about it, and on Christmas Eve I spoke of it to my mother, asking her if she considered that it was anything I might have done, or if I had neglected her, to make her seem so moody. But my mother laughed at me and patted my cheek.

"La, lad!" she said. " 'Tis but natural. All women are like to be a bit touched when they're carrying their first around. 'Twill be right enough when the bairn's born, you'll see."

"Aye," I said. "I'd thought 'twas something such, but you know 'tis a poor dull place for her none the less. Not at all like the gay life she's used to in Portsmouth. I've wondered if perhaps I shouldn't have brought her to it more gradually."

She shot me a sharp look, then smiled a little and nodded.

" 'Tis quiet enough, I'll warrant," she replied. "Maybe you're right. I'll pass the word to your uncle, and you chip in to help, and we'll make tomorrow's party a merry one. There's naught like a jolly party to bring a lass back to her right senses!"

This seemed sensible to me, and I went to bed that night relieved at least to have spoken my mind. I had confidence in my mother's judgement, and I counted on the morrow's party to do the work which I had been unable to accomplish.

That Christmas is one which I am not likely to forget soon. It had been my mother's original intention to have none but the immediate family at dinner, but after our talk she extended the party to include my uncle and all his family, the elder Rushes, as well as Edith and Moses. Besides these she also invited Nathaniel Hoyt, who had of late been most attentive to my sister Alice, and the Clements, father, son, and daughter Rachel, to whom last my cousin Davie had been paying court for nigh a twelvemonth past. Indeed, we lacked only the presence of Stiles and Toby to make our company complete, and, though the former had stated most emphatically that they did not intend to come out again until the winter was over and done with unless they were forced to, I almost expected to see them push in at the front door, the wet snow clinging in dripping gouts to their leggings and little icicles hanging from their scraggly beards.

But though that did not happen, there was no lack of hilarity. Edith and Moses arrived first, for Edith was to help out in the kitchen. They brought with them their two youngsters, Alan, aged four and one-half, and Amos, going on two, nor would my mother have heard of their being left at home. Alan took great joy in the tall tree which I had cut and set up in the corner, and he spent much of the day helping Dorcas and Purity trim it, while little Amos, who had developed a cough in the night, and plainly felt none too well, lay upon my mother's bed and howled.

The others came in by twos and threes, as did several of our neighbours to wish us "Merry Christmas." The twin bowls of flip and toddy were nigh worn out with shuttling back and forth to be filled and refilled, and by four in the afternoon, when at last we gathered at the long board, we were indeed all in a merry mood. My uncle had gathered Dorcas under his wing and insisted that she take place beside him at the opposite end of the long table from my mother. It was like old times to hear his booming laughter filling the great low-ceilinged room, and to see Dorcas, happy once more in the midst of such gaiety, laughing back at him.

When the dinner was finished the table was pushed back and a space cleared for dancing. Edith took the children home to put them away in their beds, returning shortly to join the dancers, the music for whom was supplied by Donald, who was no mean hand with a fiddle. For my own part I danced but once, with Purity, and thereafter spent the evening sitting by my wife's side and taking as much enjoyment from the watching as from the doing.

It pleased me, too, to see that it was doing Dorcas a world of good. Even though she could take but little part in it, just to be in the midst of things raised her spirits amazingly. She sat in the great chair, whilst I perched myself upon its arm; her hands were clasped about my elbow, her cheeks flushed, her eyes shining, and her lips parted in happy laughter, so that I was amazed at the change in her, and told myself that we should have to take advantage of every opportunity to repeat the performance, if only for the benefit she derived from it.

It was well after midnight before the last guest had waved good night and trudged away through the crunching snow. But not until the last one had gone could I persuade her to go to bed, although her eyes were heavy with weariness. When at last it was all over, it came over her with a rush, and she suffered me to lead her away gently to our chamber and help her from her things.

When I had seen her snugly tucked away under the covers, I left her and went below to help straighten up the kitchen and the common room, to bank the fires, and lock up for the night. We worked for near an hour, putting things to rights, washing dishes, and finally, as we finished, first Alice and then Purity went off to bed, leaving my mother and myself to lock up and blow out the lights. My mother made herself a last glass of flip to serve for a nightcap, and pulled a chair before the fire.

"Well, lad," she asked, cocking an eye at me, "d'ye think it worked out as planned?"

I was enthusiastic over the results, and she chuckled wisely.

"Aye," she began, "the lass—"

There came a sudden thundering at the door that caused her to break off suddenly and look around, startled. For a moment we both stared at the door in surprise, wondering who could be about at such an hour. Then the pounding came again.

"Answer it!" she commanded, sharply. "Don't stand there gawping!"

I crossed the room and flung open the heavy door, standing back as Moses Rush stumbled in, his face white as if he had seen a ghost, his eyes staring, and his breath coming in short gasps as if he had run all the way from his house to ours. For an instant he stood panting in the middle of the room, staring at us dully, and in the instant my mother was at his side.

"What is't, man?" she said, shaking his arm roughly. "What brings ye back? Is't one o' the lads?"

He looked at her almost stupidly for a moment before he could find his tongue. When at last he spoke his voice was so thick and heavy with emotion that I could scarce recognize it.

"'Tis Amos," he said. "He's sick!"

My mother peered at him sharply and shook his arm.

"Aye?" she prompted him.

"He was right enough," said Moses, "when Edith took them home. He'd a cold but no sign o' fever. When we got in we found him all dry and hot, and when he cried he could but make choking noises in his throat!"

My mother turned away without a word and went to her room. In an instant she was back with a cloak about her shoulders, and a bag beneath her arm. In that moment it seemed to me she had aged ten years, for all the life and laughter had gone from her face, leaving it tired and old and lined.

She took Moses gently by the arm and pushed him towards the door.

"Ye'll come back with me," she said.

At the door she turned to me.

"You go up and fetch Doc Webster down to Moses'," she commanded. "Don't let him put ye off. Tell him—"

She paused and drew in a deep breath.

"Tell him," she went on, "that I think it's come!"

With that she turned and, dragging Moses after her, disappeared into the night.

I should prefer to pass lightly over the events of the next few weeks, for I cannot yet think of them without an overwhelming sense of grief. Still, as they had a considerable bearing upon our future life and movements, I cannot ignore them, however briefly I may speak.

Within the week little Amos passed along, and before ten days more had passed his brother had followed him. As long as it had lasted my mother had attended them, nor would she leave their bedside. Now and again, when exhaustion became too much for her, she would allow herself to be relieved by Dougal or Anna or Edith or Purity; even then she would not leave the room, but would stretch herself upon the low couch which, at her insistence, we had carried down and placed within the sickroom. For an hour or two she would cat-nap, and then she would be upon her feet again, comforting, soothing, ministering to their childish needs, as if by her very energy she might pull them through.

But it was no use. In the end, when Dr. Webster sadly shook his head and turned away from little Alan's bedside, she collapsed, and we had to carry her home to her own bed. In the morning when she woke she complained of a soreness and dryness in her throat, and by evening we had another patient upon our hands.

The first appearance of the sickness in our midst had been the signal for other cases, it seemed. Indeed, it almost appeared as if a malignant spirit, having spared us for so long, was determined to wreak a treble vengeance upon us for his oversight. The pestilence swept down upon us in a wave, as shocking and unnerving as it was sudden. Within a week after the announcement of Amos' death there was scarce a house in the length of Pembroke Street, from Cochran's at the Suncook mouth, up the hill and along the plain to my uncle's, at the Rumford line that had not one or more stricken. At Buck Street there were but two houses which were not visited, and at Isle-a-Huckset* an entire family of seventeen was stricken at once. At Blunt's there were three cases; at Mann's, four; at McConnell's, one. Old John Fife, who lived alone and was past seventy, came down with it and might have died before he was discovered had not the younger Holt gone out hunting into his upper pasture, and grown suspicious that something was amiss when he saw that no smoke was coming from the old man's chimney.

In the midst of all this we had our share. My mother's sudden collapse was a blow to us, and at my uncle's house, though the children escaped, my aunt finally gave way after attending for two weeks to her little niece, Susan, Donald's youngest. Then to add the final crushing burden to our woes, Old Dougal first, and then Anna, both of whom had worn themselves thin with their devoted attention to my mother, fell ill.

Until that time I had tried to keep Dorcas quiet and out of the entire business, despite my sister's criticism; for out of consideration for her condition I did not think it wise for her to expose herself. Now, however, there was nothing else for it. With three of the household abed we needed every hand we had to care for them. Not one of us might be spared. There was something which each of us could do, and much as I regretted the necessity I could not but ask her aid.

It was little enough she could do, as it appeared, for as I have already hinted she knew nothing of cooking and suchlike. Still she could fetch and carry when needed, and she was able to take her turn at watching at the bedside, thus releasing one of the other girls to more urgent duties. Despite her own recent bereave-

* Present Hookset.

ment Edith came up to be with us and help out, so that between us, I believe, we did all that could be done.

In the end, however, all our efforts proved fruitless. It was Dougal who went first, after a short swift illness; and on the night he died I went upon my knees at his bedside and cried, for if ever a man had proved himself a true friend, he was that one. Anna did not survive him by three hours, and I could not but wonder then if any would be spared. We tried, of course, to keep this awful news from my mother, but I think she read it in our faces, for when we came to her in the morning she put the question to us straight, and we were forced to confess it. At the news she turned her face to the wall and asked us to leave her alone.

In the week that followed, it almost seemed as if she might recover. At first the news of Dougal's and Anna's deaths had been a blow, and she sank low beneath it. Then all at once she rallied, and I thought perhaps their passing and the sorrow which it plainly brought us might have given her a stronger will to live, if only for the sake of those of us who must remain behind. Even old Dr. Webster was optimistic. But in the end, it proved, our confidence was for naught.

I was awakened one morning while it was still dark, by Dorcas shaking my shoulder, having turned over the sickroom vigil to her and Purity at midnight.

"Jamie!" she was saying. "Jamie! Wake up!"

I opened my eyes sleepily and took one glance at her pale face in the flickering light of the candle she held. In the next instant I had flung aside the covers and was on my feet.

"Fetch the girls!" I cried, and as she went to do my bidding I ran at once to my mother's room.

I found her lying very still and thin beneath the white coverlet, and for an instant my heart almost stopped beating with the fear that I was come too late. But when she heard my step upon the threshold she opened her eyes and looked at me.

I flung across the room and dropped to my knees beside the bed, clutching her poor thin hand to my breast.

"Mother!" I cried. "Mother!"

Behind me I heard my sisters come into the room, and felt rather than saw them come to stand upon the other side. In the darkened corner I could hear a stifled sobbing, though whether it was Purity or Dorcas, I could never say. My mother opened her eyes again and looked up at us, each one, with a tremulous smile.

"My children!" she whispered.

She turned her gaze upon me, and I felt my tongue cleave to the roof of my mouth and a great lump rise in my throat.

"Take care o' the girls, lad," she said. "And God bless ye!"

She closed her eyes then, and I had to strain close to hear her next words.

"Alan!" she whispered, and I could hear the breath coming harsh in her throat. "Alan!"

Then after a long pause she spoke once more in a louder voice. "Wait, Alan!"

And all at once I felt her thin hand go still in mine, and saw the sweet face relax as if in sleep. I put my head down upon the bed then and cried without restraint, for I knew at last that she was gone.

3

It was over so swiftly that now, looking back upon it, I am forced to wonder that it could affect us so. Even then I was not unacquainted with the harshness of life. A man was born, lived his span, for good or for evil, and died. That was the end. Sorrow, regrets—these were but vain folly. The dead could not live again in our world, and for those who remained life must go on. Death has passed close to me before and since. I myself have heard the rustle of its wings. Yet never has it so borne me down. My father's death, harrowing though it was, was comparatively swift, and over in the telling. That I had not been forced to witness it no doubt helped to alleviate its horror and to reconcile me to his loss. I was able to think, not of how death had come to him in the midst of awful suffering, but rather of how he had looked when he had taken my hand and bade me good-bye before he rode from the Hall of Kintulloch.

This, however, was different. At one moment we were alive and anxious, struggling with all our strength and will to save another, and with all our hopes pushed on to dizzy limits by the fear we could not admit. In the next moment it seemed that life had gone from us too. We had fought; and we had failed. All our fine hope gave way to blind apathy. The one who was gone seemed to have taken that part of us that was living with her. Though we still lived indeed, we scarce knew it. We moved about our daily tasks, more from habit than from anything else. We rose in the morning and dressed ourselves. We attended the cattle in the barn and the fires on the hearth. We cooked. We ate. We went to bed and slept. But we did these things without thought; without any motion of the will.

In the end, I think, this dulling of the senses with sorrow was a blessing in disguise, for it blurred impressions and destroyed, for the moment, our sense of time, so that later it was easier to forget the misery and anguish of the days that followed. For my own part, at any rate, I find that the sharpest memories of that bitter time are lost in the swirling mists of my own wretchedness.

We buried my mother two days later in the little cemetery near the meetinghouse, the Reverend Whittemore droning off the solemn service in his great rumbling voice while a bitter north wind whistled through the bare branches of the tall elms overhead. When it was done I turned and stumbled blindly towards home, unmindful of the great white flakes that swirled about me, striking cold and wet against my face, and clinging lightly to my clothes.

The snow that came that night was doubly welcome, for it meant hard work and a chance to occupy my mind with other things than brooding. Our investments in the masting trade had already run high. Nearly half the winter was gone. If we were to take a profit from the business the men must work at top speed, and it was for me to see that they did so. Almost every waking minute of the day I was forced to devote myself to the task.

I was fortunate in this, I believe, for the work kept me away from the house and occupied my mind to the exclusion of everything else. At night, when I would come home to supper, it was almost always to tumble into bed immediately after, too tired to lie awake tossing and spending the night in meditation of our loss.

By the same token, however, it also blinded me to events which were even then shaping themselves within the house. The little things that took place during the day I was not there to see. The little undercurrents of anger, distrust, and hatred which were in the air of an evening, I could feel vaguely, though I was too tired to notice them. It was true, I saw but little of the lass Purity, for she almost seemed to avoid me, and would find work in the kitchen whenever I entered the front door. Alice turned silent and snappish; but Alice was my sister, and I gave her no more thought than most brothers do their sisters. Dorcas, on the other hand, worried me not a little, for she grew daily more morose and apathetic in public, and more picking and nagging in private. But this, I thought, was most likely due to her approaching confinement. Women with child, I had often heard, frequently do strange things, and sometimes even become temporarily slightly unhinged. Doubtless this was just such a case. When the child was born all would be well. She would be free of all her moodiness and vapourings. The care of the baby would fill her time and give her that which she now lacked—something to keep her occupied. Everything then would be serene once more. She would become her old sweet self. All this nagging and quarrelling would cease; the air would clear, and the house might once more seem like home. It did not occur to me that there might be other forces at work to destroy the harmony of the household.

It was thus matters stood one late March evening when I returned home from the mast yard. It had been a hard day, for there were still a dozen of the great sticks to be cut and yarded before the snow should begin to melt and the ice to go out. We were working against time, and I had had to stay late to see that everything was done. It was long past suppertime, and I was tired and hungry when I came at last to the house.

As I pushed open the front door I was surprised to see that no place was laid for supper at the table, and the fire in the great fireplace was low and neglected. I wondered for an instant if the baby had arrived, for he was expected at any moment now. But even as the thought occurred to me I heard the sound of voices raised in anger from the kitchen.

"I don't care!" I heard Dorcas' voice say, and I thought I detected a note of hysteria in it. "I didn't want this! I didn't know we'd have to live away off here! I'm sorry I ever came now!"

There was a low laugh, and I heard Alice's voice replying.

"Maybe we aren't all sorry!" she said.

I went through the passage and found them facing each other across the kitchen table, while Purity stood near the fireplace looking from one to the other of them with troubled eyes.

They looked up as I came in, and Dorcas cried out, "Jamie!"

"What's this?" I demanded.

Alice shook a finger across the table. "She said—" she began.

I cut her off somewhat sharply.

"What does it matter what she said?" I snapped. "Can't you see she's all worked up? She's not herself. She's not responsible for her words. What have you been doing to her?"

My sister looked at me in amazement.

"What have I been doing?" she exclaimed. She laughed derisively. "How can you be so stupid? Can't you see she's more herself now than she's ever been? That's what she's thought of us all the time, only she hasn't said so. Now she's mad, all the fine high manners are gone, and she becomes herself flying her true colours!"

"Be quiet!" I snapped.

But she was not to be stopped by mere words.

"Why, 'tis easy to see," she continued, her voice rising as her anger increased, "she's nothing but a common ordinary little sl—"

I leaned across the table and slapped her across the mouth.

"Will you be quiet!" I roared.

She fell back a step or two and stared at me in blind fury. Then she turned on her heel and, with head high, strode to the door. There she turned and faced the room again.

"All right," she said, her voice trembling with rage. "I'm going. I'm going right out of this house, and I'm going to Nathan'l. We were going to be married anyway when he'd cleared his lot and raised his cabin, and I don't suppose a month or two'll make any difference. You can have all this!"

She cast a glance about the room, and shot a malicious look at Dorcas.

"I wish you joy of it!" she concluded spitefully.

She started to turn, and I think I would have made some reply, which would scarce have helped matters, had I not heard Purity cry out behind me.

I turned just in time to see Dorcas fall forward against the edge of the table, and slide heavily to the floor.

I was at her side in a flash, slipping my arms beneath her shoulders in an effort to raise her. Purity was not far behind me, and between us we managed to get her across the room to a great high-backed armchair that stood by the fire, half dragging, half carrying, for she was not light in her condition. Over my shoulder as we struggled I called to Alice, who had turned back, startled by the sudden turn of affairs.

"Fetch brandy!" I commanded.

"I—" she began.

But I cut her short.

"Fetch brandy, by God!" I thundered.

She gave me one frightened glance and went straight to the cupboard and fetched out the high black bottle that Rob Rogers had smuggled down out of Quebec as a present for my mother. I took it from her without a word, and at a jerk of my head she turned away and went out of the room.

Dorcas choked slightly as the hot liquor which I forced between her teeth trickled down her throat, and an instant later her eyes opened. She waved away the cup of tea which Purity offered her, but nodded when I suggested that she get to bed; and so Purity on the one side and I upon the other supported her into the great main-floor chamber, which we had taken over for the time being to save her the necessity of climbing the steep stairs.

When we had set her upon the bed I sent Purity from the room and helped her to unfasten her stays and get into her nightdress. She volunteered no information, and I thought it best not to press her, at least for the time being. When at last I had seen her safely tucked in and made comfortable, I kissed her gently upon the cheek and went out.

I found Purity alone in the kitchen setting out a supper of bread and beans, with a shoulder of cold mutton for meat and a can of ale to wash it all down.

"I thought ye might be hungry," she said as I came in.

I smiled at her, for I liked her thoughtfulness.

"Aye," I said. "I was hungry when I came in, but I misdoubt this business has taken my appetite away."

She looked away quickly, and I sat down and drank a draft of the ale and tasted the beans. I found my appetite not so impaired as I had thought, for that first taste had brought it back; and I did not speak again until I had mopped up the last bit of juice with a bit of bread and drained the ale can to the bottom. I sat back then and looked at her.

"What was it about?" I asked finally.

She shrugged.

"Little enough," she replied. "In truth, Jamie, I can't remember justly if 'twas Dorcas saying the house was cold or Alice wondering how folks ate in Portsmouth who could not cook that started it. But, whatever 'twas, one word led to another, and then you came in."

It was evident that it was no great matter, but I was annoyed that my sister should have so little sense as to plague Dorcas at this time.

"That Alice!" I said, shaking my head. "Can't she leave the child alone? This is no time to be plaguing her!"

As there was no reply to be made to this, Purity made none. I got up and fetched my pipe from the mantel and loaded it from the jar in the cupboard. When I had settled myself with it before the fire it was Purity who broke the silence.

"Why don't ye take her away, Jamie?" she asked.

"Take her away?" I said, surprised.

She nodded.

"Back to Portsmouth," she replied. "She's not meant for this sort of life. She'll never be happy here, and neither will you so long as she's like this."

I looked at her in amazement. It was the first time it had ever occurred to me that the girl might have any thoughts of her own. It struck me there might be a good deal in what she said.

"How can I take her away now?" I demanded gruffly, to cover my surprise. "She's in no fit state to travel. Why, the baby might arrive this very night!"

She started to speak, but I went on hastily.

"Besides," I said, "I can't leave the work. We've put more money into this masting business than we'd a right to, and it's up to me to get it back."

I shook my head.

"No," I said, "I couldn't do it before the spring, anyway. And the young un'll be here by then and there'll be no need."

"But if there is need," she said softly, as if shy of suggesting it, "ye'll do it then?"

I smiled across at her.

"Perhaps, lass," I said, "perhaps."

She rose then and laid her hand upon my shoulder.

"Think about it," she said, and in the next instant she was gone.

I sat for some time before the fire, after she had gone, turning the suggestion over and over in my mind, and looking at it from every angle. At last I knocked the dottle from my pipe, took a candle from the wall bracket and made my way slowly up the stairs.

There was a light showing beneath my sister's door. I knocked, and when she answered I went in.

I found her sitting on the bed, staring sullenly at a great pile of clothes and trinkets and a row of empty boxes and portmanteaux.

"Packing?" I asked.

She bounced to her feet and tossed her head haughtily.

"I am," she replied, and began to cram things into the nearest case.

"Well, stop it," I said shortly. "Don't make things worse than they are."

"I'm leaving, I'm leaving, I'm leaving, I'm leaving!" she replied, at each repetition thrusting a new dress or wrap into the box.

"Look here," I said. "Don't you think you'd best talk to Nathan'l about it first? He might like a little warning. Especially as he hasn't got his cabin ready or the lot cleared."

She tossed her head.

"Nathan'l 'll be glad to have me," she declared.

"No doubt, no doubt," I replied a little dryly.

She whirled on me angrily.

"What do you mean by that?" she demanded.

"Why," I said, "only this: This is a small town, and the man who takes a wife here wants everything open and aboveboard. If he can he'll avoid giving the neighbours a chance to talk. You know there'll be talk about this. It'll hurt Nathan'l as much as it will you. And after all it isn't necessary."

I saw that she hesitated, and was quick to follow up the advantage.

"Besides," I said, "it isn't as though this were to be permanent."

She looked at me quickly.

"I don't know," I went on, "that Dorcas can ever be really happy here."

"You'll take her away then?" she said sharply.

I shrugged.

"That remains to be seen," I replied. "The baby may make a change in her. She may be content to stay, then."

Her face fell.

"But what does that matter?" I continued. "We're all well enough off to do as we please. Mother left everything in my hands, naturally; but she expected me to make a fair division with you and Edith, and I'll see it's done. If it's Nathan'l Hoyt you marry, lass, you'll come to him well dowered."

She looked at me, a little bewildered and a little confused, scarce knowing what to say. I laughed.

"So you see, lass," I said, " 'twill be best not to be too hasty. Let the bairn be born, and let me finish the work I'm on, and after that we'll set up things to everyone's taste."

And with that I tapped her lightly on the shoulder, kissed her cheek, bade her sleep upon it, and gave her a very good night, shutting the door lightly behind me as I went out.

Three days later our son was born—dead.

Perhaps I should have been more bowed down with sorrow than I was, but anxiety for the mother prevented this. Dorcas herself came near to death then, and though I must take shame to confess it the loss of the baby seemed to me a minor matter by comparison.

It was four days before I was at last allowed to see her, and then I scarce could recognize her, so drawn and haggard was her pale face against the pillows. I crossed the room and sat down upon the edge of the bed, taking her thin hand in mine, and gazed into her wide bewildered eyes.

"I'm sorry, my sweet," I said.

She closed her eyes momentarily and shook her head.

"It doesn't really matter, Jamie," she replied in a voice scarce louder than a whisper. "I can tell you now, I didn't really want a baby!"

Her words came as a shock to me, for though I had consoled myself with the thought that at least she lived, still I was by no means happy in our loss. I stiffened involuntarily, and she must have felt it, for her eyes flew wide and she gripped my hand in both of hers. Looking down at her, I could see the terror in her eyes and in the trembling of her lip.

"Jamie!" she gasped. "Jamie!"

I could not remain cold to such an appeal. She lay so pitifully helpless and weak among the coverlets, and her fear was so apparent, that I felt no matter what her attitude I could not desert her. What difference did it make how she felt? It was done, and no regrets would mend it. She needed me now as she had never needed me before. I must not fail her. I dropped to my knees beside her.

"My dear," I said, "don't be afraid. I'll not leave you."

She lay back with a tremulous sigh, and her relief was plain to be seen.

"Oh, Jamie, Jamie!" she whispered.

"What is it, dear?" I leaned close.

"Take me away, Jamie," she said in a voice scarce audible even in that silent room. "Take me away, please!"

I squeezed her hand gently and leaned over to kiss her.

"I shall," I whispered. "I shall as soon as you get well. We'll go to Portsmouth and live in a house as big as the Governor's."

I thought it might make her laugh; but when I straightened up she turned her head away quickly, and I saw that she was crying.

4

Once the decision was taken and my mind made up to the move I became fretful and impatient to see the plan put into effect, for it seemed to me then, as it has always seemed, that there is no such suspense as that which comes between the thinking and the doing. Had it been possible, I believe we should have packed that very night and the next day set out for Portsmouth.

There were a number of factors, however, which prevented our immediate departure. Dorcas was not yet in a condition to be moved. There was the settlement of the estate, the matter of my sister's wedding, the final readjustment of our business affairs, and above all the completion of the masting job upon which I was then working.

It was this last that proved the most exacting. With the single exception of Alice's marriage to Nathaniel Hoyt, the other matters were such as could easily be disposed of in a day or two. Even the impending nuptials need not have delayed us, for the date could have been set at any time, leaving us free to go and return for the ceremony. But the masting would admit of no neglect. Not for a day did I dare to leave it, lest by the delay thus engendered we might stand to lose all that we had invested, and more besides.

Each tree we took needed from four to seven days, depending upon the distance at which it stood from the mast yard, to be cut, trimmed, peeled, hauled, and yarded; and the more trees we yarded the greater would be our profits. Cutting, hauling, and yarding must go on as long as there was enough snow to skid the logs. When the snow began to go there would be a short breathing spell until the ice had disappeared from the river, and the brown water swirled high among the willows along the bank. Then the great sticks would be rolled with greatest care into the swift water, and started on their journey to the sea. Until the last log had splashed down from the bank and slowly started southward I could not think of leaving.

When this was accomplished, however, it would become imperative that I leave almost at once, for by the terms of my agreement with my uncle the duty of disposing of the timber once it reached the coast fell to me.

Hitherto, this end of our business had been left to him. At least once each year he had journeyed to Portsmouth and Newburyport to draw new contracts, and to sell that part of our crop that had been floated on speculation. Of late these annual journeyings had irked him, for he was no longer as young as he once had been and he found travelling tired him. During the summer past, since I was already upon the ground, I had undertaken to attend that part of the business for him, thereby proving that I was capable of doing it; and now that I intended to take up my residence in Portsmouth, it was decided that my cousin Davie should take my place in the woods, while I was set to watch our interests upon the coast. In this way not only should I be enabled to retain my active connection with the business, but the business itself would gain through having a permanent representative in constant touch with the market.

The question of the estate itself was not more difficult to settle, resolving as it did to a simple matter of agreement as to the

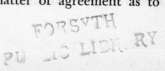

method of division. In general ours is a poor province. Ready money is scarce among our people of the interior, but for those who have a little capital to invest Nature has provided, in our forest, a source of immeasurable profit. We, having placed our money at my uncle's direction, were now in a position to realize the wisdom of his counsel.

In the years since our arrival we had prospered beyond all our expectations. We had hoped to gain a living from our investments. Instead we found ourselves wealthy—if not by the standards of London or Edinburgh, at least in the eyes of our own people. The property was considerable. Little by little we had added to our real holdings. Besides the original hundred acres on the Suncook side of Soucook Brook, upon which the house stood, we also held some two hundred more upon the Rumford side, as well as an additional hundred-acre timber lot across the river. Further, there was a half-share in the lumber and milling business—the real source, of course, of our income—not to mention the final item, a cash reserve that was already more than treble that which we had brought with us from Scotland.

As the son of the family, all this had passed quite naturally to me, with the tacit understanding that I would make a fair settlement upon each of my sisters; a task which I promptly proceeded to carry out to the best of my ability. All of the land I divided between them; giving Alice, who wished to remain in Suncook, the house and all the acreage on that side of the brook. To Edith, who was already established in Rumford, I gave all the land which we held in that township, as well as the timber lot across the river. Our half of the business I divided into four equal shares. Two of these I retained for myself, giving one of the others to each of the girls. Of the money I gave a thousand pounds to each, retaining the balance; a fair division, I felt, as the land would be of greatest benefit to them, while I, who must now reestablish myself in a new home, would have need of ready money and a good income.

With our major problems thus settled and laid aside, we suddenly found ourselves brought face to face with another minor one. We had failed, in our preoccupation, to give a thought to Purity Stiles.

Now, during the years that Purity had been a member of our household she had grown to be as one of us. In eight years we had shared our lives with her; eaten across the same table, slept beneath the same roof, felt the same joys and sorrows. We had watched her grow from a thin, wild-eyed little creature of the woods into a well set up lass of eighteen, whose wide grey eyes and small mouth, set in a delicately oval face, if not beautiful, were at least comely enough to make any man stop and look twice. There was not one of us, I know, who did not look upon her with much the same sort of affection as we would have had for a younger sister. Not one of us would willingly have slighted her; and yet here we had made our dispositions and laid our plans without ever a thought for her. What was she to do now that the only home she had known was about to be broken up? Was she not entitled to a share in the estate, having been so long one of us? These were the questions that popped into my head when the thought of her first came to me.

I went into a hasty conference with my sisters, and found them quite in agreement with my point of view. Whatever happened, we decided, she should not lose for want of generosity on our part. Alice set aside a twenty-acre section of river bottom in her favour, while Edith and I contributed to a purse that totalled some eight hundred pounds, old tenor.

But when it came to the matter of presenting the packet, neither Edith nor Alice would help me out. It was my idea, they said, and it was for me to carry it out. So, seeing that there was no way out of it, I took the deed and the money in the one hand, and my courage in the other—for I am no sort of a hand at all where matters of formality are concerned—and one evening after supper told the story and thumped the packet on the table in front of her.

She looked from one to another of us in bewilderment, and I thought her eye looked suspiciously moist.

"Oh!" said she. "But I can't accept it, you know!"

"Why not?" I demanded, gruffly, for I was determined not to be put off by foolish feminine scruples.

"Why," she said, and looked confused, "I—I just don't think I should."

"Nonsense!" I replied. " 'Tis what mother would have wanted."

She gave me a long look and reached out her hand for the packet.

"If you put it so—" she said, and I handed it across to her.

But though that was settled, we were soon to discover that it was only half our problem. The matter of what was to become of her was still in suspense. We could scarce leave her to live alone, young as she was; and yet we seemed utterly unable to suggest a solution that was acceptable. Both Edith and Alice offered her a place in their homes, but both of these offers she gently but firmly refused. I myself sounded her out in the matter one evening when the others had retired and she and I were alone in the kitchen.

"What do ye plan, lass," I said, "when Dorcas and I have gone our way, and the family's all broken and scattered apart? You can't just step out into the world alone, you know."

She shrugged, and gave me an indifferent stare.

"I don't know, Jamie," she replied. "This has been home to me."

"There's no need to leave it," I said. "Alice will be glad for you to stay."

But she shook her head. "It wouldn't be the same," she said.

"Why don't you pick out some nice young lad and marry him?" I suggested.

She gave me a peculiar look.

"Who?" she demanded.

"Well," I said haltingly, for this was more than I had bargained for, "there's Ben Holt."

She snorted scornfully.

"That big lump!" she said. "He has no more gumption than a sack of meal!"

"How about John Stark, then?" I demanded, for John had but just returned home, ransomed only the month before by Captain Stevens in Montreal.

"His face would sour me before the year was out," she replied.

"He's no beauty, I'll admit," I said, "but there's no greater heart in the province!"

She shook her head again.

" 'Tis no use, Jamie," she said. "Besides, nobody's asked me yet, and a girl can't do the asking, you know."

I looked at her in amazement.

"Surely that should be easy," I replied, "a pretty lass like yourself!"

She gave me another of those peculiar glances.

"Indeed," said she, "I have not found it so!"

"Well!" I exclaimed surprised. "Now what do ye mean by that?"

But she only laughed and picked up a candle.

"Good night, Jamie," she said, and left me there staring after her perplexed, for I could swear that she meant more than her words.

After a minute, however, I gave it up with a shrug. It was no use, I decided, to try to force her. She would make up her mind in her own good time, and in the meantime there was naught the rest of us could do but sit by and hope that something would turn up before the first of May.

The answer came with the spring thaw, floating down the river behind the breaking ice; though I must confess I did not then recognize it as the solution of the problem.

As the ice went out and the snow began to melt away in great patches in the woods, the streams filled with grey, rushing water, and the mutter of the river rose to a threatening roar. The slight lethargy that had come over the masting camp following the yarding of the last stick gave way to tense excitement, for now the real gamble began. At the crest of the flood, when the last of the ice had gone grinding down, the great logs would be committed to the care of the river. A crew would ride along the river bank, to be sure, keeping pace with the twisting, bucking, plunging, rolling monsters as they raced towards the sea. It would be their duty to do what they could to see that they arrived safely at the river mouth; but should one of those great sticks catch sideways in the boiling current of Amoskeag or Isle-a-Huckset falls all the men upon the river would not be able to prevent its splintering to kindling.

We watched the rise of the river with some anxiety, for if the water rose above the banks it was like to sweep our logs away before ever we were ready, and our profits with them. Who could tell in what rocky pasture or wooded hollow the receding waters might leave them? Day by day the swirling waters crept higher, and although there were still huge chunks of ice drifting down from above, I sometimes wondered if it would not be best to risk the ice and send the logs on down. I saw Captain Kimball ride by with his eye upon a single hundred-and-fifty-foot stick that he had floated down from Contoocook. For a day I was tempted to follow his example, but only for a day; for on the morrow came word from Amoskeag that Captain Kimball's mast had jammed across the rocks at the falls and floating ice had smashed it in four places. Poor Kimball, they said, was ruined.

The day came at last, however, towards the end of the first week in April, when the brown water ceased to rise but flowed steadily some six inches below the crumbling bank. Here and there an occasional small chunk of ice raced by upon the swift current, but none seemed large enough to cause trouble. I gave the word, and the first log plunged off the skids, splashed in the murky waters, spun, turned broadside to the current, and, slowly at first and then more swiftly, gathered way and began to drift off towards the sea.

All the forenoon we worked steadily, until by midday eight of the monsters had gone their way; each with an escort to keep it company upon its downward journey. As I sat upon the skids and ate my dinner of cold pork and biscuit I thought upon this with some satisfaction. Two days like this and all the logs would be gone. Thereafter I should be free until my sister's wedding, near the end of the month. Timothy Stevens, who had gone down-river with the first of the masts, had his orders. He would gather the others in a certain cove, not far from the river mouth, and hold them there, ready against my coming, so that I need have no worry for them. Once the last log had gone I had only to attend to my personal affairs until I arrived in Portsmouth.

So ran my thoughts until a shout above the roar of the river attracted me, and I looked up to see the men all standing and staring and pointing upstream.

Our skids were built at the foot of a long stretch of boiling rapids, difficult to run with a canoe in normal water, and considered well-nigh impossible with the river at its present stage; yet when I jumped to my feet and looked I saw that this was what was happening. A big canoe, loaded to the gunwales and expertly manned by two men, had appeared suddenly around the bend as if shot from a gun. Even now they were more than half-way down, their sharp prow plunging deep into the foam-crested waves, the rushing water threatening at any minute to engulf them. It did not seem possible that so frail a craft could survive in the midst of such swirling, crushing force, yet as I watched and doubted they were through and racing past.

We had built our skids to take advantage of the river's current, so that it was impossible for anyone to land there in a canoe, but they waved their paddles as they went by and pointed downstream to our landing. It was not until then that I recognized Jed Stiles and Toby.

They came ashore in the little backwater where we had our landing, some fifty rods below. I left orders for the men to go on with the work and scrambled down to meet them. They had stopped in Rumford and heard of our misfortunes of the winter, and about these they were duly sympathetic and sober, though aside from that they were in exuberant spirits, and these they could not long keep corked. The winter had been a good one for them. They had made a rich haul in furs—richer than either had anticipated. Their canoe was loaded from end to end with pelts, leaving them scarce room for feet, and they were bent upon a celebration. They were bound, they said, for Haverhill, where they would dispose of their furs, that being the easiest available market. Thereafter they would head for Portsmouth or Boston, they were uncertain which, to shake the pine needles from their hair and have a taste of civilization.

"Well," said I when I heard this, "don't drink up all your profits, for if I'm not mistaken you'll have a problem on your hands when you get back to Suncook."

"Eh?" said Stiles. "And what's that?"

"Purity," I replied. And then went on to tell him of the situation.

He chuckled when I had done.

"I'll leave it to you, lad," he said, laughing. "You'll see she comes to no harm!"

"But look here now!" I protested. "I don't see what I can do. She'll not listen to me. You'll have to do something."

But he only laughed.

"I'll put my trust in you, lad," he said, as he bent to push the canoe off into the river again. "Maybe we'll be back in time for the weddin'."

I watched him go with mixed feelings of exasperation and envy in my heart. It would be pleasant, I thought, to be so footloose. On the other hand he should be more thoughtful of his own.

I might have saved my worry, however, for within a week he was back. I had misjudged him, it seemed, for no sooner had he arrived than he drew Purity aside and had a talk with her. That evening, when the others had gone off to bed, he announced their decision.

"Well," said he, staring into the bottom of his can of ale, "ye can set your mind at rest, lad. The matter's settled."

"What?" said I. "Why, that's fine! I hope ye've made a good arrangement, for Purity deserves the best."

He gave me a peculiar look.

"Oh, aye," said he, "she'll be well enough looked after. She's to come back with me to the cabin and take care o' my old age."

He grinned. I must have shown my surprise.

"You don't mean it?" I cried.

"Indeed, why not?" Purity wanted to know indignantly.

"Why not?" I exclaimed. "Reason enough why not! Do you know there's not a settlement for fifty miles? There's not a soul. You'll see but Toby and your father! Why, lass, you'll die of loneliness!"

"And is that confined to the backwoods?" she asked.

I would have demanded what she meant by that, but her father spoke quickly so that I had no chance.

"That's the decision, lad," he said. "Ye'll have no more need to worry over it."

"But, my God, Jed!" I cried, swinging to face him. "You can't do it. You know it's not the place for her."

He shrugged.

" 'Tis what she wants, lad," he replied, "and I'm not one to stand in her way. She'll be safe enough, ye need have no fear."

Since it was evident that nothing would change them I said no more, and presently we all went off to bed in silence. Perhaps I should have been happy that the responsibility was no longer mine, but instead of that I found myself most unaccountably gloomy through the rest of the month.

They did not wait long after the wedding but left almost immediately pausing only to kiss the bride and drink to the health of the happy couple. I helped Stiles carry their meagre baggage down to the canoe, and at the last minute Purity burst into tears and threw her arms about my neck. I kissed her good-bye gently and handed her to Stiles, who settled her amidships among the baggage while he took the bow and Toby the stern. As they pushed out into the stream and turned their faces northward I felt the weight of an ineffable sadness, as though something that belonged to me and was a part of me had been taken away. I wondered if I should ever see them again. For a moment their canoe showed, bright against the dark overhang of the banks. Then they pushed around the bend and were gone. I turned and made my way slowly back to the house.

Our own departure was not long delayed. The next day we got off to a good start. I was up with the dawn harnessing the chestnut to the chair I had bought in Portsmouth, and gathering the baggage about the door. At sunup the youngest Foster, whom I had engaged to drive the heavy luggage as far as Exeter, arrived with his father's cart. After I had helped him load we all sat down to a hearty breakfast, with Alice radiant and blushing in the place of honour at the head of her own table, and Dorcas, at the far end, equally radiant at the prospect of returning at last to her beloved Portsmouth.

The breakfast over, I sped young Foster on his way and bundled Dorcas into the chair. Alice I kissed upon both cheeks, and I gripped Nathaniel's hand.

"Take good care of her," I said.

I climbed up beside my wife and gathered the reins.

"Come back soon and often," Alice called as I chirped to the horse and the wheels grated on the roadway.

We both waved, and then I had to turn my attention to the horse, who had been long in the barn and was full of life.

At the turn of the lane I looked back once more and saw Alice and Nathaniel standing in the doorway waving good-bye. In the next instant the woods cut off the view, and I bethought me then how I had once before looked back upon a house I was leaving, and remembered how little I had thought that I should never see it again.

5

Dorcas was in high good humour as we set out. The prospect alone of being, once and for all, shut of Suncock and returning to her own Portsmouth had raised her spirits beyond all measure.

Our actual departure lifted her to the supreme pinnacle of delight. Each step of our journey seemed to give her greater joy. With each passing mile the cloak of gloom which she had worn through all these trying weeks slipped further from her shoulders. She laughed; she sang; she prattled of her plans for the future. And, saddened though I was at the thought of leaving, the sight of her, gay and happy once again, was no small consolation to me; and was, I thought, well worth the sacrifice. By the time we reached our destination we were become as blithe and merry as a pair of newlyweds.

We went straight on arrival to my father-in-law's house, where that old rook, after showing due sympathy for our sorrows, promptly drew me aside and broached the matter of a small loan. So pleased was I with my wife's improvement that I had not the heart to refuse him; and accordingly I advanced him a generous sum—an act which I have never since ceased to regret; for neither did I ever again see the colour of my money nor was I free, from that day forth, of his touches and importunities.

My first duty, as soon as we were comfortably, if temporarily, settled, was the disposal of our masts, which even then awaited my instructions in a cove near the mouth of the Merrimack. As it proved, this presented no insuperable difficulty. Nearly half of the great sticks were already contracted for; the rest I easily disposed of, at an even better price, to Nathaniel Meserve, who had a contract to supply a firm of shipbuilders in Bristol with masts, yards, and bowsprits. Indeed, so pleased was the good colonel with our timber that he promptly engaged with us to supply him his entire stock of masts, yards, spars, bowsprits, and planking for the forthcoming year.

With this accomplished I was at last free to attend my personal affairs. Comfortable as we were beneath my father-in-law's roof, I was nevertheless anxious for the freedom and dignity of our own establishment. Moreover, it was plain that so long as we remained within his house, the old fellow would continue to levy a heavy toll upon my purse.

The location of a suitable house, however, was no simple matter, not so much from any lack of available dwellings as from the constant pressure of social affairs. Portsmouth welcomed us back with open arms. Dorcas was immediately whirled up in a round of parties, routs, and levees, and though I steered as wide of all such as I might, I could not avoid them entirely. There were callers to receive and calls to make, and for this my presence was required. The Governor received us graciously and expressed the wish to continue our discussions concerning the possible colonization of the north country: a command I could not well ignore. The Louisbourg boys greeted me with shouts of triumph and dragged me off to the tavern, with the result that I found scant opportunity to go in search of a house.

Find it I did, however, by dint of an hour here and a half-hour there. With the aid of George Stapleton and young Stephen Sparhawk I managed to locate a comfortable house of suitable though modest size on Pleasant Street not far from where the Warner mansion stands; and this I was able to purchase at a reasonable price.

Dorcas, I think, was somewhat disappointed that I had not chosen something more pretentious, but I pointed out I was not anxious for ostentation, and that the house I had located was in keeping with our means. She consoled herself with the thought that it was hers, and that there at least she would reign a queen in her own right. There followed a month of bustle; of buying of furnishings; of painting and decorating and carpentering and joining, until, in spite of its small size, I firmly believe there was no house more elegant in the town. All the while Dorcas was in a pother of impatience and apprehension, lest this be wrong and that be not quite right. But when, towards the end of June, we at last moved in and settled ourselves amongst all the dainty china and tapestry and spindle-legged furniture, I think she was completely entranced with it.

Our removal to our new quarters was the signal for a fresh round of parties and entertainments. Three times a week at least, it seemed, my wife felt it necessary to entertain old friends or new acquaintances at tea or supper, with music or at the cards. This in itself might not have proved excessive perhaps had not those thus entertained felt it incumbent upon themselves to return the compliment. As a result there was scarce an evening which we had to ourselves.

I do not consider myself unsocial, though it may be true that I am not as gregarious as some. Among my own people, among the men and women of the backwoods and the frontier, I had never found it difficult to be as free and easy as any. But here there was an undercurrent of insincerity and pretence which bewildered me and kept me constantly upon the defensive. Accustomed as I was to the open, easy manners of the country and the tavern, I found it quite impossible to assume the mincing affectation of the fashionable drawing rooms in which I now found myself. If I took a pinch of snuff I did so without any of those false flourishes which make of that act such a ritual. If I crossed the room I walked as God made me to do rather than attempt the strut which was then so much the thing among the bucks and beaux of London. I wore my clothes plainly, and affected none of those frills and furbelows which distinguished the latest mode. In short, a plain man of simple tastes, with an affinity for solitude, I found myself suddenly thrust into the midst of a society which outdid itself in a hectic attempt to be as gay and yet as formal as that of London and the fashionable watering places.

As may well be imagined, I found myself none too happy in this situation. I felt conspicuous and ill at ease in the midst of all the glitter. I doubt not there were many who looked upon me as a clumsy yokel. More than once I heard a lady titter or saw a dandy raise his eyebrows at something I said or did. Nevertheless, there were those, I believe, who liked me for my very bluntness and simplicity; most of these, to be sure, among the older people: the Meserves, the Langdons, the Ameses, and the Sparhawks. These found my manners good if not in the very latest convention, and I believe their friendship went far to help my cause. The Louisbourg Boys stood firmly behind me and accepted me as one of themselves; a fact I found greatly to their credit since they were macaronis to a man. This together with the fact that Dorcas was never so gay and happy, enabled me to put a good face upon it and to take the life as it came.

When, as happened occasionally, I found the perpetual round growing too much for me and affecting my temper, I would plead pressure of affairs and run down the coast on business, or perhaps pay a visit to Suncook to consult with my uncle and my cousins upon matters of more or less importance. At first Dorcas protested this, saying it was not polite to our guests in me to run away so. But I pointed out to her that without the business she would be unable to entertain her guests at all; and from that day on she never mentioned the matter again.

It was upon one of these latter occasions that I broached to my uncle the possibility of obtaining the royal warrant to cut the King's woods. It was some time since he had last applied for this and been refused; and in the interval we had prospered and become known in the Province. Moreover, the deputy, Major Young, who had refused his request had but lately resigned his commission and removed to Philadelphia, and the new deputy had not arrived, though I was given to understand that he was expected momentarily, the commission having been sold either in Boston or in Halifax. This, together with the fact of my own acquaintance with Governor Wentworth, made me feel that we had an excellent chance of success. When I spoke of it, however, my uncle frowned doubtfully.

"Na, lad," he said. " 'twas tried once and I mind they turned me down."

I told him my thoughts upon the matter, and still he shook his head.

" 'Twould be a fine thing," said he, "if it might be done, for of late we've had a fine plague o' inspectors, and I tell ye, lad, there is more than one of them is not above marking off a crop of good red pine as white from the King's woods, and confiscating it for their own use. But even could ye get it, lad, 'twould most like cost us more than 'twould be worth."

"D'ye think so?" I cried. "Then I'll not agree with you, for I doubt 'twill cost us more than a hundred and fifty pounds. 'Twould be a small price to pay for protection from such as you describe."

My uncle looked at me still doubtfully.

"And if we cannot get the contract?" he demanded.

" 'Twill still be worth that much," I replied, "and if I should do so well as to get the contract you need have no fear, for there will be profit in't."

My uncle was thoughtful for a long time after that, and sat sipping quietly at his pint of beer. But at last he appeared to come to a decision, and his face cleared.

"Ye may be right, lad," said he; "at least 'twill do no harm to try. But mind ye, pay no more for it."

So enthusiastic was I over this prospect that I returned post-haste to Portsmouth, where I arrived late, having covered the entire distance between Suncook and that city in a single day, stopping only to rest my nag and to take a bite to sup for myself.

When I came to our house in Pleasant Street I found it dark, and I imagined that Dorcas either was out or had retired for the night. In either case I knew that there would be no supper for me there; and as I had a prodigious appetite I drove on to Stavers' in Buck Street, where I anticipated the appeasing of my hunger with a tender duck or a brace of the juicy lobsters for which the tavern was renowned, and the drowning of my thirst in a quart of Stavers' bitter ale.

There was no one in the long, low-ceilinged taproom when I arrived, and it was Stavers himself who showed me to the booth at the side of the room not far from the great fireplace.

"Have ye seen the new captain has come to be Deputy Surveyor?" he asked, as he spread the silver and cloth before me.

"I've been away," I replied.

"His name's your own," he said. "I thought ye might know of him."

I shook my head.

"A Ferguson?" said I. "I had not known there were any this side of the water. Would he be of Balquhidder, now? I have relatives among them."

Stavers shrugged.

"He lodges here," he said, "but I've not heard him say if he's from Bally-what-it-is-ye-said, or where."

"What's he like?" I asked.

"Oh," he replied, "he is o' the army. Tall, wi' dark face and eyes. Well set up, and a nasty set to his mouth, and that about him says he cares not a damn for our small society. Very high and mighty like."

"So!" I said. "And how came he here?"

He shrugged again.

"'Tis said," he replied, "he came from Halifax where he was stationed on half-pay. I've heard he gave four hundred pounds for the post."

"Four hundred pounds, ye say?" I demanded in surprise at the sum.

He nodded, and I whistled.

"He'll need to work fast," I said, "to show a profit on that, for unless I miss my guess there's trouble making in the north e'en now."

Stavers nodded, and I thought of my plan to obtain the warrant. Here was the man to issue it, for undoubtedly the Governor would turn over the handling of such business to him, as he had to Major Young before him; the two of them sharing the proceeds of the office. If Captain Ferguson had been long in Halifax he must know the precarious state of affairs, for by all rumour there had never been peace in Nova Scotia; nor could there be so long as the infamous Abbé Le Loutre lived. This being so he would be doubly anxious to regain his money as quickly as possible, and to that end would be quick to issue warrants to those who were prepared to pay this price.

"Where is he now?" I asked.

Stavers shrugged.

"He'll be out now, I'm thinking," he replied, "but I doubt not he'll be back ere long."

At that moment there came a commotion at the door, and, turning, I saw George Stapleton enter accompanied by Stephen Sparhawk.

Stapleton caught sight of me at once, and, coming over, flung himself down in the seat opposite me. Stavers took their orders and went out into the kitchen to see them filled.

"Have ye seen your namesake?" asked George, a lazy grin spread upon his handsome face.

I shook my head.

"I heard he'd come," I replied. "Stavers was speaking of him but now."

"Ye know him, of course," said Sparhawk.

I shook my head.

"As far as I know," I said, "I have never laid eyes upon him."

"The devil ye say!" Sparhawk exclaimed.

George laughed.

"Now that's a coincidence," he said. "Ye've something in store, my lad. Splendid devil. He's set half the female hearts in town aflutter already, and all the husbands to gnashing their teeth. Be advised by little Georgy, son, and guard your lady from the elegant stranger."

I laughed.

"I've no fear for Dorcas," I said.

George raised his eyebrows and assumed an expression of mock rebuke.

"Hoity-toity!" said he. "Ain't we sure o' ourselves! Wait until ye've clapped your eyes upon this one, my lad!"

"I find it hard waiting," I replied dryly. "He sounds a wondrous sort indeed!"

"Aye," said George, " 'tis what he'd have us all believe, I doubt not."

There came the sound of voices from without, and Stapleton cocked his head and sat listening.

"Unless I miss my guess," he said presently, "you'll have your wish ere long. The man's outside now. I can hear his voice."

The sound of talking outside drew nearer, and almost before George finished speaking the door was flung open and the voices boomed into the room upon a gust of wind.

"In the morning," said someone.

"There he is!" said George.

I turned in my seat and saw a tall man standing in the doorway. His back was towards me, and he was talking to some friends outside, so that his head was turned away and I could catch only a glimpse of a swarthy jaw above the epauletted shoulder of his immaculately scarlet coat.

Beyond doubt here was a dandy. The hilt of the sword that spread his coat tail was edged in gold, and there was an enormous signet ring upon the little finger of the hand that rested on it. The lace at his cuffs was of the finest, and the queue that dangled from beneath his small three-cornered hat was wrapped and tied in the latest fashion.

For all I had said I did not know him, there was something vaguely familiar about him: a sort of arrogant swagger, that set my mind to racing back into the past in an effort to place him.

The touch of a hand upon my sleeve brought me round again to face my companions. It was George, who was upon his feet.

"Rest where you are," he said. "I'll fetch him over."

He was away before I could stop him, and I watched him thread his way among the empty tables and touch the stranger's arm. At that moment Sparhawk drew my attention with a remark upon the sultriness of the weather, so that I did not see the stranger turn in response to George's greeting. Neither did I see them cross the room nor hear their steps approach. I was suddenly startled to hear George's voice booming cheerfully in my ear.

"Here he is!" he said. "Captain Ferguson, may I present our own Mr. Ferguson, late of Suncook, now of Portsmouth?"

I turned and half rose, a word of greeting rising to my lips. But the words I might have said were never spoken, for at sight of the other's face I stood frozen in amazement.

Whether he was as surprised as I, I shall never know. For the barest fraction of a second I thought a blank expression flickered across his darkly handsome features, and for a fleeting instant there was that old furtive look in his eyes. In the next moment a sardonic smile twisted his thin lips, and his strong, slender fingers closed about my own limp hand.

"God's blood!" said he. "This is a surprise! Why, 'tis little Jamie, no less!"

I could find no words with which to reply, but only stood gasping in astonishment. And well I might; for the man who stood before me now, an almost mocking smile upon his twisted mouth, was my own cousin Hubert!

¶ 1 "Hubert!" I cried, as soon as I could find my voice.

George Stapleton, who had stood looking from one to the other of us in surprise, laughed.

"So ye do know each other!" he said.

"Know each other!" I exclaimed. "Why, man, 'tis my own cousin."

"The devil ye say!" said George, and laughed again.

Hubert flashed his twisted smile upon him, showing a brilliant set of strong white teeth, and then coughed discreetly behind an immaculate hand. I had a momentary flash of a white, frightened face; a pale blob in the mist, staring at me across the water as a ghostly brig cast off and began to slip gently seaward upon the black swirling tide. I wondered that this resplendent creature could be the same shivering wretch whom I had last seen that night so long ago.

"It is years since we met," I said.

"Why then," cried George, "ye'll let me stand a drink to your reunion!"

Hubert shot him a sardonic smile and inclined his head ever so slightly.

We made way for him at the table, while George rapped upon the partition of our booth and bellowed to Stavers to fetch a bowl of his most potent flip. My cousin, after seating himself comfortably, removed his hat and set it carefully beside him upon the table, after which he examined the set and condition of his immaculately dressed and powdered peruke in a small pocket mirror which he produced from the pocket of his waistcoat. This done, he gave me a long searching look across the table which missed no detail of my dress.

"Ye seem to have done comfortably for yourself, Jamie," he said.

"Comfortably!" George gave a snort of laughter. "Why, man, the fellow's more than comfortable, I'll warrant ye! Already he's gained a name for himself as one of the shrewdest operators in lumber in the Province. And if Benning Wentworth hasn't got him marked for a partner in a land grab, I'll eat your hat and the lace with it!"

Hubert's eyebrows went up, and he looked again at my plain blue coat. The look of faint amusement in his eyes gave way to one of patent interest.

"So?" he said, softly.

"What of yourself, Hugh?" I asked. "I'd not have looked to see you in Portsmouth—much less in the coat you're wearing."

Again that twisted smile flashed upon his handsome features.

"That would be a long story," he replied.

George glanced at me sharply as Stavers set a brimming bowl upon the table and dipped out four mugs of the bitter flip.

"Will ye want your lobsters now?" said the latter when he had finished.

I looked at the others.

"I was having a bite to sup," I said. "Will ye join me, gentlemen?"

Stapleton shook his head hastily and cocked an eye at Sparhawk.

"Stephen and I have but just finished dinner," he said.

Sparhawk opened his mouth as though to say something, but evidently thought better of it for he caught George's eye and closed it again with a snap. I glanced at Hubert. He nodded.

"Thank you," he said. "I believe I will."

I gave his order to Stavers and bade the latter hold my order until my cousin's was ready.

When he had gone, stumping across the room with his heavy drover's tread, George seized his mug and leapt to his feet.

"I give ye cousins," he cried, "a happy reunion!"

We stood up with him and drank, and as we did so my eyes met Hubert's above the rim of the cup, and the look I saw there seemed composed of curiosity and speculation, with not a little sardonic humour thrown in on the side.

George drained his cup, and it thumped down upon the table. With an ostentatious flourish he drew from his waistcoat the enormous chronometer—which I knew his father had given him upon his latest birthday, and which he took great pride in displaying—and examined it carefully, holding it so that we all might have a look.

"Upon my soul!" said he, "half after nine!"

He bent a frowning glance upon young Sparhawk.

"Come, Stephen," he said, "we must not keep the wenches waiting."

Sparhawk looked blank.

"What wenches?" he asked, in evident bewilderment, then added, "Oh!" and stood up in some confusion.

George grasped him by the arm, winked at me, and inclined his head to Hubert.

"Your sarvant, sir," he said. "Till tomorrow, Jamie."

And with that he turned and whisked his companion out through the side door, and was gone.

When we were alone my cousin and I faced each other for some moments in silence. I could not tell what thoughts passed behind that sardonic mask; but my own were clear enough. Before me rose a picture out of the past: a picture of a foppish, callow youth, a strutting, swaggering, self-centred, would-be beau, with irritating manners and a lofty way of looking down his long swarthy nose at his country cousins. I wondered if the characteristics that had once been so strongly his had since been rubbed off or submerged. Outwardly there had been but little change. Without doubt he had acquired polish. The posturing and braggadocio which had marked his youth had given way to that suave arrogance so frequently to be found among officers of the regular establishment, especially in their dealings with provincials. He had grown taller and had filled out somewhat, so that even had his dark, aquiline features not fulfilled the promise of his childhood, he would still have cut a handsome figure in his bright scarlet coat. He had the form as well as the air of a man born to wear clothes and wear them well, and he had made the best of it. His dress was impeccable.

Of the man himself I could tell but little in that brief survey. He had the manner of one who has seen much of the world and is at home in it. He had the easy air of a man to whom all men are friends. He smiled readily, if thinly. There was a quizzical look about his eyes; yet they could be amazingly frank and open upon occasion. There was that in his appearance which made me understand young Stapleton's reference to Portsmouth's feminine hearts. Indeed, one would imagine that he was more popular with women than with men. Yet I was to find, on further acquaintance, that he could be pleasantly ingratiating among men as well. In short he seemed an extremely presentable and acceptable person. But with it all there was always, behind his eyes, that light glint of mockery, that made me wonder as to his sincerity.

It was Stavers who interrupted this mutual scrutiny and put an end to our silence. He came himself with the lobsters, steaming upon twin platters, which he set before us, and scurried away after the ale.

"Well," said Hubert, sniffing the faint aroma of hot salt and lobster shell that rose from his plate, "who would have thought to see you here?"

I cracked a claw.

"Why not?" I asked, not without suspicion, for I found it hard to believe that this could be coincidence alone. "Had you no idea of where I might be found?"

He gave me his dark smile and shook his head.

"None," said he. "When I came back to Edinburgh the old gentleman said no more than that you had gone to the colonies."

" 'Twas not because he did not know," I said dryly. "He alone in Scotland knows where we are to be found."

"Knew," said Hubert shortly.

"Knew!" I said quickly. "He's not dead then!"

Hubert nodded.

"He's dead," he said simply.

"I'm sorry," I said, as sincerely as I might, and indeed I was truly shocked, for my uncle, though gouty and dyspeptic, was not an old man, and I would have given him many more years of life.

My cousin waved his hand airily.

"Spare your sorrow," said he. "He was aye crabby towards the end."

It seemed scarce a gracious way to speak, but it was no affair of mine. I even wondered if, in his shoes, I might not feel the same.

"You must have a tale to tell," I said, in an effort to swing the conversation into other channels.

He looked at me suddenly, so sharply that I was taken aback.

For a moment I thought he meant to make some reply; but Stavers' arrival with the beer interrupted him, and when the latter was gone he made no move to speak what was in his mind.

"Tom Ogilvie told me how father died," I said, suddenly remembering. "He came back and found the barn in flames— What happened to you?"

His eyes avoided mine, and for a moment he hesitated. I was filled with mistrust of him; but when he spoke his voice shook slightly, and I laid it to pent-up emotion and memory of that night, though I know now that in that I erred.

" 'Twas a near thing," he said. "They fired the barn as I came over the hill, and I thought they'd seen me. Naturally I ran."

"Naturally," I said. "Why did you not come to us in Glasgow?"

"They were on my heels," he replied. "I had no more than time to find a ship and go aboard."

"Aye," I said, "I saw you."

"And I saw you," he replied.

I reached for my beer, satisfied.

"Well," I said, lifting the mug, "here's a pleasant visit."

He seemed to relax suddenly, and when he picked up his mug I saw that his hand shook. He laughed.

We ate our lobsters in silence. When they were done and I had paid Stavers I turned to Hubert.

"It is late," I said, "and I have come a long journey today. We have much to say to one another. Will ye be my guest at supper tomorrow: say, eight o'clock?"

He took the hand I held out, and appeared to think.

"Dorcas will be anxious to meet you," I said, urging him.

He looked at me questioningly.

"Dorcas?" he asked.

"My wife," I said.

He smiled crookedly.

"I see," he said. "We must not disappoint the ladies, eh? At eight o'clock then?"

Dorcas was inclined to be peevish with me the next morning for having stayed so long away from Portsmouth.

"You might have had some thought for me," she complained.

"I'm sorry," I replied humbly, knowing not what else to say, for when angry or upset she had a knack for twisting my words in such a way that anything I said was wrong.

Being unable to find anything with which to quarrel in that simple apology, she merely sniffed and was silent. But when I told her that we should have a guest at supper she rounded upon me.

"Oh!" she cried. "Have you no consideration at all? What if I had already engaged for something else?"

"But you had not?" I asked, laughing.

She tossed her head.

"No," she said hesitatingly, "but—"

"Why, then," I said, "there is no harm done."

"But—" she began.

"Have done!" I interrupted her sharply. "Our company tonight would not interfere with aught else you might have planned."

"And who is this company you've asked for tonight?" she demanded. "Some of your up-country bumpkin friends, I doubt not!"

I laughed.

"Hardly!" I said. " 'Tis my cousin, Captain Ferguson, the new deputy surveyor of the King's woods."

"Captain Ferguson!" she exclaimed. "Not *the* Captain Ferguson?"

I nodded.

"Who else?" I replied.

"Oh!" she cried. "Why did you not say so before?"

"You did not ask," I replied.

She was all contrition at once.

"Oh, Jamie," she cried, "can you forgive me? I'm such a beast at times!"

I kissed her gently and patted her cheek, and she hurried away, then, to the kitchen to give orders for the meal.

It rained that day, a grey, dreary drizzle, turning the streets to rivers of mud, and making deep puddles in the hollows of the walks. Toward evening a wild wind came up from seaward, the skies opened, and the rain set in in earnest. It was a miserable night, and I began to fear lest my cousin might not come.

I was wrong in that, however, for at eight sharp a sedan chair deposited him upon our doorstep. I went out into the front hall, and found him handing his hat and cloak to the serving wench.

He turned upon me with a snarl.

"A fine night you chose to hale me out," said he. "Icod! for tuppence I'd ha'—"

He stopped short, with a little intake of breath, and I saw his glance go past me up the hall. I turned and saw that Dorcas had followed me as far as the drawing-room door, and that she stood there now, the soft light from the room behind flooding out around her, creating a picture of loveliness that might well make any man gasp.

Hubert flashed me a quick look of surprise.

"My wife," I said quickly, suddenly inexplicably confused. "Dorcas, my cousin, Captain Sir Hubert Ferguson."

Dorcas held out her hand, and Hubert went to her, his eyes never once leaving her face.

"I begin to believe, ma'am," he said, bowing low over her fingers, "my cousin has been far more fortunate than I."

The dinner went off much more smoothly than I had any right to expect. Dorcas was a gay and charming hostess, and Hubert was an affable and entertaining guest. He complimented Dorcas upon her table, and me upon the wine. He kept us entertained with endless stories of his adventures, both in the colonies and abroad. Indeed, so pleasant and congenial did he make himself that I began to wonder if I had not misjudged him.

We lingered over the meal, and it was nearly ten when Dorcas finally excused herself and withdrew, leaving us alone with the port between us. When she had gone I filled his glass and my own and settled back in my chair.

"Well," I said, "now we may talk freely at last."

He gave me a dark look as he took a sip from his glass.

"Does it matter," said he, "what's past and gone?"

I shrugged.

"No," I said slowly, "I suppose it does not. Yet I've a natural curiosity to know the things that happened to you from our last parting in Glasgow, and how came you here in the coat you're wearing."

He tightened the corners of his mouth in a slight smile.

"And what of yourself," said he, "or should I ask?"

"My tale is simple enough," I said, and went on then to tell him as quickly and briefly as I might what had befallen me.

"You've had it easy," said he, when I had done.

I smiled, but made no reply. He picked up the bottle and replenished his glass, then sat for some moments savouring the aroma of the rich old port. I rang for another bottle. When it had come, and the serving wench had withdrawn once more to the kitchen he began to speak.

"Well," said he, "to begin with where we left off, we made a quick passage to Lisbon. We were not stopped upon the way, though there was a King's ship hailed us off the Rinns, and I tell you I knew fear then."

He paused a moment there, and chuckled at some reminiscent thought.

"I did not lack for ready cash," he went on, "when I went ashore. If you remember, I was even then a fair hand at the dice, and on the voyage I found the crew not backward to try their luck with me. I found my pockets fair filled with Portuguese moidores, and 'twas these eased my way through Spain to France.

"I had company in Paris. The city was become overnight a Scottish capital, and as we had all been in arms together it was all very fine. At first it was not hard to get along. There were the dice and the cards, and the French were free enough lenders, so long as there was any prospect of another expedition. But after a time, when this began to appear out of the question, things began to grow somewhat more difficult. 'Twas then I thought to write to my father, despite his warning that if luck went against us I could look for no help from him.

"Either the letter I sent to him, by the hand of a friend, did not reach him, or his mind was not to be swayed by my plea. At any rate, I got no reply. Things went from bad to worse, until in the end I grew desperate. I was in debt. My clothes were old and shabby. I had not two shillings to rub together in my pocket. Had it not been for the kindness of a certain lady I would surely have starved. Even she turned from me in the end, her fancy being taken by an Irish dog with the tongue of the Devil who poisoned her heart against me."

He paused and sighed gustily, and in that sigh I read not so much a broken heart as wounded self-esteem.

"In these circumstances," he continued, "I began to toy with the thought of taking service with the French. But on the morning of the very day I meant to present myself at the barracks, I received a packet, in my father's hand, which enclosed a sum of money and a letter in which he told me that he had managed to procure my pardon from the King, and that if I were prepared to forswear my allegiance to the Pretender, and take oath to support the House of Hanover, I might return once more to Scotland.

"I believe the old man had really missed me, for there were tears in his eyes when he met me upon the quay in Edinburgh. It was the only tender emotion I ever saw him display."

He paused and gave me a quick look.

"He told me then," he went on, "that Kintulloch had been forfeit and had passed to him, as the only loyal member of the family."

I laughed a little bitterly.

"Loyal!" I cried. "There was no loyalty in't. He knew which side his bread was buttered."

Hubert shrugged, and smiled cynically.

"He played the right horse to win, you mean," said he.

"Call it what you will," I said, " 'twas treachery!"

My cousin laughed.

"If 'twas treachery," said he, " 'twas to my advantage. He settled a small allowance upon me, and stipulated only that I find some decent occupation to fill my time.

"I had no stomach for the bank. And as you know I was never aught but bored at Kintulloch. I made inquiries and found a captaincy was vacant in Lascelles', and this I persuaded him to purchase for me. I think he would have preferred that I remain with him, but after Paris I found Edinburgh deadly dull. Fortunately I was able to plead my new duties, though these were by no means as arduous as I made them to be, and the result was that I spent most of my time in London. I played a lot at White's, where I came off winner as often as not, though to do this I was forced to borrow heavily against my future. For my allowance was too miserably small to allow me to live decently as a gentleman should. When, at the end of two years, father died I found that there was not much left.

"As I said, I had never any great affection for the business, and as this also passed to me at his death I determined to dispose of it. This I did, to good advantage, to an Edinburgh syndicate, and forthwith returned to London with money in my pocket.

"For a time I played successfully, but in the end I had a run of miserable luck; and one morning I awoke to the realization that by selling my horses, and my niggers, and everything else that was of value I might just pay my debts and escape with a few paltry guineas to my name. As luck would have it, it seemed that nearly all of London was aware of this condition in my affairs. When a man's luck is down, you know, there's none will lend a farthing on his chances. There was nothing left for me to do. What remained of my fortune I risked at White's upon the turn of a card with young Freddie Cavanaugh. My luck was in, and I won. But the young fool fancied he saw me cheating, and I was forced to kill him to vindicate my honour.

"It was my misfortune that those who were with us at the time were mostly Freddie's friends, and these started rumours flying until, I tell you, I was put to it to maintain my position. When it was over I would not have cared to remain in London even had I been able to afford it."

"Do you mean," I cried, shocked at his callous recital of the business, "you shot him down in cold blood?"

He gave me an angry look, and drew himself up.

"My dear fellow," he said in a supercilious tone, "nothing so crude! I gave him six inches of cold steel in the guts in Lincoln Fields at dawn, as honour demanded. And the bastard died cursing me for a cheat to the last!"

"Was he altogether wrong?" I asked, unable to resist voicing that small part of my thoughts.

He bounced to his feet in a fury.

"Do ye call my honour in question, sirrah?" he demanded.

I grinned up at him.

"I would be no such a fool," I replied, "I am no such a fine hand with the steel as yourself, I misdoubt. Besides you have the reach of me."

He sat down then, still eyeing me balefully, but I could not but notice that despite his defiance he could not make his eyes meet mine. I pushed the bottle across him.

"Go on," I said. "What happened then?"

He poured himself another drink and drained it before replying.

"There was not much I could do," he said at length. "I thought something of returning to Kintulloch, but hearing that the Forty-seventh Irish were about to be sent out to Halifax, and that some of the officers did not relish the thought, I contrived to have myself transferred to that regiment. I have been in Halifax ever since."

"Well enough," I said. "But that does not explain how you came to Portsmouth."

He gave me a crafty look.

"Major Young had a nephew in Halifax," he said, "a lieutenant in Phillips's. The major meant that he should succeed him, and I doubt not 'twas all arranged to that end. But Arbuthnot—that's the major's nephew—could never keep a good thing to himself. He talked too much in the mess."

He paused significantly.

"What do you mean?" I asked.

"Why," said he, " 'tis plain enough. 'Twas too good an opportunity to allow to pass. As soon as he mentioned the vacancy, and boasted that he would have it, I took steps to find out how much he would bid upon it. When I had that information, 'twas all I needed. I wrote at once to your governor, applying for the place and overbidding him."

"But, your fellow officer!" I protested.

He waved an airy hand, and gave a loud snort of derision.

"God's blood!" cried he. "Would you have me be completely a fool? He was but a silly young jackanapes who knew not how to keep his mouth shut; a man without the sense to make the most of his opportunity! 'Twas a scramble raising the money, but I managed one way and other, and here I am."

I wondered what had been the methods by which he had managed but he made no move to enlighten me, and I did not press the matter.

I was not a little shocked at his recital. To be sure, there was little in it that was directly in his disfavour. Many a man has been unjustly accused of cheating. I had not sufficient knowledge of the fact to judge that matter on its merits; and certainly such an accusation could scarcely be satisfied but on the field of honour. It seemed to me that there were allusions to several affairs that were none too savoury. And yet I bade myself remember that his life had not been, like mine, a life in which the right path was always clearly indicated. He had experienced extremes of fortune that might have tried the patience of a saint. And who was I to say that in his shoes I would not have done the same? After all, he was not the first to sow wild oats. He was not the first young man to run through a fortune before achieving the sober judgement of maturity. I told myself that I must not judge him too harshly.

"Well," said I, after a pause of some moments, "we are glad to have you with us."

He gave me again a twisted smile that was full of mockery, and suddenly I felt false and insincere. I flushed and started to rise.

"Shall we join Dorcas?" I mumbled.

But he reached out and laid a hand upon my arm.

"One minute," he said, "did I understand our friend last night to say that you operated extensively in lumber?"

I nodded.

"From the stump?" he asked.

I nodded again, wondering what was in his mind.

"You and I can make a good thing of this," he said.

"What do you mean?" I demanded.

"Why, 'tis plain as your nose," said he. "I see to it that you receive the warrant to cut the King's woods—at a price. I also see that no other warrants are issued in the Province. No one else will be able to supply the navy's needs. You and I will share the profits."

He sat back with a superior air of condescension and waited for my reply.

Here was the thing that I had been trying to persuade my uncle that we should have, practically thrust upon me, yet I cannot say that I received it with enthusiasm. There was a side to the arrangement that I did not like the look of. I shook my head, for my decision was quickly taken.

"I'm sorry," I said. "We do very well without the warrant. I doubt if we could take care of such an increase."

"God's blood, man!" he cried. "Are you plain fool? 'Tis the greatest opportunity that's like to come your way!"

"Are you fool yourself?" I replied. "Do you think it will not be obvious to everyone what's happened? Our names will be linked as 'tis. Such a combination would be the ruin of us both."

He smiled derisively.

"I might've known," said he, "that your first thought would be for your reputation, Jamie. Or is it just your native caution?"

"Call it what you will," I replied stiffly, "I care not. There are some would call it honesty."

He gave a snort and shrugged.

"Ah, well," said he, "there will be others not so scrupulous, I misdoubt."

I shrugged.

"No doubt," I said, "if you are foolish enough to persist in such a course. But 'twill pay you, cousin, to consider the possibilities. You may profit for a time by such an arrangement, but do you think the Governor is like to let it continue once he has heard of it?"

He laughed.

"Benning Wentworth," said he, "strikes me as a man who will allow anything for the sake of a dollar."

"I'll not deny that," I replied, "but remember this too; Benning Wentworth is a knowing man. If you show him the way to dispense with you at a profit to himself, you may cheat yourself."

He gave me a sudden sharp look.

"Igod!" he exclaimed, "Jamie, you've a better head on you than I thought. 'Tis a possibility I had not considered."

"Consider it then," I said.

With that I rose and led the way into the drawing room, where we found Dorcas awaiting us.

"I thought you would stay the night there," she said, as we entered.

Hubert bowed.

" 'Twould be a privilege to spend the night beneath the same roof as yourself, ma'am," he said gallantly, "even if 'twere to sleep upon a table."

She flushed at the compliment.

"Where are you lodged now, Captain?" she asked.

He pulled a long face.

"At Stavers'," he replied, "but I must confess I find it none too comfortable."

She threw up her hands in polite horror.

"Oh, la!" she cried. "Why, 'tis disgraceful! James Ferguson, what can you be thinking of to let your own cousin be so poorly lodged? Captain, you must move in with us at once, until you can find lodgings more suited to your taste. I could not think to let you stay another night in that awful place! Say but the word and I will send our black Pomp for your things."

He bowed gratefully.

"'Tis most kind of you ma'am," he said. "I should be most pleased to accept. But tonight—"

She made a move towards the bell at her elbow, but he reached out his hand and stopped her.

"But not tonight, dear lady," said he, I thought something over-hastily. "That would be too much."

"Oh, no!" she began.

But he was firm.

"Shall we say tomorrow?" he asked.

"You'll not go back on us?" she said. "After all, 'tis but right you should be our guest."

He bowed.

"Tomorrow it shall be," he said.

They both looked at me expectantly.

It had come so abruptly that I scarce knew whether or not I approved the invitation. Yet on the face of it Dorcas was right. It should not be said that my door was ever closed to my own flesh and blood. Even had I disapproved there was naught I could say.

"By all means," I said.

I thought he smiled a little derisively before he turned from me to bow his head above her finger tips. I accompanied him to the door and helped him into his great cloak. With his hand upon the doorknob he paused.

"Good night, cousin," he said, and I saw the mocking lights had come on again in his eyes. "Till tomorrow."

He turned to go, and then turned suddenly back again.

"Oh, I say!" said he, "I am a bit short at the moment—don't know if I've enough to settle with Stavers. Would you make me a small loan—say fifty pounds? There's a good lad!"

It was on the tip of my tongue to refuse this final bit of impertinence, yet I could not bring myself to do it.

"I'll send it to your lodgings in the morning," I said grace-lessly.

"Thanks," said he, and bowed, and again I saw that mocking glint in his eyes, and the sardonic twist at the corners of his mouth.

"Until tomorrow, then," he said, and in the next instant he had turned and was swallowed up in the darkness of the night.

2

It must be said at the outset, in justice to myself, that I was none too pleased with the turn which events had taken. As a child I had felt no great affection for my cousin. Even then I had felt instinctively his fundamental selfishness and insincerity; and now, as a man, I found him matured perhaps but otherwise not greatly changed. There was not the least doubt in my mind that he was a rogue; albeit a rogue of somewhat admirable qualities, for he was honest in his roguishness, at least. He took no pains to disguise his egotism or to hide the fact that he made no move without first consulting his own interest. His own story, told in his own words, was scarcely reassuring; and he had told it with a devil-may-care gusto which in itself conveyed a warning to those who heard him of what they might expect at his hands. It is hardly to be wondered at that I mistrusted him.

There was little I could do about it, however. After all, he was my cousin, and my wife had done the only natural thing in inviting him to our home. In the morning, although I did so, I fear, with rather bad grace, there was naught for me to do but to send black Pomp with a purse and a letter and the trap to fetch Captain Ferguson back to the house.

If I expected aught unpleasant, however, I might have spared myself my misgivings. From the very day of his arrival beneath our roof Hubert was a changed man. He was affable. He was gay. He was witty. He minded his own affairs, which were few enough. Overnight, it seemed, he dropped his sardonic pose, and adopted a confidential one in which he hinted that the world had used him badly. This, knowing the man, I was inclined to discount, for I held that for his misfortune he had none but himself to blame. Dorcas, however, took it all in, and was frankly sympathetic.

Indeed, between them, there soon sprang up a spirit of friendship and camaraderie, which I was glad enough to see—for it improved Dorcas' temper to have someone to amuse her—and which surprised me not at all. The man was far and away the most colourful figure our small community had seen, and I knew that it pleased Dorcas to bask in his reflected glory. He took her riding and walking and entertained her in a thousand little ways. He squired her to parties which I was unable—or unwilling—to attend. For me it was an ideal arrangement, for he had all the taste for gay society which I lacked, and which Dorcas so demanded. My friends might wag their heads behind my back, but I had no fear. I was not such a fool as to place much faith in Hubert. I knew that family scruples would have but little influence upon him, were he inclined to play the part of gallant lover. But I had perfect faith in Dorcas, and so long as it amused her to play with him I saw no possible objection. Hubert was not of a kind to take the attentions of any woman so seriously that a rebuff would mean more to him than wounded vanity, and this I felt might have a salutary effect.

His attitude towards me also seemed to undergo a change. He was no longer patronizing, but instead became affable and friendly, the complete personification of good-fellowship. Only once after his coming did he refer to his scheme for monopolizing the King's timber, and when I firmly refused to have anything to do with the affair, he dropped all further mention of it. Neither did he carry out any of the alternatives which I feared he might. It would have been a simple matter, by plaguing us with his inspectors, to force us to come to some agreement with him. Perhaps he did not see the possibility. At any rate, he did not act upon it. Instead he became very much interested in our affairs, questioning me closely about the business and our methods of operation, what was my part in it, what did it return me annually, and so forth. Much to my gratification, he allowed himself to be guided by my judgement, for I pointed out to him that the best way for him to regain his purchase money was to issue warrants to all who could show a bonafide contract to supply naval needs on the basis of a percentage of the profits therefrom. He seemed to consider this fair enough, though I must admit that even this seemed scarcely honest to me. However, so long as our system of purchase of public office remains in force, there can be no end to such evils.

It was in this way we obtained our warrant, for I had the good fortune to receive, from Colonel Meserve, contracts for masts, and timber for two King's ships which were to be constructed in his yards.

Nor did Hubert's efforts to please stop there. Almost, he seemed to make a deliberate effort to prove that I had misjudged him. He went out of his way to gain my trust and affection. If we sat late of an evening over the port, the next afternoon he would appear with three or four old bottles to replenish my cellar. Once, returning from a hasty trip to Boston, he brought Dorcas a dozen pairs of fine gloves, and myself a new fowling piece of handsome workmanship. As time went by I found my doubts of him disappearing. I caught myself, more and more often, wondering if I had not, perhaps, judged him too harshly.

I do not mean by this that he was entirely changed. Outwardly he remained the same. All his little irritating airs and mannerisms, he retained. He assumed an attitude of mild contempt for our provincial society. His tongue continued sharp and ironic. But with all this he conveyed the impression that it was but a pose, and that beneath his hard exterior there beat a heart that was great and warm and filled with gratitude for our hospitality.

I was not a little surprised, at first, to discover this, and was somewhat inclined to mistrust it. But as time went by and he grew daily more frank and open, I took shame to myself for such unworthy thoughts, confessed myself convinced to Dorcas, to whom I had at first recounted my misgivings, and accepted him as one of ourselves.

I found also, to my surprise, that he displayed an active interest in the country and the people; and on more than one occasion I took him with me on business trips. On these excursions I endeavoured to teach him something of the finer details of his own work, pointing out the ways in which the laws pertaining to King's woods might be avoided, by those who wished to avoid them, as well as the ways in which unscrupulous inspectors might cheat honest people of their rights. Thrice during that fall and early winter he accompanied me to Suncook, where he renewed his acquaintance with my sisters, and showed great interest in our joint holdings. On these occasions we frequently spent one or more days hunting, and about this I found him surprisingly enough quite enthusiastic. He proved himself an excellent shot at the birds, but with a musket on deer he was well-nigh helpless. In spite of all his enthusiasm, however, I could not but note that he was always happy to return to the gaiety of Portsmouth, and no sooner had we settled in again than he and Dorcas would be off upon their round of parties, with myself tagging along upon occasion, just frequently enough to please Dorcas and to keep tongues from wagging.

It was early in February of that winter that the colony was set by the ears by an affair which to my mind reflected little honour upon the English and their relations with the Indians. This was the murder of the two Indians Sabatis and Plausawa by a white resident of Stevenstown, one Peter Bowen. Although I had no connection with this affair, beyond my own acquaintance at first hand with the unsavoury characters of the principals involved, its effect upon me, both immediate and remote, as a member of the community, was such that an account of it could not well be here omitted.

As may be recalled, during the spring of 1752 the two Indians, Sabatis and Christo, after spending some days in the homes of Josiah Miles and James Lindsey of Canterbury, suddenly slied away after stealing two negroes; the one named Tom, belonging to Mr. Miles, and the other named Peer, the property of Mr. Lindsey. Three days after their departure the negro Tom, having managed to make his escape, returned, his arms bound behind his back, a living witness to this piece of Indian treachery.

Needless to say this affair, coupled with the infamous attack upon the trapping party in which Dan Stinson had so untimely lost his life not long before, aroused the northern settlements to a fever pitch of indignation. This indignation became impotent rage when in the following spring Safatis returned, this time with Plausawa, and once again demanded shelter of Josiah Miles.

There can be no doubt that there were many in the settlement who would have been overjoyed at the opportunity to deal out to these scoundrels the punishment their arrogance deserved. Fear and sober judgement, however, prevented; for those who knew Indians and their ways saw only too plainly that such a course would bring swift vengeance from their brothers in the north. It might be thought strange that Josiah Miles would be willing to take them once again into his house. But Miles himself explained this, reasonably enough, saying that he feared to offend them lest one day returning from his work in the fields he find his wife murdered and scalped and his house in ashes.

All during that spring and summer the Indians were, off and on, unbidden guests in Josiah's house. They ate his food. They drank his rum. They wrapped their stinking blankets about them and slept off their drunken stupors upon his kitchen hearth. Not infrequently they threatened both himself and his wife with violence.

The climax was brought about one morning, not long after the first of August, by Mrs. Lindsey, whose black Peer had never returned, having been sold at a good price to a French officer at Crown Point. Hearing that Sabatis was then at the house of Josiah Miles, Mrs. Lindsey put on her shawl and set out to give the "red villains" a piece of her mind. Now Mrs. Lindsey had a considerable reputation in the town as a woman who was quite able to speak her mind on many subjects, and frequently did so. I have heard it said by some that hers is without a doubt the sharpest tongue north of the great bend of the Merrimack. There is no doubt that she made good use of her powers upon this occasion, for Josiah Miles returning home from the fields for his dinner found Plausawa standing over her in a threatening posture with a hatchet held suspended above her head while Sabatis held his own wife terrified in a corner, his long knife naked at her throat.

This was too much for even the mild-mannered Josiah. He promptly grasped his musket, and pointing it at the two Indians ordered them at once from the house.

As may be imagined, they were in a sullen mood when they left, taking with them their packs and such furs as they had left and two of Josiah's best Sunday shirts. They went straight to the river, and set out upstream in their canoe. A few miles north, in the lower part of Stevenstown, they met with two white men, Noyes and Thorla by name, who had come up from Newbury in search of some cattle that had been turned out to graze that spring. These two, thinking it likely that they might meet with some Indians with whom they might be able to trade, had brought with them a supply of rum for that purpose. They did not know Sabatis and Plausawa, and when they saw them asked if they had any furs to trade. At first the Indians said they had none, but after some talk admitted that they did and offered to trade for rum. By this time, however Thorla had had an opportunity to observe their mood, and he refused to deal with them. They were angry, but, seeing that the white men were determined to do no business with them, they turned and went.

It was not long after this that the man Peter Bowen appeared, returning to his home in Stevenstown from Contoocook. Noyes and

Thorla told him of the Indians and warned him against them, but he, having already more rum in his belly than was altogether good for him, announced loudly and with great bravado that he "was not afeared of any savage that lived," and that he would "druther fight an Indian than eat."

Some time later, Noyes and Thorla, going to the house in Stevenstown where they were to lodge for the night saw Bowen, accompanied by the two Indians, staggering towards his own house, a heavy jug in either hand. For the greater part of that night the sounds of a great carousal issued from the Bowen cabin. But that was the last time that anyone saw either of the Indians alive.

No one, however, thought to be suspicious of their sudden disappearance. Those who gave it a second thought merely assumed that they had arisen early and gone on their way before anyone else in the town was stirring.

Unfortunately Peter Bowen was not the sort of man to keep such a business to himself. Twice accused of thievery, and rescued from conviction only by withdrawal of the charges, Bowen was himself none too savoury a character. He was an enormous man, heavily bearded, with a frightfully twisted nose; a braggart, a blusterer, a bosom companion of such men as Shem Sanborn and Joseph Merrill, and most emphatically of their sort. Having done the deed, he could not resist the temptation, when next he came to Contoocook, of getting thoroughly drunk and bragging about it.

According to the tale he told in the presence of witnesses, after taking the two Indians into his house he proceeded to fill their mugs with rum until they were in a state of some considerable befuddlement. When, after a time, he thought them sufficiently moistened, and their suspicions allayed by the warmth of the liquor in their bellies, he got up, excused himself on the grounds of nature, and staggered from the room. Once in the hall, however, he merely opened and slammed again the outer door to make it appear that he had gone outside, then, quickly turning, took up the Indians' muskets, which they had, with careless faith in their host, left standing in the vestibule, and drew the charges from them, leaving only their primings intact. With this much accomplished he slammed the outer door again and returned to the room in which his wife was entertaining his savage guests. There they continued their carousal until the small hours of the morning.

In spite of the late hour which they had kept the night before, the Indians, the next morning, expressed a wish to make an early start upon their homeward way; and Sabatis persuaded Bowen to help them by carrying their baggage on his horse to the place by the river where they had left their canoe.

To make the story brief as possible, they had not gone far when Sabatis proposed to run a race with the horse. Bowen, being himself a man of considerable guile, suspected some treachery upon the Indian's part, and insisted that Sabatis take a head start. They ran about a quarter of a mile, and on the way Bowen, by holding his horse in check, allowed the Indian to keep in front of him. Sabatis seemed much amused that Bowen's horse could run no faster, and made a great joke of it. After that he went along in apparent good humour for some distance without speaking.

When at last they came near where the canoe was left, Sabatis again proposed a race, suggesting that this time the horse be unloaded of the baggage and be given a head start. Bowen refused the advantage but agreed to start even. No sooner were they away, however, than the Indian dropped behind, and Bowen, hearing a snap behind him, turned to find the other's musket pointed at his head, and a tiny wisp of smoke rising from the priming pan. The charge having been drawn the night before, of course, the weapon missed fire; and Sabatis, seeing himself caught in the act, flung it aside and ran for his life. The horse, which had been so slow before, now proved as swift as death. Before the Indian had gone a dozen steps Bowen had ridden him down, and after hacking him several times in the back with his hatchet until he fell, Bowen dismounted and finished him off with a chop across the neck.

So much being done Bowen knew that there was yet Plausawa to deal with. Leaving Sabatis lying in his blood in the pathway, he went back to meet the other. Plausawa, seeing him coming along the trail, realized at once that Sabatis had failed, and, without hesitation, he too threw up his musket and pulled the trigger. Once again the weapon merely flashed in the pan, and Plausawa finding himself in exactly the same position as had Sabatis, a few moments before, went down on his knees and begged for mercy.

There was no softness in Bowen's heart, however. The lust to kill was upon him. Moreover, he knew that there would be no peace for him so long as Sabatis' companion lived. Without a word he raised his hatchet and split the other's skull.

His deed accomplished, I presume he grew apprehensive of the consequences. He made some slight attempt to hide the bodies beneath a small bridge near by, washed the blood from his hatchet and his clothing, and returned home with the Indians' packs and weapons to prove that murder is not entirely without profit.

If this business itself was amazing, the public reaction to it, once it became known, was even more so. Overnight Bowen found himself transformed, from a man who had every right to fear the shadow of the hangman's noose, to a popular hero—a public benefactor, who had rid the community of two dangerous reptiles, and who, had the people had the power to enforce it, would have received, through the assembly, a bounty for his good work.

To understand this it should be borne in mind that the affair came as a climax to a long series of treacherous and hostile acts, committed by the Indians themselves, despite the peace which they had pledged themselves to keep, and which had aroused the English to a fury of indignation. Revenge was sweet, and the man who had obtained it was the hero of the hour.

There were some, however, and of these I was one, who recognized the possibilities of the business. It was inconceivable that the Indians of Saint Francis would allow the murder of two of their number to pass unavenged. Neither was it likely that they would be satisfied to take the life of the guilty man alone. I for one was suddenly very thankful that I did not live in Stevenstown. In my opinion the only move that could prevent retaliation was the swift trial, conviction, and hanging of the murderer; not because I was the least in sympathy with two such villians as Sabatis and Plausawa, but rather because I felt that only thus could we demonstrate to the Indians our own good faith, and so, perhaps, keep peace. Surely the life of such a scoundrel as Bowen was but a small price to pay for the peace of a province.

Popular opinion, however, was all against this point of view, and from August until the following February no move was made to see justice done in the matter. Indeed, the move was made then only because Governor Shirley of Massachusetts, hearing of the affair in a roundabout way, became suddenly alarmed. It appeared that about the first of February Captain Lithgow, commanding at Fort Richmond, on the Kennebec, wrote to Governor Shirley that the Indians were restless, and that it had come to his ears that they were determined to take the warpath and avenge the murders. Shirley, who customarily took the lead in such matters, wrote at once to Benning Wentworth, forwarding the affidavits of several citizens of Massachusetts, who had been visiting in Contoocook at the time, and who had heard the story from Bowen's own lips, and recommending that justice be done immediately.

Now, as everyone knows, Governor Wentworth was always quick to heed the recommendations of his good friend, the governor of Massachusetts. Indeed, there were many—no friends of his —who referred ironically to New Hampshire as a province of the Bay Colony. However that may be, Governor Wentworth acted promptly upon the recommendation. A warrant was issued for the arrest of Bowen and another, John Morrill, who was said to have had some small part in the affair; and the two men were brought to Portsmouth and lodged in the jail.

Such a hubbub of excitement as this move created can scarce be imagined. The entire Province was at once split into two camps— those who supported the Governor, and those who opposed him— with the opposition far and away in the majority. The date of the trial was set for the twenty-first of March; and on the day before, the town was jammed with those who had come from all parts of the Province to hear it. There were some, however, who came for another purpose. Near midnight on the twentieth about a hundred of these, neighbours of Bowen, for the most part, from Rumford, Contoocook, Canterbury, and Stevenstown, gathered before the jail, smashed in the doors, and turned the two men free.

What happened then is a matter of record which I need not repeat in detail. Bowen and Morrill disappeared from sight. An abortive and half-hearted attempt was made to arrest the leaders of the mob. On the recommendation of Governor Shirley, Benning Wentworth attempted to appease the Indians' wrath with presents to the dead men's families. The results, of course, were inevitable. The Indians took the gifts in good faith, and at once set about a series of raids at Stevenstown which did not cease until almost a score had been killed or carried away in captivity, and the settlement abandoned for the second time. But it was an occurrence of the night of the rescue which, insignificant though it seemed at the time, was for me at least to bear most heavily upon the future.

There was little sleep to be had in Portsmouth that night, what with the shouting and hurrahing up and down the streets and about the jail. Hubert and I went out about midnight and watched the break from across the way, for it was well known what was to happen; after which Hubert suggested ale and lobsters at Stavers' before retiring. I was nothing loath, for the combination of late hours and cold night air always seems to produce in me a prodigious appetite. Accordingly we made our way thither and pushed our way inside.

Stavers' low-beamed taproom was packed near to overflowing, and we were put to it to find a table. A wink at Stavers, however, did the trick and in a few moments we found ourselves seated at a small table in the corner at no great distance from the short bar.

Stavers took our order quickly and pushed away, promising that we should have our lobsters in next to no time. Scarce had he disappeared in the crowd, however, when someone lurched heavily against our table, and I turned to see Shem Sanborn standing unsteadily over me; beyond the least shadow of a doubt very much the worse for liquor. I had known that both he and Merrill had found work as drovers between Portsmouth and Rumford, but I had scarcely thought to see them here. Now as I looked up Sanborn stood sneering down upon me belligerently, teetering drunkenly back and forth, the while his friend Merrill stood close behind him eyeing me uncertainly and plucking nervously at his elbow. But Sanborn was not to be distracted.

"B'Jesus!" he hiccuped. "Here's a bit o' luck! And what do ye think o' this night's doings, me lad?"

" 'Tis a sorry piece of work," I said coldly, "and a disgrace to the Province, to my way of thinking."

"Christ's blood!" he cried. " 'Tis what I would ha' thought ye'd say, ye poor lily-livered louse, ye!"

And with that he launched into a foul stream of invective, cursing me and my ancestors in no uncertain terms. I listened to his filth for a moment in silence, until I saw curious eyes begin to turn in our direction. Then I lifted my mug of ale, and flung its contents in his face. He reeled back a step, then shook his head in

amazement. The foolish, drunken grin which he had worn until
then was wiped from his face, to be replaced by a twisted expression of rage and hatred. In the next instant he gave a bellow of
fury and lunged forward. But at that moment Stavers' black Cas-
sius, whom he kept in reserve for just such an emergency, burst
through the surrounding crowd and grasped him about the neck
from behind.

There was a brief struggle, but big as he was Sanborn was no
match for the enormous negro. As if by magic a way opened
through the crowd, and he went skidding ignominiously across
the floor and out the door to the accompaniment of howls of merriment from the assembled company.

Hubert watched the performance with a curious eye. When it
was done he turned to me.

"You've an enemy, it seems," he said simply.

I nodded, and told him he had guessed rightly.

"Who is he?" he asked.

I told him what I knew of the man, who he was, how we had
met, and of the various encounters which gave Sanborn the right
to dislike me.

"H'm-m!" he said thoughtfully, when I had finished. "I do not
envy ye. He has the look of a bad enemy about him."

What reply I might have made to this, I do not know, for at
that moment our lobsters arrived, and I for one turned my attention to them, forgetting the affair, and giving Sanborn no further
thought.

3

It has been suggested, by certain of his political enemies, that
the real reason why Governor Wentworth failed to act in the matter of the murder of the two Indians, until he was prodded by
Governor Shirley, was his preoccupation with schemes of land
speculation, which blinded him to certain of the finer aspects of
his official position. Whatever might be the truth of this I could
not say. I do know, however, that he was deeply interested in land.
He had but just realized the possibilities of the thing, and was
like a child with a new toy. Although his manipulations had not
yet reached the proportions which they were to assume in the late
fifties and early sixties, just before his death still he had worked

out his system even then, and already, in the years since 1750, had approved the grant of ten townships.

His system was simple and effective. As soon as the report of a good tract of land reached his ears, he would send to have it surveyed and its possibilities reported upon. When this was done he would call in some of his friends, in number anywhere from six to twenty, and to these he would propose the formation of a company to develop the site. These friends, forming a nucleus, would bring in others of their acquaintance, to a number seldom exceeding thirty or forty. A petition for the grant of the tract in question would then be drawn up and presented to the assembly. Here it usually passed rapidly, as a matter of course; for it was the policy of that body to pass all such petitions whose proprietors were able and willing to abide by certain provisions of the law; namely, that a road be built within a reasonable time from the nearest established settlement to the tract in question, that three free lots be set aside for the building respectively of a town hall, a church, and a school, that two lots be assigned as a cemetery, and that a minister and a schoolteacher be maintained there at the proprietors' expense on lots to be designated for their use. A time limit was also imposed, usually six to ten years, in which a certain number of families must be settled within the town or the grant be forfeit. Both to meet this time limitation and to attract others to the land, it was frequently the custom for the proprietors to offer a certain number of lots free to any who would agree to settle upon them. The rest they were free to sell at whatever price they could obtain. The Governor's interest in all this, and the anxiety he showed to see the land granted, were due not only to a substantial fee on each petition granted, but also to the fact that he was empowered to set aside a reservation of five hundred acres of the best land for himself.

It was not long after our arrival that, at one of the sumptuous levees which he so frequently held, the Governor surprised me by taking me aside into a small anteroom where, after questioning me closely again about my travels in the upper part of the Province, he asked me point-blank if I was possessed of any nonsensical scruples concerning this matter of land speculation.

Now, although I had had no experience in the business myself, I had a number of acquaintances who had. Archibald Stark of Derryfield, father to John and William, the late James Rogers,

Rob Rogers' father, and a number of men whom I knew in Rumford had tried it on a small scale, and I had observed that in each case it had proved profitable. I had often thought about it in connection with our own business. In my capacity as spotter I had had ample opportunity to observe the upper valley of the Merrimack and the lake region to the east of it, as well as the valleys of the Pemigewasset and the Asquamchumauke. My journey in company with Stiles and Toby had opened my eyes to the amazing fertility and undoubted value of the Upper and Lower Cohos intervales and the valley of the Connecticut. I knew that there were many who looked upon speculation as something unscrupulous, but this viewpoint struck me as absurd. I observed that those who had the opportunity to speculate were prompt to take advantage of it.

Something of this I told the Governor, and he laughed to hear me so outspoken and clapped me upon the shoulder.

"Would ye be interested," said he, "to take a hand in a project which some friends of mine are sponsoring? I think it might be managed."

I replied that it looked an excellent thing to me, and said that I should be glad of the opportunity; to which he answered that he would see what could be done about it, and thereafter led me back into the ballroom, where I saw no more of him until it came time to take our leave.

I gave the matter little thought, for in truth I hardly believed that aught would come of it; but within a week he summoned me to a conference, which was attended by several others of his friends. And when the meeting had adjourned I found myself, at the cost of some hundred pounds, old tenor, included in a list of petitioners for the grant of a town to the north of Stevenstown to be called New Chester.* Before the winter was over I found myself included in two more: Lower Ashuelot† and Marlborough.

If I was at a loss to account for this sudden burst of generosity on the Governor's part, I was soon to be enlightened as to its causes. It appeared presently that favourite among his projects was the exploitation of the Connecticut valley to the northward of Number Four, most particularly of the rich intervales of the Upper and Lower Cohos. The Lower Cohos he had already had

* Now Hill.
† Now Swanzey.

surveyed, and a road thither had been laid out and was even then under construction; a fact greatly resented by these Indians who looked upon these intervales as their own particular hunting grounds. The Upper Cohos he knew, as yet, merely from hearsay, though the descriptions which had come to his ears must have been glowing in the extreme to account for his excessive enthusiasm. As I was one of the few men in the Province who had visited that region, and perhaps the only one in Portsmouth, I began to realize why he had singled me out for his favours.

He came to the point in the early spring, when work upon the road to the Great Oxbow * had just been resumed. He summoned me to his chambers and asked me if I did not think the time was right for the development of the Upper Cohos. I replied to him that in my opinion any further northward expansion at the moment would be likely to bring about fresh displays of hostility on the part of the Indians. Indeed, I said that it would surprise me greatly if the moves already made towards the settlement of the Lower Meadows did not produce some such demonstration. I added, however, that I was confident of the future of the region, and that some day I felt it would be well worth his attention.

He appeared to think this over for some moments, pacing up and down the small room, one hand held behind his back, the other tugging at his great pendulous lower lip, and a scowl upon his heavy features that told me he was none too pleased with my report. Presently he turned, however, and planted himself ponderously before me.

"There will be others aware of this?" he demanded.

I nodded. "Undoubtedly," I said.

"Why then," cried he, "would it not be wise if the land were surveyed and granted now, lest someone else recognize its value and forestall us?"

"But," I protested, "the grant will be forfeit. 'Twill be years before a settlement can be made there."

"Ye may leave that to me," said he. "I will suggest to the assembly that in this case, owing to the difficulties involved, the time limit for settlement be extended."

"In that case," I said, "there might be some advantage in it."

He beamed upon me and slapped his ponderous belly in satisfaction.

* Lower Cohos.

"Good!" he exclaimed. "If ye've some friends would care to have a share in it, bid them be here a fortnight hence. We'll form our company then."

I was not the least unwilling to do his bidding in this. I have already told something of my enthusiasm for that north country, and here, it seemed to me, was the opportunity that I had hoped would one day be mine to have a hand in its development. We formed a company of fifteen, which included many of my friends; among them Stephen Sparhawk, Robert Rogers, John and William Stark, George Stapleton, and Warren Ames. To add stability and the weight of prominent names, Meshech Weare, Jotham Odiorne, Samuel Langdon, Theodore Atkinson, and Nathaniel Meserve were invited to participate. At our first meeting the amount of the bond which each would be required to post was decided upon. It was also determined that, before any petition could be drawn up and presented, the proposed site should be surveyed and accurate markings established. Since we wished to keep our plan as much as possible to ourselves until such time as the petition could be presented to the assembly and passed upon, it was considered best that this work be entrusted to no outsider, but should be carried out by volunteers from among our own number.

This decision did not allow great latitude of choice. Besides myself the only one of us who had ever been there was Rob Rogers. He was thoroughly familiar with every step of territory from the Kennebec to Lake Champlain, and from the great bend of the Merrimack to the Saint Lawrence, and even beyond. Certainly he was better qualified than I to act as guide. As luck would have it, however, personal affairs prevented his making the journey, which meant that, whether I wished it or not, I must go.

As a matter of fact, I was glad of the opportunity to escape from Portsmouth, which I had begun to find exceeding dull, and to get back to my beloved woods. And when Stephen Sparhawk volunteered to accompany me as surveyor, I was delighted.

But if we looked for a quick departure, we were destined to be sadly disappointed. No sooner was our decision taken than the Indians made the first of their attacks upon Stevenstown, whence they carried off Nathaniel Maloon and all of his family save one; the eldest son, who was working in a near-by field, saw the Indians seize his father, flung down his hoe, and escaped into the woods.

When news of this was received in Portsmouth the Governor would not hear of our leaving, and accordingly we delayed our departure for some weeks. Then, the word being given that all was clear, and that we might be on our way, it turned out that Sparhawk had undertaken some business which he must complete. When this was done I, in my turn, delayed matters with a trip to Hampton, where I had a lumber contract to renew. It was August before we were ready to go again; and again the Indians delayed us with a second attack on Stevenstown, in which they killed a man and a woman, and carried off two others captive to Canada.

I have rarely seen a man so indignant as was the Governor at this news. He fretted and fumed and stamped about his chambers in such a dudgeon that for a time I feared he must succumb to apoplexy. He swore that he would sweep the Indians from the Province; and though it seems a shameful thing to say, I must confess that he seemed more enraged at the delay it caused us than at the death and capture of a few unknown settlers. Within three days he had called out the militia and posted two troops of horse and a company of foot at Number Four. In spite of this, however, the Indians continued their mischief, and early in September it became necessary to abandon Stevenstown. This, it seemed, satisfied the savages for the time being; after one or two more appearances in which they did no damage, they drew off and were seen no more.

By October the trouble seemed over. It was late to undertake such a journey. Nevertheless, it was essential that the survey be made as soon as possible in order to prevent any other group from laying a prior claim, and if it were to be made that year it must be at once. Accordingly, though the Governor protested it, on the first of October Sparhawk and I announced our intention to be off.

All the while that this was going on, my own affairs at home had undergone a subtle transformation. Although it was not a thing that I could put my finger on, I was none the less aware of an indefinable change; of an incomprehensible air of tension and strain, for which I was at a loss to account.

Hubert had been with us for something over a year, and so much one of the family was he become that his presence seemed the most natural thing in the world. His manner toward me continued ingratiating and beyond reproach. He even went so far as to make

me a confidant and an accomplice in his manœuvres to escape
the attentions of Portsmouth's giddy belles, who, he complained,
would give him scarce an instant's peace, and with whom he professed himself bored to distraction. In this he always excepted Dorcas, of course. She, he said, was the loveliest of creatures, and he
invariably added with a great sigh that I was a lucky devil to have
made such a catch. He professed to envy me greatly; though in this
I wondered if he were not merely being polite; for with the rest
of our townsgirls he was not the least flattering in the private opin-
ions which he unfolded for our ears alone, comparing them most
unfavourably with the beauties of London and Bath and Tun-
bridge Wells.

It was Dorcas who worried me. During that winter her manner
changed imperceptibly. She grew snappish and picking, returning
almost to the nagging way she had had before we left Suncook.
Try as I might, I scarce could please her. She found fault with
everything I did or proposed to do. Nor did she confine her criti-
cisms to the privacy of our own chamber, but frequently spoke so
shortly to me in Hubert's presence that he was constrained to take
my part against her, and stand up in my defence.

This of course was a gradual business, starting about Christmas
time, when it seemed my choice of presents was unfortunate, and
nothing I had bought for her seemed to please her. From then on,
it grew steadily worse. I thought that perhaps she was growing
bored, as women will, with her surroundings; and that perhaps a
change might do her good. Accordingly, when Hubert announced
in April that business would take him to Boston for a fortnight, I
sent her with him to shop and visit with friends and relatives in
that city. On her return, however, she was, if anything, worse, so
that I could not but feel that I might have saved my money.

The prospect of my northward journey seemed a matter of indifference to her. But as the summer dragged along and I did not
go she grew more and more morose and moody, and developed an
unaccountable streak of nervousness and irritability. She greeted
each tentative announcement of our departure with the sharpest
sarcasm. I grew frankly worried about her, but there was nothing
I could do would please her. She would have none of my attentions. The best meant words met with sharp retorts, and my every
utterance was twisted to a meaning I never intended. Indeed, if
the truth be known, it was she who was largely responsible for my

final determination to go before the snow flew; for, the thing weighing naturally upon my mind, I spoke of it, I suppose, more frequently than need was. One day at dinner she flew out at me furiously.

"In God's name," she cried, "why don't ye go and have it done with?"

I looked at her in amazement. Hubert, who was with us as usual, chuckled.

"One would almost think by the way you speak," he said, "that you wished to be rid of him. Beware, Jamie! The lass may have a lover!"

She turned upon him, and for a moment I thought she meant to snap at him too. But instead she remained silent, and her mouth drew down to a thin, tight line.

"If 'twill please you," I said—somewhat stiffly, it is to be feared, for my patience was nigh exhausted—"I will!"

And with that I excused myself and withdrew in search of Sparhawk. The next evening I was able to announce the definite date of our departure.

With so much settled the air grew somewhat clearer. I was extremely busy, putting my affairs in order for my absence, and it frequently happened, in the week that followed, that I did not get home for supper. On these occasions it was my habit to drop in to Stavers' for a bite to sup late in the evening. It was on such a night that I was surprised, upon entering the taproom, to see my cousin Hubert seated at a table near the fire, with Joseph Merrill at his elbow.

They were evidently deep in conversation when I entered, but at the sound of the door they both turned and looked up. Merrill was plainly startled, and made as if to go hurriedly. But Hubert caught him by the sleeve and dragged him back. His words came loud and clearly to my ears.

"And mark ye!" he said threateningly. "If aught of harm comes to my cousin through you, I shall see you hanged, my lad!"

And with that he released the man with a slight shove that sent him scurrying on his way.

"Here's strange company for you," I said, dropping into the chair that stood vacant across from Hubert.

"The fellow'd heard that you were going north," he said. "He tried to find out from me your route and the day of your leaving."

"The devil you say!" I exclaimed. "And how could he have heard of it when there's none but Stephen and myself and the others of our company that know it?"

He shrugged.

"I told him naught," he said.

He knew naught beyond the day and our ultimate destination, but I did not think it worth while to remind him of this. If he thought he had done me a favour with his threat, it was kindness to let him continue of that mind.

"That's a fellow you should watch," he said. "I'd not trust him beyond my sight."

I thanked him with some dryness, and said I had no fear of that precious pair. I reminded him that I had had some dealing with them in the past, and that I had no high opinion of their wits. He said he was pleased to see that I took their hate so calmly, as it showed me in a good courageous light—at which I laughed and said that if he but knew it I had about as much courage as a field mouse.

Nevertheless, although I made light of it, I was glad of the warning, and gratified to have been able to discover what my old enemies were up to. There would be sufficient danger in this business, I felt, without their adding to it. I spoke of it to Sparhawk, and he agreed with me that, in the light of this, it would be a wise thing to slip away quietly and to make all haste upon the road. Accordingly, in the dark hours before the dawn of a morning, two days before our scheduled departure, we crept down to the river bank and gently lowered our canoe into the water.

Only Hubert had come down to see us off. I gripped his hand and bade him farewell.

"Look well after Dorcas," I said. "The lass has worried me of late. I leave her in your hands."

He smiled that peculiar twisted smile of his and looked at me, though in the dim light of the stars I could not see his eyes.

"You may count upon me," he said. "I will take good care of her."

Ten minutes later we were heading northward up the river, in the foggy dark. The landing place was lost to sight behind us, and there was no sound but the rhythmic chunk and splash of our paddles as we dipped them in the inky water.

AMBUSH

¶1 Young Sparhawk was an excellent strong paddler, and we travelled swiftly at first. By the time the high, cold light of the approaching dawn had driven the last pale stars from the sky we were already nearing the mouth of the Newichwannock, up which we were to turn.

Our way lay up the latter and into the Salmon Falls to the three ponds at its head, whence a long carry would take us across to the waters of Great Winnepiseogee Pond; a route I had chosen, not only because it was the most direct water road, but also because it seemed to me that Sanborn and Merrill, expecting me to pay a visit to Suncook in passing, would be less likely to watch it.

In spite of our haste, however, it took us four days to reach Winnepiseogee; partly because there were more carries than I had anticipated, but mainly because low water made upstream poling difficult and often impossible. Indeed, more frequently than not we were forced overside to drag our flimsy craft up through the shallow rapids.

Once in the Great Pond, however, and clear of all possible pursuit, we were able to proceed at a more leisurely pace. Another three days took us over the carry to Great Asquam Pond, and down through Little Asquam and the outlet to the Pemigewasset. From here we pushed on northward up the Asquamchumauke and over the long carry to the Connecticut. As we approached the broad meadows of the Great Oxbow we moved more cautiously, lest we find there some lingering band not yet returned to Saint Francis and their Canadian haunts.

But, as it proved, this was unnecessary. We swung down from the hills, and the great valley opened before us and lay spread out at our feet. In the bottom meadows the ripe river hay made golden splashes in the afternoon sun along the banks. The hillsides, already touched with frost, arose on either hand like walls of flame, shot through with red and gold and orange; here and there the deep green of a single pine or a clump of spruces, blended a touch of sober contrast to the dazzling display of colour. No sound save the whisper of the mighty river far below broke the stillness. Save a flock of geese, winging their way southward high overhead, there was not a sign of life to be seen. Throughout the length and breadth of the valley no smoke rose in the still air. There were no tracks on the carry trail or by the river's edge. Only the month-old ashes of an Indian fire on a spit of sand at the mouth of a brook betrayed the fact that man had ever been there.

In spite of these reassuring signs we did not relax our vigilance. Experience had long since taught me that Indians were most likely to appear when least expected. Not until we had passed the mouth of the Passumpsic did we breath freely, for this was the usual route by which the raiding parties from Saint Francis came to the Connecticut. Even then we did not cease to go warily, for they had been known to take an alternative way down through the lakes at the head of the Connecticut.

Three weeks, almost to a day, after our departure from Portsmouth, we poled our canoe up through the last short stretch of rapids at the head of the fall, and came out into the great sweeping bends and long still reaches of the Upper Cohos. The last thirty miles, from the mouth of the Passumpsic, had proved the hardest of all. In the two and a half years since I had passed this way, I found that my memories of it had dimmed. I had forgotten that long sweep of swift water that tumbled down, mile after mile, close hemmed between steep wooded hillsides. We had come down swiftly then, riding easily if precariously upon the crest of the flood with no more effort than an occasional flip of a paddle or swing of the body to keep us upright and true in our course.

But now we had to pole against that same current; slow, laborious, back-breaking work. And to make matters worse, although the other rivers along which we had journeyed had been still low after a summer of drought, early autumn rains, far in the north above us, had raised the Connecticut to its springtime level, and filled the long narrow chute from bank to bank with rushing, tossing, growling, roaring, white-capped, roily water. For three days we struggled against the stream, fighting our way inch by inch, step by step, upward; a pole jammed between slippery rocks; a tense moment when time hung trembling in the balance, and it seemed uncertain if we would go forward or be swept back; then a slow agonizing gain of a yard or so, the other pole jammed among the rocks, and the performance repeated, again and again, hours without end. Breaking our camp with the dawn each day, gathering sticks for our supper fire in the dark, we counted ourselves lucky to make ten miles a day.

It is scarcely to be wondered at, then, that when at last we left the ceaseless thunder of the rapids behind, and came out from between the dark encompassing hills into the broad meadows and rolling pine flats of the intervales, the place seemed a veritable haven of peace and beauty to us. It was fine to be able to speak again in normal tones; to hear the whisper of the light wind in the spruces; even just to listen to the silence. No longer did steep forbidding slopes threaten us on either hand. We were able, once more, to see beyond range of gunshot. To east and west the lush, gold-brown meadows spread, backed at a little distance by the cool green of the pines, and topped, still farther beyond, by the hills, rising in gentle curves, their flanks aflame with autumn colour. Before us the river lay, calm and flat, its current barely perceptible against the ruffling breeze. A few alders, hanging from the western bank, dipped their black branches in the blacker water, and their coarse leaves, dried now and curling at the edges, rattled lightly in the wind. In the deep water beneath the high overhanging east bank, a monster trout rose greedily to a piece of floating bark, sucking the dark surface in smoothly without a sound, and sending a ring of ripples widening in all directions. Beyond a bend in a marshy shallow, where a tiny spring-fed brook entering made a sort of backwater, a great blue shitpoke * stood upon one leg and eyed our approach solemnly for a moment before spreading his wings and leaping off into graceful, slow, laboured flight.

When we landed upon the west bank and climbed the steep shoulder of a high hill that rose sharp at the head of the fall, the whole valley lay spread at our feet, stretching away as far as we could see; the sleek black river twisting and writhing down its length, crossing and recrossing the bottom, turning and doubling upon itself, like some enormous serpent. Northward, in the middle distance, a mountain looming on the west bank thrust a massive shoulder out to force a bend; while farther beyond, and a

* Heron.

little east, two identical bald-topped peaks thrust abruptly skyward, closing off the view beyond. Westward the hills came closer
in upon the river, rising steeply from the level of the meadows.
But on the east the flats were wider, more extensive, and behind
them the slopes rose, more gently at first, and then sharply and to
greater heights, until they became in themselves small mountains.
Over the tops of these mountains, and through the clefts between
them, we could see, away to the south and east, other, greater
mountains, range upon range, marching away, one behind another, into the distance, their caps already tipped with snow, their
sides brilliant with colour.

We spent a long time on that hillside, carefully searching every
inch of the country before us for any sign that others were in the
valley. But as far as the eye could reach not a thing stirred. Unless
they had been warned of our coming, I felt sure, there were no
Indians there. No smoke was visible against the hillsides or hanging in the shadowed bottom. No birds rose in wheeling flocks to
reveal a disturbing presence. Within earshot, no squirrels or jays
scolded.

My guess proved correct. Though we returned to the canoe and
pushed on northward, following the sweeping curves of the slow-
flowing river, we saw no sign of human occupation. A paddle of
nine miles or so brought us to the mouth of the little river, upon
whose banks Stiles and Toby and I had camped before. Here we
turned away from the main stream and pushed our canoe across
the flats and as far up the bright, gin-clear waters of the tributary
as was comfortable. There we camped at the point where the little
stream tumbled out from between steep hills. It was an ideal site,
for the water was clear and cold, and there was a level spot beneath
the tall pines beside it, high enough so that it was unlikely to be
flooded in the event of a sudden rise in the water, and low enough
to be protected from the wind in case of a storm. Moreover, I
viewed it with particular satisfaction because it was located well
off to one side, and any savages passing up or down the river would
be unlikely, unless they smelled the smoke or were otherwise
warned, to suspect our presence.

Our camp was quickly made. We unloaded the canoe upon the
stony shingle, and cleared the ground above. Sparhawk set to
gathering great armfuls of fragrant balsam tips for our beds, while
I hastily knocked together a rough open-front brush and bark

shelter. Then, while Sparhawk built a fireplace of stones, which he carried up from the brook bed, I set about collecting wood for the night's fire. Next day, after taking Sparhawk to the summit of a near-by hill where he set to making a rough map of the valley and familiarizing himself with its landmarks, I came away, leaving him there, and went to work to get in a good supply of dry, clean birch and maple, that our fires might be as hot and yet as near smokeless as was possible.

In the days that followed we were both kept busy with our own appointed tasks. As much as I was able I helped Sparhawk with the survey, though this was slow work, as it required two pairs of hands; and I, as cook, guide, and chief provider, was required to spend at least half my time at other and, to my mind, more enjoyable matters. There was the woodpile to maintain, and the larder to supply. But in the end we worked it out to some sort of system, helping each other on alternate days, he running his lines on one day and I setting my snares and hunting or fishing the next.

Almost immediately the problem of supplies came heavily to the fore. Although we had come well supplied with such staples as flour, meal, bacon, tea, and the like, we had depended upon the country for fresh meat, and as hunter for the party I soon found the going difficult. During my previous visit I had found game plentiful enough, though even then I believe the cycle must have been well started on its downward trend, for now I needed all my skill to find the game, to say nothing of bringing it in. Foxes there were, and wildcats a plenty; and sometimes at night long after we had retired we would hear the wolves howling upon the hills across the river, though none of them ever came near enough to bother us. But edible game was almost as scarce as hen's teeth. By hunting far back in the hills I managed to kill a bear, whose fat I tried out on the spot, and whose coarse rank meat required two trips apiece to pack to camp and a day's parboiling before we could eat it. Acorns were scarce, and there had been no beechnuts that season, which might have accounted for the absence of the deer along the hardwood ridges. And though I scoured hill and dale it was four days before I came upon a sign, and a long week before I could drag into camp a small spikehorn buck. During the time we were upon the intervale I shot but one other deer: an old doe, whose meat was rank with the flavour of the alder buds upon which she had been feeding. Rabbits, too, were scarce, and though I set more than a dozen snares for them in the most likely spots, I caught no more than twenty in all the time we were in camp; of these, nine were mangled or devoured in the traps by fox or wildcats before I came. Partridges were as yet plentiful enough but wild, so that they were difficult to approach, and though I blazed away at many of them I missed more than I hit, and I came in time to have considerable respect for the sagacity and cunning of a bird which I had heretofore only regarded as stupid. One thing alone was plentiful and easily to be had. The river teemed with trout and salmon; and fish, in all the forms in which it may be prepared, quickly became the one staple article in our diet.

For five weeks we stayed in that camp, taking our time with the work. As the days went by, the nights grew longer and sharper, until in the last week before we left we found ice in the brook in the morning when we went down to wash and fill our kettles. Twice in that time we had days of heavy rain followed by high winds, which stripped the leaves from the trees; first the birches, then the maples, and last of all the oaks, so that in the end the valley appeared as when I had first seen it, all brown and grey and bare.

Sparhawk did his work well. He ran his lines high on either side of the valley, down to the head of the fall and up to the mouth of a sizeable, dark-watered stream that seemed to flow from the very flanks of the twin bald peaks that rose in the north. He laid out town lines with blazes, taking particular pains to mark well the corners; a great pine here on the bank of the brook, a peculiar flat-topped rock there upon the hillside, a great red oak with a three-way fork elsewhere. He drew maps of the proposed sites, as well as maps of the valley and the country round. And at last, one day, it was done.

That was a cold morning, the coldest we had had, with dull threatening skies and scarce a breath of wind. There was the smell of snow in the air, and I remember thinking that we were likely to see some winter ere we saw home again. Sparhawk had a few last details to clear up before we left, and while he was attending to these I broke camp and packed the duffel in the canoe. It was not much of a task, for we had but little equipment, and we had run through nearly all our supplies. I was done before he had gone an hour from the camp, and because our supplies were so low I decided, rather than wait and shiver, to try once more for a deer. Even a small one would see us comfortably through.

About a mile north of our camp there was a small stream flowing down out of the hills into the Connecticut. A little way up this stream there was a marshy pocket in which such deer as were in the country seemed to like to gather, for more than once I had seen their tracks there. It was my plan to hunt along the ridge behind the camp and drop down into the hollow to see if I could not jump one. The whole walk, going and coming, should not take above an hour, and if I started anything I felt that I could use my judgement as to whether or not I should follow it.

I set out carelessly enough, but had not gone above two hundred yards when I was startled, in passing through a little thicket, to come upon a spot where something heavy had lain out. From the way in which the young growth had been trampled I did not think it could have been a deer, but the ground was hard at this point and I could not be sure. I thought likely it had been a bear, though I could see no sign beyond the trampling to indicate this was so. Since it was obviously not what I was looking for, I paid but slight heed to it, and went on my way, presently forgetting it.

My luck in the hollow was about what I had expected. There had been deer there the night before and early that morning. But by the time I arrived they were all gone, and their tracks leading due eastward toward the mountains indicated that they were bound for other parts; indeed might already be there, for all I knew.

I returned to camp, where I found Sparhawk awaiting me, and we sat down to a meagre meal of the last of our smoked venison and corn bread, washed down with icy water from the brook. When we had done I suggested that it might be a good plan to take a long start, and to work as far down the main river toward the head of the falls as we could, so as to be able to run through the entire stretch of fast water on the morrow.

Sparhawk agreed to this suggestion and we pushed off at once. We were in excellent spirits, full of the pleasant consciousness of work well done. We had accomplished all that we had set out to do, and, as far as we knew, no one had so much as guessed our presence in the valley. At first I had kept a sharp lookout. But as the days had gone by and there was still no sign that any other human soul had come within miles of our camp, I had relaxed my vigilance somewhat, and taken to searching only along the river bank for signs that a canoe might have been landed. But no such signs had appeared; and of late, with the winter season approaching, and the threat of snow growing ever more real, I had grown perhaps somewhat negligent, for I felt that no Indians would be likely to venture so far afield so late in the season.

We made our camp that night at the mouth of the little river that flows down from the west and falls into the Connecticut at the head of the long stretch of swift water below the Cohos. On the way down I had shot a squirrel, which I meant to use for bait, and remembering a deep pool a little below the end of the first fall, I determined to drop down in the canoe and try my luck.

It lacked an hour of sunset when I left Sparhawk gathering firewood, and, ballasting the canoe with a rock in the bow, and taking my fishing pole, dropped down on the current the half-mile or so that separated our camp from the pool. My luck, it seemed, was with me at the outset, for no sooner had I baited my hook with a strip of the dark, red, squirrel meat and dropped it into the boiling eddy at the head of the pool than it was taken with a heavy rush by a good-sized trout; and for the best part of twenty minutes I had my hands full of the effort to bring him, flapping, ashore. After that, however, an hour passed before I felt another strike. Then, in quick succession, I landed three more; two trout that might have weighed two pounds apiece, and a small grilse of perhaps six pounds.

The sun had long since set, and the twilight shadows were growing deeper when I brought the last fish out upon the rocks. A light, almost nebulous mist had begun to rise from the surface of the pool, and when I looked off downstream I could see it hanging in thin white streaks in the blue dusk against the dark background of the spruces. As soon as I saw it I carried my fish down to the canoe and put away my hook and line; for it has been my experience that, when the mist rises from the water of an evening the trout and salmon cease to feed, the fisherman might as well start on his homeward way. He will take no more fish that night.

With the canoe lightened of its baggage it was no very difficult trick to pole it up through the stretch of rapids above the pool. I kept in close against the east bank, having it in mind to stay there until I had reached the sharp bend above, where a clear little stream tumbled down out of the eastern hills. There I meant to use the sweep of the current around the bend to help me cut across to the west bank, and take the straightaway along that shore to the camp.

By the time I had reached the bend, however, it was nearly dark. The current that came sweeping down was swift and treacherous, and even alongshore I was finding it difficult to see the rocks upon the bottom, let alone find a foothold for my pole. I decided quickly, that it would be hazardous to attempt the crossing here, and that it would be wiser to continue on up the east bank to the dead water above the fall, where I could cross at my leisure. It was a simple, sensible thought, and one that was but the result of ordinary intelligence. Yet upon just such slender threads do all our lives depend. Had I clung to my original design it is highly doubtful if I should be alive today to tell it.

At the point at which we had camped, the river came down in a great sweeping loop like the upper half of the letter S, flowing first straight out of the northeast, then twisting about to flow almost due east. At the bottom of this loop the brook upon whose bank we had camped came dropping down from the west, so that its course formed an almost straight line with that of the river below the bend. At the point where their waters joined, there was a deep V-shaped bay, where the river current meeting that of the brook formed a sort of back eddy and a small whirlpool. A short, stumpy point of land thrust down between the brook and the bank of the river. This point was high and covered with brush, and its banks were steep and the water beneath them deep. There was no landing place there. But on the south bank of the brook, where the waters met, there was a narrow sandy shingle and a level strip of woodland between the river and the steep hillside behind. It was a good landing place, and an excellent camp site, and it was here that we had made our camp. Across the river was a wider sand bar, on the inside of the curve, but there the water was shallow and the landing not so good. Moreover, it would have been necessary, to reach a possible camp site, to clear a way through thick willow scrub. Below the bar the water again grew deeper, and the banks on either side were overhung with alders, in whose tangled branches drifting brush and debris had caught. Fifty yards or so below, the dead water quickened and plunged over the head of the incline into the long stretch of boiling rapids that continued, broken only by occasional pools, to the mouth of the Passumpsic, miles below.

It was dark night when I poled the canoe up over the last sharp pitch of swift water, and with a hearty shove sent it gliding free of the sucking current, and into the dead water. As I laid aside the pole and took up the paddle I could look up the stream and across to the camp. A bright fire burned against the backlog, casting eerie shadows among the trees beyond. Against its light, at the water's edge, I could see Sparhawk's figure silhouetted where he crouched, industriously washing a pan in the shallow water.

As I looked it came over me that there was something strange about the scene—a faint, indefinable premonition that everything was not as it should be. For one thing, the fire was much too big. At the start of our expedition I had had to curb Sparhawk's boyish tendency to build great roaring campfires too hot to approach, let alone to cook over. But once I had pointed out this difficulty to him he had almost leaned over backwards in his efforts to keep them small—at least until I had prepared the meal. Now, however, he had tossed on great armloads of wood, until he had built up a bonfire that was a veritable beacon.

Neither could I understand why he should be washing a pan. I myself had washed all our cooking pots before packing them away. There should be no need to wash anything, yet there was no doubt that this was what he was doing. Not only was he washing it, but he was doing an unnecessarily thorough job of it and taking an impossibly long time. He would take a handful of sand and scrub and scrub on one side, and then turn it over and do the same upon the other. After this he would repeat the performance. And all the while it was apparent that he was giving it but little thought, for from time to time he would raise his head and peer off anxiously through the darkness in my direction.

All this I saw in the few moments it took to pole the canoe clear of the rapids and take the first two or three strokes of the paddle in his direction. The thought which occurred to me naturally was that perhaps he was worried about me. I had been some time gone, and it would not be strange if with the coming of darkness he had begun to grow anxious. I had the canoe, and had any accident occurred in the heavy water below, it was not only likely that I should be drowned but also inevitable that he would be left stranded in the heart of the wilderness without transport and with the scant supplies: a situation distressing enough in itself, but doubly so in the face of approaching winter. This could explain his apparent uneasiness, and I leapt to the conclusion that such was the case. The roaring fire, the waiting at the waterside, the anxious watching, were all the acts of a man in the first stages of panic at being left alone in the wilderness. My first instinct, no sooner had this thought occurred to me, was to reassure him of my safety. I stood up in the canoe and shouted.

"Hallo!" I called. "Did you think me lost?"

If I expected an outburst at the sound of my voice, I got more than I bargained for. He jumped to his feet wildly, and began to make frantic gestures in my direction, the pan upon which he had been so diligently scrubbing still clutched in his hand.

"Go back!" he shouted. "Go back, in God's name! Get away quickly! Indians—"

I heard no more, for at that instant the brush along the shore on both sides of the camp seemed to burst into flame, and the crash of shots drowned out whatever words he may have said.

Out of the corner of my eye I saw a figure rise from the brush behind him, the red and white and yellow paint with which its face and chest were hideously daubed standing out plainly in that sudden blinding flash of light. I saw an arm rise and fall, and saw Sparhawk go down in a heap upon the wet sand. At the same instant the air about me was filled with a sound of rushing and buzzing as if a swarm of angry bees had been suddenly loosed about my head. I felt the canoe lurch beneath my feet as a slug ripped splinters from the gunwale. The wind of something passing felt cool upon my cheek. There was a sudden searing pain across my side. Then, all at once, a smashing blow on the shoulder knocked me off balance. In the next instant I was floundering in the water.

I never knew how cold water could be until that moment. For what must have been the barest fraction of a second I was completely immersed, and in that moment the cold which caught the breath in my throat and stopped the gasp that rose involuntarily to my lips was like a blow to the belly. It seemed an age that I was under water, yet when my head broke the surface, the canoe, floating bottom side up, was no more than three yards distant. Instinctively I splashed in its direction, and quickly discovered my mistake, for instantly more shots rang out along the shore. Again the air was filled with that ominous buzzing, made doubly wild by the high-pitched whine of ricochetting bullets upon the water. A ball struck beside me, splashing my face, and I drew a deep breath and dove quickly.

It was difficult to move in that icy water, let alone hold my breath, and yet, with my life depending upon it, I managed it somehow. With the clearness that sometimes comes to us in moments of great danger I remembered the brush-choked alders that lined the east bank. If I could but reach these there was a bare possibility that I might yet escape unseen. By a bit of good fortune I was not more than a dozen feet from them at the time the first shots were fired. I made a swift calculation of their direction, and still beneath the surface, swam towards them. My lungs seemed bursting, and I could feel my very vitals growing numb with the cold. It seemed impossible that I could make it, yet there was no alternative. Let me but show my head again upon the surface and I was a dead man. I had no wish to die, even though it seemed inevitable that I must either drown or freeze if I did not come up soon. But such is the urge that drives us that, even though it seemed I could not bear it another instant, still I kept on. And just as I thought that at last I must give up and open my lips for that gasp of air for which my lungs were screaming, my groping fingers touched the slimy bark of a thick alder. I prayed hastily that I might be well in under the brush, and with such caution as my haste would permit I thrust my head above the surface and sucked greedily at the sweet cold air.

2

I found myself well within the fringe of brush that hung down from the high bank, not completely concealed, perhaps, but so far back that the slight disturbance with which I had broken the surface passed unnoticed by those across the river. The far shore, a moment ago so quiet and innocent appearing, had suddenly become apparently alive with yelling, whooping warriors. Some were running off downstream along the shore with torches in their hands. Others crashed through the brush towards the campfire. Two canoes appeared suddenly at the mouth of the inlet, and set off with quick strokes down-river in pursuit of my own overturned craft. On the strip of sand where he had fallen I could still see Sparhawk lying, a motionless, inert lump against the flicker of the fire. None of the Indians paid him the slightest heed.

As quietly as I could, and being careful to make no more disturbance than I could help, I moved back among the brush and debris until I felt that I was well hidden. The water here was about four feet deep, so that I had to half crouch, half kneel, in order to lie still with only my head above the surface. The five Indians in the canoes passed me rapidly going downstream. The others crowded in by the campfire, and I was at once struck with the smallness of their numbers. At their first volley it had seemed to me that there must be hundreds of them. The shore, I thought, must be lined with them. But now, in the light of the fire, there seemed to be no more than fifteen or twenty in all.

As I lay and watched, numb with the cold, I had ample time to think what had happened. It was obvious that the attack had been planned, for they were in full war paint, and I knew that such preparation was not to be accomplished in a moment. Indian vanity made each brave as particular of his appearance, before partaking in a raid, as the flightiest belle on the night of the Governor's ball. I knew that often they would spend hours gazing at their own reflection in some still pool, while they fussed and fumed to see that each hideous daub and slash was marked just so, and that the colours, red, green, and ochre, or even plain black and white, were of just the correct shade.

Perhaps it was this hint that sent my thoughts ranging back over the events of the day for some sign that I might have missed, and suddenly as sunlight breaking through the clouds I thought of that trampled thicket on the hillside behind our camp that morning. Intent as I was then upon bagging a deer, I had carelessly passed that warning by. With scarce a thought I had attributed the broken twigs and crushed ferns to a bear. Now I saw how negligent I had been in my judgement. Not for almost a month had I seen any sign of bear about our camp. And I knew the reason well enough. With the approach of winter they had drawn back onto the high hills, searching out rock caves and windfalls in which to hibernate, making their preparations for the long winter's sleep. Had I thought about it carefully this must have been my conclusion. No wild animal had trampled that thicket. Rather, the indications were that even then our enemies had discovered us, and were only awaiting their chance to attack.

In all likelihood they had not long been aware of our presence. Probably the discovery had been made by a lone scout who had gone back then to their camp to report his discovery. Perhaps they had meant to attack us there, and were only awaiting the opportunity to find us both in camp at once, when our own departure had forced their hands. At any rate, it was apparent that they had followed us down the river, and had decided to attack the moment they had observed our landing. Evidently they had not seen me go off in the canoe, and had arrived to find Sparhawk the sole occupant of the camp. Indianlike, they had apparently decided that I might be lured in by an appearance of innocence. Doubtless they had forced, or attempted to force, Sparhawk at the point of their muskets, to foster that appearance while they lay in ambush for my return. But in his own way the latter had tried to warn me. That was the meaning of the great fire, of the vigil at the waterside, of the ceaseless scrubbing. When he saw that none of these was effective he had risked his life to call to me! I blessed him beneath my breath, and prayed that they had not killed him.

It could not have been above twenty minutes—though to me it seemed as many hours—before the savages who had gone off downriver returned with my canoe. As they approached the shore they held aloft a paddle and a soggy something which I presently recognized as my own beaver-skin cap. The others crowded down to the shore to meet them, and for some moments they all stood there in deep discussion, some gesturing vigorously downstream, the others shaking their heads in violent disagreement. I gathered that some maintained that I had been carried down by the current, while the others thought that unlikely, and wished to continue the search for me.

Presently two braves got into a canoe with torches and pushed across to the sand bar. They climbed up through the willow scrub onto the bank, where, after a moment's hesitation, they turned and came in my direction. It was apparent that they meant to search the brush, and then and there my labouring heart almost ceased to beat. By sinking in the water so that only my nose and eyes were above the surface I could hide fairly effectively beneath a tangle of sticks and twigs that had caught in the mass of alders. I was shivering violently, however, with the cold, and the greatest effort of will could not keep me still. There was a light breeze blowing which counteracted it to some extent, but which I thought would be scarcely enough to hide from their sharp eyes the ripples which my shuddering body sent forth along the surface. Even if they overlooked this I doubted if they could fail to hear the clicking rattle of my chattering teeth. I was afraid to submerge myself entirely for fear I might come up too soon, and, by the disturbance I must make in so doing, betray myself to them.

I watched them approach until they stood upon the bank over me, the dim light of their flickering torches casting grotesque shadows among the branches of the alders and out upon the surface of the water. For a moment they stood directly above me, and I thought that they meant to come down through the brush to the water's edge. But their Indian laziness saved me; and after a minute or so, in which they both stood peering down intently through the tangle of boughs, they turned and moved off downstream.

So great was my relief that I almost cried out. Then all at once I saw a new danger. They had not cared to work down to the water's edge at this point, but if they did so at any point below my discovery was equally certain. I was losing much blood from the wounds in my side and shoulder, and it was plain to me that this must discolour the water below me. So long as they stayed high upon the bank their torches, which were but feeble, would only reflect upon the surface, without showing any difference in the colour of the water. But let them once come down close enough to the water's edge to see the blood and it would be all over with me.

For what seemed hours I lay and watched the light of their torches flickering and bobbing below, and awaiting so tensely their shout of triumph that I almost forgot to shiver. Then presently, all at once, they appeared to give it up and went back, cutting across the meadow above to the canoe.

If I thought that I had lain a long time there in the water, awaiting a chance to drag myself out upon the bank, I was to find now that my wait had only begun. The two Indians who had searched my side paddled back across the river, drawing my attention with them again to the far shore, where I saw that Sparhawk had at last come to his senses. Even as I looked a pair of braves dragged him towards the fire. I saw that several of the others were busy cutting short sticks from a clump of near-by willows; and for an instant I had the horror-filled thought that they meant to torture him. Then I remembered that of late years this practice had come to be frowned upon. Prisoners, whether ransomed or sold to the French, were more profitable alive than dead, and so must not be wasted to gratify a mere whim.

What they did, however, was bad enough. They tied his arms and legs about the trunk of a great tree, and beat him with the willow withes until he was again unconscious. After that they cut him down and bound his hands and arms brutally behind his back, trussing him up as thoroughly as any Thanksgiving turkey. I had to stifle my impulse to cry out with each blow as if it had landed upon my own back. I could do him no good, and any move on my part would only betray my own hiding place. At least I could take some small consolation in the fact that they had not killed him.

When they had finished with this sport they sat again about the fire and appeared to hold some sort of council among themselves. I gathered that there was some difference of opinion among them, whether they should push on downstream then and search for my body, or whether they should remain where they were until morning. By this time it had become almost a matter of indifference to me which they did. I was faint and dizzy with the cold and loss of blood, and I believe that only my wounds, which at first had been numb but now set out to ache and throb in a way I would not have believed possible had I not felt it myself, kept me from losing consciousness and drowning. As it was, I managed to lock my arms across a half-submerged alder branch, and to prop my chin upon another, so that my body was supported by the armpits and my head rode clear of the water. But for this the numbing cold must have forced me long since to let go my hold and surrender to the river. Now I prayed silently that the group that wished to push on might prevail.

After a discussion that seemed to last for hours (though I could not say in truth how long it was, as twice I dropped off into momentary unconsciousness) my prayer was answered. There came a sudden burst of activity across the river. Several of the Indians went off up the inlet and reappeared in their long canoes. The rest busied themselves with the looting of our camp, each making a bundle of such of our scant equipment as he could lay his hands upon. Now and again a brave would hold up for another's admiration some particularly choice object, such as my musket, which I had left standing against a tree, or one of Sparhawk's bright red blankets, which his mother had woven for him. Whatever else they might be, they were thorough, for they left not a thing where the camp had stood. Blankets, pots, pans, guns, ropes, axes, gunny sacks, even Sparhawk's papers I saw going to their canoes. In less time than it takes to tell it they had cleaned the spot bare, so that only the trampled brush and the tracks in the sand remained to indicate that a camp had ever stood there. Then at last, after another moment or two of discussion, they embarked, and one by one the canoes shoved off downstream. Long after they had gone I lay where I was, my fevered imagination suspecting some trap. Then, with infinite difficulty and much pain, I dragged myself to shore and up upon the bank. There I collapsed at once, face downward, in the long meadow grass.

I do not know how long I lay there. When I opened my eyes it was still dark. The sky was overcast, so that I had not even the light of a single star to show me where I was. For a time I lay where I was, motionless, even my numb brain refusing to work. I did not know what had happened to me or how I came to be lying out there in the meadow grass. Then bit by bit the incidents of the night came back to me. For a moment everything seemed remote and vague, like a part of some awful dream, whose horror remains though its details elude the memory. It seemed impossible that all this could actually have happened, and yet my clothing was cold and wet and clammy to the touch. And when I moved I knew that it was real enough; for a flash pain went stabbing through my side, and when I tried to place my left hand on the hurt I found I could not move my arm for the wound in my shoulder.

No sound save the whisper of the river and the rustle of the wind in the bushes broke the stillness of the night, though I strained my ears to catch the least rattle that might indicate the return of my enemies. The chill wind that blew down across the meadow made my wet buckskins cling clammily about my body and turned me numb with the cold. Little by little it began to dawn upon me that my troubles were not yet over. There was still danger here for me. At any minute the savages, having failed to discover my body below, might return in search of me. But even before that, unless I found some means to restore my sluggish circulation, I might find myself freezing to death. A fire here was out of the question, even had I the means of making one; for though my flint and steel were still in my pouch, I had not a scrap of dry tinder, and it would be impossible to find any in the dark. Even if I could, by some miracle, kindle one, I should not dare, for its light would certainly betray me to any who might be watching. Ironically enough I could still smell the smoke of our campfire, which the Indians had left burning across the river; and when I craned my neck I could make out a faint spark of it, still glowing on the farther bank. But the width of the river separated me from it, and I knew I had not the strength to swim across.

With a supreme effort I dragged myself to a sitting position and took stock of my situation. There was no doubt that I was in a bad spot. Even if they did not return, my outlook could scarcely be said to be bright. The most accessible settlement from my present position, and perhaps the nearest, was Number Four. It would not be impossible to build a raft, which, barring an accident in any one of half a dozen falls along the way, might float me down. But my enemies were below me on the river, and any attempt to reach Number Four by that route would be fatal. Stevenstown had been abandoned, and though I remembered Stiles' cabin at the forks of the Pemigewasset, I dismissed it at once; for with the northern settlements being given up it seemed to me likely that they too must have withdrawn, though I had heard naught from them since Purity's departure from Suncook. My only alternative was Canterbury, nearly a hundred miles through trackless wilderness. There was no other choice. Northward lay Saint Francis. On the west there were the French; and on the east, nothing but forest.

It would have been a desperate choice for a man uninjured and well equipped. For me, wounded, with no more than the clothes I wore to cover me and the knife in my belt for a weapon, it was but a slender hope. Once before, I had come up through those mountain passes. It was barely possible that I might be able to find my way back through them once again.

There was one ray of consolation. In the mountains I should be safe from pursuit. If my enemies returned, as I did not doubt they would, they would undoubtedly find my trail and start to follow me. But, let me once gain the protecting shelter of those craggy hills, I knew that their superstitious fear of invoking the mighty wrath of the Great Manitou would force them to abandon the chase.

How much time I had before this pursuit would begin, I could not tell, but I felt that it could not be long. The thought spurred me to action. With difficulty I staggered to my feet, and with a last regretful glance at the fire still smouldering across the river, I set my face southeastward and stumbled off across the meadow.

3

I had known it would not be easy when I turned my face from the river and started the long journey towards the mountains. But I had not taken a dozen steps before I realized how well-nigh impossible was my plan. Sitting there upon the bank, shivering with the cold, it had seemed barely practicable. Until I moved I could not realize the extent of my weakness. My wounds had stopped their bleeding, and their fiery pain had given way to a dull, pulsing ache that, so long as I lay still, made them seem less than they were. The thought of death at my elbow made me forget my handicaps and estimate my powers overhighly. But when I had dragged myself erect and taken my first few faltering steps the hopelessness of the situation almost overcame me.

As I struggled to my feet the hole in my shoulder reopened, and I could feel the warm blood from it sliding down around my torn armpit and across my ribs to my waist. Every bone in my body cried out in protest at the effort of each single step. The wound in my side, though it was by far the less damaging, became like the touch of a white-hot iron against my flank, hurting me so that, had it not been that the effort of walking required every ounce of my strength and concentration I must have screamed aloud in agony. Even as it was, I had scarce gone forty rods before I found myself sobbing with pain and impotent anger at my own weak helplessness.

I cannot recall today all the details of that night's ghastly journey. For the most part its picture is blurred in my mind: a jumbled nightmare of whipping branches, clutching brambles pain, and black darkness. One or two moments of it stand out with vivid clearness. The rest is lost in a red haze of agony. Once I remember finding myself in the midst of an alder swamp, where I stumbled about for what seemed hours, creeping under low-flung branches, clambering over others, squeezing my tortured way between still more, while the knee-deep mud sucked at my legs. Twigs scratched at my face and tore my clothes. Roots and creepers and low-fallen brush tripped me. Once I must have rammed my injured shoulder against some dead and broken stub, for I recall a blinding flash of pain that shot across my chest and my side; and when I opened my eyes I found that I was lying face downward in the muck.

How I managed to get back on my feet again is still a mystery to me, though I seem to recall that this was only one fall among many that I took that night. A little later I remember with what joy I felt the solid rising ground once more beneath my feet, and sensed the thinning of the trees about me as I left the alder thicket behind and entered the comparatively open growth of hardwoods.

I must have wandered considerably from the straight path, for it took me an unconscionably long time to go what I have since discovered was little more than two miles. Under the circumstances, however, I think this is not to be wondered at. Not only was I weak with loss of blood and fatigue, but there was not so much as a star in the sky to guide me, and the night was so black that I could scarce see my hand before my face. The wonder is that, with only the sound of the river behind me and the slope of the ground beneath my feet to show the way I should turn, I did not become completely turned around and miss my objective entirely. I think I learned then something of what it must be to be blind.

Gradually as I went along, fighting a way through trailing branches, stumbling over fallen sticks and rotten logs, entangling myself in blowdowns, the roar of the river died away to a whisper and the pitch of the ground grew increasingly steeper. Trees and stumps and rocks and bushes were beginning to take a ghostly grey form when at last I half slid, half fell down over a steep bank and found myself standing on the edge of a clear rushing little stream.

To say that I was pleased to come there would be to put it mildly to say the least. I knew that it could only be the small river that fell into the Connecticut at the bend in the rapids above the pool where I had fished the previous evening. It had been a part of my scheme to find it and follow its course south-eastward into the mountains, for this, I knew, would be the most direct route. If I had come upon it somewhat higher than I had intended, so much the better. I was that much nearer home.

In the light of the half-dawn I forced my way through the brush at the river's edge and surveyed the situation. Downstream was a long straightaway, with the bright water tumbling rapidly to what was evidently the head of dead water. Canoes might come up so far, but there was no sign that any had done so. I took a moment to reflect that if the Indians returned they would probably rest on the site of our camp until daylight, when they would begin the search for my trail. If this were so I should still have an hour or so in which to lose myself.

Above me a bend hid the river from view. I made my way up to it and saw with dismay that above it lay another swampy stretch of alder thicket that extended for several rods on either side of the stream. If it was anything like the last, it would take me hours to negotiate it, and any such delay might well mean death.

Despair swept over me. The temptation to throw myself down upon the bank and give up this mad flight was well-nigh overwhelming. I toyed with the thought. After all, why not? The Indians had taken Sparhawk alive. Might they not do the same with me? Was it not better to live a prisoner than die a fugitive—perhaps of starvation or of the cold, or perhaps even to be pulled down by the wolves?

But even as I hesitated, mulling the idea over in my mind, it came to me that I no longer had any choice in the matter. I remembered suddenly all the tales of men who had escaped the savages only to be retaken. The rage which even so temporary a defeat seemed to arouse in them was not to be satisfied by mere thoughts of reward. Such a blow to their childish vanity could only be wiped away in blood, and with the most devilish tortures which their imaginations could devise. I remembered the look of stark horror on Dan Stinson's face when I had found him, and the almost indecent way in which his features, freed of the scalp's supporting strength, had sagged and fallen apart. I remembered how I had turned away and been violently ill when at last the men in my uncle's fort had mustered the courage to go down and bring in the horribly cut and mutilated remains of James Carr from across the river. Whatever form death might take, it would be far preferable to that.

I wasted no more time in thought, but did the only thing possible. Turning away sharply from the river, I climbed the steep slope on the north side. There I swung about and took a course that paralleled the stream well above the swamp. Now that it was growing lighter with each passing moment, I found the going easier. I found that I could dodge around or under obstacles, and despite my weakness, so long as I avoided brushing my hurt shoulder against trees and brush, I could maintain a fairly swift and steady pace.

It took me less than half an hour to pass around the upper side of the swamp and find a tiny spring-fed brook, running down off the hillside into the main stream below. Here I paused, for I suddenly remembered a trick that had often been played upon me by gunwise old bucks when the chase became too hot for them; a trick that now, with myself in the role of the hunted, might stand me in good stead.

Above and below, I noticed, the bed of the brook was stony. With care it would show no tracks. And there was a chance that the pursuers, having come so far only to have the trail end, might take the wrong turn. Even if they did not it was likely that they would divide, and thus cut down by half the number of my enemies. I stepped into the water, taking care to avoid any small patches of sand and mud, and, searching out the deepest and swiftest water in which to walk, struck off downstream.

I found that it was not so easy as I had anticipated. Gnarled alders interlaced their branches above the stream. The stones underfoot were, often as not, covered with moss. The high banks came close on either side, frequently tempting me to reach out my hand to steady myself upon them. But I could not afford to make even one mistake while learning the game. Let me but break one twig, or scrape the moss from but one stone, or leave a single mark upon the bank, and my trick was worthless.

Because of the moss and slime upon the rocks the footing was treacherous and slippery; yet I durst not fall for fear of leaving some telltale mark behind. In consequence I made slow time over the hundred yards or so that separated me from the river. Once there, however, I found the going easier. This bright-watered mountain torrent gave the moss no chance to grow upon its rocky bed, and at the same time it was so wide that I had no fear of leaving my mark upon banks and branches. My only problem became one of speed; my only care, to avoid leaving wet footprints on dry rocks or in the little pockets of sand that sometimes gathered along the edges of the pools.

I did not stop to look back, but pressed forward with all possible haste. The nearer I could come to the mountains in the next few hours, the better would be my chances. As I stumbled on I saw that the clouds overhead had begun to break and hang in vaporous streaks across a chill blue sky. A few minutes later the early sun broke through, shining straight in my face and sending its welcome warmth into my chilled blood. Presently a heavy mist began to rise from the surface of the stream, blotting out even the near-by banks. For the first time since I had hauled myself up out of the river I began to feel that some kindly Providence was watching over me.

Providence or no, however, I could not afford to slacken my pace. I had no way of knowing that I was being pursued—only a sort of instinct that urged me onward. It was possible, of course, that the Indians had not returned; that, having failed to find my body below, they had assumed that I was somewhere at the bottom of the river and abandoned the hunt. Still there was always the possibility, and I knew that if they once caught sight of me my death would be but a matter of hours. In that moment I would have given all I possessed to be able to look back along the river, to see around all the bends and turnings by which I had come, and know whether or not they were there.

The power of second sight being denied me, there was naught for me to do but to keep on despite the aching of my wounds and the dizziness of fatigue. I will not go into the details of that agonizing day's journey. They are as fresh in my mind now as if they had taken place but yesterday, but to enumerate them could serve no useful purpose. Sufficient to say that by midmorning I had gone perhaps eight miles from our camp on the river. I had passed a number of tributary streams, flowing in upon both sides, any one of which I might have followed in the same way in which I followed the little river. I counted upon them, however, to confuse the enemy, and stuck to the straightaway course. Three times the river itself forked, to my infinite pleasure since each division of the stream increased my chances for escape. At the first fork I bore to the right, since that direction carried me southward towards the settlements. At the second I chose the lesser branch and kept to the left, around the base of a high hill. At the third, where the river was become but little more than a brook, I turned left again, so that I faced nearly due east, and climbed steeply after passing through a small cedar swamp.

At the top of the first sharp pitch I came upon a tiny pond, scarce larger than a good-sized pool. It was shallow. Even in the middle it looked to be no more than three feet deep; and its bottom, like many another of our mountain tarns, was comparatively solid; a mere ankle-deep film of mud upon a base of stone. What dismayed me at sight of it was a thin fringe of ice that completely encircled the pond, varying in width from a few inches at some spots to three or four feet at others.

If ever man was in a dilemma it was I at that moment. If I stepped out upon the bank to go around the pond I should leave tracks that would undo all that I had so far done. Similarly, if I should attempt to wade the pond and broke any of that fragile, brittle border in so doing, my pursuers would be quick to see it.

Still there was no choice for me. The fringe narrowed away to the width of my foot at the outlet, and I found that by some extremely gingerly stepping I could just scrape through without breaking it. Once in the pond, however, I was not much better off, for I had to walk with infinite caution, lest the waves caused by my passage smash the paper-thin ice to bits along the shore. But I made it, for all my fear and trembling, and was relieved, on reaching the mouth of the inlet, to find that because of the motion of the water no ice had formed there. Had I not been so near to exhaustion I must have felt some pride in that accomplishment, for if my pursuers were to come so far the absence of track along the shore together with the unbroken ice in the pond would go a long way towards convincing them that I had not passed this way.

For half a mile above the pond the brook came down swiftly, tumbling about the foot of a steep hill. After the first long swooping drop, however, it began to level off; little by little the hills on either hand spread out, and presently I found myself standing at the lower end of a long wide basin; a basin whose level floor was choked from side to side, and from one end to the other, with one of the darkest, dankest, most forbidding cedar swamps I have ever seen. And through the middle of this swamp, twisting and turning, and looping and doubling upon itself, in a sluggish, meandering course, ran the brook I was following.

Even today the thought of that dank, mucky hollow between the high hills has the power to make me shudder. But strangely enough I was not then dismayed. I suppose that I was too near worn out to care. The horrors of the night before, my almost helpless weakness, the agonizing pain of my wounds, and the distance I had already come, all combined to dull the movement of my sluggish brain. I was no longer capable of feeling anxiety or horror or fear or despair.

Perhaps that is why I stumbled onward when a saner, more thoughtful man would have stopped, hesitating to attempt the passage of such a rank jungle. My feet moved automatically though my mind no longer worked, driving me on up the brook bed, deeper and deeper into that tangled wilderness, when a moment's sane thought must have made me wonder at the wisdom of it.

That must also account for my failure to hear the sound of falling water until I had come around a sharp bend and found the beaver dam before me. I had not counted at any time upon the possibility of finding beaver along the stream, though if I had thought of it at all I must have realized the inevitability of it: there was scarce a brook in this part of the Province but had its colony of the animals. I stood in midstream, the icy water gurgling and sucking about my knees, and stared in dismay at the barrier of sticks and mud that stretched, chin-high, across my path.

It was a big dam, and as I looked at it dully I could feel my heart sink into my boots. There would be deep water behind that. What was I to do now?

But even as I wondered I let my eyes go across the dark surface of the pond beyond, and suddenly my heart skipped a beat. I could feel exultant hope returning. Above the dam, perhaps twenty yards, the stream split. One fork came down from the east, its water backed up deep and dark, some six or eight yards wide, to a distant bend and beyond. The other fork came from the southwest, just as deep and just as dark, but half again as wide. It was evident, from the height of the dam and the way the water was piled up behind it, that there was a long stretch of deadwater on either fork.

It was the point of land dividing the two forks that took my eye. It was high enough to be dry, and almost at its very tip a great black spruce had been blown over, roots and all, so that its top lay in the water and its butt made a tangle of brush and roots and trunk as high as my head upon the bank. There was shelter there if I could but reach it. Even if the Indians should come in so far; even if they stood upon the dam, they would not be likely to find me in that tangled mass. Of course they might cross the fork, and in that case they could scarcely miss me. But that was a risk I must run. One thing was certain: I could go no further; rest, I must.

I climbed up on the dam, being careful to keep in the spill where the water tumbled over the twisted sticks. When I stood on top I could not see the bottom. I prayed that it might not be too deep for me to touch, for I doubted my ability to swim now. There was a little fringe of ice along one shore, and a little breeze ruffled the water, black with the colour of the swamp roots through which it flowed higher up.

I hesitated for a moment, and then, drawing a deep breath, plunged in. I went deep, and gasped involuntarily with the sudden chill. But then I felt my feet touch the soft bottom, and found myself standing in water to my armpits.

It was not easy to move, so cold was it; but move I must or drown, for I knew I could not stand that icy chill for long. I set my teeth and ploughed ahead, keeping close in along the eastern bank. At least the water grew no deeper. At the mouth of the fork I swung across, heading straight towards the point. At my first step the water came over my shoulders, and at the second it touched my chin. My third step plunged me in water over my head, and I kicked my feet out behind me and struggled with my good arm to make some headway. The tip of the spruce was not more than five or six feet beyond my grasp, but it might as well have been as many rods for all I seemed to gain upon it. I could feel myself growing dizzy and faint, and the outlines of the shore began to blur before my eyes. I felt that the end had come at last, when all at once first my hand and then my knee scraped bottom and I stood up thigh-deep in the water.

I have a faint recollection, after that, of stumbling ashore, careful even then in my half-consciousness to avoid leaving tracks in the mud at the water's edge, and of burrowing deep among the dead spruce boughs and brush to the solid ground. After that I must have fainted for a time, for I remember no more.

I awoke suddenly to hear the scolding chatter of a red squirrel in the tangled branches above me. My first impulse was to shout at him; to wave my arm and throw something to frighten him away. I did not want to be disturbed. I wanted nothing more than just to lie there on my back and rest.

But suddenly I remembered where I was and what danger I was in, and the thought struck me motionless. What was it, I wondered, that had so set the squirrel to scolding? I remembered how Toby had tried to teach me to listen to the jays and squirrels and crows and to study what it was that had set them off. According to him, if you listened closely you could tell, for they had their own language; and indeed I was more than half inclined to believe him, for he would listen to a jay or a squirrel scolding in a hollow and tell, without going down to look, if it were a man or a bear or something else that had started him. But I could never do that. Nor could I understand why this squirrel should be chattering. I was sure it was not for me; for I had been there lying still too long. And if it was not for me it was for something else. Suddenly I thought I knew what it might be.

Very carefully, so as not to break any twigs or set anything to moving, I twisted around on my side and turned my head, so that I could peer out through the brush at the dam. There, sure enough, crouching on top of the muddy brush, his head turned off downstream, was an Indian.

At that distance I could make out every detail of his war paint and dress. Despite the sharpness of the air he was naked, save for a breechclout and a pair of worn moccasins. Painted horizontally across his chest at exact intervals were three white bars. An ochre stripe ran across his face from ear to ear, passing over the bridge of his great hooked nose. Below this stripe his whole face was painted alternately white and vermilion, and there were vermilion circles about his eyes, like enormous spectacles. His head was shaven, save for a single scalp lock that dangled behind one ear. The lower end of this was braided, and bound in some sort of skin, and a single feather drooped from it dejectedly. For weapons he had a tomahawk stuck in his belt, and I saw with impotent rage that he carried my own good flintlock; the one my uncle had given me when I had first arrived in Suncook.

It was fortunate that he was looking the other way, for it gave me a chance to work lower in the brush for better cover. I kept my eye on him, however, and saw that after a moment he stood up and was joined by a second Indian. For two or three minutes they stood there arguing, though I could not hear their words for the sound of water rushing over the dam and the jabber of the squirrel above my head: a jabbering that had redoubled in its intensity since I had shifted my position.

I was afraid they would notice the little beast's fury and look my way, but they seemed to take his scolding as directed at them, and paid no heed. After some moments of argument, accompanied by gestures upstream and down and not a little shaking of heads and grimacing, they separated. One stepped off onto the west bank and started up along the main stream, evidently searching for some sign that I had passed that way. The other took the opposite side and worked up the fork.

It was this latter whom I had cause to fear. He might see me if he looked across at the brush heap. Or he might take it into his head to cross and search my side. I had no way of knowing how far up the dead water went, but if it ended around the bend there was but little doubt that he would cross and search back along this shore.

I watched him with my heart thumping in my throat. Once when he came almost opposite me he came down close to the bank and looked at the water. It was plain that he had no relish for getting his feet wet. I was glad to see that his heart was not in his work, and that he was making but a superficial search. Nevertheless I did not breathe easily again until I saw him come morosely back around the bend and go back to his stand upon the dam.

A few moments later his companion returned along the west shore. They talked a few minutes with many shrugs and shakings of the head. I gathered that they did not think I had come this way and were ready to give up the search. And, sure enough, after a minute or two of talk they stood up and clambered back upon the bank. Without a sign of hesitation they turned and struck off downstream, keeping close to the edge of the brook, yet taking pains to keep out of the water.

I watched them as long as they were in sight, and then rolled over on my back and chuckled with relief. Whatever dangers might lie ahead of me, I had, at least, left the one most dreaded behind. Let come what might now, the Indians would bother me no more; and, somehow, in that moment, I had confidence in my own ability to cope with the woods.

I lay for some time where I was, scarce daring to move lest they might change their minds and return for further search. But when half an hour had passed and there was no more sign of them I plucked up my courage and crept on hands and knees from my hiding place.

My first care, now that I knew I was at last free of any pursuit, was to care for my wounds. I went down to the brookside and there, after an agonizing struggle, slipped out of my shirt and undershirt and stood naked to the waist. The wound in my side, as I suspected, was little more than a bullet burn. The shot had passed at an angle across the skin of my side, laying open a wound perhaps six inches long that was painful and bloody but by no means serious. I washed it carefully and, cutting a strip from my linen drawers, bound it up.

My shoulder, however, was a different story. The bullet had gone in under the armpit, tearing a gaping hole in the flesh and muscle, just below the shoulder joint, and coming out at the back. I could not use my arm, and the least motion of it set me sick with pain. Moreover it was in a place well-nigh impossible for me to reach with my one good hand. Nevertheless, I did my best, washing it as well as I could and then binding it after a fashion with what remained of my drawers. This done I cut the useless sleeve from my buckskin shirt and strapped the arm tightly against my side, so that it could not swing loose, and hooked the fingers of my left hand in my belt. When I finished I pulled my shirt on again awkwardly and lay back to consider my next move.

For a man wounded and ill equipped I had come some considerable distance. A walk of some eight miles, nearly all of it over stony brook beds, through icy water that varied from ankle- to waist-deep, is a task to wear down the strongest of men, let alone one already weakened by exposure and loss of blood. I had come near collapse from exhaustion. My short rest in the brush had refreshed me somewhat, but was obviously not enough. Now to add to my troubles the air was turning colder. The sun that had shone for a brief while that morning was hidden again behind a bank of slate-grey clouds, and a chill wind was beginning to blow from the north. Moreover I was beginning now to feel the sharp pangs of hunger gnawing at my vitals.

Three things, then, were obviously necessary before I could go on. I must find some means to warm myself, for unless I did I was like to perish of the cold before I could even reach the mountains. I must find food somehow or starve. And I must rest. I no longer needed to fear the Indians, for failing to find my trail that first day they would waste no more time upon me. The threat of snow was too strong to be ignored, and they would be anxious to return to Saint Francis as quickly as they could. Cold, hunger, and exhaustion were the enemies I must face now.

The spot I was in was hardly suited to those needs. I might find rabbits in the swamp, but dry wood would be scarce, and the north wind whipped up along the brook bed through the basin in a way that would make any shelter hard to find. Plainly I must keep going until I found a better place than this.

I found my feet with some difficulty, for my short rest had stiffened me, and struck off eastward along the bank of the fork. I had not gone forty yards when I realized why my two Indians had been willing to give up so soon. The swamp was a well-nigh impenetrable tangle of fir and cedar, with half-frozen mudholes interspersed with great boulders, and every open space grown shoulder-high with briers. For the best part of an hour I struggled through this hellish mass; tripping and stumbling in the mud, sliding down the face of boulders, tearing my face and hands and clothes on brambles. I had hunted through similar bogs before, but I was whole then, with the full use of my body, and I was warmly clothed and well fed, and I had slept well the night before. Now I began to understand how men could get lost in such a place, and how quickly, once they were lost, they would become exhausted with their struggles to find a way out. I made up my mind that if it meant I had to walk four times as far, thereafter I would stick to the high ground and leave the bogs and swamps alone. I was thankful that I had not blundered into such a spot during the night. Dark as it had been, I should never have fought my way clear before the pursuit overtook me.

Gradually at first, after about a mile, and then more rapidly, the ground beneath my feet became firm and began to rise, and at last I came out of the cedars onto the side of a low ridge covered with spruce and firs. On my left, to northward, the fork, a mere trickle here, scarce more than a step across, ran down through a shallow hollow from a pocket between two hills. On my right the ridge climbed in a long, low hogback to the crest of a second ridge that ran north and south.

I liked the look of the hollow whence the brook sprang. There would be good water there. The north slope would be a protection against the wind. The firs and spruces with which it was filled would provide firewood and brush to make a rude shelter as well as a bed to sleep on. It was a likely spot for small game. Already I had noticed a number of rabbit runs, and as I stood looking I heard a partridge drumming somewhere below. I could not hope to find a spot better suited to my purpose, and I turned my face towards it with a sense of satisfaction despite my fatigue and hunger.

Luck was with me. I had not gone thirty rods towards the hollow when a fat partridge rose with a thunderous whirring of wings from beneath a near-by fir. He did not fly far, and I could hear him clucking and gabbling in the brush not far off as I cast about for a stick.

I remembered how, as a lad, we had hunted these foolish birds with clubs; how they would sit stupidly in a tree, bobbing their heads at us until we could approach within throwing range. It had been no great trick, and I did not see why I could not do it now.

I found a stout stick, about as thick as my wrist and not too long, and crept towards where I had seen him come down. He had run a little way evidently, for he was not there, and I stood still listening. A rustle in the leaves on my right attracted my attention, and I turned my head to see him standing clear of the brush, his wings dragging, his tail spread like a turkey cock, and his ruff up, one eye cocked upon me curiously, uncertain whether to fly or strut a challenge. It was a long throw, but in my eagerness I determined to take a chance. I drew back my arm and took

careful aim. But my movements must have been too sudden. He took three hopping steps and rose again, with a roar of wings.

I had no time to be chagrined, for even as he rose three others rose with him, two on my left and one in front. Those beside me towered high and went sailing off over the tops of the trees, but the bird in front settled himself on a branch in a tall pine and sat ducking his head at me curiously. I wasted no time in hesitation, but flung my club. He spread his wings to fly, but I had been too quick for him. The stick caught one of the outspread wings, breaking it, snapped his legs out from under him, and he fell squawking to the ground, where I pounced upon him, forgetful of my own hurts, and wrung his neck.

Encouraged by this success I gathered up the club once more and went off after the others. But they were too wild, and I could not get near them; so that presently I gave it up, mindful of the passing time, and pushed on into the hollow in search of a place to make my camp.

I found what I was looking for in the lee of a ledge of rock that rose sheer upon the face of the hill a little above the bed of the brook. The flat surface faced south, affording protection from the wind and a reflector for a fire if I could make one. A pole and bark shelter facing that ledge, its back towards the brook, and its floor six inches deep in balsam tips, would make as snug a camp as a man could wish for.

I hung my bird in the fork of a birch, and set to work at once to make the shelter. There was no lack of dead timber, and I had no difficulty in finding a dozen poles as thick as my arm and of varying lengths. These I broke down to uniform size by catching an end between two close-growing trees and swinging my weight against the longer end. When I had as many as I felt I needed I dug their butts into the hard ground, some six feet in front of the ledge, and leaned their tips against the rock face. Then using these as rafters I piled brush and bark and more poles upon them until I had thatched a rude lean-to, its face to the rock wall and its back to the wind. The sides I built up in similar fashion so that the interior was completely sheltered; and at the top, between the edge of the roof and the rock I left a space of eight or ten inches to carry off the smoke of my fire. When I had finished I stood back and surveyed my work with pardonable pride. The lean-to was far from perfect, as I could see, but considering my weakened condition and the lack of tools to work with I could not but feel that I had done well enough.

My next task was to gather fir balsam tips to make my bed. This proved simple enough, for there were hundreds of the trees upon the hillside and I had but to stand and cut. A half-hour served to pile the inside of the shelter high with them. Firewood was no less a simple matter. As is always the case where many evergreens are crowded together there were many dead standing trees, some two to four inches in diameter, and these, with thin roots part rotted through, are easy to break down and provide fine wood for a quick hot fire. There was also an abundance of down wood, dead logs, and stumps, some of which I dragged in to use when once I had kindled a good blaze.

Tinder, however, proved more of a problem. I had to hunt over more than an acre before I could find a rotted spruce log whose heart had just the right degree of punky dryness to take a spark from the flint and steel; and I had to go high on the hill to find any birches large enough to provide bark.

With all these materials gathered within the shelter I took my bird from his notch in the sapling and carried him down to the brook, where with some difficulty I plucked and drew him. By this time it was near dark, and I returned to the lean-to with my belly jumping with impatience. On the way I cut a green stick to serve as a spit for my supper.

If I had thought that all I had done thus far was labour, I was soon to find that the hardest task of all was yet to come in the kindling of my fire. Back at the shelter I dragged in a two-foot length of half-rotted spruce to serve as a forelog. This I laid some twenty inches in front of the rock that faced the interior of the lean-to, and scooped out earth and leaves from either end of the space thus formed to make a draft. In the midst of this space I crumpled a handful of the dry spruce punk. Next I tore a roll of birch bark into thin papery strips and gathered a handful of small twigs and shavings into a pile. After that I stuck my knife in the ground beside the punk and rummaged in my pouch for one of the spare flints I always carried there. When I had found it I lay down upon my stomach, holding the handle of the knife between my teeth, and began to strike sparks from the back of the blade into the punk with the flint.

For the better part of an hour I lay there, striking off sparks and cursing, and when at last I was rewarded for my pains by the faint glow of a spark that caught among the tindery shreds of rotted wood I was as wet with sweat as if I had been ducked in the brook. My work was not done yet, however. I had to blow gently upon the spark, taking great care not to blow it out, until I saw it redden suddenly and spread. Then I seized a strip of the bark and held it among the tinder, blowing like a grampus all the while. A thin streak of smoke arose, and the bark crackled and curled. Then all at once it burst into a tiny flame.

I sat back and heaped on the rest of the bark and twigs, watching the orange fire lick up through them. Little by little I nursed it from a pinpoint of flame to a brisk blaze, and then sat back to rest and enjoy its delicious warmth.

My hour of rest had still not arrived, however. A heave of my empty belly reminded me that I had not yet eaten, and that there was still the bird to be prepared. Taking up the green stick, I spitted him upon it, and seared him quickly in the crackling flames. This done I stuck the end of the stick into the ground, so that the bird was held up to roast slowly and thoroughly. While I waited for it to cook I turned attention to my bed, cutting off the balsam feathers eight to ten inches long and sticking them upright in the ground, row after row, so that when it was done I had a bed as soft as a man could wish for. Every now and then I would stop work on the bed and turn the spit a little, so that my supper would not be too much done at any one spot. When it was finished I lifted it off the spit and fell upon it like a hungry wolf.

I never until that moment realized how little meat there was upon a partridge. This bird had been a fat one in prime condition. With his feathers on he had looked more than a meal for three hungry men. When I had plucked him I had thought he must surely satisfy at least my hunger. But when, after cooking, I had laid aside the wings and legs and neck against the morning, I found there was pitifully little left. I ate the breast and side meat, the dollops along the back, and the gristle about the tail. I even ate the skin and picked the bones cleaner than any dog could have done. When it was finished I felt a little better, but I could have eaten another just as large. For a moment I toyed with the idea of finishing what I had laid aside and trusting to luck to get another for breakfast. But a moment's reflection showed me the folly of this, and I resolutely and, as it turned out, wisely put the temptation aside.

With a good, if somewhat meagre, meal beneath my belt, a roof above my head, and a fire to warm me, I began to feel that the world was none so bad a place to live in after all. I laid a couple of heavy butts across the fire and banked the ashes up around them and lay back upon my fragrant bed to savour its pleasantness to the full. The full warmth of the fire was reflected into the lean-to by the rock wall; and the sloping roof, as I had planned it should, in turn reflected it down upon me, so that presently my wet clothes began to steam out dry, the warm blood began to circulate once more, thawing out my frozen bones, and I began to feel a languorous sense of well-being steal over me.

I had heard tales of men lost in the wilderness, starving or freezing to death, or meeting with some disaster or other, and their whitened bones being found by hunters in the spring. Now I began to pooh-pooh these stories to myself. My confidence in my own woodsmanship returned in leaps and bounds. Why, I told myself, this was none so bad. Any man with a lick of sense could do as well. The secret was not to become panicky; never to hurry; rest, and eat and keep warm, and all the while work slowly towards the settlements. It would not be hard. Those birds I had set up that afternoon: if I had not been so fatigued and anxious I should have knocked down at last two more of them. And there were other ways of obtaining food that only required a minimum of skill and a little patience.

From such whistlings in the dark I went on to lay my plans. Plainly enough, what I needed most was rest. The journey before me should not be attempted until I had regained some measure of my strength; though I must not delay too long lest the winter catch me before I could get out. A supply of food, too, would be necessary, and I must find some means of obtaining it. There would be rabbits in the hollow and down by the swamp. A half-dozen snares, set at likely spots along their runs, should net me all I could eat. There were more birds upon the hillside. After I had set my snares I could spend the day in careful, serious hunting. I should have no difficulty, I told myself, in getting a number of them. Some of these I would smoke. They would help to carry me on my way, through regions to the southward where game might not prove to be so plentiful. With luck I might even devise means of getting a deer, though this would prove more difficult. If I could, however, I should be well supplied with meat. I should have to do no more hunting until I reached the settlements. It was on this thought that I fell asleep.

I awoke with the dawn, chilled to the bone. At first glance I thought my fire had gone out, but close examination showed that I had banked it well. When I raked away the ashes I found a handful of red coals glowing among the charred stubs. A few strips of bark and some twigs soon rekindled the blaze, and presently I was warm again and confident.

I finished what was left of last night's supper, and after that lay dozing luxuriously in the fire's warmth, watching the red flames lick upward along the blackened rock.

Presently I stirred myself: there was work for me to do. I sat up and began to cast about for something to use for loops for my snares. At first I considered my buckskin jacket, but this, I decided, I should need to keep me warm; and at last I hit upon my leather leggings. Underneath these I wore a pair of heavy homespun breeches and woolen stockings, and I felt that, though they were of great service in protecting my legs against briers, they more than any other article of my clothing could be dispensed with.

I suited action to the thought and, stripping off the garment, proceeded to slit one leg of it into a dozen narrow thongs suitable for the purpose I had in mind. Armed with these I banked my fire once more and went down into the hollow towards the swamp in search of runs on which to set the snares.

I had not far to go. Even before I came within sight of the bog I began to find runways. Choosing those which carried the freshest sign I set my traps with care, marking each with a blaze or a bit of rag in a near-by tree so that I could not fail to find it again. After that I went up onto the hillside and hunted for partridge.

All that day I hunted the hillsides without setting up more than four or five birds. The first one I managed to knock down with a well aimed throw. The second I hit but did not hurt, and the rest were so wild that I could not even approach them. I did, however, manage to kill a fat old hedgehog which I knocked down out of a high beech tree, which he was girdling with his teeth. I skinned him out then and there upon the hill, having no desire to fill myself with his quills on the way to camp, and wrapped the carcass in what remained of my leggings. On the way back I visited my traps to find that of the eight but one had been sprung, and this one I had set so low that the animal had been able to gnaw through the thong and get free.

I reset the snare and readjusted the others, returning somewhat dejected to camp. All day the sky had been hung with lowering, lead-coloured clouds, and it seemed to me a storm must be brewing. That would explain why the game had not been moving, for it has always been my experience that when a storm is in the air most of the animals of the forest take to their dens and hole up until the threat is passed. As I approached the lean-to I noticed that now and again an occasional whirling flake of snow would spat against my cheek; and as the flakes became more and more frequent I found my spirits sinking lower and lower until I became downright apprehensive. A snowstorm here at this time might prove well-nigh fatal to me.

There was a ray of consolation, however, in finding my fire still smouldering in its ashes. I raked the coals out on top and fed them on bark and twigs until they had burst into flame. After that I plucked and cleaned my bird and gathered a supply of firewood for the night. Back again at the lean-to, somewhat disconsolately roasting hedgehog and bird on greenwood spits, I had to admit that I had not done so badly. At least if I could do as well every day I should not starve.

When I judged the meat to be finished I set the bird aside against the morrow and attacked the hedgehog. I found the meat tough and stringy and with a rank flavour, but fat and nourishing. I was too hungry to be particular, and despite its somewhat rancid taste I relished every bite of it. My spirits rose somewhat with my belly full. Perhaps, I thought, the storm would blow over. These first snow flurries frequently did. Then the hunting would be good again, and in the meantime I could at least keep warm. I made my preparations for the night, and when, in response to nature, I stepped outside the lean-to I found the snow had begun in earnest. It would be a bitter night, I thought, and returned to build up a roaring fire to toast my back. A little after, I fell asleep, for my roaming upon the hillside had not been easy and I was comfortably tired. When I awoke in the grey of the dawn the wind had shifted. The snow had stopped, and in its place had come rain—not the swift roaring downpour that is over in a moment, nor either the drizzling mist that wets nothing, but a cold, steady November rain, the kind that sometimes continues without let-up for days on end and soaks everything through and through. Already the roof of my lean-to was dripping like a sieve, and the fire I had worked so hard to build was out.

4

I breakfasted on the remains of the hedgehog, though, cold, its rancid taste was nigh enough to turn my stomach; and as I munched the stringy meat I considered what I ought to do. This rain had upset all my fine plans, and, as I well knew, it might go on indefinitely. So long as it continued there could be naught but misery for me here. With the woods soaked through there was no chance for me to rekindle my fire; nor should I be able, without an axe, to keep it going. My lean-to was not meant for shelter in such a downpour, and there was nothing I could do to make it watertight. More and more, as the minutes passed, the cold rain seeped through my impromptu roof, until finally I felt I might as well have been sitting outside in the downpour for all the shelter it provided me. To remain there with neither heat nor shelter would be foolish. I had rested somewhat. My belly was full. And I had food for a day at least. It was better, I felt, to keep moving under the circumstances.

When I had made up my mind there was nothing to prevent my acting at once upon my decision. Two minutes sufficed to make a bundle of the bird, which I was now more than thankful I had already cooked, and to examine and readjust the dressings on my wounds, which with the return of wet weather had begun again to make themselves felt.

I left the camp without a backward glance, wasting no time in regrets, and went straight down to the edge of the bog where my snares were set. Here again I was doomed to disappointment. Apparently very few rabbits had been stirring during the night. One of the snares had been sprung, evidently by some animal much heavier than the game I had anticipated, perhaps a fox or a bobcat, for the whole thing was carried away, and though I searched carefully in the vicinity I could not even find the thong.

Another had been sprung and robbed by fox, cat, or wolf, for it still held the mangled and worthless remains of a small rabbit. The rest had not been touched.

I gathered up the remaining snares and set out, striking up onto the ridge and following it southward. All that day the rain clouds hung low on the mountains to south and east, so that had I not previously had the opportunity to make a good survey of the land I might have had difficulty in finding my way. As it was, however, I had little trouble.

I did not hurry myself that day, for I felt that I was still weak and that I should do better to conserve my strength as much as possible and avoid exhaustion. At about midday I ate a little of my partridge and pushed on. All day long the steady rain continued without let-up, and the coming of night found me soaked to the skin; my teeth chattering together with the bitter cold.

I was high on the north slope of a mountain by then, and by a stroke of good luck I managed to find a shallow cave beneath an overhanging ledge that provided some shelter from the rain. I did not sleep much, however; from time to time I would doze off, only to awake to find my arms and legs numb with the cold and my wounds aching violently. I would sit up then and stamp the circulation back into my feet and slap my one good hand upon my thigh until the feeling was restored to my fingers. Then I would lie down again to rest until the performance must needs be repeated. When the dawn came I finished what was left of the bird and set out again, feeling that anything was better than lying there to freeze.

During the night the rain had stopped, and though the sky remained overcast the clouds rode high. I fought towards the top of the mountain, with the hope of obtaining a view of the country to southward, and the exercise of climbing warmed me. I was too much weakened, though, to make much speed, and it was well-nigh noon before I reached the summit of the hill. The view I gained from there both heartened and disheartened me; for though I could see the mountains spread in a vast panorama before me, so near that it almost seemed I might reach out and touch them, so could I also see all the wild, rugged country through which I must pass to reach them.

Directly below me, at my feet, lay spread the broad valley of the Ammonoosuc. On my left, to eastward, beyond a tumbled ridge, I could see the snow-clad flanks of Agiochook, unmistakable by its bulk, even though its crest lay hidden in the clouds. Southeast, over the top of a nubbly ridge, I could make out the cleft by which Stiles and Toby and I had come north so long ago. All across the south there stretched an almost unbroken chain of rugged mountains, but to southwest, seeming so close that I might almost reach out and touch it, was the deep notch whose mere mention had seemed to strike terror into Toby's heart. I remembered that, when I had looked into it before, it had seemed to me that this must be the direct way into the headwaters of the Pemigewasset, and then and there I made up my mind that that would be my route. I cared not what the Indians said. It was plain enough that, whether or not it led to the waters of the middle fork, it was the most direct route south. One thing was certain, at least. There I should be safe from attack, for no Indian would dare to follow me.

It was not difficult going down the south slope of the mountain into the valley. I arrived at the river bank about midafternoon. But it almost seemed to me that I might have stayed on the mountaintop, for the river was swollen with the rain, and I could see no way across. After a couple of hours' search, however, I found a spot where the stream ran out over the broad lip of a pool. Here the water was spread wide across a stony bottom, and though the current was swift it was no more than thigh-deep. With the aid of a stout birch pole to brace against the bottom I finally made my way to the farther bank, where I flung myself down and lay a long time panting with exhaustion.

It was hunger that finally brought me to my feet. I had eaten the last of my bird that morning, and if I wished to fill my belly that night I must move quickly, for the dusk was already closing in. I remembered half a dozen long shadowy shapes that I had seen lying against the bottom while I was hunting for a likely spot to cross the river. I knew them for salmon, on their way to the spawning beds, and it occurred to me after a moment that the pool above my ford might hold one or more of them. Moving cautiously and keeping my head down lest they see me, I crept around to the head of the pool and looked out over the bank. Sure enough, there against the sandy bottom below me were four long black fish, lying like logs against the white sand of the bottom.

My problem then became one of how to catch them. I was not long in doubt. One of the things Toby had taught me years before, when I first came to Suncook, was how to spear fish through the ice. I had neither ice here nor a proper fish spear, but I did not see why it could not be done. I scoured around in the brush until I found a tall, slender sapling just stout enough to serve my purpose. This I cut off about eight feet long, and whittled one end down to a long, sharp point. I should have liked to have some fire to harden the tip, but as I had neither fire nor the prospect of any, this would have to do.

Armed with this weapon I began my stalk. I found it not so easy as I had anticipated, for there was no cover on the bank by which I could approach near enough to strike. I had to get down on the sand bar and wade out towards them, very slowly and gently; one step and a wait, and then another slow, dragging step, until I could get within striking distance.

I singled out the largest of the fish for my prey and moved towards him. He let me get almost within reach, and then with a gentle flirt of his tail moved away some four feet or so and lay there gently finning himself from side to side. I was waist-deep then in the icy water, and I had to stand motionless until he became reassured and would lie still. I must have waited twenty minutes before he appeared to settle again into his sleeping position against the sandy bottom. Then very cautiously I took a long step towards him, raised my arm, and struck, driving the point of my rude spear into his body just behind the gills.

He turned with a wrench that near tore the spear from my hand. But I was ready for him, and I turned with him, catching the butt of the spear under my armpit, and levering him up, in an effort to pitchfork him back over my head onto the bank behind me. At the top of the swing, however, the spear broke, and he dropped in the shallow water by the shore. I was on him in a flash, kicking and scraping with my one hand to get him up on shore before he could get away. More by good luck than by good management I planted a lucky kick that sent him flopping out upon the sand, and there I fell upon him, fastening my fingers in his gills.

I hauled him up upon the bank, and held him up to admire; a lusty young grilse of six or seven pounds. I had no means of cooking him, and the woods were still too wet to hope for any dry tinder. But I was in no mood to be fastidious. My appetite could not wait. Scarce stopping to clean him, I cut off a sizable chunk and wolfed it raw.

I ate about half the fish before my stomach finally showed signs of rebelling. By this time it was dark, and I strung what remained of my catch on one of my rabbit snares and went in search of a place to sleep. I found what I was looking for in the shape of a great wind-fallen pine, under whose massive trunk there was just space enough for me to lie. I hung what was left of the fish in the tangled roots, that reached grotesque arms skyward, and crept beneath the tree where I promptly fell asleep.

Towards midnight it began to rain again, but such was my exhausted state that I did no more than roll over into a somewhat drier spot and doze off again. About dawn I was awakened by a scrabbling sound above my head; but, as I raised myself to see what might be causing it, I was suddenly seized with a terrific griping in my belly and a violent flux of the bowels that would not be denied. I managed to stagger away into the brush, where I relieved myself. A few moments later, I returned to see an enormous lynx making off through the bushes with what remained of my salmon protruding from his mouth. But I was too weak to care.

It is from that moment that I count my real troubles to have begun. Weakened as I already was with hunger, exhaustion, and my wounds the flux that came upon me then simply added the final straw. I lay for a long time beneath my log, before I could find the strength to drag myself down to the river's edge to attend my hurts. When I had taken away the rude dressings I discovered that the constant wettings had softened the edges of the wounds. They were open and running; beginning to fester and give off a nauseous stench. I bathed them and redressed them as best I could, and then, after a long rest, dragged myself to my feet and started on my day's journey.

That is the last day of which my memory remains clear. I pushed my way steadily southwestward through an overgrown tangle of spruce and ground hemlock, across long level, boggy stretches, and over steep brush-choked slopes. I remember after a long morning crossing another swift-running river, and not long afterward stumbling into the midst of a great covey of grouse. But though I tried to knock one of them down, I had not sufficient strength left in my arm. I would throw my stick and see it land with a thump, only to see the bird rise with a frightened squawk and a thunderous whirring of wings to sail off over the treetops and away. I remember watching the last bird fly away, to dip mockingly across the crest of a low ridge, and thereafter throwing myself upon the ground in despair.

After that I have no consecutive memory of events. How many days and nights I struggled through the woods I have no way of knowing; perhaps three, perhaps four, but certainly no more, for I had not the strength. Occasionally I have vivid, fragmentary recollections, of the period. Once I came to myself in the pitchy darkness to realize that I was standing, waist-deep, in a rushing mountain torrent. Again I remember a deer bounding out of the brush at my feet, while I sat down upon a near-by log and wept.

For all my delirium, however, there must have been a sane side of my mind that kept me pressing doggedly towards my goal, for I seem to remember finding myself standing by the shore of a small lake near dawn, and looking up to the mountains rising in sheer cliffs on either hand. I remember thinking then that I had gained the notch on the other side of which lay the Pemigewasset, and the road to the colonies, and going down upon my hands and knees on the sandy shingle to drink. Overhead black clouds raced across the mountain side, now showing patches of sky above, and again brushing the tips of the tall firs close against the lake shore. As I bent down to drink, the clouds lifted, and I thought I caught the reflection of a face peering down at me from the mountain side.

Involuntarily I looked up, to find that it was not my imagination. There against the cliffside, high above me, jutted a great frowning head. To my fevered imagination it seemed to be glaring down upon me, and the movement of the clouds across it made it seem to live and move. For an instant I sat petrified. This was why Toby had shown such a horror of the place. There was substance to his legends. This was the abode of the Great Manitou, and I had aroused his wrath! I could almost see the great stone jaws move as a wisp of cloud streamed by, and the wild shriek of the wind in the trees above me became his voice as he pronounced judgement upon me!

A sudden uncontrollable panic swept over me. I leapt to my feet and went crashing away through the brush along the lake shore, heedless of direction, caring only to be gone from that accursed spot. When, near the foot of the lake, I stopped and looked back at the mountaintop the face was gone.

What I next recall must have come some time afterwards, for I was standing upon the wooded bank of a swift-flowing river. Not far below me stood a big doe, and from the way her head dropped and the listlessness of her gaze it was evident that she was hurt and near the end of her rope. I could see that the hind leg on the side that was away from me was twisted and dangling uselessly.

There was no compassion in me then, though in ordinary circumstances I must have felt sorry for any beast in such distress. Now I saw only that here was meat, meat for the taking, and my belly was tied in tight-balled knots with hunger. Neither did I stop to think, so befogged was I with fever, that only a hunter's bullet could have smashed that leg.

I reached out and grasped the heaviest stick that I could find at hand to serve me as a bludgeon. The movement must have startled the animal, for she leapt down from the bank and bounded across the river on her three good legs. A wave of despair swept over me, and I sank to the ground. But in the next instant I was on my feet again, for I saw that she was unable to get up the steep bank on the far side. Heedless of my footing, I gave a hoarse croaking shout and flung myself down the bank into the river bed. My foot struck a rock, and I bounded forward without looking where I was going. Not until it was too late did I feel my foot slide between two stones. My ankle caught and I was thrown sideways. I felt a sudden stab of pain in my leg as the bone snapped, and at almost the same instant my head, unprotected by my injured arm, crashed against a rock. Stars dashed before my bewildered eyes. And then, all at once, everything went black.

When I opened my eyes it was near dark. A man was bending over me, and in my feverish eyes his face seemed all eyes and teeth. I could feel his hand groping beneath my shoulders and all at once I knew that this man was an Indian. I must, I thought, have gone back towards the Connecticut. Men who are lost often travel in circles, and that would be natural. This was one of my enemies who had stayed and waited for me, and now he was going to scalp me and leave me there to die. The idea went through my head crazily, like a flash of light. I flung myself sideways and wrenched out my knife, lunging at the dark figure beside me. But before I could reach him powerful fingers closed upon my arm. Something struck me a blow upon the head, and once again the welcome darkness engulfed me.

❨ 1 For a long time after that I knew nothing of what went on around me. Sometimes I would seem to awake to find myself lying on my back in the wet brush, the roaring noise of a great river pounding at my ears, and a wildcat tearing at my soaked bandages and clawing at my wound. I would cry out then with pain and horror, and would fight fiercely to keep the beast away, until another wave of darkness would sweep over me shutting it away. Again I would hear voices and feel hands lifting me. A little later I would be running through a hellish tangle of windfallen spruce, my hands and face and clothing scratched and torn by the sharp dead branches, while foul-smelling mud dragged at my ankles, and a mob of yelling, painted savages ran at my heels, pelting me with clubs and stones until I fell exhausted, when it would all seem to melt away and be forgotten, and I would feel cool hands upon my brow and soft lips against my cheek and hear my wife's voice speaking to me, calmly, soothingly, more sweetly gentle than I had ever known it to be before. After that I would seem to sleep, only to awake again to find myself floundering in icy water up to my chin, while on the bank near by I could see the Indians sitting in silent ominous rows in the flickering torchlight, waiting for me to come to shore.

How long this went on, I could not tell. But in the end I opened my eyes to find myself lying on a bunk in what seemed the main room of a good-sized log cabin. It was some minutes before I could realize that this was not a part of still another fevered dream. The rough table and benches in the middle of the room; the curtained bunk against the far wall; the huge stone fireplace, with its cheerful blaze and the blackened kettle hanging from the massive lug pole—these seemed no more real than had the Indians and the wildcats and woods and water of my delirium, and the wild whistle of the wind outside only helped to heighten the impression of unreality.

But when I tried to raise myself upon my elbow to gain a better view of the room the stab of pain that went through my shoulder assured me that it was real enough, and I lay back to ponder where I was and by what means I could have come there, when by all rights I should by now be lying stiff and cold in the mountains.

The bunk in which I lay was a wide one with deep sideboards. It had been filled eight inches deep with soft fragrant tips of balsam and the whole covered over with an enormous bearskin, making as comfortable a bed as could be desired. Over me there were a pair of fine blankets of bright red wool. My left leg felt heavy and uncomfortable, and when I tried to move it I could not. I lifted the blankets away and saw that it was bound from the knee down in a sort of heavy cast of clay and willow splints. At the same time I discovered that I was wrapped in a nightshirt of flannel that had originally been meant for a much larger man than I. There was a neat linen bandage about my middle, binding the wound in my side; and, though I could not see it, I could feel that my back and shoulder were similarly bound. The dressing at my shoulder, near enough for me to smell it, gave off a faint, aromatic, rather pleasing odour of crushed herbs. Whoever it was that had found me, it was evident, wished me no harm.

The effort involved in the attempt to raise myself had driven home one point solidly and indisputably; I was near weak enough to fall easy prey to a rabbit. The exertion had left me faint and dizzy, and for an instant I feared I was about to slip back into that nightmare state of semiconsciousness from which I had but just awakened. I lay back feebly against the pillows and gazed about the room, half hoping to find there some hint to my whirling brain of where I might be or by whom I might have been found.

There was little enough. The cabin was divided into two rooms by a pole partition at the head of my bunk. A curtain hung across the door cut off my view of the other, but the room in which I lay was spacious enough and cheerful, despite its scanty furniture. It was some fifteen feet wide by twenty long. On one side was the bunk which I occupied at the moment, a curtained window, and a cupboard. Across the room was a similar bunk, built against the wall, the door, and a second window. The enormous fireplace filled almost the entire end of the room. The only furnishings were the roughhewn table, with its two long benches, made of split logs set upon pegs, and two rustically made armchairs. Hanging on various pegs about the room were a musket, a shot pouch and powder horn, elaborately carved, and somehow vaguely familiar, a man's rough homespun coat, a short bearskin jacket, and a fox cap with the brush attached. Under the farther bunk there was a pair of small beaded moccasins such as might be worn by a woman or a child. It was such a cabin as might have been occupied by any frontier family. Yet I did not think it possible I could have won all the way to Canterbury. Probably, I thought, some hunters had found me and carried me in to the settlements.

If it was not already dark outside, night was evidently approaching, for the curtains had been drawn at the windows, and the room was lighted by two tall bayberry dips that stood in wooden holders upon the table and by a pewter bear-oil lamp upon the window shelf. Not a sound betrayed the presence of another person, but that there was someone within call was indicated not only by the lights but also by the fact that wooden plates and horn cups were laid at the table for three, and that from the kettle that bubbled merrily over the fire came the appetizing aroma of venison stew.

I became aware of this last quite suddenly, realizing all at once that I was famished, and my mouth began to water, so that I forgot to wonder at my rescue and began to lick my lips and swallow in anticipation.

It was while I lay thus, sniffing and swallowing and mentally rubbing my stomach over the fine meal I was about to have, that the door opened and a girl stepped inside. She was carrying a bucket of water, and her back was towards me, so that I did not at first recognize her. But when she turned to close the door behind her I caught a glimpse of her face in profile, and cried out in surprise. Although it was near two years since I had seen the child, she had not changed, unless it was to fill out somewhat and grow more lovely.

"Purity!" I gasped.

At the sound of my voice she set down the bucket quickly on the shelf by the door, and turned her head towards me, the little particles of snow that had caught in her hair glistening in the candlelight. She took off the coonskin coat in which she had been wrapped, and I saw that she was dressed in shirt and breeches like a boy. She must have read disapproval in my look, for she hesitated and glanced down at herself, blushing with pretty confusion. But before I could speak she had recovered her poise and was crossing the room towards me. She came to stand beside my bunk and laid her hand upon my forehead, then ran her fingers through my hair.

"How do you feel?" she asked.

I gave her a feeble smile.

"Fine," I lied. "Is this your cabin? How did I get here?"

She did not answer me at once, but stood looking down at me, her fingers twisting and turning in my hair.

"I thought you'd be gone," I said, "like the others in Stevenstown."

Instead of answering, however, she startled me by sinking to her knees beside the bunk and bursting into tears.

"Oh, Jamie, Jamie," she cried, "I had begun to think you'd never be yourself again! It's been so long!"

I was touched by her evident concern, and with an effort I slipped my good arm about her shoulders and drew her head down upon my shoulder.

"There, now," I said with as much strength as I could muster. "Has it been so bad as all that?"

Neither of us saw the door open nor was aware that there was another in the room until we heard him laugh.

"Bad!" boomed Jed Stiles' hoarse voice. "God's blood, I'd say ye were bad! Why, ye were like a catamount in a trap. It'd take the three of us to hold ye every time we'd go to change your wounds."

Purity bounced to her feet, her face flaming.

"Jed!" I cried, partly with genuine surprise, and partly to cover Purity's confusion.

"His fever's gone, pa!" she cried. "He's going to be all right."

He gave her a glance that was fondly amused and came across to stand beside her.

"How do you feel, lad?" he asked.

"Fair enough," I said, "but hungry. How about some of that

stew, Mistress Purity? It's been so long since I tasted anything but raw fish and hedgehog meat I didn't know such things existed any more."

"Long!" exclaimed Purity indignantly. "I'll have you know, Mr. Ferguson, it's been no such thing. You may not know it, but for the last ten days you've been living on the finest chicken broth in the Province! I've had to kill six of my ten chickens just for you!"

I looked at her soberly, for I knew how fond she was of her hens.

"You shouldn't have done that," I said, then stopped abruptly and looked at Stiles.

"Did she say ten days?" I demanded.

He laughed outright at the look of incredulity on my face and nodded.

"Ten days tomorrow," he replied, "since Toby brought ye in upon his back."

"But, what—how—" I began.

He turned to drag up one of the rough chairs, speaking at the same time to Purity.

"Fetch the brandy, lass," he commanded. "Then get the lad a biscuit and a bowl of broth from the stew. 'Tis food will do him most good now!"

She ran to do his bidding, returning in a moment with a tall black bottle that had obviously never seen the colour of a Boston fog, for it bore the stamp of the French government. Stiles reached a horn cup from the table and splashed it three-quarters full. With a great hand he propped my head up while I drank. The liquor burned my throat, and I could feel its warmth shooting through all my veins. I choked a little over the last few drops, and tears came to my eyes. He sat back in his seat and laughed at me.

"Ah," he said, "you'll have to learn it all over again!"

"Let's see you do better on your back," I retorted.

"I could do better standing on my head," he gibed.

I did not bother to reply. I wanted to know what had happened.

"Tell me," I demanded.

He tilted his chair back and took a long pull at the bottle.

"Let's see," he said musingly, cocking one eye at the rafters overhead. " 'Twas ten days ago. On a Sunday, it was. Toby went out for deer."

"Hunting on the Sabbath!" I exclaimed. " 'Tis a ten-shilling fine, half to the informer! I'll have the law on him, Jed."

" 'Twas a lucky day for you," said Jed soberly. "He wounded an old doe towards evenin', but she gave him the slip."

"Why," I cried, " 'twas the same I was chasing when I fell!"

Jed nodded.

"He went out next day," he went on, "to see if he couldn't pick her up, for he'd an idee where she'd crossed the river. Sure enough, 'long towards afternoon he came on her track, and a bit after he found yours. A mite further on, he come on where you'd both gone down int' the river, and there you both was; her laying tuckered all out in the fur bank where she'd been a-trying to climb up, an' you down in the stream bed with your leg wedged between two rocks and twisted clean around, and your head against another, and blood all over you and everywheres."

He chuckled.

"He said you woke up," he continued, "just as he was about to pick you up, and yanked your knife and fit him like a young catamount."

I grinned shamefacedly.

"I remember," I said. "I thought he was an Indian and was going to scalp me."

"You was half right," said Stiles.

"I meant one of those other Indians," I replied.

"What Indians?" he demanded. "Say, what happened to you, anyway?"

But Purity appeared at his elbow before I could reply, a steaming bowl in one hand and a plate of hot biscuits in the other.

"Never mind that now," she said crisply. "Do you want to put him out of his head again, pa? There'll be plenty of time for that later."

Jed laughed, and reached out his hand for the bowl.

"Oh, all right," he said.

But Purity held the plate and bowl away out of his reach.

"No, sir!" she exclaimed. "You're too clumsy. You'd have half of it down his neck. I'm going to attend to this."

He got up, laughing good-humouredly, and gave her his chair.

"Just as you say, lass," he said. "I'll wash."

He turned to go into the other room, but paused with his hand on the curtain and fixed me with a belligerent eye.

" 'Tis the best care you'll ever have," he said, and disappeared.

When I met Purity's eyes over the steaming spoon she held out to me I was well ready to believe it.

Toby came in just as I finished my supper, filling the room with the faint half sweet, half sour Indian smell of him. He greeted me impassively, and as soon as Purity had fed me the last spoonful of stew he stripped away my blankets, without the least thought of propriety, and examined my dressings. When he straightened up with a grunt of satisfaction I was relieved to see that Purity had left the room.

"Jed says I almost stuck my knife in you, Toby," I said.

He looked at me impassively and nodded, but I could see his huge belly shaking with inward laughter.

"Most do," he said.

"I'm sorry," I said. "I always seem to be trying to kill you, but I don't mean it."

His lined and wrinkled face split into a wide grin at that.

"Two time Toby lucky," he said. "Maybe three time no good!"

"There won't be any third time if I can help it," I said.

The others ate their supper not long after that. When they had finished, Stiles and Toby dragged chairs over beside my bunk and Stiles rummaged about until he found a pipe for me. I knew they wanted to hear the story of what had happened to me, but I would tell them nothing until Purity had finished with the dishes and come to sit beside me on the bunk. This, I told myself, was not from any sentimental reasons, but rather because I knew she was curious as the rest and I had no wish to tell it twice over when once would do.

When they were settled I told them the whole thing from the beginning: how we made the trip from Portsmouth; how we had done our work at the Upper Cohos; how I had failed to recognize the Indian sign behind our camp; and how they had fallen upon us. When they learned that I had come all the way wounded and afoot from the Cohos with neither food nor fire and only a knife for a weapon, Stiles and Toby looked at each other in amazement.

"Little white man damn tough!" said Toby.

Stiles spat and grinned.

"Hell," he said, "he was born to hang!"

When I came to the face floating among the clouds upon the mountain side I could see Toby roll his eyes; but Jed hooted with laughter.

"Manitou, my foot!" he shouted. "Why, God's blood, man, 'tis but a stone face in the cliff! I have seen it myself. When ye're better able to get about than ye are now I'll take ye there and show it to ye. 'Tis only to be seen from one spot at the head of the lake."

But I had had all I wished of that spot. I said as much. Stiles continued to laugh until Purity shot him a warning glance.

"Be still, pa!" she commanded.

He looked confused.

"Sorry, lad," he said apologetically. "I meant no harm."

I shook my head at him, and grinned a trifle wanly, I fear.

"What are you doing here, anyway?" I demanded. "Stevenstown's abandoned, you know. I thought you'd be gone."

He shrugged.

"Shucks!" he said. "I know all these Indians. I've known 'em all my life. I traded with 'em before I come here, an' I been tradin' with 'em since. I've always treated 'em square, an' they know it. They like me, all except maybe a few like Titigaw an' Christo. They wouldn't come here an' attack me—not without warnin' anyway."

"Oh!" I said, and fell silent. It was a thing I had not thought about. As trader to the Indians he was, of course, on better terms with them than most. Doubtless he knew well enough how long it would be safe to stay.

After that we remained wrapped in our own thoughts for a time, until all at once an idea struck me.

"What day is it?" I asked.

"Tuesday," said Purity promptly.

Stiles got up and took a stick about four feet long from the corner. I saw that it was covered with notches. He examined it closely for a moment before he spoke.

"December the fourteenth," he said finally.

"The fourteenth!" I exclaimed, making as if to rise, only to sink back with a groan as the wounds stabbed me. "How long before I can be gone?"

Stiles looked at me wryly.

" 'Bout the first of April," he said slowly.

"But I must go before then!" I cried. "Why, they'll think me dead."

Stiles chuckled and seemed about to say something, when Purity leapt to her feet.

"They'll be the happier to see you alive," she said, and turned to the others. "Come, now! 'Tis time for bed."

She shooed Stiles into the other room, and pushed Toby towards the door. I remembered that Stiles had said that Toby had his own cabin.

When they were gone she came over to my bunk and made a great pretence of smoothing my blankets.

"Don't mind them," she said, soothingly. "They don't mean anything. Last week it snowed five days steady. The snow is four foot on the level now, but as soon as it settles a mite we'll get Toby out to Rumford or Suncook with a message."

I caught her flying fingers with my good hand, and pressed them to my lips.

"You're a sweet child, Purity," I said.

For an instant she stood, her hand in mine, looking down upon me with an amused smile. Then all at once she bent down and kissed me.

" 'Child,' he calls me still," she said.

And before I could say anything she had flipped the curtains to across my bunk. I heard her feet patter over the floor and saw the room go dark as she blew out the candles one by one. An instant later there was a creak from the bunk opposite.

No man ever had more gentle care than I in the days that followed. Every day Toby would attend my wounds, and Purity, who was constantly within call, overwhelmed me with tender kindness such as I had never before known her to be capable of.

In spite of all this, however, it was a month before I was able to leave my bunk and hobble to a chair before the fire. Perhaps the degree of my exhaustion had something to do with it. Perhaps my system had been so weakened that it was slow to recover. But, whatever the cause, my wounds did not heal as they should; neither did I regain strength rapidly. Probably because I had to keep to my bed anyway, the bone in my leg knit quickly enough, so that when, about the end of January, they finally allowed me to get up and move about, I found that I could hobble around fairly well with the aid of a stick. The bullet burn on my side, being nothing more than a scratch, filled up without trouble and left barely a scar to show where it had been, but the hole in my shoulder mended but slowly, despite all Toby's herbs and potions. Indeed, to this day I am troubled with it, for when the weather grows cold and rainy it will ache me like a sore tooth; and I have never since been able to lift that arm above my shoulder.

January brought a series of blizzards, one after another, and the weather continued bitterly cold throughout February, so that it was March before I was able to be out of doors again. I was anxious to be off, for I knew that Dorcas and my friends in Portsmouth must, long since, have given me up for lost. But after the winter's hibernation I was soft and my strength was slow to return. Moreover, I had to consider my hosts' feelings. They had picked me from the very jaws of death and nursed me back to life again. I felt that I owed them more than I could ever repay, and it occurred to me that to hasten away at the very first moment of my recovery might seem to them, and especially to Jed who was sensitive in such matters, ungrateful.

There was one, however, who observed my restlessness. One afternoon in mid-March I returned to the cabin after a walk down to the river to find Purity and Toby in deep conversation. As I entered Purity looked up.

"Toby thinks he can get to Rumford now," she said, "if you want to send out word."

I looked at the old Indian eagerly.

"Will you do it, Toby?" I asked.

He shrugged.

"Can do now," he replied. "Snow not too deep."

I spent that evening writing letters for him to carry. I sent one to my sisters in Suncook, and another to Dorcas. These were easy enough to write, but I sat up half the night composing a third to young Sparhawk's family. At least, I was able to assure them, he had been taken alive. A fourth letter I wrote to the Governor, reporting to him, as fully as I could from memory, all that we had done upon the intervales, and at the same time giving him an account of the attack together with my own escape and rescue.

In the morning before the sun had climbed above the ridge to eastward Toby set out with my letters in a packet. I had given him a note to Alice, asking her to let him have what money he needed for his expenses beyond Suncook, and he was to go on to Portsmouth and wait there for any reply. As we shook hands at the door I urged him to hurry. He grinned.

"Toby go quick," he said, and belched rumblingly in appreciation of the breakfast Purity had given him.

I watched him swing away down the path towards the river and turn when he came to the bank, going off across the snow-covered field that Stiles meant to plant to corn in May. At the far end of the field, just before he entered the woods, he turned and waved once, and then was gone.

The days dragged a little after that. Before the week was out I was watching anxiously for his return, though I knew it must take him at least a fortnight to go and come. I noticed, too, that Purity seemed somewhat distraught and a little moody. Now that I no longer needed her care she had taken to going for long walks alone in the near-by woods, but she had remained cheerful and gay. Now, however, she turned suddenly silent and morose. I feared that perhaps it was my fault, and that she was overtired. She had had her hands full keeping house for two such hearty gluttons as Toby and her father, and I thought that perhaps the added burden of my care had been too much for her to carry. It was with this thought in my mind that I tried to cheer her one evening by saying that I would be going soon, and that after that she would find life easier.

Jed, who had had a long day on the traps, was snoring gently in his bunk—for as soon as I no longer needed her close attention Purity had moved into the back room—and we were toasting our feet before the great fireplace. Purity did not smile, but gave me a long look.

"Will you be glad to be going, Jamie?" she said.

I was at once covered with confusion, for I had not meant any words that way.

"That's not a fair question," I replied, stammering. "Of course I shan't be happy to part from such friends as you have been. You know I'll not soon forget all you've done for me. But—"

"But all the same," she said, "you'll be just a little happy to be gone."

"That's not so!" I cried hotly. "I shall be sorry. But at the same time I shall be glad to get back to those others who love me and who must surely have thought me dead. Surely you can understand that, child."

She did not reply, but sat silent for so long a time that I feared she was offended. But when she spoke presently I knew that she had been thinking of other things.

"It will be lonely here when you've gone, Jamie," she said.

"Lonely!" I cried with indignation, for it was what I had always thought. I had never approved of her coming there. "Of course 'twill be lonely. 'Twould be lonely for anyone but an Indian and a hermit! 'Tis no place for you, lass. Why don't you come out into the world and find yourself a good lad to love you and look after you as it should be done? This is no natural life for a girl like you!"

She smiled a little.

"Who would have me?" she said.

"Who would have you?" I retorted. "And who would not, I'd like to know? Why, I could name a dozen offhand would consider themselves lucky to make such a find! If I were not married myself I'd have you before another beat me to it. 'Fore God I would!"

I sat there breathing hard through my nose, indignant at the very thought. She looked at me and smiled gently.

"Would you, Jamie?" she asked.

There was that in her tone that confused me and set me to blushing furiously.

"I—" I began.

But she shook her head and cut me short.

"No, Jamie," she said, "it won't do. You see there's none I'd want."

"But how do you know?" I cried. "You've seen none but the lads at Suncook!"

She shook her head again.

"It's no use, Jamie," she said. "There was one once I might have had, but he'd have none of me."

"The devil you say!" I exclaimed, for I could not imagine to whom she referred. She had never shown the least interest in anybody in Suncook that I knew of.

"Tell me his name and I'll wring his worthless neck for slighting you," I cried.

She stood up, laughing at my ferocity.

"No, Jamie," she said, "I'll keep his name for my secret. You might do him hurt if I told."

With that she bent down and brushed my cheek with her lips. "Good night, Jamie," she said. "If you can guess his name I'll tell you!"

In the next moment she was gone through the low doorway into the back room, leaving me staring after her in complete bafflement. What in the devil's name had she meant by that, I wondered. Then all at once a flicker of suspicion flashed in the back of my mind. It didn't seem likely. Yet it might be. Could it have been myself she meant? I sat for a long time gazing into the fire, thinking, going back over the past. At last I got up somewhat heavily and shook my head. Only a fool could think that, I told myself as I undressed and rolled into my bunk. Still I noticed that she avoided my eye in the morning, and slipped away from the house as soon as the breakfast things were done.

It was two weeks before Toby returned at last, bearing a short note of rejoicing from my sister, a message of thanks and sympathy from the Sparhawks, and two fat packets: the one bearing the Governor's seal, and the other addressed in Dorcas' hand.

The Governor's letter I found to be written by Winston Fisher, with whom I was slightly acquainted, and whom I knew to be one of Wentworth's secretaries. The Governor, Fisher said, was deeply sympathetic for my troubles, and thankful for my safety. He himself was swamped with work at the moment, but he had asked Fisher to write that the project for the settlement of the Upper Cohos, as well as that for the Lower, had been abandoned temporarily. It was to be regretted that all I had gone through must be in vain; but circumstances forced the issue, and there was no choice. There followed a great many pages of explanation, which I found chiefly interesting as news, for they indicated that great things were happening in my absence:

War [said Fisher] is now inevitable. Our own troubles during the latter part of the summer and fall, we know now, were but a part of a general movement all along the frontier by the French and Indians. . . . An actual battle was fought in the West, at a place called Great Meadows, where Colonel Washington, of Virginia, whipped a strong force of the enemy, who were evidently bent upon invasion of that Province. . . . The French have sent out Baron Dieskau with numerous troops; and in retaliation the King has despatched General Braddock to Virginia, with orders to drive the French from the Ohio. Braddock is to command all the forces in the colonies, and he has called a conference of Governors at Alexandria in Virginia to consider the plan of campaign and the quotas in troops and money of each Province. . . . Governor Shirley has already set out from Boston to meet the General, who is expected to arrive daily in Virginia; and Governor Wentworth expects to follow him almost at once. . . .

No one knows exactly what plans the General has in mind. Expeditions against the French on the Ohio and at Crown Point are certain, and further expeditions against Niagara and Beausejour in Acadia are probable. There was a rumour that an expedition would be sent against Quebec by way of the Kennebec and the Chaudière, but this is now considered unlikely. The Province has already been pledged to raise five hundred men, and there is much contention and jealousy as to who shall command, though the choice seems to lie between Colonel Meserve and Colonel Blanchard. . . . Everything is in a state of great confusion and disorder, between the uproar of recruiting and almost daily disputes in the assembly. . . . We are finding it difficult to get recruits for the Provincial regiment as most of the lads, in Portsmouth at least, are anxious to join Pepperell's 51st, which has lately been placed on a footing as regulars, and are to receive the King's pay and be furnished with uniforms. . . .

I tossed this letter over to Stiles when I had finished reading it, for I could see that he was fair aching to hear the news, the snatches I had read him having served greatly to arouse his curiosity. He carried it over beside the fireplace, and gathered the others around him, while I broke the seal on Dorcas' letter:

My dear husband;

I find it hard to tell you how gratified I am to learn that you are alive and well; not dead as we had all long since imagined you. At the same time I am sure you can appreciate what a shock it must have been to me when that filthy old man you sent appeared at our door announcing that he had a letter from you. If it had not been for Hubert I do not know what I should have done. He has handled things admirably, but I have been confined to my bed ever since.

Hubert has been with me since you left, and I cannot tell you what a tower of strength he has been to me. When you did not return by the first week in December we began to grow apprehensive that something had happened to you. And when the New Year came and went with still no word from you we gave you up for lost. Hubert has had to look after everything, for I have had neither the strength nor the heart for it.

But now all that is past. You are alive and safe and we are all rejoicing in that. Please thank your friends for me, and give my kindest to Mistress Purity, who, I feel sure, has shown you the tenderest care and attention, and to whom, I know, much credit for your recovery is due.

I know that your wounds still trouble you, and although I am naturally most anxious to see you I do not feel that I should urge you to hasten to me before you have regained your full strength and are fit for the journey. Rest where you are until you feel strong enough. Whenever that may be, you may be sure that both your cousin and myself will be waiting to welcome you with open arms!

In the meantime, dear husband Jamie, believe me ever your faithful, dutiful wife and your most humble, obedient servant,

DORCAS DREW FERGUSON

Portsmouth, March the 22nd 1755

P.S. I have had some considerable repairs made upon the house, as well as bought a chariot and three blackamoors, a male and two female, at considerable cost. I hope you do not think me too extravagant.

I could not help but think it was a strange letter for a man long considered dead to receive from his wife. What I had expected, I could not now say; but I was certain that this was scarcely it. Still, I had to recognize the fact that Dorcas must have been distraught when she wrote it. To have a husband return from the dead does not happen to every woman, and it occurred to me that it must be disconcerting to say the least.

I looked up at Toby, as I finished it.

"What did you do?" I asked him. "She seems to have a pick on you."

He shrugged impassively.

"Not know!" he said. "Toby come door just when tall Englishman in red coat leaving. Toby see you woman stand behind. She see Toby first and holler. 'Who there?' she say. Englishman him turn, say, 'Begone, fellow!'" Here the old man's voice cracked in a ludicrous imitation of Hubert's foppish speech. "'No got for beggar!'"

He stopped and drew himself erect proudly.

"Well?" I demanded.

"Um say," he went on, " 'Toby not beggar. Toby got um letter for Jamie squaw!' "

"What did they say to that?" I asked.

He gave me a curious look.

"She say, 'Man mad. Hugh dear, make go 'way.' But him look surprise' and say, 'No! We find out about this.' Then him reach out hand and say give him letter. Him take it and show her. He say, 'Is his hand?' She give look and squawk like chicken. 'It is, it is!' she holler. 'He not die, Hugh.' Then she fall down on floor like fool white woman and make sleep."

"She fainted," I said. "Then what?"

"Big Englishman," Toby replied, "turn and holler in house, ' 'Gustus, 'Gustus!' Then him turn Toby, say: 'You go 'way now. Come back tomorrow. She give answer then.' "

"Is that all?" I asked.

He nodded.

"That all," he said. "Toby go 'way. Go back next day. Black man give letter. Toby come back here."

My first impulse was to leave at once; to get back to Portsmouth as quickly as I might. But neither Stiles nor Toby would hear of it. They pointed out that I was scarce strong enough yet for such a journey, and Toby insisted that we had not yet seen the last of winter.

There followed a wait of two weeks while I slowly gathered strength for the journey southward. Almost daily I accompanied Stiles or Toby into the woods, visiting a trap line, gathering wood, hunting, or fishing. With each passing day I felt myself growing a little stronger, and almost began to consider myself able to make the trip. But one day I went with Stiles up into the notch through which I had come, to see the stone face on the mountain. It was a long walk, and it was after dark before we returned to the cabin. I was exhausted, more than I should have been; and I knew then that I was not yet ready to go.

Throughout this period of waiting Stiles also exhibited great restlessness. He talked incessantly of Louisbourg, in which expedition he had taken an active part, and of the expedition which it had been proposed to send against Quebec in '46. He was full of tales of army life and of the wild doings of himself and his comrades, and from this I knew that the news of the forthcoming campaigns had aroused him, and that he was secretly aching to be off.

One evening I taxed him with this, and he grinned sheepishly.

"Well," he said, "I might 'a' ben thinking of it. They'll be needin' experienced men if they're a-goin' to drive the Frenchies out o' Crown Point."

"But what about Purity?" I demanded.

His face fell, and I could see that it was the first time he had given his responsibilities a thought. Then almost at once he brightened up.

"Shucks!" he exclaimed in evident relief. "I know she'd be safe enough if I was to leave her with you folks."

I threw up my hands in a gesture of despair. What could one do with such a man? Toby, who had sat silent in the corner until that moment spoke.

"You go, I go," he said.

Stiles swung about towards him.

"Will you?" he cried. "By God, I'll show you some fun!"

He slapped his knee and roared with laughter.

But with all his assurance it was plain he had not yet made up his mind. First he would be all for going. Then when he had thought it over he would seem to change his mind. I was puzzled, at first, by his vacillation, until suddenly it dawned upon me that probably for the first time in his life he had found a place to which he had grown so attached that he hesitated to leave it. Mid-April came and went, and still we made no move to leave. I had regained my strength by then, and I knew that I was fit at last to make the journey. I resolved, to myself, that unless Stiles had reached a decision before the first of May I would be off alone.

I could not foresee that our hands would be forced, nor the way in which this would be brought about.

It came on a bright afternoon near the end of the month. I was sitting outside the cabin door on the bench that was placed there, enjoying the warmth of the spring sunshine on my body. Inside I could hear the occasional rattle of a pot as Purity went about her preparations for supper, and now and again I would hear Stiles' voice mumble something. Toby had gone off up the east branch of the river to try for some trout.

All at once I was startled to see a man step out of the woods on the far side of Stiles' stump-strewn cornfield, where the river trail came in. He was a short man, clad in light buckskins, and though I could not at that distance make out his features I could see that he carried a long musket in the crook of his arm. As I watched him a second figure appeared in the trail behind him, and I caught my breath. Even without the sun glinting upon the naked coppery torso or gleaming on the shaven poll, I could have told he was an Indian by his walk. I got up quickly and went into the cabin.

"Jed!" I said, breathlessly. "There's two men coming across the field: an Indian and a white man."

Purity looked up at her father quickly and then turned back to her cooking. Stiles heaved himself up off the bunk on which he had been lying and stretched lazily.

"Only two of 'em, you say?" he demanded. "They don't mean no harm then."

"Can you trust them?" I demanded.

He gave me a quizzical grin and shrugged. He went to the door, and I followed close at his heels. But I noticed that he took his gun, for all his fine words, and stood it just inside the door within reach of his hand.

The two men had almost reached the house by this time, and I saw that while the Indian was tall and barrel-chested the white man was small and wizened, and his little black eyes peered brightly out of a face all tracked and wrinkled with tiny crow's-feet. His nose was long and sharp, and his mouth was thin and humorous. There was an air about him that told me he was a Frenchman even before he opened his mouth. When he saw Stiles in the doorway he gave a great shout.

"*Holà*, Jad!" he shouted. "By Gar damn, you still here, eh?"

Stiles waved indolently, but I noticed that he did not move out of the doorway.

"Howdy, Jules," he said. "What brings you down this way?"

The two men came up, and the Frenchman held out his hand.

"Not against you, my frien'," he said.

Stiles shook hands with him and stood aside for them to enter.

They came in, and the old Frenchman bowed low to Purity with a grin that showed him to be toothless. He looked about the room swiftly, and his eye fell upon the flintlock by the door. He wagged his head at Stiles and chuckled.

"You not trus' your ol' frien' Jules, eh?" he said half accusingly.

Stiles shrugged.

"You know how things are now," he said.

The Frenchman laughed and flung himself into a chair before the fire. The Indian took a squatting position by the wall, just inside the door, and fixed me with bright birdlike eyes.

"Come, my frien'," said Jules. "Ees thees your 'ospitality? 'Ave you no more of those fine brandy w'at I bring you las' time I come? My frien' an' me we 'ave come long way today from almos' Stevenstown. We 'ave thirst lak grrrand fire!"

Stiles went silently to the cupboard and brought down the black bottle and four cups. He poured a drink for the Frenchman and another for me. Then he poured one for the Indian, who tossed it off before he could pour his own. The Indian held out his cup for more, but Stiles shook his head.

"Not now," he said.

The Frenchman spoke gutturally to the Indian, and the latter shrugged good-naturedly and sat back again, resuming his bright scrutiny of my person. Jules held his cup aloft silently, and we all drank. When he had drained the mug the Frenchman tossed his upon the table and looked inquiringly from me to Stiles and back again. Stiles presented me by name, and I learned that the Frenchman was Jules Caron, a trader from Quebec.

"The lad was set upon by Indians on the Cohos intervales last fall," said Stiles, watching the other shrewdly. "He made his way down here afoot and with two bullets in him. Toby found him in the river just above the forks."

The Frenchman looked at me in frank amazement.

"From Upper Cohos wounded and afoot!" he exclaimed. "By de blood of de Virgin, 'e does not look so strong, eh?"

He turned to the Indian and chattered at him in the Abenaki tongue. The Indian looked at me in obvious surprise, and then began to talk rapidly. They talked for some minutes, swiftly. Then old Jules turned to me.

"You know per'aps w'at 'appen, eh?" he asked.

I shook my head.

"Only that we were attacked," I replied.

He nodded.

"In November," he said, "two Englishmen come to Saint François. They are frien' to Thomas Titigaw: one a beeg man wit' black *barbe* an' little eye, an' the oder 'igh but not fat an' wit' scared look. These man say to Titigaw two strange English come to Upper Cohos an' camp to mak settlement there. They say English will build fort. Titigaw take eleven brave an' go. W'en 'e come back 'e bring wan preesonair an' say oder man wounded, die in woods."

"Do you remember the names of the men who brought the word to Titigaw?" I asked.

He shook his head, but this mattered not to me. The description fitted Sanborn and Merrill perfectly, though I could not imagine how they could have discovered where we were.

"How is my friend now?" I asked.

Jules turned again and spoke to the Indian. Presently he turned back to me.

"Thees man, Rowi," he said, introducing the Indian with the savage corruption of the French Louis. " 'E tell me all about. 'E say your frien' safe now in Saint François. Soon 'e think Titigaw sell 'im to Bigot."

I thanked him.

"Ask him," I said, "if he will tell my friend that I am safe."

He nodded and spoke to the Indian.

" 'E will tell 'im," he said. "Your frien' 'e think you die. 'E will be glad to 'ear you 'ave escape'."

He turned abruptly to Stiles.

"You 'ave 'ear, eh, my frien'?" he said. "Now maybe we 'ave war?"

Stiles chuckled.

"I heard something about it," he replied.

"Hah!" said the other explosively. "You 'ave 'ear, but I 'ave 'ear more! I will tell you about after the suppair."

The conversation then drifted away to talk of furs and hunting, and it appeared it had been as bad a season in Canada as it had here. Trade goods were spoken of, and comparative prices in Canada and New England; and after a time the tension that was in the air at first decreased and then went away. I was amazed that men who must soon become enemies could appear so friendly.

But I must say that they were amiable enough, and since Stiles seemed to trust them, I saw no reason why I should not pretend to.

About dusk Toby came in, to be greeted vociferously by Jules, and with reserve by Rowi. There was another drink around, after which Toby settled himself upon the opposite side of the room from the Indian, and the two sat staring at each other in beady silence.

Not long afterwards Purity served us a fine hot supper, which put the Frenchman in a high good humour; and for an hour thereafter, while I helped Purity with her dishes, he kept us entertained with his rollicking French songs, sung in a booming baritone, surprising in one so withered and small.

Presently Purity withdrew to the back room. When she had gone I took down the pipe Stiles had loaned me and, filling it with some of Jules's rank Canadian leaf, joined the others before the fire. As I drew up my chair Stiles turned his glance upon the Frenchman.

"Well, what's the news?" he demanded.

Old Jules gave an explosive laugh.

"De news!" he exclaimed. "Hah! Dat ees fonny! You 'ave ask' de right man for news, my frien'. Ol' Jules knows more dan your own Governor!"

"So?" said Stiles.

"Yaiss! So!" said the other belligerently. "Look you, my frien', I am sent down into your Province of New 'Ampshire to fin' out w'at I can about w'at you do. Now I know not only w'at you do, but w'at also do all your oder province'. Een Quebec eet ees known w'at ees all your plan': thees General Braddock 'oo goes agains' Duquesne; thees pompous Shirley's plan agains' Oswego; your General Johnson 'oo will march agains' Crown Point an' Fort Saint Frederick. All thees we know, an' more, for knowing eet do we not know w'at will 'appen w'en they come? We will be ready!"

"Um!" said Stiles. "Maybe."

He gave the other a quizzical look.

"Maybe like hell by Gar damn!" exclaimed the Frenchman. "Your officers an' Governors are all fools! 'Ere in your own New 'Ampshire ees proof of thees. Your regiments are order' to Crown Point, an' w'ere you t'ink dey rendezvous?"

"Where?" asked Stiles.

"Stevenstown!" Jules exploded. "At Stevenstown, because your officers an' Governor t'ink eet ees by Cohos intervales dat de bes' route ees to be fin'!"

"No!" I exclaimed. "But, my God, man, that will take them away to the north!"

Jules leered at me, and looked at Stiles.

"You see," he said, "even your young men know eet ees not so! But your generals and your governors—" He snapped his fingers in the air. "Pouf! They are fools!"

"You can't tell me about generals," Stiles said. "Seems like when a man gets to be a general, or even a colonel sometimes, what brains he's got goes away!"

Old Jules swelled visibly, and seemed about to say something more. Then suddenly he appeared to shrink in upon himself. He looked at Stiles, and then at the bottle.

"Put de brandy away," he said. "Eet mak ol' Jules's tongue wag too free."

Stiles chuckled, and they sat in silence for some time. Then presently the Frenchman began to speak again.

"You go?" he said to Stiles suddenly.

Stiles shrugged.

"Hadn't thought much about it," he said.

I glanced at him sharply, but bit back the exclamation that rose to my tongue.

"W'y you don' come to Canada?" said Jules, after an instant's silence. "We pay een gol'. We 'ave plenty brandy. An' our officers are not fools!"

"But he couldn't do that!" I exclaimed. "He's an Englishman."

The old Frenchman turned slow eyes upon me.

"W'y not?" he said. "W'at difference eef 'e ees English or French? Wan ees as easy for killing as another. W'at difference it mak' w'ich side shoot at you so long you get bes' pay?"

Stiles laughed.

"Sure!" he said. "What difference does it make?"

I looked at him in amazement and some disgust, and might have had something of my mind to say, but he turned away from me quickly and spoke to the Frenchman.

"I dunno, though, Jules," he said. "I think not. I had enough at Louisbourg. All I want now is to stay here in peace an' quiet."

Jules looked at him queerly.

"W'at you say," he said, and shrugged. "You 'ave your chance."

"Thanks," said Stiles. "I'll keep it in mind."

He stood up and stretched, yawning.

"Guess I'll turn in," he said, and crossed to his bunk.

Jules and Rowi stretched out in their blankets on the floor in front of the hearth, and I noticed that after he had blown out the lights Toby, instead of returning to his own cabin, lay down near the door. The sinister air of the early afternoon seemed to have returned, and I tossed and turned for some time in my bunk before I was able to get to sleep.

When I awoke with a start it was daylight, and the others were already up and moving about. Jules and Rowi were attending to their packs, while Toby prepared breakfast at the fireplace. Purity, though I could hear her moving about in the other room, had not yet come out.

We ate a silent breakfast at the rough table. When it was finished the two travellers shouldered their packs and stepped outside the door. Toby, following, handed them their muskets, and I knew from the look in his eye that he had drawn their charges in the night. They took them without a word, and Jules turned to Stiles.

"You don' change your min', my frien'?" he asked.

Stiles shook his head.

"No," he said, "I guess not."

The Frenchman shrugged.

"Well," he said, *"à la bonne chance!"*

Very solemnly they both shook hands all around, and swung off down the trail towards the river. They crossed upon the rude log footbridge that Stiles had built across it, and a moment later disappeared in the woods on the far side.

2

They had scarce disappeared from view when Stiles beckoned Toby to him. He pointed after them.

"Follow them," he said. "Make sure they're heading out of the country."

Toby nodded comprehendingly and, picking up his long flintlock, set out along the trail at a jog trot. In a few moments he too had crossed the footbridge and was swallowed up in the far woods. I turned to Jed.

"What was that for?" I demanded. "You don't think they mean us mischief, do you?"

He shrugged.

"If they've a company lying out there," he said, gesturing towards the dark woods to westward, "now's the time they'll choose to attack—and it's likely they're not alone. We'll hear from Toby soon if they're not."

"But I thought they were friendly," I protested. "You said they'd not attack without warning anyway."

He gave me an impatient look.

"How much warning do you want?" he asked dryly.

I had no answer, for I had not thought of it in just that way before. Yet now that he spoke of it it was plain enough that that was what had been intended.

But he gave me no time to brood upon it. He turned into the cabin, and I could hear him talking to Purity.

"Watch the door," he was saying. "If anyone comes, bar it. You know what to do. We'll be back in a minute or two."

He came back with his gun in the crook of his arm, and jerked his head at me. I followed him down the little side path that led to Toby's cabin.

I had seen the Indian's hut before, but this was the first time I had been inside. I was surprised at the neatness of it, for I had never thought of Toby as an orderly person. It consisted of a single room, scarce larger than half the main room of Stiles' cabin, and was built of peeled spruce logs, neatly chinked with moss. At one end was the fireplace with its blackened lug pole, and the ashes of yesterday's fire lying white and dead against the soot-smeared hearth. At the other end was an enormous bunk built up a foot or so above the floor, and covered with a pair of thread-bare grey blankets, none too clean. There was no other furniture. Along the back wall hung an assortment of old greasy coats, shirts, and breeches. There was a pair of beaded moccasins toed in under the bunk, and in one corner was a small keg of powder, with a heavy bag of shot hanging from a peg above it. From pegs by the fireplace hung a battered skillet and a horn mug. A black-ened kettle still hung from the lug pole.

There was no window, only the door and chimney serving for

ventilation, and the room was filled with a stench that was at once rotten and vaguely familiar. I looked about, half expecting to see something dead, but beyond the haunch of venison that hung, covered with flies, in one corner there was nothing to be seen; and though that was strong it did not account for this overpowering smell. I saw Stiles looking at me and grinning.

"What in the name of God is it?" I demanded.

He laughed and jerked his head towards the roof. I looked up and saw that the room had been ceiled with birch poles, so that there was a sort of shallow loft overhead.

"He keeps his pelts, green and cured, up there," said Jed.

He did not wait for any comment, but strode to the bunk and ripped the blankets off, tossing them to me.

"Here," he said. "We'll have to be quick. Spread these out and dump his stuff into 'em. We'll take it all up yonder."

He jerked his head in the direction of the other cabin.

"Toby'll come back there."

I set about doing as he said, while he found the trap leading to the loft and swung himself up. I could hear him moving about on the poles overhead and cursing at the darkness. Then presently he began tossing down the furs.

In no time at all we had Toby's scant belongings packed in his blankets and the furs baled, ready to go. Stiles looked around.

"Guess that's all," he said.

He looked at the pile of stuff in front of the cabin.

"It'll take three trips," he added.

He leaned down and hoisted the two huge bales of furs onto his back with no more effort than he would use in lifting a baby.

"Bring along that kag o' powder," he said, "and the bag o' shot too, if you can manage it. Don't strain your shoulder though."

I picked up the articles he indicated with some difficulty, and staggered along behind him, up the path to the main cabin. Within a half-hour all the rest of Toby's belongings had been brought up and stowed. The little cabin in the hollow beside the spring stood drear and abandoned, looking as if it had not been occupied in years.

It was getting on to dark and the purple shadows were deepening in the wooded folds of the hills when Toby came back. Stiles met him at the door, standing to one side for him to come out of the grey dusk into the rich, yellow light of the candles.

"Well?" he said.

Toby looked tired, and I knew he must have gone a long way. I had never seen him look that way before. He was panting as if he had been running hard.

"They go," he said, between panting breaths. "Toby follow um over ridge." He gestured westward past where the bulk of Mooselauke loomed. "They come little river an' go down towards Ammonoosuc."

"Maybe they'll meet friends at the Oxbow," said Stiles.

But Toby shook his head.

"Take packs with um," he said. "Not do that if comin' back. Um cut 'cross from Ammonoosuc to Connecticut at Passumpsic. Go back Saint Francis first. Come back later."

"Why would they come back here?" I asked, for I could see no reason for it.

Jed looked at me impatiently.

"Old Jules talked too much," he said. "He never could hold his tongue. Every time he takes a drink everything in his head runs out his mouth. He'll remember that. The quicker we're gone from here, the better."

The next two days were filled with activity. Everything imperishable in the cabin—pots, traps, axes, clothing, buckets, snowshoes, even the frames of the windows—had to be securely cached away in the woods. Everything else was packed and stowed in the two long canoes. When the enemy came they would find only the empty shells of the two cabins.

On the evening of the second day the work was done, and everything was in readiness for the start. We slept that night on the bare shells of the bunks, the balsam tips long since turned brown beneath us, and only a single blanket each to cover us. As I lay in the darkened room, listening to the measured breathing of Stiles and Toby, I was conscious of a profound sense of regret at this hasty departure. Not until then did I realize how happy had been my stay.

We set out the next morning, April 28, at dawn, and went that day only as far as the falls of the Pemigewasset* above the mouth of the Asquamchumauke where we camped for the night. The

* Livermore Falls.

next day we pushed on downstream, making all possible haste, for Stiles was anxious to come early to the camp at Stevenstown.

We knew we were approaching the camp long before we came to it, for the tap of hammers and the ring of axes in the woods carried far in the light air. I could see Stiles begin to grow excited. Then all at once we swept around a bend and saw it spread out before us in a great field on the right bank above the river.

There must have been nearly a hundred tents pitched in a long double row along the river bank. On a little knoll behind the tents were three new peeled-log cabins, and a dozen fires were smoking in the long street. On the sandy shingle by the river forty or fifty men were hammering away at battoes in various stages of construction. In the field between the cabins and the tents perhaps a hundred more were wheeling and filing in awkward imitation of military drill.

As we swung around the bend the men hammering upon the boats stopped work to stare. Someone shouted, and men on the bank turned to look in our direction. Heads popped out of gaping tent flaps. Up at the cabins a door slammed. A man came out and looked, then turned and disappeared inside again. As our keel grated upon the sand of the shingle I heard someone call my name, and looked up to see John Stark's homely face, twisted in a dour grin, peering down at me from the bank.

"Come ashore," he said, "and identify yourselves. I have to make sure you're not a pack of Frenchmen come to spy on us."

He came sliding down the bank as we stepped out upon the sand, followed by two rather slovenly-looking individuals, one tall and ungainly, the other about medium height and stout, and both carrying long muskets in the crooks of their arms. I had never seen either of them before.

Stark came forward to me with outstretched hand.

"I thought it was a ghost at first," he said. "But when I saw you slap at that fly I knew it couldn't 'a' been."

The men who had been working on the boats had begun to crowd around us curiously. Stark turned to them, drawing himself up with an air of stern authority.

"Get back there, now," he commanded. "Get on with your work. This ain't none o' your affair."

One by one they began to turn away. I heard someone in the crowd say, "Hi, Jamie," and looking saw Thomas McConnell of

Suncook among them. I waved my hand at him; but Stark was speaking, and I turned back to hear what he was saying.

"We're the provost guard," he said. "Cap'n Rogers is acting provost marshal. He's put me in command here at the landing. I'll have to ask you a few questions. It's a matter of form."

"Rogers!" I exclaimed. "A captain! That's not Rob?"

He nodded.

"Why not?" he said. "He's a good one."

"Well," I replied, "I don't know why he shouldn't be. I was just surprised, that's all."

"There's a lot of things about this camp 'll surprise you," he said. "Where'd you come from?"

"Pemigewasset forks," Stiles cut in. "We figgered 'twas time to clear out."

Stark nodded soberly.

"It's a wonder to me you stayed so long," he said. "You stopping?"

"We might stay over a day or two," Stiles replied noncommittally.

Stark looked from one to another of us, his gaze finally resting on Purity.

"How're you, Mistress Purity?" he said. "You're looking good."

He probably knew he was understating the case, but Stark was never one to show his enthusiasm.

He turned to Jed.

"An army camp's not hardly the best sort of place for a girl," he said. "Some of the officers 've brought their wives though. They all bunk in one of the cabins yonder. I guess Mistress Purity can bunk in there with 'em till you're ready to go."

Stiles nodded.

"That's all right," he said.

"We better go on up and see Mrs. Blanchard," Stark said. "She sort of looks after the women, the way the colonel looks after the men."

He turned and motioned Purity up the bank before him. I picked up her light pack from the canoe and followed. Stiles and Toby moved to come along, but Stark turned and shook his head.

"You two 'd best stay with the canoes," he said. "I'd leave these fellers if I could trust 'em, but they'd be just as like as not to forget they was guards."

He turned to the two men.

"You fellers stay here and watch the landing," he said.

The taller of the two spat a brown stream of tobacco juice and nodded.

"All right," he said.

Stark puffed up the bank behind me.

"There's something about an army camp that's demoralizing," he said as he scrambled up beside me. "It don't seem to make a difference how honest a man is before he comes. As soon as he gets there he turns thief."

I began to laugh. He braced his stocky legs and faced me belligerently.

"What's funny?" he demanded.

"This camp," I said.

He looked around, soberly, as if searching for something to laugh at, and then looked back at me inquiringly.

"What's wrong with it?" he said.

"Why," I said, "I'm not a soldier, and I don't suppose I know much about it, but I've seen army camps in the old country; and they never looked like this."

He looked about him again, and then looked back at me, waiting for me to go on.

"Take uniforms, for instance," I said.

He spat disdainfully.

"There ain't a one in the camp," he said. "What'd we need them for?"

"Well," I said, "how do you know who's in the army and who isn't? A stranger—a spy, say—could come right in here, and no one 'd ever know the difference."

He shook his head. We began to walk slowly up the street between the tents towards the cabins.

"We all know who's in our company," he said. "Ain't that enough?"

"But what about the other companies?" I asked.

He shrugged.

"That's the other fellers' lookout," he said.

"Well, then," I said, "how about discipline? I take it you're an officer here?"

"I'm a lieutenant," he replied.

"Well, who'd know it?" I demanded. "You dress the same as

everyone else. How's anyone to know you've got more rank than the next man?".

"The men in my company know it," he said, "and that's all that matters. I don't try to boss anybody around that don't belong to me. Why, hell, they wouldn't take it!"

I threw up my hands in despair.

"Maybe we ain't got discipline the same as regular troops," he said. "But when you think of it, why should we? These boys ain't soldiers. They're farmers, mostly, who've come out to fight. And when it comes to fighting you'll find they don't need all that discipline. Remember Louisbourg."

"I'm not likely to forget it," I replied, "with Stiles talking it at me all day long for the last month. He was there, you know."

"Was he now!" Stark demanded. "Well, do you suppose he'd want to sign up again?"

I shot a sideways glance at Purity, but she was busy looking around her at the unfamiliar scene.

"You might ask him," I said.

We had come to the cabins by this time, and Stark led the way to one that stood a little behind and to the right of the others. Despite the bright warmth of the day the door was closed. Stark knocked, and a grey-haired, motherly-seeming woman opened it and stood in the doorway drying her hands upon her apron.

"Here's another boarder for you, Mrs. Blanchard," Stark said. "Can you find a place for her?"

"Why, yes, I guess so," she said, looking from Purity to me. "I don't think I've seen you before, young man."

Stark hastened, with some confusion, to introduce both Purity and myself to her. When she heard our names her face fell.

"Oh!" she said. "I thought maybe 'twas bride and groom. We've several of 'em here, you know. The boys, some of 'em, seems like, just can't wait till the war's over!"

She brightened a little as a thought struck her.

"I'm glad to see," said she, "that there's one man in the Province with a lick of sense. Most of 'em don't stop to think how 'twould be on a new wife if they was to be killed first thing right off like that!"

I could hear John Stark choking back his laughter.

"Mistress Purity came with her father, ma'am," he said.

"Oh!" she said, a little disappointed. But a look of determination came into her eye. "Don't you worry, young man," she said. "I'll look after your young lady for you! If you want to see her you'll find her here, safe and sound."

I said, "Thank you, ma'am," very gravely, and bowed.

"Come in, child," she said to Purity, who was blushing furiously.

I handed her the light pack, and Stark and I turned away and started back towards the river.

We found Stiles and Toby the centre of an excited crowd. Stiles was standing up on the forward thwart of one of the canoes and was holding up a fringed buckskin shirt.

"What'm I bid for this elegant doeskin jacket," he was saying. "What'm I bid? Do I hear sixpence? I hear sixpence. Who'll make it eight? Who'll make it eight? Eight I got! Nine? Eight I got! Nine? Nine I got! Ten? One shilling! There's a man knows a good thing when he sees it, by God! One shilling I got! Will anyone make it one and one? One and one I got! Anybody one shilling tuppence? One shilling tuppence? One shilling tuppence? One and tuppence I got. Any more? Any more? Ha'penny? By God now, it's gettin' hot! One shilling tuppence ha'penny I got, anybody bid higher? Anybody bid higher? No? Going—going—gone, by God, to the long-laiged cuss over there with the grey beard, for one shilling tuppence ha'penny! Let's see your money, mister."

Stark pushed his way through the crowd.

"What's going on here?" he demanded.

"Auction," said a lad at his elbow, a farmer from his looks.

"We're signin' up," said Stiles. "Figgered this was as good a way as any to get rid of our extry junk."

"You most done?" Stark asked.

"All finished," said Stiles. "Sold our furs to a sutler from Rumford, and auctioned off one or two things like that shirt. The rest o' what we got we're goin' to want."

"I hope you left one of the canoes for me and Purity," I said. "We'll need it to get as far as Suncook."

At mention of his daughter's name, Stiles' face fell.

"Jesus!" he said. "I forgot!"

Then his face brightened.

"You'll look out for her, won't you, lad?" he asked.

I laughed.

"You needn't fear for Purity," I said. "There's not a home in Suncook she couldn't stay in if she wanted. She's in a position to choose."

Stark glanced at me.

"How about you signing up?" he asked.

I shook my head.

"Not me," I replied. "My wound still bothers me. Besides, I think too much of my hide to go where you're going."

"What do you mean?" he demanded.

"I don't like the idea of going to Crown Point by way of the Cohos intervales and Lake Memphremagog," I said. "That don't make sense to me."

Most of the crowd had drifted away by this time; but those who had not, turned and eyed me curiously. Stark looked at them and frowned. Then he turned and looked at me sharply.

"You came down from the north," he said. "Where'd you hear that?"

I told him then about old Jules and his visit, omitting any mention of his offer to Stiles, as I felt it could do him no good. When I was done Stark gave a low whistle. Knowing Stiles, and his acquaintanceship in Canada, he evidently did not think it strange that the Frenchman had stopped there. It was something else that was bothering him.

"So they know about it?" he said.

I nodded. "They seem to know all about it," I replied.

"This is a case for the colonel," he said, and turned away. "You come along with me."

He started up the bank once more, but paused halfway up, and looked back at Stiles and Toby.

"Haul your canoes up and bring your packs," he said. "We can sign you up at the same time."

Stiles scratched his head doubtfully.

"I dunno," he said. "I did have some idee of signin' up with Eb Eastman."

Stark shrugged.

"Suit yourself," he said. "I only thought maybe you'd like to be with me and Rogers. We can't pay you any more, but I'll guarantee you'll see more action."

"Rogers?" said Stiles. "Hell, why didn't you say so before? I'd ruther be with Rogers than Eastman any day. I thought you said he was provost marshal."

"That's temporary," Stark said. "He's for the Ammonoosuc to build a fort next week."

"Whoop!" Jed shouted. "That's my man! Come on!"

He clapped Toby on the shoulder, and started scrambling up the bank. Stark grinned dourly and turned to lead the way once more back to the cabins.

The cabin to which Stark led us this time was the central one of the three. When he came to the door he rapped smartly, and without awaiting a reply pushed it open and entered. We followed close upon his heels, blinking our eyes in the sudden change from bright sunlight to comparative dark.

But presently, as my eyes grew accustomed to the dim light, I began to make out my surroundings. The interior of the cabin was almost bare, save for a couple of bunks against the wall and a plain deal table in the middle of the room. Behind the table sat a stocky, grizzle-haired man, who might have been in his late fifties. He was frowning at us dourly, as if he resented our sudden intrusion but did not know quite what to do about it. Him I set down in my mind as Colonel Blanchard, in command of the New Hampshire troops.

But there was a second figure in the room: a tall, broad-shouldered man with a great beak of a nose and almost popping eyes. He had evidently made some attempt at a uniform, for he was dressed in a knee-length buckskin coat that had been dyed green, and on his head he wore a peculiar sort of round cap with a curly feather that stuck up in the back and drooped over the crown like a squirrel's tail. His dark eyebrows were drawn together in a black scowl, and his small mouth was pursed up petulantly. But at sight of me he broke into a laugh and strode forward, grasping my hand and pumping it heartily.

"Jamie, by God!" he exclaimed. "I heard you were dead."

"They can't kill me!" I said. "I'm too tough!"

I stood back and looked at him. Here was a new Rob Rogers. He had always been a big man, but now he had filled out across the shoulders and drawn in at the waist, so that he gave an impression of immense strength. In his dark eyes was a new power: the light of confidence in his own ability to command. Looking at him, I had the feeling that here was a man who had fallen into the very thing that suited him. If ever a man was born to be a soldier it was Robert Rogers, and I think subsequent events have borne out my judgement of the man. Whatever one may think of his private life or of his morals, none but the most prejudiced will deny he is a born fighter.

All this passed through my mind in a flash, before Stark spoke.

"Here's a couple of recruits," he said.

"You've come to sign up, Jamie?" Rogers demanded. "I can give you an ensign's berth if you want it."

I shook my head.

"Not today, Rob," I replied. "I've a bullet hole in my shoulder as big as your fist, and it's not healed yet. I'd be no good to you." I jerked my head at my companions. "Jed and Toby 'd like to go with you, though."

He gave them a quick look and chuckled.

"Good," he said. "The more we get, the better. But how about you? You won't change your mind? All I can offer now is the ensigncy. But maybe later we'll find something, eh, colonel?"

He looked at Blanchard for confirmation, but the latter merely grunted noncommittally. It was evident that he was bewildered by what was happening.

"I'm sorry, Rob," I said. "It's no use. Stiles 'll tell you I'm not fit for it yet."

He looked so disappointed I was almost tempted to change my mind. But then I thought of Portsmouth and Dorcas. Stark broke in at that moment.

"Jamie brings news might be of interest to you and the colonel," he said.

Blanchard pricked up his ears. Rogers looked at me curiously.

As quickly as I could I went over the story of the Frenchman's visit again. When I had done, Rogers turned to his superior.

"You see?" he demanded. "They know it already. I told you it couldn't be kept a secret. It was a fool idea even if it didn't take us halfway into Canada and back!"

Blanchard seemed to ignore him. Instead he turned to me.

"From what you said," said he, "I gathered that you do not approve of the route chosen to send the army to Crown Point. Why?"

"Because," I replied, "it takes them fifty miles north of Crown Point. It's all hard country to travel. And the Indians at Saint Francis know it too well. They'd have half your men murdered and scalped before you got beyond Memphremagog."

"You've been that way?" he asked.

"I've been over enough of it to know it is impracticable," I replied. "And I have been through to Crown Point once by a more direct route. There are no trails. I think you'd have trouble getting through even there."

"Is there any way you think we might get through?" he asked.

"None that I know of from here," I replied. "As far as I know the best way to reach Crown Point is through Albany." I jerked my head at Stiles and Toby. "These gentlemen," I said, "have crossed and recrossed a number of times. They might know of something that I do not."

The colonel looked at them with raised eyebrows. Stiles shook his head.

"You see it, colonel?" said Rogers. "These men know the country. What they tell you is the truth. How much chance do you think we'd stand to get through, now the Frenchmen know we're coming?"

The colonel shrugged.

"We have our orders," he said.

Rogers exploded.

"Orders!" he roared. "From a nitwit assembly! Why, most of them couldn't find their way to their own backhouse on a dark night! And they expect us to cross two hundred miles of black wilderness, full of savage enemies, who know we're coming, and with no communications!"

"They're our orders, none the less, Mr. Rogers," said the other. "What do you expect me to do?"

"Do?" roared Rogers. "You might at least protest! Write the Governor a letter with this information you've just heard. Mr. Ferguson 'll bear it to him, and use his influence. I happen to know he has some!"

The colonel looked doubtful.

"I'll think about it," he said.

"Think about it, hell!" said Rogers. "Go ahead and do it! It'll cost you no more than ink and paper, and it might be the means of saving this regiment to do some good in the campaign! You'd like to see some action, now wouldn't you, sir?"

Colonel Blanchard reached out a listless hand, and took up pen and paper.

"All right," he said, "if it'll stop you always pesterin' me!"

Rogers herded us all out the door as the quill began to scratch wearily. Outside, he shook hands all around.

"I'll have to go back and see he finishes it," he said. "He'll change his mind in the middle if I don't."

He turned to Stark.

"Bring 'em all to my quarters later," he said.

And with a wave of his hand he was gone again through the low doorway.

That evening Rogers held open house in his tent down by the river in our honour. Word of our arrival appeared to have gotten around swiftly, and it was gratifying to me to see how many of my old friends from Suncook, Rumford, and the neighbourhood dropped in to shake hands and congratulate me on my escape. Dick Rogers was lieutenant in his brother's company, as was John Stark. Noah Johnson was ensign. Will Stark was with a company from Londonderry. Phin Virgin was a sergeant in Eb Eastman's company. Amos Eastman was in the ranks. And there were dozens of others. The Exeter and Portsmouth companies were out on practice patrols, so that I saw none of my friends with them; but I learned that George Stapleton and Warren Ames were lieutenants with the latter, and that Homer Odiorne and Peter Davis were also with the company.

Pleasant as it was to see old friends again, I was none the less anxious to get to Portsmouth, and so would consider no delay. Rogers, fearing that I might have some difficulty handling the canoe with my injured shoulder, offered to send Stiles with me if I would wait until the next afternoon, by which time he would have completed his enrolment in the company. There was nothing below us, however, which should give us any trouble—no portages to be made, no rapids which we could not run; and the thought of waiting irked me. Consequently I refused the offer, and by midmorning Purity and myself were waving good-bye to our friends upon the bank as we drifted down around the bend.

There was little enough for us to do, beyond steering the canoe, for we had a good stiff breeze at our backs, and such slight rapids as we had to run all had channels clearly marked by the smooth slick slide of swift deep water. Purity seemed thoughtful and not inclined to conversation. Several times I commented upon things seen in the camp, the beauty of the weather, or the war; but each time she answered me in monosyllables, and at last I gave it up.

When, towards noon, we passed Rumford, however, I made another determined effort, for I knew that within the hour we should be in Suncook, and that there was an important matter to be settled before we arrived.

"Have you thought where you're to stay, lass?" I asked her.

"Have I thought of aught else?" she demanded—a little bit-terly, I thought. "I had not thought my father would go off so, without a thought for me."

"Your father," I replied, "has been so long without responsibil-ity that you cannot blame him now if he does not take to it readily. Besides," I added, "he was not entirely thoughtless. He begged me to look out for you."

"That was an imposition," she said. "I'm sorry he did it."

I snorted. "An imposition!" I cried. "After all you have done for me? Why, lass, you know there can be no thought of imposi-tion between us!"

She did not reply. Neither did she look back. I waited a mo-ment, and then went on.

"There are three homes in Suncook," I said, "where they will be only too glad to have you back. Either Edith or Alice would be only too delighted to see you. And I know I need not speak for Uncle David."

She paddled several strokes before replying.

"I suppose I should go to Mr. Ross," she said. " 'Twas where I started. 'Twould be strange that I should come back after so long. But somehow Suncook does not seem the same."

"I did not say," I replied, "that our house in Portsmouth would always be open to you. I wanted you to take that for granted."

"I loved Suncook once," she said. "There are a hundred things I remember about it. But when your mother died it all seemed changed. I know I should hate it now."

"Will you come to us?" I asked.

She did not speak for such a long time that I began to fear I had somehow offended her. When at last she did reply it was in such low tones that I could scarcely hear her words.

"Would you mind?" she said.

"Mind!" I cried. "Why, child, I would be not only pleased but honoured!"

She swung about on her thwart to face me so abruptly that for a moment I thought the canoe might go over, and her smile was as rarely happy as I have ever seen.

"Would you, really?" she asked.

"Of course!" I said.

"Then I will come to Portsmouth!" she announced.

"You will be welcome there," I said.

A few minutes later I ran the bow of the canoe out upon the familiar shingle at the mouth of Soucook Brook and stepped ashore. On the hill we could see the house my mother had built, a thin wisp of smoke curling from its huge chimney, and hanging blue in the air against the green of the farther hills. I slung Purity's light pack across my good shoulder and, taking her arm in my hand, guided her up the path.

3

It would be needless for me to describe the welcome that awaited us in Suncook. Alice, when she opened the door to us, flung her arms about my neck and wept for joy, while my young niece and nephew sat upon the floor and watched in round-eyed wonder, not knowing what it was all about, but certain that it was an occasion for great solemnity. Nothing would do but Alice must send her serving girl running to Edith's and my uncle's to tell them of my arrival. Edith came at once, with a shawl about her head; and not long afterwards my uncle arrived, having left his plough standing in the field.

The word spread rapidly through the town, and that evening there was such a flood of visitors to the house as to rival a gathering of the clans. There were toasts drunk and greetings exchanged, and the air rang with shouts of welcome. And over and over I must needs tell my story, again and again, from beginning to end, until I grew sick of the sound of it.

To say that I was touched by all this would be sheerest understatement. Actually I was overwhelmed. Such sincere good will raised a lump in my throat and left me with a guilty feeling at my own haste to be gone; but I could not forget that there was still my own family awaiting me in Portsmouth. They too, I felt, would be anxious to see me, and it was a duty to them, if nothing more, to be on my way. Purity, I think, rather scandalized everyone with her determination to go with me, but no argument would change her mind; and, having once pledged my word, I could not well add my voice to those of my sisters, even though I began to have doubts as to the wisdom of the move. Consequently, the next morning at dawn my uncle came with his cart for our canoe and luggage, and with much embracing and great reluctance we said good-bye and set out upon the last leg of our journey.

My uncle carried us as far as the Lamprey River in Charming Fare,* Chester, where we took again to our canoe. That night we rested at the ordinary in Newmarket, and the next morning set out across Great Bay, with a fresh breeze in our faces, for Portsmouth.

From Newmarket to Portsmouth by water is a fifteen-mile paddle through Great Bay and the Piscataqua, with little current to help, and though we got an early start, what with first the wind and then the tide against us, and my injured shoulder to hold us back, it was dusk before we reached our destination. We left the canoe at the landing place near the ferry to Kittery and walked up through the growing darkness towards the house.

It was not until that moment, walking up through the well kept streets in the dark twilight beneath the rows of tall elms, with the spotless, white-painted houses standing back aloofly on either hand, their yellow-lighted windows gleaming out at us like critical eyes, that I realized the roughness of my own appearance. After my flight through the forest there had been little enough left of my clothes. My shirt was in tatters, and my breeches not much better. My moccasins, although I had made them myself with the greatest of care, had failed to withstand the constant soaking and had gone to pieces completely, so that when Toby found me I was barefoot. There was little left to salvage.

My friends had done their best to provide for me. Purity had made me a new shirt of buckskin and patched my breeches. Toby had taken great pains over a new pair of moccasins of moosehide and a great fuzzy cap made of the pelt of a spotty bobcat, that en-

* Present Raymond.

gulfed my ears and enlarged the appearance of my head to thrice its normal size. Stiles had provided me with a pair of leggings, much too large for me, and a powder horn and shot pouch of his own making. At the camp at Stevenstown, Rogers by an obscure process of reasoning based upon some claim I might have against the Province for the attack I had suffered within its borders had seen fit to equip me with a new musket out of those supplied for the regiment by the provincial assembly. But, well meant though their efforts had been, the result was a makeshift rather than anything else. I looked more an animated scarecrow than a respected and respectable citizen of the town returning to his home.

Something of this, I say, occurred to me as we made our way up through the dimly lighted streets. But the full force of it did not strike me until I stood before the door of my own home. Even in the growing dark it was plain that the house had been freshly painted, and as we came up the street I could see that a small ell had been built on at the back. The lawns were immaculately groomed, and from the window of the dining room came the sound of light laughter. I could not help but run my hand across my bearded chin somewhat sheepishly before I lifted the bright polished knocker.

The door was opened by an enormous blackamoor, resplendent in a livery of purple velvet trimmed in gold thread, his massive legs encased in stockings of the finest white cotton thread. The apparition left me speechless, and I suppose my own appearance must have been something of a shock to him, for he glowered at me a moment in surly suspicion.

It was he, at home and confident of his position, however, who recovered first.

"Ain't nobody home," he growled, and made as if to shut the door in my face.

But I forestalled him by thrusting the butt of my musket over the threshold, whereat he flung the door open wide and took a threatening step in my direction. I presented the muzzle of my gun at his middle waistcoat button, and he stopped short, his black jaw hanging slack and his eyes rolling white in his head.

"You're new," I said, sharply enough, I fear, for I was weary and out of patience, "and you don't know me. Under the circumstances you may be excused your impertinence—"

A querulous voice, which I at once recognized as Dorcas', called from the dining room:

"Augustus! Who is that? Augustus! Who's there?"

"Stand aside," I said. "Go tell your mistress that the master has come home again."

He gaped at me for a moment without moving until Dorcas called again.

"Augustus! Why don't you answer?"

"Jump," I said, "or I'll have you out fighting Indians within the week."

He turned then and went heavily down the hall.

There was a moment's silence after that. I stepped on inside and held the door for Purity, swinging it shut behind her. She did not look at me as she came in, and suddenly I felt unaccountably confused.

"I shouldn't have come," she said.

"Nonsense!" I replied. "Why shouldn't you? Besides, you don't have to stay if you don't want to."

She gave me a strange look, and then tossed her head. I thought she was about to say something more, but at that instant there came a scream from the dining room, followed by a dull thud, a wild scraping of chairs, footsteps, and the noise of people all talking at once. An instant later the tall figure of my cousin Hubert stepped through the door and came towards us, closely followed by the giant Augustus. As I stepped forward to meet him I saw that he was scowling angrily. He scarce noticed the hand I held out to him.

"In God's name!" he cried. "What kind of way is this to do? Why did you not send word ahead of your coming?"

"How would I send word?" I said, mildly reproving. "There was none to send. Besides, I came as fast as any messenger."

"Well," he said truculently, "you should have let us know. You've thrown Dorcas into a fainting fit, and upset our guests!"

"Damn your guests!" I said, for I was ill pleased with my reception. So wrothy was I it did not occur to me to note the incongruity of his "our guests." "Who are they?"

"Some people from Boston," he said, surlily, "relatives of Dorcas. You don't know them."

"I don't want to know them," I snapped. "I don't like my wife's relatives. Tell them to go home. Tell them to go back to the tavern where they belong."

"Isn't that somewhat unusual?" he demanded.

"Why shouldn't it be unusual?" I said furiously, for I was past caring for convention. "There're a lot of things unusual about this. Here's a husband come back from the dead. Isn't that a little unusual?"

He had been turning away; but at that he stopped short and faced me abruptly, and I saw that he was white to the lips.

"What do you mean?" he demanded.

"Only what I say," I replied. "Don't you think it unusual? Here's a man set on by Indians, and he escaped to come home almost a year later. There's nothing very ordinary in that, is there?"

"If you're implying—" he began.

"What would I imply?" I cut in. "Is there anything I should imply?"

Suddenly I had a flash of memory in which I saw Joseph Merrill bending over a table, at which sat Hubert, and looking over his shoulder at me with that expression of guilty fear which he habitually wore whenever we met.

"You give me ideas, Hubert," I said.

I saw him bite his lip as he turned away, and called him back.

"On second thought," I said, "let them stay. You were quite right about that."

He was relieved and pleased at the concession, for he smiled.

"I'm glad you said that," he said. "It might have been awkward otherwise. They're staying here."

"Here!" I exclaimed, thinking of our only two guest rooms. "That does make it awkward!"

He looked at me dully, not comprehending, and suddenly I remembered that I had neglected to present Purity. I turned and beckoned to her, and she came forward from where she had been standing in the shadows by the door. When I looked at him again I could see, by his expression of bewilderment, that he had not until that moment noticed her.

"This is Mistress Stiles," I said, "an old friend. Her father has joined up for Crown Point, and she is to stay with us until his return."

It was funny to watch him as he greeted her. The look of bewilderment on his face became one of incredulity at my words, and this was replaced by almost amazed admiration at her soft beauty as she came into the yellow lamplight. As he bent over her hand he gave me a glance of sly suspicion.

"There was a spare room built over the new wing," he said.

"Is it fit for a guest?" I asked.

"Why, of course," he said.

I thought he was about to say something more, but he stopped abruptly and waited for me.

"Then she shall have it," I said, "until these others are gone." He nodded.

"Go back now," I went on, "and see to your guests. Have two places set for us. Tell Dorcas we will be down as soon as we have changed and freshened up. 'Twill be less shock for her than if she sees me so."

He bowed agreement, and turned away. I turned to the giant Augustus, who had listened to the conversation with drooping jaw and wide eyes.

"Here, you," I said, "you heard the talk. Show Mistress Stiles to the new room. And when you've done that fetch towels and water for us both."

"But, boss!" he began.

"Jump!" I said.

"Boss!" he wailed. "Ah cain't!"

"You can't?" I demanded, astonished. "Why not?"

"Boss!" he said. "Mistress Dorcas done had all yo' things moved back in that there room. She done said as how 'twas goin' to be yo' room!"

"Well," I said, "don't be a fool. Move 'em back again!"

"Yas suh," he said, plainly doubtful.

He shook his head and lifted a candle from the hall table.

"Jamie!" said Purity. "I'm not hungry, Jamie. I'd rather just go to bed."

"Nonsense!" I scoffed. "You've had a long day. You must eat. I'll meet you here in twenty minutes."

"But I've nothing to wear!" she protested.

"That's silly," I said. "Wash up and come as you are. I shan't be dressing up."

She might have said more, but I cut her off.

"Run along," I said.

I watched them mount the stairs and go off along the hall. Then I turned and took up the other candle. I stood my gun in the hall corner behind the door. After that I too went up the stairs.

It was half an hour before Purity appeared again at the head of the stairs, clad in a gown of some dainty pink stuff that had neither hoops nor panniers, but was remarkably fresh and unmussed for all the packing it had undergone. I thought I had never seen her looking so handsome, despite her obvious weariness.

She came down the stairs with apparent reluctance, and I was quick to drop her a compliment upon her appearance, for I felt that unless I said something quickly she might be inclined to feel that her presence at such a time was an intrusion. She received it with a sweet smile, and took the arm I offered her without a word.

We found the dining room a blaze of light from a dozen candles set in silver holders on the white-clothed table. As we entered Dorcas rose and faced us, her hand gripping the back of the chair. No smile of welcome lit her face, and her eyes were dull and staring.

"Jamie!" she cried.

I saw that she was still white, and I cursed myself for the thoughtless way I had broken in upon them. Of course it had been a shock to her. She had not yet recovered her poise. I dropped Purity's arm and went to her, my hands outstretched.

"My dear!" I said.

She smiled a little then, but her eyes were still dull, and there was no answering pressure in her hands. The kiss she gave me was lifeless. Abruptly she drew back and turned.

"Do you know my cousins from Boston?" she said, formally. "Marcia and Bradley Drew. My husband."

I made an elegant leg to Marcia Drew, a buxom, black-haired, black-eyed little wench, who replied with a coquettish nod of her head and a dazzling flash of white teeth. To her husband I nodded, somewhat stiffly, for I was not prepossessed by his appearance. He seemed a foppish sort, dressed in a plum-coloured coat and heavily buckramed waistcoat that stood out before and at the sides like a lady's skirts. His periwig was powdered and pomatumed and curled at the sides, and the queue was caught up in a square black bag into which he had put a lavender sachet which filled the room with its overpowering stench. His manners were more ladylike than his wife's, and he was for ever mincing about and talking in lisping tones, and punctuating his conversation with the most foul language, as was the style then in London, or at least so he believed. I could place him now, for he and his wife had come up to Portsmouth for our wedding.

A little sickened by the company, I presented Purity as briefly and simply as I might. Hubert bowed again with smooth dignity. Bradley simpered like a girl of thirteen. And Marcia was haughty. But Dorcas came forward and held out her hands, greeting her with that oversweet enthusiasm with which women proclaim their enmity.

When we had taken our places at the table nothing would do but I must retell my story for the benefit of the Drews, who plied me until I was weary with questions, so that there was little opportunity for other conversation. When the meal was finally finished I hoped we might all be allowed to go our ways; but I was soon to find that this was not to be. First we must pay homage to Dame Fashion and play at cards and coffee in the drawing room. At this, however, I rebelled and went to sulk before the fire. Presently Purity excused herself, saying that she was wearied by the day's journey, and not long afterwards Hubert, who had been somewhat stiffly aloof all evening, also withdrew. Marcia and Bradley I thought would never leave us, and finally I had to point out to them that Dorcas and I had much to discuss, and that I hoped they would excuse us. Since they could not well ignore this suggestion they drew themselves up—rather huffily, I thought— and departed in the direction of their own room.

Not until their steps had died away from the landing above and their bedroom door thumped shut did Dorcas turn upon me with the first spark of animation she had shown all evening. It took no more than a glance to tell me that she was furious.

"How could you?" she demanded. "How could you be so?"

I looked at her, bewildered. This was hardly the reception I had anticipated.

"How could I be how?" I asked mildly. "What have I done but live? I did not think to find you angry for that."

She stamped her foot impatiently.

"Oh!" she cried. "Don't pretend you don't know what I mean.

All evening long you've scarce bothered to be civil to Marcia and Bradley. And you've hurt Hubert terribly."

"As for your cousins," I retorted, for I was growing impatient myself, "I think they scarce deserve civility for all the consideration they have shown us. And why should Hubert's feelings be so hurt?"

"Do you deny the dreadful thing that you implied?" she demanded.

"He told you that, did he?" I said.

She made no answer, but stood tapping her foot angrily upon the rug.

"I implied nothing," I said. "If he chose to misconstrue my words he must look to his own conscience for the answer."

"His conscience!" she snorted. "Do you think it pricks him? How do you think Hubert could do such a thing? What motive would he have?"

I shrugged.

"I don't know," I said lamely, and was at once furious with myself for falling upon the defensive.

"It's ridiculous," she stormed, "to imagine such a thing. And poor Hubert is so sensitive. I think you owe him an apology."

I controlled my anger with an effort. After all I did not want to quarrel with her on this my first night home.

"Very well," I said. "If it will make you any happier, my dear, I will apologize to him in the morning, though I still maintain that I meant naught but what my words said."

I held out my arms to her then, but it seemed she was not to be placated so easily.

"And that strumpet!" she went on. "To think that you would bring her here!"

I looked at her in angry astonishment at that, and restrained myself from slapping her face only with the greatest effort.

"Mistress Purity," I said stiffly, "is no strumpet, but an old friend and a trusted one. But for her it is likely that I would not be here now. I owe my life to her, and in view of that I think it the very least we can do to offer her our utmost hospitality. I'll ask you to remember that, my dear, for if I hear of any affront put to her while she is here I shall have to ask you to leave this house. I cannot in honour stand by and see her wronged!"

As I spoke she sank slowly down into the chair behind her and sat staring at me in wide-eyed wonder, as well she might, for it was the first time I had ever presumed to speak so to her. So infuriated was I that I did not see the quiver of her lip, but turned at once upon my heel when I had done and strode towards the door.

My hand was on the knob when a stifled sound behind me made me turn, and I saw her still sitting, dully bewildered, as though I had smitten her across the face, with two tears trickling down across her cheeks and her breast heaving spasmodically as a great sob struggled to come out. I had been furious a moment before, but when I saw her so, confused and hurt and beaten, my heart softened within me, and I went to her, falling on my knees beside her and taking her in my arms.

"There, my dear," I said, "is this a way for husband and wife to meet again when death has all but come between? You know I love you more dearly than anyone in all this world. Let us not quarrel now."

I drew her to me then and showered kisses upon her tear-streaked face. For a moment she lay still and unresponsive in my arms; then slowly, almost reluctantly, I felt her arms go about my neck. After a little I rose and led her gently, my arm about her waist, upstairs to our room.

13

THE KING'S SHILLING

〖 1 As I look back upon that period immediately following my return to Portsmouth the thing that strikes me most forcibly is that I should have been so blind that I did not see that which was so painfully obvious to my friends and neighbours: my wife's infidelity.

Time and the interposition of events have deadened the shock of discovery and lent perspective, so that I can now think of it with neither anger, nor sorrow, nor even disgust, but only a sense of pity for her. I know now what I was too fatuous to believe at first—that it was not for myself she had married me, but rather for what I had to offer; for the money that was mine, and the position which I had attained. In the very beginning, children though we were, she had played with me, like the coquette she was. Doubtless that would have been the end of it, had I become the graceless yokel she believed me that night when we met again, after six years, in James Osgood's taproom in Rumford.

My bloodied nose, my cracked and bleeding lips, my blackened eye and swollen jaw, must have revolted her fastidious soul then; for whatever one may say of her she was like a cat in that respect. Yet as soon as her father had carried her the tale of my standing in the Province she had become at once all smiles and sympathy, and I, in my infatuation, had been only too ready to believe that these were meant for me alone.

After our marriage, I have no doubt, she was as good a wife to me as any, until the day I brought Hubert, resplendent in scarlet coat and gold lace, to the house. After that, I am ready to believe, so carried away was she by her new passion that she forgot the bargain she had undoubtedly made with herself in marrying me, and, figuratively speaking, threw herself into his arms. Hubert was not one to refuse an amour. And there was advantage for him in such an affair. Perhaps, in the beginning, he never meant it to go further than that. And yet I feel certain that he too, for what was, for him at least, a considerable time, fell under the spell of her charm.

It may be said that I was a fool to throw them together as I did. Another man, perhaps, might not have done as I did. Yet, in my own defence, I submit that in the light of reason it was not unnatural. I loved my wife. I believed firmly that she loved me, and while I trusted Hubert scarcely at all, the beginning and the end of my faith were in her. I knew that in trivial matters she was weak and flighty and vain and selfish. Yet these faults I considered to be the result of her upbringing by an overindulgent parent. Fundamentally I felt that in the face of a crisis she would show sufficient strength of character to rise above them. In the meantime I foolishly continued to indulge her whim. And I was proud of her.

It was this very pride, this very faith in Dorcas' integrity, that blinded me to what I should have seen, and stopped my ears against all warnings. Until the time of my departure for the Cohos, while I doubt not the affair was already well begun, there was naught about it to start idle tongues to wagging. But in my absence it must have made itself apparent, for on my return I could not but notice a certain diffidence with which my friends greeted me. One even—old Colonel Atkinson, who was then approaching seventy—attempted to warn me, though I would have none of it. This happened one evening in Stavers' taproom, a few days after my arrival. I came in late for a glass of ale before going home after a long evening conference with Colonel Meserve in the matter of contracts, and found the tall old gentleman leaning against the bar with Jotham Odiorne and Meshech Weare. As I had not seen him since my return I made haste to cross over to him and offer him my compliments.

"Young man," he said in his high-pitched old voice as he took my hand, "I am glad to see you back. I do not make it a rule to meddle with other people's affairs, but there is that here which demands your attention."

"What is that, sir?" I asked in all innocence.

"If I may come straight to the point," he replied, "I refer to this unfortunate affair between your wife and your cousin."

I stared at him in amazement.

"This is the first I had heard of it," I said.

"It is common gossip in the town," he replied.

"I had not thought you one to listen to old wives' tales, sir," I told him.

A spot of high colour appeared upon his withered cheek.

"This is no 'old wives' tale', as you are pleased to call it, sir," he said, "but a matter that is plain for any man to see or hear, provided he be not deaf or blind or a plain damn' fool!"

Anger at this old womanish gossiping took possession of me, driving out my amazement.

"Sir," I said, "Captain Ferguson is my cousin. Dorcas is my wife. In both of them I have the utmost confidence. Furthermore, may I remind you that I live beneath the same roof with these people, quite aside from their relationship to me, and am therefore in a better position than anyone to know what goes on between them?"

He snorted testily at that.

"In a better position," he growled, "to have the wool pulled over your eyes!"

"Colonel Atkinson," I said stiffly, "you are a man whom I have always felt honoured to call my friend. Moreover, you are an old man—too old a man to be called upon the field of honour. Nevertheless, sir, I must warn you that if you persist in this malicious pettifogging I shall be forced to call you out!"

He pressed his thin white lips together at this, and anger blazed in his eyes, so that for a moment I thought that he would issue the challenge himself. But instead he shrugged his old shoulders, and turned back to the bar.

"Let the fool look after himself," he said harshly.

I ventured no reply but, turning on my heel, strode from the room, never daring to look back lest I be tempted to return and follow my threat with action. I never saw him again but there was a coolness between us, even though time proved him right.

I walked the streets for some time after that before I felt sufficiently cool to go home. The thing, I told myself, was ridiculous. It was impossible. Nevertheless, it impressed me sufficiently to make me mention it to Dorcas that night in the privacy of our chamber.

She was combing her hair before the mirror, and when I spoke the brush she held hovered an instant in mid-air. She spun on her seat to face me.

"What did you say?" she demanded.

I told her again what Atkinson had said, and for a moment she just sat staring at me and biting her lips. Then all at once she burst out in a fury.

"Oh!" she cried, stamping her foot. "How could he? How could he suggest such a thing? The nasty old meddler! Why, you don't know what it's been to have Hubert here! You don't know how sweet he was, and what a help, when everyone thought you were dead! I don't know what I should have done without him to help me! He tended to everything! And now they say these nasty things about him, and about me too! How can they be so rotten?"

Her indignation seemed so real, her virtue so outraged at the very suggestion, that I was convinced that it was genuine. She seemed almost on the verge of hysterics, and I made haste to reassure her.

"What does it matter?" I said as soothingly as I could. "I told him I did not believe it, and I don't!"

She stopped crying abruptly and dried her tears.

"Oh, Jamie," she cried, "you are a dear!"

And with that she ran to me and threw her arms about my neck, kissing me peckishly upon the cheek, for which I was most foolishly happy.

Our lives flowed along swiftly enough in those first few weeks after my return, for there was much to do. In the first place I found it necessary to straighten out various tangles in our business affairs which had cropped up during my absence. At the same time, I was forced to hustle to keep up with the increased demand for lumber. With war in the offing there had come a boom in shipbuilding up and down the coast. From Meserve's yard in Portsmouth, and from the yards across the river in Kittery, the clattering tap of hammers sounded ceaselessly from dawn till dark. During the month immediately following my arrival our business, already doubled, doubled itself again, and I was kept running from morning to midnight and more, sealing contracts and arguing terms, while my uncle, in Suncook, was hard put to it to find men to fill his crews.

My investments in land, of course, had to be written off as uncertain, for, most of them being along the frontier, all settlers' activities upon them had come to a standstill, and more than one of them had been temporarily abandoned. It was to inform myself upon this, and reassure myself as to the safety of my investment, as much as to deliver Colonel Blanchard's letter, that I called upon the Governor almost at once upon my return.

I found him in a state of great agitation at the added responsibilities which the coming campaign laid upon him, and at that moment much perturbed by the assembly's seizing upon the moment to oppose him in certain measures concerning his own salary, which had always been a bone of contention between them. He roused himself from this state long enough to greet me rather curtly and say that he was glad to see me safely back. I asked him the questions that were uppermost in my mind, and he assured me, testily, that he would certainly do his utmost to see that the assembly granted an extension of time upon such grants as we had been forced to give up by the war. He reminded me that he too had an interest in those grants, but added grumblingly that God alone knew what the assembly would be pleased to do. They paid little enough attention to his recommendations!

I gave him the letter which Colonel Blanchard had written, and he read it with an impassive face, and tossed it aside when he had finished. For half an hour after that he questioned me closely about the country between the Connecticut and Crown Point. Did not the end of Lake Memphremagog fall somewhere near the Lower Cohos? And was there not a river which ran thence, navigable for battoes, into Lake Champlain near Crown Point? What was the best way across? Could not the journey be accomplished almost entirely by water, with but one or two short carries? I was not surprised at the extent of his misinformation, for he but echoed the popular view. There was not one man in a hundred in the Province who knew what lay beyond the outermost settlements, and I daresay that fewer knew it by more than hearsay. I doubt if there were more than twenty of us, all told, both of New Hampshire and of the Bay Province, who had made the journey overland from the Connecticut.

I answered him to the best of my ability, and when he had done I told him that Captain Rogers, who was then building his fort at the mouth of the Ammonoosuc, or Jed Stiles or Simon Toby, the Indian, both of Rogers' company, could tell him more than I, as all three of these were better acquainted with that region than myself. He only grunted noncommittally at that, and went on to question me about the Frenchman who had come to Stiles' cabin. Where had be obtained his information? What did he know? Could he have learned anything through Stiles? Was the latter to be trusted?

I assured him that Stiles could have told him naught, since I could swear that he had not been long enough away from the cabin all winter to have learned what was going forward. After that I went on to tell him all that old Jules had told us. When I was finished he sat in gloomy silence, moodily staring at the littered top of his desk.

"The devil!" he exclaimed at last. "The man's information is uncommonly exact! I shall have to consult with General Shirley about this."

And with that he rose, giving me thus to understand that the interview was at an end. I was tempted to ask him if he still meant to send the Hampshire troops overland, but refrained, for I knew that he would think it prying in me. Instead I walked with him in silence to the door, where he shook my hand and I took my leave. I never knew how much this interview influenced the decision of those in command, but I like to believe that it was the information that I brought which caused the orders to be changed some weeks later and sent the Hampshire regiment overland through Massachusetts to the general rendezvous at Albany.

It was some weeks after this—six or seven, I do not just remember which—that an event which I believe we had all been anticipating at home occurred.

I had had an easy day of it, comparatively, and had managed for once to get home for an early supper. On this particular evening, however, Hubert, who was rarely delayed, was late. I recall we waited until well past eight, and then we three, Dorcas, Purity, and myself, went into the dining room and took our places at the table.

Dorcas, I thought, was nervous and inclined to be cross. I remember that at the instant he appeared in the doorway she was in the act of lifting a glass of wine to her lips.

"It's come," he said, to no one in particular. "Sorry to be so late."

I turned to look at him and saw that he seemed rather pleased than otherwise.

"What's come?" I asked.

"My orders," he replied. "I've two days to finish business here. After that I must be off for Halifax by way of Boston."

I heard Dorcas give a little gasp behind me, and at the same time heard the wineglass smash against her plate as it dropped from her fingers. I turned to see her leaning against the table, her face gone white as ashes. For an instant I thought she was about to faint, and Hubert must have had the same thought, too, for we bounded about the table, one to each side of her. But she waved us away.

"It is nothing," she said, "a passing weakness. I will be all right."

And with that she sat down and called for another glass. In another instant she was herself again, gay, happy, almost flippant in her determination to speed our guest cheerfully upon his way. But the gayer she was the more gloomy I became. The thoughts that Atkinson had put into my head came back upon me overwhelmingly. In that moment I was near the truth. If Hubert, as she said, meant naught to her, why had the announcement of the arrival of the expected orders so upset her? The wonder was that they had not come before. If she did not love this man, then why should his departure come as such a blow?

These thoughts persistently returned to me throughout the evening, though I tried to put them from me; and as a result I was but poor company, I fear. Neither did brooding upon what seemed to me the obvious conclusion improve my temper; so that when at last we came into our own bedchamber for the night I said a thing of which I might well be ashamed.

"Well, madam," I said bitterly, closing the door and placing my back against it.

"Well, sir!" she mocked. "Jamie, what's come over you tonight? You've been as glum as a preacher all evening."

"Can you deny," I demanded, "that it was the news of your lover's forthcoming departure that made you pale and drop your glass?"

"Jamie!" she gasped. "Can you think such a thing?"

"I not only can," I said grimly, "but I must. What else am I to think? Was it not plain enough to be seen?"

She tossed her head angrily at that, and swept across the room to her dressing table.

"You slander Hubert!" she said.

I laughed.

"And you slander me," she went on, not turning her head to look at me. "I cannot tell you why the spell should come at just that time, but I can explain my dizziness, even to you!"

"Think fast," I said, "for I shall be hard to convince!"

"I had not wanted to tell you until I was sure," she replied, "but I—I think I'm going to have a baby."

For an instant I stood rooted in amazement, my jaw hanging slack and all the belligerence gone out of me. Then suddenly I was overcome with shame. I went to her and went down upon my knees to beg her forgiveness. But she turned away and would have none of me, and presently I crept off to bed feeling that I scarcely blamed her.

Whether it was the reaction or not I could not say, but in the two days that remained of my cousin's visit with us I must admit to a greatly increased feeling of fellowship and good will. Nothing that he might ask was too much for me to do. I made him a present of the black Augustus, as well as of a brace of fine pistols that I had purchased for my own use, some time since, of John Pine, at the sign of the Crossed Guns on Ann Street, Boston. Before he left he begged me for a loan of a hundred pounds, which I gave him, though I must admit to an expression of surprise, for it was commonly known that he had made an excellent thing of his office as deputy surveyor and his expenses for living, staying with us as he did, amounted to almost nothing. I was to learn later that he had gambled heavily with certain bloods of the town. And no sooner was he gone than his tailor, his hatter, his glover, his boot-maker, his card maker, and sundry other creditors set up such a clamour for the debts he left behind him that I felt in honour bound to pay them, though their total came to something more than thirteen hundred pounds! Moreover, so pleased was I at having my suspicions finally lulled that, although I considered this a typical bit of Hubertian scoundrelism, I paid them gladly. Indeed, I almost felt myself fortunate, under the circumstances, to have come off so lightly.

Dorcas, too, seemed her old gay self once more. And Purity, who had hitherto been somewhat distant to him, became cordial and even friendly. These two got out their needles and thread and went over his entire wardrobe, patching, mending, and sewing on buttons, though I believe Purity did most of that, for Dorcas could never lay great claims to being a seamstress of any particular note.

On the evening before his departure I made it a special point to come home early. I found Dorcas and Hubert sitting upon the settle in the drawing room. Purity was nowhere to be seen. As I entered Hubert rose and came towards me.

"Dorcas has just been telling me the good news," he said as he wrung my hand. "You don't mind?"

"Of course not," I said.

The old sardonic smile played about his lips for an instant.

"I shan't be here," he said, "to stand godfather to the boy."

"If it is a boy," I replied.

"But of course it will be," he said, so sharply that for an instant it was almost as if he were offended. "Will you promise to give him my name as well as your own?"

"Why—" I stammered, for I hardly knew what to say to that. But Dorcas gave me no opportunity to refuse. She clapped her hands.

"The very thing!" she cried. "James Hubert will be his name."

He laughed at that.

" 'Tis settled then," said he. He reached out a hand for the bell. "We'll take a cup on that, eh, Jamie?"

He left the next morning at dawn, and for once Dorcas, who was rarely out of bed before midmorning, arose in time to see the sun rise. I went with him to Stavers', whence he was to ride with the postboy, while his baggage went on ahead by the freight wagons with Augustus. When he had swung up upon his horse's back and settled himself in the saddle, he gave me his twisted smile and reached down his hand.

"Good-bye, Jamie," said he. "It's been like old times, being with you again."

He laughed then, as if at some small private joke, and wheeled his mount with a wave of his hand. A moment later he was gone, leaving me staring after him through the grey morning fog as long as I could hear the ring of hooves upon the cobbles.

That summer and fall were as full of excitement and hope and despair for those of us who stayed at home as for any who went off to the wars. In July, almost on the heels of Hubert's departure, came the news of General Braddock's defeat and death at the hands of the French and Indians in the forests of Pennsylvania. The effect of that news upon our self-esteem was much like that of a bucket of ice water thrown upon a drunken man. In the enthusiasm of the moment no one had dreamed that the end of summer would not see the end of war. In the West, it was taken for granted we should beat the French as easily as a squirrel would pouch a beechnut. By autumn Crown Point and Niagara would be ours, and there would be naught for them to do but sue for peace.

But instead of this our first word was of British troops in full flight before a handful of coureurs de bois and savages—and those, mind you, not the raw provincial levies of the colonies, but seasoned British veterans; regular soldiers, accustomed to the most rigorous campaigns. The gloom and fright that settled upon our frontier colonies may well be imagined.

Word came in from the other parts of the campaign but fitfully. Everything at Albany seemed in the utmost confusion. By the first of August the expedition against Crown Point had not even gotten under way, while the Oswego expedition seemed to have been swallowed up entirely in the forests to westward of the Hudson. Only in Nova Scotia was there any sort of success, and that was but a poor campaign. About the end of August word came down from Halifax that the Acadian French, having proven themselves untrustworthy, were to be transported in a body and distributed piecemeal throughout the colonies from Maine to Georgia. But this could scarce be called a triumph. Indeed, no matter what was done upon a small scale—the building of the forts above Albany, the northward movement of General Johnson towards the Lakes, our successes in Acadia—there was no lightening of the cloak of pessimism that had fallen over us. The general feeling was that if these devilish Frenchmen and their savage allies could so easily defeat a column of picked and hardened troops, what might they not be expected to do to our own poorly equipped and scarcely trained levies? Even word of the arrival of some of Braddock's regulars at Albany did nothing to relieve our fears.

Early September, however, brought a second and more agreeable surprise, for on the eighth of that month General Johnson met, with his raw troops, a powerful force of French regulars and savages under command of Baron Dieskau, and defeated them at the south end of Lake George. This was undoubtedly cause for rejoicing—though for some of us it was also cause for sorrow, for in the fight that followed at Bloody Pond fell George Stapleton and Homer Odiorne.

After that we lived from day to day in hope of hearing that Johnson had pressed on against Crown Point while there was yet time, or that Frontenac had fallen. To the amazement and indignation of the taproom tacticians, however, Sir William, instead of pressing his advantage, was content to rest upon his laurels and fall back upon Fort Edward. And the crowning blow came at the end of the next month, when Shirley returned from Oswego, confessing his expedition a failure. They had built a sort of rude fort upon the shores of Lake Ontario, and there they had sat themselves down to glare across the lake at the French until approaching winter set them scurrying for home.

Our own household reechoed but slightly to these triumphs and failures. There was talk, of course, a plenty, for there was no other topic of conversation when guests came to call; but on the whole the war touched us but slightly.

Twice we heard from Hubert—he wrote both times addressing his letters to Dorcas: first from Boston, which he described glowingly as it appeared in the midst of preparations for the campaigns, and again from Albany, whither he had gone, he said, to join the staff of Governor Shirley at that gentleman's request. Officers of the regular army, it appeared, were a rarity then in the colonies, and the Governor had no intention of letting one slip through his fingers—most particularly not to return to Halifax, where, he maintained, they had much more than enough of them.

The winter set in late in November, and the troops began coming in in squads and groups to end their short enlistments. Every evening found Stavers' taproom full to overflowing of barroom generals and men "who were there," talking and arguing and discussing what "would have happened if," or what "should have been done but for." I found these gatherings often hilariously amusing, and since Dorcas, with the approach of her time, grew more and more difficult of temper, I found myself spending more and more of my time there, often returning homeward reluctantly about midnight or later, knowing full well that, no matter how gentle or tender or considerate I might try to be, she would have naught but fault to find with me. In ordinary circumstances I should have been quite out of patience with her, and I doubt not we should have quarrelled incessantly. But when I thought of her condition I made allowances for her, and accepted her abuse without retort, only hastening to leave the house as soon as I might. Indeed, had it not been for Purity, who seemed to grasp the situation without the least difficulty, and who, surprisingly enough, seemed to have gained some measure of Dorcas' confidence, we should have had an even more difficult time of it. She could soothe my wife's ruffled feelings and restore harmony to the home with a far more gentle touch than I, and whenever the storm clouds gathered upon Dorcas' brow I beat a swift retreat, leaving her in command.

This was the state of affairs towards the middle of January when, after an evening spent in tactical discussion with ale mugs, tankards, and bottles for troops, Stavers tapped me upon the shoulder and said, with a wink, that there was a negro wench at the side door asking for me.

I went at once and found it was Dorcas' Lizzie, shivering outside the door, a shawl thrown over her head. She grabbed my arm and thrust her black face close to mine, her eyes popping wide with excitement.

"Yo better come quick, lil mister," she said. "Your missus is a-hollerin' and a-screamin' sumpin wicked. I reckon her time's done come!"

I wasted no time on questions, but set out towards the house as fast as my heels would take me, cursing old Dr. Sweare with every third step. Dr. Sweare had attended the births and deaths and illnesses of all Drews since the beginning of time apparently, and upon our arrival in Portsmouth I had seen no reason to employ another. By all our calculations the child should not be born before the first week in February, but I had noticed that Dorcas had been growing uncommonly big, and mentioned the fact to Sweare. He had laughed at my suggestion, and told me not to worry, giving me the old assurance that he had never lost a father —at which he had laughed heartily, though I found I could no longer see anything funny in it. The child, he had assured me, would arrive on schedule, and I had believed him. Now as I raced up the steps to the door I breathed a swift prayer that he had arrived in time.

I came into the drawing room just as he came down the stairs.

"Doctor!" I exclaimed breathlessly. "Is she all right? Is it—"

"It's a boy," he said, "a buster, too."

"But you told me—" I began, but could get no further.

He gave me a quick shrewd look and pursed his old lips.

"Premature," he said shortly. He nodded towards the stairs. "You'd best be goin' on up. She'll be lookin' for ye."

I helped him on with his heavy coat and clapped his hat upon his head. Scarce had the door slammed shut behind him, when I was bounding up the stairs three at a time towards the room in which she lay.

2

Often in the days just before James Hubert's birth I had looked forward to the event with the feeling that by some mysterious sort of alchemy it was to bring the most profound changes in our lives, setting us all off on new courses that were destined to be happier, pleasanter, more agreeable to contemplate. On that day the world was to change. During the long months of waiting, time had stood still, and the effects upon each one of us had been inevitable. We had grown irritable and snappish. But, once let it be over with, time would move on again, along its smooth, unruffled way. The suspense would be ended. Dorcas would become her old gay self once more, and there would be no more quarrelling. In the house there would be only sweetness and light, and we all should be pleasant to one another again.

But it was not long before I learned my mistake. Save that a new hand ruled the house, there was not much that was different. Certainly Dorcas lost none of her querulousness. If anything, it rather increased. Having no longer the discomfort of carrying the child upon her belly she actually felt better, I think; but so strong had the habit become that she could not stop complaining, even though she could find little to complain of.

I had hoped that the care of the child would occupy her mind to the exclusion of herself; but this, it appeared, was a vain hope. Though she was as ridiculously adoring as only a fond parent can be, she could never learn to tend to all the thousand and one little demands that a baby makes. She might feed him when he was hungry, for this was a relief to her too. But beyond that she would not or could not go. To change him when he was wet and bathe him when he was dirty and soothe him off to sleep when he was fretful were things she was completely incapable of doing. And when he filled the house, as any healthy baby will, with lusty bellowing it came near to driving her to distraction.

Indeed it was a lucky day for little James Hubert when I brought Purity home to stay with us, for from the very beginning she took charge of him. It was Purity who bathed him and changed him and tucked him into his crib at night. And later, when he left his mother's breast and turned to solid foods, it was she who cooked for him. She taught him to speak his first gurgling words, and when he finally began to walk it was to her knee and not his mother's that he took his first tottering steps.

In the middle of February, Hubert came to pay us a visit, bringing the latest news of the war, though, indeed, there was little enough to be said on that score, most of the troops, except a small handful at Ford Edward on the Hudson and at the new fort, William-Henry, on Lake George, had been mustered out and sent to their homes for the winter. Only one small fragment of what he had to say was of interest to me especially. This was that one of the companies that had volunteered to stay the winter at William-Henry was that captained by Rob Rogers—a fact which did much to explain why, although our Hampshire troops were all come home again, I had found so few of my friends among them.

He went on to tell of plans that were going forward for the coming year. Even now there was no official war, though the formal declaration was expected to come from England any day. Meantime poor Shirley, who had lost much of the confidence of the various colonies through his blundering of the season just past, was going doggedly ahead to outline his campaign. So far, according to Hubert, this consisted of expeditions against Duquesne and Niagara, through Frontenac, as well as Crown Point; and also again, the pet project, a thrust at Quebec by way of the Kennebec and Chaudière. The Colonial governments, however, lacked enthusiasm, and unless word of help from overseas arrived shortly it was doubtful if they would support the scheme. In the meantime there was a rumour about that Shirley was to be relieved of his command and recalled to England, though who would replace him was still a matter of speculation and argument. Some said it would be Sir William Johnson, who had been made a baronet for having lain in a funk in his tent at Lake George, the while Colonel Lyman, of Connecticut, fought and beat the doughty Baron Dieskau for him. But this was thought to be doubtful, for it was well recognized that our New Englanders were jealous of their "rights" and would be unlikely to fight under the command of a Yorker.

It was upon this last that Hubert and I almost came to blows.

"Rights!" he scoffed. "You Yankees are plain fools! You prate of rights while the wolf is gnawing at your heels. The French are upon you, yet you are too busy quarrelling among yourselves to fight them!"

I shrugged at that.

"We will defend our own," I retorted, "but you cannot expect us to raise men and money to fight Pennsylvania's battles."

It was well known that in Philadelphia the Quakers had steadfastly refused to lift a finger in their own defence, although it was their frontier which had thus far fared the worst.

Hubert shook his head.

" 'Tis no more than you seem to expect the crown to do," he said. "You are too niggardly to provide for your own defence, and yet you expect troops and money to be sent from England for the purpose. Why, 'tis common talk in Boston that Massachusetts will raise neither money nor men until she is reimbursed for her expense in the last campaign."

"No, no," I replied, "you are hardly fair. Such a campaign as the last—or any campaign, for that matter—is an expensive business. Were the colonies to bear the whole burden 'twould raise our taxes beyond what we can bear. These colonies are a mighty asset to the crown. It is but just that we should expect the crown to bear a share of the cost of keeping them British. I, for one, would as lief be a Frenchman as to pay dear for the privilege of being British!"

He drew himself up, very haughty and supercilious at that.

"Aye!" said he, "I mind now you have not always been friendly to the crown."

"Hoity-toity!" I cried. "Does the pot call the kettle black? No one has ever questioned my loyalty to the crown—on the right head! But neither has anyone heard me express any fondness for the Dutchman that wears it now. I seem to recall that you once bore arms against the crown yourself. At least I do not blow hot and cold with the wind."

444

He turned fiery red and, I believe, would have made some angry retort; but Dorcas laid a hand upon his arm and stopped him.

"For shame, Jamie!" she scolded. "Are these the manners of a host?"

She was right enough, and I admitted my fault, apologizing for it.

"After all," I said, " 'tis not a thing we should quarrel over. 'Twill not be settled at our dinner table!"

He acknowledged the apology sourly, and we moved into the drawing room. A few moments later we were at it again upon another subject.

"What is needed," he said, "is a strong force of regulars. Let us have trained soldiers enough and we will soon show the Frenchmen a thing or two."

"Aye," said I sourly. "Send us lobsterbacks to eat our provisions and lord it over us and be quartered upon us in our homes— as they will be, mark my words—and then expect us to pay for them!"

"Then how would you suggest the crown help?" he replied sarcastically.

"Let the crown send us the money," I said, "and we will send the men."

"Bah!" said he. "The provincials are no better than a rabble. You cannot win battles if you rely upon such troops as those."

"They will fight," I said, "though their tactics may be rough."

He laughed.

"Who was it took Louisbourg in '45?" I demanded hotly, for I was stung by his attitude. "Were there any regulars there? And how many were there at Lake George? Who was it fled when Braddock fell?"

"Pother!" he cried. "You know nothing of military science!"

"I have no need to," I replied, "when I have the record so clear before me."

From all of which it may be seen that we talked in circles, for neither of us was entirely wrongheaded; and as is the case with most such arguments there was something of right on each side.

But all his visit was not spent in argument. From the very moment his letter arrived, heralding his coming, Dorcas brightened noticeably, although I was too pleased at seeing her gay again to put two and two together. He made much of little James Hubert, and was obviously pleased that we had fallen in with his suggestion. The entire month of his visit was a round of gaiety and parties, in which I did my best to participate with a good grace, seeing that it would be for so short a time.

He was full too of stories of the campaign. Those of the camp and field he reserved for my ears alone, for many of them were unfit for feminine ears; but to Dorcas he sang the praises of Boston and New York and Albany, and told tall tales of the gay social life of those cities, especially of the last, which surprised me for I remembered the place as a sleepy Dutch town without much capacity for such doings. It appeared, however, that as army headquarters the place had blossomed. Many of the officers had brought their wives and set them up there where they might be near them, with the result that the city was full of lace and ruffles and pretty-pretties, and rents had rocketed sky-high. As soon as she heard of this Dorcas clapped her hands together delightedly.

"Jamie!" she cried. "Why don't you go? It really is your duty, you know. I'm sure Hubert could arrange to see that you have proper rank!"

"Why not, old man?" said Hubert. "There's a new regiment to be raised for the crown, the 62nd—Royal Americans, they're to be called. They'll have status as regulars. For a matter of three or four hundred pounds I can get you a lieutenancy."

I shook my head. My wounds had healed by this, and I was feeling my old self again, but I could not feel any enthusiasm for such a service. I had no illusions as to the glory of being shot at.

"No," I said. "Thanks, but I think not."

Purity, who was present, smiled; but Dorcas began to pout like a spoiled child, and Hubert looked superior.

"Afraid, are you?" he sneered.

"Hubert," I said, "I have been shot at, and I have been wounded, and I tell you frankly I did not like it. If that is fear, then I must be afraid."

"I might arrange a staff berth at headquarters," he said contemptuously.

"No doubt you could," I replied. "You seem to have done well along those lines for yourself. But if it's all the same to you I'd rather not. You yourself have said that I know nothing of military science. I would be worse than useless as an officer of the line, if that is so. Until I find some branch of the service in which my own peculiar talents and knowledge will be of use I will prefer to stay at home, caring for my family and tending to my business. I flatter myself that the service I do in that way is a hundredfold more valuable."

"You coward!" Dorcas exclaimed.

I turned to her coldly.

"My dear," I said, "your poor opinion of me has long since ceased to hurt. You may as well save your breath."

I rose in the midst of a silence that was almost painful, and started towards the door. Before I went out, however, I could not resist one last thrust. I turned.

"And, madam," I said to Dorcas, "when and if I do find such a service as the one of which I just spoke, and when and if I do go off to war, you and James Hubert will stay at home like respectable folk, and not go gadding off about the provinces in search of sociability."

I passed the matter off thus lightly upon the surface; but in spite of my assurance, I found the business weighing upon my mind. Dorcas' thrust had struck home. No matter how cold our relations, I could not feel happy to have her regard me as a coward. Hubert spoke to me once again before he left, repeating his offer, but I refused to listen. But when he had gone his way hardly a day passed but Dorcas taunted me for it; so that I was fair put to it to keep from enlisting in self-defence. About a month after he had gone, a letter came from Hubert saying that he had made inquiries and could assure me of a lieutenancy in the Royal Americans; but I tore it up without bothering to reply, though my every inclination was to accept his offer.

If the temptation was strong then, it became ten times worse as spring drew near. In March a strong force of French and Indians, coming from Fort Frontenac on the north side of Lake Ontario, swooped down upon Fort Bull, which guarded the western end of the Great Carrying Place, so called, from the Mohawk to Wood Creek and Oswego. Now it is probable that, this being a small affair, we should never even have heard of it but for the fact that the entire garrison of thirty, with the exception of two or three who managed to hide themselves in the near-by woods, were slaughtered. Those who had been in garrison at that point had all been selected from Shirley's regiment—the 61st. In consequence, both Shirley's and Pepperell's having been recruited mainly from about Boston and Portsmouth, and many of those who had fallen being well known in the neighbourhood, it was but natural that a particular interest in the affair should be felt there. Indignation ran high. There was a grand clamour for revenge. Men swept away by their anger began to volunteer for the coming campaign, determined now to teach the French dogs a lesson.

At almost the same time recruiting began in earnest, both to raise new troops of provincials and to fill out the ranks of the regulars depleted in the preceding year. At any hour of the day one could find crowds milling about in Buck Street and the Square, listening eagerly while a recruiting sergeant bellowed to make himself heard above the rattle of the drum and the squeal of the fife, which was always a part of his show. Many a young yokel, carried away by the lurid promises of glory and adventure, of rum and meat in plenty, and thoughts of a swashbuckling life of ease and fun, or blinded by the bright uniforms and roused by the martial thump and fervour of the music, pushed his way forward to take the King's shilling. And, looking on, I could understand why they might, for even I, to whom this was by no means new, felt the urge to raise my hand and step forward.

For all the feeling of tensity and excitement, however, it was noticeable that it was mainly the hotheads who stepped forward. It was not until the middle of April that news came which fired the general enthusiasm to the point where sober-headed gentlemen, who at another time might have thought twice about it, rushed to volunteer. This news, which so caught at the popular imagination, had indeed a businesslike ring. In the first place, war was declared. Secondly, the busy but ineffectual Shirley was to turn over his command to Webb and Abercrombie, who were to make general preparations for the summer's campaign. Later the Earl of Loudoun would arrive, with, so rumour said, 15,000 picked troops, and a shipload of gold to finance the campaign.* Finally,

* Governor Shirley did not receive the formal notice of his own relief until June. The Earl of Loudoun, however, received his orders on December 25, 1755. Intimations of the change were received in the colonies as early as April 16. It is reasonable to assume that there must have been some fairly accurate rumours even before this.

the colonies were to raise and equip a similar force. In the face of such overwhelming numbers the French must surely give way. By autumn they would be swept from the continent, and we should have peace again. On street corners, in taprooms and drawing rooms men talked and argued with enthusiasm, and the war spirit rose in the breast of every farmer and merchant in the land. Now we would show the French dogs! Volunteers clamoured for admission to the ranks, until groggy recruiting sergeants rubbed their eyes and wondered if they had not died and gone to their own particular heaven!

In the midst of all this martial fervour it is not to be imagined that our home was untouched. I count myself as susceptible as the next. Certainly I was not a bit better. But if I did not at once rush to enlist it was rather my Scottish stubbornness than any scruples which prevented me. Scarce a day went by but Dorcas nagged at me, and with the support of so much public clamour I doubt not she actually came to believe herself when she called me coward. In those days our quarrels were frequent and bitter, for I could not sit by and hear her lectures without reply. Indeed, so fed up was I upon discordancy at home and the clamour of the town, that after each quarrel I would slam out of the house, half determined in my mind to leave it all and go away to Suncook or even farther, just so that I might have peace.

It was upon one of these occasions, when I had flung out of the house after some particularly hard words between us, that I made an encounter which changed the whole current of my life. It was late in the afternoon, and the day was hot and still. My anger had left me thirsty and overheated, so that I turned my sulky steps towards Stavers' taproom, where I looked forward to a glass of cold ale to quench my temper. As I approached the wide door another man turned in before me, and though I could not see his face I could not help but notice him, for he was of medium height and stocky build, and he was clad in a suit of deep green buckskin such as I had never seen before, and on his head he wore a small Scotch cap at a rakish angle, with a black ribbon dangling down behind.

We set our hands upon the door at the same instant, and he turned to look at me, whereupon we both cried out in pleased surprise, for here was no other person than John Stark, whom I had thought to be miles away at Lake George.

"Jamie!" cried he. "The very man I'd hoped to find."

He took me by the arm.

"Come have a pot of ale," he said.

"What are you doing here?" I asked, as we entered arm in arm. "I thought you were at William-Henry from the last I heard."

He grinned.

"What are any of us doing here?" he demanded. "I'm recruiting. Have ye ever seen aught like it?"

"Tell me of it," I said. "What is it like in the army?"

He looked about him. The long room was packed to overflowing with soldiers and civilians in all stages of sobriety and befuddlement, arguing and gabbling and shouting orders.

" 'Tis noisy here," said he. "Let's go where we can hear ourselves think."

He caught hold of Stavers by the arm as he was passing.

"Have ye a room for us?" he demanded.

Stavers bobbed his head and led the way to one of the private dining rooms that ranged one side of the main tavern.

"Rogers will be along presently," said Stark. "He'll be looking for me."

"I'll tell him where ye are," said Stavers.

When he had taken our orders and gone Stark turned to me.

"Well," he said, "you're not in it?"

"Not yet," I replied, "though it isn't as if I hadn't a chance."

And I told him of what had passed between me and Hubert and of the rift it had made in our household. When I had finished he laughed.

"And who can blame you?" he demanded. "A man likes to pick his own way, not to be driven through life by his wife and relatives!"

He stopped laughing and eyed me soberly for a moment.

"But I've the place for you," he said, and shook the green buckskin fringe of his sleeve before my face. "Ye see this coat?" he demanded. "D'ye know what it is?"

I shook my head.

"I never saw it before," I said.

" 'Tis the uniform of Rogers' Rangers," he went on, almost as if he had not heard me speak. "There's the service for you."

"I never heard of them," I said. "What makes you think that that's the place for me?"

"Because you're a woodsman," said he. "Listen! I'll tell you about it. Come the end o' June there'll be sixteen thousand men at the forts on the Hudson and Lake George, waiting to move up against Crown Point; and not a one of 'em hardly has ever seen an Injun before. Most of 'em never laid eyes on deep woods in their lives. All right! Now the French are building a new fort at Ticonderoga at the outlet of Lake George. Whoever's in command has got to have scouts to watch 'em and tell him what they're up to. He's got to have men that know the woods, so they can go and find out where the Injuns are, and how many they've got. He's got to have men who can sneak up through the brush and catch a picket napping and bring him in for questioning. He's got to have men who can slip in and worry 'em and get away again. Only woodsmen can do that."

"Well," I said, "it sounds reasonable enough to me."

"It's plain common sense," said he. "Most of 'em don't see it. They look at it like your cousin. They think it's the regulars will win the war. But what they don't see is, the regulars won't even start if we don't have rangers to go ahead and find the enemy for 'em. Regulars aren't cowards, but they're not used to brush fighting. If they can see anything to fight, they'll fight; but when they're being shot at and can't see who's doing it they don't know what to do. They get scared and run. Nobody ever told 'em to hide themselves and shoot from cover. That's not in the tactics books. They think it's cowardly. But it has to be done here."

He paused for breath. I merely nodded. What he said made sense.

"Shirley saw what was needed," he went on. "Johnson don't approve of it because he thinks his Injuns'll do as well, but Shirley knows you can't trust Injuns. He begun looking around for a man to take the job. All winter Rogers has been working out of Fort William-Henry, scouting and ranging and bothering the French all he could. Shirley heard of him and sent for him. His orders were to form one company of permanent Rangers, Rogers to command, other companies to be formed as needed and approved. It's your service, man, because you're a woodsman, and you'll need no training, and that's what we've orders to get. When the other troops are fiddling their thumbs in garrison, you'll be out on active duty, always going. There's nothing quiet about this job, mister."

I had never heard Stark so enthusiastic upon anything before. I grinned.

"You sound as though you liked it," I said.

"Like it!" he exclaimed.

A tap at the door cut him short, and he rose to open it. I looked up to see the huge bulk of Rob Rogers fill the doorway. There was no doubt that the military life agreed with him, for he had filled out and there was a look of wild confidence about him. There was no doubt he was a man who could command.

"Ho, Jamie!" he cried. "Stavers told me ye were here.'"

He swung upon Stark.

"Have ye made him a convert yet?" he demanded.

John spat sourly.

"The man's a natural Scotchman," said he. "He'll not commit himself."

Rogers turned back to me.

"Come," he said. "He's told ye about it, I can see that. I can offer ye no better than an ensigncy now, for I've but the one company to begin with, and John here and my brother Dick are bespoken for lieutenants. But if that means aught to ye, there'll be other companies made up before the summer's out, and I'll see ye have a lieutenancy in one."

I hesitated only an instant. Then I bethought me of my cousin's superiority and my wife's scorn. I remembered the words I had used to them, that when I went it would be in a place that suited my talents and was of my own choosing. I should never, I thought, find a better. I thrust out my hand.

"I'll take you," I said. "Here's my hand on't."

3

If I thought that this action on my part would please any member of my household it was not long before I was disillusioned. I made all haste homeward from the tavern, but my announcement at supper was received with a frosty silence. Purity said never a word, but only stared at me incredulously. Dorcas set down her fork abruptly.

"What?" she demanded.

"I've done it," I repeated. "I've taken the King's shilling."

"You've listed!" she exclaimed.

"Your pardon, ma'am," I replied stiffly. "I have accepted a commission as ensign in Captain Rogers' company of rangers."

"With Rogers!" Purity exclaimed. "Why, then you'll be with father."

I nodded.

"I hope so," I said.

Dorcas snorted angrily.

"Provincials!" she sneered. "Oh, Jamie, how could you be such a fool? What can you hope to gain from such a connection? And when Hubert has been so generous, too! How can you turn your back upon his offers?"

I looked at her coldly, not a little put out at her attitude.

"You are devilish hard to please, ma'am," I said. " 'Tis months now you've been urging me off to the wars, and now I tell you that I'm going it seems you're not satisfied. If you'll remember I once said that when the time came to go 'twould be only in a capacity in which my talents and knowledge would be of use. I have chosen my service with that in mind. Neither have I thought to gain from it. There is more profit to be taken at home than with the army, as you well know."

Far from being rebuked, she only appeared the more angry at what she was pleased to consider my stupidity.

"But provincials!" she exclaimed. "Have you no thought for your family's standing, Jamie, that you can turn away a commission as lieutenant of the regular establishment to become a paltry ensign of provincials? How will I ever face my friends if it becomes known?"

I came near to choke over my beefsteak at that.

"If you think, madam," I said, "that I go to the wars and risk my neck for the sake of our social prestige, you are sadly mistaken."

"You might have some thought for me," she replied testily. "I can see that it would make but little difference to you whether you were regular or provincial. But you should consider how much better would be my position in Albany as the wife of an officer in the regular army."

"Albany!" I exclaimed. "Who said anything of Albany? Not I surely!"

She looked at me with a peculiar expression that was half defiance, half apprehension.

"I should go to Albany, of course," she said. "I would want to be near you."

"My dear," I said, somewhat mollified, "my duties will take me far from Albany. Once we have gone on to the forts I shall probably not return before the end of the campaign. Then it may be nearer to come straight to Portsmouth. With our movements so uncertain 'twill be better if you stay at home, as a good wife should, and think no more of Albany."

"I might know you would take such an attitude," she said bitterly.

I glanced at Purity, who was obviously embarrassed at this exchange, for she kept her eyes averted and her cheeks were pink. I checked the remark that sprang to my lips and looked away.

"There is nothing more to say," I replied. "The thing is done. Let us have no more discussion of it."

I was early at the tavern the next afternoon to sign the rolls; yet, early as I was, I found Stark and Rogers before me with a handful of recruits. Between the orders he had that morning received to go to Number Four, as soon as his company was complete, and the great quantity of rum he had consumed throughout the day, Rogers was in high good humour. In spite of his potations, however, he seemed none the worse. Indeed, but for the aroma of the liquor, which hung about him like a fog, a stranger would never have guessed his state. Certainly there was no falter to his step, no thickening of his speech, no glazing of his eye. Rather his natural swagger and conceit seemed more pronounced. He gasconaded without bluster. He boasted without arrogance. Drunk he may have been—but magnificently so, not stupidly.

As he read to us the orders by which the company was raised and the articles of war by which we were to be bound, I had a new opportunity to study the man and remark the changes that had come over him since the day when he had courted my elder sister. In those days he had been a boaster and a poser with naught to support his vanity, so that he cut a laughable figure. Now he could boast with reason, for already his name was mentioned as that of a partisan fighter more wily than the Indians themselves. He had made good his bragging, yet, characteristically, he was not pompous with his success. He could be petulant or flippant or audacious or insolent as he chose; yet he was offensive only when he intended to be so, and he showed a knack for reading men's thoughts and emotions, be they his subordinates or his superiors, and turning them to his own account, that was nothing short of uncanny. He had always had an air of command, and now dressed in his green buckskins, his broad shoulders filling the fringed coat, with his round cap set jauntily on one side of his head, the curving plume that curled above it from in back sweeping the smoke-blackened beams of the taproom ceiling, this air seemed to be accentuated beyond measure. Looking at him through the smoke haze of the tavern, I could visualize him in action in the forest, and I was glad that I had not been swayed from my purpose to join him by my wife's protests.

He finished reading his orders:

". . . from time to time to use your best endeavours to distress the French and their allies, by sacking, burning, and destroying their houses, barns, barracks, canoes, battoes, &c; and by killing their cattle of every kind; and at all times to endeavour to waylay, attack, and destroy their convoys of provisions, by land and water, in any part of the country where you may find them."

He looked around at all of us, to see if there were any comment to be made or questions to be asked. But no one spoke. He turned and slapped the papers down beside him upon the bar and called for ink and a pen.

"All right, my lads," he said as soon as Stavers had complied with his commands. "Step up and make your sign."

He pointed a thick forefinger at a blank space near the head of a list that I could see was already well over half full, and shoved the quill in my direction. I signed, and noted that I was to receive pay at the rate of five shillings per day, New York currency, as ensign; as I laid aside the quill Stark thrust a roll of Spanish dollars at me.

"What's this?" I asked.

" 'Tis in the articles," he replied. "Each man to receive an allowance of ten Spanish dollars upon enlistment for clothing, arms, and blankets."

I dropped the money into my pocket and watched while the others signed. Seven of the men Stark had brought with him were able to stand and write their names; but the other four were so far gone in rum that they had to be held up by Rogers, while John, who himself seemed to be none too steady, guided their hands. When they had all signed Rogers pushed them over into an unoccupied booth.

"Drunk," he grinned, as he came back to the bar. "Let 'em have it while they may. 'Twill soon be shaken out of 'em once they're on the way."

He took up his papers and counted the list of names laboriously.

"Forty-two," he said at last, and rubbed his hands together in satisfaction. "We'll need eighteen more to fill."

"Dick and Jed will get that many upcountry," Stark said.

Rogers nodded and called for rum.

"Our orders are for Number Four as soon as the company is complete," he said. "Serjeant Stiles will be in tomorrow from Rochester and Durham. And we're to meet Dick at Exeter Friday with the Rumford and Canterbury men."

Stavers brought the rum, and Rogers thrust a mug into my hand and thumped my back.

"You're in the army now, my lad," he said. "We'll have one short drink to a swift campaign and a merry one!"

He tossed off the hot liquor without so much as the quiver of an eyelash.

"You have it now?" he asked of me. "We muster Friday at half after two on Exeter common. Be ready to march. John, here, will tell you what equipment you'll need."

We shook hands, and after I had arranged with Stark to meet him on the morrow to confer in the matter of my personal supplies, I took my leave of them and made my way homeward with a lighter step. The move was made now. There was no turning back, and somehow I found myself vastly relieved.

This was upon a Tuesday morning. The Wednesday and Thursday that followed were strange days for me.

Abrupt as my decision had been, I was something put to it to set my business affairs in fit order to be left behind. I was fortunate in having such a friend as Colonel Meserve, for he offered to look after my interests with his own. But for that, I believe, I should have felt uneasy at leaving; as it was, I was able to go, confident that nothing would be neglected.

But there were other matters requiring my attention as well. On

Wednesday I went to get myself properly equipped with green buckskins, two pair of moccasins, a tin plate, a horn mug and spoon, blankets, smallclothes, powder horn and shot pouch, a fine musket, a knife and hatchet, a bullet mould, and a sack to carry all in. On Thursday I undertook to see to it that my wife and child would be provided for in my absence, and drew up a legal-seeming will in the event of anything happening to me. Here again I was fortunate, for I found young Sam Livermore, who was but lately come to Portsmouth, only too willing to act as my attorney, and I knew that matters left with him would be well attended.

Purity, who was frankly disapproving of the entire business, nevertheless sat herself down, and by dint of almost constant knitting, made me a woollen jacket to wear beneath my coat upon frosty nights, for which I was later most extremely grateful. As I accepted it from her hands I thought that her lips trembled and she was dangerously near to crying; and I was touched at this evidence of her affection for me. Beside it I could not help but notice Dorcas' attitude, which was indifferent to say the least. Not only did she not approve of what I had done, but in some obscure way she actually felt that I had done her an injury; and so incensed was she at this fancied wrong that I could scarce get her to speak to me, even to the very eve of my departure. Try as I might, neither pleading nor cajolery nor threats would move her from that position. I had made up my mind to this thing myself, she said, and if go I must, she at least would have no hand in it. Nor would she give me such comfort as is due a man when he fares forth from his house upon any journey. Not by word nor by look did she indicate that she cared any longer what might become of me, so that in the end, as may well be imagined, my leave-taking was but a sorry one.

In the meantime, Wednesday night, Jed Stiles—now Serjeant Stiles—and Toby came down from their recruiting trip to Rochester and Durham and the eastern settlements with fifteen of the needed eighteen recruits.

"Christ!" swore Stark to Rogers, when he saw them trooping in. " 'Twas never so easy! Your brother will be raising at least as many in Rumford, if not more. We'll have to draw lots to see who's to be turned back."

But Rogers grinned.

"Be damned to that!" he said. "We'll have need of every man. We're authorized for sixty, and there'll be more companies raised before the summer's out, mark my words. Until then I'll pay every extra man out of my own pocket."

That evening they stayed in the tavern, where both of them got roaring-drunk. But the next day Stiles left Toby at Stavers' and spent the day in our kitchen (he would not come into the drawing room, which he said was too high-toned for him) and talked with Purity.

The next morning I arose in the grey dawn and dressed myself as quietly as I could, so as not to disturb Dorcas. When I stood ready to go I shook her gently by the shoulder. She opened her eyes and looked up at me sleepily.

"I'm going now," I said.

"Good-bye," she answered, and turned upon her side.

For a moment I stood staring down at her, feeling not angry but only hurt, and somehow guilty and bewildered, as if perhaps I had actually done her some hurt. Then, because I could not help it, I bent down and kissed her cheek.

Downstairs Stiles and Purity were waiting for me in the hall. It was then she gave me the knitted jacket; I took it from her, thanking her and thinking, in spite of myself, how much more gentle and gracious and unspoiled she was than my own wife.

"Take care of yourself, Jamie," she said.

And with that she kissed me upon the lips. I could feel Stiles plucking at my sleeve.

"Come along," he said gruffly. "Mr. Stark will be anxious to be away." (Rogers had gone on ahead the night before with half the men.)

As I turned I squeezed her hand.

"Bless you, child!" I said. "Keep an eye upon them for me while I'm gone. I doubt not Dorcas'll need a level head to guide her."

She opened the door and held it for us, and I could not but think how lovely she looked standing there, a great cloak wrapped about her, the yellow light of the candle shining through her disheveled hair from the table behind her, and the grey morning mist swirling in about her from the darkness outside.

"I'll do my best," she said, simply.

We said good-bye then, and turned away into the darkness.

When I looked back once through the drifting mists she was still standing there, framed in the doorway, a black figure, sharp against the bright glow of the candle within.

When we came to the tavern it was to find Stark all in a great sweat. For an hour past he had been trying to rouse up Toby for the road, but the best he could get was a rumbling snore and a series of foul belches rank with rum.

"Get your man up, serjeant," he blustered, all the fine military man at once. "He's your charge, God's blood! If I'd my way there'd be none of these red devils in the service. Have him ready for the road in five minutes."

With that he strode outside with his stocky strut to await us in the tavern yard with the men lined up before him.

We did not join him in five minutes, nor yet in twenty; but at the end of a half-hour we had a groggy and very ill tempered Indian ready for the march by means of a half-dozen buckets of icy water and a little amateur blooding on Stiles' part, who seemed well accustomed to the business. Stark fumed and fretted with impatience to be off, but there was naught he could do, unless he wished to set out ahead; and this he apparently preferred not to do. For all his impatience, however, I could not see that it mattered greatly; the distance to Exeter was not above seventeen miles, and we were not due upon the common before afternoon. There was not a one of us to make the march but could have done it on the level road in four hours or under.

In the end we were ready at last, and with the stumbling old Indian in our midst to keep him from lagging behind we set out in rough order across the whispering cobbles of the innyard. As the first rays of the sun tinged the sky pink in the east behind us, we swung out upon the Exeter road above the town, and turned our faces westward towards the war.

14

LESSONS IN WAR

[1 We came early into Exeter, a few minutes past noon, to find that Rogers' first lieutenant, his younger brother Richard, was already come before us from the neighbourhood of Canterbury and Rumford with a score and some odd of recruits for the new company. We were scarce given time to snatch a bite before young Caleb Page was tooting upon his bugle to summon us to muster upon the common.

That afternoon, until dusk, we drilled beneath the tall elms, learning to wheel and turn and carry our arms as soldiers should. And when night fell, under the sharp guidance of the few veterans among us, we made our first encampment, much to the amusement and edification of the townsfolk, for Rogers, maintaining that 'twas only thus we should learn, ignored the village and set out pickets and chose his site, just as he should have done it in the field.

That night, at the evening muster, Captain Rogers read out to us his most recent orders, which called upon him to proceed as quickly as he might to Number Four, upon the Connecticut, with a scout of his own choosing. In accord with these he picked fifteen of the score of veterans among us, and with Lieutenant Stark as his second in command, set out before dawn the next morning. The rest of the company, he left under the command of his younger brother, Lieutenant Dick, a man as big as himself yet without the extreme moodiness or the force of personality. I was named second in command of this detachment, and our orders were to march immediately and by the shortest possible route to Albany.

That day we marched to Dunstable, where we lay the night. On the next we came, by half-forgotten Indian paths, to Monadnock Number One,* a long march; and on the third we came an even longer way to Deerfield on the Connecticut. Thereafter we moved

* Rindge.

more slowly, following an old Indian trail up into the heart of the Berkshire Hills, through a place called by the Indians Pontoosuck, and thence across the northern Taconics into the broad valley of the Hudson, where on the eighth day after our departure from Portsmouth we came at last into the provincial camp that lay between Greenbush and the Hudson, across the river from Albany.

I for one must confess that I was delighted at the sight of that vast grey sea of tents that spread confusedly in every direction across the flats. Of all the recruits I, perhaps, stood least ready for such a march as we had made; for I was soft with town living, and out of touch with outdoor life. Not since before the ambush upon the Connecticut had I seen so much of the woods, and it must be admitted that a week of marching, frequently as much as thirty miles in a single day, had left me footsore and weary.

Nor was marching all we had accomplished in our way. No sooner had we left Dunstable behind than I realized why Rogers had chosen this route for us. Too far south to be in any danger of attack, and at the same time far enough north of the beaten track to approximate conditions as we would find them in the field, the entire route proved an ideal training for recruits. Every step of the way was drill for us. During the day we marched, in accordance with the special tactics worked out by Rogers for the ranging service, in single file, an interval of six feet between each man and the next so that a single shot might not bring down two men in the event of an ambush. Guards went before and to the rear, in constant touch with the main column, and flankers marched at twenty yards on either hand. When we came to soft or swampy ground we crossed it in line abreast, so that a possible enemy upon our trail might have more difficulty in tracking us. At sundown scouts were sent ahead to choose a camp site that would be difficult to approach, and no day's march ended before dark; so that an enemy must track us after nightfall in order to overtake us. At night pickets were set out in regular order, and the detachment lay upon its arms, while Lieutenant Rogers and I divided the night between us, turn about, as officer of the guard; so that, weary though I was, I had regularly but half the sleep I needed to refresh me for the next day's march. In the morning we were up before the dawn and standing to arms, for this is the hour when Indians prefer to attack. And with the coming of daybreak we were again upon the road, swinging along at a steady league an hour. By the time we reached the Hudson I had begun to realize that this service I had chosen was to be by no means easy.

My recollections of our entry into that camp are but a hodge-podge of sights and sounds and smells. We came into the main highway between Albany and Kinderhook a half-mile below the camp and, turning, presently found ourselves passing through the first rows of dingy grey tents. Men lolled about upon the ground, loafing or mending harness. Beside several of the tents I saw racks upon which other harnesses were hanging, and the stench of horse manure was heavy in the air; so that I guessed that these must be the teamsters who helped supply the army. Before one tent a group was openly playing at the cards, although, as I was later to learn there was a strict camp ordonnance against it. The teamsters—not being attached to any force, it seemed—held themselves above camp rules.

A little farther on we passed the Rhode Island encampment. There the men flocked out to the street to watch us go by—tall, lean, sour-countenanced fellows, as mean, I doubt not, as they looked; for though I have seen many of them it has never been my good fortune to meet a native of that Province that was not sour-spoken, ill tempered, and always on the lookout to see what he might steal or cheat his fellow men of. I suppose there must be some honest souls among them; but, as I say, it has never been my good fortune to see one.

Upon the edge of this encampment, where it gave way to the tents of a Jersey regiment, I saw a company kitchen tucked away between a row of privies upon the one hand and a slaughter shed upon the other, in the midst of such a stench as turned my stomach just to pass it. Startled at first at the sight of such ill judgement, I soon grew used to it, for in our passage through the camp I saw the same, or similar sights, not less than four separate times by count.

The truth was, there was no sign of order in this camp. Regimental commanders made their dispositions as they pleased with scant regard for one another, while the men did much as they wished. There was a great hubbub of shouting and cursing, and the streets were filled with men hurrying about various errands or loafing in the way. Down by the river a group of men added to the uproar by shooting at bottles floating in the water. Every man seemed to go about with an air of truculence, bearing a chip upon his shoulder; so that, though I saw no actual brawling, I did not envy the provost marshal his task.

In the midst of all this we came into the parade, where Lieutenant Rogers wheeled us into line before the commander's tent and, leaving me in charge, proceeded to make his report. For some moments we stood waiting his return, the centre of an idly curious throng that poured out to greet us and see what was happening. Apparently our little company, handsomely uniformed in green buckskins, was a new sight among this motley mob, for there were but a few of the older established regiments among the provincials that had any pretence to similarity of dress; and this oddity was the source of not a few sarcastic comments on the part of the onlookers.

"Purty little fellers, ain't they?" said one hard-bitten Rhode Islander in a loud voice. "Keepers o' the privies, or some such, like as not."

A burst of laughter greeted this crude sally, and the lanky Narragansett man swelled with pride at his own wit.

He spat. "Haw, haw!" he roared. "I want the little feller out front fer my detail."

I could feel my ears grow red, and heard the men stir restlessly behind me, at the laugh that went up.

A stocky little man, in a faded blue coat, not much taller than myself and nearly as broad as he was tall, thrust his way through the throng.

"Shut up!" he said to the tall Rhode Islander. "Can't you see these men are on parade? Why don't you give 'em a chance? Stand back there."

The thin man spat but made no answer. Neither did he move back. Nevertheless I could see by the look in his eye that he stood somewhat in awe of the short man. Whoever he was, the latter had evidently established for himself a measure of authority in this bedlam. He turned to me and looked at me out of hard grey eyes. There was a slight smile on his heavy features.

"Putnam's the name," he said. "Captain Israel Putnam, of Connecticut. Your servant, sir!"

I introduced myself, and told him who we were. He eyed the company speculatively.

"H'm-m," he said, and stroked his chin. "So Rogers got his ranging company, did he?"

"You see it, sir," I said.

"Well," said he, "I can't say I admire the man, but I'll say he has the right idea. 'Tis such a company we've needed for a long time."

"Captain Rogers is an old friend, sir," I said stiffly; for I could see there was no love lost here, and I felt that I should make my own position plain from the beginning.

He eyed me with a twinkle in his eye.

"I'll not quarrel with a man for the friends he makes," he said. "I don't get along well with Rogers myself, but that's naught against him. If there's aught of help I can give you, you'll find me among the Connecticut troops, on the north side o' camp."

He nodded with that and, turning on his heel, was gone before I could thank him. Nor could I call after him, for at that moment the crowd before us parted to let through a stout man, in bright blue coat and buff breeches. Even had Dick Rogers not come treading close upon his heels, I should have known from the attitude of the onlookers that here was someone in high authority; for they fell away before him and touched their forelocks respectfully. I turned and called the company to attention.

The stout man gave me no more than a quizzical glance out of a merry eye as he passed, though young Rogers tipped me a wink and a nod. Out of the corner of my eye I could see them pass behind me and go slowly down the line, the stout man nodding vigorously and asking questions while Rogers replied in monosyllables. At the end of the line they turned and came back towards me. As they came I could catch their words.

"'Tis a likely-seeming company, lieutenant, I'll be bound," I heard the elder man say. "They'll be veterans of the last campaign, of course?"

I could hear Rogers' chuckle.

"There are five veterans among us, sir," he replied, "including myself. The rest are new recruits."

The other stopped short.

"God bless my soul!" he exclaimed. "You don't mean it? Why, 'tis a miracle, no less. You should have a care how you tell it, lest you be drafted from the ranging service and set up for an instructor."

"I have no fear of that, sir," Rogers smiled. "My commission reads for ranging service for the duration of the war."

The other coughed loudly, and blew his bulbous nose as if it were a trumpet.

"Harrumph, hah, howuff!" he sputtered. "Perhaps you are right, sir. Perhaps you are right."

They had come abreast of me by now and stopped. The stout man eyed me curiously.

"Ensign Ferguson, sir," said Rogers, "my second." And then to me: "Colonel Ruggles, in command here."

The colonel nodded with dignity.

"Mr. Ferguson, sir," he said.

"Your servant, colonel," I replied.

He turned back to Lieutenant Rogers.

"Your brother—the captain—is gone to Number Four, you say?" he asked.

The lieutenant nodded.

"At General Shirley's orders," he replied.

Ruggles sighed gustily.

"A pity," he said, and shook his head. "I should like to meet him. He has been well spoken of, of late."

He stood a moment in silence, looking down at the ground.

"Ah, well," he went on presently, "all in good time, all in good time. Your men are weary with their march, no doubt. You'd like to see them in their quarters, lieutenant, eh?"

Rogers nodded.

"If it is not too much trouble, sir," he replied.

"No trouble at all, lieutenant," the older man said, " 'pon my word!"

He appeared to think a moment.

"I'm going to put you between the Rhode Island troops and the river," he said at last. " 'Tis the best place available now. And I doubt you'll be with us long. You'll come with me tonight across the river to pay your respects to the general."

"As you wish, sir," said Rogers.

"Good," said the other. He let his eye sweep the circle of curious faces about us until it hit upon one that was familiar. "You," he said, "Serjeant What's-your-name."

"Ray, sir," said a stolid-looking man, drawing himself up.

"Serjeant Ray," said the colonel, "yes, yes. Show Lieutenant Rogers the space between Colonel Greene and the river."

The serjeant touched his forelock.

"Right, sir," he replied.

The colonel turned back to Rogers.

"I'll look for you at my tent at seven, lieutenant," he said. "I'll see the general is expecting you."

He bowed ceremoniously from the waist.

"A pleasure, sir," he said in reply to the other's thanks, and, turning, was off to his own tent.

Serjeant Ray led us back the way we had come, and showed us to a narrow strip of level ground behind where we had passed the sour-faced Rhode Islanders. Many of these latter came down to watch us make our camp in truculent silence. But as our men paid them but scant heed, they had little to say and presently drifted back to their own quarters, leaving us alone. This pleased me just as well, for I was too weary to wish for any problems of order in Lieutenant Rogers' absence across the river. All was quiet while he was gone; I was glad nevertheless when he returned about midnight and I was able to turn over my duties to the serjeant of the guard and retire.

One of the first things I had intended to do upon arrival in Albany was to search out my cousin Hubert. This, however, I was unable to do the first day after our arrival, for there was much in camp that needed my attention. In the morning we were issued such necessities of camp life as tents, powder, shot, provisions and stores, and it fell to me to see that these were properly set up and stowed. In the afternoon General Shirley, accompanied by General Winslow and several members of his staff, came over to review us and inspect our camp, which, because our service was a distinctly new departure in the military art, had aroused much interest and curiosity.

Next day, however, by noon, I found a few hours for my own affairs; and accordingly I brushed myself up and set out immediately after dinner to find a boatman who would ferry me across to the Albany side.

I had little difficulty in this, for boats were constantly passing to and fro between the camp and the city. My first thought on landing was to go straight to the regular encampment, for it was there, I thought, I should be most like to find him. At the outskirts of the camp I was duly challenged, in military fashion; and when I had made my wants known to the sentry he summoned a corporal of the guard, who forthwith conducted me to the officer of the day in the centre of the camp. As we went along I could but contrast the scene here with that across the river. Here the white tents stood in neat rows, each company with its own parade and sanitary arrangements, so placed as to be both inconspicuous and inoffensive. Everything was set up with the utmost orderliness and precision, and I could not help thinking it would be well if some of our own officers and men could be better drilled in such matters.

In spite of all this, however, I could not be comfortable all the time I was there. From the sentry who challenged me, through the corporal, to the officer of the guard himself, I could sense condescension and impatience with a benighted provincial. Even the privates we passed upon the street gave me looks of arrogant contempt, which they only half attempted to veil, so that by the time we reached the guard tent I was seething within.

The officer of the guard was a young lieutenant of the 44th foot, a dazzling young fop, with highly pomatumed hair and a delicate nose. He did not look up when the corporal brought me in, but went on tending to some sheets that were spread upon a table before him. Not until he had finished his leisurely survey did he let his eyes rise and go first to the corporal, then to me, and back again.

"Yes?" he asked in a haughty voice.

"'Ere's a gent, sir," said the corporal, "says 'e's lookin' for a Captain Ferguson, sir."

The lieutenant glanced at me lazily, grimaced and touched a lacy kerchief to his delicate nostrils. The meaning of his gesture was unmistakable, though I knew he could find nothing offensive about me, for it was less than an hour since I had bathed. I supposed, however, it was his way of showing his opinion of all provincials, and I restrained myself with difficulty.

"Er—would you mean Major Ferguson?" he demanded.

"'Twas Captain Ferguson last I knew," I replied shortly. "Captain Sir Hubert Ferguson."

He grimaced again, as if in distaste at my abruptness.

"Oh!" he said. "That would be the major. Promoted, y'knaow,

only last week. May I ask what might be your business with the major?"

"Sir Hubert," I said, in my haughtiest tones, "is my cousin. My business with him would hardly be of importance to you, sir."

He bounced to his feet at that with an expression of almost ludicrous astonishment and incredulity upon his delicate features.

"Oh, I say, my dear man!" he cried. "In God's name why didn't you say so in the beginning? I took you for one of these bleddy provincials, what with your get-up and all, haw haw!"

I smiled slightly.

"It so happens," I said, "I am one of those 'bleddy provincials.' James Ferguson, sir, ensign in Rogers' company of Rangers. Your servant."

His jaw dropped still lower at that, making him look all the more like a horse. And for once he forgot to flourish his lacy kerchief.

"But stap me!" he cried, and stopped short.

I could see he scarce knew what to do in such a case. Half, I could see, he felt he should turn on his arrogance once more; and yet in the way in which I had caught him out it was difficult for him to pretend to dignity again. So at a loss did he seem, indeed, that I could not but pity him his blundering.

"No matter," I said. "If you will but tell me where I may find my cousin I will give you my thanks and be off. I should not have bothered you now, but I am newly arrived and am not, as yet, acquainted hereabouts."

"Of course," he said, relieved that it was to be so simple after all. "You will find him at General Shirley's headquarters, where he is in charge of the commissary for the regular forces. Anyone in the town can direct you there."

I thanked him gravely, and left him mopping at his bedewed forehead with his dainty lace. The corporal, in whose estimation I had risen wonderfully, to judge from his expression as we walked through the camp, accompanied me as far as the picket where he had found me. There, taking my arm and pointing back along the street into the town, he gave me detailed instructions for finding the General's headquarters.

"When ye find the 'ill, sir," said he, "ye cawn't miss it. There'll be blokes an' orficers comin' an' goin' in an' aht by the 'undreds."

I thanked him and gave him a half a crown for his trouble,

telling him to drink a beer for me with it, and thereupon took my leave. As he had predicted, I had no difficulty finding the place, a small brick house of moderate size set a little way up the hill from the river. As soon as I clapped eyes upon it I knew it for what it was. Regular officers in lace and gold braid and powdered wigs mingled with provincials in blue and buff of colony militia, or in plain grey homespun. Soldiers and civilians crowded the porch and the street in front. Messengers and orderlies came and went. There was an air of controlled confusion over everything. Doors slammed. The drone of voices was audible even in the street, but the sound of words was indistinguishable.

I pushed my way through the crowd on the porch and entered a sort of large reception room. Here, if anything, the crowding and confusion were worse than on the porch. Everyone was talking at once, but through the uproar only occasional words came to my ears.

". . . a thousand lashes, and he took but a hundred before they cut him down. I give you my word I never saw a back so cut! Major Orde extended clemency and commuted sentence to a week in stocks. The serjeant's been grumbling ever since!"

"Devil take the wench." This from a tall, handsome young ensign of foot, who for all his worldly airs seemed scarcely out of his teens. "I care not what she says. I tell you I never clapped eyes on her in my life!"

". . . and the next time I looked the fellow's hair was gone . . ."

"Major Raley's compliments, and tell the General the latrines have been removed as he ordered."

" 'Twenty-five quid,' says I. 'Done,' says he."

"Oh, my deah!"

". . . six yoke of oxen, b'Jasus, a half-mile from the fort an' wid all their tongues cut out!"

In the corner a burly, grim-visaged man in a rusty coat and white breeches was arguing vehemently with a smiling captain of regulars.

"But I must have more boats," he was saying.

"By all means," said the other. "Why don't you build them?"

The burly man clutched at greying temples and rolled his eyes to heaven.

"Build them!" he fairly screamed. "Build them! Great Christ!

And what will be happening at Oswego if I stop to build boats now?"

"Sh-h-h!" said the other, looking around apprehensively. "If you please! Not so loud, colonel!"

"Sh-h, bah!" bellowed the older man. "I want boats, I tell ye, more boats; and if I have to tell all Albany where I'm bound to get them I'll shout it from the housetops. D'ye understand that, my fine popinjay?"

I pushed my way through to a table near the wall where a serjeant sat glowering sullenly at the throng.

"Would I find Major Ferguson here?" I asked.

He did not bother to look up.

"Busy," was all he said.

I took a crown from my pocket and held it in the palm of my hand so that only he could see it. He stood up.

"Follow me," he said.

He led the way down a hall and stopped before a door.

"Wait there," he said, opening the door and holding out his hand.

I gave him the coin.

"What name?" he asked.

"Tell him 'tis his cousin, James Ferguson, of Portsmouth," I said.

He nodded and closed the door behind me. I could hear his steps going back down the hall.

I found myself in a small anteroom, equipped with a single wooden bench and a solitary window through which I could look out upon a dishevelled back yard. I sat down upon the bench to wait, wondering if the serjeant meant to give Hubert my name. I had my own doubts of that, but this seemed as good a place to wait as any. Certainly I had no chance of seeing him out in front.

I must have waited all of an hour before the door opened and Hubert appeared. Save that he wore a major's coat he had not changed. His lips still wore that same half-mocking smile. His dark eyes were coldly insolent. He did not seem surprised to see me.

"Oh," said he, stopping upon the threshold, "it's you!"

"Were you expecting someone?" I asked.

"Frankly," he replied, "I was."

"I'll not keep you," I said, rising.

"Don't be a fool," said he. "They'll keep. You were always much too touchy, Jamie."

He took me by the arm and propelled me through another door into what appeared to be an office and pointed to a chair.

"Headquarters for the service of supply for the King's troops," he said. "Your own stores will come through here, for the new Rangers are to be provisioned by the crown, you know."

"That's so," I said. And then, as the thought struck me: "You seem well informed. How did you know I'd signed with Rogers?"

He shrugged.

"Dorcas wrote me something about it," he said, "and you wear the uniform."

"I'm glad to know," I said dryly, "that one of us is to hear regularly from her. Thus far I've not had a word."

The sardonic smirk came and went in a flash. But he made no answer to my remark. Instead he shifted the subject.

"Why did you not come to me?" he asked. "I could have made a soft place for you here."

"I prefer to take my service in the field," I said stiffly.

His laugh was openly mocking at that.

"Well then," he said, "there were still the Royal Americans. They're recruiting entirely in Pennsylvania Province, but I could have arranged a lieutenant's commission for you—at a price."

"I want none of your Pennsylvanians," I replied. "I'm serving now with men I know and understand. Moreover, you know my objections to serving with a regular regiment."

"That's where you're wrong," said he. "Colonel Bouquet's entire intent is to train this regiment for Indian warfare."

I shrugged.

" 'Tis gratifying to know," I said, "that someone has learned a lesson from the last campaign. Nevertheless I am happy where I am."

"But you'd take rank as a regular, man!" he persisted.

"I see no advantage," I replied. "I am no King's man, but a plain provincial only."

He chuckled.

"There are some," he said, "would hold you King's men for that you eat the King's bread."

" 'Tis not so I read my commission," I retorted, "and if you hold such views I'll thank you not to speak of it before my men. They feel as I do, and if 'twere hinted that 'twas otherwise they'd leave us in a body."

"Gad," he exclaimed, laughing, "but you provincials are touchy folk!"

" 'Tis not touchy precisely," I told him, "but only that we care not overmuch for the King's men we have seen among us."

He eyed me speculatively a moment, through narrowed lids, and then nodded.

"You may be right," he said. "No doubt you will be more useful where you are."

He ventured no explanation of this remark, but rose as if to indicate the interview was at an end.

"I'd not hurry you," he said, "but I'm a busy man."

He walked with me to the door.

"I'll try to see you again before we move up," I said.

"Come and take dinner with me day after tomorrow," he said. "You'll find my quarters on the hill beyond the Schuyler house."

I said that I would if I could, and that if I could not I would let him know; and with that we shook hands and said good-bye.

As I came out into the front room and started through the press of the mob towards the door I felt myself suddenly jostled roughly to one side. I looked up to find myself face to face with Shem Sanborn.

"Here!" I cried, and clutched at his sleeve, for this was the first time I had laid eyes on the fellow since my return to Portsmouth the year before, and I wished to confront him with what I had heard from the Indian Rowi.

But he was too quick for me. He slipped away towards the door by which I had just entered the room; and before I could follow, the crowd had closed in between us. There was naught I could do but stand staring after him.

"What's the matter, young feller?" said a voice in my ear. "You look as if ye'd seen a ghost."

I turned to find the grizzled man in the rusty coat who had argued so boisterously about the boats an hour before standing beside me.

"That man," I said, "he's a common murderer!"

He raised grey shaggy eyebrows at that.

"Do ye say so!" he exclaimed. "An' one o' Major Ferguson's favourites too!" He began to laugh dourly.

"Major Ferguson!" I exclaimed.

He looked at me quickly. "Would ye be acquaint with the major now?" he asked.

"He's my cousin," I replied.

He did not answer at once, but regarded me quizzically for a moment. Then he began to smile.

"I have heard it said," he remarked, "that we cannot help the relatives the good Lord chooses for us."

The serjeant at the table stood up at that moment and began bawling at the top of his voice.

"Colonel Bradstreet! Colonel Bradstreet!"

"Yo!" bellowed my companion.

The serjeant pushed his way through the crowd and thrust a sheaf of papers into Bradstreet's hands.

"The orders for the boats you required, sir," he said.

The colonel nodded and stood for a moment reading the papers while the serjeant pushed his way back to his table. In the interval I had an opportunity to study my new-found friend. So this was the man the raising of whose regiment along the coast had caused so much scandal from Falmouth to Providence. If so, I could well understand why Bradstreet's Battoemen were already beginning to make a name for themselves.

He finished his reading with a grunt of satisfaction and, thrusting the papers into an inner pocket, turned to me.

"Ye must fight for everything in this town," he said.

He glanced at the now closed door of Hubert's office, and then looked back at me.

"Ye made a charge a bit ago," he said, "that might be serious. Would ye care to tell me of it? I might be able to advise ye."

I nodded.

"Come outside," he ordered.

I followed him out onto the broad grass-bordered street, and we moved a little distance away from the building and the crowds and sat down in the shade of a tall chestnut. He listened gravely as I told my story and gave my reasons for suspecting that it had been Sanborn and Merrill who had set the Indians upon us. When I was done he sat a moment in silence, pulling speculatively at the grass before him.

"Ye've naught but an Indian's word for this," he said, "—an enemy Indian at that; and even he, as you tell it, did not say 'twas he."

I nodded.

"That's so, sir," I said.

"Well then, my lad," said he, " 'tis my advice to you, forget it—but keep a weather eye open."

"But I've no doubt of it," I protested. "And I've witnesses to the Indian's story."

He shrugged.

"Ye cannot prove it," he replied.

I remembered one other time when this very matter of proof had thwarted justice. Yet it was plain enough that his advice was sound.

"But what does my cousin do with such a scoundrel?" I demanded.

He looked at me speculatively.

"I do not know," said he, "how you regard your cousin, the major, so I'll not say the old adage that comes first to my mind. There's no gainsaying Sanborn's a fine teamster; and so's the man Merrill, I mind. In his capacity as commander of the service of supply the major has need of such."

The explanation was reasonable. I said as much. The colonel scrambled to his feet, and held out his hand.

"I'm sorry I cannot advise ye differently," he said. "Ye may find the sharp eye will stand ye in good stead yet."

I shook hands and thanked him.

"My kindest to Captain Rogers when ye see him," he said.

I watched him go away up the street with the feeling that at least I had made one friend this day. In Portsmouth I had heard that he was testy and tempery, and I knew he was not popular in the army. My first impression of him in the room at headquarters had rather confirmed this; yet when I had talked with him he had seemed kindly and understanding. I turned away with the thought that 'tis thus men are misjudged.

I had some trouble finding a boatman, as it was near the hour of parade, and not many were abroad. At last, however, I found an old Dutchman in a leaky rowboat who agreed to ferry me straight to our camp for the exorbitant price of a shilling, New

York. He was a slow rower, and it took him full a half-hour to reach the shingle below the camp, so that the evening muster was just dismissed and Rogers was entering his tent as I came upon the parade. At sight of me the lieutenant turned and came towards me.

"Are you ready to move out in the morning?" he asked.

"In the morning?" I echoed.

He grinned.

"The morning, aye," he said. "We're ordered up for Fort William-Henry at dawn."

2

It was amazing the way, once we had left the town behind, the farmsteads ceased and the woods closed in. From Albany to the village of Cohoes at the falls of the Mohawk our road had been dotted on either hand with prosperous-seeming small farms, neat and spotless after the Dutch fashion, basking peacefully in the warm spring sunshine, as if there were no such thing as a war within a thousand miles of them. But to the northward of the Mohawk the scene changed abruptly. There a few scattered buildings huddled close to the river, within sight of the town. Behind them the flats were cleared and cultivated; but where the hills began the fields stopped, and all beyond was forest—dense hardwood growth, with here and there, in the hollows, a scattering of pine or spruce or a little cedar. Now and again, as we marched, we came upon occasional clearings, brush-choked now and abandoned, with perhaps a heap of charred timbers and ashes in the centre to show where once a cabin had stood. Twice we passed cabins still intact though deserted, their empty windows seeming to follow us like sightless eyes as we went by; their sagging doors gaping open like mute mouths trying vainly to cry out their tale of horror and desolation.

There was nothing new in this sight to me, for I had seen it at Stevenstown and elsewhere upon our northern borders. But never before had I come upon it so suddenly, so abruptly, within so short a distance of a civilized centre. Our settlements pushed out gradually, imperceptibly, now here, now there, like fingers in the forest, so that in going northward from established villages into the wilderness the change came slowly and naturally, and our frontier was no sharp-drawn line such as this, but rather a broad belt that might be a dozen miles in width.

That, I supposed, was the Englishman's way. These Dutchmen appeared to do differently. Not until the land behind was settled and in cultivation did they press forward. I doubted not that these few cabins would prove, upon investigation, to have been occupied by English colonists rather than their more phlegmatic neighbours. It seemed to me a sharp observation; yet when I spoke of it to Dick Rogers, as we marched side by side, he laughed.

"You must not forget the savages," he said. "Remember 'tis but an easy journey from Crown Point for such as they. Even the Dutchmen will not put so much trust in the French as to push their settlements too nigh."

"But there were settlements along the river," I replied, remembering the tiny villages upon the Hudson, that had been there even when Stiles and Toby and I had come that way almost a decade since.

Rogers nodded.

"There were," he said, "but they never grew. Nor will they until the Frenchmen have been driven back upon the Saint Lawrence. They're military posts now, as you'll see tomorrow. Tonight we'll stop at Half Moon."

I could see that he was not greatly taken with the idea, and that he cared not at all to discuss it; so I let it drop, and presently my mind slid away to other thoughts. I thought of my cousin Hubert—I had arranged with Captain Putnam of the Connecticut troops to notify him of my inability to take supper with him— and of his apparent connection with the scoundrels Sanborn and Merrill. From what Colonel Bradstreet had said, it was evident that he favoured them, though I myself had told him what he might expect of them. Still, I supposed he might have forgotten our discussion of the point at Stavers', in Portsmouth. It was some time since it had taken place, and I guessed that in his position it was necessary for him to make use of what material offered. There was no denying that the two were good teamsters. At the same time there was a dark thread of suspicion in the back of my mind that would not be dismissed. I knew enough of my cousin's early history to realize that he was not to be trusted too far; and Colonel Bradstreet's words had hinted that he was none too well favoured, even then, in certain quarters. It was the first time that it had occurred to me to consider Hubert in the light of a menace to myself, and even as I thought of it I dismissed it as ridiculous. Nevertheless the thought persisted, and in the end I made up my mind to keep a watchful eye upon him and upon his two associates in so far as it was possible to do so.

We came early in the afternoon to Half Moon, a distance of some fourteen miles or so, where we halted for the night. After Rogers' warning I was not surprised to find the little village unchanged in the eight years since I had seen it. The tiny fort had been strengthened somewhat—so that the little cluster of houses that formed the town seemed to huddle closer to it than ever. A few farms on the outskirts had been abandoned, and on the flats below preparation was going forward rapidly for the vast camp which was to shelter General Winslow's army before the month was out. But aside from this there was little change.

The inhabitants themselves were jovial and happy. The prospect of a permanent camp upon their doorstep relieved their fears. No longer need they dread the savage war whoop. No raiding party, they were convinced, would dare molest them now. What matter if the war went on? They at least would be left in peace to till their fields and work their farms. Small wonder that they greeted us with open arms and cheerful faces and gave us of their best without complaint. They did not know yet what it was like to have an army in their midst. Before the summer was out they were to complain bitterly that savages were a thousand times preferable to the vast provincial rabble that swore and stole and stank fit to drive them from their homes, and with it all swaggered about as if they owned the place and everything that was in it.

We pushed on, the next morning, nine miles to Stillwater; and in the afternoon, fourteen more to Saratoga, where there was another fort. That night we slept for the first time behind walls, for Indian raiders were active hereabouts.

During the night it rained, and it was still overcast in the morning, when we lined up for our departure. Lieutenant Rogers went down the line inspecting us critically.

"You'll remember the things you've learned these two weeks past," he said, "for you'll have need of it from here on. Guards and flankers will keep sharp watch for suspicious signs. And mind you, no straggling if you want to keep your hair. If you've a mind to relieve yourselves, wait for the regular halt."

It was simple advice, and sound, and it was given out to all who passed this way; yet it was amazing how many ignored it—and paid for their carelessness with their scalps.

Fort Edward proved by far the largest and most military of all the posts we encountered in our northward march. We came into it in the wet dusk after a long day's marching in the drizzling rain, our wet buckskins clinging clammily to our backs, our pack straps chafing tender shoulders, and only the tiny post at Fort Miller, which we reached in midafternoon, to break the dreary monotony of the dripping woods. As we came out upon the river bank and saw the geometrically patterned walls looming through the streaming murk with their earthen glacis, and an abatis of logs fringing it about, a mutter of pleasure and satisfaction swept through the ranks. Even to our inexperienced eyes this looked the real thing, and there was not a man of us but felt that at last we were getting near to the war. Soon we should cease this futile marching and get down to business.

It was necessary for us to curb our impatience, however, for during the next three days it rained steadily, the while we cooled our heels at Fort Edward. There was no sense, said Lieutenant Rogers, in moving up while this weather held. We should but be kept in camp at Fort William-Henry, and we might as well do our waiting here in comfort as expose ourselves to the wet to no purpose. On the fourth day, however, the weather cleared, and we were able once again to take the road. It was late afternoon, when the purple shadow of the mountains lay across the deep valley, that we pushed at last through a hollow between two sharp hills, and saw before us the narrow reach of Lake George, stretching away to the north and east, its dark waters dotted here and there with tiny, wooded islands, and the rugged, forest-clad headlands closing in upon it on either hand in the distance. Closer, although the sight of the fort and the camp itself was shut off from us by the tops of intervening trees, we could see the smoke of camp-fires rising, blue in the evening air. And as we followed down the road towards it, the sounds of the camp came sharply and clearly to our ears: the tap of hammers; the barking of a dog; the ruffle of a drum; the desultory crack of muskets upon the target range; and now and again a man's voice raised in quavering song.

We were welcomed effusively enough at the fort. No sooner was the report of our arrival carried to the commanding officer than we were bidden to wait upon him in his quarters to take a glass of toddy with him, an invitation which we lost no time in accepting, for the march had been a hard one and the evening was cool. Leaving Serjeant Johnson to oversee the making of our camp in the appointed spot near the lake shore, Dick Rogers beckoned me to join him, and we repaired at once to the fort, where we were promptly shown into the colonel's quarters. We found the room already crowded with other officers, and Colonel Bagley himself, a jovial, ruddy-faced Bay Colony man, presiding over the toddy bowl. A log fire burned upon the hearth, and the room was thick with tobacco smoke.

At our entry the colonel left his duties at the bowl and greeted us with outstretched hand.

"By God, gentlemen!" he exclaimed, when the first formalities had been disposed of. "I am glad to see you, upon my soul! If ever a company of Rangers was needed, 'tis needed here. We've the Devil's own job to be done—three sloops to build as well as a matter of six hundred whaleboats! The fortifications to enlarge and repair, and land to clear! And all the while the Frenchmen and their savages like flies about us! I declare, I've had to detach three of my own companies to the ranging service, but they can't seem to lay hands on the sons of bitches, though they come and go about us as they will."

Both Rogers and I clucked sympathetically and remarked that his task would seem to be no light one, whereat he laughed.

"Aye, gentlemen," he said. " 'Tis no fit life for soldiers; but with your help, and that of rum and the Devil, I trust we'll have all ready for my Lord Loudoun when he comes to lead us against the mounseers."

He called to an orderly to fetch us drinks.

"You'll be anxious to see your men bedded properly," he said when they had come, "so I'll not detain you. Drink up, and remember you're always welcome here, whether you come on duty or no. I'll send your orders in the morning, though I warn you you'll be expected to carry on your ranging duties on your own without help or orders from me for the most."

He was as good as his word on that score. In the morning came down from headquarters a long screed of orders, by which our routine in relation to the rest of the camp was set, and whose chiefest concern appeared to be that we keep at least one party out upon the scout at all times. We were not to come to him with matters of discipline, or such, but were to deal with these ourselves. All prisoners and any information as to the enemy's movements and intentions, which we might come upon in our scouts, were to be placed in his hands at once; and each week a detailed report must be made to him in writing for forwarding to the high command at Albany. In addition, at least half the command, not out on scout, must be held in readiness at all times to undertake such orders as he might see fit to send down. But aside from these emergency measures, we were, it seemed, to be left largely to our own devices: a sort of independent command within the camp, with obligations to act only in the common good.

It was surprising to me how quickly our little company settled into the routine of the camp. On the third day after our arrival Lieutenant Rogers took out the first scout of ten men, leaving me in command of the camp. All went well enough, with one small exception. This occurred when a sentry, apparently asleep at his post, paid for his carelessness with his life and his scalp. Colonel Bagley sent down orders to me to take out a party in pursuit of the marauders, but though we found their trail readily enough, they scattered before we could come up with them, and we were forced to give up and return to camp empty-handed after chasing them nearly ten miles down the east shore of the lake.

Within the week Rogers returned with one captive, whom he had taken from beneath the very noses of the French at Ticonderoga, and after making his report to the colonel set out again with eight men. Three days after his departure I was surprised and not a little pleased to see John Stark and six of the men who had gone with him to Number Four appear in camp. He had, it appeared, set out with Captain Rogers for Crown Point, but when they were a day's march on their way he had come down sick with a flux, and the captain, fearing that they might delay his march, had sent him overland to Fort Edward with the six to guard him. Three days later Captain Rogers himself appeared, having lain a full day in sight of Crown Point and done some damage there among the enemy's cattle. On the following day the lieutenant returned from his scout, so that for the first time since the company had mustered at Exeter we were all together once more.

By this time it was nearing mid-May, and I was growing more and more impatient of inaction. Hitherto there had been only myself and Richard Rogers to command the company, so that but one of us could be out at a time. As Rogers was experienced at the game, it was but natural that he should be the one to go, while I was left in camp. But now, with our full complement of officers in camp, there was no reason why I should be left behind. If ever I was to take the field, I decided, it was high time I began to learn my duties. I determined to ask Captain Rogers to allow me to accompany the next scout. When I spoke of it to him he laughed, but agreed that I was right; and in consequence, a few days later, when Rogers set out with eleven men in whaleboats I was one of the party.

There was little indeed to mark that expedition either as a great success or as a conspicuous failure. We brought in but one prisoner, and had a slight brush with the enemy. Yet, since it is typical of the average of my experiences during the next four years, its account must be here set down. Summer and winter, rain or snow, in bitter cold or blazing heat, this was my routine, the background against which all the more outstanding events hereinafter recounted were to occur.

May the 20th came up grey and overcast. We embarked at dawn in two whaleboats, Rogers taking the lead in his boat, and following down the east shore. After the canoes to which I was accustomed the heavy battoes seemed unwieldy and hard to handle, but there is no doubt that in still water they were the most satisfactory method of troop transport.

Towards midmorning the clouds burned away and the sun came out, hot and strong, to shine upon our unprotected heads, so that the men, who had hitherto complained of the flies, could now turn their grumbling against the heat. I must confess I was, at the time, not a little perturbed at this seeming ill spirit. But I have since learned by experience that this is a thing common to all soldiers; when they are not fighting they must ever be grousing, and he who croaks the loudest is like to be the best fighter when it comes to a skirmish.

A little before noon we came to an island in the Narrows, upon which a lookout was constantly kept, and here we hauled up our boats and rested until nightfall. Shortly after dark we set out once more, with muffled oars, and a short while before dawn put into a deep bay on the northeast shore. Here we hid our boats in the brush a little distance from the shore, and after waiting until past daylight to make certain our landing had not been observed we struck north, towards the summit of a hill overlooking the French position.

In that jumbled, unfamiliar country I should speedily have become confused had not Rogers kept me close at his elbow and been at great pains to point out the lie of the land with the assistance of several charts and maps which he carried with him. As it was I flatter myself that I had a fair picture of the general outline of the region in my mind's eye by the time we had reached the outlook on the hill.

Exactly what I had expected to see, I do not now remember, but I shall not soon forget the surprise I felt when I looked down from that vantage point upon the scene of activity spread out below. Until this moment the French had seemed as something remote and inactive. The bustle and energy of our own camp had so filled my mind that I had not given thought to what our opponents might be doing. In the security of our camp at William-Henry it had seemed as if we must surely sweep triumphant over such puny obstacles as the mounseers might place in our way. But now, beholding them in their own camp, I began to have my doubts.

The whole point swarmed with scattered groups of men, so that I could scarcely begin to estimate them. But when I asked Rogers what he thought their numbers might be he shrugged and guessed somewhere about a thousand and fifteen hundred. Even had they not been so many, however, it would be a difficult task to attack them, for their position was strong. At the very tip of the high point, where the inlet from Lake George joins the waters of Lake Champlain, they had begun the construction of a strong fort of stone, logs, and earth. Before this the entire point, from Lake Champlain to the outlet from Lake George, had been cleared of trees for a distance of several hundred yards. Midway of this clearing a line of earthworks and trenches traversed the point, and between this line and the fort stood the French camp. From the woods below us came the ring of axes, and the occasional crash of a falling tree, indicating that the clearing was being pushed still farther back. From the slopes of the point came the tinkle of cowbells, indicating that in view of recent depredations of Rogers and his men, the cattle were being held in close proximity to the fort. Along the bank of the river flowing from Lake George we could catch occasional glimpses of the road that led through the outpost forts to the landing at the lake. As we watched, carefully hidden in the scrubby brush, we could see a detachment of white-clad regulars swing along it, going towards the fort. Plainly the French were not idle. I glanced at Rogers.

"Well," I said, "what next? They're looking out for their cattle, it seems. And they look to be shy of travelling the road alone."

He grinned and shrugged.

"We'll stay here for the present," he replied. "Later we'll drop down to the road and see what we can do. Meantime you make as good a sketch as you can of those works."

He waved an arm towards the fort.

"Don't show yourself, though," he warned.

I was glad of something to do, so I squatted down on my heels and with a stub of lead, cut from a bullet, and a piece of birch bark, I drew as accurate a plan of the fort and the point as I was able, considering my lack of artistic talent. It was done long before we were ready to move, however, and after I had shown it to Rogers for his approval there was naught for me to do but sit and kick my heels with the others until dusk.

That night we rested on the mountain. And next morning we crept down to the road between the fort and the first outpost. Twice we had to drop and lie flat in the brush to let swift bands of Indians run by, padding silently on moccasined feet, the wet scalps slapping at their belts. At sight of them I involuntarily gripped my musket, but Stark's hand on my arm was a warning that kept me quiet.

At the road Rogers spread us out in the bushes on either side, with orders not to shoot unless he gave the signal. Two men he sent to watch the road from the post, and two to watch the fort and the clearing. Two more he set to guard our rear.

Shortly after this a large detachment of regulars, some 118 in number, passed out from the fort in the direction of Lake George; but as they were too strong for us, we lay close in the bush and let them by. A few moments later another detachment, numbering some twenty-two came along from the direction of the out-posts. Our lookouts had warned us of their approach, and we were ready. As they drew abreast, Rogers gave the signal to fire, and we poured a sharp volley into them.

Had I thought about the matter at all, I suppose, I must have been horrified at the thought of it. Yet at the moment it seemed the natural thing to do. These men were armed. They would do the same to us if they could see us first. We were enemies, sworn to kill each other on sight. I aimed at the leader and pressed the trigger.

As the smoke of our blast rolled out across the road I was amazed to see that not more than eight or nine of them were down, though I had expected to see at least half of them in the dust. Vaguely I remember thinking that several of us must have picked the same man, for to miss at such point-blank range was almost out of the question. In the next instant the rest had broken and were fleeing up the road, while Rogers, with a wild whoop, burst from the brush at the roadside and dashed in pursuit. The rest of us followed suit, but quick as we were they were too swift for us. Rogers grappled with the hindmost man and, tripping him, flung him to the ground. Several of the rest of us came up at that moment and helped him bind his prisoner, after which we went back to where the ambush had taken place, to find the dead Frenchmen already scalped by two of our men who had stayed behind for the purpose.

"We'll have to travel now!" said Rogers.

He lined us up and counted heads to see that we were all present.

"All right," he said, then. "Follow me."

And, turning, he plunged from the road, running diagonally eastward away from it.

I shall not soon forget that run, though in days to come I was to undertake many like it. We trotted with no slackening of pace for the better part of an hour, until I thought my lungs must burst and my feet felt like blocks of lead. But not until we had cleared the shoulder of the hill on our left did Rogers halt. Then he held up his hand for silence. I could hear nothing for the thumping of my heart, but Rogers' hearing seemed to be keener than mine. He nodded.

"They're coming," he said. "We'll scatter here. Each one of

you pick your own way. We'll meet at the boats at nightfall. Any man not there by then will be left behind."

He gave swift instructions to each man, the best route to take, sending the prisoner with Toby, and turned to me.

"You stick with me," he said.

Already the men were striking out one by one into the woods. Without further words Rogers turned and plunged back the way we had come. I followed him without question. Indeed he did not give me time to speak, even had I been so minded.

We had not gone twenty yards before the crashing of the pursuit became audible even to me. I was beginning to fret, when Rogers turned suddenly and whispered over his shoulder.

"This way!"

I followed him blindly, trusting to his judgement, fifteen yards off the trail and flung myself down beside him in the lee of a huge fallen log. Almost as I did so the first of the pursuit went by, so close that I could have thrown my musket among them. For the most part they seemed to be Indians, though I counted a number of Frenchmen, dressed not so differently from the savages themselves. Thirty I counted, and wondered if there might be more, when Rogers plucked at my sleeve and jerked his head.

"That's all for now," he said, "but there'll be more along later. Come on!"

He rose to his feet and began running again, to the southward this time. I followed him without a word, wondering how the others might have fared.

At noon we stopped on the bank of a small brook that wound its way through a swamp, and for the first time I had opportunity to speak.

"We've lost them," I said. "Is it customary to abandon the men like that?"

He sensed the censure in my words, and grinned dourly.

" 'Tis one of the rules of the Rangers," he said, "that you must remember: when you are hard pressed, scatter. It makes it that much harder for the enemy. I'll wager ye'll find all the men at the boats by nightfall. The Frenchies won't lay a finger on one of them."

And as it proved he was quite correct. We pushed on through the swamp that afternoon and took our time to skirt up along the lake shore to the cove where we had hidden the boats, moving carefully lest we come upon a searching party looking for our scalps. It was shortly after sunset when we found the hiding place, and replied to the soft challenge that greeted us. Five of the men, including Toby and the prisoner, had already found their way there, and in the next hour and a half the other six came in one by one, dropping down the mountain side, or coming up the shore like ghosts in the dusk. When we were all there Rogers sent two men down to scout the lake. They were back in a moment.

"They're on the lake," said one of them.

Rogers nodded.

"I thought they'd be," he said. "We'll wait for dark. The moon rises late tonight, so 'twill be an easy getaway. Listen for the signal, then pick up the boats and carry them down. And mind ye, make no sound, for I'll cut the throat of the man with my own hand who stumbles or rattles an oar."

The dusk crept in upon us gradually and turned to darkness so black that I wondered if we could find our way to shore. But at the signal the men rose silently and grasped the gunnels of the boats. Rogers led the way, feeling carefully for each twig that lay athwart the path, and an instant later the boats floated without so much as a ripple.

"Every man for himself, now," said Rogers as he took his place in the sternsheets of his boat.

"We'll meet at the Narrows?" I whispered, from mine.

"With the Devil's luck," he replied. "Stick to the shadow of the shore if you can."

And with that his boat pushed off and was swallowed up in the blackness. In less than an instant I had no inkling of where he might be. I whispered the word to my men, and in a moment we were pulling silently out along the shore.

For half an hour we rowed in silence, only the drip and swish of the muffled oars making the least sound in the dark. I was worried about the other boat, more than about an enemy, and it was this rather than any sense of watchfulness that kept me on the alert, and made me catch the faint sound of paddles on the left. I peered in that direction, straining my eyes with the effort to make out whence the sound had come, and after an instant was rewarded with a sight of a blot of blackness against the only slightly lighter blackness of the night. That it was a boat, I could not doubt, and that it was moving, was plain, though on a course that was parallel to ours and in the opposite direction. This could not be Rogers, I thought. Hence, it must be the enemy. And by their course they must pass within thirty feet of us. If they had not already seen us, they soon would. What was I to do? I was half prepared to order the men to fire when an idea struck me. I turned the tiller, turning the boat boldly out into the lake on a course that would cross their bows, and sang out:

"*Qui vive?*"

There was an instant's startled silence, and I could feel the men staring at me in consternation. In that moment I managed to hiss them lightly into silence.

"Brevard," came the answer, after an instant's pause. Whoever this Brevard might be, he was obviously a young man, and one not too sure of himself. I blessed my stars.

"*On les a trouvé?*" I demanded.

"*Pas de chance,*" came the reply, sourly. "*Et vous?*"

"*Rien!*" I said, trying to sound equally disgusted. "*Je vais essayer à l'autre côte.*"

"Row!" I whispered to the men.

"*Bonne chance!*" came Brevard's voice behind us as we swept out into the lake.

As we pulled away I bore gradually southward, until by the time we had lost the Frenchman in the blackness astern we were headed straight up the lake. It was a good hour before a word was spoken; then one of the men whistled.

"Christ!" he said. "I thought the Frenchies was right in with us!"

A chuckle ran down the boat. I laughed.

"Row," I said, "or they may be yet."

We came into the Narrows at dawn and found the other boat awaiting us in the shadow of Tongue Mountain. As we pulled alongside the men in my boat began pouring out the tale of my ruse. But Rogers cut them short.

"We heard," he said. "We were hugging the shore, and thought the Frenchy'd spot us, but your talk gave us our chance to slip by."

He gave me an approving look.

"You're a Ranger now, my boy!" he said.

3

That campaign of the summer of 1756, upon which so many of us had rested such high hopes, never materialized. Colonel Webb's arrival in June, to take over the command from General Shirley pending General Abercrombie's coming, was the beginning of a series of disappointments arising out of misplaced faith. Webb proved but a timid fellow, afraid to act for fear of censure. Indeed, subsequent events were to prove him no better than a craven coward in the face of the enemy. But at the outset we had great expectations of his leadership.

It was fortunate that General Abercrombie should arrive not long after; for aged and blundering though he was he proved at least a cut above Webb. He did undertake various reforms in the organization of the forces then in camp, and moved for the raising of additional troops. Moreover, his rank as a general officer commanded for him a degree of respect that had been lacking in the case of his predecessor.

So far as any active steps towards the completion, or even the commencement, of the summer's campaign went, however, he soon proved himself nearly as timid as the colonel. Such work as had already been done, such lines as we then held, were all very acceptable, and should be maintained, of course. But as to any advance upon the enemy—it was simply out of the question. Such things must wait upon the orders of the commander-in-chief, and he, alas, was not yet come! In the meantime, nothing could be done.

Such was the attitude of General Abercrombie—or "Aunt Nabbycrombie," as the men came, disrespectfully, to call him. Nor would any amount of pleading or threatening or cajoling on the part of our own leaders, who saw the summer slipping away from them in idleness, move him. He sat him down, with true Scots stubbornness, and from his position he would not budge. And in the meantime the men in camp must kick their heels and fret and fume with the inaction, for which there was no remedy to be had.

My Lord the Earl of Loudoun himself, Governor of the Virginia Colony, General-in-chief of His Majesty's forces in America, Colonel Commanding the Royal Americans, &c., &c., did not arrive before the first of August. Even then it was not too late for action, for the boats were built and ready, General Winslow's army of some seven thousand lay encamped at Half Moon, while another five thousand were divided between Forts Edward and William-Henry. Everything was in order for an advance. For a short time even those who had given up hope began to hope again. But my good Lord, after a first flurry of meaningless activity, confined himself to a series of inspections and a vast deal of letter writing, and straightway fell into a violent feud with our retiring commander, the Governor of Massachusetts, General Shirley; so that the remainder of the season passed, not in coming to grips with the French, but in bickering and dissension and bitter denunciation, the one or the other, until the troops fair sickened of the spectacle, and more than one farmer, listed for the defence of his family and his holdings, took thought of all that he might be accomplishing in his fields at home, and left in the night without so much as by your leave.

Nor was this either a beginning or an end to our troubles in camp. In the enforced idleness in which the men were held the jealousy and friction that was ever present between provincial and regular could not but grow and become an increasingly sore problem. When my Lord Loudoun, in accordance with his own orders, handed down the ruling by which all provincial officers, when serving in conjunction with the forces of the regular establishment, should take rank only as eldest captains, there arose a storm of fury and protest in the colonial ranks that bid fair to tear the army asunder. Under such an arrangement, it was pointed out, any regular major in the field might assume command of the entire army, over the head of anyone in the provincial ranks. For a time it seemed likely that the army, as a man, would pack up and go home. Indeed, such a move was forestalled only by a compromise on Lord Loudoun's part, by which provincial officers retained their rank, subordinate only to regulars of similar grade.

But all our difficulties were not so simply compromised. The problem of discipline alone was enough to drive an officer to drink. Regulars might be ruled with an iron hand; but not so our provincial levies. Orders they would take from none but their own officers. Nor would they take them from these unless they were in the mood. Theft, desertion, insubordination, laxness in duty, and drunkenness were rife within the ranks. Among the regular troops any of these might be punished by the lash, while the first two as frequently as not called for a death sentence. But among the provincials penalties for infractions of military law, as set by assemblies, jealous of the rights and liberties of their constituents, were laughable. A dose of the stocks for insubordination, a ride on the wooden horse for drunkenness or laxness in duty, a week in irons for desertion, and riding out of camp on a rail, or a mild flogging in extreme cases, for theft—these were the maximum penalties that provincial officers could exact. Small wonder that provincial discipline was bad!

By the same token it is scarcely to be wondered at that the provincial camps were in a constant state of disgraceful disorder. Our men were not soldiers, in the professional sense. They had listed to fight, and fight they would, as they had ample opportunity to prove later. But they understood naught of long encampments or of the degree of sanitation that must be practised there. They had not the orderliness of the regular soldier, and in consequence within a week their camps were a mess. By the end of a month they were filthy. And before the summer was out they were a stinking shambles, resembling nothing so much as a charnel house in which a man's breath gagged in his throat while his stomach rebelled.

Nor were the officers primarily to blame for these conditions. Even had they been sufficiently experienced to instruct the men, they had not the power to enforce the rules of cleanliness that they might lay down.

The results were, of course, inevitable. By the middle of July fully one-third of the men at Fort Edward were ill with fever and flux, or were otherwise unfit for duty. At Fort William-Henry the proportion increased to more than half. Towards August the smallpox appeared in the camp at Half Moon, and spread rapidly to the forts. By mid-August we were burying as many as eight and ten a day at the lake, while at Fort Edward the mortality was only slightly less.

Much of this, to my way of thinking, might easily have been avoided in an active campaign. In the field there would have been less chance for friction to develop. The men would have had less time to dwell upon petty jealousies. There would have been less inclination to mischief. And, though I am not acquainted with the science of the matter, I know it to be true that men in active movement are less prone to sickness and ill health than those who perforce lie idle in a camp.

Certainly this was true of the Rangers, at least. We, who were allowed no idle moments but were kept constantly upon the move, were better disciplined, aside from the regular troops, than any unit in the entire army; though in fairness it must be admitted that this was in part due to the fact that Rogers, not being responsible to any provincial assembly for his men, could make his own regulations and see that they were carried out. By the same token our camps were kept in better order and with a sharper eye to sanitation than was the general rule. And if we were not entirely immune to the ravages of disease, our activity at least enabled us to spend much of our time away from the plague-ridden air of the camps, so that our casualties from this source were light by comparison.

Towards the end of June, General Abercrombie arrived in Albany, and Rogers at once went down to make his report to him. He returned within the week with an order in his pocket for the raising of a second company, to be commanded by his brother. Dick, now captain by virtue of the general's commission, chose as his lieutenants Noah Johnson and Nathaniel Abbot, while Caleb Page was appointed ensign. With the officers chosen, he then proceeded to Portsmouth to begin the raising of his company, which he accomplished within the month, and was forthwith ordered to the Mohawk to take part in the expedition then under way against Fort Frontenac. In the meantime in the first company John Stark was advanced to the post of first lieutenant, I was commissioned second lieutenant in his place, and Jonathan Burbank succeeded me as ensign.

Throughout the season we engaged in repeated scouts, with the constant expectation of a general attack being made upon the enemy. Indeed, it was not until Lord Loudoun's announcement in October, that no further advance would be made that year, that the hope was given up entirely. In the meantime I accompanied Rogers on at least half a dozen occasions on expeditions which carried us deep into the enemy's country; and my scouts with Stark were at least as many. Upon one occasion we carried our boats across the mountains to the South Bay of Lake Champlain, and after rowing down the lake, past the forts at Ticonderoga and Crown Point, waylaid two lighters laden with supplies for the forts, and took eight prisoners, after which we hid the boats in the woods and made our way back to Fort William-Henry on foot. At another time we proceeded well down Lake Champlain, halfway between Crown Point and Saint John, where we lay upon a point intending to waylay the enemy's boats; but this we were unable to do, and accordingly we withdrew. After a further unsuccessful attempt to take a prisoner near the fort, we were obliged to retire in haste to our own lines. Upon still another occasion we took captive a sentry to the French picket guard, stationed upon the road which led between Ticonderoga Fort and the advanced outpost upon Lake George, by the simple expedient of walking up to him in broad daylight. When first we appeared, marching towards him, he challenged us.

"Qui vive?"

"Des amis," replied Rogers gruffly.

The man hesitated an instant while we drew closer, and then, not recognizing any of us, cried out in alarm, *"Qui êtes-vous?"*

"Rogers!" replied the captain, as we drew abreast of him.

And with that we seized him and made off as quickly as we could in the direction of our boats, returning thence in triumph to Fort William-Henry.

Our prisoner proved a mere lad, with dark hair and great black eyes, and a long sallow face, who sat in sullen, silent fright beside the captain upon his thwart, while the rest of us pulled at the oars in the face of a stiff head wind. Little by little, however, Rogers gained his confidence. He shared with him the bit of corn biscuit that we stopped to eat at midafternoon, and gave him rum from his flask to warm him.

Presently he became convinced that we meant him no harm, and began to reply to Rogers' questions—in monosyllables, at first, and then, when the rum had loosed his tongue, at greater length.

He was, he told us, of the regiment of Languedoc. He had come out from Brest in the previous year with Baron Dieskau, and had been present at the Battle of Lake George, in which, he said, the French losses had been heavy.

From personal matters Rogers led him, with the skill of a mas-

ter, to speak of other affairs of greater importance within the French lines; so that, without his realizing it, he gave us much useful information.

There were, he said, at that time, at Carillon, as the French called their fort at Ticonderoga, some thirty-six pieces of ordnance: twelve eighteen-pounders, fifteen twelve-pounders, and nine eight-pounders. He told us that Monsieur de Montcalm commanded in Canada that year; that the forces at Carillon consisted of three thousand French regulars, and some two thousand Canadians and Indians; that Monsieur de Montcalm had already drawn off for the winter with one battalion of regulars, and that Monsieur the Chevalier de Levi commanded in his place. He said that the advanced guard upon the west, towards Lake George, were all drawn in to the foot of the falls upon the river running down into Lake Champlain; that the other guard, upon the east, at the old Indian carrying place across the lake from the fort, consisted of six hundred men, but that this was to be withdrawn November first; that the French were in two camps, one of five battalions and sixty Canadians at about half a league from the fort, and the other under the fort in which the rest of the army was encamped; that there were barracks in the fort for five hundred, and he thought this number would be quartered there for the winter; that most of the Indians had gone off for the hunting, but that most of these talked of returning for the winter; that the French had, on Lake Champlain, one schooner and some two hundred battoes, and half a dozen more on Lake George; that the Canadians were commanded by Messieurs La Corne and Columbie; that they had discovered four of our whaleboats, hidden in a cove on Lake Champlain; and that the French were well informed of all our moves—from what sources, he did not know, but he believed the letters to come from someone in Albany, for he had overheard Monsieur de Bourlamaque make some joking allusion to the "Albany Post" in speaking to Monsieur de Bougainville.

At this point he appeared to realize how much he had told us, for he turned abruptly silent again, and greeted all our questions with naught but sullen stares. Only once again between that point and the fort did he venture to speak again; and then it was to say that we had deceived him; that he did not believe that any one of us could be the infamous Captain Rogers.

Rogers grinned and asked him why he thought so.

"Because," the other replied, "you have not the appearance, nor have any of these others. Neither do you act like him. This Rogers is a fiend, terrible to look upon. It is said that he scalps the wounded alive, and that he tortures his prisoners with hot coals to make them talk. I have heard it said that he will not hesitate to eat the flesh of his own dead comrades, and that this is why he will come alive out of the woods when another man would die!"

I half expected Rogers to fly into a rage at such a pack of slanderous lies, but instead he laughed.

"You flatter me, monsieur!" said he. " 'Tis gratifying to know my enemies hold me in such awe! But it seems I have heard similar stories of your own La Corne and Marin and Rigaud. Tell me, are all these true?"

The youth looked at him for a moment in all seriousness, and seemed about to speak. Then he saw that Rogers was laughing, and he shrugged with a sheepish grin.

"Ah, m'sieu," he said, "it is plain someone has been lying!"

And thereafter he said no more.

Towards the end of September, Rogers' company of Rangers was withdrawn from Fort William-Henry and encamped at Fort Edward, on the island. Captain Dick, who had returned from the Mohawk, was set to temporary duty at the lake, pending the raising of two new companies, to help hold the forts during the winter months. At Fort Edward, Rogers himself was set to watch the road between the fort and Saratoga, and a further order was sent down calling for a continual patrol of one officer and twenty men to be constantly in the woods between Fort Edward and the South Arm of Lake Champlain. These orders somewhat curtailed Rogers' own activities, for much of his time was required at or near the fort. At the same time he was expected to keep out scouts in the direction of Crown Point, with orders to bring in such news as might be obtainable of the enemy and his doings. Only once in October was Rogers himself able to lead a party out, and, since the Wood Creek patrol to the South Arm was to be taken turn and turn about, it was obvious that if we were to do all that was expected of us, sooner or later I must go out. Consequently I was but little surprised, one evening towards the end of October, to be summoned into Captain Rogers' tent.

"Can ye handle an expedition down the lake?" he demanded as I was ushered into his tent.

"Aye," I said, trying not to show my eagerness, for I was impatient to lead out a scout of my own, "I can."

"Good," said he. "These are your orders. You will take eight men of your own choosing. You will cross to the South Arm and take one of the boats which we have hidden in the mouth of Wood Creek. You will go as far down the lake as you are able. You will mark what the enemy is doing at Ticonderoga and Crown Point; and if you can annoy their shipping or bring in a prisoner so much the better. Here is your warrant to draw upon the commissary for such supplies as you may need. I will expect you back by the fifteenth. You have it?"

"I have it," I replied.

He grinned then, and relaxed from his official manner. He reached down and fumbled beneath his cot with a long arm.

"Then we'll drink to success," said he, and pulled out a black bottle.

With the rum still warm in my belly I went back to my own tent and sent for Jed Stiles. He came within the quarter-hour, pulling back the tent flap and ducking his head for the low doorway.

"Jed," I said, "we're going out down the lake in the morning. I want you to get Toby and a half a dozen others of our platoon, fit men all, and have them here within a half-hour."

"Aye, sir," he said, touching his forelock in imitation of a regular's salute, and bobbing went out.

He was back in less than twenty minutes with the men, who came in one by one and lined up at the end of the tent. I saw that he had chosen well, for besides himself and Toby there were John Morison, Alexander Grant, Ebenezer Call, Phillip Richards, Jacob Bump, and Phinehas Virgin—all men who had served on scouts before with Rogers, and all of whom were well known to me. I nodded with approval.

"We're for down the lake tomorrow," I said, when they were all within, "with orders to get as far as we are able. I'll warn you now we're going to try for a look at Saint John. You all know this is my first scout. If any one of you is not willing to follow me, now is the time to speak."

I waited to see if any would refuse to go, for I wanted no one with me who was unwilling; but none spoke.

"Good!" I said at length. "Your confidence is satisfying to me. We'll leave at dawn. You men will be before this tent with full equipment at five. You'll get your rations then. I want Stiles and Toby to come with me now to the commissary. The rest of you may go."

Stiles and Toby and myself poled across the river in the dark in one of the great unwieldy battoes that were provided for the purpose; for the footbridge had not then been built. At the fort we drew our rations, and carrying them in gunny sacks set out on the return to the island. As we stepped out of the commissary shed, however, I saw a figure I knew well step back among the shadows and disappear around the corner. I stopped short and gripped Stiles' arm.

"Jed!" I said. "Yonder was Shem Sanborn."

Jed nodded. "Aye," he said, "I saw him. And 'tis not the first time. He teams supplies this way now."

"He was watching us," I said.

Stiles laughed. "Your nerves are jumpy!" he scoffed.

"No!" I retorted, stung. "That's not true. I'll swear the man was watching us."

"Go on!" said Stiles. "And if he was, what then?"

I shrugged. "Why, nothing," I replied, "except that I like it not. Never a time have I laid eyes on the man but bad luck has followed."

"Stuff!" Stiles exclaimed. "Ye'll be telling me next the man's bewitched ye!"

I laughed, for it was ridiculous to suppose that aught of harm lay in the man's power. Yet I could not rid myself of the idea that the sight of him had in some way foreshadowed trouble. I slept but fitfully that night, and even in the morning the thought lingered.

But I had no time to brood upon it. The men gathered at my tent before the dawn, and I had to see to it that each received his proper ration for the journey we were about to undertake. When all was at last in readiness Rogers himself came down to see us off across the river. As I stepped out of the battoe onto the mainland he reached across the gunnel and shook hands.

"Good luck," said he. "We'll expect ye back by the fifteenth."

And he watched us swing away along the river in the grey swirling mists of the morning and disappear into the woods on the north side of the fort.

We marched, in accordance with our orders, straight to Wood Creek, where we came about midafternoon. There we rested in hiding until dark, when we launched our boat and rowed north, down the narrow arm of the lake.

The night was cold and overcast, so that the men were pleased to keep moving and we made good time. Before light we landed upon the west shore, at a distance of some two miles below Ticonderoga. There before dawn we hid the boat securely in the brush, and disposed the men in hiding for the day. This done, I left Stiles in charge of the detachment, with orders to fall back upon Fort Edward in case I was not returned by midnight; and with Toby I set out to reconnoitre the fort and the surrounding country.

I had chosen my landfall purposely, with this in mind, for just to southward of Ticonderoga Point, across the estuary formed by the outlet from Lake George is the hill from whose summit I had overlooked the fort on the occasion of my first scout with Rogers. The French were lately become well aware of the strategic importance of this hill, and frequently maintained a picket guard upon its summit. But in spite of this I knew that Captain Rogers, on several occasions since its establishment, and Captain Putnam at least once, had used it to make a reconnaissance of the fort. It was my intention, if possible, to imitate them on this occasion.

Toby and I approached with circumspection, crossing the summit of a higher hill in the direction of Lake George, and approaching our outlook from the southwest. We might have spared ourselves the trouble, however, for when we came out upon the rocky ledges near the top, we found only a handful of cold ashes, indicating that the picket guard had been withdrawn at least a week since.

All that day we lay close upon the hill, watching all that went on below us. It was evident that the French were making ready for the winter. The posts in the valley, with the single exception of the guard maintained at the sawmill, were all drawn in. The camp which had stood on the cleared ground at a little distance from the fort was abandoned, and only a few tents still remained close by the walls. Across the lake, at the old carrying place, there was no sign of the large outpost that had spent the summer there. All day long, boats came and went in the direction of Crown Point and the north end of the lake. Those coming southward appeared to be heavily laden with stores for the winter, while those northbound were filled with troops for whom there was no accommodation. Judging from the number of tents still beneath the wall, and adding to this the known capacity of the barracks within, I estimated that their numbers were still in the neighbourhood of two thousand; while a further encampment, at a short distance from the fort, indicated the presence of some two hundred or more Indians.

I kept a careful account of all these matters in my orderly book, and at dusk we returned to where our own party was hidden. Stiles reported that one large scout of fifty had passed them going up the lake, evidently destined for Fort Edward's vicinity, but our men had lain close in hiding, and the French had gone by without seeing them.

As night drew on, the skies cleared and the stars came out bright and shining, although there was no moon. I should have preferred it had the weather remained overcast; nevertheless I determined to attempt to slip past the fort under cover of the darkness. Accordingly, about nine o'clock, we set out with muffled oars.

We kept close along the east shore, hugging the shadow, and keeping a sharp watch for possible guards upon the shore. Evidently, however, the French considered the time for such expeditions past, for we passed unchallenged. Ten o'clock brought us opposite the fort, which we could see, looming black against the sky, across the narrow channel, and I must confess that when I saw the movement of a sentry's hat against the stars, as he followed his round of the walls, my heart was in my mouth. But I steered the boat as close as I might in the shadow of the shore, and in twenty minutes we had slipped by and rounded the point on the east, in whose shelter we were once again safe from discovery.

We rowed that night a good distance down the lake, and lay the next day not far from Crown Point, where I repeated, in so far as I was able, my tactics of the day before. Here I was not so fortunate as to gain such a point of vantage, but I was able to gather things here were much the same as at Ticonderoga, though the force in garrison was smaller by half. Apparently, now that the fort at Ticonderoga was completed, that at Crown Point had suffered in importance, and become little more than a storehouse and stopping-off place between the former and Saint John.

The next night we passed Crown Point, much as we had slipped past Ticonderoga, with bated breath and thumping hearts, for though there were those among us who had done this very thing time and again, before, still there was ever that element of danger in the thing, the possibility of discovery, that made each single accomplishment of the trick an achievement in high adventure. We reached the north end of the lake after five nights more of rowing, despite the stiff winds that frequently blew in our teeth. A few miles from the outlet of Isle aux Noix we hid our boat in the brush at the bottom of a shallow bay in the west shore and, skipping around the outpost at the end of the lake, headed directly for Saint John.

For three days we lingered in the neighbourhood. On the second day it came on with a cold drizzling rain, and we took shelter in a large barn not far from the town, where we hid ourselves in a loft above the haymow. We had not been there above an hour when a man and a girl came out from the house, ostensibly to tend the stock. They neglected that duty, however, and dallied for some time in the hay, after which the girl went back to the house leaving the man to their original purpose. No sooner was she gone than we crept forth and seized the fellow and, slipping out the back way, carried him off into the woods, where, when we had put a sufficient distance between us and the farm, I made shift to question him.

He was, it proved, a serjeant in the regiment of Béarn, which, with that of Guienne, was stationed, partly in the fort at Saint John, partly at Chambly, and the balance scattered about in quarters upon the inhabitants of the valley. Monsieur de Montcalm, he said, had gone off to Quebec, after giving orders for the withdrawal of the greater part of the troops from Crown Point and Ticonderoga to winter quarters, leaving only the regular winter garrisons which were made up of the battalions of Languedoc and La Sarre, together with some Canadian militia, a handful of coureurs de bois, and some two hundred Indians, all of which last were at Ticonderoga. From all that he was able to tell us it appeared that, so far as the French were concerned, at least, the war was over for the remainder of the year.

Having written his information in my notebook, I sent him under guard of Call, Richards, and Bump to the place where we had hidden the boat, with orders for them to await our arrival there. After which, with the rest of the men, I went down the river to the vicinity of the fort at Chambly. There we lay in ambush upon the road leading from Chambly to Saint John, and about dusk fired upon a party of twenty who were coming down to the fort. Four of the party fell at our first fire, and the rest of the company, disconcerted by the sudden attack, and evidently believing us to be more than we were, turned tail and fled.

We lost no time in leaving the neighbourhood, but on the way back found time to set fire to a half-dozen barns and houses. As may be imagined, the countryside was in an uproar as the alarm spread, and parties were everywhere searching for us.

This delayed our return to the boat not a little, and in the meantime Call, Richards, and Bump were forced to lie extremely low with their prisoner. Three times, so Richards reported to me, searching parties came within musket shot of them, and it was only by sheerest luck and the utmost vigilance on their part that they were not discovered. It was nothing short of a miracle that the boat was not stumbled upon.

By the middle of the next afternoon, however, we came up with them; but not before we ourselves had been sighted by a large mixed party of farmers and soldiers. They had of course fired upon us at once; but we, taking to our heels, had escaped with only one of our number slightly wounded; he having a bullet burn across his back side, which did not incapacitate him.

The pack was in full cry now, for the French had followed quick upon our trail once they had laid eyes upon us, and we were put to it to get our boat launched before they were upon us. It was only by the very skin of our teeth that we succeeded in doing so, and we were pulling away from shore, our prisoner lying trussed in the bottom like a pig going to market, when the first of our pursuers burst through the bushes and levelled their muskets upon us. We were quick to drop our oars, however, and fire into them, scattering them for a few moments; just long enough to enable us to pull away out of gunshot range.

It was fortunate for us that there were no boats nearer than Isle aux Noix, for had it not been for the delay occasioned by their having to go back for them, it is doubtful if we could have escaped. As it was we did so only by dint of furious rowing, making no attempt whatever at concealment, until darkness overtook us, when we took shelter on an island near the mouth of Missisquoi Bay. There we lay all that night and the next day, watching the procession of boats that kept marching up and down the lake, keeping up a constant search for us. When night fell we again launched our boat and crept cautiously up the lake. Thrice, in the course of the night's journey we sighted other boats, prowling along the shore. But our luck held, and we landed safely before dawn upon a wooded point about halfway to Crown Point, where we lay again in hiding. As soon as it was dark we pressed on again, planning to lie the following day upon the east shore, in a place some miles above the fort where, upon an earlier occasion, I had gone with Rogers.

But it was there I made my great mistake, for though we rowed with all possible speed the first faint grey light of dawn found us still upon the lake, a mile or more short of our objective. There was nothing to do but put in to land before the light became too strong for further concealment, and accordingly I turned our bow into a shallow cove in the lee of a low brush covered point.

As we pulled in towards the shore I had an uneasy feeling that all was not right. But it was the metallic click of a musket being cocked that gave me warning. Even before I had identified the sound I acted instinctively. I flung the tiller hard over, so that the boat sheered off sharply. At the same instant I ordered the men down and threw myself into the bottom of the boat.

We were not a moment too soon. Even as we ducked, a volley crashed out from the bushes lining the shore. For the most part the bullets whistled harmlessly above our heads. One, however, passed through my hat and tore splinters from the gunnel. Another pierced the side of the boat and passed through the muscle of John Morison's upper arm.

There was no time to lose in thought or hurried counsel. Our one hope of escape was apparent to all; to get away from that spot before our assailants had time to reload and fire again. There was no need for commands. Each man moved instinctively to his place and fell to rowing, while I grasped the tiller and headed the boat out into the open lake.

We had not cleared the point, however, before the enemy had tumbled into their own boats, which they had had concealed in the mouth of a small creek at the foot of the cove, and came in pursuit. Three boats, they were, and I noticed that they came on fast; faster than we were able to row, weary as we were from the night's journey.

Indeed, I could not help thinking that we were in a very ticklish situation. We could not go on up the lake, for in that direction the fort at Crown Point barred our way. Neither could we go north, the way we had come, for that way was barred by further parties who were already on the lookout for us. The west shore alone remained a hope of refuge, and it was for this I steered, urging the men to row for their lives.

It is fortunate that the lake, at this point, is not wide, or we should never have gained the farther shore. Two of the pursuing boats seemed unable to do more than match our speed, so that we kept well ahead of them. But the third boat was either lighter or more strongly manned, for little by little it drew away from its companions and lessened the breach between us, until at mid-lake they were scarce more than a musket shot behind. Unless we thought of some way to stop them they would be upon us before we gained the shore, yet we could not wait and fire upon them, for this would give the other boats the opportunity to close up with us.

The thought came to me suddenly that our prisoner would be of use to us here. Certainly if we gained the shore we should be unable to take him with us. I leaned down and pulled him out from under the thwarts.

"Can you swim?" I asked.

"No, m'sieu," he replied.

"Well," said I, "there is no time like the present to learn."

And with that I dragged him out and forced him to stand upon the stern thwart, so that his uniform must be plainly visible to those in the pursuing boat, the while I cut him free of his bonds. When I had done this I pointed astern.

"Yonder are your friends," I said. "If you flap your arms in the water—so—you will be able to keep yourself afloat until they come up to you; though I should advise you to shout to them loudly that you cannot swim, lest they leave you for one of the other boats."

"But, m'sieu," he said, blankly, "I do not understand!"

"You will," I replied, and gave him a great shove that sent him flying overboard. "Over you go, my lad, and don't forget to shout for help!"

He landed with a great splash and came up sputtering and thrashing at the water with arms and legs. Thrice he called to his fellows for help and twice his cries were cut short in a gurgle as his head sank beneath the surface. For a moment I believed the oncoming boat would pass him by, and in that moment I felt that I had murdered the man. But, to my vast relief, as they drew near the boat swerved close, and I saw one of its occupants lean over and exchange a few words with him. In another instant three of the crew had shipped their oars and were helping to pull him in over the side. As they did so their boat lost headway and dropped behind.

It was but a brief delay, but it was enough. By the time they had resumed rowing we had widened the breach between us considerably. And by the time we reached the western shore they were still some distance away.

We made no effort to save the boat, nor would it have been of any use. Instead I led the men directly into the woods and away from the lake. With solid ground underfoot and the dense forest all about us I began to feel that there was yet some chance for us to escape. But we must separate.

With this in mind I called the men to me one by one as we jogged along, twisting and dodging circuitously in order to shake our pursuers from our trail. As we ran I gave each man his instructions to strike southward, keeping well back from the forts and picking his own way, to rendezvous in three days' time at the head of the Northwest Arm of Lake George. At intervals of about a half-mile I sent them packing; first Richards, then Bump, then Virgin, then Call, then Grant, and Morison, and finally Stiles and Toby, until at last I found myself running alone with the pack still at my heels.

I made a wide circle to northward, leaving a plain trail in the fresh-fallen leaves to draw the pursuit from my companions, and came at last to a ridge of rocks overlooking the lake. Here I turned south along the ridge, taking more pains now to hide my trail, and after a short distance turned once more to westward, striking into my own trail behind my pursuers, from which point I backtracked to a small brook where I took to the water and waded for more than a mile through the heart of a dense alder thicket before I felt that at last I had shaken off immediate pursuit, and was free to make my own way south.

There is little to tell of that southward journey. I struck directly for Lake George, skirting the area of the French patrols about Crown Point, and paralleling the trail to Ticonderoga until I came to Rogers' overland route between Lake George and Lake Champlain. Three times I had to lie hidden in the brush while scouting parties of the enemy passed, and once, when I was almost at the lake, I had to turn aside quickly to avoid meeting with a company of near two hundred coming north along the shore.

It was about noon of the third day when I came to the meeting place at the head of the Northwest Arm behind Thunder Mountain. Richards and Virgin I found already there, and John Morison, grown feverish with his wound, which there had been no time to bind. Virgin had come upon him dazed in the woods, and had brought him in, else we should have lost him. During the afternoon the others came in, in ones and twos; stubborn Ebenezer Call and dour Alexander Grant together, then Jacob Bump towards evening, and a little after dark Toby.

That left us all present and accounted for save Jed Stiles. At first, I must confess, I felt but little anxiety on his account, but disposed the men for the night, undertaking to stand the watch myself, for they were all exhausted with the one possible exception of Toby, who seemed utterly tireless. But when, by midnight, Stiles had not appeared I began to grow uneasy, and I became definitely worried at dawn when he was still missing. Aside from the fact that I counted him among the best of friends, he was also a man we could not afford to lose; for there was none in the service who knew the country better or had so broad a knowledge of the French and their Indian allies, unless it should be Rogers himself.

There was nothing we could do, however, but wait. To search

back along the trails he might have taken would be well-nigh hopeless, and would require a much larger and better provisioned party than ours. Moreover, even then, it would be like searching for a needle in a haystack, for each of us had taken his own route, and like as not Stiles had left the trails to strike out across country for himself.

Hour after hour we waited until at noon I felt we could wait no longer. Our provisions were run so low that we could not afford to spend another night in the woods. The men were near exhausted, and after all my duty to bring them in safely did not end with the loss of one man. Moreover, John Morison's arm was festering, and the man was green with pain.

Accordingly I gave the order to march with great reluctance. As I did so, however, old Toby stepped aside.

"Toby stay," he said, almost defiantly. "Go look for friend."

It was against all regulations, and he knew it well, else he would not have been so stiff about it. But I had neither the heart nor the inclination to rebuke him.

"I can't leave you any supplies," I said.

"Toby find own supplies," he replied.

I shrugged.

"Very well," I said. "If you do not find him within four days, come to Halfway Point. If you find him, take him there. I will try to come out myself to meet you. Of if I find that is not possible I will see that boats are sent."

He nodded.

We shook out our packs for our last grains of corn meal and scraps of venison jerky, which we made up for him into a small bundle, for I knew that with any luck at all we should be at Fort William-Henry by nightfall. When this was done we shook hands.

"Good luck," I said.

He replied nothing, but turned away, and in an instant was swallowed up in the brush upon the hillside. When he was gone, I gave the word reluctantly to march, and we set off stumbling up the lake in the direction of the fort.

It was barely possible that he had come out nearer to the fort than to our rendezvous. He might even have been forced to strike for Fort Edward. There were plenty of possibilities. But as we marched I felt I knew that, no matter how long Toby searched or we waited, we should not be like to see Jed Stiles again in this life.

4

We came late that night into Fort William-Henry, where we were made welcome by Captain Dick Rogers, who commanded the Rangers there; and he listened with interest to my account of our scout. There was no word here of the missing Stiles. Neither had he reported in at Fort Edward, where we came about the middle of the next forenoon, having left the lake at dawn.

It was with a sense of utter failure that I went to make my report, for Stiles' loss weighed heavily upon me. Rogers, however, did not appear to share my pessimism. He heard me out with evident approval, interrupting me only occasionally with questions as to the enemy's dispositions, their morale in winter quarters, and so forth. When I had done he nodded.

"You have done well," he said. "I would not have expected so much of a first scout."

"Saving your presence," I said, "I cannot feel that my expedition was so successful, for it was accomplished at the expense of one-ninth of my total force, and I do not believe that anything I learned was worth the loss to us of such a man as Serjeant Stiles."

He gave me a shrewd look.

"Is it Serjeant Stiles you regret?" he asked. "Or is it Jed?"

"He was my good friend," I replied, stiffly, "as he was yours. I cannot but feel that it was my own rashness which was responsible for his loss."

He did not reply for a long time, but sat looking at me curiously.

"Yes," he said at last, "he was my good friend, too. I also lived with him upon the trail, camped with him, got drunk with him at the tavern. But what of that?"

He was watching me through narrowed eyes, but I was too wrought upon to see that he was deliberately leading me on.

"What of that?" I cried indignantly. "Can you be so callous to the loss of a friend?"

I half expected to see him angered at my words, but instead he relaxed slightly and smiled.

"You are new here, comparatively," he said, "and you have yet much to learn. One thing has thus far passed you by. These men who have this year died of the pestilence, those we have occasionally lost upon the trail, the few who have been killed in various engagements while we waited for the campaign to begin, were all persons remote from you. You did not know them, so you were able to think of their death dispassionately, without emotion, looking upon them only as numbers in the aggregate force. Now comes the loss of a close friend, and the first hard lesson of war is brought home to you. Bullets do not respect persons. They find friend and foe alike. Remember that every man in this army is a friend to another; and that for every man that is lost there is one who feels as you do now. Yet for all that we must all go on fighting, seeing the war to its end, or admit defeat."

"Would not defeat be better than all this killing?" I demanded, for I was bitter, and his words failed to soothe me.

He shook his head.

"No," he said. "I have been in this from the beginning. Stiles is not the first friend I have seen go. Sometimes I have felt as you do now, wondering if it is worth the price. But the answer is always the same."

"We didn't have to start it," I said.

"Did we not?" he asked. "Do you remember Dan Stinson? As I recall it he was a friend of yours, too. Do you remember Elizabeth Call, murdered by the Indians before the war at Stevenstown, or the Maloon family, carried off captives into Canada? That's what we started to fight about. Those are the things we all want to put an end to. But if we cry quits now they will go on as before, and there will be the whole thing to do over. All the blood that has been spilled thus far would be wasted."

I was somewhat mollified, for I could see the truth of what he said, though I doubt not many among the regulars would have thrown up their hands in horror at the suggestion that we fought for aught but loyalty to the crown.

"Nevertheless," I said, "that does not alter the fact of my responsibility. I cannot but feel that I must have been in some way at fault."

He nodded.

"You have one quality of a good officer," he said. "You show a proper regard for the lives of the men under you. Too many are inclined to take them lightly. At the same time we must not lose sight of the fact that in war men are expendable. Some will be lost. Would it make you feel better if I said that I did not think you were in any way to blame? There are hazards in this service that are unavoidable, and this is one. I would say that it was proof of your capacity to lead, quite aside from good fortune, that you came off as well as you did."

"Thank you," I said dryly. "I still claim the responsibility."

"Well, then," he burst out, turning suddenly impatient, "what in the devil's name d'ye want me to do about it?"

"I would feel better in my mind," I said, "if I might be allowed to go back and look for him."

He looked at me speculatively for a moment, then nodded.

"At least," he said, " 'twill do no harm; and it may be that 'twill do some good. I will consider the matter, and give you my orders according to my decision tonight. When Mr. Stark comes in, will you send him to me at once?"

With that he made a gesture of dismissal and turned to a heap of papers spread out before him upon the table. I turned and went out into the dank November drizzle, feeling no better than when I had gone in.

I left the next morning at dawn in company with Stark and thirty men, going by way of Fort William-Henry, where we procured boats. That night we camped at the point where I had agreed to meet Toby, and before daybreak the latter came in—alone.

It was obvious that he had not failed for lack of trying. He was on the point of collapse from exhaustion. His buckskins hung upon his squat frame in stained tatters. His great floppy black hat, which he wore constantly—for he steadfastly refused to don the regulation cap save on parade—drooped disconsolately. He was the very picture of utter dejection, and he stank like the living dead.

Until he had eaten he would say nothing. But after he had wolfed the food we set before him he told us a tale which, even I could realize, gave but a faint idea of what he had been through.

He had, he said, scoured the lake shore from the Northwest Arm to the outlet, without success. From there he had gone northwest in a great half-circle, almost to Crown Point and back, through swamps and gullies, along wooded hillsides, across the crests of ledgy ridges. He had searched along the banks of brooks and the shores of several ponds. A score of times he had come upon sign that might have been left by any one of our party. But not once had he discovered any trace that he could identify for certain as having been left by our missing comrade; nor did he find any trail that might lead to him.

In the face of such expert failure it must have seemed incongruous to the men that we should continue to search. Nevertheless, throughout the next day we ransacked the woods along the lake from Tongue Mountain to the outlet, spreading our line out to almost a mile in depth. By noon of the next day even I was ready to admit that it was no use. At the midday halt Stark came and sat down upon a log beside me.

"We waste good time with this searching," he said.

I made no reply.

"Stiles was a better woodsman than you or I," he went on. "If something had not happened to him he would be in long ere now. 'Tis in my mind he has been taken."

" 'Tis an ambush I fear," I replied. "He may have been shot from hiding. He may be even now lying wounded in the forest, starving, too weak to make his way."

Stark shook his head.

" 'Tis not likely," he said. "Did ye hear aught of shooting after ye separated?"

I remembered that I had not, and shook my head.

"The country is not so great but some of ye'd have heard it had there been any," he went on. "And, furthermore, if it had happened the Indian'd have found the sign. 'Tis hard to shoot a man, even to wound him, in the woods without leaving some trace of it."

There was cold logic in what he said, but I was too full of regret and self-reproach to make answer. He saw that I was distressed, and did his small best to cheer me as he could.

"Come, lad," he cried, clapping me upon the shoulder, "buck up. 'Tis the fortune of war. It might as easily have been yourself, or any of the others. Ye've no need to take it upon yourself. There is no blame to you."

He paused, but I did not reply.

"At least," he went on, "since we find no sign of his death, 'tis like he lives—unless he fell among the savages."

With this small encouragement he left me to see to his men. I knew that what he said was true; yet there was always the chance that Jed had fallen in with the enemy's Indians, and the thought made me shudder; for on more than one occasion I had seen their handiwork upon a victim. It was no help to remember that there was no corps of English more hated by the red men than the Rangers. It was a sad day for any of Rogers' men when they came into their hands.

We abandoned the search that afternoon, for it was plain that we were getting nowhere, and Stark had his orders to continue on to Ticonderoga on reconnaissance. I returned with Toby and five of the men as an escort with the boats to Fort William-Henry, thence going overland to Fort Edward, dreading every step of the way for the duty that was to be mine when I came there: the task of notifying Purity of her father's loss.

I hope I may never again have a letter so difficult to write as that one. It took me the better part of an entire day, and if I started it once I must have torn up a hundred sheets of foolscap to make a new beginning. In the end it was but a poor business, stating the details of what had happened, and voicing my regrets. I had not the courage of my convictions at the finish, for in my effort to lighten the blow somewhat I fear I held out more hope that he was alive than I myself could muster. Then, before I could again decide to change it, I signed it hastily, sealed it, and sent it on its sorrowful way to Portsmouth; after which I lived for days in deep regret that I had not torn it up and done it over.

The three weeks that followed this business were uneventful. For the most part I was kept occupied with the patrols that scoured the forest between Fort Edward and Wood Creek. As this was but a short distance and one that could be covered by two patrols in a little more than half a day, I spent much of my time in camp, and so came more in contact with army life than I had at any time since early in the summer. On several occasions I encountered my old enemies, Sanborn and Merrill, who were engaged in bringing up winter supplies from Albany for Fort Edward and William-Henry. But, though my blood boiled at each new sight of them, I took thought of Colonel Bradstreet's counsel to bide my time, and held myself in check; though I kept a weather eye open for any sign of treachery on their part.

In the meantime the men were moving down into winter quarters. The regulars had been withdrawn, to be quartered upon the inhabitants of Albany, Philadelphia, and New York, despite indignant protest. Nearly all the colonials had gone home. General Lyman remained at Fort Edward. My friend Captain Putnam was stationed at William-Henry. The Rangers were increased from sixty to a hundred men, each company; and two new companies were authorized and raised, under the command of Captains Spikeman and Hobbs, and sent to the lake for the winter, while Captain Richard Rogers' company joined our own at Edward. As the cold weather drew on the vast scattering of tents about the fort disappeared, and as many of the men as could be accommodated were crowded within the buildings. Those who could not be accommodated inside the structure were quartered in barracks on the island in the river opposite.

This overcrowding was not without its bad effect. With the coming of autumn and the departure of many of the troops there had been a noticeable improvement in the general health of the men. The number of cases of smallpox and camp fever in the hospital tents diminished, and new cases became more and more infrequent. Had we been able to remain in the old camp a few weeks longer, all might yet have been well. Winter, however, would wait upon no man. It was necessary to get the men under cover, and as was inevitable in those crowded quarters the pestilence broke out again with renewed fury. At one time almost a half of the troops at Fort Edward lay stretched upon their backs with the fever. Even among the Rangers was this true, and through the month of November the loss from the smallpox in our ranks was greater than it had been during the entire summer.

Under these circumstances the wonder is that we did not all come down with the sickness at once that first season. Indeed, taking the campaigns together, there were but few of us who escaped it entirely; and I took my turn with the rest.

As nearly as I can remember it was about the first of December when I felt the first signs of approaching fever. On that morning I awoke with a parched throat and throbbing head. Every bone in my body seemed to creak. My legs felt heavy. And there was such a griping in my belly that I thought my bowels were being tied in knots. I paid little heed to these symptoms, however, laying it rather to the flux, from which the entire camp suffered intermittently, than to anything more serious.

The next day I felt somewhat better, so that I did not report the matter, but continued on duty. On the third day I felt about the same, and on the fourth Rogers ordered me out with eight men, to supplement the regular patrols.

According to our instructions, we were to lie out near the point where the South Bay of Lake Champlain narrows to pass between two perpendicular rocks, and from there observe what parties of the enemy passed upon the lake in boats, the ice not yet having formed. In obedience to these orders I went directly to that spot and established my lookout, placing our camp at a discreet distance from the lake, where we could light a small warming fire without too much fear of detection.

For two days we lay there, in which time but one small party passed, going north, evidently from a scout within our lines. As my orders were to report only large parties moving south, we did not molest them, but let them pass without revealing our position. On the third morning, however, a party which I estimated to number some two hundred appeared from the direction of Ticonderoga, whereupon we withdrew quietly and hastened with all possible speed towards the fort with the warning.

Now, from the time we had left the fort I had realized my mistake in not reporting myself for the sicklist. On the march out my head had buzzed and ached, and my feet had developed a curious trick of not going where I wanted them, so that I had some difficulty in keeping to the broad pathway. If the men noticed it, none of them spoke. Perhaps my imagination exaggerated my weaving gait. Perhaps they thought I had peered too long into the rum jug the previous evening. However that may be, I came well enough to the camp at the narrows. Once there I lay half the time shivering with an ague, and the other half burning with a fever. By night I could not sleep, while by day I had difficulty keeping my eyes open.

But it was on the return journey that my real troubles began. From the very start my head felt light as a bucket of swansdown and as large as a good-sized pumpkin. From my hips down my body had the numbness of lead, yet when I walked I seemed to float through the air as lightly as a feather. Moments of black dizziness alternated with spells in which all my senses were sharp and abnormally clear. By the time we had covered half the distance to the fort I was staving off delirium by sheer power of will.

This was my condition when the trail dipped abruptly into a wooded hollow and started across the bottom, and it was here that we met Toby, whom I had sent forward as advanced guard, hurrying back to meet us. Something in his attitude must have warned me that his news was important, and I suppose it was this that jerked me back into the world of reality; for all at once I was keenly aware of all that took place about me, and my mind worked with the utmost clarity.

Toby made a swift gesture behind him as he came up.

"Frenchmun come," he said quickly, holding up the fingers of both his hands. "Ten Injun, two Frenchmun. Come fast."

I saw what I might not have seen in normal circumstances; that though our position was not, perhaps, ideal, it would be better to form an ambush there than to fall back to the hillside, lest they discover the signs of our passing and take warning. Quickly I disposed the men, equally on either side of the trail, and waited.

Scarcely had we taken our positions when the first man came by; an Indian, stripped to the waist despite the sharpness of the air, and hideously daubed. He was travelling fast, and paying slight attention to the trail, though he was quite evidently intended to be an advanced scout. I knew that it would be some moments before he discovered our sign, so I kept cover, and let him pass. A moment later, scarce fifty paces behind their advanced guard, came the main body, swinging along at a dog trot, obviously hurrying, glancing neither to right nor to left. I waited until they were well abreast of us, then gave the order to fire.

They had been coming along in good order, one Frenchman in the lead, and the other bringing up in the rear. But our first fire threw them into confusion. Five of their number went down at the volley; and of the rest, those in front turned to fly, while those in the rear pushed forward, so that for an instant they milled uncertainly in the trail. It was while they stood thus hesitant we burst upon them from our hiding place.

The skirmish that followed was brief but savage. I stepped out of the brush with the others, to find myself confronted immediately by an enormous Indian, whose face was streaked with vertical bars of red and yellow. My dizziness had come back upon me, yet even today I can recall with precise clearness every detail of what happened. To me, it was like two men fighting in a dream, their movements so slow and unreal that they seem unable to reach one another. He had his tomahawk poised to strike, and I brought my musket up to parry the blow. Our movements, slow as they seemed, must have been swift enough. I can remember the sparks that seemed to waver out from the blow, as the edge of the tomahawk turned upon my gun barrel. At the same moment a musket butt swung down from somewhere on my right, and the man's gaudy daubs were mingled in a bloody pulp. He went down without a sound, and I followed him an instant later from a crack on the back of the head that sent me spinning.

When I opened my eyes a moment later the field was ours. Both the Frenchmen lay dead in the path, as did five of the Indians. Two Indians, including the advanced guard, had escaped in the woods, and we had three prisoners, two of them slightly wounded and the third unharmed.

What it was that had hit me, no one seemed to know. But there was a lump at the back of my head as large as an egg. Strangely enough the blow seemed to have cleared my mind, for I was less dizzy when I scrambled to my feet than I had been while I was struggling with the Indian. I knew, however, that this was not likely to last for long; for already I could feel the fever spurting through my veins. A hasty calculation told me that we had lost a half-hour in our skirmish. The scout which we were to report could not be many miles behind, and it was plain that if we were to reach the fort in time for Rogers to act upon my information, we must hurry. I ordered one of the men to search the dead Frenchmen and set the others to gathering up the dead men's muskets. When they had done this I lined them up with the prisoners in the centre.

We were ready to start when the man I had detailed to search the Frenchmen came forward. In his hand he had a packet wrapped in oiled silk and bound round with a gold thread, sealed heavily with wax. That the packet contained letters was evident, though why they should be unopened was more than I could at the moment understand.

" 'Twas all he had on 'im," my man said.

"No money? No marks of identification?" I demanded.

I saw his eyes waver at the first, but he lied valiantly.

"None, sir," he replied.

I let it pass. If he found a few handfuls of small silver that way, why should I take it from him? Certainly the Frenchman would have no further use for it. I could feel the pounding again in my head, and my tongue swelling in my mouth. The men before me wavered slightly. I knew that I must move on, if I were not to remain here for ever. I slipped the packet into my pouch, and gave the order to march.

We made a rapid journey of it, despite my dizziness, reaching the road that runs between Fort Edward and Fort William-Henry a little after noon. By this time my condition was obvious, even to the men, and Toby had taken charge; for I was no longer capable of commanding, moving as I was in a complete daze.

As luck would have it, a convoy of empty wagons came along the road, going down from William-Henry, soon after we came to it, and Toby commandeered one of these to ride us in, in style, although the driver protested strenuously. The next thing I remember, I was in Captain Rogers' quarters.

I must have come in upon my feet, appearing somewhere near normal, for the captain was standing talking to me.

"What?" he said. "Speak up! How many did you say there were?"

"About two hundred," I replied, not knowing what I had said up to that point.

He spun about on his heel and looked at me sharply.

"What?" he demanded. "What in hell are you talking about? What's the matter with you?"

He thrust his face close to mine, and I could see he was angry, dizzy as I was, for his features were all puffed and blotchy as they were when something riled him.

"Him sick."

I heard Toby's voice as in a dream coming from somewhere beside me.

Rogers looked at me again, sharply, and then seemed to blur and go away. I could hear his voice and Toby's, seeming to come from somewhere away off. I heard Toby tell him about the French who had come out from Ticonderoga, and of our march back to the fort. He told of our meeting with the two Frenchmen and the Indians on the trail, but I do not recall that he mentioned the packet I had gotten from the dead Frenchman; nor did I speak of it myself. I had a vague feeling that there was something I ought to say, but could not think what it was. Presently I became aware of Rogers' voice addressing me again.

"How d'ye feel?" he was saying.

"All right," I replied, listlessly enough, no doubt.

"All right!" he scoffed. I felt his hand touch my forehead, and heard him exclaim. "God's body! You're hot enough to cook eggs on. Here—let's have a look at you."

Fingers fumbled at the fastenings of my jacket, and in an instant I felt the cold air upon my chest.

❪ 1 ❫ I lay five weeks in the lazaretto, after a purge and a bleeding which alone would have sent a man to bed for a week. During the first ten days, they tell me, I was in a constant state either of coma or of violent delirium. However that may be, I know that for a time I was prey to dreams and hallucinations in which the face of everyone I had ever known rose before me in all manner of weird antics, the which, fantastic though they were, were none the less horrible in their reality. On the eleventh day the fever passed its crisis, and from then on I lay in a sort of dazed stupor from which I rallied slowly, until at the end of the fifth week it was deemed safe to release me and send me to my quarters for further confinement, until I should recover my strength.

Throughout this period I was attended, night and day, by the faithful Toby, to whose care I probably owed my life. Having had the disease early in his youth, he was immune to it, and Rogers appeared glad enough to let him act as my orderly. No matter at what hour of the night or day I might awake, I would find him always beside me, ready to wait upon my slightest wish.

Such an illness does not leave a man strong and fit for duty upon the first day of his release. I knew that I was skinny and hollow-cheeked, and my knees were shaky as I walked across the parade and down to the river on Toby's arm; but I was not prepared for the way Stark and Rogers, who had ferried across from the island to greet me, stared. I looked, so they told me, like the very shadow of the living death. But there was no question that they were glad to see me alive and on my way to health once more.

They led me to my quarters and there made me lie down at once, showering me with attentions and not allowing me to lift a finger to do anything at all. When I expressed a wish for a pipe of tobacco, which I had not been allowed to have since the beginning of my illness, Rogers jumped to his feet and asked where my pipe and Virginia might be. Nothing would do but I must let him prepare it for me!

Laughing, I pointed to my pouch; and he took it up, fumbling about in it for the tobacco, which lay in a small bag near the bottom. As he pulled it forth some one or two other articles came out with it and rolled upon the floor: a pair of socks, a balled kerchief, a packet of snuff, and a second packet done up in oiled silk and bound about with gold thread heavily sealed with red wax. Rogers apologized at once and went down on his knees to gather them up. But as he picked up the sealed packet he frowned and turned it over in his hands.

"What's this?" he asked.

"Why," I said, puzzled, for the circumstance in which the packet had come into my hands for the moment escaped from me, "I don't know. Open it, and let's see."

Kneeling there upon the floor, he broke the seal and unwrapped the silk, drawing out several folded sheets of foolscap, closely written. He gave them one hasty glance and then looked back again more closely with startled eyes. All at once his face went purple and puffy, and I could see the great vein bulge at the back of his neck.

"God's body!" he roared. "Where did these come from?"

I looked at him stupidly, uncomprehending.

"I don't know," I said. "What is it?"

He thrust the papers at me.

"Look!" he said.

I looked down at them and saw that the first sheet was an enumeration of all the English forces then in commission in the colonies, together with their dispositions and the officers commanding. A second sheet gave vital information as to plans for the winter and the coming campaign, while the rest consisted of plans of Forts Edward and William-Henry, showing the location of the various guards and pickets, enumerating the strength of the garrisons, and pointing out the weakest points about them.

I racked my brain to think how these had come into my possession, the while Rogers stood over me, frowning, black as a thundercloud. It was Toby who gave my memory the jog. He looked over my shoulder.

"Um-m!" he grunted. "Him come from Frenchmun."

"By God," I cried, "that's so!"

Suddenly I recalled the circumstances of that fight, and of all that followed, as clearly as if they had been but yesterday. And as quickly as I could I told Rogers of it.

"Why did you not give me these before?" he demanded.

I shook my head.

"I don't know," I said. "I remember now thinking there was something I must tell you. But I could not then think what it was."

He nodded, but seemed uncertain what he should do.

" 'Twill be easy enough to prove where they came from," I said. " 'Twas Obe Carter took them from the dead man and gave them to me."

He nodded again, and seemed somewhat mollified. I handed the papers to him, and he went over them again, more carefully this time.

At last he looked up from them, and announced that it made but little difference now. Since these papers were written, he said, almost the entire picture was changed. William-Henry and Edward had both been strengthened against the winter, many of the troops had been moved because of the difficulties of quartering. Even the colour of the staff at Albany had been changed somewhat. Moreover, as the papers had been intercepted there was no harm done. At the same time, however, he said he would keep them and see that they reached the proper hands, as they might be the means of catching a spy who was obviously well placed, to say the least.

This out of the way, he stuffed the letters into his pocket and proceeded to more pleasant topics. Among other things he told me was that my Lord Loudoun had ordered the raising of five more companies of Rangers, all to be placed under his command, and he went so far as to promise me promotion to a first lieutenancy if I cared for it when they should be raised and in commission. On this note both he and Stark took their leave. A day or two later, though I did not see Rogers himself again before I left, I received from him an order for a month's leave, to become effective as soon as I was in proper condition to travel home.

It was several days after this before I felt strong enough to do more than sit by the fire or lie upon my bunk, and nearly a week before I could get up and move about my cabin freely. But on the fourth day I received an unexpected caller.

Considering the season of the year—it was by then almost mid-

January—the weather outside was unusually mild and springlike: one of those rare days that sometimes fall in the middle of winter between two viciously cold spells. The sun was shining, drawing mist from the roofs of the row of cabins in which I found my quarters. The snow melted and ran down from the ridgepoles, forming thick icicles that dangled dangerously from the eaves, and the air was almost balmy.

Notwithstanding this, Toby had taken the precaution of building up a roaring fire on my hearth, before going out to attend to some other duties, so that I soon found myself sweltering in my tiny room. In order to temper the heat somewhat I tried opening the door; but this made too strong a draft, and after a moment or two of discomfort I rose and took the frame of glazed paper out of the window, letting the sunshine stream in. Then I dragged my table and chair over beside the window and, fetching ink and paper, sat down to write a long overdue letter to Dorcas, giving her a detailed account of all that had befallen me since my last, and forewarning her of my present home-coming.

In the midst of this I was surprised to hear a woman's voice outside asking the way to my quarters. Without standing upon ceremony I leapt to my feet and went to the door. As I laid my hand upon the latch there was a knock from without, and I opened it to find myself come face to face with Purity Stiles!

2

To one who examines the facts from a distance it may appear strange that in all the time I had been away I had heard but thrice from home. But to me, on the spot, it had not seemed a matter for great wonder. As I have said, communications were of the most difficult; and Dorcas had never shown any great inclination for letter writing. Neither, I fear, had I proved myself much better, though the duties of camp and field were such that I had scant opportunity for scribbling.

Dorcas' first had come to me as a dutiful reply to one of my own early letters. The second had reached me in July, and the third had arrived in mid-October, not long before the fatal expedition in which we had lost Jed Stiles. In each of these she had begged to be allowed to come to Albany—"to be near you," as she had said. To the first of these I had returned a sharp refusal, saying that for all she would see of me in Albany she might as well stay in Portsmouth, as I came but rarely down the Hudson. But to the third I made no reply, being busy with matters of duty, and feeling that, since she already knew my views upon the subject, my silence would be the more emphatic. Since I had heard nothing further I had naturally assumed that she had accepted my wishes with wifely resignation, and that as she sent me no word to the contrary all was well with my household in Portsmouth.

Imagine my surprise, then, at finding myself thus suddenly face to face with Purity Stiles in the midst of this snowbound camp!

"Purity!" I cried.

At sight of my face, all hollowed out by the fever and scarred and pitted with the marks of the pox, she had hesitated. But at the sound of my voice she threw herself into my arms and lay sobbing upon my breast.

"Oh, my poor, poor Jamie!" she cried.

I closed the door awkwardly with one hand, and with my other drew her into the room and led her to the only comfortable chair, which stood before the hearth.

"There, child," I said in a clumsy effort to soothe her, " 'tis naught now. Here! Sit you down and let me fetch you some brandy."

"You've been ill," she said as she took the chair.

" 'Tis over now," I replied, "and I am well again."

I saw that she looked doubtfully at me, and her lips trembled.

"Let me fetch that brandy," I said hastily, and turned away.

When I returned with the liquor in my horn cup she seemed to have composed herself somewhat. She took the cup from me with a steady hand and sipped at it with a wry face.

"What brings you here, child?" I asked. "I thought you safe in Portsmouth. Did you get my letter?"

"Letter?" she asked, and shook her head before I could reply. "No, 'tis three months since I have had a word from anyone, even father. We left Portsmouth before the end of November, and—"

"You left Portsmouth!" I cried. "Dorcas too?"

She nodded, looking a little bewildered.

"Why—yes," she said, hesitantly.

I sat down upon my bench by the table with a groan and took my head in my hands. It was plain what had happened. They had left Portsmouth before my letter had arrived. And, there being none there to forward it, had never received it.

"What's the matter?" she demanded.

The horror of the news I found myself thus suddenly called upon to deliver thrust from my mind any annoyance I may have felt with my wife for having disregarded my wishes. For the moment I could be conscious only of the difficulty of the task that lay before me.

She must have noticed my hesitation, for her eyes flew wide in apprehension.

"What is it?" she demanded again. "What is wrong, Jamie? Is it father?"

I nodded.

"I have sorry news for you, child," I replied.

"He's dead?" she said in a flat voice.

I nodded.

"I fear it," I said.

She looked at me with an ashen face, and her eyes were like those of a whipped puppy.

"No!" she whispered. "No, it can't be!"

I went to her then and, kneeling beside her on the floor, told her the whole thing as it had happened.

"The fault is mine," I said when I had finished.

But she shook her head.

" 'Tis nobody's fault," she said. "You say you did not find a trace of him?"

"Not a sign," I replied.

"Then it is just possible that he still lives?" she asked.

"Barely possible," I said, and could have bitten out my tongue for my weakness; for her face showed what store she set by my reply, and I knew how slim were the chances.

"If he had been killed in the pursuit," she said, "you would have found him?"

"Probably," I replied.

"Then he was taken," she cried. "He is alive!"

"If that were so," I said, "his name would be in the list of prisoners for exchange. I have seen the list, and his name was not there."

"It must have been overlooked," she said.

I shook my head.

"That is unlikely," I said. "It is more probable that he was never turned over to the French. They were Indians who followed us, and they do not love the Rangers. If he fell into their hands there could be no room for hope!"

But she was not to be swayed in her determination that he lived.

"My father," she said scornfully, "had more woodsmanship in his little finger than a hundred dirty Indians! He would not let himself be taken by them! There is more in this than we know! He lives, Jamie! I tell you he lives! I feel it here!"

She clapped her hand upon her heart.

But I could not share her enthusiasm. I shook my head.

"Pray God you are right," I said.

We sat thus for a time in silence, each with his own thoughts, until, happening to look down, I saw that her shoes and the bottom of her skirt were wet and caked with mud. With an exclamation of annoyance at my own stupidity, I sprang to my feet.

"But you are soaked!" I cried. "Take off those wet things, and let me dry them for you."

I gave her a blanket to wrap about her and heavy socks to put upon her feet, and turned my back while she stripped off her wet clothes and dropped them in a little pile upon the hearth. When I turned back she sat wrapped in my blanket in the armchair, with her feet upon the footstool, toasting them before the fire. As I hung the things beside the hearth I remembered that she had told me nothing of herself as yet.

"You have not said what brings you here," I remarked.

She laughed. "To Half Moon," she said, "I walked upon my snowshoes; but from there I had a ride in a supply sledge."

I made a gesture of impatience.

"You know that is not what I mean," I said. "Is Dorcas in Albany?"

She nodded. I must have shown my annoyance, for she looked stubborn.

"If you had been a better correspondent—" she began.

"Better correspondent!" I interrupted. "I am a soldier, not a scribbling clerk! I have not time to be forever writing letters like my Lord Loudoun!"

"If you had been a better correspondent," she went on as if she had not heard me, "she might have stayed at home. It was when she received no reply to her last that she made up her mind to come."

"But, damn it," I cried, "she knew how I felt about her coming to Albany! Must I keep telling her?"

She smiled. "If you have something you want a woman to know," she said, "it is best to keep telling it."

I saw that she was not my ally in this. I shrugged.

"Well," I said, "what then?"

"Well," she mimicked, "then, when we got to Albany we heard from Major Ferguson that you were ill; and only the other day I met Captain Rogers, and he told me of your recovery and convalescence. I came at once to see you as soon as Major Ferguson could get me the pass."

"But Dorcas?" I said, bewildered, for it seemed to me that she was the one who should have come.

"Dorcas has been confined to her bed with a bad cold this last week," she replied, "or she would have come herself."

I was indignant.

"A cold indeed!" I snorted. "And yet she allowed you to expose yourself to all manner of things: cold, Indians, pestilence!"

She looked at me contritely.

"You are angry with me for coming?" she asked.

"Angry!" I exclaimed. "Bless you, no! 'Twas sweet of you, but—"

I stopped, thinking still that it was strange Dorcas should not have come herself.

"But what?" she asked.

"But you shouldn't have done it," I said for lack of a better thought, and feigned cheerfulness about it.

"Tell me," I went on, anxious to change the subject. "Where in Albany did you find lodgings? They say rooms are so scarce, what with the regulars stationed there, and one thing and another, that you can't get them for love nor money."

It may have been my imagination, but I thought she flushed slightly.

"Your cousin, Major Ferguson, was kind enough to put us up," she replied. "He has taken a small house upon the hill near the Schuylers."

"What!" I cried, staring at her in unbelief. "You don't mean she's living there?"

Purity nodded. "Of course," she said. "Why not?"

"Why not?" I raged. "Why not, indeed! Has she no thought for propriety? Doesn't she know there's only one thing more gossipy than an old woman, and that's an old soldier? Albany's overrun with 'em!"

"But, he's your own cousin," she said.

"My own cousin, be damned!" I cried. "I wouldn't trust him five minutes out of my sight!"

I thought then that she looked at me a little strangely, but I laid it only to bewilderment and childish naïveté, and I was too much agitated in my mind to pay much heed. That Dorcas should have come to Albany at all was bad enough. But that she should accept the hospitality of a bachelor officer, even though he were my own cousin, infuriated me. I did not think that there was aught behind it but innocent carelessness. It did not occur to me to doubt my wife's fidelity. Rather, I felt, she was sincerely ignorant of the damage she might be doing her own good name. But it was this very childish innocence, as I believed it to be, that angered me more than any mistrust could have done. After all, I told myself, she had reached an age where she should know better! I stepped to the door and bellowed for Toby. When that faithful shadow appeared, like the genie of the lamp, I drew him inside and slammed the door.

"Look," I said, "we go to Albany tomorrow. Take the passes and see that they are stamped, and make arrangements for transport on a supply sledge if you can. Let Rogers know."

"Rogers go on scout," Toby said.

"Stark then," I replied.

"Stark go too," he said, "and Captain Spikeman and L'tenant Kennedy."

"Well, then," I persisted, "notify whoever's in command. The passes are in order, and Rogers told me to use 'em when I could. I can now; and I'm going to."

Toby grunted and went out.

I noticed then that the sun had gone down, and it had begun to turn cold, for the window was still open. I replaced the frame with its glazed paper in the sash, and threw a couple of logs upon the fire, which blazed up brightly, setting the kettle on the hearth to bubbling merrily. I reached out and hooked the kettle off.

"Here," I said, "let's have a dish of tea."

The wait, however, was welcome as it gave me a chance to think; a chance hitherto lacking, for my mind had been occupied with the problem of getting Purity safely down to Albany. Now that I saw the house I was more than ever annoyed at my wife's thoughtless flouting of the conventions. It was small, almost too small for decency in the circumstances; and I thought she could not realize the harm to which she exposed her own good name, as well as mine, by so thoughtlessly accepting my cousin's hospitality. Moreover, I was displeased at her evident disregard for my wishes. Her flouting of my command to keep herself in Portsmouth, it seemed to me, showed scarcely the respect due a husband. Whatever might be her motive for coming, she knew my expressed views on the matter. Yet she had deliberately chosen to ignore them.

The more I thought upon these matters, and the longer I cooled my heels in that daintily furnished room, the angrier and more annoyed I became with her; so that when she finally came I was, to say the least, scarce in a loving mood.

As she swept in at the doorway it was plain what had delayed her, for she was powdered and painted in the height of fashion, and so bedecked and beribboned in ruffles and frills and furbelows, more appropriate to a court ball than to midafternoon in a garrison town on the edge of the wilderness, that looking at her I felt half ashamed for her of her vulgar display. In that moment I realized abruptly how far apart we had grown in the years since our marriage, for she no longer had the power to move me by her very entrance into a room.

My own appearance must have been something of a shock to her, for she moved but a step or two from the door before she stopped and stood staring. I knew that my face was emaciated and pitted with the pox, and that my clothes hung awkwardly upon my skinny frame, and I had expected her to be startled at the sight of me and perhaps even horrified; but I had not looked to see distaste upon her face. So evident was her aversion that I myself was shocked.

I might have loved her even then and forgiven her all her airs and haughtiness and wilfulness had she condescended to show the least affection for me. Instead she stood looking at me coldly with an expression that told only too plainly what was in her mind; so that I felt the anger mounting within me and a wave of bitterness swept over me.

"Well, madam," I said irritably, "do you stand and stare as at a ghost? I assure you that I am that same man you loved and married four years since. God knows I have been a good husband to you!"

She tossed her head defiantly, and caught up my remarks with a swiftness that should have told me of her secret had I been of a less trusting nature.

"Do you say I have not been a good wife?" she demanded. "What cause have you to doubt me?"

Even then I did not think there was aught of harm in her, but only wilfulness. Nevertheless, I was determined that for once she should learn who was master in the house.

"Nay," I replied, hotly, for my temper was getting the better of me. "I have not said that I doubted you, though well I might when you lay yourself open so deliberately to gossip! 'Twas bad enough in Portsmouth while I was gone—"

She cut me short with a weary gesture.

"Oh, Portsmouth!" she said, as if the town which she had once thought so admirable was now beneath her contempt. "Will you never forget Portsmouth? It's so provincial! Surely you couldn't take those scandalmongers seriously!"

In my anger I blundered blindly past the opening she herself made for me.

"Albany is a garrison town," I said, "and could give Portsmouth odds and still best her at scandalmongering. I have a place to maintain in this army. If you have no more consideration for your own name than you have shown in coming here, I'll ask you to remember that and act accordingly."

"But after all," she protested, as if trying to reason with a small child, "Hubert is your own cousin."

"Cousin or no," I replied, "he is none the less a man. Moreover, I expressly forbade your coming to Albany. That you are here shows you have scant respect for me as your husband. If only to assert my proper authority I must ask you to pack your things and send them to my quarters at the tavern at once."

"And if I refuse?" she demanded defiantly.

"Then, by God, madam," I swore, enraged beyond all endurance, "you are no wife of mine, and I'll have you whipped through the streets for a common harlot!"

At that she went suddenly white and ghastly, so that the paint on her face stood out horribly in contrast with the sickly pallor of her skin, and she looked old and flabby beyond her years, and panic-stricken as well. Her air of bravado departed abruptly, leaving her weak and trembling. Her shoulders sagged, her mouth drew down at the corners, and all at once she burst into tears.

"Oh, Jamie, Jamie!" she sobbed. "Is this the way you greet me? How could you say such things to me? How could you? How could you?"

It was her tears, I think, rather than her words that made me feel all at once horribly ashamed of myself and angry for the hurt I had done her. I was never strong enough to stand by in anger while a woman wept. I went to her, suddenly full of contrition, and took her in my arms, where she clung to me, sobbing upon my shoulder.

"There now," I tried to comfort her. " 'Tis not that I believe these things myself, but I must try to show you what people will say since you seem not able to see it for yourself."

"B-but that awful tavern!" she sobbed. "Surely, Jamie, you'll not make me go there."

I looked at her astounded. Was this all that she had gathered from my tirade? I could feel myself growing angry and impatient again, but the sight of her tear-streaked face softened my heart within me.

"Eh!" I said. "If that's all that worries you I'll take a house of your own for you. Since you're here you might as well stay."

She stopped her sobbing abruptly, and smiled at me through her tears as if she could not believe her ears.

"Oh," she cried, "do you mean it?"

And when I nodded, she threw her arms about my neck and half smothered me with kisses before I could break away.

"I'm sorry, Jamie," she apologized, "if I did wrong. But I did want to be near you. And Hubert was kind to offer to keep us. You can't deny that! You will forgive me?"

Without waiting for my answer she broke away and flew to the door.

"I'll run and pack," she said. "You get ready and meet me in an hour. I know just the house I want!"

And with that she was gone all at once in a swirl of silks, leaving me bewildered with a mixture of feelings; glad that I had smoothed things over and made her happy once more; and yet perplexed at her callous behaviour and evident disregard for any but herself.

3

The house upon which Dorcas had set her mind was a large one—much too large a one, to my way of thinking, for her needs. Nevertheless, despite the landlord's fee, which I had every reason to consider exorbitant, I took it for the sake of peace in the family. Nor indeed had I much choice in the matter, for houses for the renting were as scarce as hen's teeth in Albany at the time, what with men and officers billeted throughout the town; and this one, as it proved, was only vacant through the chance that the captain who had previously occupied it with his family had suddenly been called to Boston to join Lord Loudoun's staff. Had I not taken it I doubt if we could have found another in the city, and having given my word in the matter there was naught else I could do.

There was one great advantage in it, however; it had a pleasing location. It stood in its own spacious grounds in a quiet section of the town at the edge of the hill overlooking the river, not far from the Schuyler mansion, and not above a quarter of a mile from Hubert's quarters. There was but one other house visible from its lower floor, and that stood some rods distant, only its Dutch peaked roof showing above the trees and shrubbery that lay between.

It was this very isolation that appealed to me, for I had my bellyful of soldiering, and looked forward to a quiet rest with as little as might be to remind me of my own place in the army. There I was able to look out the window without seeing a streetful of uniforms, or to sleep the clock around without once being wakened by the rattle of drums, the blaring of a bugle, the shouting of profane commands, or the thud of marching feet.

There were other advantages as well to the solitude, notable among them that it allowed little James Hubert, now just past his first birthday and growing more darkly like his mother with each passing day, to play and rest undisturbed under the watchful eye of Purity, who was nurse and second mother to him, Dorcas having not the patience to bear with his wailing for more than a few moments at a time.

We moved in bag and baggage, Dorcas, Purity, James Hubert, and myself and Dorcas' three blackamoors, on the second day after my own arrival in town. Dorcas at once wished to hold a housewarming; but I put my foot down upon this, giving two excellent reasons why I would not have it: first, that I was more in need of rest than diversion; and second, that I had none of the proper clothes for such an occasion. I think it was the last that finally brought her to the light of reason, for though it made her pout to know that she was not to have the pleasure of dragging me upon a round of routs and parties, still she would have preferred not going out at all to being forced to appear in the fashionable world of Albany with me in my smoke-stained buckskins. She did not sulk for long, however, for as it proved Hubert was willing and only too pleased to be allowed to squire her about to the various affairs with which the officers of the regular establishment whiled away the winter, and for my part, I may be censured for it, but I was as well pleased to see it work out so happily for all concerned.

My worthy cousin I found not much changed, and I had ample opportunity to observe him; for when he was not on duty at headquarters or leading Dorcas off to a dinner party or a dance he was making himself comfortable in our parlour. He had prospered, evidently, with the war, for some of the leanness was gone from his face, and he did not lack for fine feathers. He had managed somehow to maintain his important post under General Abercrombie—the same he had held under the late lamented Governor Shirley—though he had been unable to extend himself to my Lord Loudoun's staff, as he had tried to do.

His rank as major he retained, though I found out it was on a basis of half-pay; a fact which puzzled me mightily, for it was plain enough that in these days he never lacked for ready money, and he lived far beyond the meagre pay he received from the crown. At first I thought perhaps he might have sold some of his holdings at home; but this I soon realized was scarcely likely, as at his present rate he would run through anything he might get from them in less than three months. Neither could it be entirely from the profits of his position, in the form of spoils, for had this been the case he would never have dared to flout it so for all to see. That he was flush, there could be no question, for not once during my stay did he approach me for a "small loan." By the same token, however, neither did he offer to repay to me any of the moneys I had already advanced him, which by now amounted to a considerable sum.

For my part I speculated upon the matter somewhat idly for several days, before deciding that his luck at the tables must have taken a turn for the better, and that his profits came from gambling: a likely enough conclusion, for, in common with most of his brother officers he spent much time over the cartes, and I knew that vast sums frequently changed hands at these sittings.

The time whiled itself away swiftly enough. For the first few days I was tired with the exertion of the journey and of moving Dorcas, so that I cared to do little but sit close by the fire and talk to Purity. By the end of a week, however, my strength had so returned that I felt the need to get about a little now and again. Several times I accompanied Dorcas and Hubert to informal affairs, more for the sake of propriety than for any pleasure I took from them. On these occasions I could not but feel that Dorcas was uncomfortable and a little ashamed of the ragged figure I cut, so that after I had gone with them often enough to smooth appearances, I refused all further invitations, and divided my time between the house and the pleasant taproom of the Crown and Garter tavern in Broad Street, not far distant. It was in this latter place that I encountered an acquaintance of my former visit to the city.

I had grown restless at the dinner table, and shortly afterwards, Dorcas and Hubert being bid to cartes at the General's, I slipped into my greatcoat and turned my steps towards the tavern. As I entered the door I collided with a heavy man who was on his way out. He had his head turned over his shoulder and was talking to a younger man in the uniform of a colonel of regulars, so that he did not see me at once. But I knew him the moment he turned his head.

"Colonel Bradstreet!" I exclaimed.

He peered at me a moment in the dim light without recognizing me. Then all at once his face brightened.

"God bless me!" he roared. " 'Tis the young ensign, Rogers' man, Ferguson!"

"The same, sir," I replied, "only it's lieutenant now."

"Is it now?" he said. "Well, well! They tell me ye've been doing great things up there to northward, you Rangers."

He turned to his companion.

"Here's the lad," he said, "can support your arguments."

He took my arm and pulled me inside into the light, introducing me to the other as we went.

"Colonel Schuyler, Lieutenant Ferguson."

I shook hands with Schuyler, recognizing him now, for I had seen him several times going in or coming out of the great house on the hill.

"Your servant, sir," he said, bowing as easily as if a colonel's epaulets had never brushed his shoulders.

There were not many officers of the regular establishment, I knew, would stand thus in public and acknowledge an introduction to a provincial in tattered buckskins, and I liked him at once for his independence. It had been my experience hitherto that provincials appointed to the regular service were like to be more hoity-toity than Englishmen themselves.

"You weren't with Rogers last week, by any chance?" he asked.

"No, sir," I replied, "I have but just recovered from the pox. I've been in Albany the last fortnight on sick leave."

He raised his eyebrows.

"So?" he said with a distinct Dutch inflection. "Then perhaps you have not heard?"

"Heard?" I asked. "No, sir, I have heard nothing. What is it?"

"Why," said he, "we have not the full details of the affair as yet, but the report is that Rogers and seventy-four of his men were set upon near Ticonderoga last week by a great force of French and Indians. Rogers fought a desperate battle until dark rescued him, and then drew off with only half his force."

"Here," said I, forgetting his rank in my excitement, "this is news. Who were the casualties? D'ye know their names?"

He frowned in thought.

"Only three officers," he said. "Rogers himself was wounded slightly, and a Captain Spikeman and Lieutenant Kennedy killed. I think there was another as well, an ensign, though I can't think of his name at the moment."

"Was it Page?" I demanded, "Caleb Page?"

"That's it," he said, brightening with the recollection. "That's the man."

"I'm sorry," I said slowly. "Spikeman and Kennedy I did not know well. They were with the new company. But Page was a neighbour of mine at home, a fine lad. 'Twas a shame he had to fall."

We had moved over near the bar, and now stood leaning upon it. My companions were silent for a moment. Then Colonel Bradstreet thumped the mahogany.

"Shall we drink a cup to the memory of Ensign Page?" he asked.

Colonel Schuyler nodded, and I followed suit. The drinks were called for, set up, and drunk.

"Heard you aught of Lieutenant Stark?" I asked, when we had set our glasses down.

"Stark?" said Bradstreet. "Why, yes, 'twas John Stark directed the fight after Rogers was wounded."

I was pleased to hear that at least one of my friends had come off well, until I remembered how Stark had set his cap for Elizabeth Page, young Caleb's sister.

"Poor John," I said, " 'twill go hard for him. 'Twill be his duty to break the news at home."

We stood for some moments in silence, each with his own thoughts; then glancing up I chanced to see a significant look pass between my companions. Bradstreet, seeing I had intercepted the exchange, laughed easily.

" 'Tis a dispute we have between us," he said eyeing me curiously. "Ye may be able to help us settle it. 'Tis my contention that Captain Rogers' methods have shown up but poorly in this affair."

"Poorly!" I said, falling straight into his trap, for from all I had ever heard Bradstreet advocated exactly the same sort of warfare. "Poorly, you say? Why, my God, sir, the wonder is not that he could bring back so few, but that he could bring back any of his force at all. If it were not for the way he trains his men to fight like Indians from behind the trees and bushes, I'll warrant you none would have returned. A like force of regulars would have been cut to pieces, and well you know it!"

He laughed and clapped me on the shoulder, leaving me completely mystified, and turned to Colonel Schuyler.

"You see?" he said. "Here's our champion!"

Schuyler smiled and turned to me.

"He's been trying you," he said. "You see, lieutenant, 'tis this way. There is a group of us, mostly all regular officers, that meet at my house upon the hill. There are a few among us who maintain that in this wooded country we must adapt our troops to the methods of warfare in use among the natives if we are to prevail against them and the French, who have been quick to learn their ways. The rest hold to the old school, that the manœuvres we learned upon the drill field are the best in warfare, no matter what the conditions."

"Why!" I said. "But that's ridiculous! Anyone who knows conditions here should see that!"

He nodded.

"Exactly," he said. "But not all of us have seen the conditions. Many of us cannot imagine them as they are. You are a man who knows what woods fighting is. You have seen English troops fighting as Indians do, and doing it well. Maybe you can convince some of these stiff-necked fellows that they are wrong."

"But—" I stammered, and flushed, "I—I don't want to make speeches. I'm not a tactician."

"Oh, no!" he said, smiling. "No speeches. Just come up to the house. Join the party and get into the conversation, and when the matter comes up—as it will, mark my words—tell them what you've just said to me. 'Tis the one idea our officers must learn if ever we are to drive the French back to the sea."

I looked down at my ragged, smoke-stained buckskins.

"But I'm hardly dressed for it," I said. "I can't go calling in these. I'm afraid your aunt wouldn't appreciate it, sir."

He grinned at that. Everyone knew that Madam Schuyler was the social dictator of Albany. From her place in the big house she ruled the city's society with an iron hand.

"Nonsense!" he snorted. "You'll find us no such sticklers up there."

And Bradstreet laughed and clapped me on the shoulder again.

"You'll find uniforms and gold lace aplenty," he said, "but you'll also find plain folk like ourselves, and none so fancy-dressed either. 'Tis not the clothes they care about at the big house, but the man wearing them."

"Well," I said, mollified by their evident cordiality, "if you're sure no one will mind my appearance—"

Schuyler gave a snort.

"Mind your appearance!" he exclaimed, and taking my arm he steered me towards the door.

"Come on," he said.

It was a bitter night outside. A sharp wind whipped the fine-powdered snow from the banks beside the footpath full into our faces, and pinched our nostrils with its' biting cold. Underfoot the snow creaked at our passing.

I was glad enough when I saw the yellow lights of the Schuyler house gleaming through the dark before us with a promise of warmth; and I think my companions shared my feeling, for they quickened their steps at the sight. We hurried up the path and climbed the low porch. Colonel Schuyler did not stop to rap, but opened the heavy front door quickly, and stood aside for us to enter.

In the vestibule I gave my coat and hat to a lackey in a green velvet livery and, turning, saw a small, elderly woman coming out of the adjoining drawing room to greet us. Her hair, beneath the tiny lace cap that she wore, was white as snow. There was humour and understanding in the little lines about her mouth and eyes, and despite her evident age—she must have been near to seventy—her cheeks were as fresh and rosy as a girl's. She bore herself both with pride and with vigour, and yet with such an air of graciousness that I was attracted to her at once. I did not need her nephew's introduction to know that here was the well re-nowned Mrs. Schuyler.

"Aunt," he was saying as she came up, "this is Mr. Ferguson, one of Rogers' men, and a friend to Colonel Bradstreet."

She gave me a little smile and a curtsy, which bound me slave to her then and there, and I made her as elegant a leg as I knew how.

"Your servant, ma'am," I said.

She gave me her hand, and I bent over it.

"Upon my soul," she said, banteringly, "a New Englander, and with the manners of a polished gentleman! You'll pardon me if I say so, young sir, but the combination is rare."

Her smile took the sharpness from her words, and I saw that she was but teasing me.

"I fear you do not know us well, ma'am," I said.

"Oh, la!" she exclaimed. "I know you well enough. Many's the one of you I've welcomed at this very house when Shirley was in command, and always they were glum and always shrewd and sometimes sharp and never able to agree on anything at all."

I laughed. "Ma'am," I said, " 'tis only what we at home say of Yorkers! And you'll admit it takes two to disagree."

"Hark to the lad," she laughed. "You must come and see me when all these others are not about and tell me of your New England, for I can see you love it well."

"Who's about, Aunt?" Schuyler asked, interrupting.

"Oh," she replied, "my Lord Howe is at the tables with Colonel Delancey and Colonel Haldimand and a dozen others, and Colonel Haviland and Major Craven are in the drawing room baiting poor Henry Bouquet. You'd best go in and rescue him. The poor man always gets so excited in an argument!"

Colonel Schuyler chuckled. "He'll have a champion in Mr. Ferguson," he said. "Will you come in?"

But she shook her head.

"I'm for bed," she replied. " 'Tis high time old ladies retired."

She turned to me. "You'll come again, Mr. Ferguson?" she asked.

I bowed. "I would be delighted," I replied.

" 'Tis a promise," she said. "Good night."

And with a smile and a nod she turned and was gone up the wide stair.

I followed Schuyler and Bradstreet into the long drawing room that ran down the full length of one side of the house. It was a pleasant room, elegantly furnished after the English fashion, and lighted with a single huge chandelier of crystals that hung suspended from the centre of the ceiling. At the far end of the room was an enormous fireplace, on whose hearth a bright fire crackled merrily. On a table near the fireplace were a punchbowl and a collection of glasses, and a group of officers, brilliant in scarlet coats and gold lace, gathered in a small knot before the fire. Through a door that opened on one side, midway of the room, I could see another group, officers, civilians, and their ladies, gathered about a number of small tables, playing at cards. As we moved down the length of the room Schuyler fell back beside me and took my arm.

"You must not take my talk to heart," he said. "So long as you are a guest here I want you to do what pleases you. Would you care to take a hand at the cartes?"

I shook my head. "Thank you," I said, "I think not."

I saw a ghost of a smile flicker about his lips and, lest he misunderstand my motives, hastened to explain.

"It is not that I have any scruples against it," I said, "but only that the cartes bore me. If you don't mind I'd rather join you in your discussion."

He nodded. "Excellent!" he exclaimed. "Let it be so!"

As we approached the end of the room the group about the fire resolved itself into its individual parts. Half leaning, half sitting upon the end of the long table that ran down the middle of the room was a young man in civilian dress: a mere lad, scarce out of his teens, I judged. By his features I guessed that here was a close relative, if not a younger brother, to Colonel Schuyler; and indeed my guess proved correct, for the colonel introduced him as his brother Pedrom. Leaning against a corner of the fireplace, nearest the punchbowl, stood a tall, powerfully built man in a captain's coat and high jack boots of the sort that went out of fashion long since, but are still useful for horseback travel upon our muddy roads. He held a half-consumed glass of punch in one hand, and his eyes were blue and twinkling. I needed no second glance at his face to know that he was an Irishman. Before the fire, his back to it and his hands thrust beneath his coattails, stood a tall spare man, with a face that was square-cut and ruddy and divided evenly in the middle by a long thin nose. On a settee placed at right angles to the hearth sat a captain and a haughty-seeming major, while in one of three chairs that stood ranged in a semicircle opposite sat a thin-lipped, sharp-featured colonel of regulars. Behind the settee, and leaning upon it, stood a younger man—a lieutenant by his coat, and one of the most exquisitely pink and white bits of foppish splendour I have ever encountered. Indeed, so elegant and immaculate were they all that I began again to grow uneasily conscious of my own somewhat ragged state.

But I could not go back then, had I wished it. As we drew near I could hear the spare man before the fire speaking earnestly in a harsh voice that bore a heavy Teutonic accent.

"I tell you, shentlemen," he was saying, "it iss only so we shall accomplish anysing on dis terrain! Ven ve eqvip de men lightly,

where he put it all I could not say, for he showed not the least effect from the others he had drunk. While the maid was away fetching it Captain Monypenny, a close friend of my Lord Howe's, came in. I rose to my feet.

"Excuse me a moment," I said. "I've someone I want you to meet. I'll see if he's come in."

Before he could reply I was on my way across the room.

"Good evening, captain," I said as I approached. "Is his Lordship about?"

Monypenny turned a chalky blue eye upon me.

"Ah, there, Ferguson," he replied. "I believe he is, somewhere here."

"Good," I said. "I've Captain Rogers over here, and I thought he might like to meet him."

Monypenny's white eyebrows went up.

"Not the celebrated Captain Rogers?" he exclaimed. "My soul! He's talked of nothing else this past week. I'll fetch him. Where are you sitting?"

I showed him our table, and he turned towards the back of the room, where I knew were a number of private dining rooms. I went back to our table.

"Not here?" said Rogers.

I nodded. "He'll be along," I said. "I sent for him."

Rogers grinned. "He must be somebody," he said. "I saw you ordering the captain to fetch him."

"If he's not," I said, "he will be, mark my words. He's sympathetic to our viewpoint. He thinks all our troops should be trained like Rangers. And he has power. If you need help with your troubles, this is the man to talk to."

He nudged me under the table, and I looked up to see Captain Monypenny threading his way towards us, closely followed by my Lord Howe. I stood up, and Rogers stood up also.

"Captain Rogers," said my Lord Howe, when I presented him.

"Your servant, sir," said Rogers. He swept a hand to the table. "Will you join us?"

Howe and Monypenny sat down, while Rogers bellowed for cups. His Lordship seemed amused, for he smiled, and looked at Rogers' wounded arm.

"You've had an accident, captain?" he asked.

Rogers looked down at the black silk sling and scowled.

"No accident, my lord," he replied gruffly.

Howe looked puzzled.

"The captain took a ball through the wrist," I hastened to explain, "near Ticonderoga. He thinks the French were deliberately set upon him, and so regards it as no accident."

Lord Howe raised his eyebrows.

"Deliberately set upon him?" he said. "How can you know that, captain?"

"Easy enough, sir," Rogers replied. "They couldn't have found our rear and taken their position so quick, if someone hadn't told 'em right where to look."

I thought Lord Howe looked interested.

"So?" he said. "Is this your first instance of information passing to the enemy? Have you any idea how it might be done?"

"Well," said Rogers, "the expedition was no secret. I suppose there are plenty of ways it could be done. Not long ago Mr. Ferguson, here, shot a Frenchman and took a batch of papers from him giving plans of our forts and dispositions and numbers of most of our forces. I've wondered sometimes if there might not be some connection."

I sat up and banged the table with my hand.

"By God!" I said. "I'd forgotten about those."

Howe looked at me quickly and turned back to Rogers.

"Mr. Ferguson turned those papers over to you?" he asked.

"That's right," said Rogers.

"And what did you do with them?" Howe said.

"I turned 'em over to Captain Abercrombie," Rogers replied, "the general's A.D.C."

His Lordship nodded.

"Make a note of that, Albert," he said to Monypenny, then turned back to Rogers. "This should have attention," he said. "I'll speak to Abercrombie about it."

He went on then to ask about the battle, and for the better part of an hour we sat and talked tactics and strategy. At last, however, Lord Howe turned to Captain Monypenny.

"What time do you make it, Albert?" he asked.

Monypenny consulted a huge repeater which he pulled from beneath his waistcoat.

"I make it ten of seven, sir," he said.

"Bother!" said Howe petulantly. "I'm afraid I shall have to

leave you gentlemen. I'm bid to dinner at the general's, and I fear 'twill be deadly dull. Come to the house later on, Ferguson, and bring the captain with you."

He turned and gave his hand to Rogers.

"If you're to be in town a few days, captain," he said, "I'd be pleasured to see you. Mr. Ferguson will bring you to my quarters."

He bowed with great ceremony and turned away.

When he was gone Rogers raised his cup to me with a grin.

"Well!" he said. "You do get about, don't you! Why didn't you tell me you knew Lord Howe this afternoon?"

"You didn't ask me," I replied.

Rogers stayed in Albany a full fortnight, in which time I had him several times to the Schuylers', where he made a sensation, as much for the amount of rum toddy he could consume in the course of an evening without so much as turning a hair, as for his famous exploits. My Lord Howe was deeply interested in the Rangers, and spent many hours closeted with him, in deep discussion of tactics, equipment, and all the various problems that were unique with our service. Indeed, so impressed was he with what he heard from both Rogers and myself, that before we left he made Rogers promise to take him upon an expedition, that he might observe at first hand how our methods worked.

For my part I was more than pleased when Rogers summoned me one afternoon to his quarters at the tavern and told me that we would return the next morning to Fort Edward; for I felt myself to be fully recovered and fit for whatever duty might come my way—and I was already growing bored with idleness. As soon as he had told me I made my way back to the house to pack my few necessities and break the news.

I found both Dorcas and Purity out—the one to tea at Mrs. Delancey's and the other upon some household errand—so that I went straight to my packing, which I finished in the space of an hour. Neither had come in by the time I was done. I left a note for Dorcas, telling her the news, and went out to take leave of my acquaintances in the town.

This was not quickly accomplished, for I had made a number of new friends, and their quarters were scattered. However, by six I had seen all save the Schuylers, whom I had saved for last because of the feeling I had for them. It was about a quarter past the hour when I lifted the great knocker at their door.

Colonel Schuyler himself greeted me in the entrance hall.

"Ah, Ferguson!" he said as he caught sight of me. "You're just in time. You'll stop and take potluck with me, eh?"

"You'll excuse me, colonel," I said. "I'm ordered back to duty in the morning, and I think I should spend my last night at home. I came to say good-bye."

"I'm sorry to hear that," he said. "We shall miss you."

I heard a step in the doorway, and looked up to see Mrs. Schuyler standing there.

"What's this I hear?" she demanded. "You're not leaving?"

There was a note of anxiety in her voice which made me realize, with sudden shock, that the good old soul was become truly fond of me. I nodded soberly.

"I'm afraid I must," I replied.

"Oh, this war!" she exclaimed, and turned to her nephew.

"Go fetch Lord Howe, Peter," she commanded.

The colonel left without a word, and Mrs. Schuyler came over to me. Taking my face in her hands, she kissed me with infinite tenderness; and I saw that there were tears in her eyes.

"God keep you, boy," she said. "Don't forget us when next you are in Albany."

I could do no more than squeeze her hand, for there was a lump in my throat that prevented speech. It was fortunate that at that moment the colonel returned, followed closely by my Lord Howe. Otherwise, I fear, I might have burst into tears, so moved was I at her kindness and her obvious distress.

"What's this?" said Lord Howe, coming to me. "Colonel Schuyler tells me you're ordered out."

"I'm for Fort Edward in the morning with Captain Rogers, my Lord," I said.

"I wish I might go with you," he said. "One grows tired of inactivity."

"We would be honoured to have you, sir," I replied.

He smiled and shook his head.

"I cannot now," he answered. "Some other time. It is a promise."

He turned to Mrs. Schuyler.

"Is the supper ready yet, ma'am?" he asked.

" 'Twill not be for an hour yet," she replied.

"Good!" said he. "I will have time for a last walk to his door with Mr. Ferguson."

He called for his hat and cloak and donned them, the while I took my final leave of the colonel and his aunt. A few moments later we were walking down the ice-crusted pathway, with one of Colonel Schuyler's blackamoors going on ahead with a lanthorn to light our way.

I could see that his Lordship had something on his mind that he wished to say, and walked in silence waiting for him to speak. We were halfway to my house, however, before he broke his silence.

"I have seen the papers you took from the Frenchman," he said finally. "They are in Captain Abercrombie's hands."

As there seemed to be no answer to be made to this, I said nothing.

"That was a bad business," he went on presently. "You should have turned them over to Captain Rogers sooner, lieutenant."

"I would have," I replied, "but the fever was on me. I did not know what I was about, sir."

He nodded. "Of course," he said. Then after a moment's hesitation: "What was this Frenchman like? Was there nothing that might have identified him, or told us what might be his connections behind our lines?"

"No, my Lord," I replied. And I went on to describe the man, not very vividly, I fear, for I found that my own memory of him was but hazy.

When I had done, he shook his head.

"That will not help," he said. "Have you any idea how such a packet might have been passed into his possession?"

"My Lord," I said, "it might have been done in any one of a dozen ways. The men have orders not to go beyond the pickets, though many do, and some are taken. Supply sleds and wagons often pass between the forts unguarded. There are settlers between the Hoosicks and the river that seem not to be molested by the enemy's Indians. Any of these might have relayed the packet. Or the Frenchman may have come to Albany itself. The thing is not impossible."

He nodded. "Yes," he said, "all that is true, but of little aid. You will be on the ground at Fort Edward and William-Henry.

Keep your eyes opened, and if you see anything suspicious report it to me at once."

"I will, my Lord," I said.

We were by then come to the wide gate where the driveway turned in to the house I had taken, and were about to turn in when a rattle of hooves and the creak of runners in the loose snow brought us up short. As we stopped, a trim cutter, drawn by a sleek grey colt, whirled in front of us and passed up the drive. In the light of the sidelamps I could make out the darkly handsome face of my cousin Hubert, framed in a fur cap and muffler.

He caught sight of us standing by the roadside and waved a greeting. I nodded and waved in return, but my Lord Howe simply looked after him, as if he had not seen him.

"Who was that?" he asked.

"Major Ferguson," I replied, "my cousin."

"Ah," he said, and gave me a peculiar sidelong glance.

I would have gone on up the drive, but he made no move. Instead he only stood there for some moments, apparently in deep thought, the while he flicked a lump of caked snow with his long stick. When, presently, he spoke I could see that he was troubled.

"Lieutenant," he said, giving me my rank as he frequently did, in contrast to so many of his brothers in the regular establishment, who would not recognize that provincial officers had any standing at all. "Lieutenant, there is a thing I must speak of, though it is against my policy to meddle in those personal affairs of others which do not concern me."

He hesitated a moment.

"You may speak freely to me, sir," I said.

"I am sure of it," he replied. "I have taken a liking to you, sir, and am pleased to think of you as a friend. I should be something less than a friend if I did not tell you something of what is in my mind."

"I am grateful for your friendship, my Lord," I said, "though I assure you I can conceive of no necessity for you to prove it."

He gave me that peculiar hesitant glance again.

"Can you not?" he demanded. "Can it be you have no idea?" He saw that I was puzzled, and went on. "No, by God, I believe you have not!"

"Sir," I said, "you are keeping me in suspense."

I laughed, but he did not smile. Instead he glanced up the driveway after the cutter, towards the house.

"Well," he said, at last, "I will not say too much, for you might not thank me if I did. But this much I must say: It often happens that while we may see clearly, either from a distance or after the passage of time has lent perspective, those things which contribute to our lives, frequently we are unable to see them when they happen because we are too close. Sometimes this blindness to our own affairs brings ruin to our whole life. May I suggest, sir, as a friend, that you look about you, at your personal affairs and see if there is not something there that demands your immediate attention? I believe you will see what I mean if only you will look."

I was completely puzzled, for I could think of nothing in my life that could draw such an explosion of confidential advice from anyone, much less from my Lord Howe, who had always struck me as the most balanced of young men.

"I am afraid I do not understand you, sir," I said, "unless you will give me some more direct hint. What is it that I must look for in my personal affairs? What is the disaster that threatens?"

He saw that I was smiling, and thumped his stick savagely upon the banked-up snow.

"No," he said with decision, "I will say no more. Already perhaps, I have said more than I should. The hint I have given is enough, if you will consider it, to open your eyes to a condition that is obvious to all the rest of us. As the person most deeply concerned, once you learn what it is, you will thank me for going no further into it. It is possible that in spite of all the evidence I may be mistaken; and if this is so, no harm will be done. On the other hand if I were to say more it might cause an irreparable breach between us."

With that, before I could make any further query, he seized my hand and wrung it heartily.

"Good night," he said, "and good luck. My good wishes to Captain Rogers when you see him in the morning, and tell him I will accept his invitation to go on an expedition as soon as I can find the time."

He stood back abruptly and saluted me with his stick, and an instant later he was gone.

I stood for some moments, watching him hurrying back the way we had come, his long legs bobbing grotesquely in the light of the lanthorn. When he had turned the corner and disappeared from view, I walked slowly towards the house.

To say that I was puzzled would be too mild a statement. I was perplexed, bewildered, amazed, and incredulous. I could not think of anything in my life that could be the subject of such a warning. As I walked towards the house I racked my brain to think what it might be. Lord Howe had said it was plain to many, but it was not plain to me. In spite of my late illness I was by now sound in mind and body. My military career, if not brilliant, had at least been consistent, and was sufficiently satisfactory to my superiors for promotion. I liked good rum as well as the next man, but I took no more than most of my fellows. Indeed, if anything, I might be considered abstemious by comparison with many. I could not think of a time when drink had made me obnoxious. As for my family life, all seemed serene there. True, of late my wife and I had grown something indifferent to each other; yet I could not believe that this was obvious to an outsider. Nevertheless, I made a mental reservation to remedy that as soon as possible; a word to Dorcas, a reassurance of my affection, and I felt sure that all would go smoothly there once more. I blamed myself for having neglected her. Still I could not think it was this to which my Lord Howe had reference. As I climbed the stoop I was no nearer the solution of the problem.

I found Hubert in the front hall and Dorcas upon the stairs, dressed in her best bib and tucker, with Purity putting a few final touches upon her hair.

"What's this?" I demanded, looking from one to the other. "You're not going out?"

"Yes," Dorcas replied, "we're going out."

"Didn't you get my note?" I said—none too gently, I fear, for I saw all chance to put my good resolution into effect go glimmering. "Where is that black she-devil? Can't she remember a thing?"

"Don't be such a beast, Jamie," said Dorcas, admiring herself in the hall mirror. "I got your note."

"But my last night!" I protested. "I wanted—I mean I thought—"

My voice trailed away dully. I wasn't sure just what I had thought, but I was aware of a sharp sense of disappointment.

"Oh, Jamie," Dorcas cried petulantly, "don't be a prig! You know Colonel Gage is giving a dinner tonight. He's expecting us. You can't expect us to drop out at the last moment."

She slipped into her wrap and went past me to the door, letting her finger tips brush my cheek lightly as she passed. They were halfway down the walk to the gate before a thought struck me.

"Look here," I called, "Colonel Gage isn't expecting you for an hour and a half yet. You don't have to go so early."

Dorcas laughed. "We have to call for some friends of Hubert's," she replied, and turned back to be helped into the waiting cutter. Hubert climbed in beside her and, with a wave of his hand and a flash of teeth, drove off. I shut the door and turned back to find Purity looking at me strangely. I was dashed, disappointed, and unaccountably annoyed. A variety of emotions were struggling within me, and I fear I was more than a little curt.

"Well," I snapped, "what the devil are you looking at me like that for?"

For an instant her expression was almost as though I had slapped her across the face. Then all at once she burst into tears, and fled up the stairs, leaving me staring after her in utter bewilderment.

5

I ate a solitary supper that night, for Purity did not come down to the table. Nor can it be truthfully said that at the outset I much missed her, for I was still ruffled by the events of the evening and in no mood for small talk. As the hot food warmed my vitals, however, my humour grew somewhat mellower. I had, I told myself, been overhasty. Whatever I may have felt about Dorcas' behaviour, there had been no need for me to snap at the child. I began to regret the sudden access of temper that had led me to it. Indeed, by the time I had dallied for an hour with the port I was in half a mind to go straight to her room and apologize for my boorishness. In consequence, my pleasure may be imagined when, on coming into the drawing room, I found that she had come downstairs to sit before the fire.

I went straight to her chair and leaned upon the arm.

"Purity," I said, "I spoke harshly to you before supper, and I did not mean it. I was upset. Will you forgive me?"

She did not look up at me.

"It does not matter," she said. "I know you did not mean it."

"But it does matter," I replied. "I was unjust, and I want you to know that I am sorry."

She gave me a smile then.

"Of course I will forgive you, Jamie," she said, "if it means so much. I had already forgiven you, but if you ask it I will do it again, and gladly."

I gave her shoulder an affectionate pat.

"Good lass," I said.

"I knew you were upset," she said, and looked away into the fire.

She said no more then, but sat silent, staring into the glowing embers upon the hearth, while I went to the cupboard and got down my pipe and filled it. Not until I had settled myself comfortably in a chair opposite and had a good coal going in the bowl did she give a hint of what was in her mind. Then she turned to me.

"Jamie," she asked suddenly, "what am I to do?"

"Eh?" I said, startled. "Do? What do you mean?"

"What I say," she replied simply. "What am I to do? I can't stay here for ever."

"Why not?" I demanded. "What's to keep you from staying on here? Why shouldn't you stay here as long as you want? You know Dorcas could hardly manage without you. And who'd look after the boy?"

She looked down at her hands that lay folded in her lap, but avoided meeting my eyes.

"Dorcas would not miss me," she said, "and as for young Jamie, there are nurses aplenty to be found."

"Well, what is it?" I persisted. "What makes you feel you cannot stay?"

I was struck by a sudden thought.

"Is anyone bothering you?" I demanded. "Has my cousin annoyed you?"

She laughed at that.

"He might," she said, "but I will not let him."

"The devil you say!" I exclaimed. "I shall speak to him!"

"Oh, no!" she said hastily. "Please don't. I am not afraid of him."

"Then why?" I persisted. "Why do you feel you cannot stay? Don't you like it here?"

She stopped smiling, abruptly.

"No!" she said, almost harshly. "No! I hate it! I don't belong here! Everyone treats me like a child, and I'm not a child! And I have to sit by and watch things happening without ever doing anything."

She broke off abruptly, and sat staring at the fire.

"What things do you have to watch happening?" I said, puzzled.

She started to speak, then seemed to check herself.

"Oh," she said after a moment's hesitation, "people going out, and all, while I never do anything."

It wasn't like her to care for such matters, and I had the feeling that it was not what she had started to say. But she gave me no chance to interrupt her.

"If daddy were here," she said, "I'd ask him to take me up to the fort with him."

"Nonsense!" I said. "He wouldn't do it. He couldn't. There's no place up there for women—not for your kind, anyway. Such women as are there aren't— Well, they aren't nice."

She made no reply, and I went on hastily, thinking I saw my advantage.

"I know it's hard to sit still here," I said, "not knowing what's happening or going to happen. But it can't last much longer. This year we're bound to drive the French back, and the war will be over. You wait till the end of this campaign, like a good child, and then—"

But I got no further. She stamped her foot and interrupted me with an angry exclamation.

"I'm not a child!" she stormed. "I'm not a child. I'm a woman grown, and I won't be treated like a child always!"

Looking at her then with her eyes blazing with anger, her delicately rounded breasts heaving with her emotion, and the bright colour flooding her cheeks, I realized, all at once and for the first time, that it was true. But I had always thought of her as a child, from the first day I had seen her, wide-eyed and shy as a wild thing, in my uncle's house, and it was difficult for me not to think so still.

"I'm sorry," I said lamely; "I didn't mean to upset you. You know you've always been a little girl to me—I suppose because we grew up together. I forget you've grown too."

"That's just it," she snapped pettishly. "You never do see what's happening around you."

For some reason I thought then, suddenly, of the little bird-faced major I had encountered on the road to Blairgowrie, near the Bridge of Cally, so many years since. Vigilance and caution, he had said, were next to valour the best qualities in a military man. Twice today I had been accused of lack of vigilance, or so it seemed to me. My Lord Howe had hinted at it; and now Purity came out with it boldly. But in what way I had been careless or what it was that I could have missed by it, I could not imagine.

"What do you mean by that?" I demanded.

But she avoided my eyes.

"Nothing," she said, looking away into the fire. "I was just angry. I didn't mean anything."

I looked at her for a long moment in silence, while she pursed her lips primly and studied the carpet before her with altogether too much intentness. The more I looked, the more uncomfortable she became; and the more uncomfortable she appeared, the more convinced I was that she could solve the riddle for me. At last I could bear it no longer.

"Look here!" I burst out. "You are the second one who has said much the same thing to me today."

And with that I went on to tell her what my Lord Howe had said to me that very evening.

"What do you think of that?" I concluded. "And what did you mean by what you said?"

She did not take her eyes from the carpet.

"I don't know what he meant," she said.

She was not very good at subterfuge. I could see plainly that she had a very good notion of what he had been driving at. But I could also see that she was determined to say nothing.

"But you must know what you meant yourself," I persisted.

"I only meant," she said, not once looking up at me, "that you never noticed me."

I was annoyed at her evasion, and so I missed the implication of her words.

"I thought I might at least count upon you," I said somewhat bitterly. "If you call yourself so much my friend, why do you not tell me what is this thing I ought to see for myself, instead of beating about the bush and evading all my questions?"

I had half expected to goad her into some angry retort wherewith she might let drop some hint that would solve the mystery. But I was not prepared for what happened. Scarcely were the words out of my mouth, when she burst once more into tears.

I was amazed and shocked to see that my words had such an effect upon the child—for child I still considered her in spite of myself. I grew angry with myself for my clumsiness, and cursed myself for a stupid blunderer. It occurred to me that perhaps she had not meant anything by her own words. Women, I have found, frequently speak in haste, without thought for what they are saying. Perhaps she did not know what my Lord Howe had meant. Perhaps I had misjudged her there. I remembered what she had said—that I never noticed her—and gathered from it then at least that she was lonely. And small wonder. Since her father's disappearance I was the only friend she had in the world.

I was touched. I went to her and dropped to my knees beside her chair, slipping my arm about her shoulders, and drawing her head down upon my breast, while I tried to comfort her and stop her sobbing.

"There now," I said, awkwardly trying to be soothing, "I did not mean to hurt you, Purity. You know I'm as fond of you as I am of my own sisters!"

But this, it seemed, was not the right thing to say, for at the words she only broke out in redoubled weeping, until, in desperation, I began to kiss her—the which, indeed, is the only way I have ever found to stifle a woman's sobs.

I placed my finger beneath her chin and raised her tear-stained face to mine, kissing her full upon the mouth. But no sooner had my lips touched hers than I was startled by a loud exclamation from the doorway behind me. I scrambled to my feet in some confusion and faced about, to see Dorcas standing there, her lips pursed grimly in anger, her little foot tapping at the carpet, and my cousin Hubert looming in the hallway behind her, an expression of sardonic amusement flickering across his darkly handsome face.

For an instant we faced each other in strained silence. Then, because I thought I saw what was in my wife's mind, I attempted a feeble explanation.

"The child was upset," I said.

Even in my own ears the words sounded inane and flat.

Dorcas sniffed audibly and moved a few steps into the room, her back straight and stiff, her head up, nose and chin in the air, as full of dignity and outrage as a dowager duchess whose carriage has become mired.

"She might well be upset!" said she shrilly. "The ungrateful minx! Is this the pay she gives me for my kindness? After all I have done!"

"Oh, damn my soul!" I cried impatiently. "Don't be such a fool! I've known the child near all my life. We are like brother and sister together. Would you have me stand by and see her weep without trying to comfort her? You make much of nothing, my dear!"

She turned upon me with angry eyes.

"Brother and sister, indeed!" she sneered. "You need not come your smug Scots hypocrisy on me, sir! Yon was no brotherly kiss, I'll warrant. I've eyes in my head to see with."

Up to this moment Purity had stood silent beside me, but now she dropped a small curtsy.

"'Tis one thing we all have, ma'am," she said, "eyes to see with."

At the moment it seemed to me a silly remark, for it meant exactly nothing, and I wondered that Purity could be so stupid. Yet her voice as she spoke was strong and sure, and the effect upon Dorcas was amazing. She fell back a step and went deathly white— with anger, as I thought.

"Oh!" she cried. "Such insolence!"

I looked from one to the other in utter bewilderment, for I could not couple the actions of the two women with anything that had been said. By her sudden advent into the discussion Purity seemed to have become the mistress of the situation, for she stood straight at my side, looking defiantly at Dorcas, who in turn glared back at her with fury and, I almost thought, something of fear in her eyes. Behind Dorcas, Hubert stood, darkly impassive. His handsome features were devoid of any expression as he looked at Purity. But a flicker of speculative interest showed in his eyes, and a thin ghost of a smile pulled at the corners of his mouth as he drew an enamelled box from his waistcoat pocket and helped himself, with an elaborate gesture, to a pinch of snuff.

"You will leave my house," said Dorcas in a voice so harsh with emotion that I scarcely recognized it as hers. "You will leave my house the first thing in the morning!"

"She will not!" I said, for by this time I too was become angry with all this foolishness. "I gave my word to her father that she would be well looked after in this house so long as she cared to stay, and that word I will not break, even for you."

She looked at me haughtily.

"Then I shall leave," she said, as if she were delivering an ultimatum.

But my Scotch stubbornness was aroused.

"Leave then, madam," I said, "if you will. My word has been passed and cannot be withdrawn, whatever you may do."

She looked at me as though I had slapped her across the face. "Oh!" she cried. "This is intolerable!"

She swayed a little, and I thought she might be about to faint. I started forward and held out my hand, as if to catch her, but she turned abruptly to Hubert.

"Please!" she said to him. "I do not think I could manage the stairs alone. Will you see me to my room, Hugh?"

My cousin gave me a glance that seemed to contain both triumph and amusement and lent her his arm. An instant later she swept from the room, leaning heavily upon him, and I could hear their steps as they went slowly up the stairs.

That at the time I missed entirely the implication of the whole affair seems to me now but the sheerest stupidity. Still, there are those who are kind enough to say that because of my own forthrightness I am slow to perceive duplicity in others.

When they were gone I turned ruefully to Purity.

"Well," I said, "this is a pretty kettle of fish! I fear I have not improved matters."

I had expected to see her hurt and downcast, even indignant, but I was totally unprepared for what I found. To my amazement she seemed cheerful, gay, almost pleased!

"Poor Jamie!" she said, smiling. "She will not leave you."

I had to admit the probable truth of her statement, for fond as I was still of Dorcas, I had but few illusions left concerning her, and I knew that her chiefest thought was for her own comfort. Her father had long since sold out his house and property in Portsmouth and taken to living here and there in taverns, where he found congenial company. There was slight chance that she would exchange her present luxury for such a life as that.

"But I may have done you hurt," I said. "She does not easily forget a slight, be it real or fancied. I fear she will not be pleasant with you."

She smiled. "I have no fear," she replied.

"You must not stay on my account," I said. "If you would rather leave, I will not stand in your way."

She looked at me soberly.

"Do you want me to go, Jamie?" she asked.

"Do you count me so poor a friend?" I demanded hotly. "Of course I do not!"

She laughed gaily. "Then I will stay!" she cried.

And with that she leaned forward quickly and kissed me full upon the mouth. In the next instant she was skipping across the room.

"Good night!" she called.

She was laughing at me over her shoulder, not watching where she went, so that she did not see Hubert come into the doorway until she ran full into his arms.

For one startled instant she stood there in his embrace, for she would have fallen if he had not caught her. Then, before she could wrench free, he bent his head, and with a mocking expression kissed her lightly upon the cheek.

With an exclamation she drew back and, so swiftly that my eye could not follow the movement, slapped him a stinging blow in the face. In the next moment she had slipped past him and was running up the stairs, while he stood below in the doorway rubbing his cheek and staring after her with an expression of rueful admiration upon his dark features.

"Hoity-toity!" he exclaimed. "The minx has spirit as well as looks. I envy you, my lad!"

He cocked a supercilious eyebrow at me and chuckled as he took a pinch of snuff.

"You may save your envy," I growled at him sourly, for I found myself suddenly unaccountably furious with him. "There is naught save friendship 'twixt Mistress Purity and me."

His finely plucked eyebrows went up unbelievingly.

"So?" he drawled. "In that case I might have a try for her myself. She'd be a dainty piece, I'll warrant you!"

"Oh," I cried furiously, "get out! Get out!"

He laughed and took up his hat from the table.

"Very well, sweet coz," he said, and made me a sardonic leg. "I leave. Sleep well, for only sleep will improve that vile temper of yours!"

And he went out, laughing hugely at his little joke.

For full a minute I stood staring after him, unable to move for my fury. Then, as my blood began to flow less hot, I went to the sideboard and poured myself a generous drink of brandy to remove a foul taste from my mouth.

(1 I confess it was not without misgiving that I left Albany the next morning with Rogers. I had experienced Dorcas' temper in times gone by, and, though I was shamed to admit it even to myself, I did not put it past her to work out her spite upon the defenceless Purity. I might have spared myself the worry, however, for though Dorcas wrote to me no more frequently than before, Purity kept me constantly in touch with affairs in Albany, and, if her reports were to be trusted, the matter was not again mentioned.

The winter passed quietly enough for us at the forts, with little to upset the routine of scout and fatigue. Immediately upon my arrival at Edward I was ordered up to join my company—under Stark, now a captain—at Fort William-Henry, where we sat through the long winter evenings secure behind the log walls listening to the booming of the ice outside upon the lake.

Only once were we shaken from this customary rut. This was towards the end of March, when a warm spell had cleared the ice of snow, and a sentry making his rounds upon the walls spied the flicker of a fire some distance down the lake. Scouts sent down to investigate returned with the news that a large body of the enemy were encamped beyond the point. Our own numbers were not above four hundred, officers included, and as the reports estimated the enemy at something over a thousand, Major Eyre, in command at the fort, deemed it the better part of valour to hold us all behind the walls and await developments. Our company of Rangers was called into the fort from the cabins which we occupied by the lake shore, and assigned to somewhat cramped quarters in the barracks with the regulars—a fact which did not endear them to us. A messenger was dispatched posthaste to Fort Edward to warn the garrison there of our position. And everything was put in readiness for a siege, with the garrison divided in two parts, each taking watch and watch while the others slept upon their arms.

It was past midnight before we heard the tramp of feet approaching along the ice. Evidently the enemy believed themselves unobserved, for they came on, judging from the sound of their approach—it being too dark to see—in massed column. We waited until they were close upon us, and then at a command from the major, poured a volley into them from all the cannon on that side of the fort.

Whether our fire had any killing effect upon them or only frightened them, we never knew. We heard no cries or groans, but only, after our ears stopped ringing from that first sharp thunderous clap, the thud of feet retreating in haste. They did not again molest us in that night.

The next day, however, they appeared again upon the ice, and we made out their numbers to be in the neighbourhood of fifteen hundred. About midmorning they filed off into the woods about us, being sure first to keep at a safe distance, and then under cover of the trees closed in to the edge of the woods, whence they kept up a continual fire of musketry throughout the day until nightfall without any other effect than to waste their ammunition while we sat snug behind the stout walls.

That night they came on as before along the ice, and again we drove them back with the cannon. A little later, however, a flicker of flame warned us that they had gotten to the battoes stored along the shore. A party of regulars sallied out in an attempt to save the boats, but it was too late, and they were forced to return to the fort with three wounded. We managed, however, with careful shooting, aided by the light of the flames from the boats, to keep them from firing the storehouses and our own Rangers' cabins lying outside the fort, though we could not prevent their setting fire to two sloops which lay icebound in the lake.

The next day being the Sabbath, they paraded for our benefit at a safe distance from the fort, showing their numbers to advantage and carrying scaling ladders to signify their determination to assault. After an hour of this they sent down an officer under a flag of truce to offer us terms: safety as prisoners of war if we surrendered, or slaughter by their Indians if we would not. To this Major Eyre replied that we would hold the fort to the last man, and the French officer returned to his superiors with the jeers of the garrison ringing in his ears.

Their whole force then advanced openly to the attack, and we made ready for a fight, for there was little question in our minds that if they came on boldly they could overpower us by sheer weight of numbers. Apparently, however, they had not the stomach to face our guns, for they stopped at a safe distance, seeing their bluff to have failed, and loosed a volley of musketry in our direction which fell far short, the balls skittering upon the ice of the lake and lodging in snowbanks along the shore. So contemptuous were we of this exhibit that we did not even fire a reply.

That night they crept in again and fired the hospital and the sawmill, as well as two storehouses that stood close against the walls of the fort, so that for a time we were put to it to keep the barracks within the fort from taking light from the flying sparks. But by midnight the fires had died down, and it had begun to snow heavily.

All the following day it snowed, and the enemy did not stir; but towards dawn on the following morning they made one last attempt to burn the remaining boats, cabins, and storehouses. They succeeded in firing a sloop which stood in stocks near the shore, as well as a number of our cabins. But we caught them with a heavy fire before they were able to get clear of the blaze and stretched several of their number in the deep snow.

On Wednesday, four days after their first appearance, the dawn came up grey and cold, with the snow lying three feet deep upon the ice. For a time we feared another attack; but as the light strengthened a shout went up from the lookout upon the walls.

"They've given up!" he shouted. "They're going home!"

Those of us who were within earshot of his call rushed up to the walls and looked where he pointed. There, already far northward down the lake, we could make out a long winding line of bobbing black dots, pushing their tortured way through the hindering snow. In an hour there were but a few of them to be seen, and a little later we had only the blackened embers of the burned boats and buildings, and the few bright stains of blood, already turning dark in the snow upon the lake, to remind us of what had happened. The enemy's casualties we could not know, but that they had been heavy we were certain. Our own loss was but seven wounded; all but two of these but slightly.

It was not long after this that Lord Howe came out for his promised expedition. Rogers had been ill with the smallpox since before the attack on the fort, and as Stark was away at the time with beating orders, it fell to me to take him out. I took him down the lake with sixteen men in boats, the ice being just out, and landed upon the eastern shore, whence I took him to the top of the mountain overlooking the fort at Carillon and let him spy out the enemy's positions for himself. He was pleased as a boy with the undertaking, and overjoyed when, in the return march, I showed him our method of moving in extended order and demonstrated to him the way in which we scattered when an enemy pressed hard upon our heels.

I should have liked to talk with him further about the warning he had given me in Albany, but I found him a changed man in the field—not a martinet, to be sure, but none the less a strict disciplinarian and a stickler for military etiquette—so that I did not feel it my place to mention the matter; nor did he speak of it himself. Once we were back at the fort he congratulated me upon the way I had led the expedition and spoke enthusiastically of the Rangers. He reassured me of his esteem, indeed, but not once did he mention the thought that was uppermost in my mind. Two days later he shook hands with me and took his leave, to return to Albany; and though I was to see him again on several occasions, it was always in his official capacity, and I was not destined to talk with him as a friend again for almost a year.

It was the middle of April before Rogers returned to duty; and not long afterwards orders came for all but one company of Rangers and nearly all the regulars to go down to New York. This was a surprise, for we had been of the general opinion that a determined attempt on Ticonderoga and Crown Point would be made that summer.* We soon learned, however, that this was a mistake, my Lord Loudoun's plan being to leave the forts under a skeleton guard, while the main force of the army was directed against Louisbourg.

However much we disapproved such a plan, which must leave our northern boundaries open to attack, it was not for us to question it; and consequently towards the end of the month we set out, bag and baggage, for the coast.

* 1757.

We went down fast, making the march from Fort Edward to Albany in two days, and embarking the next morning for New York. In Albany I had only time to look in upon my family and inform them of the new orders, before I was whisked away again; but from all indications Dorcas and Purity had patched up their differences, and all was serene once more. In the morning when we cast off, both Dorcas and Purity, accompanied by Hubert, drove down to the river's edge in my cousin's chair to wave me farewell; and, the last I saw of them, Hubert was helping the ladies back into their conveyance while we scudded off to southward before a stiff breeze.

We might have spared our haste. It was near the end of June before we were finally embarked upon the transports. In the meantime the command of the company came down to me through Mr. Stark's falling ill in his turn with the smallpox, and I was put to it to keep the men, who had scarce laid eyes on a civilized habitation in the year past, out of mischief. In the end we came through it better than I had expected, for though we gained a reputation among the Yorkers as thieves and hellions, when we sailed we had lost but six by desertion and three by arrest, while the number of broken crowns and aching pates among us was less by proportion than among the regulars.

There is no need for me here to recite the details of that heart-breaking campaign. The blundering, the stupidity, the utter blindness of our commanders in that summer is a matter of history. On the first of July we landed at Halifax. On the third the bulk of the Rangers were set to hay-making at Schitzcook, while the remainder stood guard, and the rest of the army passed their time in drilling or hoeing vegetables at Halifax.

For a full month we lay thus in idleness, doing only what we might better have been doing at home; twelve thousand men under arms with nothing better to do than twiddle their thumbs and fall sick like flies of smallpox and the flux. Even the officers of the staff grew restless. Sir Charles Hay was placed in arrest and stripped of his rank, for remarking that the crown's money was being wasted on cabbages and parades. Rogers himself was twice reprimanded severely for leading out scouts without orders, only to take the taste of inactivity out of his men's mouths.

But the fault lay not wholly with the command. Our fleet, without which we could do naught, did not arrive until near the middle of July. Then we were hampered by the fogs that lay low over the coast. Day after day everything lay under a dank grey blanket, that hid even the dark green walls of spruce that hemmed us in to shoreward, and covered land and sea for miles to north and south. So long as the coast was cloaked in fog, how were we to know if the enemy were prepared to receive us? Our scouting craft could gain no advantage.

At last, however, a little past the first of August the order came down for the troops to embark. A wave of excitement ran through the ranks. The fog still lay thick across the harbour, and a dank drizzle fell; but even this could not damp the men's enthusiasm. Here was action at last.

All day we loaded—men, arms, ammunition, and supplies— until at last, by nightfall, all was in readiness. We lay in the harbour that night prepared to sail with the dawn; but though the morning found the rain stopped and the fog lifted somewhat, still we did not move.

What delayed us, I never learned; but whatever it was, it was providential. About midmorning the signal to sail was flown from the flagship. One by one the anchors came up, dripping mud, from the harbour bottom. White sails bellied in the wind, and the great ships came about, falling into line as neatly as a company of soldiers on parade, to follow the heels of the flagship out the harbour mouth.

Scarce had we cleared the point of land outside, however, when from our place on the fourth ship in line we spied a tiny sloop come bearing down for the Admiral's ship to come about upon her weather side and hang there a moment while some words were exchanged. A moment later a boat put over from the sloop and danced across the green tumbling water towards the great high-sided man-o'-war. I heard a sailor behind me grumble.

"What's the matter?" I asked him.

"'Twill be messages for the Admiral," he replied. "More delay, you mark my words."

I mark his words as prophetic. Sure enough, scarce had the sloop's boat touched her side when a pennant fluttered at the flagship's masthead; and as one craft the line of ships came about and lay with heads to the breeze, their white sails flapping idly.

A moment later another flag went up, and in reply the chains thundered from half a hundred hawsepipes as the anchors sought bottom once again.

An hour, two hours we lay there wondering what it was all about. Then, in response to a third signal, the anchors came up once more, and the flagship, sweeping down along the line, headed us all back into the harbour again.

That night we lay bewildered upon the ships, and in the morning marched ashore again to set up our camp where we had left it. Not until the third day afterwards, however, did we learn what had so abruptly upset our plans. The sloop, it seemed, came from Newfoundland, bearing letters taken from a French ship lately captured. From these it appeared that Louisbourg was prepared for our coming. Twenty-two ships of the line and a number of frigates lay in her harbour—a total of near fifteen hundred cannon—and seven thousand men lay behind the thick walls of the great fortress. Though we had men and artillery to outnumber them on land, our ships were too few. With such an armada they would have destroyed us before ever we could set a man ashore. Even the dullest among us could see that the projected expedition against Louisbourg was at an end, and all our summer's labours were lost.

Another fortnight we were held in camp, and then once more embarked upon the transports. It was on the day of our embarkation that we were all saddened by the news of Dick Rogers' death by smallpox at Fort William-Henry. We had suffered much with this pestilence during the summer, and each company had had its share of losses, though casualties among the officers had been few. This was but the second time one of our captains had been carried off, and as he had been well liked we were all distressed at his end. Somehow, I believe, we should not have felt so badly had death come to him in the course of his duty; but to go out in this way seemed to us horrible in the extreme. To Rogers of course it was a crushing blow, for, though he had other brothers, Dick had been his favourite. He tried his best to hide his grief, but we were all well aware of it, and carried ourselves accordingly.

On the day after embarkation the entire fleet got under way once more, passing out one by one through the broad channel to the open sea, where the men-o'-war swung northward towards Cape Breton, where Admiral Holbourne was determined to attempt to lure the French out to some sort of engagement, and the great covey of transports turned southward, under the convoy of a few frigates.

We stood southward in a long line down the coast for two days until we came in sight of Cape Sable. There a small sloop came winging northward to hail my Lord Loudoun's flagship and put a boat aboard her. How the news circulated among these widely separated vessels, I have no way of knowing, but within the hour every man in the fleet knew that she was a dispatch boat from Governor Pownal of Massachusetts Bay, and that she carried important news.

All morning and a good part of the afternoon, we lined the decks, eyes on the flagship, speculating idly on the nature of the tidings. Then about midafternoon a pennant ran to her masthead summoning the ranking officers of each ship forward for council. As there were none but Rangers aboard us, this meant that Rogers must go up, and accordingly a boat was put over the side for him. A half-hour later we saw him clamber up over the great bulging side of the flagship and drop across her bulwarks.

Through the afternoon the enforced idleness of shipboard bred rumours like flies. We were ordered to put about and sail up the Saint Lawrence against Quebec. We were to land at the mouth of the Kennebec and proceed overland against that mighty stronghold. A French fleet had attacked New York, and now lay between us and Boston. And, most farfetched of all, for the word of it could scarcely have come to us through the Governor of Massachusetts, Admiral Holbourne had met and defeated the French fleet outside Louisbourg, and we were to put about and take the fortress. But not one of these hinted at the truth.

About dusk Rogers returned, and as he came over the side his face was mottled with anger and black as a thundercloud. He ignored all our questions and went striding savagely across the deck, the curious throng opening a path before him as he went, falling back on either hand, as if the men by some sixth sense knew that it would be dangerous to impede him now.

"Officers to my quarters," he bawled over his shoulder as he paused at the hatchway, and the next instant dived below.

In the tiny cubbyhole that was his cabin below he sat in dour silence, clenching and unclenching his fists, until all his officers had crowded within. Then he spoke in a voice that was low yet vibrant with his anger.

"William-Henry has fallen," he said.

We looked at one another in dismay. But he did not wait for our questions.

"Montcalm attacked with all his force on the fourth," he said in the same low, curiously hoarse voice, "Colonel Monro was forced to surrender on the ninth. According to the terms the garrison was to be escorted in safety to Fort Edward, after they had laid down their arms. These terms were disregarded, and the savages set upon them, as soon as our men had been disarmed."

An exclamation of horror ran round the room.

"Was there no relief from Fort Edward?" I asked.

Rogers turned his puffy eyes upon me and stared for a long moment.

"None!" he said, finally, and his very tone was an indictment.

Someone in the back of the room cursed.

"But surely Colonel Webb—" I began.

But Rogers made a gesture of impatience.

"Colonel Webb did not stir from the safety of the fort," he spat. "Nor would he risk any of his force. The man's the rankest coward ever came out of England!"

A growl of assent went up from the others in the cabin.

"The sick and wounded," Rogers went on, "were butchered in their beds, and the Indians set upon the rest as soon as they marched out of the camp and took the road for Fort Edward. Those who could escaped to the woods, but hundreds were slaughtered in cold blood."

I had a sudden sharp vision of the French and Indian horde moving southward. If the account were true, Webb would be but slight hindrance to them, and once Fort Edward fell naught but a few small posts stood between them and Albany. I think the same thought occurred to others in the room; but Rogers gave us no opportunity for questions.

"Even the dead," he said, "were not left in peace, but were dug up and scalped!"

It was these words that betrayed the deep personal source of his bitter fury, for if this were so his brother's body must have been among those thus violated. None of us cared to speak at that moment. Rogers rose to his feet, his great head near brushing the low rafters of the cabin, his face dark and bitter in the smoky light of the swaying lamp. He raised his fists to the ceiling and turned his eyes to heaven.

"By God!" he thundered. "They shall suffer for this!"

And strange to say, his words were prophetic, though not in a way that he could foresee; for in the spring we heard that many of the western Indians had taken the pox from those poor mutilated bodies and carried it away to the plains and forests where it became a scourge upon their people, wreaking vengeance a thousandfold upon them for the atrocities committed that dark day.

2

It has long been a thought of mine that it takes disaster, or something near it, to arouse in the British mind recognition of a sorry state of affairs. Certainly it was so in this case. Few, even in the provinces, let alone in high places at home, realized how badly our cause was faring until the fall of William-Henry shocked them to it. But that calamity was enough to bring even the most obtuse of cabinet ministers to the certainty of what must befall unless immediate and potent action were taken.

Thus, even before fall, forces were put in motion that were eventually to result in the utter rout of the enemy; but we in the colonies knew nothing of it until spring. So that all through the winter of 1757–8 there raged a controversy, in the northern settlements at least, the elements of which were impotent fury, disgust, bewilderment, fear, and black despair. There were those hotheads who would rush forward and lay siege to the French strongholds with no more preparation than to grab musket and powder horn from behind the door in passing. There were those who held that nothing could stop the French. Let them once open a way to Albany, they said, and they would pour a horde of savages upon us, and the whole coast from Maine to the Carolinas would echo their savage whoops and the groans of their victims. There were those who would have us drive out our British allies and take matters in our own hands. And there were those who only stood and wrung their hands and cried that they knew not what to do.

But in the midst of all this clatter of dissenting voices there was one point upon which all, or nearly all, agreed—and this was in the placing of the blame. Wherever one went Lord Loudoun's name was to be heard upon men's lips. Some cursed him for a craven. Some damned him for a fool. But few would stand up and defend him.

To my mind, weighing all the evidence, this seemed grossly unfair. Lord Loudoun may have blundered in some respects—such as in leaving the craven Webb in command in his absence. But for the most part he had but followed his orders. It was not Lord Loudoun's fault that news of the plan leaked out of London and found its way to Paris in time to put the three French fleets in Louisbourg harbour before the end of June, as we later learned had happened. It was not his fault that Admiral Holbourne had been unable to sail from England until it was too late, and then with an insufficient force. But for these accidents Louisbourg must surely have fallen before us. As for his personal bravery, even if it had not been already proven his conduct in this affair should have acquitted him of those charges. Only that spring Admiral Byng had been tried, sentenced, and executed on a trumped-up charge of cowardice before Minorca: a fate which Loudoun must have shared had the charges against him been true. His orders were to attack either Louisbourg or Quebec at all costs. That he chose, in the face of what had happened to Byng, to disregard these orders when it became apparent that neither venture could succeed, should have relieved him of all stigma. Yet there were few in the colonies would see it so, and only his recall in the following spring stilled the outcry against him.

In the meantime the confusion on the frontier was indescribable. Why the French did not follow up their advantage is a mystery. Certainly they would have met with little resistance from Webb. But perhaps they did not know this, or overestimated his strength. Had they chosen to go forward they could have taken Albany with but little difficulty and, with the key to the Hudson in their hands, have made their own terms and ended the war then and there. That they did not is a matter of history. Within a fortnight of the fall of William-Henry, Montcalm was back in Ticonderoga with all his force, and the English scouting parties were once again pushing northward to the blackened ruins that were all that remained of the fort on the shores of Lake George.

We landed in New York in the midst of cheers, for the city

that had reviled us for a pack of thieves and kidnappers * welcomed us back as protectors, no one then being certain what the French would do next. Almost immediately the Rangers were re-embarked on sloops and sent up the river to Albany, whence we were marched overland to Fort Edward. Indeed, so swiftly did we move that I had not even the opportunity to notify my family of my passing; and I was out scouting towards Ticonderoga before ever they were aware that I was no longer in Nova Scotia.

Conditions in the camp at Fort Edward were appalling. Most of the militia, for whom Webb had called too late, were come in and were lying idle there. All were disgruntled and grumbling, the men claiming—and rightly, to my mind—that they had come out to fight, and that if they were not to fight they should be allowed to return to their harvests, then rotting in the fields. Some few were sent back. But most were kept on despite their protests. Hundreds deserted in disgust, and on one occasion an entire regiment of Yorkers, attempting to desert in a body, was fired upon, and the entire camp was placed on the verge of mutiny until the regulars were called out and order was restored at the point of the bayonet. Most of the men had neither tents nor blankets nor pots to cook in, and those who had these were forced to share them. Discipline, as always in such times, grew harsh, and the thwack of the cat and the screams of the flogged men ran continually through the streets of the camp.

Fortunately for me, I learned of these things more through hearsay than experience, for I was kept almost constantly out on scout from the moment of my arrival. Nor was this an easy assignment, for with the French in such numbers at Ticonderoga they were extremely active, and buzzed about our outposts like flies, attacking our pickets, lying in ambush upon the road between Albany and the fort, and making raids southward into the settlements. For a time there was some talk of a counterattack. But by the time anything could be agreed upon it was too late, and in November the bulk of the troops were drawn off for the winter, and we settled once more to our cold-weather routine.

* Loudoun had surrounded the city with regulars on the eve of his departure and sent press gangs through the streets to fill the crews of the transports, which had been sadly depleted by wholesale desertions to privateers, who were bringing in many valuable prizes.

Strange as it may seem, in all this time I heard but little from my family, and, but for Purity's occasional notes, in which she expressed concern for the state of my health and wardrobe but was extremely laconic as to news, I should have been completely in the dark concerning them. The years had not improved Dorcas as a letter writer. Nor, I fear, was I much better; though, indeed, I had an excellent excuse, being kept far too busy for scribbling. It was as well for my peace of mind that I had faith in Purity's word, for when she wrote that all went quietly and there was little to report beyond that Dorcas had bought a new pair of gloves, or little James Hubert had taken his first steps, I accepted it without question and went to my work with a mind free of worries. As for my tiff with Dorcas, on the last night before my departure, I had completely forgotten it, and had anyone asked me I would have said that she had too.

Despite my preoccupation, however, there is little to be told of the winter's campaign. Until November the enemy stayed in full force at Ticonderoga and kept their scouting parties out constantly, so that a Ranger's life became a hazardous one: scarce a scout went out but fell in with them, and more often than not we were outnumbered. If the odds were at all even and the ground favourable, we were like to stand and fight, so that there was not a man of us but soon became adept in the art of bush warfare. But we ran as often as we fought, and this was good for us, too, for we learned what is important to a soldier almost above all else —to retreat in good order. If it was possible to do so, on these occasions, we preferred to scatter and meet again at some designated spot, as has been described. But frequently we were surprised so suddenly that this was not possible, and on these occasions it was our practice to form in two ranks, always taking advantage of such cover as the ground afforded. Then, if it were possible to hold our ground at all, the front rank would fire and fall down, reloading while the rear advanced and repeated the manœuvre. If, on the other hand, we were forced to retreat, the front fired and fell back, reloading as they went, while the rear, in their turn, stood, fired, and fell back. In this manner such a constant fire was kept up upon the enemy that frequently they were unable to come forward in the face of it, and a few men might hold off a large party until the coming of darkness could relieve them and enable them to scatter. Indeed, so successful were these tactics that Rogers embodied them in a set of "Rules of Conduct for the Ranging Service," which was adopted as a basis of training, first for a group of officers, volunteers from the regulars, which Lord Loudoun sent up to Rogers for instruction in this method of war, and finally for several of the light regiments which underwent a drastic reorganization under the recommendations of Lord Howe, Lord Loudoun, and General Amherst.

About the time that these gentlemen came to us, my Lord Howe also paid us a visit, and went with Rogers upon a scout from which he returned well satisfied. At that time he was but just come back from leading a belated relief to the German settlements upon the Mohawk, and I myself heard him say that, had he had but an hundred Rangers at his disposal upon that occasion, he could have caught Beletre and his savages at work there and prevented much of the havoc which they wrought upon the defenceless settlers.

After my Lord Howe had gone back to Albany we settled quickly enough to the winter routine: a dull round of scout and report, rest and scout, a business so monotonous as to grow tiresome in the extreme. Indeed, though I was out almost daily, either with my own detachment or under the command of Stark or Rogers, from early November until the end of March, only twice did anything occur worth recounting here: the first for what seemed to me an opportunity lost; and the second for the beating we received.

About the middle of December we were ordered out, with a party of some 150 men, to reconnoitre the fort at Ticonderoga, and to get such information as we might of the enemy's activities and designs. Colonel Haviland—the same with whom I had clashed so sharply at the Schuylers' in the matter of light troops versus heavy for this type of war—was in command at Fort Edward, and though he sneered openly at our scouts, I noticed that he kept us out regularly. Indeed, it was by his orders that we took the field upon this occasion.

Rogers took his own company and Stark's, and set out at once on receipt of his orders for Lake George. As Stark's lieutenant, I was naturally one of the party, though I should have preferred to stay at the fort, toasting myself by the fire, for I had come back but the day before from a scout to South Bay, and was heartily tired of all this marching in and out.

We went that day as far as the halfway post, that had stood on the road to Fort William-Henry, and there lay for the night. Until this moment we had been experiencing unseasonably warm weather. But no sooner had we left the fort than it turned suddenly cold, with a blustering north wind, and began to snow. By dark it had fallen three inches, and in the morning we awoke to find ourselves near buried beneath a foot and half of it.

As is always the case when the seasons go awry, some of the men had not prepared themselves for the inevitable. Upon our waking in the morning Rogers lined us up and made a hasty inspection, with the result that eight men were found unfit to go on, six of them having lightened their packs by leaving out their blankets, while the other two were weakened by the flux. These men were sent back, with orders for the punishment of those who had come ill equipped, while the rest of us pursued our journey northwards.

That day the snow stopped, and though the slaty sky hung low above our heads and the wind droned dismally in the trees, we were comparatively comfortable. At night, however, the temperature began to drop steadily, and by morning the cold was bittersharp and the wind cut through even our thickest clothing like a knife. By night of the third day eleven men of Stark's company and eight of Rogers' had frosted their feet or fingers or faces and were unfit to go on. Rogers, who was still bitter at his brother's death and warmed by the spirit of vengeance, cursed them for a pack of old women, unfit to serve with men, and sent them back. The next morning we pushed on again, our numbers reduced to 123, officers and men together.

We lost no more men from frostbite, although the weather remained bitterly cold through all the time we were out. As the lake was not yet frozen over, we had to march along the shore; a slow task, for the brush was thick and the footing in the deep snow—we had no snowshoes, having left these behind—was treacherous. Nevertheless, though we went but slowly, we came in good time to our objective, and lay within a hundred rods of the fort, upon a little knoll, this being Christmas Eve.

About an hour after we had taken up our position a serjeant of marines * passed up the road from the fort going towards the

* The Troupes de la Marine were regulars attached to the naval establishment and recruited in Canada.

mill, and was gathered in. It being my party that took the man, I led him at once to Rogers, who began to question him closely as to the forces both at Ticonderoga and at Crown Point. At first the fellow was surly; but when Rogers offered him rum, and he saw that no harm would come to him if he behaved himself, his tongue loosened and he told us that there were at that moment but four hundred in garrison at Ticonderoga and not more than a hundred and seventy-five at Crown Point. Monsieur de Montcalm, he said, was in Montreal; and he added that he did not know if the French meant to attack the English forts during the winter, but that a number of Indians were expected as soon as the ice would hold them to plague the English, and that their bakers at the fort were, even then, busy baking bread for them.

When I heard how small was their garrison I could not help exclaiming. Rogers looked at me.

"Well?" he said. "I suppose you're thinking a thousand men could take the forts, eh?"

"Say seven hundred," I replied, for it was exactly my thought. "Why, 'tis the opportunity of a lifetime! If we could but get Colonel Haviland to send the men up, Ticonderoga and Crown Point, too, could be ours before ever Montcalm in Montreal knew what was happening."

Rogers' eyes flashed, but he grinned sourly and spat when I mentioned Haviland.

"That louse!" he said. "Look ye, I agree 'tis an opportunity not to be missed, but d'ye think Haviland 'd have aught to do with it? Seven hundred's half his garrison. Would he take the responsibility of sending so many out without authority from his superiors? And how many Frenchmen d'ye think 'd be here by then, eh?"

Even then it was plain from his tone that he had small use for Haviland; but I doubt if even he was aware of the feud that was to spring up between them before the winter was over. For my part my enthusiasm was not so easily damped.

"We might try it," I said. "Give me two men, and I'll have the word to Haviland by tomorrow night."

He cocked an unbelieving eye at me.

"Would ye fly?" he said, and before I could answer went on. "No. 'Tis out of the question. Even if you made it (which I doubt you could) and if Haviland ordered the men out (which I doubt he would), you'd need a week to get 'em back here. And what would I be feeding the men in the meantime?"

"But—" I began.

But he cut me short with an imperious gesture.

At the same moment a man came up from the group that lay along the trail below. Rogers looked at him inquiringly.

"There's a hunter on the trail," the man reported, "going towards the fort."

Rogers was on his feet in an instant.

"We may not take the fort," he said, "but we'll have some fun with 'em."

He turned to me.

"Go down," he said, "and chase yon hunter. Mind you don't take him till you've reached the edge of the woods. There show yourselves and shoot off a few guns to let 'em know you're there. See if you can draw some of 'em out."

I was away at once, for this was an order, and I saw what was in his mind. If we could draw some of them out we would divide their forces, and if we divided them enough, even so small a command as ours might contrive some means of taking the fort.

I put my men onto the trail upon the hunter's heels, who, as soon as he caught sight of us, ran straightway towards the fort as if the devil were after him. He was a squat fellow, however, and not a fast runner, so that I had small difficulty in doing as I was bid. We let him gain the clearing and go a few steps towards the fort, and then we fell upon him and carried him to earth with much shouting and yelling and banging of muskets.

After a few moments of this horseplay we picked him up out of the snow and rushed him back to the shelter of the woods. There we found Rogers come down with the rest of the company, lying ready among the trees, doubled up in laughter.

We were doomed to disappointment, however, for our ruse did not work. They must have heard us and observed what we did, but not a man ventured out from behind the protecting walls. As soon as it became apparent that they did not mean to stir out in pursuit, we set about finding what damage we might do to them, setting fire to two sheds and several large stacks of wood which they had collected against the winter. Late in the afternoon we discovered a pen containing nearly a score of cattle, which we slaughtered, hoping thereby to embarrass them some-what for provisions. As I gazed upon this scene of carnage, a thought occurred to me, and I sought out Rogers.

"You could feed the men for two weeks upon that meat," I said.

But he shook his head at me so sharply that I did not persist. His reasons were doubtless sufficient, for in such matters he was not often mistaken. Nevertheless, I could not but regret what seemed to me a lost opportunity.

We hung about the fort, thereafter, until darkness shut in and made it impossible to accomplish any further damage. One party, under Stark, made an attempt to close in and burn the houses that stood close under the south wall of the fort, but the enemy firing off their cannon drove them back, and an hour or so later we began our homeward march, arriving, three days later, at Fort Edward.

Rogers' guess, as it proved, was better than mine, for despite his report of the scanty numbers of the French garrisons at Crown Point and Ticonderoga, nothing was done. Rogers was bitter about it, and blamed Haviland, holding that he was remiss in his duty. Indeed, he blamed the unfortunate colonel and his kind —Braddock and Abercrombie and Webb and the other old army men who would not see that conditions here were different—for all the failures of the war. Nor was he in the least reticent to say so.

"What can you expect?" he would bellow across his rum of an evening in the officers' common room at the fort. "What can you expect when hidebound dummies in scarlet and gold lace are set to the command of men? We run their errands and pull their chestnuts, and act as eyes and ears. We tell 'em when the French have got their britches down. But do they act? Not they! They sit about upon their powdered arses and say the weather doesn't suit 'em or the flies are too thick. And when someone at court de-mands to know why something isn't being done, they holler it's the damned provincials can't be got to do a thing! My God!"

Of such charges as these, of course, Haviland in his capacity as commander of the garrison could take no official notice, if only for the sake of dignity, and the more particularly so since Rogers was careful to name no names, but only to speak by innuendo.

Nevertheless, it was plain enough at whom his gibes were aimed, and I should not have been in the least surprised had the colonel chosen to disregard the second article of the seventh section of the articles of war, which forbade duelling, and called him out; which of course would have made a very pretty scandal indeed.

Instead of this he let it be known unofficially and in private, though he was well aware that it would get about and, indeed, so intended, that he considered himself a gentleman—which he was in the strict sense of the word only—and, as such, not bound in honour to make any reply to such a one as Rogers, who was but a low fellow. At the same time he was not surprised, he said, to hear what Rogers had to say. Everyone knew what sly dogs these provincials were. They screamed to the crown for help against the French and Indians, and when it was sent refused to cooperate, even expecting the crown to bear the full expense of the war down to the last farthing. When, he went on, they did take the field under protest they made the world's worst soldiers, cowardly, undependable, insubordinate, and dirty; and the worst of them, the most undisciplined, the most thievish, the most mutinous and rascally of the lot, were the independent companies of Rangers, commanded, if command it could be called, by that arch rogue who, everyone knew, had only joined the army to escape a charge of counterfeiting—Captain, as he called himself, Rogers. Moreover, said he somewhat as an afterthought, it was a well established fact that these so-called Rangers shirked their duty. When sent out upon scouts they were known to go only so far as an island in Lake George, where they lay about in idleness for the required length of time, and then returned with falsified reports to account for their activities.

When a report of this reached Rogers' ears he flew into such a towering rage that it was only with difficulty that we restrained him from going to the fort to give the other a thorough drubbing with his bare fists.

This was but the beginning of a quarrel between the two men that was remarkable for its bitterness, and which lasted throughout the war. Whenever they met they snarled insults at each other, and I am firmly of the belief that blood would have been shed on several occasions had not others, less hotheaded, been present to separate them.

Such a hatred between commanders could not be without its

reflection among the men, and before the new year the fort was divided into two camps, with the Rangers and provincials on the one side and the regulars on the other. Haviland, of course, as commander of the post had the upper hand, and he was not a man who would hesitate to use his power for his own purposes. He kept the Rangers running upon a succession of errands and impossible assignments, and though he could not interfere with discipline within our camp, his methods when he caught any of us within his bailiwick were harsh in the extreme, as witness an occasion when a Ranger, one of Captain Bulkley's company, was caught stealing a tub of butter from the regulars' commissary. The man was sentenced to two thousand lashes of the cat, although the usual punishment for such an offence was but five hundred. When news of this matter reached the island, the men were only prevented from crossing the river in a body and rescuing their companion by Captain Shepard's confronting them with a loaded musket in his hands and threatening to shoot the first man who set foot in a boat. When the man died of his beating it was considered best to give out that he had been dismissed from the service and sent home, else nothing would have prevented an active mutiny. Subversive as it was of discipline, and deplorable on that account, the feud was nevertheless not without its brighter side. If it did nothing else it kept the life of the camp from growing too drearily monotonous.

All this is not related simply as idle gossip, but rather because of the bearing which it may or may not have had upon the disaster which befell us in March. Rogers always maintained, and maintains to this day, that we were deliberately sent into a trap. And though I am not of that opinion, for I cannot believe that even Haviland would stoop to such a trick, nevertheless it cannot be denied that in sending us out as he did he behaved with extreme carelessness. Indeed, he might well be charged with negligence, and if treachery was not among his crimes, at least the suspicion of it will always cling to him.

About the middle of January an order came up from my Lord Loudoun to Rogers for the raising of five new companies of Rangers. It was at this time that I came to know my own ill fortune to be serving as first lieutenant to John Stark, for he, it appeared, was Rogers' champion recruiting officer, having a most persuasive way with him, as I myself could testify. And now, with five new companies being raised, it fell to him to go off recruiting, while I remained behind in command of the company, to my intense disgust, for I should far rather have been in his shoes.

There was naught for me to do, however, but accept my fate with the best grace I might. Everything went along evenly enough for a time, but about the end of February Captain Putnam, the same who had befriended me upon my first arrival in Albany, was sent out upon a scout. At the same time the entire garrison was ordered to parade before the fort, and general orders were read, among them an order to Rogers to hold himself in readiness to lead out a party of four hundred Rangers as soon as Putnam should return.

I did not see Rogers as soon as we were dismissed, but when I had got my men across the river to the island and returned to my own quarters I found Toby there, awaiting me with a summons to Rogers' cabin. I lost no time in obeying, and on entering found Captains Bulkley, Brewer, Shepard, and Burbank and Lieutenants Moore, Pottinger, Campbell, Crafton, and Phillips already there before me. As I entered Rogers, who was seated at his writing table looked up, his face puffy and congested; and I knew at once that he was in a towering rage.

"You heard the orders," he said, and his voice shook with anger in spite of his visible effort to control it. "What did you make of them?"

Shepard, who had frozen his ear on a scout the day before fingered the swollen organ gingerly, and made a wry face.

"Four hundred of us," he said. "That ought to be quite a party."

"It all looks merry to me," said the half Dutch, half Indian, Lieutenant Phillips.

"I don't see anything wrong with it," was Brewer's comment.

Captain Burbank, stout and stocky and always good-natured, so that he was a favourite among the men, laughed.

"We ought to have some fun," he said.

Rogers shot him a sour look, and his little mouth was pursed up petulantly.

"Yes," he said derisively, "we should! Now it's spread all about the fort we're going. D'ye realize, gentlemen, there's not a sutler's servant or a drummer boy doesn't know we're ordered out? How long d'ye think 'twill be before the French discover it?"

He stopped and looked at us with slightly popping eyes, while we stared back in sudden consternation. Such a thought had not before occurred to any of us.

"Are your wits all dull?" he bellowed at us. "Can you tell me you saw naught that was out of the ordinary in those orders? Haven't you all been here long enough to know the usual procedure? Have you ever heard such an order read in public before?"

He stopped and glared from one to another of us.

"Have you, Mr. Ferguson?" he demanded.

I started at his direct question.

"No, sir," I replied.

"Have you, Mr. Bulkley?"

"No, sir," said Bulkley.

"Have you, Mr. Pottinger?"

"No, sir," was the reply.

Rogers threw up his hands.

"Of course you haven't. By God!" he roared. "And why? Because it isn't done. That's why! Because this damned, treacherous, dirty, sneaking dog Haviland wouldn't send the word straight to the enemy, but he'd make a big loud noise about it, hoping that some word of it might reach their ears! That's why! Because this is his way of doing us in. This is the way a fine gentleman works! By Jesus, I tell you, it stinks!"

By the very force of his fury he had convinced most of us in the room at that time. Lieutenant Campbell looked sick, and a little shamed, for he had come to us out of the 42nd Regiment of regulars, and the others looked little better.

"But what can we do?" said Burbank.

"Do?" bellowed Rogers. "Do? There's not a damned thing to do but go forth to the slaughter like obedient sheep, and hope we can outwit 'em. I've half a mind to lie out on Hoop Island, as 'tis said we do; but 'twill be a fair guess we'll be watched this trip!"

"Let me go down to Albany, captain." It was Lieutenant Campbell who spoke. "I can explain the whole affair, and bring back a countermanding order."

Rogers turned upon him, snarling.

"And have it said that Rogers was afraid to lead his men out?" he demanded. "Why, man, we'd be laughed out of the service in no time."

No one ventured to reply to this, and he sat for some minutes eyeing us in silence. When he spoke again it was with restraint and some determination.

"No, gentlemen," he said, "there is nothing we may do but accept the orders as they stand, and hope that by the exercise of the utmost vigilance we may be able to guard against surprise."

I thought of the little sparrow-faced major then. "Vigilance and caution," I could almost hear him saying. But there was no time for reminiscence. Rogers was still talking.

"It must go without saying," he said, "that our suspicions must not go beyond this room. Whatever we may think, the men must not hear of it. It would make them nervous and jumpy in the field. I will expect you gentlemen to say nothing. Have your men in readiness to go out as soon as Mr. Putnam comes in. That's all, gentlemen."

As we filed out into the night and scattered towards our own quarters, Brewer fell in beside me.

"What do you think of it, Ferguson?" he said.

"I think it's all stuff," I replied. "Captain Rogers' feud with the colonel has got him jumping at shadows. 'Twas a mistake for Haviland to have the orders read in public, but I'd not say he did it deliberately."

I heard Brewer chuckle dryly in the darkness.

"I've always heard you were a trusting sort," he said.

It was about three days after this that one Potter, a servant to a sutler named Best, was taken by a flying party of the enemy's Indians in the road from Fort Edward to Albany. Potter, it appeared, was on his way down the river on some errand for his employer, and had managed to get a ride with the driver of an empty supply sledge. About two-thirds of the way between Fort Edward and Fort Miller this Potter, having lately been ill of the flux, felt the call of nature so irresistibly that he must needs stop at once to relieve himself, and both the sleds halted to wait for him. He had been gone but a few moments, when the drivers of the sleds heard him cry out, and without waiting to investigate they whipped their teams into a frenzy, and fled with the war whoop ringing in their ears.

This news in itself was upsetting enough, for Potter was fully aware of all our plans. But an aspect of the matter that, for no logical reason, struck me as sinister was that the names of the teamsters who so precipitately saved their skins were Sanborn and Merrill. Somehow, I could not forget that my every contact with these men had brought disastrous results, and I could not help but wonder, though I do not claim to believe in signs, whether this might not also be an omen of evil. Needless to say a rescue party of Rangers was dispatched as soon as the word was brought to us, but by then the enemy had too fair a start, and we were unable to overtake them.

It was a fortnight before Putnam returned, and then it was with the loss of one man who had deserted to the French from his camp at the narrows. According to Captain Putnam's report, he had approached to within eight miles of the fort, and found the enemy active. Scouts which he had sent out, had gone within six hundred yards of the fortifications, bringing back the report that there was apparently a strong force of regulars and Canadians in the fort itself, and a camp of more than six hundred Indians outside.

I was in Rogers' quarters when an orderly brought the news, and I must admit that even I was startled at the fury with which he received it.

"By God!" he roared, thumping his fist upon the table. "That settles it. This thing must go no further, whatever they may say!"

He snatched up pen and paper from the table before him, and glared at me with a bulging eye.

"Mr. Ferguson," he said, "go fetch me Captain Creed."

Captain Francis Creed was one of Lord Loudoun's volunteers from the regulars, an officer of Colonel Haviland's own regiment and a fine straightforward young fellow, albeit something of a grand dandy; very different from his commanding officer. I could not imagine what would induce Rogers to call for him at such a time, but it was plain it was not a moment for questions, and I jumped to obey.

I found Captain Creed in his quarters in the cabin which he shared with Captain Burbank, and returned with him to Rogers' without delay. The latter gave us a glance and a grunt as we entered and jerked his head to the bench beside the fireplace.

"Sit down, gentlemen," he growled. "I will be with you in one moment."

We sat in silence, waiting for him to finish his writing, the only sounds in the cabin being the steady scratching of the quill upon the paper, and the captain's heavy laboured breathing as he struggled with the wording of his missive—such things being more exhausting to him than any amount of marching or fighting. When he was done he sanded the paper with a swish, and folding it in four put the address upon it. Not until then did he glance in our direction.

"Mr. Creed," he said, "you're an officer of Haviland's. The colonel may be willing to listen to you."

He tapped the note which he held in his hand.

"I have here written," he went on, "my protest against the expedition which the colonel proposes I should lead at this time. I have every reason to believe that the enemy is fully informed of its proposal. Captain Putnam's report indicates that they are in such strength at Ticonderoga as to make such an undertaking not merely inadvisable but foolhardy in the extreme under the circumstances. All this I have set down here. I am going to ask you to deliver it to Colonel Haviland, and to use your influence with him."

Captain Creed stood up and reached out his hand for the letter.

"I'll do my best," he said.

Rogers saw him to the door and closed it gently behind him. When he turned he found Serjeant Clough, his adjutant, staring at him in open-mouthed surprise. He frowned.

"Here you, Clough," he said, "run over to the fort and see if you can find out what's become o' those four barrels o' powder we were supposed to get yesterday. And mind you, not a word o' this to anyone, d'ye hear?"

The serjeant touched his forelock, bobbed, and was gone. When we were alone Rogers dragged a chair over to the fire and sat down heavily with a sigh.

"Ah, Jamie," he said, "be grateful for your luck! You don't have to deal with yonder brassbound fool!"

I made no reply, though I sympathized with him, and he sat silent for some moments.

"There's rum in the cupboard there," he said presently. "Fetch it down, and we'll have a drink. I need it."

I brought the squat black bottle from the cupboard shelf, and a pair of horn cups, which he slopped full. One he pushed towards me, and the other he held aloft.

"It may be our last together," he said; "we might as well make it a good one. Here's luck!"

"Luck," I replied. "We'll need it."

He drained his cup at a gulp, while I sipped at mine somewhat more gingerly. When he had done he flung his cup into his bunk and, kicking his chair back, stood up and began to pace the room thoughtfully.

"Are your men ready to go out?" he asked.

"As ready as they'll ever be," I replied. "We had thirty-two report sick this morning."

He whistled.

"Thirty-two!" he exclaimed. "They're skulking. They've no stomach for this job, and I don't blame them."

"I looked at them all with Mr. Pope, the surgeon," I said, for I knew that what he said was not so. "'Tis mostly the flux."

"'Tis fear affects their bowels," he growled in reply.

He strode to the table and fumbled among the papers that were strewn across its surface.

"Where the devil did that woodenhead Clough put those returns?" he mumbled, more to himself than to me. Then, as he found them: "Here they are. Let's see. 'Parties out—Captain J. Rogers to South Bay with forty men, Captain W. Stark to Saratoga on patrol with fifty men; the sick lists, Captain R. Rogers' company, twenty-three, Captain J. Stark, thirty-two, Captain Shepard, twenty-eight, Captain W. Stark, thirty-one, Captain Bulkley, thirty-seven, Captain J. Rogers, twenty-one, Captain Burbank, twenty-seven, Captain Brewer, twenty-four.' With casualties, ninety-two, since the companies were completed in the fall, that's a total of four hundred and five out. That leaves"—here he did some rapid calculation on his fingers—"let me see, four from seven's three—three hundred and ninety-five effectives, not counting our volunteers, who can't be considered for such a service, and officers out recruiting."

He chuckled, and glanced at me.

"Say three hundred and ninety," he said. "Mr. Haviland 'll have to support us with some regulars if he wants us to follow the orders."

There was a knock at the door at that moment, and in response to Rogers' shout Captain Creed entered.

"Well, sir?" said Rogers.

Captain Creed shrugged.

"I'm sorry, sir," he replied. "Colonel Haviland insists that the orders be carried out as read. You are to be ready to march within the hour, sir."

Rogers grinned wolfishly.

"So!" he exclaimed. "Very well. My compliments to Colonel Haviland. Tell him illness, casualties, and patrols have reduced my present strength to three hundred and ninety effectives. Ask him if he will fill that number with regulars. Ask him also if he wishes me to divide my force."

He stopped and looked down at the floor.

"It might be more convenient," he said bitterly, "for him to murder us all in a lump, than have the thing to do twice."

Captain Creed saluted stiffly.

"I will tell him what you say, sir," he said, and was gone.

Rogers stepped to the door and bellowed for the serjeant of the guard.

"Fetch Clough," he roared when that worthy had come running. "Tell him, 'Never mind that powder now.' Call all commanding officers here for a conference; seconds to turn out the companies meantime, ready to march at once!"

The man left on the run, and Rogers turned to me.

"You may as well stay," he said. "Phillips will turn out the men."

In less than ten minutes the commanders and acting commanders were assembled and Rogers was busy giving orders. A quarter of an hour later Captain Creed returned, and without a word laid a paper before him. Rogers picked it up and read it; and as he read his face grew purple and congested with rage.

"By God!" he swore. "Gentlemen, listen to this:

"To Captain Rogers, commanding his Majesty's Independent companies of Rangers at Fort Edward. Sir, Owing to the illness which has depleted the ranks of the regulars it is not considered advisable to support your scout with any men from their ranks. Neither should all the Rangers now in garrison be taken. You will therefore take with you only such men as are available after leaving the equivalent of two full companies. As your men are under arms and ready you will leave within an hour of your receipt of this order, and will report your departure to me. Signed, William Haviland, Colonel commanding at Fort Edward. Given under my hand this 10th day of March 1758."

He stopped, and there was a moment of such dead silence that his heavy breathing was audible throughout the room.

"God!" said someone at length.

"It's murder," said another.

"Murder or no," said Rogers, "those are the orders. We're allowed a hundred and eighty men. I'll call for volunteers."

Instantly the tiny room was in an uproar. Everyone pushed forward and endeavoured to catch his eye.

"Me!" shouted Burbank.

"I'll go," said Bulkley.

"Count me in," said Shepard.

"And me, and me," said both Brewer and I in the same instant.

Rogers held up his hand, smiling grimly.

"Gentlemen, gentlemen," he said, "we can't all go. I'm pleased to see your spirit, but I'll have to choose from among you; and I'll ask those not chosen not to feel slighted at the choice. There'll be need for commanders here too."

He stopped and looked from one to another of us, as we stood ranged before him, each trying to catch his eye.

"Captain Bulkley," he said at length, "Lieutenant Moore, Lieutenant Crafton, Lieutenant Ferguson. Each of you gentlemen will choose your own seconds and an ensign each. You will each draw forty men—volunteers if you can get 'em—from the ranks, and report to me with the men ready to march in a half-hour."

There were a few murmurs, some of protest, some of approval. Those of us who had been chosen turned to go out, when Captain Creed's voice rising above the muttering brought us about in curiosity.

"If I might have your permission, sir," he was saying, "I would like to be allowed to go with you."

For a moment there was a dead silence. Then someone, I could not see who, laughed. Rogers gestured impatiently for silence.

"That's not a thing to laugh at," he said. He looked steadily at Creed. "You know what it means, sir?" he asked.

Creed nodded. "I understand the risks, sir," he replied.

Rogers shrugged. "You'll have to ask Colonel Haviland," he said. "I doubt he'll approve."

"I have already asked the colonel," said Creed.

"The devil you say!" said Rogers in surprise. "What did he say?"

"He gave his consent, sir," Creed replied, without the flicker of an eyelash.

Rogers shrugged. "All right," he said, and started to turn away.

"Sir," said Creed, catching his sleeve, "Lieutenants Kent and Campbell, and Mr. Wrightson, also begged me to ask your permission for them."

Rogers began to laugh.

"By God," he said, "there seem to be some fire-eaters among you at that. And I suppose the colonel gave his permission for them also?"

"He did not object, sir," said the captain.

"Very well," said Rogers. "We may show you some real fighting before we're through. Tell them to get ready and report here in a half-hour."

I did not wait to hear more, but hurried out to collect my men, finding them already standing under arms by Lieutenant Phillips' command. My call for volunteers brought a gratifying response, and after choosing the men I picked Phillips and Ensign Ross to accompany me. This done, I set the serjeants to apportioning rations, powder and shot, while I went to prepare my own equipment. Within the half-hour the entire expedition was drawn up and ready before Rogers' cabin, and twenty minutes later we filed out of the fort turning our faces northward, into the wind, and took up the trail towards Lake George.

The march out was not remarkable. We lay the first night at Halfway Brook, on the road from Fort Edward to Lake George, and the next day marched as far as the first narrows on the lake, making our camp on the east side of the lake at a point where the steep slope of the mountain covered our rear, and the ice of the lake lay unbroken and clear of any obstruction for some distance before us.

Notwithstanding the strength of this position, however, Rogers was nervous. No sooner was the site chosen than he sent Lieutenant Crafton and a scouting party on down the lake on skates, for, but for an occasional patch that lay glaring silvery in the moonlight, the wind had swept the black ice clear of snow. At the same time he posted double sentries on the landward side of our encampment, and kept several patrols continually going to and fro upon the ice throughout the night. Only the smallest fires were allowed, and these were confined to the thickest part of the woods, and further hidden by being kindled at the bottom of pits scooped with our snowshoes in the snow, which in the shelter of the trees lay some four feet deep. As the night was bitter there were few who slept. For my part, I was fortunate to command one of the early patrols, on the return from which I found myself so thoroughly exhausted that I wrapped myself in my blanket and was soon nodding over the fire, only awakening to find another day had come.

In spite of the cold we could not have wished for a finer morning. Indeed, I would not have wished for one so fine, for by my experience it is easier to march and keep a good watch when the sky is overcast and the glare of the sun upon the snow and ice does not dazzle the eyes.

We set out before sunrise, marching in extended order, myself in charge of the advance, Lieutenants Moore and Crafton in charge of the flankers, and Ensign White bringing up the rear; the whole party keeping close in against the shore to be the less easily observed from the hills. Lieutenant Crafton had returned about midnight with the report that, so far as he was able to ascertain, there was no enemy between us and the French advanced posts at the foot of the lake. We had no assurance, however, that they had not come forward in the night, and in consequence I had picked my own party with the utmost care, choosing men in whom I had complete confidence—some of them men I had known at home, but all of them men who had proved their mettle on previous expeditions. There was Nathaniel Maloon, whose family had been carried off from Stevenstown before the war: a great-eyed, sombre youth, without a spark of humour in his make-up. There was Ebenezer Call and his brother Phillip, whose young wife had been murdered in the same raid: a bitter, vengeful man, whose hatred for the Indians was only surpassed by his contempt for their French masters. There was David Stinson of Epsom, a cousin to Daniel, a great good-humoured hulking fellow, not overly bright but yet a creditable woodsman. There was redheaded David Mc-

Clary, one of the "wild Irish" of Londonderry, whose sharp humour and violent temper made him perhaps the most feared and respected man in the entire corps. There were Timothy Eastman of Rumford, and Asa Cook of Canterbury, and Joseph Bean of Chester, as well as a half-dozen others whose names I do not at the moment recall. And of course there was Toby.

With this party I set out about a quarter-hour before sunrise, leading the main body by some six hundred yards. As long as we kept the crest of the eastern ridge between us and the sun, we had little difficulty seeing everything that lay before us upon the lake. But when the sun rose above the trees, its slanting rays beating down upon the smooth glare ice, my eyes soon began to smart from peering ahead to detect the slightest movement that might betoken the presence of an enemy. Indeed, so painful did it presently become that I found myself half wishing an enemy might appear; then we might take to the shelter of the woods and there obtain relief.

Whether it was in response to this unuttered wish or not, I could not say; but we were not gone five miles when an exclamation from Toby, who was following close upon my heels, brought me up short.

"What is it?" I demanded.

He pointed ahead, and following the direction of his finger I made out a black dot moving across a patch far ahead.

"Dog," he said.

At that distance, even under the best conditions, it would have been difficult for me to identify that moving spot. With that glare in my eyes it was utterly impossible.

"Maybe it's a fox," I said.

Toby shook his head emphatically.

"No fox," he said insistently. "Dog!"

It was difficult to believe, yet I had had other proofs of the excellence of the old Indian's vision. The others had come up and halted behind us. At Toby's announcement a murmur ran through them.

"Where there's dogs there's generally men," said McClary.

"Quiet!" I said. "What kind of a dog, Toby?"

"Injun dog," he replied.

I thought of the lean, sharp-nosed, vicious mongrels that infested every Indian encampment and made scouting such a hazard with their yapping at everything that moved. Once seen, that breed could not be mistaken.

"McClary, Carroll," I snapped, "go back to Captain Rogers and report what we have seen. Ask him to get the men up off the ice and hold them until I can investigate and make a report."

The two men saluted and, turning, trotted back the way we had come. One man I left in the brush at the lakeside, with orders to watch the dog as long as he remained in sight, and then to report to me which way he went. The rest of us took to our snowshoes and circled up through the wooded slopes to approach the lake again at the point whence the animal had appeared.

Those woods were still with the absolute silence that comes only to the deep forest in the dead of winter. Not the least sound betrayed the presence of a living creature. The ice that lay along the branches of the trees, melting at the warm touch of the sun's rays, dripped soundlessly into the soft snow beneath. Even the slight crunching of our snowshoes underfoot came to our ears as a light whisper, deadened and diminished by a great distance. No breath of wind shook the drooping branches of spruce and balsam. Once a rabbit bounded silently, like a grey-white ghost, from beneath a small fir and floated away in long leaps, leaving only the wide-spaced marks of his tracks in the snow to assure us of his reality.

Under other circumstances I might have found pleasure in this quiet solitude. But now there seemed something sinister about it; something evil and unnatural, as if the very trees themselves were awaiting some devil's signal to burst out in hideous clamour. There was a tension in the air that made my scalp tingle, and sent little shivers racing up and down my spine.

This of course was pure imagination on my part, for, suspicious though it was, the fact of a dog crossing the ice was not conclusive proof that his masters were about. Yet so strongly had my imagination been wrought upon by the anticipation of the expedition, that I peopled each clump of bushes with painted savages, and saw an enemy behind each shaggy tree trunk. Almost, it seemed, our every move was watched by unseen eyes.

Nor was I alone in this sense of insecurity and foreboding. The men were nervous and jumpy as a flock of chickens who have seen a hawk's shadow pass upon the ground. Of us all, Toby alone was not fit to start at shadows, though even he, I think, believed a trap had been laid for us ahead, for he led us cautiously in a long circuit, that carried us near a mile up the flank of the mountain from the shore, and brought us back again to the spot where the dog had appeared, stopping every now and again to stand staring at some queer-shaped stump or clump of bushes as if he expected to see them move or in some other way betray the hiding place of an enemy.

We might have spared our caution, however, for though we found the dog's tracks, clear and unmistakable in the deep snow, we saw no trace of human feet. Spreading out, we scoured the mountain side for some hundred yards back from the shore, but found nothing. We backtracked the dog for a full half-mile, until we were satisfied that, wherever he had come from, he had not brought his masters with him. It was possible that they were hidden upon the farther shore, which we dared not approach across the open ice for fear of showing ourselves. But a careful scrutiny with perspective glasses of the rather open woods upon the hillside and the brush that lined the lake front revealed no sign of life, nor even of anything that might be shaped like the crook of a human arm or leg.

I for one was satisfied that no enemy lay waiting for us there, and Toby, in whose eyes I placed more faith than all the perspective glasses I might assemble, agreed. It seemed likely that some party had come part way up the lake. They might even now be lying in wait for us further down, while their dog, all unbeknown to them, slipped off in search of game, and so betrayed them. But at least it was safe to say that they had not come this far, and this was the report I carried back to Rogers.

He heard me with evident relief, for I believe it was in his mind, if possible, to avoid a fight upon this expedition, the chances of the enemy's turning out in force being too great to risk. Nevertheless, he heeded the warning of the dog, and after dispatching Lieutenant Moore with a party to march through the woods along the east shore, and sending me ahead to do the same upon the west, he called the main column in off the ice, and set them to marching northward, under cover of the forest, upon snowshoes—a mode of travel that was a sore trial to the little group of volunteers from the regulars, for they were unaccustomed to it and were soon exhausted by it. In respect to them, however, I must do them the credit to say that not one of them complained.

As much cannot be said for our own men. More accustomed to

small flying parties and swift daring raids, they grumbled at the size and seeming uselessness of the expedition; they cited its hazards, and in the same breath cursed our cautiousness, which they found irksome in the extreme. But though I grew annoyed at their mutterings and growlings, at the same time I was become enough a campaigner to realize that it signified only boredom and forecast with what sullen ferocity they would fight if it came to that.

We moved slowly during the morning, keeping patrols out constantly ahead to feel out the country and make sure no traps were set for us. By noon we had reached Sabbath Day Point, and here we rested, Rogers deciding that to go further by daylight was too risky. By his orders we sought out such cover as we could find, and there lay awaiting the darkness. Nor were we allowed to kindle a single fire, though the cold was intense, lest the enemy learn our presence from the smoke.

I have known hours to pass slowly, both before and since, but I hope I may never see them drag quite so interminably as they seemed to do that day. The frost nipped at our faces, but aside from slapping them to bring back the circulation, there was naught we could do for them. When we became hungry our bellies cried aloud for hot food and drink, but we had naught to give them save cold rations and a little rum. Our volunteers, worn out as they were from the morning's march, rolled up in their blankets, and were soon asleep; but few of the rest of us were able to follow their example.

Darkness came at last, however—the black, pitchy darkness of a moonless night—and Lieutenant Phillips was sent forward down the lake on skates with fifteen men as an advanced patrol. The rest of us marched in close order upon the ice, keeping well in against the western shore, in the deeper darkness of its shadow. Captain Bulkley commanded the advance guard, scarce ten rods ahead of the main column, and yet completely hidden from view. Ensigns Ross and Wait commanded the flankers. And Ensign M'Donald covered the rear.

In this order we moved forward some miles, until I estimated we were coming near the end of the lake, when all at once a low whistle came to our ears. Rogers held up his hand, and his whispered command to halt was relayed down the line.

"That's Phillips," he said, and whistled in reply.

A moment later Phillips himself came in with the report that he had discovered a fire high on the flank of the hill on the east shore, or thought he had.

"Ain't you sure, man?" asked Rogers.

"Can't be sure, cap'n," was Phillips' reply. "If it's fire they've hid it good. Comes and goes like it was reflectin' from th' snow. Maybe 'tain't what I think 'tis."

"We'll find out," said Rogers. "Mr. White?"

"Here, sir," said White.

"Go forward with Mr. Phillips and see if you can help him. Let me have your report as soon as you make up your minds," said Rogers.

The darkness swallowed up the two men in an instant, and Rogers ordered the rest of us to squat down upon the ice and rest. For my part I found the wait both hard and cold, and the rest scarce worth the discomfort, but at the end of an hour Phillips returned and reported that both he and White were agreed it was a fire that he saw.

"All right," said Rogers. "Advanced guards and flankers in. Everybody on shore to stow packs and blankets. Quick now."

Such an order could only mean that we were about to attack, and the prospect immensely cheered the men, who were grown weary of inaction. In less then ten minutes packs, blankets, sledges, and all other heavy gear had been hidden in the brush upon the lake shore, and a party told off to stand guard. The rest of us moved off swiftly, even eagerly, in the dark.

We had gone barely half a mile when we met Ensign White and his party returning.

"Didn't I tell ye to stay where ye were?" demanded Phillips.

"That's right," said White, who was possessed of a Yankee humour, and never addressed his superiors as "sir" if he could help it. "Th' men got cold waitin', an' I figgered 'twould be better if they kep' a-movin', so I come t' meet ye."

Phillips muttered something that sounded suspiciously like a curse beneath his breath, and White and his men fell in with the rest. We plodded on for another half-hour, until Rogers grew impatient. White and Phillips had their heads together and were arguing in violent whispers when the captain cut in upon them.

"Where in hell is this place?" he demanded.

"By my reckonin'," said Phillips, "it sh'd be right about here, or p'r'aps a mite further."

" 'Tain't," said White. "It's back a ways. Ye passed it."

"My God!" exclaimed Rogers. "Mr. Ferguson, take two men and go forward a half-mile. See if you can see anything that looks like a campfire."

I took Toby and McClary and did as I was bid, but though we went further than he had ordered we saw never a sign of a glow upon the hillside to betray the presence of an enemy. I returned to the column and reported my failure, to find that Phillips and White had been sent up on to the hillside with a party. It was a little better than an hour before they returned to report that they had discovered nothing.

"No tracks?" Rogers demanded.

"Mister," said White, before Phillips could reply, "if there was tracks up there you couldn't see 'em. It's blacker 'n the inside o' my aunt Abbie's outhouse. Might be tracks all over th' mountain side, but we didn't see none of 'em."

"Bah!" said Rogers. "You never did see anything but a patch of bleach snow, maybe, or fox fire." *

" 'Twas fire," said Phillips stubbornly.

Indeed, as it turned out, he was right at that, for a party set to watch for our approach, as we afterwards learned, had built a fire to warm themselves; but hearing us coming they had extinguished it and returned to the fort. None of us believed this at the moment, however, and we returned to where we had left our packs, cursing Phillips and White for plagued blunderers, and there spent the remainder of the night shivering in our blankets.

In the morning Captain Rogers called a conference of the officers and put the question to us straight whether we should push on along the ice of the lake towards the enemy's advanced posts, or whether we ought to take to our snowshoes and circle in behind the hills, to intercept their communications between the outer fortifications and the fort, and there perhaps trepan some of them.

It was the unanimous opinion that we should take to snowshoes, the risk of discovery being less that way, and the chances of

* Wood that has rotted in the damp sometimes turns phosphorescent and emits a glow colloquially called fox fire.

success greater. Accordingly we set out at once from the west shore, keeping a long wooded ridge of mountains between ourselves and the French advanced posts. Before we left the ice, however, Rogers sought out Captain Creed and his fellow volunteers.

"We will be travelling by snowshoe," he said, "in deep snow, a way of travel that is not familiar to you, sir. No one will think the less of you if you choose to await our return with the baggage."

Captain Creed smiled. "Thank you, captain," he said. "I appreciate your thoughtfulness, but for my part I would prefer to go along, if I may."

Rogers looked at the others, who nodded. He shrugged.

"Very well," he said. "Mr. Ferguson, show the captain the best way to tie his raquettes." *

I did my best to instruct Creed and his fellows in the art of tying on a snowshoe; but it is a knack that comes only with practice, and at best they made a poor job of it; so that during the morning's march we were frequently held up while one or another of them picked himself out of a drift, recovered his unwieldy footgear, or fashioned a new knot to hold perhaps a mile or so.

At noon we rested on the back of the ridge, about opposite the French outer posts, and overlooking the valley of a small brook that ran down behind the ridge to join the river flowing between Lake George and Lake Champlain. There we ate a cold midday meal, and waited until past midafternoon—that the enemy's daily scout in this direction might be returned to the fort before we set out once more.

By now, however, we were well into the enemy's territory. Indeed, we were in a part of it he often much frequented, so that it behooved us to go warily. Captain Rogers divided the party in two forces, the first of which marched under the command of Captain Bulkley, and the second he commanded himself. In addition Ensign M'Donald commanded the advance guard, while Ensigns Wait and White held the rear. We marched with the little brooklet gurgling under the ice that covered it upon our left, and with the steep slope of the mountain, silent and snow-covered, rising sharp upon our right.

It was not the easiest path, for the deep snow hampered our movements, and the undergrowth was thick enough to be a nuisance. Walking upon the ice that covered the brook would have

* Snowshoes.

been easier, and Captain Creed ventured in a half puzzled, half questioning way to suggest this. Rogers gave him his bulge-eyed stare, and grinned.

"Easier?" he said. " 'Twould be easier, ye say, to follow the ice? And what if the enemy did as we are doing now, and followed upon the bank? We'd be in a pretty mess, eh?"

Creed gazed down into the shallow gully through which the brook flowed and was forced to admit, though not without some reluctance, that this was so.

"O' course 'tis so," said Rogers. "And 'twould be an end to all of us. For my part, if we are to meet them I prefer the higher ground, even though it be more difficult."

"There's sound common sense in that," said Creed.

"Aye!" said Rogers. "And another thing: Mark my words, if the enemy should come this way he'll be upon the ice; for he'll not think to find us here, but will rather be counting upon cutting in behind us on the lake. That way the advantage will be with us."

And so it proved, surely enough. We had not gone above a mile and a half when word came back from the advanced guard that a party of the enemy's Indians, close to a hundred in number, was coming upward along the brook.

This was what we had long been anticipating, but we had not expected their numbers to be so few. Indeed, Rogers was frankly sceptical.

"How many?" he demanded, seizing by the arm the messenger who had brought the word.

"Ninety-six, sir," the man replied, "by Mr. M'Donald's count."

"Bah!" snorted Rogers. "They'd not come after me with so few when they must have word my own force numbers four hundred! Mr. M'Donald must have skipped every third man, or else there's others behind."

"I counted 'em meself, sir," said the fellow stubbornly, "an' ninety-six was all there were. As for others behind, they may be there, but we've had no sign of 'em if they are."

"Here's luck," said Rogers, turning to Captain Creed. "Perhaps they don't know we've come, after all. This may be no more than a scout sent out for news of us."

He began to give rapid orders in a low voice.

"Mr. Pottinger, support Mr. Wait and Mr. White," he said. "Conceal the men along the top of the bank, so that when I signal they will fire down into the enemy in the brook. Remember that you will be upon the left flank, and do not let them get around you. Mr. Ferguson, do the same for Mr. M'Donald. And ask Captain Bulkley to do the same as you go by. Remember that yours will be the right."

I saluted and was away at once, as fast as my webbed footgear would carry me. As I passed Captain Bulkley I relayed Rogers' orders to him, and went on to the advanced guard, where I found M'Donald had already got the men into position behind the trees and brush that lined the edge of the gully. There was little for me to do.

"Good work," I told him. "Where are they?"

He was a stocky, fat little man, with flaming-red hair and a pair of humorous blue eyes. He looked at me now, a little disappointed, I thought, at having another set over him, yet smiling cordially enough.

"They'll be coming up the gully in a minute," he replied. "I called the advance patrol back."

I nodded, and looked over his dispositions. The men were well concealed and ready. Indeed, though it was yet lacking two minutes of the time the first word of the enemy's approach had come to Rogers, the entire company had laid down their packs, faced left, established contact along the line, and fallen into position, using every scrap of cover that the forest afforded. Had I not been well aware of our numbers I should never have guessed, even from my place behind the lines, that such a force lay hidden there. I joined M'Donald behind a large oak, and lay down to wait. Presently a messenger came down the line from Rogers.

"Captain says no one's to shoot till he gives the signal," he said.

After that there was no more movement among us, and the stillness of the forest settled in upon us like a heavy hand.

Ever since our departure from Fort Edward I had been nervous and alert. Now I found myself grown suddenly calm though curious. Thus far my experience had been largely confined to small scouts. There had been but little fighting, and that little had been with small bands, the total number on both sides never exceeding threescore. Now I was about to take part in something that would more nearly approximate a real battle, and I found myself wondering if it would differ, and if so in what way, from those lesser engagements. Would such a force be as easily broken as a small party under like conditions? Would they stand and fight, or would they break and run? If they stood, could they hold until reinforcements came to them from the French outposts, not two miles distant over the ridge?

These considerations flitted through my mind as swiftly as thought, but suddenly the tightening of M'Donald's grip upon my arm drove them from me. I glanced at him and then looked where he was staring. There was a movement in the brush below, and then, all at once, they came into view: first a squat, bandy-legged Canadian in a dirty white blanket coat, with hood drawn over his head; then an Indian in smoke-stained buckskins, his head half hidden under an enormous fur hat beneath which his dark painted features appeared both ludicrous and evil. He was followed by another and another. As they trotted along the ice their black eyes darted here and there, to right and left. Snowshoes slapped upon their backs. Their muskets were carried before them at the ready.

Along the bank not a twig stirred. I found myself counting them as they passed: . . . nine, ten, eleven, twelve, thirteen . . . twenty-one, twenty-two . . . forty . . . fifty-three, fifty-four . . . sixty, sixty-one (I began to grow restless) . . . eighty-two, eighty-three, eighty-four, eighty-five . . . ninety. Somewhere far up the line a musket cracked.

Below me the line stopped—wavered uncertainly. I threw up my musket and drew bead upon a tall savage with particularly evil features, and a brass gorget upon his breast. I squeezed the trigger. Smoke belched from my gun, but the sound of the report was drowned in the crash of the volley that burst from the brush along the gully's edge. I saw my Indian spin and go down. Then the scene below was blotted out in smoke.

I leapt to my feet, reloading hastily. The smoke began to drift up the gully, and in the rifts I saw confusion below. Dark bodies sprawled in the snow, some lying motionless as they had fallen, others writhing jerkily in agony. Still others dragged themselves painfully along, leaving a trail of crimson behind them in the fresh whiteness of the snow. As I stood uncertain, staring down at that scene, I felt suddenly sick to my stomach. A band of men came running down the gully, stumbling over the dead, trampling the wounded, running heedlessly in blind panic. Yet there were some who kept their heads. A bullet whacked into the trunk of the oak above my head, causing me to duck involuntarily. Behind me I heard Rogers' voice bellowing.

"After 'em! Head 'em! Head 'em! Ferguson, M'Donald, get in there!"

In blind obedience to that voice I left my shelter and stumbled clumsily down into the gully. Out of the corner of my eye I saw other green-clad figures following my example. Bulkley passed me at a run. Others swarmed behind him. The savages were turning now, stopping to fire and then run again. Beside me a man buckled abruptly in the middle and plunged headforemost into the snow, flinging his musket ahead of him as he fell. I glanced at him as I ran, seeing him as though from a great distance, and knowing at once from the grotesque way in which he lay without the least movement that he was dead. I shouted, and ran on.

The gully became crowded from bank to bank with the green jerkins of the Rangers; men running without heed to orders, anxious only to overtake the fleeing savages. Then suddenly something seemed to go wrong. Those in the lead seemed to stop abruptly. Others piled up behind them, pressing them forward, while the fire in front swelled from a few scattered shots to a steady, crackling roar.

"God!" I heard someone near at hand shout. " 'Twas only their advance!"

The angry whine of bullets filled the air. I saw the men in the front rank wither, and begin to drop. Smoke drifted out from among the trees in front. Captain Bulkley, almost immediately in front of me, turned and waved his arms.

"Back!" he shouted, endeavouring to make himself heard above the crash of musketry. "Back! Get back to your positions!"

I saw his head jerk as a bullet took him in the back of the neck, and he went down, his head half torn from his shoulders, the blood pumping out in a fountain from the severed arteries, staining the snow about him crimson.

"Back!" I shouted, taking up his cry. "Get back!"

Slowly the disorder gave way to some semblance of organization. We had been wild in our pursuit, but this sudden reappearance of danger seemed to bring us back to our senses. Things about me were no longer a meaningless jumble, but took shape and regularity. I saw clearly, though remotely, as in a dream, all that happened. Up on the slope Crafton and Moore were gesticulating, shouting. Near by Lieutenant Campbell ran down the line, his lips moving, soundlessly in all that uproar, kicking, shoving, striking out with clenched fists at the more obtuse who did not yet understand what it was they must do. And all of a sudden I realized that I was doing the same.

"Back, get back!" I was shouting. "Take cover! Fall back on your former positions! Rogers is covering you up there. Get back now, before 'tis too late!"

Gradually, little by little, we brought order out of chaos, and, step by step, slipping from tree to tree and from bush to bush, we fell back to the high ground, where Rogers and the rest who had not surged out in pursuit stood ready to cover us with their fire.

But it had been a costly mistake. Of all our number near fifty lay abandoned in the snow below. Captain Bulkley was gone. Lieutenant Moore dropped at the foot of the bank, and Campbell fell halfway up. Pottinger had gone down before their first withering blast.

Back on the crest of the bank I looked about me, safe for the moment. Rogers stood a little distance away directing the defence of our position. Someone touched me on the shoulder. I looked up. It was Toby. He pointed at my side.

"You hit," he said.

I put my hand down and felt something warm and wet. I took it away and looked at it. It was stained crimson with blood. I looked down to see that my jerkin and my legging from the waist down was soaked with it. Yet I had not felt the ball strike, nor did I feel it now—only a sort of numbness in my side.

"It is nothing," I said, and loaded my musket with elaborate care to prove it.

He might have said more, but a renewed burst of firing in our front distracted our attention, and a fresh attack all along the front required all our concentration.

They came in waves, through the brushy tangle below, in such numbers that for a time it seemed the woods were alive with them. But our position was strong, and we were well placed among the trees for our own protection. At one moment they could be seen running towards us, slipping from tree to tree, coming within thirty yards of our front. Despite the cold, sweat rolled down my face and got in my eyes, as I worked—load and fire, fire and load—

with feverish haste. Acrid powder smoke stung my nostrils, and the barrel of my musket grew so hot that in order to hold it for aiming I must needs first scoop up a handful of snow to rest it on.

A wave of smoke drifted between me and the enemy at a moment when it seemed to me that in another instant they would be upon us, and I prepared to receive them hand to hand. But instead when the grey blanket drifted past it revealed them once more in full flight. Our concentrated fire had been too much for them.

This time, however, there was no pursuit. We had lost too many and were too weak to attack, even in their confusion. There was a momentary lull, while men prepared for the next attack, which we knew could not be far off. I sat up and leaned my back against my tree trunk. Rogers was crouching behind a spruce a little way off. As I sat up he looked at me, and I saw his eyes drop to my side and then come back to my face.

"How is it?" he called.

I told him the truth.

"I don't even feel it," I replied.

He looked worried.

"Well, hold on," he said, "we've lost all the officers we can afford now. There must be near eight hundred of 'em down there."

I wondered vaguely how he could tell. To me it had seemed there must be thousands. In the confusion I did not think it possible anyone could estimate their numbers. But it was certain we had come foul of a large force. I looked about me and missed the volunteers.

"What's become of Mr. Creed?" I asked.

"I sent 'em all back," said Rogers, "with Serjeant Huckins. They've had trouble all day with the snow. If we should be broken we might scatter; but they'd be in a bad fix."

I nodded.

"Get about now," he went on. "Tell your men when the next attack comes to fall back slowly on the hill until they get the steep of it at their backs."

He waved an arm backwards towards the two steep, wooded knolls that rose upon the ridge behind us. I nodded again.

"Watch your flanks," he said. "That's where they'll try to get at you."

Without waiting for an answer he turned and scuttled away,

stooping low and dodging from bush to tree to boulder towards the centre of our line.

Scarcely was he out of sight when a rattle of musketry in front indicated that the attack was about to be renewed. A bullet whacked the trunk of my tree on the other side, and another ploughed the snow a yard away. I left my cover and dropped back, zigzagging awkwardly in my clumsy snowshoes, until I reached the company line. McClary was the first man I found.

"Keep in touch," I ordered. "Watch the right: they may try to flank us. When they come on, drop back against the hill."

He passed the word along, and I could hear the men all down the line repeating it. I sent Toby, who had followed me, down to the left to round up stragglers, and send them back. By the time the first wave of Indians was to be seen flitting through the brush below, we had formed a solid front.

We met that attack staunchly, the first confusion of the fight being worn away, and fell back in orderly fashion until we had the steep of the hills close at our backs. This is not to say that we any of us had time to stand up and look about us. We were each one busy with his own problems, for they pressed us close, and we fired and fell back, each man minding his own affairs and leaving his neighbour to the solution of his own difficulties.

With the smoke lying thick among the trees, it was often impossible to see whether the enemy was still before us or whether they had broken; and often as not we had to fire blindly. Now and again we could catch a snap shot at an arm or a leg or a paint-daubed face half seen through a momentary rift, but for the most part we had no way of knowing the effect of our bullets.

When I felt the rising ground behind me I went up it a few paces and then passed the word left and right to stand where we were. There was a great pine a little on my left, with trunk enough to shelter twenty men; and I decided that this must be, for the time being, my headquarters. I dashed for it, the enemy's lead whining above my head and rattling in the bushes, and flung myself behind it. To my surprise I found its shelter already occupied by Creed, Kent, and Wrightson.

"Hey!" I cried. "I thought you'd gone."

Creed snapped a shot around the tree.

"We had," he replied, shouting to make himself heard above the crash of battle, "but we saw you hard pressed and came back."

"Good man!" I muttered, and aloud: "Where's Huckins?"

"I sent him to find Rogers," said Creed.

I nodded. "Here's where you find out how we fight," I said.

He grinned. "I've discovered why your officers carry muskets like private soldiers," he replied.

The crackle of musketry was by now almost continuous though, as far as I was able to make out, the advance had stopped and the enemy was firing from cover. It was hard to see anything directly in front of me, but there seemed to be some movement off to the right in the brush. I called Creed's attention to it, and we both fired at once. Judging from the commotion that ensued both shots took effect.

In a lull that fell momentarily I heard a shout go up from our right.

"They're climbing up to get behind us!"

By craning my neck I could see that a number of the enemy's Indians had swung around our right, beyond musket shot, and were climbing the hill beyond. Before I could give an order, however, I heard Rogers' voice behind me.

"Who's in command down there?" he demanded.

"Mr. Phillips," I replied.

"Well, send down word to Mr. Phillips to take his men and get up on the hill," he said. "Tell him to get there first. Don't let those Indians get there if you want to get home."

I passed the word to McClary, who ran down to where Phillips lay in the snow behind a clump of brush. The latter wasted no time in questions, but leapt to his feet, and with a handful of men at his heels raced for the summit of the knoll. We could not see what happened, for the crest of the hill hid them from our view, but presently there came the sound of heavy firing, and a moment later we saw several of the enemy's Indians tumbling down in flight. In the meantime Rogers had come into the shelter of our tree. He nodded to Creed, but said nothing about his return.

"All right?" he said to me.

"I think we've stopped them for the moment," I replied.

"They'll be back," he said, "as soon as they find their flanking movement has failed."

He stopped and gritted his teeth.

"God damn Haviland!" he swore. "If I'd the four hundred he promised me to begin with we'd have broken 'em before this!"

He made an effort to peer through the smoke and brush to the right to see what was happening.

"They tried the same thing on the left," he said. "I've sent Mr. Crafton that way."

He seemed to be talking more to himself than anyone, and I did not venture a reply. He appeared to think a moment, and then turned to Creed.

"Mr. Creed," he said, "will you and your gentlemen be so kind as to go up and support Mr. Crafton?"

Creed smiled at the formality with which Rogers had worded his request, and bowed.

"Yours to command, captain," he said, and turned to Kent and Wrightson. "Come along."

Rogers had already turned back towards the centre, and was slipping from cover to cover. But the three gentlemen of the regulars scorned such tactics. They stood up together and marched out from our shelter, large as life, making a bee line for the hill where the rattle of Crafton's defence could even then be heard.

I was horrified, and cried out in warning, "Take cover, take cover," but I doubt if they heard me. Creed and Kent went steadily onward, until the curve of the hill hid them from view. But Wrightson went no more than a dozen paces before he appeared to trip and fell face downward in the snow. I watched to see if he would move, but when he did not I concluded that he was dead.

There was no time to do more, for the enemy, seeing an officer in scarlet go down, chose that moment to renew their attack, and again the roar of musketry swelled, the woods filled with a dense cloud of smoke, through which it was impossible to see more than a few feet. I stood half clear of the great pine, loading and firing as rapidly as I could, until a quick movement a little to my right attracted my attention, and I turned to see the foggy smoke open and to find myself face to face with a swarthy, bearded Canadian in the blanket coat that was with them almost a uniform. He had his arm drawn back to split my skull with his hatchet, but I managed to drop my powder flask, with which I was just priming my musket, and swing the gun up in time to catch the blow upon the barrel. The flat of the hatchet slithered across my knuckles, where they gripped the barrel, sending needles of pain almost into my elbows; but I instinctively clung to my weapon and swung the muzzle into his face. I pulled the trigger and saw the black-bearded features disappear in a cloud of white powder smoke.

I felt rather than saw him fall, for I must needs turn at the instant to face a savage who came at me around the tree. But it was Toby who saved me from his knife by emptying his musket into the fellow's belly. I evened matters an instant later by clubbing my musket and swinging with all my strength upon a third, who at that moment leapt upon Toby with upraised tomahawk. My weapon took him beside the head, splitting it like a pumpkin, and striking upon the lock; and the weight of the gun, with the force of my swing, rather than the strength of my arms, snapped the stock off short.

But there was no time to look for another weapon. The smoke was clearing, and it could be seen that they were upon us in full force. The white blanket coats and dirty brown buckskins were everywhere in little knots. There was no time to see what our own men were doing; no time for aught but to fight as desperately as I knew how. I laid about me with my broken musket, finding the heavy barrel made an excellent club. Behind me on the hill, in the quieter intervals I could hear someone shouting.

"Back!" It was Rogers' voice. "Up on the hill! Fall back!"

In my snowshoes I could not obey without tripping, for to do so would have meant turning my back to an enemy too close for comfort, and I could not walk backwards without catching the tails. I had visions of myself borne under a mass of hacking, struggling savages, as I had seen others fall that very day, and I resolved to sell my life dearly at least; when, suddenly, relief came in the form of McClary and Phillips and Toby, who flew among my assailants with whirling hatchets and laid about them with such fury that they broke and fled before them.

The whole attack had taken but a few minutes, but I had lost all sense of time. When I saw the savages turn to run, I flung my broken weapon away, then turned and ran in my turn, only to find myself suddenly seized by the neck and hurried along by my faithful Toby, while McClary and Phillips panted at his heels.

A little way up the hill I saw a musket lying in the snow, and stooped to pick it up, only to toss it aside when I found it was a French fusee, whose barrel my own bullets would not fit. A little later I picked up an English gun with the initials J. B. cut into its stock. I remembered that Joseph Bean had so marked his gun, and for a moment I wondered what had become of him. But it was no time for coherent thought. Bullets whining past our ears quickly drove curiosity elsewhere.

We ran as quickly as we could, making hard going of it up the steep slope in the deep snow, and it was to our good fortune that the enemy who pursued us found the going fully as hard and so were unable to fire upon us more than they did, else we might not now be alive to tell it. Halfway up we passed Wrightson's body, the scalp already torn from his head, and I saw that my first guess had been correct; for a ball that must have been near the size of a baby's fist had entered beneath his left shoulder and passed out his chest, tearing nearly half the side away. We passed other bodies on the way, but most of them I could not recognize for the positions in which they lay.

We found Rogers and what was left of the command at the top of the hill, and there we made still another stand that sent the Frenchmen to cover; though by now they had learned the game, and kept up a steady fire as they advanced, forcing us to drop back little by little, the while we fired automatically as machines. Bit by bit they drove a wedge between us, taking advantage of the little hollow between the two knolls held the one by Phillips and the other by Crafton, and forcing the main party, under Rogers and myself, back on Crafton's position.

How long this took, I could not say, for I had lost all sense of the passage of time; though the whole engagement could not have lasted above an hour and a half, it being past midafternoon when we ambushed their advance guard. The first hint that came to me that the seemingly endless round of load and fire, duck, and load and fire again, could not go on for ever, was a voice at my elbow, harshly croaking.

"It's coming on dark," it said.

I looked around and was amazed to see Rogers, his face blackened with powder. His voice had been so hoarse and strained I could not recognize it.

" 'Twill be dark soon," he said. "Time for a getaway."

I looked about me and saw that what he said was true. Dusk hung heavily in the air.

"They may rush us first," I said.

He did not reply, but looked down to the right.

"They've taken Phillips," he said.

The knoll to which we had been driven was slightly higher than the one Phillips had held, and now, following the direction of his gaze, I found we could look down upon it. It was swarming with Canadians and Indians. As we watched I saw Phillips thrust up upon a stump. Someone waved a white rag. Others must have seen it too, for all along the line the firing died down, and for a moment there was silence.

"They've offered terms, cap'n." Phillips' voice floated up to us. "I got to take 'em, an' I'd advise you to do the same."

I saw the veins bulge in Rogers' neck, but when he replied his voice was well controlled.

"Do as you think best," he called back. "We're holding on."

Somebody cheered behind us, and a musket banged. In another instant the battle was on again. But through the smoke of it, we could look down and see all that happened on the knoll below.

There could not have been more than half a dozen of Phillips' men left, but these were dragged to trees and tied. Hands reached up and dragged Phillips from his stump. He too was dragged to a tree and his hands bound behind it. A savage stepped forward and buried his hatchet in the breast of one of the bound men. It seemed to be a signal, for all the savages on the knoll set up a hideous yowling and dashed in to hack at the poor devils, chopping and stabbing with knife and hatchet, until their victims literally hung in shreds, the while we on the hill above stared in helpless horror.

"Their terms!" said Rogers, his lips close to my ear so that he would be heard.

We set up a fire upon them that presently forced them to desist from their sport and turn their attention to us; but not until three of their victims hung in bloody, shapeless masses against the tree trunks. My last glimpse of Phillips, before the drifting smoke shut him from view, showed him standing calm in his bonds, awaiting what fate might hold for him.

As the fury of the fight redoubled and the smoke rolled across the hilltop in clouds, Rogers drew me back a little.

"We'll have to make a run for it soon," he said. "It'll be too late if we don't. Such wounded as can travel ought to get away first. Round 'em up and head for the lake with 'em. Wait for us at the sledges."

"But you're going to need every man!" I protested.

He jerked his head impatiently.

"If there's no wounded here to hamper us," he said, "we may get free. But if they stay they won't be able to get away fast enough. We'll have to stay to defend them, and we'll all be caught. D'ye see?"

"I see," I said, "but why send me?"

"Because you're wounded yourself," he snapped. "Now get on, and take that Toby along to guide."

I had not had time to think of my own wound, so furious had the fighting been. Indeed, though I had lost some blood by it, I did not think it could be severe. I said as much.

"God damn it!" he shouted, his face black with fury. "Will you do as you're told? Get out! We'll cover you as long as we can. When you hear the shooting stop, you'll know we've run for it. Look out for yourselves then!"

I went then, and with Toby's aid rounded up all the wounded I could find who could travel. As we passed southward along the ridge, past Lieutenant Crafton's detachment, I saw Captain Creed, his white teeth gleaming at me through a mask of powder stain in a friendly grin.

"Luck!" he said, and waved his hand.

I waved back, and a moment later we began to drop down on the far side of the ridge, turning our faces towards the lake. Behind us the sound of battle diminished rapidly, until we had gone about halfway. Then suddenly, like a candle that has been snuffed out, it stopped short.

When I heard that, I knew that our danger was really begun. We were about thirty, more than half the party of survivors at the top of the hill, but fortunately only five were so seriously hurt as to slow their progress. These I placed between comparatively sound men, and drew off a dozen of the best to act as rear guard, the command of which I took myself, over Toby's protests, knowing that if the savages followed up on our trail it might well become a running fight.

In this order we came some time after dark to the lake shore, and turning southward soon found the cache where we had hidden our packs and sledges. By the same token we also found Rogers, pacing upon the ice, while a little knot sat silent and exhausted behind him on the snow.

"Who's there?" he said, whirling, as the sound of our approach carried to him along the ice.

"Ferguson," I replied.

"Ah!" he said. "Good! You got through. They didn't follow you?"

"They didn't overtake us if they did," I replied.

"Lose any?" he inquired.

"Not since we left the hill," I said.

"How many are you?" he demanded.

"Thirty-one," I replied.

"Ah!" he repeated, in that same lifeless tone in which he had said it before. "That makes fifty-three. Fifty-three out of a hundred and eighty! God damn Haviland!"

A low whistle sounded on the hill above us.

"What's that?" said Rogers. "It sounds like Phillips, but it can't be. Get that Indian up there and tell him to find out what it is."

I sent Toby up to investigate, and Rogers turned back to me.

"We've got the sledges out and ready," he said. "Get the men who're badly hurt onto them. Tell the others to get out their packs and skates and put them on. We'll have to get away from here."

Steps sounded crunching in the snow, and we turned to find Toby coming up, followed by a familiar figure.

"Phillips!" cried Rogers. "How'd you get away? They had you tied when we saw you last!"

Phillips grinned painfully. Even in the half-dark we could see that he had been badly beaten. His eyes were both blackened and swollen and his face was cut in several places.

"They didn't find this," he said, and held up a small clasp knife. "I put it in my sleeve when they took me. Thought they'd do me in too, but your fire saved me, I guess. While they were busy with you I cut my way loose."

He stopped and sobered thoughtfully.

"The others were dead," he said simply.

No one spoke for a minute; then Rogers cleared his throat noisily.

"All right," he said. "Let's get going!"

We dragged out the remaining packs, and those of us who could fastened on our skates. We put the badly wounded men upon the sleds, which we proposed to pull ourselves, and Rogers

lined the men up, skating down the front of the line in a brief
inspection with me at his heels. I was dazed to see how few of
them there were.

"I want two sound men," he said when he was done, "to carry
the word to Fort Edward."

McClary and Toby came forward.

"You'll do," said Rogers.

He scribbled hastily upon a sheet which he tore from his orderly book, signed it, and handed it to Toby.

"Don't waste time," he said. "I'll look for relief at Hoop Island
by tomorrow night!"

He nodded, and they were off almost at once. Rogers turned to
me.

"All right," he said, "we'll march."

A thought struck me.

"Where's Captain Creed and Mr. Kent?" I asked.

He shrugged. "Lost," he said. "They were with us when we
started. When we came here they were gone. We didn't linger on
the way. They must have dropped back somewhere."

I looked at him in horror.

"But you can't leave them like this!" I exclaimed.

"Can't I?" he said bitterly. "What the devil else can I do? I have
to look after my men, don't I?"

I fell in beside him, and skated in silence, making no answer,
for I knew he was right.

ONE MAN'S DEATH

¶ 1 It was a sorry company that came two days later into Fort Edward. Mr. Stark, who during our absence had returned from his recruiting, met us at Hoop Island with supplies and sledges; a welcome reinforcement, for what with wounds and the cold and utter exhaustion we were well-nigh perishing, and we had no way of knowing that the enemy were not still upon our trail.

Stark was sympathetic and shocked. He had grown into a stoical coolheaded man, with a face usually as expressionless as an Indian's. But, on this occasion he made no effort to mask his fury and disgust. Nor was he alone in that. The men who came with him were loud in their denunciation of a command that would thus waste its strength out of personal spite and jealousy, and although we bade them be quiet in the interests of discipline we could not but be secretly pleased at their grumbling.

That the general public was also with us was evident upon our arrival. We entered the fort between silent rows of stolid, wooden-faced men, both regulars and provincials, who had turned out from their quarters to watch us march in. There was no cheering, no shouting, scarcely even a spoken word. Once a man somewhere in the pack said "Cor!" but after that there was only the creak of our feet on the dry snow and the slipping sound of the sledge runners to break the silence. Within a quarter of an hour of our dismissal upon the parade our quarters upon the island were overrun with officers of all ranks, come to tender their sympathy and congratulations upon the stand we had made. But with all this we heard never a word from Colonel Haviland. Some message to honour those who had fallen or regret what had happened, I believed, was surely due us; but I never heard that any such sentiment was ever expressed, either publicly or privately. Indeed, so far as I was able to discover, his only comment upon the entire affair was a sneering remark in the officers' mess that Mr. Rogers was to be congratulated upon his own escape!

Rogers was, of course, furious at this; and he swore that he would bring charges against the colonel that would drive him from the service in disgrace. I believe he did make some report; but whether Haviland's influence was too great or the high command too indifferent to act, I do not know. Nothing ever came of it.

In so far as I was concerned the whole affair was but a source of misery, trouble, and disappointment from beginning to end. On the return journey to the fort I had ventured to console myself with the thought that at least my wound might be the means of getting me a long sought-after leave. But even this was to be withheld, it seemed, for when I spoke of it to Rogers he shook his head sourly and replied that since we were now so shorthanded he could not spare any for leave but those who were flat upon their backs.

In justice to him, for all my disappointment, I must say that he was quite right. The wound was such as to deserve scant notice, the bullet having traced its way diagonally downwards across the flesh of my belly and side, leaving a gaping slash that was bloody in the extreme and hideous to look upon, but otherwise not alarming. Consequently, I spent the two days next after our return to the fort flat in my bunk, and the next week attended to light duties about the camp. At the end of a fortnight I was once more fit for duty in the woods, and Rogers lost no time in sending me out.

It was about this time that we began to hear reports concerning the coming campaign. According to rumour General Amherst was to be given the supreme command, and a simultaneous attack was to be made at three widely separated points: at Louisbourg on the east, at Ticonderoga in the centre, and at Fort Duquesne on the Ohio in the west. Amherst himself, it was said, was bringing a strong force from England to the siege of Louisbourg. The northern colonies were to raise an army of near ten thousand for the attack on Ticonderoga; while an additional five thousand were to be drawn from the southern provinces for the Ohio expedition; which last was to be led by Brigadier Forbes.

The magnitude of the plan was in itself proof of the zeal with which the home government was attacking the problem, and this went far to revive our enthusiasm and raise new hopes of victory in place of those that had dwindled so sadly at the fall of Fort William-Henry in the previous year. But the news which set us all to cheering was that of the order recalling the Earl of Loudoun, who had made himself exceedingly unpopular with his fumbling and blundering and the high-handed way in which he had quartered his regulars upon the populace. This enthusiasm was slightly damped when it was announced that Loudoun would be succeeded in command of the centre by the doddering Abercrombie. But almost immediately it was revived again by the word that the post of second in command would be filled by my Lord Howe, who was thereby raised to the rank of brigadier, and who in the short time he had been in the colonies had made himself tremendously popular with all with whom he had come in contact. For my part I was overjoyed at the news, for quite apart from considering his Lordship an excellent and vigorous leader I esteemed him as a friend and rejoiced at his good fortune. Those who knew both men and who were familiar with the workings of the general's staff predicted freely that the actual leadership and command of operations would fall upon Lord Howe; and in this they were not far wrong, as it proved, though had it been otherwise things might have fallen out better than they did.

A few days after the arrival of this news Rogers was summoned hastily to Albany and thence to New York to wait upon the general himself. I was out upon a scout at the time, so that I was not a witness to his departure; but I was in camp at his return, and chanced to meet him near the door of his cabin as he came up the path from the river. Seldom have I seen a man so evidently satisfied, from his expression, with himself and with the world in general.

"Well, captain," I said—a bit sourly, it is to be feared, since I was still piqued at having been denied my leave, and jealous that he should have been able to go while I could not—"I trust you had a successful journey."

"Major!" he bellowed jovially, not in the least put out at my surliness. "It's major now, my lad. Major Robert Rogers, Commanding His Majesty's Independent Companies of Rangers! Come in! We'll have a drink on it."

He took me by the arm and dragged me inside the cabin, flung his bag upon the bunk, and turned to the cupboard, where he rummaged about for one of the squat bottles he kept there.

"Look in the bag," he said over his shoulder, "and fetch me the packet of papers you'll find there."

I did as I was bid, and he took the packet from me after setting out bottle and glasses upon the table.

"Now where the devil?" he said, ruffling through the official-looking papers. Then: "Ah! Here we are."

He snapped one of the documents from the binding string and pushed it to me.

"Here," he said. "It's a present for you."

I took the paper automatically and looked at it dully. It was folded and had an official-looking seal.

"What is it?" I asked.

"A commission," he replied. "Captain's commission. You're to have Bulkley's company. Don't you want it?"

He looked fierce—frowning.

I laughed.

"Of course I want it," I said. "Why didn't you say so?"

"We'll make it official at parade tomorrow," he said, and poured two glasses.

The heavy odour of the rum filled the tiny cabin. He raised his glass, and I followed suit.

"The King's arms," he said.

We drank.

"There are five new companies ordered up," he said, setting down his glass. "And we're to fill the old ones. We'll be at full strength by the middle of next month: eight hundred men."

"It's true then," I said.

"What's true?" he demanded.

"All this about a strong centre attack," I replied.

He looked at me and laughed.

"You may lay to that," he said. "It's true enough, mark my words. By the first of July there'll be thirty thousand men lying at the head of the lake ready to march!"

I looked at him incredulously and whistled. Thirty thousand men! If that were so, this was the end. The French would never be able to withstand such a force.

"I saw Lord Howe in Albany," he said before I could make any remark. "He sent his compliments, and said you are to keep your eyes open."

He looked at me curiously.

"I don't know what that means," he added. "Maybe you do, but it's orders."

I nodded, but did not say that I understood it as little as did he. Several times in the next few days I pondered over the meaning of that cryptic message, but I never found the answer. And presently in the excitement of reorganization I forgot it.

The events that followed seemed to bear out Rogers' predictions. Within a week after his return men were dispatched to the lake to rebuild the camp on the site of the ruined Fort William-Henry. Skilled carpenters and boat builders were set to making battoes and whaleboats and flatboats for the artillery. Troops began to come in, slowly at first in isolated companies, and then more rapidly, regiments at a time. By June there were three thousand at the lake and six thousand more at Fort Edward. We began to grow cramped for space. Companies were filled out. Regiments were enlarged. And the Rangers were no exception to the rule.

By mid-May our five new companies were in, among them one of Stockbridge Indians commanded by Captain Jacob Nawna-wapteeonks himself. These last Rogers handled in masterful fashion, almost as if he were part Indian himself, although he had no great faith in them. They were good enough fighters, he maintained, if they were mixed with white men to steady them, and they were valuable as scouts under the direction of a white officer. Accordingly this was the method he used to send them out. It was while returning from one of these scouts, the lone white in a party of seventeen, that I had an amusing encounter that deserves mention.

We had scouted Ticonderoga from the south, returning homeward along the South Arm of Lake Champlain and striking overland towards the new camp on Lake George. Our way brought us to the road that ran from Fort Edward to the lake, at a point about midway between Halfway Brook and the camp, over a high wooded shoulder that loomed above the wagon track. I was first over the crest of the ridge, and was descending rapidly towards the road, when suddenly Toby, who was first behind me, grasped my arm and held up his hand for silence. Behind me the line of braves, grotesque in their green leggings and paint, stood rooted motionless, listening.

I listened too, though at first I could hear nothing. Then, after a moment, it came to me, a thin distant squealing and squalling, that seemed to float up to us from a great distance down the road. As we listened it drew nearer, until all at once I thought I recognized the sound, though I could scarce believe my ears.

I looked back at my Indians and saw that they were obviously uneasy. Their eyes were bulging in superstitious horror, and their jaws hung slack, as if they thought that all the demons of the forest were after them. Even Toby, whose faith in me was unbounded, looked uncertain.

I passed back a word of reassurance, and looked about me. A little below was a ledge of rock that stood out among the surrounding woods and overlooked the highroad. Motioning to my companions to follow, I made my way thither. As we went the sound grew louder, so that I knew I could not be mistaken. It filled the glen with a wild skirling, rushing up at us through the trees and seeming to come from everywhere at once. I found myself trembling with excitement as I climbed the rock and beckoned the others up beside me.

We had not long to wait. For a few minutes the wild music filled the air, growing louder with each passing instant. Then they swung in view around a bend in the road, the pipers first, as I had pictured them, their cheeks bulging with the blowing and the bags of the pipes swelling beneath their arms. After them, in column of fours, the late afternoon sun flashing upon their muskets, their bare knees swinging in time to the skirling of the pipes, and the dark green of their tartans blending with the fresher green of the light spring woods, came rank upon rank of good Scotch Highlanders.

I looked at my companions, and came near to split with laughter at the amazement in their faces, for they had never seen anything like this before. To me, though it came as a surprise, I was not yet so astounded as they, for I had heard that some of the newraised Highland regiments were coming to take a hand in our war. Nor was I surprised to hear that they had already earned a name for themselves among the French as the *sauvages sans culottes*.

As we lay upon the rock and watched them they came on to a point almost directly beneath us and there halted to rest. The devil of mischief must have gotten into me at that moment, for I saw my chance to play a trick on them that I could not resist. Raising up my voice, loud and clear so that they could not fail to hear me, I called to them in Gaelic welcoming them to our dark hills.

The effect was instantaneous. There was a stir in the ranks as the men looked at one another in astonishment at this Highland voice shouting at them out of the alien forest, and I could see their faces turning uneasily this way and that as they tried to locate me among the trees.

Then one of their officers raised his voice and demanded to know who I was. I gave him my name and rank, and scrambled down the road to them with my Indians. There again I was highly amused, for there was not a man among them had ever before set eyes upon a savage, and their interest and astonishment was plain. They were, I learned, the first battalion of the Forty-second Regiment, but new landed in New York, under command of Major Duncan Campbell of Inverawe, a tall sombre gentleman of middle age, who gave me a courtly welcome and showed much interest in my savages.

In the end, it proved, the joke was on me, for the major requisitioned me to act as a guide and advanced party for his column, thus delaying my arrival in the camp by a matter of some hours. Nevertheless, I took some pardonable pride in the fact that it was I, with my sixteen red men, who first brought the Highland regiments into the camp. Moreover I made new friends that day, and thereafter there was scarcely a day, when I was in the camp, I did not pay at least one visit to their regimental mess.

It was early June when my Lord Howe came up to the fort from Albany. He had not been in camp a day before I received a summons to wait upon him. I went at once and was most cordially received.

"Tell me, captain," said he, when once the formalities of greeting were over, "do you remember the letter you took from a dead Frenchman some little time back?"

I cast my thoughts back over the campaigns of the past several years and nodded.

"I remember," I said.

"Have you seen or heard of aught here in camp," he asked, "that might lead us to the writer of those letters?"

I looked at him in amazement, for I had thought that matter long since closed.

"What?" I cried. "Has your Excellency not found the man yet? Why, I mind it was but a week ago they hanged a Dutchman of Fort Lydiass for a spy! I thought you had him."

But he shook his head and gave a wry smile.

"Oh, we have hanged a dozen, more or less," he said, "and there was proof enough against them. But they were but small fry: runners, go-betweens, links in a chain. But we have yet to put our fingers on the source."

"You think," I said, "it is a single man directs all their activities?"

His eye gleamed, and he slapped his hand among the papers scattered on the table before him.

"Think!" he cried. "I don't think it, I know it! As surely as I am sitting here before you, I know it! I know the man. But the rascal is clever. He will not give me proof!"

"Eh?" I cried. "You know him, sir?"

I should have liked to ask whom he suspected, for I was overwhelmed with curiosity, but for once I let discretion rule.

"I know him," he replied. "I thought you too might know something of it, but I see I was wrong."

I must have looked blank, for he laughed.

"No matter," he said. "That you know naught of it speaks only well for you."

He hitched his chair forward a little and eyed me narrowly.

"I have a plan," said he, "whereby, if my suspicions prove correct, we can hoist the scoundrel by his own petard. If I may have your help it will be an easy matter to put through."

"I am yours to command, your Excellency," I said.

He waved his hand impatiently.

"I know!" he said. "I know! But these things are best done by volunteers."

"You may count on me, sir," I said.

He smiled. "Good! I shall!"

He hitched his chair forward once more, and placed his elbows upon the litter of papers on the table.

"It is not much that I shall ask you to do," he said. "Major Rogers already has his orders. You will take not more than six men and proceed to the narrows of the South Arm. There you will lie ready to observe what passes. If my suspicions are well grounded the French will appear in some considerable force early Wednesday morning and take up a position near you. As soon as they appear you will draw off. If possible take a prisoner and bring him to me. I will also ask you to write a report of what you have seen."

He made a gesture of dismissal, and I started to leave. But he called me back.

"Mind you, captain," he said, "no word of this to anyone!"

To say that I was puzzled would be to put it mildly. I could make no connection between his first words and his final orders. It seemed to me a simple scout, such as he had proposed, could be carried out without all this secrecy. Nevertheless, I knew him well enough to know that he would have excellent reason for anything he did, and I set about carrying out his orders without question.

As it happened everything fell out much as he had predicted it would. I selected the six men of my scout with great care and led them straight to the high rocks overlooking the narrows of the South Arm, where I had lain once before on a somewhat similar mission. Wednesday's dawn revealed the lake to north-ward acrawl with battoes and canoes. Counting six to each canoe and ten to a battoe I placed their numbers at about four hundred. Toby, dispatched along the shore for further investigation, returned to say that another party of fifty was approaching by that route.

Mindful of his Lordship's orders, I drew off some distance down the lake, where I lay and watched while they landed from their boats and took up a position on both sides of the narrows, covering the lake so that scarcely a gnat could have passed undetected. Once they had so settled themselves I crept in close with my party, and had the good luck to take a French serjeant of regulars, who had gone a little apart from the main body to relieve himself; after which, with my prisoner securely bound and gagged, I made all haste back to Fort Edward where I lost no time in presenting myself at Lord Howe's quarters.

I found headquarters in an uproar, and learned from Mr. Monypenny, who was lately become a major, and who was acting as my Lord's aide, that preparations were going forward to move the entire army up to Lake George. For four hours I cooled my heels in an anteroom, while messengers came and went. But presently his Lordship found a free moment and I was summoned into his presence.

"Ah, captain," he said, by way of greeting, "I see you have your man."

He took the report of my scout, which I had written out in accord with his orders, and between us we questioned the Frenchman closely.

It was little enough that he could tell us, or so it seemed to me. He was of the battalion of La Reine, which was then at Ticonderoga. Seven other battalions were expected. Monsieur de Montcalm was in command, and his present force at the fort was not above two thousand. On the previous afternoon an Indian had come in with information that Major Rogers, with fifty men, was ordered out to scout Ticonderoga by way of the South Arm. Monsieur de Montcalm had at once ordered their party out to waylay him in the narrows. He did not know the Indian. Neither did he hear from whom the message had come.

I was frankly disappointed, but my Lord Howe seemed pleased. He rubbed his hands together in satisfaction.

"Good! Good!" he exclaimed. "It could not have happened better!"

He stepped to the door and summoned the serjeant of the guard.

"Here," he said when that worthy had appeared. "See that this man is taken to Albany and held there under close guard until further orders from me."

The serjeant led our prisoner from the room, and Howe turned to me laughing.

"My good Ferguson!" he exclaimed. "You are bewildered?"

I admitted as much.

"And well you might be!" he said. "But the explanation is really simple. You see, having my own suspicions in certain quarters, I let false information as to Major Rogers' movements be circulated there, on the theory that if the French acted upon it my suspicions stood proven fact. What this prisoner has told us is simply further proof."

I looked at him amazed.

"Why, then," I said, "you have the man!"

"Beyond the least shadow of doubt," he agreed.

"You'll order his arrest, of course," I said, "and have it done with?"

But he shook his head.

"There will be no arrest for the moment," he said.

I must have looked still further bewildered, for he smiled.

"The army moves up to the lake tomorrow," he said. "As soon as General Abercrombie arrives from Albany we move against Ticonderoga. There will be no time for courts-martial. Since the fellow does not know we have him, it will be better to let him stew in his juice a little longer. Perhaps he will find other ways for us to hang him. In the meantime we have the proof. When Ticonderoga is ours the trap will be sprung, and you shall make the arrest."

"Me, sir?" I exclaimed, forgetting grammar in my surprise.

He nodded. " 'Twill be but simple justice," he said.

"But—" I began, for I could not make head or tail of this.

He held up his hand.

"No more," he said.

He turned and lifted a leather-bound box from beside his cot and set it upon the table. This he opened with a key that was hung about his neck on a ribband. Lifting the lid, he dropped my report inside, and locked the box again.

"This fellow," he said, "has been a slippery one. I have had to tread carefully and alone in order to get the proof I needed. Now that I have it I shall keep it locked up here among my personal papers until the time comes to make it public."

He tapped the box gently with a long finger.

"I need not remind you," he went on gravely, "of the necessity for secrecy. Even Major Monypenny does not know how closely I have followed this thing. I must ask you to keep strict silence upon the whole matter."

"You may count upon me, your Excellency," I said.

I left my Lord Howe's quarters scarce any the wiser than when I had arrived. But I did not concern myself greatly with the matter, for it seemed to me that it had little to do with my affairs. Indeed, I was surprised that his Lordship had been so confidential with me; but this I laid in the end to no more than friendship, for I knew that he held me in good favour. At the same time, I could not but observe that he had given me precious little vital information.

As I could not see what connection I might have with the case, beyond carrying out my Lord Howe's orders, I dropped the matter from my mind as soon as I had passed outdoors, and turned my steps towards the officers' mess, where I hoped to find Captain Carrigain, who had but lately come up from Albany, and with whom I had promised to play a round of drafts.

The captain was not there, but, to my amazement, my cousin Hubert was. I had not heard that he had been ordered up, and after the moment it took for me to recover from my surprise I pushed my way across the room towards him. He was talking to several foppish-seeming young officers, and did not see me approach. Indeed, he was not aware of my presence until I touched his elbow and spoke his name.

"Hubert!" I said.

He started and looked about at me, and I swear if ever I saw a man disconcerted it was he.

"Uh—Jamie!" he exclaimed. "What are you doing here?"

"Why," I said, surprised, "I've been here off and on all year. What's odd in that?"

"But I thought you'd be with Rogers," he said.

I shook my head, puzzled.

"No," I said, "we often go out on separate scouts. Rogers went up along Lake George. I've just come back from the South Arm."

"The South Arm!" he exclaimed. "Then—but I thought— Oh, I see!"

He looked at me sharply.

"The major's out on Lake George, you say?" he asked.

I nodded wondering, and for an instant I had a flash of suspicion. Then Hubert laughed easily.

"Well, well!" he said. "It only goes to show you can't believe everything. I had heard somewhere that the French were out along the Mohawk, and that Rogers had been ordered down after them!"

The explanation fell so glibly from his lips that it seemed wholly plausible to me. I laughed.

"Someone's been pulling your foot," I told him. "What brings you here?"

He made a gesture of impatience.

"A lot of nonsense," he replied petulantly. "Brigadier Howe seems determined to leave no one behind. Every officer and man must be at the front, he says! And what's to become of the service of supply if he keeps up a policy of that sort, I ask you."

I laughed again. "A little active service will do you good," I told him. "You're putting on a paunch."

His companions laughed, but he looked annoyed. I realized I had touched a sore spot.

"Come and have supper with me," I said. "I'll show you the Rangers in camp—and you can give me news of Albany. That wife of mine has a phobia for pen and ink."

But he shook his head.

"Sorry," he said. "I'm already engaged with the colonel for supper."

I was as well pleased, though I did not show it, for I found I took but little pleasure in his company. We talked then for some minutes, while he told me that Dorcas was well and that little James Hubert was becoming quite a lad. Purity, he said with a leer, was growing more beautiful each day.

"A little spitfire, that one," he added.

But though I resented the freedom with which he spoke I refused to be drawn into a quarrel upon that matter, and after a few more banal exchanges we took our leave of each other and I made my way across the river to my own quarters.

I ate a solitary meal that night, and promptly afterwards rolled into my bunk; for I was tired from the day's exertions. But I did not fall asleep at once. The picture of Hubert, amazed at my presence in the fort, kept rising up before me. Plainly he had been surprised, and not a little nonplussed, to see me. Could it be that Hubert was the man to whom my Lord Howe had referred?

I put the question from me at once as absurd. His explanation had been simple and plausible. I myself had heard rumours of scattered raiding along the Mohawk, and it was quite possible that someone had set a report afoot that Rogers would be sent to put a stop to them. Such false alarms were common stock in the army at that time. Still I could not rid myself of the feeling that all was not as it should be. I made up my mind that in the morning I would wait upon my Lord Howe and tell him of the conversation, and upon that thought I fell into a fretful sleep.

In the morning, however, at dawn, Lord Howe marched out before I could reach him, at the head of the main body of regulars; while I was left behind with the rest of the Rangers to await Major Rogers' return. The latter came in three days later, whereupon we all moved up to the lake. There the camp was in such a bustle of preparation that the matter quite slipped my mind. Indeed, even had I remembered it, I doubt if I could have seen his Lordship, for from the very break of day until long after nightfall he was swamped with the affairs of the army, and none but the officers of the staff were allowed to approach his quarters.

Three weeks later we were embarked in boats, sixteen thousand strong, and the great march on Ticonderoga began.

2

The troops embarked on the fifth of July from the site of Fort William-Henry. Close upon sixteen thousand troops, brilliant in gold and scarlet, in whaleboats and battoes, spread across the sparkling water of the lake from shore to shore, drums thumping and pipes squealing, made a moving and impressive sight on that bright, sunny morning. Colonel Bradstreet and his battoemen took the centre of the advanced guard, with the Rangers, some eight hundred strong, on their left, and Gage's light infantry on their right. Next came the regulars, my Lord Howe's Fifty-fifth in the lead, followed by the Sixtieth, the Twenty-seventh, the Forty-fourth, the Forty-sixth, and the Eightieth infantry. Then came the Forty-second Highlanders and two huge scows, propelled by sweeps and mounted with artillery, so arranged as to be able to cover the landing. On both flanks came the provincial regiments from Massachusetts, Connecticut, New York, New Jersey, Rhode Island, and New Hampshire, resplendent in new blue uniforms. Behind these were the battoes full of supplies and provisions for the siege, together with more flatboats with artillery; and in the rear came a guard of provincials and regulars.

By five in the evening we had made twenty-five miles to Sabbath Day Point, where we landed and made camp for dinner. About ten in the evening we re-embarked, and now my Lord Howe rode forward in his whaleboat with Major Rogers, Colonel Bradstreet, and Colonel Gage. I went ahead at this time to reconnoitre the landing place, and after approaching as close as I dared made out the campfires of the French who were stationed there. Returning as quickly as I might, I met the army about dawn four miles from the landing and reported my find. Thereupon Major Rogers, with my Lord Howe and Colonel Bradstreet, went ahead to look the ground over.

We came up with them waiting about a mile offshore, and there the army was halted while Colonel Bradstreet and his battoemen went ahead to clear the landing. Small though the defending party was, it put up a spirited, if brief, battle before retiring. For a half-hour the army lay upon their oars while the rattle of musketry and the flash of shots, showing luridly through the morning mists, came to us across the water. Then the firing seemed to die away, and presently a boat came out from shore to announce that the landing had been cleared, and that Colonel Bradstreet had gone ahead in pursuit.

A few minutes later the first boat's keel ground upon the shore, and the army began disembarking. The work went forward rapidly, and by nine the entire force was landed and stood ready on its arms to march. It was at this point was made the first of that fatal series of blunders that was to end in disaster.

It is easy enough to say, when everything is finished, what should have been done. But what seems so simple afterwards is not always clear at the time. A little less haste at that moment, a curb upon our impatience, a slow methodical advance along accepted lines might have saved us heart-rending loss and crushing defeat. But there was none among us to see it then.

Colonel Bradstreet returned shortly after the last company had been landed with the report that the enemy had retired across the river, which here swept in a great semicircle, and had burned their bridge behind them. A council was hastily called. The obvious move was overlooked. A less evident decision was taken. The orders for the march passed, and the troops lined up.

The move that now seems so logical was simple enough. The road from the landing crossed from the west bank of the river to the east in about a half-mile. It was the bridge at this crossing that the enemy had burned. From that bridge the road crossed the ground inside the river's loop, and then, at the sawmill, recrossed the stream. It would have been an easy matter, if somewhat slower, to bring up the artillery to protect the crossing, rebuild the bridge, and push on along the road. But instead of this it was decided to lead the army through the woods along the west bank of the river, following the stream's wide looping course, and coming out upon the road again below the second crossing, behind the enemy's position.

Now, the great flaw in this was that no one knew exactly what lay between us and the fort by that route. A little brook, the one on whose upper waters we had fought our disastrous battle on snowshoes not long before, emptied into the river somewhere along the way. But beyond this, I believe, not even Rogers knew the character of the ground before us. To our great dismay we were soon to find out.

Despite our prompt and early landing it was past noon before the order came for the troops to move out. We marched in three columns, the Rangers at the head of the centre column and a little in advance of the Connecticut regiments of Lyman and Fitch, which headed the columns on either flank, the regular regiments falling in behind: Gage's on the right, Howe's Fifty-fifth in the centre, the Highlanders on the left, and so on.

Our line of march could scarcely have been worse chosen had it been picked by Monsieur de Montcalm himself. Within a half-mile we came into thick virgin timber, through which we had literally to force our way. This was followed by something better than a mile of spruce bog, which in turn gave way to a tangled windfall in which tree trunks and great upended roots lay scattered about every which way like so many toothpicks tossed willy-nilly upon a table.

Even to Rangers trained and equipped for such going it was bad enough. Branches and briers clutched at our clothing. The mucky ground sucked at our ankles. Roots reached out to trip us, and the tangled trunks of fallen logs blocked our way, so that we were for ever stooping to crawl under or scramble over them. Low-hanging branches of spruce and balsam became tangled in our packs or slapped across our faces. And as if this were not enough myriad swarms of the tiny black gnats that infest our forests at this time of the year filled the air above our heads, biting the backs of our necks, getting into our eyes and nostrils, making us cough and sneeze. I hated to think what might be happening to the regulars behind us, to many of whom this was a first experience with our deep woods. I cursed the haste that had sent us off along this route.

Up forward I could see Rogers plodding along, the back of his neck red with the rage I knew must be empurpling his face. Every now and again he would slap viciously at the flies that buzzed about his ears; and from time to time the light air would carry to my ears the sound of his sulphurous cursing.

Our orders were to gain the summit of the low mountain that stood a little northward of the river bend; to stand there until the rest of the army should come up; and from there bear eastward to the road at the sawmill. It was a route that should have taken us, in good going, not more than a half-hour at the most. Yet it was more than an hour before we gained the top of the mountain. There Rogers disposed us along the eastern slope in a position of defence against possible attack, and there we settled down to await the arrival of the rest of the army.

It soon became apparent that we were to have a considerable wait. Backward, to the south, over the spruce bog towards the lake, a thick green curtain of treetops hid all movement from our sight. Indeed, had I not well known their presence I should never have guessed that a vast army was struggling towards us through that innocent-seeming leafy jungle. To eastward, through the treetops we could see smoke rising from the point where the sawmill lay hidden by the river at the foot of the falls. That way, at least, lay familiar ground, for we had often lain upon this slope with our scouting parties to raid the road that ran between the sawmill and the fort.

A quarter of an hour passed without a word from the army struggling below. Rogers began to fidget with impatience. He called up several parties and sent three of them down towards the sawmill to reconnoitre and two back to find the army and guide them to us. A half-hour later the parties that had been sent eastward returned to report that a strong force of French was entrenched near the sawmill. And a moment later one of those sent to the rear came in to report that the army was in complete confusion, the columns having fallen in upon one another and become hopelessly entangled, but that the whole was advancing slowly in our direction. A few moments later a crashing in the brush signified that some were approaching, and an instant later the head of Lyman's regiment appeared, followed closely by that of Fitch.

The Connecticuters halted just under the crest of the ridge and flung themselves down upon the ground. Colonel Lyman and Colonel Fitch came forward to consult with Rogers. The major greeted them courteously, and made room for them to sit down beside him on a log. Scarcely had they done so, however, when a rattle of musketry burst suddenly in the rear of the Connecticut regiments.

Fitch, stocky and moonfaced, looked up with a startled expression.

"Here!" he cried. "What's up?"

Lyman, more active in mind and body, was already on his feet.

"By God," he cried, "they've cut in between us and the main body! Get down there and form a front. We'll catch them in the rear. I'll take the right. Mr. Rogers, go down and take Mr. Fitch's left as far as the river."

There was no time for questions. Even before the words were out of his mouth our men had begun a circling movement, running down through the brushy woods towards the river in such a way that we formed a new front, facing back the way we had come.

In this order we began to advance, dodging from cover to cover, while the sound of musket fire ahead swelled and grew into an uproar. Patches of smoke began to drift through the woods, taking ghostly shapes in the blotchy sunlight that filtered down through the leaves. Occasional bullets began to buzz angrily overhead and to thuck viciously into tree trunks. As I walked forward I noticed how lazily the leaves, cut from the branches by stray shots, drifted down to the ground. Off on my right, through the haze of smoke I could make out some of Fitch's men closing in. And once I caught a flash of scarlet far ahead. I remember thinking that, whoever they were, we had them in a pocket, and that they could not escape us. Then a bearded Frenchmen stepped from behind a tree some distance in front of me, and I threw up my musket and fired.

The white blossom of smoke hid him for a moment from my view, and when I had charged on through it he was nowhere to be seen. In the next moment the woods were suddenly full of Frenchmen who appeared from behind trees, their hands held high over their heads, their voices raised in surrender. A number of Fitch's and Lyman's men came down and began herding them into a group, while I pressed onward with the rest of my company to see if there might not be others beyond.

As suddenly as we had come among them we seemed to pass beyond and all at once I found myself in the midst of the scarlet coats of Howe's and Gage's light infantry. I called out to my men to halt and looked about to see a lanky regular grinning at me.

" 'Ullo!" he said, when he had caught my eye. "Where'd you come from?"

"Right through them," I replied.

"Where'd they spring frum, so all of a sudden?" he said querulously. "Thąt's whut I'd like to know!"

I shrugged. "We'll soon find out," I told him. "We caught them fair and square, and they all appear to have thrown down their arms."

"Maybe they was lost too," he said.

I laughed, but as it proved he was none so far wrong. Messieurs Langy and de Trepezec, who were their leaders, had watched our approach and landing from the high rock that overlooks the lake upon the west shore. In endeavouring to cut in above us and rejoin their comrades at the fort they, too, had become confused in the deep tangle of woods, and before they were aware of it had found themselves between the two divisions of our army.

I looked about me, and noticed that the regulars were all in confused little groups, standing dully bewildered and idle while no officer appeared to call them to order. This struck me as odd, to say the least, and I turned to my lanky friend.

"Where are your officers?" I demanded. "Who is in command here?"

He shrugged. "Captain Fowler was 'ere not a minute since," he said, "but larst I see 'e was 'eadin' over there."

He made a vague gesture with his left. Following the direction he indicated I made out at some distance through the trees a little knot of scarlet coats that must, to judge from the gold lace among them, belong to officers. As I looked they would all bob down, only to lift up again. There was some waving of arms; evidently a considerable discussion going on. As I watched I saw Rogers' tall form, conspicuous in his green buckskins, come among them. Obviously there was some excitement that way, and I determined to find out for myself what it was.

Calling up Lieutenant Cobb, I gave over the command of the company to him, and turned my steps towards the group. As I came up I saw that there would be little chance of comfort in trying to worm my way into that tight-packed throng. But there was a great sad-faced soldier standing near by, eyeing them dully and with a stupid, dazed expression. I turned to him.

"What is it?" I asked. "What's all the excitement?"

"It's 'is Lordship," he said.

"What!" I exclaimed. "He's not hurt, is he?"

"'Urt?" said he, "I sh'd sye 'e was. 'E's dead, that's wot 'e is. Dead's a stone!"

"Dead!" I cried, scarce able to believe my ears. "But that's impossible! How do you know?"

"'Oo sh'd know better?" he demanded, rolling his dull ox eyes at me. "Right beside 'im, I was. 'E come runnin' up, 'e did, shoutin', 'Up an' at 'em, lads,' w'en a bullet took 'im in the 'eart and choked 'im orf like that!"

He made a wringing gesture with his two hands while I stood and stared at him in shocked and bewildered silence.

"Went over on 'is back, 'e did," the fellow went on in his droning voice, "an' kicked once or twice, stiff-legged, like a stuck 'og, an' then lay still, 'e did. An' 'e never spoke another word!"

Out of the corner of my eye I saw Rogers push his way out of the crowd, followed closely by Major Monypenny. Even at that distance I could see the latter's eyes blinking rapidly.

"We'll need a man who won't get lost to take this word back, major," I heard him say. "One of your men, perhaps."

I saw Rogers' bulging eye swing in a half-circle and come to rest on me. I was on my way towards him even before he called my name.

"Here's Mr. Ferguson," he said, as I came up. "He's the man to do it."

Major Monypenny stared at me blankly a long moment, and then said, "Mr. Ferguson—oh, yes, Mr. Ferguson!"

Rogers shot him a quick look, and then turned to me.

"Go back to the landing," he said quickly. "Mr. Cobb will take command of your company. Find the general. Tell him there's been a little skirmish up here. Tell him we've killed a few of the enemy, and taken some more prisoners—about two hundred, I guess. And tell him, too, that Lord Howe has been killed. Jump now."

"Yes, sir!" I said, and turning, I plunged into the woods at a run.

It had taken us an hour to go up from the landing. It took me almost two to go back, despite the fact that much of the way was downhill, and that I now knew the way. Every few rods along the way I found my path blocked by a sentry or an officer. "What's up? What's happened? What are we waiting for?" These questions were hurled at me with every other step I took. Nor would they let me by until I had given them some sort of answer. Indeed, I really believe that some of them almost thought me either a deserter or the forerunner of a disastrous retreat. To allay these fears I soon had a singsong account ready for them as soon as they stepped in my path.

"Runner for General Abercrombie," I would say. "There's been an engagement with one of the enemy's scouts, but they're all taken. Stay where you are. We'll be moving again in a minute."

This generally satisfied them and calmed their evident nervousness. But the necessity for repeating it time after time slowed my progress considerably. It was darkling when I came at last to the landing and made out a tent pitched by the lake shore. Instinctively I knew I should find the general there, and I went directly to it, only to be seized by the scruff of the neck and dragged backwards just as I was about to enter.

"Ho!" said a gruff voice. "Not so fast, sonny, not so fast!"

"Damn you!" I swore, struggling in the grip of the hairy giant of a grenadier who had been standing guard at the doorway. "Let me go! I've important news for the general!"

"Ho, yus?" he said, and laughed. "Think o' the like o' you to be carryin' important messages for the general!"

An immaculate young officer thrust a head out the door.

"Here!" he said severely. "What's going on? Hasn't the general given orders he's not to be disturbed?"

The grenadier dropped me like a hot potato and drew himself stiffly to attention. Before he could answer I thrust myself forward, for I had recognized, in the foppish young officer, Captain Abercrombie, nephew and A.D.C. to the general.

"I'm from the head of the column, sir," I said, "with an important message for the general."

He looked at me superciliously.

"You may tell it to me," he said. "I will see that he gets it in due time. His orders are that he is not to be disturbed at present."

"My news is for the general himself," I said stiffly, for his attitude annoyed me. "He'll not thank you if it is delayed."

I thought for an instant he was about to refuse me entrance, but before he could speak a gruff voice spoke querulously from within the tent.

"What is it, James?" said the voice. "What is all this haggling?"

Captain Abercrombie withdrew his head.

"A runner from Mr. Rogers," I heard him say. "He says his news is important, sir."

"Well, have the fellow in," came the reply.

The captain's head reappeared at the opening.

"Come in," he said, and stood aside.

I followed him inside and found the interior of the tent plain enough. A low cot stood along one wall, and in the centre was a table littered with papers, in the midst of which was a half-emptied bottle of port and a flickering lanthorn. Behind the table was a chair, and beside the chair, as if he had but just risen from it, stood a thick-set, elderly-seeming man, not above middle height, with great baggy pouches beneath his eyes and a great, bulbous, blue-veined nose. I should scarcely have recognized the general, for on the brief occasions when I had laid eyes on him before he had appeared immaculate in great powdered wig and scarlet coat, bedecked with much gold lace and ruffles. Now he was in his shirtsleeves, his stock loosened at the throat, and the top two buttons of his breeches opened to ease his ponderous belly. He had taken off his wig and tossed it upon the cot, and his shaven poll gleamed in the lanthorn's light. As I entered he looked at me heavily.

"Well?" he demanded.

"Major Rogers' compliments, your Excellency," I said. "I am ordered to report that there has been a slight skirmish up ahead."

"Ah!" he exclaimed, glancing at his nephew. "That was the fire we heard, James."

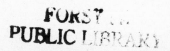

He turned back to me.

"You've come up with them so soon?" he asked.

"No, sir," I replied. "A scouting party of the enemy came between our advance guard and the main."

"And you had them, of course," he interrupted, "caught them between two fires, as it were. Were there any prisoners?"

"Yes, your Excellency," I said, "about two hundred."

He rubbed his hands together.

"So! But this is excellent, excellent!" he said gleefully. "Is that all?"

"I wish it were, your Excellency," I said, and hesitated, for I did not know exactly how I should break my news.

"Well, man," he snapped impatiently. "Out with it! Out with it! What more is there?"

"Unfortunately, sir," I said, "it was my Lord Howe who led the attack. He took a bullet through the heart and was killed instantly."

He gripped the edge of the table with both hands and glared at me incredulously.

"What's that?" he shouted. "What's that you say? Lord Howe? Killed?"

"Yes, your Excellency," I said.

For a long moment he stood staring at me as though he were unable to believe his ears. Then little by little I saw realization of the truth dawn in his eyes. He stared at me and through me. His mouth sagged. His hands shook, rattling the papers on the table before him. Suddenly his knees gave way beneath him and he sat down in the chair. All his pompous confidence and false courage seemed at once to ooze from him.

"Killed!" he said in a hoarse whisper. "Lord Howe killed! Great God!"

And with that he dropped his face in his hands and began to rock slowly from side to side.

For some moments I stood and stared at him in startled silence. Then a touch on my arm recalled me to life. I looked up to see the captain standing beside me. He raised his finger to his lips and moved his head towards the door. I nodded and, as silently as I could, turned and stumbled out into the fresh, cool air of the night.

I might have felt moved to greater compassion for the old man, so obviously crushed was he by the news I had brought, had it not been for the fact that I knew his distress to be wholly selfish. Utterly incompetent himself, it was well known that he was bitterly jealous of his subordinate's superior ability. Yet such were his orders from home that he durst not interfere with the other's authority. During their association he had fretted openly and complained that his Lordship took liberties beyond his due and rightful place. But now that Howe was dead he came suddenly face to face with his own shortcomings, and was appalled at the responsibilities that became his to bear alone.

The results of his incompetence were soon made manifest. All through that long night the troops stood upon their arms in the woods, while never a command went down to them to find out the higher ground and make themselves as comfortable as they might. In the morning a hasty council was called in the general's tent, and for an hour, if reports be true, there was not a word of agreement spoken. My Lord Howe's personality had been the mortar that had knit the army together. Quietly and unobtrusively, yet with a firm hand, he had guided the decisions of the council and controlled the destinies of us all. From the officers of the staff and the various regimental heads down through the ranks to the meanest provincial private, there was not a man of us but had felt the force of his leadership. Now that he was gone a great lassitude fell upon the ranks, and in the council petty jealousies sprang up. No two officers, it seemed, were able to agree; and the general listened to first one and then another, until it appeared he must prevail who could shout the loudest. Orders went out and were countermanded, only to go out again and be countermanded once more. And all the while the army stood bewildered and idle in the forest, slapping at flies and mosquitoes, and wondering what was to be done next.

In the end, although more than half the troops had passed the worst of the route around the west bank of the river, and the head of our columns lay within striking distance of the enemy at the sawmill, the entire force was recalled to the landing, and a new start taken along the road.

I count myself lucky that I was not forced to remain at the landing to witness that heartbreaking return. The general, although he had already decided upon the course he was to pursue, as it later appeared, suddenly decided that a reconnaissance of the enemy's position must be made; and to this purpose he dispatched his nephew, Captain Abercrombie, and a Mr. Clerk, a lieutenant of engineers. Captain Stark and myself were detailed to guide the party, and two hundred Rangers were sent along under our command as guards.

We left the landing at about nine in the morning, not long after the army had begun to retrace its steps of the previous afternoon; and, crossing the river at the site of the bridge, bore eastward up the side of the mountain that separates the foot of Lake George from Lake Champlain. We found the going easy, the way rising as it did at a fair grade through moderately open hardwood growth, and for a time we swung along at a brisk pace. But after a mile or so our two observers, unaccustomed to this sort of thing, announced, with great superiority and with a regular's vast contempt for poor, bungling provincials, that we were moving much too fast and without proper caution. Whereupon Stark winked at me and called a halt so that they might regain their wind. Thereafter we proceeded at a more moderate pace, in spite of which, no sooner had we reached the summit of the hill that lies to southward of Ticonderoga, than both Clerk, who was somewhat on the buttery side, and Abercrombie threw themselves down upon the ground, disregarding the havoc it must wreak upon their belaced and ruffled scarlet coats, and gasped for breath.

In the meantime Stark and I, having disposed our men in proper defensive positions about the summit, proceeded to make some small reconnaissance of our own. The hill upon which we stood was the same from whose summit I had looked out upon Ticonderoga on the occasion of my first scout. It rises almost due south of the fort, perhaps a cannon shot away, and is separated from it only by the estuary formed by the outlet of Lake George falling into Lake Champlain. From its summit it is possible to overlook not only the fort itself but also the entire point on which it stands, and to see some considerable distance down Lake Champlain as well, a fact of which both Stark and myself were well aware.

What we saw spread out below us now brought exclamations of surprise and some dismay to our lips. The French were evidently well informed of our coming, and were making every effort to

strengthen their defences. The ground around the fort itself, for
some distance back, had been cleared of every obstruction. About
a quarter of a mile from the fort they had constructed a huge
breastwork, to serve as an outer line of defence, that ran in zigzags across the entire width of the point. Outside this they had
cut down all the trees, for a distance of some rods, and these they
had dragged up to the breastwork to form an abatis, their butts
against the earthen wall, and their tops presenting an impenetrable tangle of sharpened branches to an attacker. Even at
that distance it appeared to me a formidable defence. And as we
watched thousands of Frenchmen appeared to swarm upon them,
making them higher and stronger and more impassable with axe
and shovel and pick.

Our exclamations aroused Clerk and Abercrombie, who presently came sauntering over to have a look themselves. Clerk
trained his glass upon the works below, and gave a satisfied grunt.

"Might be done, eh?" he said. "What do you think, old chap?"
He passed his glass to Abercrombie, who squinted through it.
Stark, who had been busy with his own thoughts, spoke up. "A
battery of artillery at this point," he said, "could make it hot for
anyone behind those works, or even in the fort for that matter."

Clerk gave him an amused glance.

"And how would you get your battery up here, my good fellow?" he demanded patronizingly. "Fly?"

Stark flushed at the other's tone.

"Give me two hundred men and two days' time," he said, "and
I'd have your battery up here."

The other laughed derisively.

"Indeed!" he snorted. "Two weeks would be nearer the mark.
You don't seem to realize, my good chap, that speed is what
counts here. Those prisoners we took yesterday report that Montcalm has six thousand men at the fort, with three thousand more
expected from Crown Point. The attack must be made before
those reinforcements arrive."

Stark looked down at the fort doubtfully.

"If there are six thousand men down there," he said, "I'll eat
your hat! As for the reinforcements, look here."

He rose and pointed away northward down Champlain to a
point where the lake narrowed to less than a half-mile in width.

"Three thousand men at that point," he said, "with artillery to support them, could hold the lake against any reinforcements that might be sent down, and bottle up Montcalm in the fort to boot. With his communications cut he'd come to heel soon enough, I'll warrant."

Clerk shrugged and made no reply, but Abercrombie snorted.

"All that's beside the point, my man," he said disdainfully. "We haven't all summer, you know. What the general wants now is a report on the feasibility of a direct frontal attack on the enemy's position."

"It appears quite possible to me," said Clerk.

I looked from one to the other aghast.

"Possible!" I exclaimed. "Why, man, where are your eyes? That position's impregnable to anything but cannon!"

Abercrombie looked bored.

"Really, my dear fellow," he said, "we know our business. Wait until you have seen regulars in action before you judge of that!"

"Why!" I cried, scarce able to believe my ears. "You must see that what you propose is impossible! The losses would be appalling! It would be sheer murder, I tell you!"

Clerk looked as though he were about to make an angry rejoinder, but Abercrombie merely shrugged.

"Oh, there will be losses, of course," he said airily; "but after all you can't make an omelet without breaking eggs, and it's what the general wants."

"Why, you—" I began. But Stark's elbow dug sharply into my ribs, and I clamped my teeth upon the words I was about to utter.

There was no further discussion between us. Clerk and Abercrombie finished taking their observations, and about mid-afternoon we began the descent of the mountain in silence. When we came to the road we found that the army was already moved down to the sawmill, where General Abercrombie had set up his headquarters. As we approached the camp we were startled to hear a sudden burst of cheering, and as we entered an amazing spectacle greeted us. Everywhere men were jumping up and down, slapping one another on the back, turning cartwheels, tossing their hats in the air. The cheering and huzzaing were deafening. We had almost to fight our way through to headquarters, where we left the two regulars. Thereafter we turned our steps towards that section of the camp occupied by the Rangers, where we came presently, still completely baffled as to the reason for all the sudden tumult, and there dismissed our men. Rogers met us at the door of his tent with a broad grin.

"What's all the cheering for?" Stark demanded as we ducked inside.

"Louisbourg's fallen," said Rogers. "A runner came in half an hour ago from Albany, and the general gave out the news at once."

He chuckled and rubbed his hands together.

"It won't be long now," he said, "before the war's over."

Stark spat. "You're as bad as the regulars," he said.

Rogers looked from one to the other of us.

"What's the matter with you boys?" he demanded. "You look as sour as last week's cream! What you need is a drink."

He reached under his cot and pulled out the inevitable squat black bottle. As he did so Stark told him what we had seen from the mountaintop and our conversation with the two regulars. Rogers looked grave for an instant, then laughed.

"What difference does it make?" he said.

Stark shrugged. "If they weren't in such a hurry!" he said, and went on to tell of his suggestion and the way in which it had been received. Rogers gave a derisive snort.

"Sure!" he said. "I'll lay odds you thought that was original! But let me tell you, Williams and Bagley and Fitch and Lyman and Bradstreet and even that woodenhead Putnam have all had the same idea, and no one'd listen to 'em. No chance! I tell you this is the regulars' show, and they're running it to suit themselves. They'll take no advice from such as us. You may as well make the best of that!"

He poured three cups full of rum, and the dark molasses smell of it filled the tent. He chuckled.

"But it doesn't make any difference," he said. "This is once we'll have our way with the mounseers!"

Stark looked dubious and sniffed at his drink.

"You don't doubt it?" cried Rogers. "Why, man, you and I know there are no more than four thousand in the fort if that, no matter what prisoners may say! The odds are four to one! Show me the Frenchman with a stomach for that, and I'll show you a liar! Not Frenchmen nor anyone else could stand before this force. Let the tin soldiers play their game as they will. 'Tis too late to spoil it now. Ticonderoga will be ours tomorrow night.''

Stark shrugged. "Let's hope you're right," he said.

Rogers gave an exclamation of disgust.

"Christ!" he swore. "To listen to you would chill the bowels of a saint! Drink up, man. 'Twill warm your guts, and put new life into you!"

And with that he raised his cup to us and drained it at a single draught.

The morning proved him not far wrong in one respect, at least: no colonial officer was called to sit upon the council. The troops were turned out at dawn, and their arms and equipment rigidly inspected. By six o'clock this was finished, and thereafter we stood about idly under arms while the various regimental and corps commanders waited upon the general for his orders. At seven Rogers reappeared among us and called the company commanders into conference.

"All right," he said, when we had assembled at his tent. "These are the orders. The regular troops will make the assault; but the Rangers and the light infantry will go forward first to drive in the enemy's pickets and clear the ground. We will follow the road to the fort until the advanced guard makes contact with the enemy. As soon as this contact is established you will form your companies on a front across the line of the road and advance in extended order through the woods towards the clearing, driving in any of the enemy's pickets you may encounter. When you reach the edge of the clearing you will halt your men and await further orders. Is that clear?"

We all nodded.

"Good!" he said. "Lieutenant Tute will take the advance with fifty men. The main body will follow at a hundred paces. That's all."

We went back to our places then, and about nine received orders to march. We set out along the road in good order. As we went I became conscious of a queasy feeling in the pit of my stomach. Our battle on snowshoes and the affair in which Lord Howe had fallen were the only actions I had ever seen involving more than twoscore on either side; and then, although I had experienced a few qualms beforehand, things had happened so swiftly that there had been little time for anticipation. Now, for the first time, I found myself about to take part in a major battle, and it must be confessed that I took small pleasure in the thought.

For more than a mile our march was unimpeded, until the ringing sound of axes at the edge of the clearing, where the French were still at work upon their defences, came clearly to us through the woods; and I, for one, began to wonder if we were to be allowed to come upon their working parties without opposition. But scarcely had the thought crossed my mind when a crash of shots rang out ahead, followed almost instantly by a spattering of return fire.

Immediately we plunged into the woods, alternate companies on opposite sides of the road, deployed, and moved forward again in line abreast, taking such cover as we might from trees and brush as we went.

But we did not at once meet with any general resistance. For a few minutes the scattering fire continued in the centre, where a strong picket had ambushed our advanced guard. But Lieutenant Tute held fast, and an instant later the enemy broke and took to their heels as our main body came up. From the direction of the fort a cannon thumped; evidently a signal gun calling in the work parties, and after that no sound save the rustle of our feet across the leafy ground or the occasional snapping of a twig disturbed the stillness of the woods.

As I moved forward with my company I found it hard to believe that this quiet solitude would soon re-echo to the thunder of gunfire and the cries of the wounded: that within the hour, and at a distance of less than a half-mile from that spot, two armies would presently be locked in deadly struggle. It seemed a fantastic thought. In an oak overhead a red squirrel forgot his fright at the recent exchange of shots and scolded at me angrily as I passed beneath. In a clump of bushes a flock of small birds fluttered and chirped. Somewhere in the distance a woodpecker drummed on a hollow tree. Sunlight, bright and a little hazy, filtered down in patches through the leafy cover and flickered upon musket barrels and the green buckskins of my companions as they moved. But the distant sound of axes came to us no longer.

Then all at once we came to the edge of the woods, and the picture changed abruptly. Before us lay a scene of complete and man-made desolation. For a distance of some hundred rods the ground sloped upwards gently, and in that space not a tree or a bush had been left standing. Everything had been swept flat as though a hurricane had passed over it.

Viewed thus from below, a number of points about the works that had been invisible from above, the day before, became apparent, and as I saw them my heart sank within me. For one thing, from above it had been impossible to appreciate the ruggedness of the ground immediately in front of the position. For another it had not been noticeable from above that the breastwork had followed the crest of a low ridge stretching from the outlet across the point to the shore of Lake Champlain.

Nor had the enemy neglected the opportunity our delay had afforded them of improving their advantage. The works themselves rose some eight or nine feet in height and were stoutly made of logs and earth with frequent emplacements along the top for cannon and muskets. In addition to this they were so constructed in zigzags that anyone approaching within fifty yards must be caught in a deadly cross fire from above.

This in itself would have been discouraging enough, but French ingenuity had not stopped there. Immediately in front of the breastwork, at the steepest part of the slope, the abatis of trees and branches which I had noted from above had been completed, presenting a tangled mass of countless sharpened stakes, a gigantic chevaux de frise, in the face of any enemy who might win so far. In front of this, for perhaps a hundred yards the ground was swept bare of anything that might conceivably afford cover; so that a charge must be open and exposed throughout the entire distance. In front of this, again, the forest had been cut down, willy-nilly, and left to lie where it had fallen; great, stout-butted timbers and slender saplings, tossed in utter riotous confusion, their tops and trunks inextricably tangled; so that an army coming upon it must inevitably break ranks to pass through it, for no formation could hold in such a maze.

Before this jungle a further attempt had evidently been made to create a second cleared strip before our approach had interrupted the work. Here too the trees had been cut away for a distance of some hundred yards. But here the work was not complete. Many of the smaller trees and bushes had been dragged up to add to the confusion of the central strip, but many of the larger trees, too stout to be easily moved, still lay where they had fallen, their stumps and butts and bushy tops affording some measure of cover for an advancing force.

This, then, was the position that was to be taken by direct frontal attack. I groaned inwardly as I looked upon it, and with a sagging heart disposed my men along the wood's front according to my instructions.

Presently a runner came down the line from Rogers with orders to keep up a fire upon the works, where we could catch an occasional glimpse of a head or a hat or an arm, and to watch for movement in the tangle of fallen trees, where he suspected some of the enemy's pickets still lurked.

For some time we followed these orders, smoking out two or three parties of the enemy from the edge of the tangled strip of brush, but without being able to drive them back into the shelter of the breastwork. These, as soon as they had sought out more secure positions, dug themselves in and returned our fire briskly; so that the long wait that followed was not without a lively sort of interest.

At last, however, I heard Rogers' shrill whistle from the woods behind me. At once I turned the company over to Lieutenant Cobb, and, keeping my head down lest I stop a potshot as I went, wormed my way back until I found him squatting in the shelter of a great red oak a few yards behind the lines. He nodded to me grimly as I slipped in beside him, but did not speak until the other company commanders had come up. When the last man had appeared he looked about at us.

"Well," he said, "are you ready?"

No one spoke. He waited a moment, and then went on.

"Good!" he said. "Here's the set-up. Bradstreet and DeLancey are on the left. Gage and the Fifty-fifth are on the right. We are the centre, and the spearhead of the advance. There are a number of the enemy hidden in that brush, and it is our duty to clean them out of it and prepare the way for the regulars who will follow us. When you get my signal you will go forward and endeavour to drive the enemy from their positions, forcing them in behind the works. When you have done this you will fall down and take cover in the brush, allowing the regulars behind to pass through you and advance to the charge. You will hold your positions there until the breastworks are taken, when you will advance for further orders. If the first charge is beaten back you will hold your positions and cover the regulars' retreat. Is that understood? Any questions?"

"Do we take scalps?" said Captain Shepard.

Rogers looked at him impatiently.

"You'll be lucky to keep your own," he said. "That's all."

He made a gesture of dismissal that sent us all scurrying back to our posts. A few minutes later his whistle rang out shrilly above the desultory popping of muskets. As I scrambled to my feet and started forward I glanced at the sun and estimated the time at a little after noon.

As we stepped out into the clear, I could see out of the corner of my eye the scarlet coats of the light infantry among the stumps far to the right and the blue and buff of DeLancey's Yorkers on my left. It was at this last point that the enemy's snipers seemed most heavily concentrated; for at our appearance a heavy fire burst out at once on that side. I saw the blue coats waver momentarily, and then go on as Bradstreet's battoemen joined them. At that same instant something buzzed angrily past my ear, and I was recalled sharply to my own part in the affair.

The fire which had begun so briskly on the left swelled now and ran all along our front, so that the jumble of fallen trees before us grew hazy and was near hidden by the smoke. From habit, rather than from any commands I gave, we used our usual tactics to advance, every other man loading and firing from cover while the rest moved up to the next cover and repeated the manœuvre. By this means a steady fire was maintained covering the advance, and the resulting roar of musketry was deafening. When, presently, the French along the breastwork added their fire to that of their comrades in the brush the din became earsplitting, so that it seemed to smash against the consciousness with almost physical impact and became by far the most terrifying thing we had to face.

In that terrific uproar it was impossible to hear one's own shouts. Even the angry buzz and whine of the bullets was drowned out. Only an occasional stirring of the air, a splinter tossed flying from a log, or the vibration of a stump against which one was crouching, indicated that the air was full of flying death. But there was no time to think of these. The senses observed them dully and registered them upon some remote portion of the mind while our bodies went forward mechanically, rising, running a few steps, and dropping again behind some stump or convenient log, to fire and rise and go forward again. Nor was it easy to see. Blue-grey swirls of acrid powder smoke obscured the field, stinging in the nostrils, smarting in the eyes. Here a man would loom out of the haze to flop down beside you, or another would pop up abruptly ahead and go scurrying away out of sight. Once a man ahead rose suddenly from behind a stump, to spin and crash forward on his face, and I saw with dull surprise that he wore the white coat of a French regular. Again one stumbled through the smoke beside me, his hands clutched tightly across his stomach, to pitch across a stump, where he hung blindly kicking for an instant. Then he rolled off slowly to one side. His knees jerked spasmodically once or twice, and after that he lay still.

Walking through those quiet woods before the attack, lying at the edge of the clearing and looking out at the French works, I had been afraid. When I had thought of what lay before me my stomach had gone suddenly weak and cold. My knees, my legs, my spine had seemed turned to an icy jelly. But now, going forward, I found I had no time for fear. Instinctively I ran and crouched and ran again.

How long it took to reach the strip of fallen trees I could not say, though it could not have been more than a few minutes. I seemed to have been running for an interminable time when the tangled barrier loomed before me. In it I fear I saw only shelter, for I flung myself upon it, shouting at the top of my lungs, though the sound of my voice went no farther than my own teeth. Over logs, under them, thrusting through branches, I drove my way. Once a Frenchman loomed before me, his musket clubbed ready to strike. Instinctively my finger crooked upon the trigger and I saw him suddenly shrouded in smoke, his head jerked sharply back, eyes staring and mouth open to the sky above, while a great red stain appeared suddenly upon his white coat. I thrust the butt of my musket into the pit of his stomach before he fell, crashing sideways, and pushed on.

All at once I found myself come out at the other side of the barrier. A puff of wind swept across the field, lifting the smoke momentarily, and we were able to see the white-clad forms of many Frenchmen scurrying, like ghosts in a fog, for the shelter of their breastwork. As we watched some of them fell and lay still, but most of them passed under the wicked spikes of the abatis, gained the front of the barricade and were helped over by their comrades on the other side.

As abruptly as it had begun the firing ceased. I flung myself down behind a thick stump to catch my breath. For the first time I had opportunity to appreciate the miracle that had brought me untouched through that veritable hail of death. It was difficult to believe that any living thing could pass through that and survive; yet looking to right and left I could see that I was far from being alone. Indeed, our losses had been surprisingly small.

But now I found that my first reaction was suddenly come back upon me with redoubled force. Had the command come at that moment to retire, I believe I must assuredly have been left behind, for my legs were all at once grown weak as water. My stomach twitched and writhed so that I was near to vomiting. My teeth chattered together involuntarily, and the palms of my hands were so slippery with sweat that I had difficulty in loading my musket.

I was not given opportunity to reflect upon these manifestations, however. As if the abrupt silence had been a signal a new sound rose from the woods behind us—the thin, reedy squeal of fifes and the rattle and thump of drums, and, forming a background for them all, the wild skirling of the Highland pipes. From the shelter of my stump I looked back to see the regulars emerging from the woods in six columns, their scarlet coats standing out brightly through the haze of powder smoke, now slightly lifted, the sun gleaming coldly upon the steel of their fixed bayonets.

As precisely as if they were on parade they moved forward. Halfway across the clear the six columns merged and became three. The pipes and drums went abruptly silent, and in the interval we could hear the officers shouting their hoarse commands.

I believe even the French were dazzled by the sight, for they did not open fire at once, but let them come on almost to the strip of fallen trees. Then at an almost unintelligible command the three columns began to move forward at a run; and, as if this were the signal for which they had been waiting, a deafening crash of fire burst out all along the enemy's front.

The impact of that smashing volley upon the close-packed ranks was terrible to see, yet they did not waver. On they came. Wherever a man went down another took his place at once. At the barrier strip they hesitated for an instant, while the rear ranks piled up against the front. Then the close order broke and they began scrambling through the tangled mass, each man picking his own best way.

It was a heartbreaking sight to watch those high-gaitered, heavily encumbered infantrymen struggling across that snarled maze of trunks and branches. Some, in desperation and disregard of their orders, flung up their muskets and began to return the fire, only to feel the flats of their officers' sabres across their backs. Others struggled doggedly onward, a scarlet wave that in an instant had engulfed the entire strip, while a steady fire poured from the breastworks above into the mass and filled the air with flying lead that tore tiny bits of bark and twigs and splinters from the down trees.

It seemed scarce any time at all before they had reached and passed me and were charging on up the slope towards the works above, yet their losses in that instant were terrific. In the tangled branches of the felled trees horribly wounded men hung grotesquely like scarlet sacks, or struggled desperately and in agony to free themselves of the clutching brush. One man, a grenadier, fell across my legs, and I grabbed him and dragged him back into the shelter of my stump. When I turned him over I saw that he had a hole in his breast the size of a turkey's egg. I loosened his tunic, and tried to make him as comfortable as I could. He thanked me with his eyes; but when he tried to speak a great fountain of blood came gushing out of his mouth and he died almost at once.

When I looked back at the fight our troops were at the very points of the chevaux de frise, struggling to break through. And it was there that the French chose to loose their cannon upon them. Out of the clouds of white smoke that ringed the tops of the works the light eight-pounders bellowed, spewing down grape upon the close-packed ranks below, tearing great gaps in them. It seemed impossible that human flesh could stand it, yet for an instant longer they fought and struggled there, trying doggedly to break through. Then all at once they broke and came staggering back towards us and the shelter of the fallen trees.

I found then that I must have been firing steadily without realizing it, for my musket barrel was hot to the touch and my eyes were smarting from the smoke. For a moment I thought we might enjoy a brief respite. But even as the thought came to me fresh troops burst from the woods and swept forward to the charge.

I have no wish to describe here all the awful details of that afternoon. Nor, indeed, could I if I would, for after those first few minutes in which my mind noted everything clearly and in its proper order my senses grew dull with noise and fury, and I fell to loading and firing and loading again, mechanically, without stopping to observe much of what went on about me. Here and there individual occurrences stand out in my mind like the recurrent parts of a hideous nightmare; a handful of Highlanders breaking through the chevaux de frise and scaling the works, only to be spitted on bayonets at the top: a regular with his belly shot away and his entrails hanging out, impaled upon a sharp branch and crying out for death; an officer, whom I recalled dimly having met at Schuyler's in Albany, his arm and breast torn away by a cannon shot, urging his men onward with his last breath; a white-faced, frightened drummer lad, scarce a year from his mother's apron strings, shivering in the shelter of a fallen tree. These things I remember clearly to have seen; but for the most part my memory of that day is no more than a welter of blood and hideous noise.

How often the regulars rallied and went forward again to the charge, I could not tell from memory. I have since heard that six separate and desperate attacks were made. And each time, as I can testify, they were beaten back. In the end I was roused from my mechanical round of fire and load and load and fire by someone tugging at my sleeve. I looked around to see Rogers at my elbow. He put his lips close to my ear and shouted to make himself heard above the tumult.

"They're drawing off the regulars," he said. "Keep your men firing to cover the rescue parties. Draw off slowly when you hear my whistle."

I nodded to show that I understood, and he was gone in the next instant, picking his way carelessly among the stumps and tree trunks, to carry the command on to Brewer and Burbank and Shepard who were on my right. In that moment I saw to my surprise, for I had lost all sense of time in the fighting, that the sun was low on the western horizon, and that dusk would soon be upon us. I saw, too, that what Rogers had said was true. The regulars were falling back. Fire on both sides was slacking off. Already rescue parties were slipping forward from among the tangle of trees and brush to bring in the wounded.

We kept up a scattered fire as long as the parties were out, more as a warning than because we had anything to shoot at. Nor did the French molest the rescuers, but contented themselves with desultory sniping at us. Little by little the field was cleared of the living and such of the dead as could be reached, and a few minutes before dark Rogers' whistle shrilled, calling us back to the shelter of the woods, where we sought out the road and formed for the march back.

We were a haggard and weary crew that came down the road in the darkness to the sawmill. To our astonishment that place was in flames, and the spot where the camp had stood across the bridge was deserted save for a single young staff officer who sat upon a stump, his coat and gold lace bright in the glare of the fire. At our approach he rose and came towards us.

"Major Rogers?" he said, as he approached the head of our small column.

"That's me," said Rogers.

"General's orders, major," said the other. "You're to bring your men back to the landing."

Rogers shrugged. "As you say," he said.

As we swung off down the road I moved up beside him.

"What is it?" I said. "We're not going back?"

He shook his head. "I don't know," he said.

"But great God, man!" I cried. "It can't be as bad as that. The loss has been terrific, but there must be twelve thousand of us left!"

"Don't tell me," he replied. "I take my orders from the general."

I fell back then beside my company and marched in silence. As we approached the landing we began to pass great piles of stores and ammunition and baggage looking desolate and abandoned in the moonlight. Once we saw a dozen cannon, just as they had been unloaded from the barges that brought them, their wheels not even mounted. The men began to mutter among themselves, in spite of our commands for silence. As we swung across the bridge to the landing place the murmur rose to a low growl. Save for a few battoemen moving about on the strand and a row of boats pulled up along the shore the place was deserted. Far out on the lake we could hear the rhythmic chunk of oars.

Rogers halted us against the line of trees that stood back from the beach.

"Rest!" he said. "Stark, Brewer, Ferguson, Burbank, Shepard, come with me."

He turned on his heel and strode towards a little knot of officers gathered about a tiny fire. The rest of us followed. As we approached, one of the officers looked up, and I recognized Colonel Bradstreet.

"All right, major," he said as he saw Rogers, "get your men into the boats. We're going back up the lake."

Rogers stood and stared at him a full minute before answering.

"They're quitting, then?" he said at last in a strained voice.

Bradstreet shrugged.

"What about those stores?" Rogers demanded, jerking his head towards the road by which we had come.

"Leave 'em," said Bradstreet.

Rogers started to speak, but Bradstreet stopped him with a gesture.

"Those are the orders," he said.

Rogers' shoulders sagged, and he turned to us.

"You heard him," he said. "Get your men into the boats. The war's not over yet by a long shot!"

·18·

"TREASONS, STRATAGEMS, AND SPOILS"

❰ 1 Of all the bungling steps of that miserable campaign the precipitate flight of the army, defeated, through the blunders of its chief, by an enemy still outnumbered more than three to one, was the most shameful spectacle. Yet let it be said at once, to the credit of the army as a whole, that there was scarcely a man, in the ranks or out, who understood the reasons for that desperate rout. For once, an entire army obeyed its orders blindly and without question—too blindly, indeed, as it presently appeared—and the net result was bitter shame. In fact it was several days before all the parts of the story could be pieced together and we were able to realize the full implications of all that had occurred. When that realization came the army's rage knew no bounds. It was well for the doddering craven Abercrombie that he had by that time taken himself off to New York, for I make no doubt that there were those among us who would have vented their anger upon his person.

Briefly, what had happened was this: To begin with, there was the hasty and ill advised attempt to circle through the woods that had cost us the life of the one officer competent to command such an undertaking. This was followed by the decision, muddleheaded to say the least, to attack with the bayonet a position that could, with the use of artillery, have been reduced effectively in the course of a day and with comparatively little loss. The attack itself had been as gallant as it was rash and bloody. Our losses had been terrific. But at the end of the day more than three-fourths of the army remained intact. Indeed, more than half had not even taken part in the battle, for by far the greater part of the provincial troops had been held in reserve in the woods without so much as firing a gun.

Why, then, if this was so, was not the army held in camp at the sawmill, and the attack renewed along more appropriate lines in the morning? There is but one answer. Throughout that bitter day General Abercrombie attempted to direct the battle from the security of the sawmill, two full miles behind the lines. Without knowledge of the terrain, without viewing the enemy's position, he tried to whip an active and strongly entrenched opponent by moving knives and forks upon a tablecloth and substituting theories for facts.

And at the end, when the broken, mutilated remains of the regulars came gallantly down the road, he took one panic-stricken glance at their battered ranks and, gathering up his papers, fled, leaving orders behind for the army to follow. By the time the troops, perplexed, bewildered, harassed, and not a little apprehensive lest this precipitate departure of their chief betoken some desperate counterattack on the part of an enemy of whose feebleness they were not aware, had gained the boats he was already far up the lake; and the world was given the spectacle of a once proud British army fleeing, like some great puppy, with its tail between its legs, before the insolent yapping of a belligerent terrier.

As I have already indicated, it was some time before it was generally recognized that this was what had occurred. In the meantime the camp at the head of the lake was in a turmoil of confusion. Each hour brought forth some fresh rumour to bewilder us. At one moment it was said we should presently be ordered back to the boats to return to Ticonderoga. In the next we were to march at once for New York and there embark for Quebec. Again we were to hasten with all possible speed to Fort Edward, carrying with us such provisions as we could and destroying the rest. Orders came for all the wounded and the heavy artillery to be sent at once to Albany. Yet none of these things were done. In the first day after our return the provincials were thrice ordered to move their camp; orders which only added to the confusion and did nothing to improve the men's temper. Others were set to lay out new lines and begin work on new fortifications to replace those destroyed by the French a year ago. By the end of the day we had accomplished nothing more than to count our losses and lick our wounds.

The week that followed brought no improvement. By the end of the second day we were all convinced that the news of Louisbourg's fall, as given out before the attacks, had been but a fiction to raise the spirits of the army. Deserters coming in from the enemy informed us that at the time of our attack Monsieur de

Montcalm had but thirty-five hundred men, and that so certain had he been that we must overwhelm him by sheer force of numbers alone, that he had ordered everything put in readiness for a retreat down the lake by boat to Chambly, intending to mine the fortifications at Crown Point on the way. They added that since our flight additional forces had come to reinforce him, raising his total strength to some seven thousand.

On the third day dysentery and diarrhoea broke out among the men so suddenly that our meagre sanitary arrangements were unable to cope with the situation. On the fourth the provincials were again ordered to move their camp. Each day the quality and amount of provisions rationed out to us grew meaner—mostly, I imagine, because near half the army's stores had been abandoned at the foot of the lake. As the food grew worse the men became ugly, disgusted, and mutinous.

As so often happens in such times as these there was little effort made to better matters by rectifying mistakes. Instead discipline became unnecessarily harsh, adding fuel to the fire of discontent; and men were flogged, picketed, and even hanged and shot for offences that in other days would be too trivial to notice. At all hours of the day we were turned out on parade to witness an execution or to see some poor devil beaten into unconsciousness, his back cut to ribbons by the cat. One man, a fellow named Hone from New Jersey, was hanged for the theft of two or three pairs of buckles of no great value; though it was said that he was a notorious thief, and so perhaps deserved his punishment. Another, a regular, was shot for stealing a pound of butter from a pile of stores he was set to guard. Sam Leach, of the Rangers, was sentenced to "five hundred lashes of the cat on his bare back" for refusing to go out upon a scout until he had received his allowance of rum. A Connecticut man received a thousand lashes for mutinously refusing to stand guard. A serjeant of regulars who stepped beyond the limits of the camp to relieve himself was taken by the Indians and escaped. He was reduced to the ranks and received a thousand lashes. A Rhode Islander was given five hundred lashes for passing counterfeit dollars which he had made himself, first borrowing a dollar from a comrade with which to make a mould! And once I saw the man Sanborn flogged five hundred lashes for the theft of two blankets from a wagonload which he brought up from Albany for the wounded.

As often as not the poor devils who were thus beaten fell unconscious before their sentence was half carried out, in which case they were dragged back to the guard tent, there to lie until they had recovered sufficiently to have the rest of their punishment meted out to them. Not infrequently they died from the effects.

Small wonder is it that under such circumstances we lost more men by desertion in a month than were killed and wounded in the battle of Ticonderoga. Every night that passed saw some small party of them slip away into the forest, and on one occasion an entire regiment clubbed their rifles and marched out of camp swearing that they would not remain another day to eat wormy, inadequate provisions.

For my own part it must be confessed that I shared the general feeling of disgust. For the first time since I had joined Rogers I began to feel that the game was not worth the candle. Indeed, had it not been for the fact that I had given my oath to serve for the duration of the war I should not have had the least hesitation in packing my few belongings and taking myself off to Portsmouth. As it was, however, there was nothing for me to do but stay and make the best of a bad business.

Little by little, however, order came out of chaos. Towards the end of the month we learned that the reports of Louisbourg's fall had not been exaggerated, and this went far to raise the army's morale. In August, Rogers gave a good account of himself against a strong party of French and Indians under the partisan Marin. As luck had it I was not present at that affair, having been ordered out to the northward of Lake George upon a scout. But I heard of it promptly upon my return and was much pleased, despite the fact that Mr. Putnam, who was lately become a major and who had accompanied Rogers, had been taken prisoner at the very start of the engagement and carried off to Canada. In September we learned that the Frontenac expedition which Abercrombie had sent out at Bradstreet's instigation, not long after the fiasco at Ticonderoga, was a success; and finally the news of the fall of Fort Duquesne on the Ohio in November removed the last bitterness from our minds and gave us hope for the future.

In the midst of these alarms and excursions my own affairs remained much as they were. My cousin Hubert I saw but once after the bloody business at Ticonderoga. After that he returned to Albany, where he had in some way managed to regain his post on the general's staff. I sent a letter by him to Dorcas, but received no answer. Neither had I expected one, knowing my wife's antipathy for letter writing. Once or twice I heard from Purity that Albany was quiet, but beyond that I had only the routine of the camp and the company of my fellow officers in the Rangers to help me pass the time away.

This must not be taken to mean that I was idle. On the contrary, the Rangers, as usual, were the busiest troops in the camp. One scout followed another, and when we were not out scouting we were detailed to chase some party of the enemy that had been reported either from the camp or from Fort Edward. Such brief moments as we enjoyed in camp were fully occupied with seeing to the replacement of equipment and the care and feeding of our men, so that for all it was routine work throughout there was scarce a minute of my time that I could call my own. I seemed to remember that once, when I was fresh come into the army, I had enjoyed this life. But now the monotony of it only bored me, though I did my best to see my duty done in a soldierly fashion.

But there was one occurrence, now that I recall it, in that summer and fall that is worth repeating, both for the part I took in the affair and for the bearing it had upon my future, which was considerable, and even came near to being the death of me.

In September, towards the end of the month, General Amherst, having settled the Louisbourg affair to everyone's satisfaction, sailed for Boston, upon a hasty tour of inspection to discover, if possible, why his subordinate on the Hudson had acted with such indecision that an entire year's campaign was wasted. I am told that he cared little for what he saw. Nor can I say that I blame him, when I think back upon the filthy conditions prevailing in the camps. I know only that he came one day to Fort Edward, where I was then stationed with Rogers, and came across from the fort to our island to inspect our camp with only the briefest of warnings.

In spite of that we managed to turn the men out in some sort of order on the parade. I remember seeing him trudge up from the bridgehead, a tall spare man of sombre countenance with high cheekbones, a sharp-pointed nose, and reddish sandy hair. At his heels trotted Colonel Haldimand, short and a little stout, who was then in command at the fort. As they approached I saw Amherst turn to the colonel and heard his harsh, peculiarly penetrating voice.

"What are these troops, you say, colonel?" he asked.

Haldimand's reply, pitched to lower tones, I did not catch. But I saw Amherst nod.

"Ah!" said he. "Major Rogers' Rangers, eh?"

His eye swept along our front and went over our heads to the officers' cabins and the tents beyond—which, if I say so myself, were neat and in order.

"A pity," he said, "they can't all be like this."

He shook hands with Rogers after that, and then, while officers and men stood rigidly at attention, passed down the line. When he had finished inspecting the troops Rogers led him on a brief tour of the camp, and a half-hour later he shook hands once more and returned with Haldimand to the fort.

It was late that evening that the event of which I speak occurred. I had gone across to the fort to attend to a matter at the commissary for Major Rogers, and, the business done, was returning to the island. My way took me across the parade past the officers' quarters, a row of cabins along the west wall of the fort on either side of the river gate. The first of these cabins, and the nearest to the gate, was occupied by Colonel Haldimand, who at that moment was closeted within with the general.

Before the door stood two guards, men of one of the Massachusetts regiments, to whom I paid but scant heed as I passed. I went around the corner of the cabin, and was about to pass out the gate when a furtive movement in the shadows, between the rear wall of the cabin and the wall of the fort, caught my eye. I stopped short and peered into the gloom. There was a window in the cabin there, evidently open, for it was one of those pleasantly balmy nights that sometimes fall towards the end of September, and in the light that streamed from it I made out the crouching figure of a man.

Obviously the fellow could have but one purpose there—to listen to the conversation that was taking place within. My action was involuntary, purely a matter of instinct. Without stopping to consider I dashed in between the cabin and the wall and flung myself upon him, raising my voice at the same time in a shout for the guard.

But it was evident he had heard me and was ready. As I grappled with him he made a slash at me with a dirk and stood up. I felt the blade catch in the shoulder of my sleeve and rip it to the elbow without more than scratching my flesh. In the same instant his head came into the square of light cast from the window and I recognized Shem Sanborn. For a moment surprise robbed me of the power of action, and in the next instant he gave me a buffet on the ear that sent me reeling against the wall of the cabin. When I regained my feet he was gone, running up the alleyway between the cabins and the side of the fort, and was swallowed up in the darkness. A moment later the guards burst around the corner of the cabin and barred my way with their muskets.

"Fools!" I shouted. "Yonder he goes! Stop him!"

They looked at me and then at one another stupidly, and then peered behind me into the darkness; but of course by that time there was no trace of the fellow to be seen. A head popped out of the window behind me, and I heard Haldimand's voice.

"What the devil's going on here?" he demanded. "What's all this ungodly noise?"

I turned to see him hanging half out the window. Behind him I could see the scarlet coat of the general himself.

"There was a fellow listening under your window, sir," I said. "I tried to hold him, but he was too much for me."

"Hah!" he said, eyeing me with suspicion. "Did you see him?"

"Yes, sir," I replied. "I happen to know him. His name is Sanborn, a teamster for the service of supply."

"Hah!" he snorted again. "You have it mighty pat, young man. Who might you be?"

"Captain Ferguson, sir," I said, "of Rogers' Rangers."

"So?" he said, and turned to the guards.

"You!" he commanded, pointing to one. "Turn out the guard. Find this man Sanborn."

He motioned to me. "You come inside," he said. And to the other guard: "You find the officer of the day."

He pulled his head in abruptly and slammed the shutters from the inside.

I went around to the door and entered. Colonel Haldimand was still standing near the window. General Amherst was seated near the table. I advanced and saluted. Amherst nodded to the colonel.

"Come now," said Haldimand, "what's all this? Out with it!"

I told him how I had been returning to our camp when I had

noticed a furtive movement in the shadows behind his cabin; how when I had gone to investigate I had discovered Sanborn. And I added that I could not be mistaken in the fellow's identity, for I would have known him anywhere, having had some dealings with him before. When I had finished the colonel sneered openly.

"A likely story," he commented.

I flushed angrily.

"Is it likely, sir," I demanded, exhibiting my torn sleeve, "that I would have done this to myself simply to create excitement?"

"It is possible," he said, "that you may have imagined yourself observed, and thinking escape impossible, have slashed your own tunic and invented this tall tale to save your own hide."

"Sir!" I said hotly. "You complicate a simple matter needlessly." And I added with bitter sarcasm, "I must needs be something of a genius to do all that you suggest in so short a time!"

He looked at the general and puffed.

"It's the way with these provincials," he said. "They'll swear to anything with damnable insolence."

Amherst smiled frostily an instant, and then turned his eyes on me without a shadow of expression in them.

"You say you know this man Sanborn," he said. "Do you know of any reason why he might be listening beneath Colonel Haldimand's window?"

"I do not, your Excellency," I replied, "but it does not surprise me to find the fellow is a spy. I doubt not my Lord Howe knew him well enough, but he was killed before he could take action."

He started and leaned forward at the mention of his Lordship's name.

"My Lord Howe, eh?" he said. "What has he to do with this?"

I told him of my last conversation with his Lordship, and he heard me out without the least expression.

"He confided all this in you?" he demanded when I had finished. "Why?"

I flushed. "I don't know, Your Excellency," I replied. "All that was said to me, I have told you."

He turned slowly to Haldimand.

"We may have stumbled on something here, Fred," he said. "His Lordship's papers should bear out the captain's story."

Haldimand shrugged. "They might," he replied dryly, "but I fear they won't. I was talking with Monypenny only the other day, and he told me that all of his Lordship's personal papers—his baggage, everything—were left behind when the army fled from Ticonderoga."

"What?" I cried, for the moment forgetting where I was. "Why, how can that be? His Lordship—"

I broke off in confusion, remembering those great, lonely piles of stores and baggage we had passed on the march from the sawmill. Haldimand shrugged.

"Nevertheless," he said, "it is so."

He and Amherst exchanged a quick glance.

A knock at the door startled us at that moment.

"Come in, come in," shouted Haldimand.

The door opened and the officer of the day entered, followed by the second guard and a burly fellow whom I recognized as the chief teamster. All three saluted and waited for the colonel to speak.

"Captain Snell, sir," Haldimand said, and then looked at the guard. "Have you found any sign of him?" he asked.

"No, sir," said the man. "We set guards to all the gates, and run down along the walls, but we ain't seen ary hide nor hair o'm."

"Did you ever see him?" demanded the colonel impatiently.

"No, sir," said the man dully.

"Tell me what you did see," Haldimand commanded.

"Well, sir," said the man, shifting a quid of tobacco from one cheek to the other, "me an' Otey Steele was standin' guard at the door like the captain ordered, and all at oncet we heerd a sound o' scufflin' an' grapplin' out back and a voice hollers 'Help, help, th' guard!' like that. Me an' Otey picks up our guns an' runs around, but all we see is this feller here pickin' hisself up off'n the ground. We sticks our guns in his face an' he cusses us suthin' fierce an' tells us to chase this other feller, an' then yer Honour sticks his head out'n the winder an' took over."

"You didn't see the other man at all, eh?" Haldimand asked smoothly.

"No, sir, I did not, sir," the fellow replied. "All I seen was this feller strugglin' on the ground tryin' to get up. I never seen no other man."

"He was gone by the time you got there," I said scornfully. "If one of you'd come around the other side of the cabin you'd have got him sure enough."

The man looked at me hostilely and made as if to spit, then suddenly remembered where he was and swallowed instead.

"Hampshire man, ain't you?" he asked, and looked at the colonel. "Wouldn't trust one of 'em a mite, sir," he said. "There ain't a particle o' honesty in any o' 'em."

General Amherst rapped sharply on the table with his knuckle.

"That'll do," he said. He nodded to Haldimand to proceed. The colonel turned to the chief teamster.

"What's your name?" he demanded.

"Clew," said the man.

"This man Sanborn one of yours?" said the colonel.

"Used to be," said Clew laconically, "but I ain't seen him hereabouts for a couple o' months."

Amherst and Haldimand looked at each other sharply.

"That would be about the time I saw him last," I said, remembering how he had been flogged.

"What became of him?" the general asked Clew.

"I dunno," the latter replied, "I heard somebody tell he was to Albany, actin' as a special messenger for Major Ferguson in charge o' supplies."

"Major Ferguson?" Amherst looked at me. "Relative of yours?"

"My cousin, your Excellency," I replied.

"Hum-m!" said Amherst, but his face gave no hint of his thoughts.

"Very well," he said. "That's all. Captain Snell, you will search the camp carefully for this man Sanborn, and bring him here as soon as you find him—if you do."

He dismissed us all with a wave of his hand, and then as an afterthought, turned to me.

"And by the way, Mr. Ferguson," he said, "you'd best stay near your quarters for the time being. Colonel Haldimand may need you. You may tell Major Rogers that these are my orders."

He nodded to indicate the interview was closed, and I saluted and withdrew.

2

The frame of mind in which I left the colonel's quarters will not be difficult to imagine. What had at the time seemed a perfectly natural action—a clearly logical procedure—had rebounded against me with a vengeance. Dragged out into the light of day, I now realized, my story sounded exceedingly thin. As I reviewed it in my own mind even I found it difficult to believe. And I had not a shred of evidence to support it. I could readily understand why Colonel Haldimand and the general must consider me either a complete and accomplished villain or a madman, or possibly both! Certainly General Amherst's last words, kindly spoken yet unmistakable in import, were enough to show that he meant to take no chances either way. At the same time it indicated that he recognized that there might be some truth in what I had said, for, had it been otherwise, I did not doubt he would have had me placed under arrest.

Indeed, the whole affair was become far too complicated for my poor comprehension. No sooner was I outside than I began beating about in my mind for anything that might serve as a clue. Could Sanborn, I asked myself, have been the spy to whom my Lord Howe had referred? Obviously the thought was so absurd that I laughed aloud as soon as it occurred to me. The man could not possibly have had access to such vital information as had been in the letter I had found upon the dead Frenchman. On the other hand Sanborn might easily have been one of the scoundrel's agents, and I for one did not in the least doubt that he was. My Lord Howe had hinted that he had many.

It occurred to me to wonder if they would catch the fellow. I doubted it; for if I knew him at all he was by now well away from the fort. Probably well on his way to Albany. As a matter of fact I rather half-heartedly hoped they would not find him. He was but small fry in the game, if my guess was worth anything. At the same time he was slippery enough. If they brought him in he would doubtless have some tall tale to explain his presence. He would probably even find some means of casting further suspicion upon me; and I realized that in the present state of affairs I might have some difficulty in proving my innocence.

If only, I told myself, I could find some hint as to the identity of the man of whom my Lord Howe had spoken, I might then be able to prove my story. But how was I to go about it? If only he had given me some clue!

But he had not—or had he? He had given certain false information to the man, whoever he was. Beyond that he had told me nothing. I suddenly remembered how startled Hubert had been to see me in the officers' mess that night. Could it be that he was the man? Certainly he had access to the information. And there was a definite connection between him and Sanborn. At the same time, what motive could he have? He had much to lose and little to gain by such a business, though I supposed the enemy paid well for such a service. I knew my cousin too well to imagine that he would scruple greatly about it. At the same time, when the evidence was examined critically there was really nothing against him. He had given a ready and plausible explanation of his surprise. And the fact that Sanborn was under his direction was nothing against him; so were a thousand other teamsters in the service of supply. I dismissed the thought as patently absurd.

I had been walking steadily during these reflections, and now I saw that I was approaching Rogers' cabin. Mindful of the general's orders, I went in and told him the entire story, but made no mention of my own thoughts on the way there. He heard me out gravely, and when I had done sat for some moments in silence.

"You can prove none of this?" he asked.

I shook my head. He rose and began to pace the cabin.

"It must be true," he said finally, half to himself. "No one but a fool would tell such a story on himself if it were not so! And I'll say this for you, Jamie, you're no fool."

"Thanks!" I said dryly. "How was I to know that Lord Howe's personal effects had been left behind?"

He nodded. "You couldn't," he said. "Why didn't you tell someone about this before?"

I shrugged. "It was not my place," I said. "I assumed that others must have been in his confidence to some degree. I thought surely Major Monypenny must know of it."

"But he didn't," he said.

"I see that now," I replied. "What am I to do? You can see what a damnable situation it puts me in."

He laughed. "By God," he said, "I do! I wouldn't want to be in your shoes. They think little enough of me as it is!"

"Well," I said, "what shall I do?"

"Do?" he said, and pursed his lips.

Then suddenly he turned on me.

"Look here," he said, "is your conscience clear?"

"What do you mean?" I demanded.

"I mean is this the straight truth you've told?" he replied.

"Of course!" I said stiffly.

"Well, then," he said, "if that's so, don't do anything."

"But—" I began.

He cut me short with a gesture.

"You have a story," he said, "which you can't prove."

I nodded.

"All right," he went on. "So have they, d'ye see? If your conscience is clear, if there is nothing that can be proved against you, you have nothing to fear. This fellow, whoever he is, will not make any accusations, even if he knows your connection with the case, which I doubt. All you have to do is sit tight and leave spy-catching to those whose business it is."

This aspect of the matter had not struck me before, and I said as much.

"Aye!" he said. "Your head was too full of this fellow. You do as I say, and I'll warrant you the whole affair'll blow over in a month. Indeed, 'twill surprise me if you ever hear anything more of it."

I stood up, and my relief must have shown in my face, for I had been gravely worried by the business. He laughed.

"In the meantime," he said, "since the general orders it, I'll see that your assignments are such as will keep you in camp. That way 'twill not go beyond us."

He kept his word with a vengeance. I was placed in charge of commissary; and from that day onward, for three months, did not set foot outside the camp.

Needless to say, this close confinement was irksome to the last degree. If I had grown tired of scouting before, I now grew a hundred times more tired of the life of the camp. At least, on scout there was some change of scene and the promise of excitement. But in the camp there was nothing but the same dull round, day in and day out. There was nothing I could do about it, however, save make the best of it.

At least I did not have to endure it alone. Poor, faithful old Toby, as my orderly, was also confined to the camp, and he, not knowing the reason for it, was even more bewildered than I. It was plain that he was fretful, for such a life was completely foreign to his nature; yet he never complained. Nor could I explain matters to him, even though I often looked up to find his eyes fixed upon me with a puzzled, almost pleading expression. In spite of his bewilderment, however, he never asked a question, but accepted the situation quietly, as if to show tacitly that whatever I might do met with his approval.

There were others who were not so discreet. I had always been as active as anyone in the service, and this sudden shift could not but be noticed. I had to bear a good deal of heavy humour and chaffing in silence, for I felt that the less said about the real reasons for my confinement to the camp the better. Of these last the hardest to bear was Captain Shepard, who plagued me in a rough-humoured way, not in the least intended to be offensive. One night he came in from a particularly difficult scout and flung himself wearily down upon my bunk.

"You picked an easy berth," he said. "Where did you get the luck?"

I remember I was in an ugly mood that night and in no mood for his banter.

" 'Tis none of my choosing," I retorted.

He cocked an unbelieving eye at me.

"No?" he said.

"No!" I replied. "Any time you want it you can have it—subject to the major's approval."

He laughed loudly.

"D'ye tell me you don't like it?" he demanded.

"I do not," I said.

He looked surprised.

"So?" he said. "Is it a feud then between you and the major?"

I shook my head impatiently.

"It's nothing of the sort," I told him. " 'Tis work that must be done, and I suppose the major likes the way I do it."

He shrugged, and went on to speak of something else, but the exchange will give some hint as to the curiosity the situation aroused.

During the first month, it must be admitted, I was nervous and apprehensive, though if anyone had asked me of what I should not have been able to say. The man Sanborn, of course, was never discovered. By what means he managed to slip past the sentries I could never tell. But the fact was obvious that he had done so.

In the second month I was more sure of myself, and by the end of the third I was convinced that the whole affair had been forgotten. If I did nothing about it myself, I thought, I should be like to be confined to camp for the rest of my service, and accordingly I went straight to Rogers and asked him if he had heard anything more concerning my case. He shook his head.

"Nary a word," he said.

"But see here," I cried, "this can't go on indefinitely."

He shrugged. "I'll tell you what," he said. "I believe the whole thing's tommyrot. Yet I can't turn you loose on my own initiative over the general's orders. You go to Haldimand and stand upon your rights as an officer. Tell him you want to be released or formally arrested, charged, and court-martialed. I'll warrant you that'll call their bluff."

"But suppose they bring charges?" I demanded.

"What charges can they bring?" he said.

The next morning, being New Year's Day, I presented myself at the colonel's quarters and was presently ushered into his presence. He appeared to be in a jovial mood, which I was pleased to see. He beamed upon me in a fatherly fashion.

"Well, young man," he said in not unkindly tones, "what seems to be the trouble?"

"I wanted to ask you, sir," I said, "if you could tell me how much longer I would have to stay in confinement of the camp?"

"Confinement?" he asked, obviously bewildered. "Confinement? What confinement? Who are you, sir?"

"Captain Ferguson, sir," I told him. "You may remember I stumbled upon a fellow listening beneath your window while General Amherst was here three months since."

"What?" he cried. "Have you heard no more of that?"

"I have not, sir," I replied, and I wanted to add that he well knew it, since anything on the matter must pass through his hands. However, with years I had learned a measure of discretion.

"Hrumph!" said he. "No more have I, though I know his Excellency meant to look into the matter when he got to Albany. What is it you want?"

"Sir," I said, "I came to ask that I either be released from the necessity of staying within the bounds of the camp, or else be allowed to stand upon my rights as an officer and demand that I be formally arrested, charged and tried."

"Hump, hump, hump, harumph!" he puffed. "So? That's it, eh? Well, humph, I see no harm in it. Surely if charges were to be preferred we'd have had 'em by now. You may consider yourself released, sir."

"Thank you, sir," I said. "Will you give me an order to Major Rogers to that effect?"

"Of course! Of course!" he said, and snatched up pen and paper and scrawled a brief order to Rogers. When he had done I took the folded paper, thanked him, and went out a free man once more. The very next day I led out a scout towards Ticonderoga, and grateful I was for the privilege, too.

It was not long after this that I began to consider the possibility of leave. It was now two years since I had seen my family, though with the exception of the Louisbourg campaign in which I had taken part, they had never once been more than a hundred miles away. Surely, I thought, I was entitled to it. But when I applied to Rogers he shook his head.

"I'm sorry," he said, "I have orders to allow no leaves save on matters pertaining to the service."

"You might send me recruiting," I suggested.

He shook his head.

"Stark and Brewer and Shepard are out now," he said. "I can't send too many for the purpose."

I must confess I was a little bitter about this, but my turn to laugh came later. In February, General Amherst arrived in New York, and Rogers promptly wrote proposing that he be allowed to come down and make a return of the Rangers to him.

This was a little jaunt that Rogers had long been looking forward to. At the time the Earl of Loudoun succeeded Shirley, and again when Abercrombie succeeded Loudoun, he had made this proposal and it had been warmly received on both occasions. Evidently then he had managed to combine pleasure with business, and found time to do a little celebrating of his own on the side, for he never tired of talking about it.

This time, however, there was a different story to be told. By return courier he received a letter from Colonel Townshend, the general's A.D.C., which began: "Sir, I received your letter with the enclosed return. The General commands me to inform you that he can by no means approve of your leaving Fort Edward."

I declare I have never seen a man so discountenanced and at the same time so put out as Rogers was then!

A little later insult was heaped upon injury when the general refused to allow Rogers' proposal to raise two new companies of Rangers until the old ones were complete. Rogers stormed and cursed, but to no avail; especially as no one but his own officers heard him. He damned the general for a nincompoop. But for my own part I could not help thinking that it was a good omen. At last, it seemed, we were to have a commander who knew his own mind!

The events of the next few weeks proved that. Preparations began at once for the forthcoming campaign, and the way in which these preparations were accomplished was enough to prove that at last we had a cool and thoughtful head in the lead.

The plan for the campaign, when it was announced, was not unlike the former campaigns in its threefold form. On the east, now that Louisbourg was out of the way, there was nothing to prevent an attack on Quebec itself. Such an attack was to be made, led by a new general whose name was Wolfe—a young man evidently, and one of whom no one appeared to have any knowledge save that he had fought with Amherst at Louisbourg. At the same time that Quebec was being attacked, Amherst himself was to lead the inevitable expedition by the centre against Ticonderoga and Crown Point, with Montreal as its ultimate objective. Simultaneously a smaller expedition was to attack Fort Niagara, on the fall of which it was to make a diversion down the Saint Lawrence towards Montreal, so that the French would be unable to set their full strength against Amherst on his northward march.

As a plan it did not differ greatly from others that had failed in years gone by. But there was a new spirit of determination abroad in the army that boded well for its success. Upon one thing at least we were determined. We had learned a costly lesson during the previous summer, and we were not in a mood to let similar blunders wreck our hopes.

It was May before Rogers had his wish: a summons to wait upon the general. As it happened it was only to Albany rather than New York, but it pleased him so that I believe he did not care. His vanity was soothed.

Also I believe his rebuff made him more sympathetic to others, for when he learned that he would be permitted to bring an aide he suggested that I accompany him.

Needless to say, I jumped at the chance, and we left that same afternoon—the fourteenth of the month, as I recall—going by canoe, and planning to make the run in two days if it were possible. Accompanying us were Toby, and Rogers' man Blount, and a fifth man who would stand guard over the canoe the while we were in Albany.

We made good time in the daylight that remained to us, and camped that night a little distance below Fort Miller. The next day we were away with the dawn and being all five strong paddlers, and having the wind and current at our backs, hoped that day to make the entire run. About midday, however, the wind shifted and blew strong in our faces from the south, so that we had a stiff paddle in the face of it. We reached the Cohoes at the mouth of the Mohawk, nevertheless, and after a short rest there and a bite to sup, decided to push on to Albany that night. Accordingly, about eight o'clock we reembarked and began the final twelve-mile paddle to the city.

It was late when we arrived, and for a time I pondered whether I should not take quarters in the tavern for that night, the more especially since our departure from Fort Edward had been so abrupt that I had been unable to send word ahead of my coming. After some consideration, however, I made up my mind that there was scant profit in paying for a house if I did not use it occasionally. Moreover I felt that under the circumstances Dorcas would hardly object to being awakened, no matter what the hour. Accordingly I shouldered my duffel, having first seen Toby bedded at the tavern, and set out up the hill.

I came presently to the house, set back from the roadway in its grove of trees. All the windows, as I had expected, were in darkness, but through the fanlight above the door, I could see that a faint night light was burning in the hallway. It would be amusing, I thought, to slip in and surprise Dorcas. Climbing cautiously onto the porch I tried the latch, and found to my surprise that it was unlocked. The door gave under my hand, and I pushed it open and stepped inside.

I dropped my duffel bag behind the door and, turning, took a step towards the lamp which burned low upon the table. As I did so I heard a faint step upon the stair above, and looking up I saw a dim figure outlined in the gloom. Before I could speak I heard Dorcas' voice.

"Hugh?" she said. "Is it you, Hugh? Darling, I didn't think to see you back before tomorrow."

I was by the table then, with my hand upon the thumbscrew of the lamp. But at the words I stood thunderstruck, scarce able to believe my ears. Nor could I speak in return. Something in my attitude must have alarmed her, for she spoke again, hastily and with a rising note of panic.

"Hugh? Hugh? Why don't you answer me?"

I turned up the light then, and spoke.

"I am not Hugh," I said.

As we stood there facing each other, the light upon my face, she gave a little stifled scream and stared at me with frightened eyes, unable to make a further sound. For a moment I could neither speak nor feel. My only sensation was one of astonishment, so suddenly had it come. But as we stared at each other I began to feel anger growing within me, filling me with hot trembling wrath. I felt suddenly resentful of all she had ever done or said to me. I wanted to cry out and curse her. But even as the impulse came upon me she swayed ever so slightly and I saw her as she was, one thin hand gripping the banister and the other pressed against a mouth grown slack now, and drooping in horror, her eyes blank and lustreless, her cheeks sagging and flabby, so that she looked twice her age. Though I could see it all now—everything that had happened in these years past—though I knew now what was in my Lord Howe's mind when he had warned me to look about me, I could no longer feel angry. I only knew a feeling of deep disgust and a little pity for this broken-down woman, this poor hollow shell of a creature that had once been so lovely. This was the girl I once had loved. If I cared now, I wondered, why was I so indifferent?

All this passed through my head in far less than the moment it takes to tell. In that instant we faced each other there upon the stairs. Then all at once she gave a little shuddering cry and swayed out towards me. I sprang forward, just in time, for she had fainted, and, in fainting, fell. Had I not been there to catch her she must have slid the full length of those steep stairs.

I carried her down and laid her upon the settle at the foot of the stairs, half wondering what to do next, for I had little experience with this sort of thing. A second step sounded above, and I looked up to see Purity descending, a candle held high over her head while she strained anxiously for a sight of what was happening below.

"What is it?" she called. "What has happened? I heard someone cry out."

"It's all right, Purity," I told her. "She's fainted." And I added, somewhat bitterly, I fear: "She hadn't looked to see me."

"Oh!" she said, surprise in her voice. "It's you, Jamie?"

"Yes," I said, "it's Jamie."

She had reached the landing by then. Something in the way I spoke made her look at me sharply. I nodded.

"I know," I said. "You'd better fetch me some brandy."

She turned without a word and went into the drawing room, returning in a moment with a glass. I raised Dorcas' head and forced some of the liquor between her teeth. Her eyelids fluttered, and a moment later she sat up. She looked at me miserably.

"What are you going to do?" she asked dully.

"Nothing," I replied harshly. "Go back to bed."

She got to her feet shakily and, taking the candle, turned away. Without a word I watched her go slowly up the stairs and turn down the hall. She would be all right for tonight, I thought. I turned to Purity and nodded towards the drawing room. She turned and entered, and without a word I followed. In so doing I could not help but notice the difference between the two women. Purity had blossomed out. Dorcas had faded. Purity's glance was direct, her bearing proud though not haughty—assured and self-confident. Now that it was gone I could see that Dorcas' air of simplicity and dependence had been but a cloak to hide her real character. I wondered what could be the outcome of this mess. I was totally bewildered.

Purity sat down before the fireplace, and I came to stand before her.

"How long have you known of this?" I demanded.

She shook her head.

"I think I suspected it from the first," she replied, "from the time I came to your house in Portsmouth, though I was not sure of it until we came to Albany."

I stared at her in shocked surprise.

"As long as that!" I exclaimed, and I fear my voice expressed not only incredulity but contempt as well; for it seemed to me that if she had kept their secret for them she was but a poor friend to me, and somehow this affected me more bitterly than the fact itself. "Why did you not tell me?"

She dropped her eyes before mine.

"How was I to tell you?" she asked. "You would not have believed, and I could not prove it. You would have thought me a meddler and a bearer of tales, no better than an old gossip. It was plain enough to all the rest of us. We could only hope that one day you would see it for yourself."

"We?" I said.

"All of your friends," she replied. "Lord Howe tried to give you a hint. And if you will remember I did, too, that same night."

I thought back to that night and remembered that it had seemed she was trying to tell me something; something I had never found out. I remembered too, and with a spasm of bitterness, the scene Dorcas had made because she had come in and found me with my arms about this child. I realized now the hypocrisy of that, and all at once I felt my shoulders sag.

Purity looked at me compassionately.

"Poor Jamie!" she said. "Does it hurt so much?"

I shrugged. "No," I said. "Somehow, I don't know—I don't seem to care. Yet I am confused. I don't seem to know what I should think or do or feel."

She looked at me with troubled eyes.

"Poor Jamie!" she said again. "If this were all!"

"Eh?" I said, startled, for I must confess my mind had gone wandering. "All? Why, what else could there be?"

She hesitated for a moment, and I thought she was about to say something. Then she appeared to change her mind. She shook her head.

"I cannot tell you now," she said. "Perhaps tomorrow, or the next day."

"See here!" I said fiercely. "He hasn't been bothering you too, has he?"

She laughed, almost gaily, I thought.

"Oh, Jamie!" she cried. "You are a dear!"

She stood up then and laid her hand upon my shoulder.

"You are tired," she said. "Go to bed now and sleep. There will be time enough to worry about this tomorrow."

"But—" I began.

"Sh-h!" she commanded. "Tomorrow we will talk about it."

And with that she leaned forward and kissed me full upon the lips.

"That's for one who loves you," she said, almost defiantly.

And before I could recover myself sufficiently to speak she was gone, laughing, out the door and up the stairs, leaving me staring after her more completely bewildered than ever.

3

I spent a sleepless night, full of doubt and uncertainty. At one moment I was all bitterness against Dorcas for having thus betrayed my faith; and in the next I blamed myself—for surely some of the fault was mine. I had been too weakly acquiescent. I had had neither time nor inclination for all the social pleasures that were so dear to her heart; and at the same time I had not had the heart to deny her. Hubert, with all his grace and elegance and social tact, had seemed an ideal solution to the problem. But I saw now that I had been lazy as well as overfond. Had I bestirred myself to be more the stern husband and less the indulgent lover, perhaps none of this would have happened.

But, for all this, I did not blind myself to my cousin's perfidy. Ever and again, when I might otherwise have slept, I found myself starting awake, trembling with rage at his black-hearted treachery—consumed with fury at the way in which he had abused my hospitality. There, at least, I promised myself satisfaction, come what might.

The problem of what to do was no less harrowing. I had known of other similar cases in which the injured husband, by recourse to a court of law, had had the erring wife and lover publicly whipped and branded; but such measures seemed to me cruel and harsh, and the man who used them scarce better than those he sought to punish. My first impulse was to show the woman—for I could no longer think of her as my wife—the door, driving her out into the street like a common harlot. And yet some faint shreds of sentiment, some flicker of my old love for her, must have clung to my heart, for I could not entertain the thought for long, let alone put it into action. Nor could I think of any other punishment that would suit the offence.

There was divorce, of course, but this, too, was odious to me, not only from principle but also because whipping and branding for Dorcas must inevitably follow for the civil crime of adultery. Moreover there was the child to consider—poor little fellow, who must go through life bearing the name of his mother's betrayer! I began to sense, now, the hideous humour of Hubert's request that the boy be named for him!

In the end I concluded that the lad was most to be considered. If his mother and I could never again look upon each other as husband and wife, there was no reason for the rest of the world, or even for the boy himself, to know it. If she were willing to concede her error and put thoughts of her lover aside for the child's sake there was no reason why we could not live together in apparent domestic harmony. Such a life would be shameful indeed, but at least it would be no more shameful than what she had already done; and it would have the saving grace of being done for our son's sake.

Such were my own thoughts on the matter. It will be seen presently how little I realized, even then, my wife's selfishness and complete demoralization. Upon one thing, at least, I was determined. As quickly as it was possible for her to pack, Dorcas would leave Albany. She must go straight home to Portsmouth, and there live quietly and respectably until the war was over and we could straighten matters out, once and for all. It was upon this thought that I finally settled into a fitful doze just as the grey light of dawn began creeping in at the windows.

Breakfast was a dismal affair. Dorcas did not appear, and Purity and I had the table to ourselves. But she made no reference to the business of the night before, and I was in no mood for small talk; so that in the end, I believe, scarce more than two words passed between us.

After breakfast, having been ordered by Rogers to appear at headquarters at nine, I made my way thither, stopping on my way to make some inquiries on my own, only to find that Major Ferguson had been called to New York some days since but was expected back momentarily. At headquarters I spent the morning helping Rogers with certain details pertaining to the allotment of the recruits for the Rangers that Stark and Shepard were sending in. But this was accomplished with such poor grace and such fuddle-headedness that even Rogers, whose long suit was not his ability to observe distress in others, asked if I were coming down with a fever. When I replied curtly that I was not, he dismissed the matter without a second thought.

Not so Toby, however. Each time thereafter, when I looked up I would find him staring at me with stolid, black-eyed imperturbability. In spite of his expressionlessness I felt vaguely that he was disturbed.

At midday Rogers dismissed me.

"I wait upon the general after dinner," said he. "There is no need for you to be with me."

I was as well pleased and said so.

"Be ready to start back in the morning," he said.

I nodded and turned away.

On the way back to the house Toby plodded beside me stolidly, his great belly, which had grown more ponderous with the years, jerking from side to side with each movement of his short legs. We were almost at the house when he fixed me with a pair of beady eyes and asked a question.

"What matter you?" he said. "You sick?"

I smiled slightly, for his concern flattered me.

"Not sick, Toby," I replied. "Only upset. Not anything you would understand."

He looked towards the house.

"Toby understand some thing!" he said. "Toby not too old to see! Last night you come down see wife you feel good. Today you come down like man with bellyful of sour wind. Toby know wifes bad. Toby not understand English wifes. When Injun wife no good man beat her and send her home to own people. Then get good wife. You try."

I was amazed and shocked at his knowledge. If even he had seen it, was there any, I asked myself, who had not?

"You don't understand, Toby," I said, because I could think of no better reply.

He shook his head.

"No," he said. "Toby not understand."

He trotted along beside me for a moment in silence. Then he plucked my sleeve.

"Look," he said, "Englishman's scalp look like Frenchman's. Even Frenchman not tell some. Toby good scalper. Tony get bad English scalp, make 'um look like good Frenchman. You say so."

He pulled his short, thick-bladed knife from his belt to leave me in no doubt as to his meaning. I smiled and shook my head.

"No, old friend," I said. "I appreciate your offer, but this is a thing I must do myself."

He put the knife back in its sheath and shrugged.

"All same," he said, "Toby not far away. You need, you call."

I stopped then and shook his hand, for I was touched to find him such a friend.

The midday meal, if anything, was more sombre than breakfast. Toby took his dinner in the kitchen, where the help complained bitterly of his smell, and neither Dorcas nor Purity came down from above, so that I was alone at the great table. So engrossed was I with my thoughts, however, that I scarcely noticed it.

I must have dawdled over my food, for it was near midafternoon when I rose, determined to call Dorcas downstairs and have the business over with.

But first I promised myself a pipe to compose my mind, lest I be too harsh. I went into the drawing room and took down my pipe and Virginia. But scarcely had I settled myself in an easy-chair by the fireplace when I was aroused by the sound of footsteps on the stoop outside. The front door opened. Someone entered, and the door slammed shut again. As I rose I could hear the steps turn towards the drawing room. They came as far as the open door and then stopped abruptly, and I looked up to see my cousin Hubert standing surprised and startled on the threshold.

In the instant that we faced each other across the room I could see that he had not counted upon finding me there. He seemed annoyed, almost a little apprehensive. Some of his customary suavity seemed to have slipped from his shoulders, and I could have sworn that I saw a flicker of doubt pass across his handsome features. Then his lips parted in his old bland smile, and his jaunty air came back to him.

"Well!" he exclaimed. "This is a surprise indeed."

"A most unpleasant one, I've no doubt!" I replied.

"Eh? Damme, what d'ye mean by that?" he demanded, for I had put more coldness into my words than the words themselves implied.

"You know well enough what I mean," I said. "If I have been blind to your philandering in my house before now, it was because

I trusted you and had faith in my wife. Now that my eyes are opened, however, I have no mind to allow it to continue."

"Fie, man!" he exclaimed. "What tavern talk have you been listening to? Your suspicions are an insult to a most gracious lady!"

"I have the lady's own word for it, sirrah!" I said. "This is no tavern talk. My evidence is sufficient that if I chose to shoot you dead this minute no court in the land would hold me guilty!"

He eyed me a moment sardonically, and in that instant I heard the patter of running feet in the corridor beyond and the creak of footsteps on the stairs. But my attention, fixed upon the man before me, did not waver for an instant. He shrugged and moved towards the table, where he stopped and took a pinch of snuff with a flourish.

"Well?" he said. "What are you waiting for? Have you forgotten your pistols?"

All my old resentment against his haughty superiority welled up within me, and I felt my resolution to hold my temper in control slipping from me. All at once I was in a trembling rage.

"I would not waste good powder and lead on such as you," I said. "Cold steel were a better remedy for this ill!"

And with that I stepped around the table and slapped him across the face.

"I don't know," I said, shaking with anger, "why I choose to allow you the opportunity for an honourable defence. But I am no murderer. I cannot kill a man in cold blood—even so poor a man as you."

He drew back, his face livid, and clapped his hand to his hanger.

"By God's blood!" he cried. "Why do we wait?"

I had my blade out on the instant and faced him across the strip of carpet. It was at once evident where the advantage lay. With his greater height and longer reach, not to speak of his superior swordsmanship—for after all I was but a poor backwoodsman in these matters—he might have had but little difficulty in disposing of me, had I not made up in some measure by speed and fury for lack of skill and size. But no sooner had our blades crossed than the door, which he had carefully closed behind him, burst open, and Dorcas, followed closely by Purity, flew into the room.

Purity stopped still and fell back against the wall, where she stood, her eyes wide with horror, her lips ashen. But Dorcas flung herself between us and threw her arms about Hubert's neck.

"No!" she cried. "No—you must not!"

She turned to face me scornfully, at the same time shielding Hubert's body with her own. Considering the way the odds lay, the gesture was laughable; but it must be admitted I did not see it at the time.

"'Tis a sudden interest you take," she railed, "after all these years of neglect!"

"Neglect!" I cried, amazed. "Madam, no woman ever had a truer husband! If of late I have had duty elsewhere, you should remember 'twas yourself urged me to it!"

Hubert laughed with a note of superiority that was maddening.

"On my soul, cousin James," he said, "I don't see how you can expect otherwise. To leave a lovely lady so poorly attended! Is it any wonder she looked elsewhere for comfort?"

There was no doubt that he spoke the truth in part, at least, for in that moment she was lovely, with her cheeks flushed with excitement, her eyes bright with anger. But I had no eyes for her.

"Nay!" I said, for I had him there. "This is not a thing that began with my enlistment. 'Tis a thing that goes much farther back than that. A pity I did not lend an ear to Colonel Atkinson when he sought to warn me of how matters stood. It would have simplified things to have dealt with it then."

"Is it so much more difficult to deal with now, then?" he asked with a sneering laugh.

"Aye!" I replied bitterly. "For then I should have spitted you without hesitation, and turned this woman out for the baggage she was. But now the circumstances have changed. There is the boy to think of."

Dorcas laughed shrilly, with a note of hysterical exultation.

"No boy of yours, James Ferguson!" she cried.

For an instant I believe even Hubert was shocked. Then he laughed mockingly.

"You see, cousin?" he said. "What more have you to say?"

In the bitterness of my rage I scarce knew what I was saying.

"That is not all!" I cried. "It is enough, God knows! But now, look ye, not content with soiling my bed, you've gone so far as to try your filthy tricks upon a maid for whose safe keeping in my house I have pledged my word!"

Dorcas looked at him sharply, clinging to his arm.

" 'Tis a lie!" she cried. "Tell him he lies, Hugh!"

But he ignored her, shaking his arm free, and glared at me over her head.

"Faith!" he said. "You're well informed, cousin. Has our pure maid been telling tales?"

"Mistress Purity has told enough," I said, "to show me the black-hearted traitor you are!"

Now, in speaking the words I had no thought beyond the relations existing between Hubert and myself. When I called him traitor it was with reference only to the treacherous way in which he had accepted my hospitality and violated it. Consequently I did not look for the effect upon him which my words produced. He started and glanced quickly at Purity and then back again at me, and for an instant I could have sworn that I saw fear in his eyes. I thought, too, that Purity stared at me curiously.

But I had not time to think upon it. Hubert thrust Dorcas roughly to one side.

"So!" he said between clenched teeth. "This is a matter which must be settled here!"

And with that he lunged at me with his hanger.

I met his attack and parried it with ease, for in his haste he had overreached himself. But before I could follow up my advantage Dorcas had once again thrown herself between us, though this time she beat her small fists furiously upon his breast.

"There is no truth in it, Hubert?" she cried. "Tell me he lies. There is naught between you and this girl?"

Thus forced to give her his attention, he slipped his arm about her waist, swinging her away from him.

"Nay, my sweet," he said to her, " 'twas but a dalliance. I would have seen the smug wench belie her name, no more!"

And with that he pressed her back and came at me afresh.

But it appeared that we were not destined to go that day uninterrupted, for no sooner were we at thrust and parry again than there came a thunderous pounding at the door, and in the next instant the room seemed full of strangers.

Truth to tell, there were but two strangers, both officers of the regulars, to judge from their coats. The other two were Toby and Major Rogers. Rogers stepped between us and swept my sword up as if it were but a bothersome bit of brush across his path. At the same time Toby grasped Hubert from behind and held him secure.

"Have done! Have done!" cried Rogers. "Have ye not a bellyful of fighting at Ticonderoga, captain, that ye must be looking for it when ye come to Albany?"

"This is a personal matter, Major Rogers," I said coldly, "and I'll thank you to step aside and let me finish it like a gentleman."

"And see an officer o' mine spitted before my eyes?" he demanded. "Ye'd think good men were easy come by!"

"There'll be no spitting save I do it!" I replied hotly.

"Ho! Fire-eater!" he roared. "Ye've a bellyful of confidence at any rate! But, if this is an affair of honour, as ye say, why do ye not carry it on the field, according to form, and not stand here clacking swords together in the presence of a lady like tavern brawlers?"

He did not wait for my answer, but turned to Purity and made a leg.

"Your pardon, ma'am," he said. "I had not time before to express my thanks to ye for sending yon Indian. He came to us just as we were leaving the general's door."

I remembered the steps I had heard in the hall. So that was it! I lowered the tip of my sword somewhat abashed, yet none the less determined to have satisfaction.

"I am ready to meet Major Ferguson at any spot and at any time," I said.

But here one of the young officers stepped forward.

"The general disapproves of duelling," he said, "and insists upon the strict enforcement of those sections of the articles of war pertaining to it, under penalty of court-martial. I must ask you gentlemen to put up your swords and use them against the French until such time as our hostilities are at an end. After that will be time enough to settle personal differences."

"Eh, sir?" I said hotly. "And who might you be to come between gentlemen in a personal quarrel?"

He turned to me, not a whit offended, for he saw that I was angered beyond discretion, and made me a leg.

"Captain Amherst," he replied suavely. "William Amherst, sir, brother and aide to his Excellency, the general. Your servant, sir."

Somewhat mollified I bowed and introduced myself. The fourth man was introduced as a Lieutenant Hamilton. I indicated Hubert with the tip of my sword.

"No doubt you know this, Captain Amherst," I said.

Amherst smiled thinly.

"I have met Major Ferguson," he replied.

I nodded. "Since you are familiar with the articles of war, captain," I said, "you will remember that section which says that if any officer is guilty of conduct unbecoming an officer and gentleman he will be tried by court-martial and dismissed the service?"

"I remember it," he said.

"Very good, sir," I said. "This man has put such insults upon me, sir, that if I were not to resent them in the ordinary fashion I would be guilty of such conduct. If I am to be read from the service in any event, I think, sir, you might concede me the right to choose my own offence."

Amherst smiled. "The general's orders are specific," he said. "They are for you and Major Rogers to return to Fort Edward at once. There is no time for fighting."

"We will not be long in the fighting," I said.

Rogers looked questioningly at Amherst over his shoulder from the corner into which he had pushed Hubert. There was no doubt but that he was inclined to let me have my way.

"Your orders are to leave without delay, major," said Amherst. "Besides, I have told you the general's attitude towards duelling."

"Sir!" I protested. "This man has abused my hospitality, violated my home, and even attempted to seduce a young lady who is here under my protection, all by his own confession. Surely the general cannot disapprove of my settling such a score!"

Captain Amherst shrugged.

"I have no doubt of the justice of your cause," he said dryly. "But unfortunately General Amherst makes no exceptions. If you wish to bring charges of conduct unbecoming an officer and a gentleman against Major Ferguson, that is your affair. But for the present your orders are clear. You are to leave at once for Fort Edward with Major Rogers. Under those circumstances I see nothing for you to do but obey."

I bowed in resignation.

"You leave me no choice," I said.

I turned to Hubert.

"You may thank these orders for saving your skin this time, cousin," I said. "But I promise you there shall be no interference a second time."

Hubert grinned at me sardonically while he sheathed his weapon.

"A poor excuse is better than none," he taunted.

I restrained myself with an effort.

"We will let these gentlemen be the judges of that," I said. "Now I'll see you out of my house, and warn you that if I find you in it again I'll shoot you down without further words."

He bowed debonairly and took a pinch of snuff, after which he bent low over Dorcas' hand and drew her with him towards the door.

"Good-bye, my dear," he said, and his eyes, looking past her, sought mine mockingly. "Have no fear but that this will presently be settled with satisfaction for us all."

With that, and without another word to any of us he turned and left the room. For a moment no one spoke. Then Dorcas gave a little choking sound, half sob, half cry and followed after.

4

It was Rogers who recalled us all sharply to the present.

"Well?" he said, "what are we waiting for?"

I looked about at him with a start.

"I'll get my things," I said.

I turned towards the door, but Captain Amherst put out a detaining hand.

"One moment please, captain," he said apologetically. "I must beg you to understand that my interference here today has been purely a question of duty, and in no way reflects my personal feelings in the matter."

I bowed. "I understand, sir," I replied. "In the circumstances you had no choice."

He nodded gravely. "Thank you, captain," he said. "When the proper time comes I would be honoured to act for you."

I bowed again. "I will remember it, sir," I said.

He returned my bow and turned to Rogers.

"Well, major," he said, "if you have no further need of us, Lieutenant Hamilton and I will say good-bye."

They took their leave then, and I walked with them to the door. When they were gone I went upstairs and gathered up my duffel. As I came out into the hall with the bag I found Purity waiting for me. I set down the bag and took her hand in mine.

"Good-bye, child," I said. "This is a bad business, but if you will bear with it for a few days more I will write you what is best to be done."

She clung to my hand, and I could feel that she was trembling. "Oh, Jamie!" she said. "I must talk to you—I must!"

It was plain that she was upset beyond reason, and I could not leave her so. I stepped back and indicated the door of my room.

"Of course, child!" I said. "Come in."

But she hung back, shaking her head sharply.

"No, no!" she said. "Not here, I cannot!"

"But—" I began.

She cut me short. "Go," she said. "I heard Major Rogers say that you would pick up Captain Stark at the Crown tavern. I will meet you there."

Before I could say anything she brushed my cheek with her lips and gave me a gentle push along the hall.

I was surprised at her insistence, but I saw that she would hear of nothing else; so I made no protest. In the lower hall I handed over my bag to Toby, and a moment later we were away.

I was in no mood for talk; but Rogers was jovial despite the fact that the orders which sent him back so hurriedly prevented the carouse to which he had looked forward for so long.

"By God!" he exclaimed. "We've a leader at last, you mark my words!"

"You were not long with the general," I growled by way of answer.

He shot me an amused glance.

"And lucky for you I was not," he said. "Why, as God's my life, the fellow'd have had you dancing a jig on the end of his sword in another minute! I'll warrant he had the reach of you by six inches."

I made no answer to that, and we walked along for some moments in silence. Then, presently, he reverted to his former topic.

"Yon Amherst," he said, "there's a man of action! You'll see no grass grow under his feet. 'Good day, major,' says he, when

I come in. 'I hear Mr. Stark has just come in with sixty recruits. Does this fill your companies?' 'It does not, your Excellency,' says I. 'It leaves us short by a hundred men.' 'Very good,' says he. 'Here's a beating order for a hundred men. I leave the details to you, major, but I want your companies complete and ready to march with the army by the fifteenth of next month. Is that clear?' 'It is,' says I. 'Good!' says he. 'In the meantime I want all the information as to the enemy's activities that you can get me. You will go back to Fort Edward tonight and start your parties out as soon as you arrive there.' 'Would it be all the same to you, sir,' I says, 'if I started in the morning?' 'No,' says he. 'You will start tonight. And you will take your men with you. The sooner scouting resumes, the better. That's all.' And just to make sure he sends his brother and Lieutenant Hamilton with me!"

When I still made no answer he shrugged resignedly.

" 'Twas at the corner we met the Injun," he said.

We were come by then to the door of the Crown, and I was roused from my thoughts by the sound of running feet behind me. I turned, and Purity flung herself into my arms. Rogers raised his eyebrows, and looked humorously wise.

"Oho!" said he. "That's how it is!"

I jerked my head towards the tavern.

"Go on in," I said, forgetting that he was my superior for the moment. "I will join you presently."

He turned away with a grin and entered, and I tried to disengage myself as gently as I might from Purity's grip.

"Come, lass," I said. "What's all this?"

But she only clung to me the tighter, and I saw that she was sobbing with fright.

"Oh, Jamie!" she cried, "Jamie! You should not have done it. You should not have let him see that you knew. Now he will not stop at anything till he kills you!"

"Nonsense!" I said gruffly. "The matter is closed for the moment. Even Hubert would not stoop to murder over such a business."

She stood back a pace and looked at me wide-eyed.

"But," she began, "but you called him 'traitor.' "

"Aye, traitor!" I growled. "I did indeed! And was it not a traitorous trick he played upon me?"

She stood then and stared at me for a moment incredulous.

"Then you don't know?" she said at last. "You don't know. But I thought you did, and so does he! I saw it!"

"Know what?" I demanded impatiently, for I was bewildered and not a little annoyed at all this mystery.

She clasped her hands together in distress and drew her breath in sharply.

"The man's a spy," she said.

"What?" I cried startled out of my sulking fit.

"He's a spy," she repeated. "And now he thinks you know!"

Suddenly I remembered all my doubts about him. I remembered how startled he had been to see me at Fort Edward, and how confused he had seemed, and how interested he had been in where Rogers was. And everything was suddenly clear. The excuse he had made me so glibly had been characteristic—pure fabrication tossed out on the spur of the moment with so much assurance that I had been completely taken in.

"How long have you known this?" I demanded.

"Nearly two years," she told me. "For a long time all sorts of strange men came to the house asking for him—he used your house for it, Jamie; but I wasn't suspicious until one night just before the fall of William-Henry. A stranger came, with a foreign accent. I thought he might be a Dutchman from the Mohawk, so I thought little of it when I let him in. Afterwards, when I had gone to bed I could hear them talking. The stranger seemed angry, and every now and then would raise his voice; and though I could not hear the words I knew they were speaking French. After that I watched more closely, though I learned little—only once when I found a purse of his filled with louis-d'or. I think he suspected me; for he was careful to give me no hint, and though I searched among his things several times I could never find anything."

"And you told no one of this?" I asked.

"I told my Lord Howe as soon as he came back," she said, "for I remembered that he was a good friend to you."

"What had he to say?" I demanded.

"He seemed much pleased," she replied; "but he told me to say nothing more to anyone—only to keep a sharp watch and see if I could learn anything more."

"That's it!" I cried. I knew now why he had called me in and so confided in me. And I saw why he wished me to make the arrest. It would suit his sense of justice. The parts of the puzzle began to fall in place rapidly.

Purity looked at me curiously.

"When he was killed," she said, "I thought someone must know. But nothing ever happened."

"The secret died with him," I said, "and besides ourselves there was no one even to suspect it."

"Oh!" she cried.

"But that is a small matter, now," I said. "We know the man! The general must be told!"

A sudden thought struck me, and I looked at her sharply.

"Has Dorcas any hand in this?" I demanded.

"I don't know," she replied miserably, and looked away.

"No matter," I said. "This is not a thing that can be kept secret for any reason whatever."

It was at that moment that Rogers came out of the tavern, followed closely by Stark.

"I thought you were coming in," he said, wiping his mouth with the back of his hand.

"Look here," I said, "I've got to see the general at once! It's important."

"Great God!" he swore impatiently. "Forget it, can't you? You heard what Captain Amherst said."

"But that has nothing to do with it," I began.

But he was not listening. Instead he turned away on his heel and started towards the landing a short distance away, walking in long strides. I had to run to catch him, and at that he was close to the water's edge when I took hold of his arm and pulled him around to face me. The waterfront was crowded, what with all of Stark's recruits drawn up there, and canoes and supply battoes coming and going. As I spoke I saw, from the corner of my eye, a large canoe draw away from the landing and turn upstream. But I paid it slight heed.

"See here," I said. "This has nothing to do with the duel."

He jerked his arm angrily, but before he could speak I went on hurriedly.

"I've found the spy," I said, "the man I spoke of; the man Lord Howe was watching for."

He stopped then and turned to face me squarely.

"What?" he said. "Why didn't you say so before?"

"You gave me no chance," I replied.

Someone plucked at my sleeve, and I turned to find Purity at my elbow, oblivious to the stares of the soldiery all about us. She was standing with her face turned away, staring up the river.

"That canoe," she said. "Shem Sanborn was in it."

"Sanborn!" I exclaimed, and hesitated. Then I remembered abruptly that we had more important things to attend to. "Well, it doesn't matter," I said. "We'll come to him in his turn."

I turned to Rogers.

"Do we see the general?" I demanded.

He hesitated a moment.

"You're sure of this?" he said.

"I am," I replied.

"All right, then," he said.

He turned to Stark, who had listened in amazement.

"You come, too," he said. "If we meet his cousin 'twill take the two of us to keep them apart!"

With that he turned and shouldered his way through the crowd back up the hill.

Stark fell in beside Rogers, while I dropped back a few paces with Purity.

"Have you told me all you know, child?" I asked, once we were fairly on the way.

She nodded.

"It is not much," I said, "but 'twill have to do. Perhaps by boldness we may trip him up."

We came presently to general headquarters, set at no great distance up the hill, and pushed our way in through the swarms of officers that continually surrounded the place. Rogers led us straight to an oak-panelled anteroom and pushed open the door. As we entered a young officer, whom I recognized as Lieutenant Hamilton, bounced to his feet. At sight of us his jaw dropped.

"Is the general in?" Rogers demanded, before he could speak.

On the far side of the room there was a second door, and from behind this came the mumble of voices. Hamilton jerked his head in that direction and nodded.

"He's busy at the moment," he said.

Rogers made an impatient gesture with his hand.

"I must see him at once," he said. "The matter is important!"

His tone was such that Hamilton moved automatically to obey. He knocked at the farther door, and the mumble of voices stopped abruptly. A harsh voice called, "Come in."

He pushed open the door and entered shutting it behind him. At almost the same instant the door by which we had entered swung open, and I turned to see Hubert standing upon the threshold.

He appeared startled to see us, and his eyes swept swiftly from one to the other of us, dwelling longest on Purity. Then as suddenly as he had lost it he regained his poise. He stepped inside and closed the door.

"We meet again," he said with a mocking bow.

It did not occur to me to wonder what he did there. I saw only that providence had played into my hands for once.

"The very man," I said. "Our business has to do with you. You may as well hear it too."

Rogers looked startled.

"Look here," he said. "I thought you said—"

"I did," I interrupted him. "This is our man."

He looked at me blankly, but my eyes were on Hubert; and I was sure he looked perturbed. But in the next instant he was as suave as ever.

He bowed. "As you say, cousin," he murmured with a mocking smile.

In that instant Lieutenant Hamilton came in from the other room looking wide-eyed and a little frightened.

"Will you come in, gentlemen?" he said.

Rogers went in first, followed by Purity, then Hubert, Stark and myself. The general was standing tall and spare on the far side of a great table; and from his scowl I could plainly see that he was furious. There was another man in the room, whom I later came to know as Colonel Townshend, his aide; but at the moment I scarcely noticed him.

The general did not wait for Rogers to speak.

"Well, major?" he rasped, "what brings you back? This matter of a duel, I'll warrant! I thought my orders to you were clear, sir! Were they not?"

Rogers gulped, and his face was crimson. Had the moment not been so tense it must have been laughable.

"Yes, sir," he said meekly.

"Well, by God," thundered the general, "what brings you back then? Why must I always be hampered with insubordination? What do you mean, sir, by ignoring my orders?"

I could see that for once Rogers was too terror-stricken to speak, and that if the situation were to be saved it must be done quickly.

"Your Excellency," I said, taking the bull by the horns. "We have not come to speak of my quarrel, but of a matter that is of the utmost importance to yourself and to the army as a whole."

He frowned around at me fiercely.

"What's that?" he demanded. "Who are you, sir?" And then as he looked at me I saw recognition dawn. "Oh," he said, "Captain Ferguson, isn't it? You're one of the gentlemen involved in this shameful business, eh? Well, I hope my brother made my views on the subject clear, sir!"

"Your Excellency," I said, "Captain Amherst made himself perfectly clear on that matter. It is another that brings us here now."

"So!" he said. "What is it?"

"If your Excellency remembers the circumstances in which we last met, 'twill be a help. 'Twas in Colonel Haldimand's cabin at Fort Edward.

He frowned, but apparently his curiosity overcame his annoyance at the impudence of my suggestion.

"I remember," he said. "You had a story to tell of my Lord Howe and a spy, or some such matter."

I nodded. "Your Excellency," I said, "I have found the man."

He gave me a long penetrating look, but not by the movement of a muscle did he betray the least surprise.

"Have you?" he said at last. "I have had Monypenny and Montresor and Townshend all working on that business for months without the least success. Who is this fellow?"

"He is in this room with us now, sir," I replied.

I turned and pointed to Hubert.

"There is your spy," I said.

Of all those present I believe only Amherst showed no emotion at the charge. Rogers' eyes, ever prominent, popped. Stark looked surprised. Purity bit her lip and gripped her hands nervously together. Hubert was white and defiant, and the venom of his glance was enough to send shivers down my spine; yet he lost none of his jauntiness. The general looked at him and then at me without the least change of expression.

"So?" he said. "Major Ferguson, is it not? I hope you realize the gravity of these charges, captain, and have evidence at hand."

I told him swiftly what Purity had told me, adding my own account of what had happened when I had met Hubert at Fort Edward before the last ill fated Ticonderoga campaign. When I had done he looked at Purity.

"Is this true, ma'am?" he asked.

She dropped him a hasty curtsy.

"Yes, your Excellency," she replied.

Hubert spoke now for the first time, and I was amazed to see that he retained all of his old assurance.

"Your Excellency," he said suavely, "must see the absurdity of these charges. There is no evidence save the word of a highly imaginative young woman, and your Excellency realizes, no doubt, how groundless such accusations can be."

For the first time the general allowed a flicker of emotion to appear in his face. He seemed annoyed. How Hubert could have known of it I could not say, but the effect of his words would seem to bear out a rumour I heard later that the general's own domestic life was not all that it might have been. Be that as it may, Amherst turned on him.

"You do not seem to realize the seriousness of the situation, major," he snapped.

"Begging your Excellency's pardon," Hubert replied, "it is precisely because I do realize the seriousness of it that I speak so. I have already pointed out the untrustworthiness of such sources of information. May I point to another bit of evidence which in itself refutes the charge? Mistress Purity admits that she told her suspicions to my Lord Howe. Anyone who knew the man is aware that he was a man of action. If he gave any credence to her suspicions, why did he not act upon them and cause my arrest at the time?"

"Your Excellency!" I protested. "I have already told you why my Lord Howe did not act."

Hubert gave me a sardonic glance.

"My cousin says that he has told you my Lord Howe's reasons, your Excellency," he sneered, "but he has no whit of evidence to prove his story! If I may be pardoned for saying so, the pot may call the kettle black. My cousin may have his own reasons for thus accusing me."

I did not miss the implication of his words, and so thunderstruck was I by it that I stood staring at him in amazement, unable to speak. The general looked at me sharply.

"So?" he said.

Hubert laughed in my face.

"Your Excellency," he said, "an agent engaged in such a business must have some evidence of his work about him somewhere—some papers or other evidence, either on his person or in his quarters. My own quarters and person are open to search for such evidence. Indeed, your Excellency, I shall demand that such search be made, that my character may be vindicated. I hope my good cousin stands as ready!"

The challenge was plain enough. I felt my face go furiously red.

"Sir!" I cried. "I am as ready as he!"

General Amherst stood looking from one to the other of us woodenly. Then abruptly he seemed to make up his mind.

"So be it!" he said. "It will be one way around an impasse."

He took up a small bell from his table and rang it. The door to the anteroom popped open, and Lieutenant Hamilton appeared.

"Your Excellency rang?" he said.

"Hamilton," said the general, "you will call out the provost marshal and ask him to take a squad and search the quarters of both these gentlemen immediately."

Lieutenant Hamilton's eyes popped.

"At once, your Excellency," he said.

"Have the provost marshal report here to me with his findings as soon as he is done," the general commanded.

Hamilton saluted and was gone.

"In the meantime," said the general, "I am a busy man. I shall ask you people to wait in the anteroom until the provost marshal brings his report."

That wait in the general's anteroom was one of the hardest I hope I shall ever have to endure. Hubert went at once to the window, where he stood with his back to the room, staring out and toying with his fobs. Rogers flopped himself down in the easiest chair and looked bewildered.

"This is a fine kettle of stew!" he said. "No one knows what's in it!"

Stark shook his head uncertainly and took to pacing the small room, his hands clasped behind his back.

I sat down upon a bench, and Purity sat down nervously beside me.

"Oh, Jamie!" she whispered. "I am afraid."

"Nonsense!" I said. "There is nothing to be afraid of."

"But I don't like it," she replied uncertainly. "All this business of a search. He was so quick to suggest it."

"They will find nothing," I said. "He is too clever for that. But then neither will they find anything in my quarters."

"Then he will go free," she whispered.

"For the time being," I replied; "but now we know him we will soon have proof, never fear. I know at least one of his men who can be made to talk."

She looked at me wide-eyed.

"Merrill?" she whispered.

A shadow fell between us, and I gestured for silence. Looking up, I saw that Hubert had taken to patrolling the circuit of the room. As he passed he gave me a sardonic smile, and spun his fob about his forefinger.

"He heard us!" she whispered when he had passed on.

I nodded. "We had best say no more for the present," I replied.

After that we sat in silence with hands clasped, waiting. Lieutenant Hamilton returned after a while and resumed his duties without speaking to any of us; and later, after what seemed an interminable period, Captain Small, the provost marshal, stout, pompous, and bandy-legged bustled in.

"Lieutenant Hamilton?" he said. "You may tell the general my report is ready."

Hamilton disappeared within the general's room, and a moment later we were all ushered in once more.

"Well, captain," said the general, when the door had closed behind the curious Hamilton once more.

Small cleared his throat importantly.

"In Major Ferguson's quarters, your Excellency," he said, "we found nothing."

I heard Rogers expel his breath in a great whoosh.

"But in Captain Ferguson's house," Small went on, "we found this, and this, and this."

Diving into one pocket after another, he produced first a packet of letters, then a rouleau, such as coins are wrapped in, and finally another packet of letters. Picking up the rouleau, he broke it open, to spill upon the general's table a pile of shining louis-d'or. After that he stood back with an insufferably smug, self-satisfied expression upon his features.

"Your Excellency!" I cried. "I think it has been established that my cousin has been using my house as his unofficial head-quarters these four years past."

He looked up at me without moving an eyelash.

"Has it?" he said.

Captain Small bustled forward importantly.

"This packet," he said, picking up one and fixing me with a bulging eye, "was taken from the pocket of a coat hanging in your closet, a coat that could not possibly have been Major Ferguson's. This"—here he picked up the other packet—"was found concealed in the mattress in your bedroom, as was the gold."

I stood aghast, bewildered, completely nonplussed at the accusation, so far was it from all my calculations. I felt Rogers' eyes on me curiously, suspiciously. Stark was frowning. Hubert was looking at me with mocking triumph in his eyes, and I realized at once that he had carefully prepared this for just such an emergency. Indeed, I doubted not that it was the very thing that had brought him to the general's quarters so opportunely. And I had played directly into his hands.

I heard Purity gasp.

"No!" she cried. "No, no! Can't you see it's all a plot to throw discredit on Jamie?"

The general looked at her, not unkindly.

"I shall have to ask you to be quiet, ma'am," he said, "or leave the room."

After that she stood with her hand pressed to her mouth, her eyes wide with terror.

The general looked down at the objects on his table. Presently he swept the gold aside.

"That does not count," he said. "Any boy might have that. The men are selling them in the streets as souvenirs."

He picked up the first of the packets, and broke the string that bound it.

"Your Excellency," I said, abruptly. "It is two years since I have been in Albany, as Major Rogers will testify. In that time I could not possibly have left anything of this sort here."

He looked up from the sheet he was reading.

"Do you recognize this?" he asked, and his face was like stone.

He held the paper out to me and I took it and glanced at it.

It was a letter, in French, addressed to Monsieur F, and it asked for a detailed account of the troops to be dispatched to Louisbourg. The date on it was May 17, 1757.

"You see it is more than two years old," he said coldly.

"Your Excellency," I cried, "it is not mine! I never saw it before. I swear it. You see it is addressed to Monsieur F. That might be either my cousin or myself, and he has been clever enough to see it!"

"But they were found in your clothes, in your quarters," he said.

"Sir!" I said. "Would I be so foolish as to keep such documents where they might be found? I beg you to remember that my cousin has had access to my quarters at times when I have not!"

The general hesitated as he considered this side of the matter. But Hubert would not give him time for thought. He gave me a smirking glance and stepped forward.

"Your Excellency," he said, "must realize that the fellow will spare no effort now to fix the blame upon me. However, if he is guilty as the evidence indicates, there will, in all likelihood be further evidence to be found in his effects at Fort Edward."

I saw Rogers start.

"By God," he said, "I'll search his quarters with my own hands! And if I find it's true—"

He glared at me, and I saw all my world tumbling about me, my friends turning against me, my name dragged in the muck; and I was so choked up that I could not speak. Rogers turned to the general.

"With your permission, your Excellency," he said, "I will start at once."

"An excellent idea, major," the general said.

Rogers turned to Stark.

"Stay here," he said, "and see how this turns out. After that report to me at Edward."

He turned away without another glance at me and started for the door. Suddenly I remembered the canoe that had swung away from the landing earlier in the day, and recalled what Purity had said of it: "That canoe, Shem Sanborn was in it!" And all at once I saw the whole rotten plot.

"Rob!" I cried. "Major Rogers!"

But it was too late. He was gone, and the door slamming behind him cut off my words.

"Your Excellency!" I cried, swinging about.

But the general held up his hand.

"That is enough, Mr. Ferguson," he said. "We can do no more about this until we have Major Rogers' report. In the meantime" —he turned to the provost marshal—"Captain Small, you will place Mr. Ferguson under arrest in the town jail. As an officer he may have his orderly to wait upon him and such counsel as he chooses. All other visitors will be subject to your own or my approval. I need not caution you to keep him under close guard."

Captain Small saluted and stepped forward to take my arm, but I pulled it free.

"You need not trouble yourself," I said. "I will go along quietly."

The general nodded. "That is all," he said.

I turned then and went slowly out the door which the captain held for me.

OUT OF THE FRYING PAN

⟨ 1 The others followed me from the room. Once we were all come into the antechamber, and the door shut behind us, Hubert made me a disdainful bow.

"I think you have no further need of me," he said. "With your permission I will take my leave."

I was too bitter against him to make any reply. He smiled sardonically and turned to Purity, and offered her his arm.

"If you are going my way, my dear," he said mockingly, "I would be pleased to walk with you."

But she turned on him, her eyes blazing.

"Oh!" she cried. "You are hateful!"

He gazed at her with evident admiration.

" 'Od's blood," he exclaimed, "but 'tis a dainty morsel! Almost I might wish myself in Jamie's shoes if 'twould gain me such sympathy."

"You need not flatter yourself," she replied coldly. "I would not care if you were slow-burned in brimstone, I would not waste my tears on such as you!"

At that he bowed with exaggerated formality, and sweeping us all with a sardonic glance, turned on his heel and strode from the room.

When he was gone I turned to Captain Small.

"If you please, captain," I said, "may I have one moment alone with my friends?"

He hesitated.

"I have a right to counsel," I went on, "and I could ask none better than Captain Stark. As for Mistress Stiles, surely there is no reason why she should be excluded."

He appeared to yield.

"If I may have your parole," he said.

"You have it," I replied.

He nodded, and led the way out of the room and across the corridor to a second small chamber which looked out upon the garden at the side of the house. I stood aside while Stark and Purity entered, and then followed them inside and shut the door.

No sooner was the door latched behind me than Purity turned and flung herself into my arms.

"Oh, Jamie! Jamie!" she sobbed. "What have I done?"

"There, child!" I said as soothingly as I could. "It is nothing. Give us a week to gather our evidence, and I will be free once more."

But she saw through my poor attempt at assurance and smiled up at me through her tears.

"Dear Jamie!" she said. "You know it is not so simple. And it is all my doing!"

I shook my head at that.

"You must not reproach yourself, my dear," I said. "The whole thing was swiftly planned and executed. 'Twas that which brought him here at just this time. Had I not been arrested here it must have happened at the fort, in which case matters must have been much worse!"

"Aye!" said Stark, gruffly. "He speaks the truth!"

I saw that she was not convinced, but there was no time now to argue the matter with her. With my arm still about her shoulders I turned to Stark.

"You do not believe this charge, John?" I said.

He shook his head and smiled in his homely droop-mouthed way.

"I have known ye too long, lad," he said, "to believe such things against ye."

"Rogers does," I replied bitterly, "and he has known me as long."

He shrugged. "Aye!" he said, "Rob was ever one to take the bit in his teeth and plunge ahead without ever looking beneath the surface of things. But 'twill be well enough with him when he finds no evidence against ye at the fort."

"But that's just it," I wailed. "I make no doubt he will find it."

He looked at me startled, bewildered.

"Look ye!" I said. "Do you remember at the landing Mistress Purity saw a canoe going up-river?"

He nodded and looked puzzled.

"Shem Sanborn was in that canoe," I said. " 'Tis he who runs my cousin's errands for him. I tell you, the evidence will be planted in my quarters ere ever Rogers reaches the fort."

He shook his head at that and smiled.

" 'Tis the curse of a fine imagination, Jamie," he said. "Ye let it run away with ye!"

" 'Tis not my imagination," I replied. "The whole thing has been too carefully worked out for that. You must not underrate him, man. My cousin is an accomplished villain!"

He looked doubtful.

"What will ye do then?" he asked.

"Will you be counsel to me, John?" I said.

He hesitated. "I have no experience in these things," he replied.

"It is not experience that matters to me now," I said. "I must have a man who knows me and believes in me; else my case is lost before it is begun. I know no one but you who will fit that description. Will you take it?"

"I must ask Rogers," he said. "Without his permission my hands are tied."

My face must have fallen then, and some of my despair shown through, for he smiled and came forward to take my hand.

"But I will do my best," he said, "to persuade him. It is not usual for a commander to refuse such a request, and I do not think he will deny me this one if I ask it."

I wrung his hand in grateful silence, unable to speak my thanks. But indeed I needed to say nothing. He understood well enough what was in my heart.

"I will go along now," he said, "and find out what has happened at the fort. With luck I will be back before the end of the week; and we will try then to think what is best to be done. They will not want to have the trial before that?"

"I should not think so," I said.

He nodded, bowed to Purity, and went out.

Scarcely had the door closed behind him, however, when it opened again and Captain Small bustled in importantly.

"I'm sorry," he apologized. "I'm afraid I must insist upon going, now."

Purity clung to me.

"No! no!" she cried.

I disengaged her arms as gently as I could.

"There, child," I said. "It will not be for long. And I'm sure the captain will let you come and see me."

"I will go with you as far as I may," she said.

I was touched.

"If you wish it," I replied.

I looked at Small.

"I am ready," I said.

He held the door, and I offered my arm to Purity and we went out.

I was surprised, when we reached the street, to see that it was past sunset and that darkness was not far distant. As we came down the steps a paunchy figure rose from the lawn where he had been squatting and came towards us. I was glad that Rogers had not taken Toby back with him.

As he approached us Captain Small bustled up.

"What's this?" he demanded. "Who is this man?"

"It's all right, captain," I told him. "This is Toby, my orderly."

The captain squinted at him through the gathering gloom and sniffed audibly.

"Humph!" he snorted. "An Indian!"

"Aye," I said, "an Indian, and a true friend!"

"Well, come along," said the captain with frank disapproval in his voice.

We made a strange little group as we walked down the hill towards the town jail. I went a little before, with Purity clinging to my arm. Captain Small followed a pace or two in the rear, and Toby trotted along behind the three of us like a faithful hound.

We were within sight of the gloomy building when a thought struck me suddenly. I looked at Purity.

"See here, child," I said. "You cannot go back to that house now."

She looked at me with wide-eyed innocence.

"I am not afraid," she said.

"I know," I said impatiently, "but I cannot hear of it, nevertheless."

"What am I to do?" she asked.

"Look ye," I said, "do you know the Schuyler house?"

She nodded.

"Go there," I told her, "and tell the whole story to Mrs. Schuyler. She was ever a good friend to me, and I'll warrant she'll take you in and keep you there. She may even think of something else that may help our case."

She nodded again.

"If this does not work, come back to me," I went on, "or find Toby and let him tell me. I will think of something else."

We were at the steps of the jail by then, and we stopped and faced each other.

"You will do as I ask?" I said.

"I will do anything you say," she said.

She held up her face to me then, and I kissed her tenderly.

"Good-bye, Jamie," she breathed.

"Good-bye, my dear," I said gruffly.

And thereupon I turned on my heel and followed Captain Small into the gloomy prison that was to be my home for eight interminable weeks.

That first week of my imprisonment was, perhaps, the hardest to endure; for I had not yet learned the necessity for patience, and I spent hour upon hour patrolling my cell, desperately hoping, scheming, planning my defence. I worried, too. I worried about Purity, for I was desperately afraid lest Hubert find some means to do her harm. I worried, lest Rogers forbid Stark to act as my counsel. But strangely enough it did not occur to me to worry much about my own plight. Throughout those long weary weeks I felt ever confident that somehow, in some way, we should find means to beat my cousin at his underhanded game. And this confidence went far to sustain me during that period.

On the first day after my incarceration Purity came to me early in the afternoon.

"See," she said, thrusting a paper into my hand after she had kissed me. "It's an order from the general! I'm to be allowed to see you as often as I wish."

I looked at it, and saw that it bore the scrawl, "R. Townshend, for General Amherst, commanding."

"Why," I said, pleased, "that's fine! How did you get it?"

"I went straight to the general this morning," she said gaily. "He was kind, and agreed at once." She sobered thoughtfully. "I think you have a powerful friend there, Jamie," she said. "And I am sure he does not like Hubert."

I nodded, but my thoughts were elsewhere.

"Did you see Mrs. Schuyler?" I asked.

"I went to her straight from here," she said. "You were right about her, Jamie. She was sweet, and said I might stay with her as long as I wished. When I told her the whole story she was furious with the general for having put you in prison. She said he should have known better, and I agreed with her! She is fond of you."

I felt as though a great burden had been lifted from my shoulders. As long as she was at the Schuylers' I knew no harm would come to Purity. I said as much, and she looked at me curiously.

"Does it mean so much to you then, Jamie?" she asked.

"My dear," I said gently, "it means more to me than anything just now!"

She seemed pleased at that, and was gaily cheerful during the rest of her visit. But when it came time for her to go she came to me and took both my hands in hers.

"You must not despair," she said. "You know Captain Stark and Toby and I will do everything we can to get you free."

"I am sure you will," I said. "But you must be careful, and not expose yourself to risks on my account."

"Dear Jamie," she said, "there is no risk I would not run for you!"

She kissed me then and left, and it was not until she was gone that I began to realize how much I depended upon her to keep my courage up.

Towards the end of the week Stark came down from Fort Edward with a face that was longer than usual.

"Well," I said, "what news?"

"Bad news," he replied. "Your guess was right. They found enough evidence in your quarters to convict a regiment."

"Rogers is convinced then?" I asked.

He nodded grimly. "He swears he'll have your guts, drawn by his own hand," he said, "after they've hanged you!"

"But he did not prevent your coming!" I said.

He smiled slightly. "I am here," he said.

We sat down then, to put our heads together and consider what was best to be done.

"Your enemies," said Stark, "are pressing for an early trial, but I think you may discount that."

"You seem sure of that," I replied.

He shrugged. "I have seen the general," he said, "and he assures me that you will have a month at least in which to prepare your defence. In fact I believe it might be more. If I am not mistaken he would like to see the campaign well under way before he comes to it. He is pressed for time now, and you are where you can do no harm."

"But," I protested, "would he keep me here all summer without some sort of hearing?"

He shrugged. " 'Tis irregular," he said; "but unless we protest 'tis my guess that's what he'll do. And if you heed my advice you'll not protest until you have a case. If you were to come to trial now you'd hang as surely as you sit there!"

There was no answer to be made to that. He looked at me and grinned.

" 'Tis as well to know how you stand," he said.

"You've made it plain enough, at any rate," I told him.

He nodded. "You see that," he said. "Then this is how the case stands."

He went on from there to sum up the evidence both for and against me. My accusers, he said, rested their claims upon letters and documents found, rightly or wrongly, in my possession. All of these documents were substantial and incriminating evidence against me. Not all of them were strong, however. Some had their weak points, and it was upon these weak points that we must, for the moment, base our hopes. For instance, several of the letters bore dates on which it could be established that I was away on scouts, and could not have received them. But the reply to this would be obvious. My enemies would say that they were received by my agents and passed on to me on my return.

The strongest point in my favour was a letter referring to information sent by the hand of Monsieur Potter, regarding Rogers' expedition before the battle on snowshoes. As will be remembered, Potter was a sutler's servant who had set out for Albany in company with Sanborn and Merrill and, according to their story, had been made prisoner not far from Fort Miller when he had gone into the woods to attend to a personal matter. From this it appeared that the whole business of Potter's capture had been engineered—with the aid of the teamsters, I did not doubt; though the letter, unfortunately, did not tell us this. Monsieur Potter, it appeared, had passed safely to Ticonderoga with the information, and a suitable trap would be laid for Monsieur Rogers and his party. The note had evidently been enclosed in a payment, for it went on to enumerate the moneys included.

This letter Stark regarded strongly as upholding my cause, for, as he pointed out, it was not likely that I would give information concerning an expedition which I myself must accompany, especially when I knew that by that information the entire party was like to be wiped out.

Such was the extent of my defence thus far, and I was forced to agree with Stark that as compared with the absolute evidence my enemies had gathered against me it was but a poor hope. Unless we could find other evidence in rebuttal I was like to be hanged out of hand. Purity came in, in the midst of his summing up, and sat upon my bunk beside me, listening without a sound.

When he had finished, I sat silent for some minutes, thinking.

"There is one," I said at last, "who helps my cousin in these things and who might be made to talk. That is the man Merrill. The fellow is a weakling, for all his length, and I'll warrant you a good scare would set his tongue to wagging at both ends."

Stark's head was shaking before I had even finished what I was saying.

"No," he said, "we'll learn naught from Merrill. The man was found dead and scalped on the road between Fort Miller and Fort Edward three days since."

I heard Purity gasp.

"Jamie!" she said. "It was because he heard us talking!"

I nodded. "As like as not," I replied. "You see the man will stop at nothing."

"They said 'twas Indians," he said, "but I examined the fellow's head. It was not the work of an Indian."

We fell into silent thought then, and for some moments no one spoke. It was Purity who at last broke in upon our reflections.

"If he kept such papers as these," she said, "that can be taken to mean more than one thing; it might be that he has kept others more definitely referring to himself."

Stark stirred uneasily.

"'Tis possible," he said. "Any man in his right senses would have destroyed such as have been found. In his possession they would have been as strong against him as against Jamie. But who can tell what such a man as he would do?"

"I'll warrant the man has others that would prove his guilt," Purity persisted.

Stark shrugged. "A fine lot of good will they do us if he has," Stark replied. "He will have them well hidden."

"But they might be found," she said, "if one were to look carefully. They will either be in his own quarters or at Jamie's house, most like."

I began to see what she was driving at, and was moved to protest.

"See here," I said. "I'll not have you taking any foolish risks on my account. You hear?"

She made a little face at me.

"I hear," she said. "You'd think a body was deaf the way you shout!"

"Well," I grumbled, "I only wanted it understood."

She looked at Stark.

"Don't pay any attention to him, captain," she said. "I don't."

Stark looked at her seriously.

"Do you think you might be able to find them?" he asked.

"I could look," she replied. "I would not be so hasty as Captain Small's men, nor look in such obvious places."

"Look here!" I protested. "I won't have it!"

"You'll not be able to stop me, my lad," she said. "This is once I will not mind!"

I protested violently but to no avail, while they discussed ways and means and possibilities; and when at last Stark rose to go I was thoroughly angry.

"Damn you, Stark!" I said. "I don't want her dragged into this."

"Whether you want it or not," he replied, "she's in! You asked me to be your counsel, didn't you?"

"Yes, but—" I began.

"There are no buts," he replied. "I am your counsel, and you can't get rid of me now. I'll handle the business to suit the needs of the case; and Mistress Purity and I will build a defence for you in spite of you!"

He shot a glance at Purity.

"Moreover," he went on, "you should be able to see, if you weren't half blind, that the lass has her mind made up in spite of anything you or I may say."

With that he bowed with stiff formality.

"I will be back," he said, "within the week. As soon as I may."

And he rattled a stick on the grating of my cell as a signal to the guard to let him out.

When he was gone I turned to Purity.

"Child," I said, "you should not do this."

But she only laughed, and would not listen; and at last she left me, more gaily than she had since my imprisonment, happy that at last there was something she could do.

I might have spared myself my fears. How she did it, I will never know, for she never told me the details, nor will she to this day; but I know that in the next four weeks she visited both houses, not once but many times, when the occupants were out, and made a thorough, systematic search of each room and cubbyhole, rummaging through closets, poking into corners and crannies, looking everywhere where papers or suchlike stuff might be hidden, even going so far as to tap the walls for hidden panels and cupboards; and yet, with it all, doing it so carefully and precisely that the search was never once suspected. As soon as I learned of it I tried to insist that she take Toby with her for protection. But this she steadfastly refused to do. The Indian odour, she maintained, would cling for hours in the house, and at once betray them. Once it was discovered they had been there, she said, there would be no chance to return.

It was a risky, heartbreaking business, yet in the end she might have spared herself the trouble, for she found nothing. Each morning she went out gay and optimistic, determined that that day she would stumble upon some clue. And in the evening she would come to me worn out and discouraged, empty-handed.

All the while Stark fretted and fussed and worried, and blew hot and cold by turns, so that I almost regretted having asked him to act for me. But there was nothing to be done about it then.

In the meantime, while all this was going on, I did not lack for company and entertainment. Not everyone, it appeared, was convinced of my guilt, and Hubert was almost universally disliked.

Captain Carrigain was a regular visitor to my cell.

"Faith!" he exclaimed, upon his first visit. "This is a nasty mess ye're in, but at least ye've no work to do! Man! If ye were on the outside now there'd be no rest for ye. This Amherst is a slave driver, I tell ye!"

He went on, after that, to tell me of all the changes that were taking place on the outside, and of the preparations that were going forward for the campaign; though he was careful to tell me nothing of importance, dwelling only upon such minor items as the way the Rhode Islanders would steal, or what Colonel Bagley had said to Colonel Haviland when the latter called him a "rough, untutored farmer." I was not listening closely, but I believe it was a quotation from Horace, and the point of the story was that Haviland was so puzzled by it that he had to ask his aide to translate it for him! Assuredly a joke after Carrigain's own heart.

Besides the good captain there was Alan Fraser, a young lieutenant of the Forty-second, whose acquaintance I had made before Ticonderoga. He was a gloomy fellow, and persisted in telling me that his father had died in a dungeon in Stirling Castle—"and never a chance for trial," he would always conclude. Yet despite his dismal forebodings, I liked the lad.

Colonel Bouquet, tall and soldierly, came to extend his sympathy in heavy accents, and to assure me that he thought me unjustly accused. So did Major Monypenny, who also offered to be a witness for me at my trial. Even the bluff and hearty Colonel Bradstreet called upon me. Indeed, I should have been flattered at the attention I received had I not more than half suspected that most of them came out of sheer curiosity. However, I did my best to receive them graciously.

When I was not having such company there was always Purity, who came several times each day, and brought me all manner of things for my comfort and pleasure. When she was away Toby was almost constantly within call, and at such infrequent intervals as even he was absent, I would pass the time by trying to get my guard, a dour-faced Londoner, to talk.

I had not much luck in this direction, however, until one evening towards the end of my sixth week in prison when Hubert came to taunt me through the grille.

"Well, cousin," said he, "how does it feel to be on the other side of the fence? You and your side of the family used to hold me up as the black sheep. Now it seems the shoe is on the other foot!"

I paid him no heed, but sat upon my bunk and feigned interest in other things; and presently, seeing that there was no sport to be had here, he flung me a parting gibe and withdrew.

Now I was not so impervious to his taunts as I had pretended, and no sooner did I hear his footsteps receding in the corridor than I flung myself upon the door and pressed my face against the grille to glare after him down the gloomy passage. As I did so my guard, hitherto so taciturn that I could scarce get a word from him, spat and moved a sideways pace closer to the door.

"Ar!" said he. " 'E's a black-'earted one, 'e is!"

I looked at him, startled.

" 'E don't remember me," he said, "but I remembers 'im, right enough! Ah've 'eard stories abaht 'im an' orl, since I come hover to this bleddy country; but there's one I could tell yer 'd myke yer 'air stand on end!"

"You knew him before, then?" I said.

"Aye!" said he. "I didn't hexactly know 'im, as yer might sye. But I did run acrost 'im, in a manner o' speakin'."

To tell the truth, I was not greatly interested; but I looked polite, and he continued.

" 'Twas in the 'Forty-five," he said.

I must have appeared startled, for he stopped and looked at me in surprise.

" 'Ere!" he said. "Wot's the matter?"

"Nothing," I said. "Go on."

" 'Twas in the 'Forty-five, like I said," he went on. "At Culloden Moor. You're a Scot, ain't you?"

I nodded. "Go on," I said.

"No hoffence!" he said. "We 'ad yer army on the run. They was scattered orl over th' countryside, poor beggars! An' the orders was to clean 'em up."

He stopped a moment and shook his head.

"There was a bloody business," he said, "but 'tweren't for us to question our orders. We done as we was told if it did turn our stomachs."

"Yes?" I said, as quietly as I could, for I was impatient to hear what he had to say.

"Yus!" he said emphatically, then continued. "I was in Moore's company then. 'E was a bloody devil, 'e was. If 'e come acrost a wounded man tryin' to crorl away, 'e'd stick 'im 'imself, 'e would."

He looked at me as if expecting some comment; but I merely stared at him without a sound, and he went on.

"Well," he said, "it 'ad turned dark on us before we was 'arf done, and we was beatin' up through a gully when we 'ears a cracklin' in the 'eather, and the captain pounces in an' drags out this 'ere same bloke as is a myjor now.

"'E was one of the Young Pretender's men, no doubt abaht it; for 'e was done up in real 'Ighland fashion, with a kilt an' a tartan an' a dirk as big as 'e was, an' Captain Moore 'ad the point o' 'is sword against 'is belly when 'e flops down on 'is knees an' cries out:

"'Don't kill me. Don't kill me, for I'll tell ye where there're fifteen more the like o' me 'idin' awye if only yer'll leave me go!'

"Well," he continued after an impressive pause, "I thinks that's kind o' strong even for Captain Moore; but duty was duty, an' after a bit 'e lowers 'is sword an' stands aside.

"'Lead on, MacDuff,' says 'e.

"'The nyme is Ferguson,' says the bloke very stiff like. The captain spits, an' orf we goes hup the gully. In a matter o' minutes 'e leads us orf by another gully, an' arfter a bit o' scroungin' abaht in the 'eather, 'e shows us a bit o' a grass-covered barn.

"'They're in there,' 'e says.

"The captain stands out an' shouts, 'Come out o' there!' An' a voice calls, 'Coom an' git us, mon,' an' there's a shot that lifts th' captain's 'at wig an' orl. 'Orl right!' says the captain. An' with that 'e snatches a brand w'ich the serjeant 'ad been carryin' to light the way, an' bingo 'e 'eaves it on the grass roof. I tell yer it fair made my stomach 'eave to 'ear them poor wretches screamin' in the flames! But w'en we come to look for the young lad, 'e was gorn! An' that's yer fine myjor, for yer!—'Ere, now! Wot's the matter?"

I cannot say that I blamed him for being startled, for I must have looked ghastly white, and I was clinging for support to the grille in the door.

"My father!" I said. "My father was in that barn!"

And I turned and stumbled over to the bunk and threw myself down upon it.

Behind me the guard said, "Christ!" in a hoarse whisper and then was silent.

It was an hour later when Purity came in and found me lying there. I had not moved. When she saw my face she started back.

"Jamie!" she cried out in alarm. "What have they done to you? Are you ill?"

I shook my head, and while she sat beside me and held my hand in hers I told her the whole story. When I had finished she leapt to her feet, her eyes blazing.

"Oh, the beast!" she cried. "How can God let such monsters live?"

In the next instant she was on her knees beside me, her arms about my shoulders, whispering soothingly, comfortingly in my ear, until before I realized it I felt better. I put my arms about her and kissed her tenderly.

"You are a sweet child, Purity," I said.

To my surprise she returned my kiss vigorously, then leapt once more to her feet.

"Jamie," she said, before I could speak, "may I have Toby to-night?"

I looked at her curiously and not a little apprehensively, for now more than ever I was disinclined to let her take risks for me.

"What do you want him for?" I said. "You are not going to do anything rash?"

She laughed lightly.

"Oh, no!" she said. "I only want him to carry some things for me."

She did not fool me; but I felt that, whatever it was, she would be the safer for having Toby along. I gave my consent, and presently she went out to find him and give him my orders.

I saw her to the door, and as the guard snapped the lock behind her he peered through the grille at me.

"Yer don't 'old it against me, do yer, gov'nor?" he asked.

"No, man," I said, "it was none of your doing."

"Ar!" he said, with a note of relief, and thereafter lapsed into silence. Nor did I urge him to talk further.

Stark came in that evening late, after the evening meal, and his face was even gloomier than ever.

"Well," he said, "what news?"

I spread my hands and shrugged.

"None," I replied. "And you?"

"Worse than that," he said. "I have questioned and cross-examined about camp till men run when they see me coming; but not a thing have I been able to turn up that might help us. And the date of your court is set."

"What?" I said sharply, for this was news indeed.

He nodded. "For the twentieth," he said—it was then the third day of July. "I have seen the general this very day and confirmed it."

"Why," I said helplessly, "that is less than three weeks!"

"Aye," he replied, "and unless we stumble on something in the meantime I fear you'll dance on air when it's over!"

We sat silent for some time, and at last, because we both realized the hopelessness of discussing my case, we began to talk about the preparations for the coming campaign. Most of the army, he told me, already lay at Fort Edward. Some few of the provincial levies were still coming in, and a strong detachment was putting the finishing touches on the camp at the head of Lake George, whither it was expected the entire army would move within a fortnight. New boats were being built and supplies were coming up rapidly. The road between Fort Edward and the lake had been widened and cleared on either side. The Rangers were as active as ever. Rogers remained convinced of my guilt, and most of the officers and men shared his view.

We had talked thus, pointlessly, for perhaps an hour when I was aroused by the sound of light footsteps hurrying up the passageway outside. A moment later came the creak of drawn bolts and my door swung open to admit Purity with Toby shuffling at her heels. She came straight to me, her eyes shining, and held out her hands.

"I have it, Jamie!" she cried. "I have it at last!"

I leapt up, filled with an uncontrollable desire to laugh.

"What?" I cried. "What is it?"

She pushed me gently down again.

"Sit down," she said. "Sit down first and let me tell you."

She sat down beside me and composed herself, the light of Stark's lanthorn casting a ruddy glow upon her finely chiselled features.

"About two weeks ago," she said, "when I first began to realize that my search would produce nothing, I began, Jamie, to follow your cousin."

"My dear!" I said, "that was dangerous!"

She laughed. "Oh, I took good care that he should not see me," she replied. "I was certain that he must have some place where he kept his letters and private papers, for I had never found so much as a note in his quarters. And I felt, too, that to follow him was the only way to find that place."

"And you found it, ma'am?" asked Stark eagerly.

"Will you let me tell the story in my own way?" she demanded. Thereafter we left her to her account.

"For a part of each day," she continued, "I lost him, and it was at that time, I felt certain, that he went to this place. He would go down towards the river, and day after day I lost him there in the crowds, nor did I dare to follow him more closely for fear he would see me."

She paused a moment for breath, but neither Stark nor I spoke.

"At last," she went on, "I found a little Dutch lad whom I could trust to be discreet, and I gave him a crown to follow him. He followed him across the river to Greenbush, to a low tavern on the camp side. Tonight I went there myself."

An involuntary exclamation of dismay sprang to my lips, but she silenced me with a gesture.

"I bribed one of the kitchen wenches"—here she blushed furiously—"telling her I was his mistress, and found he had taken a room there permanently. I got her to let me in, and while Toby kept watch below, I searched it."

"And you found—" said Stark, unable to contain himself longer.

"I found two trunks, all packed," she said, "as if he had prepared this place for any emergency. I had an iron bar with me—for I have become skilled in burglary these past weeks, my dear—and with the bar I forced the locks. One of the trunks contained nothing but clothes. But the other was full of letters and papers. I took out all I could and took a small brassbound box besides that was full of papers, and came away, for I was fearful lest he come and find me there."

"But you got away safely?" I said.

"It was as well I came away when I did," she replied, "for as I was going out the door below he came in, and he recognized me at once. He made to grasp me, but I slipped around him, and Toby caught him a clout on the head that dazed him for a moment. In that time we were away. Of course he set up a great hue and cry and raised the alarm, but your Indian knows a trick or two himself, and he brought me safely off."

Stark was on his feet in an instant.

"We must go back there at once," he said, "and seize that trunk."

"It will not be there," she said dryly.

Stark sat down again, looking almost disconsolate.

"Of course you are right," he said.

"Did you bring the papers that you took," I asked, "and the box?"

"I could not bring the box," she said, "for the guards would have taken it from me. But I brought what papers I could under my skirt. If you gentlemen will turn your faces to the wall I will produce them."

We turned away dutifully, while she rummaged beneath her billowing skirt. In a moment she spoke again.

"You may turn now," she said.

We turned and saw that she had both hands full of papers and packets of letters, and we both reached for them. She handed one to Stark and the other to me. I glanced down at those she had given me, and started violently, for the packet on top was the one I had taken from the dead Frenchman so long before; the packet that had begun the whole affair.

"Why," I cried, "see here, these are the letters I gave Rogers and he turned over to Captain Abercrombie. My Lord Howe had these, for he showed them to me."

Stark leaned forward.

"Let's see," he demanded.

I showed them to him.

"Why, so they are," he said.

"That box," I said to Purity, a thought suddenly breaking on my mind. "What was it like?"

"It was brown, and brassbound, about so by so"—making a descriptive movement with her hands. "And the lock had been broken."

"The very box!" I cried. " 'Twas the one Lord Howe kept his private papers in. Why, the whole thing is clear now. Hubert guessed he was suspected when my Lord Howe gave him false information, and after his Lordship was killed he contrived to steal the box. 'Twas never left behind as Major Monypenny thought."

Stark nodded eagerly.

"That must be it," he agreed.

I leapt to my feet and began pacing the cell excitedly.

"Why," I cried, "this is perfect! It couldn't be better! What more do we need? All we must do is show that Hubert stole the box, and the contents will convict him!"

But Stark was looking at me soberly, shaking his head.

"How will you do that?" he asked. "Indeed, if the box were found in your possession now 'twould be difficult to prove that you did not take it! I wonder that he did not plant it there himself to begin with."

I looked at the papers in my hand, and then dropped them on the bunk as though they were hot.

"That's so," I said dully.

There was a moment's dead silence. Then Purity said, "Oh, and I thought I had done so well!" in a disappointed tone, that was close to tears.

Stark looked at her and smiled.

"You have, my dear," he said. "Let's have a look at these others."

He broke the string on one of the packets and picked up the top letter and began to read without a flicker of expression, while Purity and I watched, fascinated. A half-dozen he read before he finally said "Ah!" and held the letter across to me.

"Read this!" he commanded.

I took the letter and read.

"M. F.:

"There has been some report here that a considerable portion of the garrison at Fort William-Henry is on the sick list, both with flux and the smallpox. It is important that we receive at once exact information as to the numbers so incapacitated. In your post as officer charged with the service of supply this should be an easy matter for you, in line with the forwarding of medical necessities—"

"That's clear enough," said Stark.

"Why," I cried, "it couldn't be better. It proves conclusively to whom the letter was addressed."

He handed me another.

"Some slip here," he said.

" 'Major F.,' " it began.

"You never were a major, were you, Jamie?" he asked with a grin.

He hesitated a moment before handing me another. It was an envelope, with seal broken, enclosing one of the damning letters. Across the back of the letter, in Dorcas' firm hand, had been written "For Major Ferguson—private."

"Do you recognize that hand?" he asked.

I stared at it for a moment dully, then cast the envelope aside.

"I have lost the power of pain there," I said. "There is no villainy can surprise me now."

Stark exchanged glances with Purity and rose.

"You say you have more papers like this, ma'am?" he asked.

She nodded. "They are at Schuyler's," she replied. "I could not bring them all."

"We must go over them all at once," he said.

"See here," I said, rising, "this thing is dangerous now Hubert knows the evidence we have. He will stop at nothing to get it back. Purity must be guarded closely."

Stark nodded agreement.

"Yet the papers are safest with her," he said. "So long as she is at Schuyler's, he will dare attempt nothing."

"Nevertheless," I said, "she must be guarded. I will send Toby with her. And do you send up to the fort for David McClary and Stinson and Timothy Eastman. We can trust them, and she will not be unguarded for an instant."

He nodded. "It shall be done," he said.

I turned to Toby.

"Toby, old friend," I said, "go with Mistress Purity and guard her with your life. Do not let her go anywhere but you are with her."

The old fellow bobbed his head, and his black eyes gleamed.

"Me watch!" he said. "Good!"

I felt easier then as I saw them to the door.

That night I scarcely slept a wink for excitement, and early in the morning they were all three back again, jubilant. To be brief they had found a round dozen of letters and documents conclusively proving my innocence and Hubert's guilt.

"Why would a man keep such damning evidence?" I demanded.

Stark shrugged. "Who knows?" he said. "Perhaps from vanity. Perhaps as a warrant for further reward from the French once the war is over. Perhaps he even looked forward to further enterprises of the sort in future, and kept these to serve as references."

I laughed. "Whatever the reason," I said, "we may be thankful for it."

For several hours we sat with our heads together planning my defence. At last, feeling the pangs of hunger, I leapt up.

"John!" I said. "Do you go straight to the general and make sure that the court is not postponed for any reason. Say that on my right as an officer I demand a speedy trial. After that fetch wine— the best; and meantime I will send Toby out to order up such a banquet as this old jail has never seen the like of!"

2

If the first six weeks of my incarceration in the Albany jail had dragged, the last two were endless. Keyed up as I was to fever pitch in anticipation of our coup, each succeeding day seemed longer than the last, until at last it seemed to me fairly that I must end my days there, or at the least come out an old grey-bearded man upon the day of my trial.

In addition to this I was beside myself with fear lest some evil fortune overtake Purity. In the weeks since my imprisonment I had come to realize how true a friend I had in her. She had run tremendous risks for me, and I was not ungrateful. At the same time I did not wish to see her exposed to greater danger on my account. Only in those weeks of adversity had I come to realize to the full my own fondness for her.

But I might have spared myself the worry. So long as she remained under the Schuylers' protecting wing she was safe. Nevertheless, I breathed easier when Stark, true to his word, sent down McClary and Stinson to help guard her. Timothy Eastman, it appeared, could not be spared, but I had every confidence that the two who came would attend their duties well.

Colonel Bouquet came to see me again in those last weeks, and was at once struck with my improved spirits.

"So!" he exclaimed. "You are habpy for a man who iss so soon to pe dried for dreason!"

"And well I might, colonel," I replied, "for when the trial is over I shall be a free man once more!"

And with that I told him as much as I felt proper of what had happened.

"Ah, so!" he said, when I had finished. "I am gladt, my friendt, for you. I haf never pelieve t'is t'ing off you."

The time came at last, about a week before the fateful day, when I was to be moved from Albany to Fort George, as the new fort lately begun upon the ruins of Fort William-Henry was called. The general and all his staff had gone on before a few days since, and it was for his convenience that the camp at the head of the lake was chosen as the scene of the court-martial.

According to reports the camp was already overcrowded, and living conditions there none of the best, for all that they were an improvement over those of the last campaigns. In consequence of this it was decided that Purity should remain in Albany until the last minute, when she would come on on horseback with her three guards and the accumulated evidence for my defence. I felt the safer for this arrangement, too, as I had heard that Hubert had already gone forward with Dorcas to the camp, and I felt that the farther Purity was separated from him the better for us all. With him at Lake George and her in Albany, I felt, he would find it difficult to harm her. But if they were both in the same camp his devilish ingenuity might devise some means of upsetting all our plans.

At the same time, however, I did not mean that the vigilance of her guardians should be relaxed. I was already too well and too bitterly acquainted with his cunning to believe that she could ever be entirely safe, even though Hubert were miles away. What he might be able to do at a distance, I could not imagine; but I meant to take no chances. On the day before I was to leave I had in Toby and the two guards and lectured them roundly upon the importance of their vigilance. They each promised me that they would spare no effort to see that she was kept safe out of harm's way, and that night I slept easier.

The next morning Purity was in my cell almost before daybreak.

"Jamie!" she said. "I could not let you go without seeing you once more."

I kissed her gently.

"This separation will not be for long, my dear," I said. "When this business is over and our lives are straightened out of their tangle once more, perhaps we can arrange that there will be no more of them ever—if you would like it so."

"Oh, Jamie!" she cried, and hid her face in my shirt front.

I lifted her face to me.

"You will be careful, my dearest?" I said. "Yours is the most dangerous mission now."

She nodded gaily.

"Now, more than ever, I will be careful, Jamie," she said, "for your sake!"

It was but a few moments after this that the guard which was to escort me to the lake came for me. I bade her a tender farewell then and turned her over to Toby, with a final admonition to guard her carefully. The last time I looked back, she was still standing on the steps of the grim stone jail, waving a handkerchief in a last gesture of encouragement and godspeed.

Our northward journey was uneventful. It had occurred to me that Hubert might attempt to seal matters once and for all by in some way eliminating me at this time. However, on second thought, I realized that this was hardly likely. Whatever became of me, our evidence was such that his own downfall must be encompassed unless he regained it, and he would hardly expect to find me carrying it. At the same time, as far as I was aware, he had made no effort to regain the documents that Purity had stolen from him, although he must be well aware of their importance. The thought made me nervous and apprehensive for her. Sooner or later, I felt, he must try to get them back. And the longer he delayed, the more violent and desperate would be his means. But there was naught for me to do now but wait and hope.

We found Fort Edward piled high with stores, and lightly garrisoned, the greater part of the army being already at the lake. Beyond Fort Edward I was amazed at the improvement in the road, despite Stark's forewarning of what had been done. The way itself had been widened throughout, and for three-quarters of the route the woods had been cut back on either hand to a distance of some fifty feet, with blockhouses placed at frequent intervals along the road. To be sure the work was unfinished. From a point midway between the halfway fort and the lake, a distance of some four miles, naught had been done save widening the road, the task having been interrupted by the approach of the army. But this was so near to the camp itself that the unfinished work was thought negligible for the time being.

At Fort George I was lodged in the cramped cell in the stone guardhouse, which, with one wing, was all that had so far been completed of the fort. There Stark visited me at once, and went away swearing that if he had any influence at all I should be removed at once to more comfortable quarters.

The next morning he reappeared with Colonel Townshend, who asked for my parole that I would not attempt to leave my quarters if removed elsewhere. I gave it at once and without reservation, and was presently conducted to Stark's own tent, which I was to share with him, supposedly for the rest of my days. Except for the two guards posted outside I should never have known I was under arrest.

This was on Tuesday, the seventeenth. On Wednesday we heard the first news from Albany, indicating that Hubert was at last making some attempt either to regain or destroy our evidence. This was in the form of a message from Purity saying that on the evening after my departure an attempt had been made to set fire to the Schuyler house. The fire had been laid in the wing which she occupied. But fortunately her guards had discovered it in good time, and it was extinguished with but slight damage to the house.

As may be imagined this news set me to fidgeting and worrying over Purity's safety, and had there been time I would have tried to persuade Stark to send other guards to supplement those she already had. It was too late for that, however, for by then she must be already upon the road. Indeed, if she were travelling in accordance with my instructions she should be even then arriving at Fort Edward, and we could look for her on the morrow early in the afternoon. Meantime, there was naught for me to do but sit and worry and hope that all would go as it should.

Thursday turned up bright and sultry with a thick haze lying over everything, as if it might rain if it were not so hot. Not a breeze stirred. Through the morning I lay upon my cot sweltering and listening to the clap and rattle of hammers, preparing boats and barges at the lake shore for the forthcoming expedition. On the parade not far away companies wheeled and deployed and charged and wheeled again in complicated manœuvres. On a range on the east shore several hundred men were shooting at marks. Over on the west side of camp several companies practised shooting by platoons.

Towards noon I began to grow restive, though I knew that Purity and her companions could not be expected for some time yet. By two in the afternoon I was pacing the tent, and by four I was near frantic with worry. About that time Stark came in from drilling his company in close order tactics upon the parade and made an attempt to calm me.

"Be easy, man!" he said. "There is naught to fear. They will be along presently."

"Would God I could believe it!" I cried. "But I have a feeling that something has gone wrong. John, if aught of harm comes to that child I will never forgive myself!"

It was at that moment we heard a commotion in front of our tent, and Stark stepped to the door and looked out. I heard him give a startled exclamation before he plunged outside, and I followed him to the doorway, only to find the way barred by the crossed muskets of my guards.

I did not need to go outside, however, to see what was the cause of it. Perhaps fifty yards away, coming towards the tent at a shambling, staggering run, was a man. A little crowd had gathered at his heels, and from all about us others were running towards him. And well they might, for his buckskin leggings were stained bright red with blood, and with every step he took, even at that distance, I could see the precious fluid pump from a great gaping hole in his left side. His jerkin hung in tatters from his shoulders. There was a great knife slash across his bared chest, and another across his face, and still a third had split the side of his scalp and torn away one ear. I had to look twice to recognize McClary, but when I did I cried out his name in wild alarm.

He came forward doggedly, thrusting men aside, staggering, almost falling once or twice, until he came to where Stark ran to meet him. There he sprawled face down full length in the dust and lay still. I saw Stark bend over and lift him up. Turning, he carried him up to the tent and laid him down upon the ground, where he dropped to his knees beside him and leaned over him.

In their excitement my guards forgot to bar my way and I slipped out and knelt on the other side.

"John!" I said. "It's McClary!"

He looked at me soberly and nodded.

We both looked down and saw the man's eyelids flutter.

"Quick!" said Stark. "Some rum!"

Someone in the crowd that had gathered about us reached out a canteen, and Stark took it and pressed it to McClary's lips. The man choked and gurgled. Then his eyes opened. He looked up at Stark.

"The girl!" he said. "They got her!"

I leaned forward sharply.

"Who?" I whispered.

"Injuns!" he said. "They'd 'a' got me too, but I stuck to my horse. He dropped about a mile up the road."

"What about Toby and Stinson?" said Stark.

"They—" The man's eyelids fluttered. There was no doubt he was going fast. Stark gave him another drink of rum. "They got them," he said falteringly, "dead. There must 'a' been forty o' 'em."

"Is she—" I began.

His eyes opened wide and looked at me straight.

"They didn't harm her," he said.

I felt suddenly weak. That was something at least.

"The letters?" said Stark.

"She had—'em on—her," McClary said.

Stark groaned. McClary's voice died to a whisper. Stark bent down to catch his words.

"Rum!" said McClary.

Stark gave him another drink. For a moment he lay still, his eyes closed. When he spoke his voice was stronger.

" 'Twas a white man led 'em—cap'n," he said.

There was a harsh rasp in his throat, and he went limp. Stark looked at him sharply.

"He's dead," he said.

But even as he said it, McClary's eyes opened once more and he looked up at us. With a great effort, his breath coming in great gulping gasps, he spoke.

"Shem—Sanborn—done—" he breathed.

An instant later his eyelids fluttered down. He arched his back once in great agony, and in another moment he died.

3

A low growl went up from the crowd about us, most of whom were Rangers. There must have been twenty who had heard. Stark looked up sharply.

"You heard?" he demanded fiercely.

A dozen voices growled, "Aye!"

"This may be of the utmost importance to Captain Ferguson," Stark said. "You men have my orders to say nothing of it until you are called upon. If your testimony is needed you will be called. You hear?"

There was a mutter of assent.

Stark stood up then and motioned me to return to the tent. I obeyed him willingly enough, while he gave orders for the care of McClary's body.

Search and pursuit parties were ordered out at once, and all through the night they scoured the woods on both sides of the lake, but without success. It must have been some time after the attack that McClary reached camp, for Toby's and Stinson's bodies were stiff when they were found.

In the meantime I sat in my tent sunk to the ultimate depths of despair. Little I cared now whether I lived or died. Two such friends as ever a man had were dead on my account, to say nothing of the two Rangers who had fallen. Toby, whom I had known since my arrival in this country, and whom I had come to love as fondly as if he were one of my own, was gone. In his life he had been a walking rebuke to those who held that the only good Indian is a dead one. In Purity I had found my love, only to lose her again, almost overnight. I knew now that I loved her—indeed, that I had always loved her, for I saw plainly enough that what I had taken for love of Dorcas had been but the dazzlement of a spell her beauty had cast upon me.

I lay upon my cot and cursed the war and all that it had done to me. My home was wrecked; my child revealed as not mine at all. My name was disgraced. My friends were dead, and at that better off than I. And Purity was gone, carried away through the dark woods, whither I knew not. And I did not doubt I should never see her more. Small wonder I took little interest in the outcome of my trial!

Friday, the day of my court-martial, dawned, a repetition of Thursday's hazy sultry heat. Stark, who had not come in from the search for the marauders until the small hours of the morning, did his best to rally me.

"Look ye, lad," he said, "you must not give up hope. You must fight this thing. McClary said 'twas Indians carried her off, which means no harm will come to the lass; and if you give up now there'll be none to save her."

I saw what he meant, and realized the truth of it. It was one of the remarkable things about these savage raiders that they rarely molested the white women they carried off. Perhaps they considered them ugly by their standards. Perhaps they had other reasons. But whatever lay behind it, it was true enough. On rare occasions one heard of a white girl adopted into the tribe that had taken her and married off to some buck. But as a rule they preferred to profit by their captives in another way: either by holding them for their friends to ransom, or by selling them as slaves to the French. At the same time I saw but little hope that I should survive to ransom her; and in that case what Stark said was true. I sat up sharply.

"Bring me pen and paper," I commanded.

He set them before me, and I wrote hurriedly. When I had finished I signed and called in the two guards, whom I also asked to sign. Then I folded the paper and handed it to Stark.

"This," I said, "is my will. In it I have left everything to Purity. If I am hanged I want you to ransom her. Bring her back, John, and see that she is made comfortable."

"I will do that, lad," he replied gravely, "if it is in my power."

I saw, too, what he meant by that, and my old fear came back upon me. There was more to this than just a savage raid. Hubert's hand was in it, and I feared he was not yet done.

I lay upon my cot till noon, hourly expecting the summons that would take me to face the court. But it did not come. Stark came in about midday with the word that everyone was rushed with preparations for embarkation on the following morning, from the general on down, so that the hour of court-martial had been postponed until nine that night.

Shortly afterwards I had a visitor—Colonel Bouquet, who came to wish me luck. He took one look at my gloomy features and his own face fell.

"So!" he exclaimed. "Somet'ing iss wrong?"

Stark explained what had happened, and the colonel looked concerned.

"I am sorry!" he exclaimed, and took to pacing the tent in silence.

After some moments he looked up.

"Gabtain," he said, "I haf hadt some egsperience wis—wis such matters. Vould you let me share wis you de defence?"

Stark looked at me inquiringly.

I nodded listlessly.

"I would be honoured, colonel," said Stark.

"Goot!" Bouquet exclaimed. "I shall haf to notify de general, uff course. If you will to come wis me, gaptain, I t'ink I may 'ave somet'ing t'at will help."

Stark rose hastily, and they went out, their heads together.

It was midafternoon before Stark returned. When he came in I looked at him inquiringly.

"Eh!" he said. "The Switzer is not so dull as he seems. He has an idea—just an idea, but it may help if all else fails."

"What is it?" I asked, more from curiosity than from hope.

"Just an idea," he repeated. "But, look ye, lad, one thing I will ask you to promise me."

"What?" I said.

"No matter what is said," he said, "you are to make no protest. 'Twill be for your good."

I nodded indifferently.

"Anything you say," I told him.

Promptly at nine a squad of grenadiers marched to our tent, whence I was immediately escorted to the great tent in which General Amherst had set up his headquarters. A dozen lanthorns filled the place with light, and I was placed between two guards and marched within, the rest of the squad being stationed about at various posts outside.

Inside, at one end, there was a long table, its top strewn with piles of papers. Behind this table, ready to begin, sat the court, consisting of General Amherst himself, as judge advocate, with Brigadier Gage and Colonel Haviland, seated respectively on his right and left, and with Colonel Townshend and Major Rogers at either end. It was the first time I had seen Rogers since the day I had been accused, and I looked at him curiously. He returned my stare with grim hostility, and then dropped his eyes to the papers on the table before him.

At a small table on the left Stark and Colonel Bouquet were already seated. The general motioned my guards to that side, and I was marched over against the wall of the tent, where I stood stiffly at attention.

"The prisoner may sit down," said Amherst.

I sat down in the empty chair between Stark and Bouquet.

A moment later Hubert entered with Dorcas on his arm. I was not a little surprised to see her there in a military court, but I imagined she was come to support Hubert against any accusations I might make, since she could not legally appear against me. At sight of her the court rose politely. She curtsied daintily to the general and swept me with a contemptuous glance, after which she moved to a seat at a third table which stood across the tent from our own. Hubert saluted the court and held Dorcas' chair, after which he sat down himself.

Other witnesses and guards filed in and ranged themselves about the tent. General Amherst began to rustle his papers and looked right and left at the other members of the court. At that instant a man appeared in the doorway, saluted the court and moved to Hubert's table. At sight of him I half rose to my feet, an exclamation of surprise springing to my lips, for the man was Shem Sanborn.

Stark grasped my arm and pulled me back into my seat.

" 'Tis Sanborn!" I whispered. "How can he be here?"

Stark shook his head warningly.

"He must have left his Indians," he replied under his breath, "and circled back. No doubt your cousin counts upon him to help damn you."

At that instant General Amherst rapped upon the table. At the lower end of the tent a subaltern clerk began to scribble, the faint scratching of his pen coming clearly to our ears in the heavy silence. At a little distance outside I could hear the sound of the waves lapping at the boats drawn up upon the beach. The general cleared his throat.

"The case of James Ferguson," he began, "late captain in Major Rogers' Rangers. The charge is treason."

He went on to read out the charges, upon which I had been arrested and brought to trial, in obscurely legal and ominous terms which I will not here attempt to reproduce, for they were monotonous in their heavy formality. Neither will I endeavour to record each passing detail of the trial itself, for there was much of it that was of little importance in the end.

Captain Small was called as prosecutor for the crown. He told how he had, under orders from the general, searched both my own and Hubert's quarters. He enumerated the results and produced the evidence to be marked and set before the court. The six soldiers who had accompanied him upon the search were called one by one, and testified that these documents had been found in my home, in my quarters and belongings. Major Rogers was then called upon to testify that he had found further evidence in my quarters at Fort Edward, and this in turn was produced and catalogued.

Witnesses were then called as to my character. Hubert, under questioning, brought it out cleverly that my father had served the Prince in the 'Forty-five, and that he had been killed at Culloden. I whispered an instant with Stark at that, and he leapt to his feet.

"The defence protests, your Excellency," he said.

"On what grounds?" the general asked.

"The testimony is irrelevant coming from such a source," said Stark.

"How so?" said Amherst.

"May I question the witness?" asked Stark.

Amherst nodded.

Under Stark's cross-examination Hubert admitted that he too had fought for the Prince at Culloden. Stark turned to the court.

"It would appear from this," he said, "that the witness is no better than the accused. Indeed, if anything he is worse, for the accused did not bear arms against the King, while the witness did. I move the testimony be stricken from the record."

"The major is not on trial," said Amherst; "the accused is. The record stands. Proceed."

Hubert then proceeded to damn me with faint praise. He had never suspected, he said, any of my nefarious doings, but had trusted me implicitly, even to the extent of answering many questions concerning his duties which later appeared to have been passed on to the French. It was not until recently that he had suspected anything—the occasion for that being, one evening about six months since, when a letter evidently intended for me came into his hands by mistake. He here produced one of the letters vaguely addressed to "Monsieur F." and turned it over to the court. From then on he had, with the aid of Shem Sanborn, kept an eye on me from a distance.

Sanborn was then called and sworn. I prepared myself for a new series of lies, but here the general himself created a diversion.

"Your name is Sanborn?" he asked.

Shem nodded. The general looked at me.

"Is this the man you claimed to have seen skulking outside Colonel Haldimand's window?" he said.

"That is the man, your Excellency," I told him.

He turned to Sanborn.

"Were you at Fort Edward at any time during last September?" he demanded.

"I was not," said Sanborn.

"What?" demanded the general sharply.

"Yer Excellency," said Sanborn quickly.

"Where were you?" asked the general.

"I was carryin' supplies out to the Mohawk, yer Excellency," Sanborn replied.

"You can produce witness to that effect?" said Amherst.

"I can, sir," said Sanborn. "The major will testify to it. An' I can find others."

"Let that go for the moment," said the general. "Proceed."

Sanborn then testified that, acting under Hubert's orders, he had watched me, and several times followed me into the woods where I met with French officers and gave them information. The damnable part of his story was that he was apparently well coached, for at the times he said I was meeting with the enemy I could not have proved where I was.

Stark leapt to his feet.

"Your Excellency!" he said. "I protest that this man's testimony is worthless."

Haviland, on the general's left, sneered openly.

"The defence seems to rest its case in calling the prosecution's witnesses liars," he remarked.

The words angered me.

"Your Excellency," I cried, rising. "At the time of my arrest I maintained that the entire charge was a plot against me. If I am not to be allowed to prove this you may as well hang me without further ado!"

The general rapped sharply on the table.

"Sit down!" he commanded. "Mr. Stark," he went on, "there

is some justice in Colonel Haviland's comment. Thus far the defence has attempted to produce no witnesses of its own, but has confined itself to attempting to discredit the testimony of the prosecution."

Stark bowed. "Your Excellency," he said, "until yesterday we had two excellent witnesses, as well as documentary proof, that this whole thing is a plot to put upon an innocent man the blame for a crime he never committed. Those witnesses and that evidence were set upon, yesterday, upon the road between here and Fort Edward by enemy Indians. One of the witnesses was killed. The other was abducted, and the evidence was taken."

Haviland snorted. "Rot!" he exclaimed.

"As your Excellency can see," Stark went on, paying no heed to the interruption, "this event has deprived us of our case. Nevertheless, with your permission, I will proceed to question the prosecution's witness to prove the grounds of my protest."

Amherst nodded. Stark turned to Sanborn.

"Where were you yesterday afternoon between the hours, say, of one and three?"

Sanborn looked shiftily about the tent.

"Right here in camp," he said.

"That's a lie!" Stark rapped out. "You were lying in wait upon the road to Fort Edward with a party of enemy Indians at your command to waylay a certain party which you expected to pass that way en route to this place!"

There was a buzz of amazed comment throughout the tent.

"That ain't so!" Sanborn shouted.

Amherst thumped angrily on the table.

"Mr. Stark," he said angrily, "do you know what you are saying? Do you realize the gravity of this charge?"

Stark bowed. "I am fully aware of it, your Excellency," he replied. "Mr. Sanborn evidently does not realize that one survivor of that party escaped, badly wounded, to this camp. As Major Rogers himself will testify, that survivor died in the company street in front of my tent. I was by him when he died, and with his last breath he told us that Shem Sanborn was the leader. I can produce a dozen witnesses to this fact!"

The tent was in an uproar at once. Sanborn's glance darted towards the door as if he contemplated making a dash for it. The general was on his feet, pounding on the table.

"Seize that man!" he commanded.

He turned to Stark.

"Have you your witnesses present?" he asked.

"I have two of them and myself," Stark replied. "The rest I can call if your Excellency wishes."

Amherst shook his head.

"Two will be sufficient for our purposes," he said.

The two regulars who had stood guard over the tent were called and sworn. Their testimony confirmed the truth of what Stark had said. The general sat down.

"This would seem to prove that Sanborn is himself an agent of the enemy," he said to his fellows on the court, "and would thus lay his previous testimony open to considerable doubt."

The others nodded. Haviland shrugged.

"You may take that man out," said the general to the two soldiers who now stood at either side of the bewildered Sanborn. "Keep him under close guard. We will settle his case immediately this one is finished."

They turned to go, but Colonel Bouquet was on his feet.

"One moment, blease! Your Excellence!" he cried, speaking for the first time: "I vould like to ask dot man some questions."

Amherst nodded and signalled to the guards to wait.

"Vould Mr. Sanborn care to turn der King's witness," he asked, "in return for a promise of glemency, and tell der gourt who iss hiss chief in dis pusiness?"

Sanborn looked shiftily about him. But before he could answer the general rapped once more upon the table.

"It is for the court to promise clemency, Colonel Bouquet," he said, "not for the counsel for the accused. That question is out of order."

"But, your Excellence!" Bouquet protested.

"No!" snapped Amherst sharply.

Bouquet shrugged. "One more question, your Excellence!" he begged.

Amherst nodded.

Bouquet turned to Sanborn again.

"Vass Mr. Sanborn avare," Bouquet asked, "that der young lady, whom he trebanned on der roadt, hadt been for some time der mistress of de Major Ferkuson?"

Again there came that mutter of amazement throughout the

tent. I myself half arose, furious, my mouth open, about to utter strong words of protest when Stark kicked me sharply under the table. I looked at him.

"Remember!" he whispered tautly. "Your promise!"

I sat down. "But—" I began.

Stark only shook his head warningly and looked at Sanborn. The latter, obviously bewildered and frightened, was looking shiftily from Bouquet to the court to Hubert, licking his lips.

"I—I dunno!" he said hoarsely. "I ain't sayin' nothin'."

General Amherst was thumping on the table again. Bouquet ignored him and shot another question.

"Iss it nod drue," he demanded, "that de major had a room at a zertain inn in Greenbush, vich he kept alvays and vere he met her?"

Sanborn looked truculent, defiant. Obviously he was unable to understand what the colonel was driving at—as were we all—and he feared some trap.

"How do I know?" he said. And he repeated, "I ain't talkin'."

General Amherst gave the table a final violent thump.

"Colonel Bouquet!" he roared furiously. "You will confine yourself to questions bearing on the case in hand! These matters are quite irrelevant, if true."

The colonel shrugged and bowed.

"As your Excellence bleases," he said, and sat down.

I glared at him angrily, but he merely smiled at me.

"What the devil do you mean?" I whispered, furious. "You know there is no truth in it!"

"Ah!" he replied. "That iss vhat ve know! But does everyone?"

He glanced significantly across the room, and following the direction I saw that Hubert and Dorcas were in heated conversation. Amherst pounded upon the table once more.

"Order!" he shouted. "Take this man out of here!"

The two guards led Sanborn out.

"Has the defence any further questions?" the general asked.

Stark rose. "Your Excellency," he said, "I would like to ask Major Ferguson a few questions."

"Very well," said Amherst stiffly.

Hubert was called and sworn once more. It must be admitted that he appeared very debonair and handsome, standing before the long table.

"Major Ferguson," said Stark, "is it true that you quarrelled recently with the accused over your attentions to his wife?"

Amherst rapped on the table.

"Is that necessary to your defence, Mr. Stark?" he demanded.

"It is, your Excellency," Stark replied.

Hubert nodded haughtily.

"That is so," he said. "Is it any fault of mine that I should prove more attractive to the lady than her husband?"

The court shifted uneasily. Certainly this was an unusual way of conducting a court-martial.

"You will confine yourself to answering the question, major," Amherst said.

"Is it not true, major," said Stark, "that lately there has been some difference of opinion between yourself and Mrs. Ferguson concerning your attentions to a certain young woman?"

Hubert addressed himself to the court.

"Your Excellency!" he protested. "I cannot see what this has to do with the case."

"Mr. Stark," said the general, "unless you can confine yourself to more relevant questions I shall have to ask you to retire from the case."

Stark bowed. "If your Excellency will bear with me for one moment more," he said, "I think he will see the relevancy of my questions."

There was no reply, and Stark turned once again to Hubert.

"Is it not a fact, Major Ferguson," he demanded, "that you engineered the abduction of Mistress Stiles because you feared to have her encounter Mrs. Ferguson here? and that it is your intention presently to slip away to Canada and join her there?"

Hubert whirled indignantly to face the court.

"Your Excellency," he cried, "the charge is absurd!"

"Mr. Stark!" Amherst snapped.

But at this point a third voice broke in, and we all turned to see Dorcas standing behind the table, her eyes fixed in blazing anger upon her lover.

"So!" she cried, and her voice carried in it a wild note of hysteria. "So, that's it, is it? You told me you had gotten rid of her! But I see your little scheme now! You think you're going to treat me as you've treated others, do you?"

I heard Bouquet say, "Ah!" sharply, and saw him lean forward. General Amherst pounded on the table.

"Madam!" he shouted. "This is a military court—"

But Dorcas was not to be hampered by such silly formalities as military etiquette. I had seen her thus enraged before, and I knew there was no stopping her. She would scream out her anger in one furious tantrum—and regret it later.

"My dear!" said Hubert. "You must be calm. I swear—"

But she would not listen.

"You tell me to be calm!" she screamed. "I won't be calm! You want me to sit quietly by and see you plan to leave me for a common little baggage with a pretty face because you're tired of me! But I won't! I won't! I'll see you damned first! I'll tell everything I know first! I'll tell them how you made love to me the first day you were in our house! I'll tell them how you planned to have Jamie murdered by the Indians when he went up onto the Upper Cohos that time! I thought it was me you wanted, but I know now it was the estate I would have inherited! I believed you when you said you loved me; and when you bragged about the other women you had known, I thought that I was different. But now I see you thought me just another to be tossed aside when you were through!"

Hubert had turned and was moving towards her. She drew back.

"Don't you touch me!" she screamed. "I'll tell them all about your dirty business! How you have been selling information to the French ever since the war began! How it was you who sent word to Montcalm that the garrison was short at Fort William-Henry, and half sick! I've taken your messages, and relayed them, and covered your tracks, and I'm as bad as you are. But I'll tell them! I'll tell them how you planned to have Jamie hanged for your work! how you hid those papers among his things, and sent Sanborn with others to hide in his quarters at Fort Edward! I'll tell everything I know!"

In our amazement at the revelations that poured from her lips we all sat spellbound. I think there was no one who noticed that Hubert had edged away towards the door. Now his voice cut sharply through her tirade.

"Be still!" he commanded.

She fell abruptly silent, and our eyes swung in his direction.

He held a pistol in his hand, and it was pointed directly at Amherst.

"Sit still, gentlemen!" he said. "Stay right where you are!"

For a split fraction of a second we all sat rooted where we were. Then Dorcas hurled herself forward.

To do him justice, I do not think that Hubert meant to shoot her. But he was tense, ready to fire at the first movement. As she took her first step he swung the pistol involuntarily in her direction, and I saw his finger tighten upon the trigger. There was a flash and a deafening roar. Dorcas stopped abruptly, an expression of utter astonishment on her face, and her hand flew to her throat. In the next instant Hubert had turned and hurled the now useless pistol full in the face of the court clerk, who was nearest him; and before any of us could move he was out the door, slipping adroitly between the two startled guards outside, and running towards the lake.

❨ 1 Instantly all was bedlam in the great tent. Stark, who was nearest the door, was on his feet in a twinkling and off in hot pursuit. Rogers was not far behind. Others of the court were on their feet. Someone, in leaping up, overturned the long table, scattering papers upon the floor. General Amherst was bellowing for the guard. From outside came the sound of rapid shots, followed by a babble of shouting and running feet.

I leapt across the tent to where Dorcas had fallen and turned her over gently. The shot had passed through her windpipe, tearing away half her throat and opening the jugular. She was sinking fast, but as I raised her up and held her, her eyes fluttered open and she tried to speak. No sound came, but I understood. I whispered such words of comfort as I could in her ear. Her hand came up for an instant and her fingers stroked my cheek. Then her hand dropped again to her breast. Her eyes fluttered and closed. Someone knelt facing me at her other side, and I looked up to see that it was the general himself. He looked at her an instant.

"She is dead," he said, and rose again and turned away discreetly.

For a moment I held her so. Then I laid her gently down and stood up myself.

The guard had come in, and the general was giving terse orders for the pursuit.

"May I go too, your Excellency?" I asked.

He looked at me briefly and shook his head.

"You had best stay here," he said.

He completed his orders, and the guard went out. He went over to where the table was overturned. We were alone in the tent, for all the others had joined in the chase. He looked at me.

"Give me a hand here," he said.

Between us we righted the table, and set about gathering up the papers.

Presently Colonel Townshend came in.

"He found a canoe," he said, "and went off down the lake. There are fifty boats out after him, but the fellow is as slippery as an eel."

He looked down at Dorcas and stopped abruptly. He looked at the general, and the latter nodded.

"Have her taken to my tent," he said, "and call Doctor Clement. See that she is prepared for decent burial at once."

Townshend saluted and turned to the door. Amherst turned to me.

"You will permit the liberty?" he said. "It is better that way."

I nodded dazedly, unable to speak. He gripped my shoulder briefly, in silent sympathy, and turned away. Townshend came in with two of the guards, and between them they lifted Dorcas and carried her out.

Slowly, and one at a time, the members of the court returned. Colonel Bouquet came back. But Stark remained still out. Amherst took his place behind the table—a little wearily, I thought—and rapped for silence.

"We'd best get on with it," he said.

The others nodded or were silent. Colonel Bouquet stepped forward.

"Your Excellency," he said, "I t'ink before t'is goes any furt'er an egsplanation shouldt pe made. Certain questions uf mine gonzerning Mistress Stiles vere intended burely as bait for a chealous voman, andt hadt no foundation in fact. I am sorry. I couldt not know de ressults vould be zo dissastrous."

"That is between you and Captain Ferguson," said the general.

"Your Excellency," Bouquet continued, "I t'ink de gourt vill agree t'at t'ere iss no longer any case for der crown. If your Excellence vill permit, I vill mofe t'at der case pe dismissedt."

Amherst looked to right and left. There was a general nodding of heads. Colonel Haviland shrugged as if he admitted the fact, but reluctantly. The others were even eager.

"The case is dismissed," said the general. "Captain Ferguson is declared acquitted and will be reinstated in his command."

At the small table by the door the clerk's pen scratched as the subaltern, a handkerchief pressed to his cheek where Hubert's flung weapon had cut it, wrote down the record of my innocence. General Amherst stood up.

"Captain Ferguson," he said, "a grave injustice has been done you, and you have borne yourself with dignity and restraint throughout. If you will accept my deepest apologies for all that has happened I will make it my duty to see that you are properly recompensed at the earliest possible moment."

I bowed. "Your Excellency," I said, "the establishment of my innocence and the clearing of my name are all the recompense I could ask."

There was a movement at the door of the tent at that moment, and Stark came in. The general looked at him curiously.

"Well, captain?" he said.

"The man's the devil himself, your Excellency," said Stark. "We found the canoe a half-mile down the lake, overturned. But of Major Ferguson there was no trace."

"You think he may have escaped then?" the general asked.

"I am sure of it, your Excellency," Stark replied.

Amherst nodded. "Major Rogers," he said, "you will turn out your men and beat along both shores of the lake. If you find the scoundrel, bring him in at once for trial. But do not hesitate to shoot if he makes any attempt to escape."

Rogers saluted and rose to go out.

"Hold on!" I said. "I'm coming too. I have a score to settle with my cousin!"

Rogers hesitated, and glanced at the general. Amherst nodded. "The captain's reinstatement begins at once," he said.

Rogers looked at me and grinned.

"Come on," he said.

And without further words we went out and turned towards the Rangers' section on the extreme east side of the encampment.

There was little rest for any of us that night. Rogers, grown suddenly solicitous after me, suggested that I must be well-nigh exhausted after the day's events, and would have left me in the camp; but I would not hear of it. With Stark and two hundred men of our combined companies I scoured the east shore of the lake for a distance of some six miles, as far as Long Island, but without success. At the same time Rogers and Brewer hunted the west shore to a point nearly opposite Hoop Island with similar results. Not a trace of the man could we find.

I myself would have been inclined to continue the search longer, though it was obvious that if he had won thus far our chances of taking him were negligible. But Stark pointed out that it was already well past midnight. The general assembly, preparatory to embarkation was set for two A.M., and the men must get what rest they could before that time. I agreed with some reluctance, and the search was forthwith abandoned and we returned to camp.

Upon our return I found that things had not stood still in our brief absence. Anxious to clear the entire business, General Amherst had appointed Colonel Lyman to sit in Major Rogers' place upon the court-martial, and had held a brief and summary trial of Shem Sanborn. The latter, seeing himself abandoned and likely to bear the whole brunt of the affair, promptly made a clean breast of everything, giving us enough evidence to hang Hubert thrice over if we could but lay our hands upon him. Much of what he had to say was no news to me. But one point I found to be of the deepest interest; namely, that the Indians who had been employed to raid the party on its way to my defence and carry Purity off were of Saint Francis, and had been led by Thomas Titigaw, the same who had led the attack upon me at the Upper Cohos.

Beyond this, he either knew or would say nothing of what had become of her. I lost no time in visiting him in that same dank cell in the stone guardhouse that had been my lodging upon my first arrival at the fort; but he was sullen and disinclined to talk, and so I left him to his fate. In the morning, while the troops were embarking, I saw him led out to the execution grounds near the cemetery; and a little later a crash of shots told me that Shem Sanborn was no more.

That morning, too, I was summoned by Major Rogers. The general, he told me, in view of what I had undergone, had sent down word that if I so wished I might be excused from participation in the forthcoming campaign. But that, I felt, was unnecessary. Indeed, I even considered it undesirable. In my then state of mind, only by direct action did I feel that I might preserve my sanity. Two obsessions completely possessed me: one, to rescue

Purity, for whose misfortunes I blamed myself alone; the other, to see my cousin brought to justice for the crimes he had committed against me and mine. But, for the moment, towards the fulfilment of neither of these plans was I able to make a move. Even had I known where to lay my hands on Hubert or to find Purity I should not have been able to reach them; and anything, I felt, was better than sitting idle and brooding upon this helplessness. One request I did make, however: that I be allowed one day in which to see Dorcas laid properly to rest. This was allowed without hesitation, and consèquently when at dawn the bulk of the army headed down the lake, I remained behind.

I will not go into the details of that dismal day. For all that Dorcas had done, for all that she had been, I could not view her passing without some sense of bereavement. Calculating, querulous, self-centred, and faithless though she had been, she was not without her good points. There was no denying her loveliness, and when she was in the proper mood she had been a gay and loving companion. But for the appearance of Hubert upon the scene I did not doubt but that she might have made me a good and proper wife after her own lights. We laid her to rest that morning in the little graveyard reserved to officers on the knoll behind the fort.

During the afternoon I wrote and despatched a number of disagreeable and necessary letters: one to Lawyer Drew, who was by now grown decrepit and become almost a permanent resident of Stavers' taproom, if reports were true; a second to my sisters in Suncook; a third to my landlord in Albany, enclosing rent; and a fourth to the nurse with whom Dorcas had left little James Hubert, instructing her to look after him until my return, at which time I meant to assume that responsibility myself, feeling that whatever had befallen us it was none of the child's fault. He was not, I was determined, to be penalized for what was none of his doing. The next morning I found a place in a despatch boat going down the lake, and went to join my comrades in arms.

It was obvious from the beginning that this campaign was to be no repetition of last year's fiasco. By the time I arrived, two days after the army's landing, the attack was well under way. Despite the fact that the enemy had gone to much greater pains than last year to block the road, cutting down hundreds of great trees across the way, destroying the bridges, and so on, there was no discussion as to which was the best way to approach. Schuyler's and Ruggles' regiments had been set to clear the way, with Gage's and Lyman's to support them. The bridges had been rapidly repaired, and by nightfall of the first day the greater part of the troops had occupied the high ground in the woods facing the breastwork of last year, which still stood as a first line of defence, although not so formidable, many of the felled trees having died and been burned away. By nightfall the first battery of artillery, two twelve- and two six-pounders, was in place to open fire upon the works.

The effect of this move was instantaneous. It had been the general's intention to cut a road through from the sawmills to Lake Champlain, and there cut the enemy's retreat down the lake—a move, it will be remembered, Stark had suggested the year before. Indeed, the Rangers and a battalion of light infantry had at once been directed to the task of clearing a way through the woods. But when the dawn came on the twenty-third it was seen that the French had abandoned the works, knowing them to be of small use in the face of artillery, and had withdrawn a small garrison to the fort to engage our attention, while the rest struck their tents, embarked in their boats, and under cover of darkness pulled away to Crown Point, some fifteen miles down the lake.

In this way Monsieur de Bourlamaque, who commanded the enemy, had contrived to save the greater part of his garrison. By dawn he was already well away. In the meantime, as soon as it was light enough to see, the skeleton force left in the fort began a heavy cannonade, that made a great stir in the ranks, but did small damage. Amherst was quick to see the advantage. With the bulk of the enemy gone down the lake there was little point in cutting their lines. Nor was it practicable to pursue them. He changed plans quickly and moved the army forward, in several columns, taking possession of the abandoned breastwork, which now from the other side served as a front line as well as it had done the French the year before.

Under cover of these works a system of entrenchments was begun, and all the heavy artillery brought up and laid in place for a siege. By nightfall it was apparent even to the dullest clod in the ranks that the fall of Ticonderoga was but a matter of hours.

It was at this point that I arrived from Fort George. Even before I reached the landing I could hear the dull thunder of the cannonade, which boats passing southward along the lake told us had been continuous throughout the day. The landing itself was crowded, two of the Massachusetts regiments being there to move forward the provisions, and the road was jammed with men coming and going. I pushed my way through to the sawmill, where upon inquiry I learned that Rogers and the Rangers were encamped upon the far side of the point, close by the shore of Lake Champlain. It was there I joined them.

There is little I have to tell of the final siege and fall of Ticonderoga. Unlike the previous year's campaign the work went forward methodically and logically step by step. On the day after my arrival it became apparent that comparatively few men would be needed in the actual operations against the fort. Consequently the bulk of the provincials were drawn off to bring forward boats and provisions from Lake George and to rebuild the sawmills, that we might at once begin the construction of a fleet upon Lake Champlain. The first New Hampshire regiment was ordered back to Fort George, with further orders to march at once, upon their arrival there, to Oswego to reinforce Brigadier Prideaux on his expedition down the Saint Lawrence. The second regiment was ordered to Fort Edward to cut a road from there to Wood Creek, a more practicable route between Ticonderoga and Albany than the longer way round by Lake George.

In the meantime the enemy kept up a constant cannonade which had but little effect. Colonel Townshend, the general's aide, had his head carried away by a cannonball, but aside from this our losses were comparatively light.

There was none of the bright pageantry or the brilliant rashness of the last campaign. Everything was orderly and on schedule. Consequently there was little for the Rangers to do. The third day of the siege I spent with my company, filling in the road that had been cut across to Lake Champlain from the sawmill, lest, once the fort was ours the enemy attempt a counterattack by the same route.

We completed this task about nightfall, and marched back to camp to find that Rogers had gone out with a detachment to attempt to cut the boom of logs, which the enemy had stretched across the lake to cut off our pursuit. This was a work that promised some excitement, for enemy patrols were constantly in motion upon the lake, covering the departure of occasional detachments of the garrison, and an attempt to cut the boom would probably lead to a brush with them. However, I was too weary with the day's labours to feel any envy about it. I ate a hasty supper and, wrapping myself in my blankets, lay down to sleep.

That must have been about nine in the evening, and I must have been more exhausted than I thought, for when I awoke it was broad daylight and Stark was sitting upon his cot across the tent, grinning at me.

"Your conscience must be clear," he said, when he saw that I was awake, "to be able to sleep like that!"

"Like what?" said I. "Is there aught unusual in a man asleep?"

He laughed. "Aye," he said, "when all around him is bedlam!"

I listened. If anything things seemed quieter. Even the desultory cannonading from the fort seemed to have stopped.

"Bedlam!" I snorted. "I hear no bedlam! And if you cannot sleep yet amid the ordinary noises of the camp 'tis time you saw the surgeon, man!"

He laughed again. "Wake up, man!" he cried. " 'Tis over now. You slept while Ticonderoga fell!"

"What?" I cried, sitting up. "But—"

He waved a hand in reassurance.

"Be easy in your mind," he said. "There was no need to call you. There was no action. The French mined the fort, and slipped out. A little before midnight she blew such a blast that I thought all the forest round must be laid flat. But you slept right through it!"

I looked at him in amazement. Last year close on two thousand men had laid down their lives in a vain attempt to force this place, and now it fell into our hands as simply as this! It did not seem possible.

"But," I said, "was there no fighting?"

He shrugged. "The major," he said, "encountered some of their hindmost boats after he had cut the boom, and drove a number of them ashore; but apart from this 'twas all done for us."

I leapt out of my blankets.

"I must have a look," I cried.

He followed me out of the tent.

"There's not much to see," he said. "They left it in flames."

I scarcely needed him to tell me that. Even as I stepped outside the tent I could see it for myself. From behind the grim walls great orange tongues of flame licked skyward. On the east one bastion appeared to have been blown away, but for the rest it still stood as dark and forbidding as ever. A pall of smoke hung over the whole point, making the day hazy and gloomy despite the bright sun, and a great cloud of smoke rolled away southeastward before the light breeze. Silhouetted against the dark smoke I could make out the bare white pole of the flagstaff, the lilies of France no longer floating proudly from its peak. Stark, following the direction of my gaze, grinned.

"They left their colours," he said, "but a serjeant of light infantry volunteered to go in and bring them off. That's how they found there were no more mines."

As I watched, a detachment moved out from the breastwork, armed with buckets, kettles, axes, and shovels. The fort, it appeared, was not ours yet. We had but exchanged one enemy for another, and it seemed likely that the new would require a harder fight to subdue than the old.

During the next few days we were all set hard at work to extinguish the fires, a task which took three days to accomplish, and to level the works and entrenchments which had been thrown up for the conduct of the siege. In this time Major Graham with the second battalion of Highlanders was ordered away to Oswego. A day later Brigadier Gage followed precipitately. I did not then know the reason for this, but it was rumored that Brigadier Prideaux had been killed, and that Gage was to take his place. On the third day we heard a number of heavy detonations to northward; and a scouting party sent out to investigate returned two days later to report that the enemy had destroyed all their works at Crown Point and had drawn off in the direction of Isle aux Noix.

Three days thereafter, that being the third of August, most of the boats having been brought over, Captain Brewer and myself with our companies were ordered to march overland to Crown Point and occupy the most advantageous position we could. This we did, finding both the fort and the village abandoned, and establishing ourselves upon the ruins of the fort. The following day the remainder of the army marched in and took possession.

Thus simply did Crown Point, for fifteen years a thorn in the sides of our English colonists, fall into our hands. Our total casualties for the campaign thus far were but sixteen killed and fifty-one wounded. An impressive record, when set against the blunders and bungling of former years.

Whilst all this was going on, it must not be imagined that I was wholly forgetful of my own affairs or that I neglected my obligations to Purity. On the contrary, so much was that matter on my mind, and so worried was I as to her fate, that I fear my regular duties suffered by it. By hook or by crook I managed to question each prisoner we took and each deserter who came to us from the enemy's ranks; and though I learned nothing of her possible whereabouts from them—for they all denied knowing of any Indian parties with prisoners passing that way—I did manage to get some inkling as to Hubert's activities.

He had come, it appeared, to Ticonderoga, but a few hours before Amherst's arrival, with a white handkerchief on a stick to indicate his friendly purposes. And because he claimed to have important news for General Montcalm, Monsieur de Bourlamaque had sent him on at once to Quebec by way of Montreal.

Putting two and two together from this meagre account, I drew a fairly accurate picture of what had occurred. The Indians, under Titigaw, had avoided both the forts at Crown Point and Ticonderoga, as well they might, for it is likely that M. de Bourlamaque would not let them keep their captive. They had carried Purity directly to Saint Francis, or possibly even to Quebec, where they would in all likelihood hold her pending instructions from Hubert.

With this assumption it became evident with what devilish ingenuity my cousin had worked. He had prepared his vengeance for any contingency. Had his plans carried through and I been hanged, Purity would have been a helpless captive among the Indians, and would doubtless have been easily disposed of either in Montreal or in Quebec. On the other hand, the failure of his plot against me must make her fate even more horrible, for he was not one to forget a grudge. Stark had not shot so far wide of the mark when he had accused him, quite at random, of intending to join her in Quebec! What would happen to her when that occurred, I dared not think.

The agony of spirit which these thoughts produced in me may

well be imagined, particularly when I admit that I held myself
to be, however unwittingly, the instrument of all the child's misfortunes. But for me, I felt, none of this would have happened.
I was beside myself with anxiety, and at the same time frantic
to see some effort made to rescue her. I even went so far as to suggest to Rogers that the time was ripe to send an expedition to
wipe out Saint Francis. He agreed with me in that, but said that
he would have to take the matter up with the general. In the
meantime I could do naught but bide my time with such patience
as I could muster.

For five days thereafter I wandered about the camp like a lost
soul, unable to concentrate upon my duties, indeed scarce able to
eat or sleep with impatience. Stark was sent out with his company
and my own to cut a road through the wilderness of the Hampshire Grants to Number Four on the Connecticut. But I was left
behind. Other parties went north to scout the enemy's position
at Isle aux Noix. Still others searched for a new route to Montreal
by way of Otter Creek. Ensign Hutchins, of Brewer's company,
was despatched to Wolfe, before Quebec, by way of Albany and
Boston, the Kennebec and the Chaudière. But no word came that
my proposal to lead an expedition against Saint Francis was even
considered. In the end I made up my mind to wait upon the
general myself, to demand that I be allowed to go, alone if necessary, and make at least an attempt at a rescue.

I might have saved myself the trouble of making that decision,
however. That very afternoon Rogers summoned me to his tent.

"The general has asked for you," he said when I appeared.
"You are to wait upon him at once in his tent."

I lost no time in obeying that order, and gave my name to the
burly Irishman of the Twenty-seventh who barred my way at
the general's door. The man stood aside at once.

"The gineral is expectin' ye, sor," he said. "Ye're to go in at
wanst."

I found his Excellency seated beside his table, which was scattered with the inevitable papers that seemed always to confront
a commanding officer. There were two other men in the tent:
Lieutenant Hamilton, whom I already knew, and a tall, pleasant-
seeming man about my own age, rather spare and handsome in a
dark way, with black hair. The general rose as I entered.

"Ah, captain," he said, "we were expecting you. I believe you already know Lieutenant Hamilton?"

Hamilton bowed. "I have not had the opportunity to express my pleasure at your acquittal, captain," he said. "You will permit me?"

"Thank you, lieutenant," I replied drily. "The pleasure was mine!"

They all laughed.

"This other gentleman," said Amherst, "is Captain Kennedy, of Gage's Eightieth."

Captain Kennedy bowed elegantly.

"Your servant, captain," he said.

"And yours, sir," I replied.

We shook hands, and he gave me such a flashing smile that I liked him at once.

"Now, gentlemen," said Amherst when the introductions were over, "we can proceed to business."

He turned to me.

"Major Rogers tells me," he said, "that you are anxious to go to Saint Francis."

I nodded. "I am most anxious to go there, your Excellency," I replied.

"I will not inquire into your reasons for wishing to go there," he said sternly. But there was a light of amusement in his eye that belied his severity.

"I make no doubt the major has already told you my reasons, your Excellency," I said.

He chuckled. "Aye," he said.

He appeared to think for a moment.

"Under the present circumstances, captain," he said at last, "I do not feel that I can spare the men for such an expedition as you propose, though I must admit the plan is a tempting one."

I must have shown my disappointment, for he held up his hand.

"Don't think I am not in sympathy with your purpose, captain," he said. "I am deeply. Those devils at Saint Francis have too long preyed upon our settlements. But for the present we must try other means."

My heart jumped at his last words.

"Your Excellency has another plan then?" I asked.

He nodded. "I have," he said, "and if it fails I give you my word the expedition you propose will go forward. Would you go to Saint Francis with a small party?"

"Your Excellency has only to command me," I said.

"Good!" He nodded. "You know the way?"

"I could find it, your Excellency," I replied. "I would bear east from the head of Missisquoi Bay to Memphremagog, and thence north to the Saint Francis River—"

He cut me short with a curt gesture.

"I will leave the route to you," he said. "This is the plan."

He gathered us about him.

"As you know," he said, "Ensign Hutchins has been despatched to General Wolfe by way of the Kennebec. That way is long and extremely hazardous, or so I am told. There is no way of knowing when, if ever, he will reach Quebec. Certainly he will not come there in time to fetch an answer back to me."

He looked up at us to see that we were all following him. Hamilton and Kennedy nodded.

"The short route to Quebec is by way of Saint Francis," I said. "Your Excellency wants someone to carry despatches by that road. Is that it?"

"Exactly!" he said. "But there is more to it than that."

"How would a courier be able to pass Saint Francis?" I asked.

"Listen!" he said impatiently. "Sir William Johnson sends word from the west that he has had some success in winning over the Indians of the Ohio and the lakes to the cause of peace."

I had my own opinion of what Sir William might have accomplished in that quarter, but I held my tongue.

"This would indicate," he went on, "that the enemy's Indians at least have had their stomachs full. They know which way the wind sets. I propose that you three gentlemen go to Saint Francis under a flag of truce. You will bear a proposal of peace to the Indians there. Let them lay down their arms and recognize their rightful sovereign, and I will guarantee them their lands and homes. Otherwise I will destroy their villages and drive them from the land."

He looked about at the three of us, but none of us spoke.

"You will carry their answer to General Wolfe," he concluded, "to whom I will give you letters of instruction to act accordingly. You will also carry to him other despatches which I will give you."

He sat back and looked directly at me.

"What do you think of the plan?" he asked.

"Your Excellency asks me?" I said.

"I do," he replied.

"I don't believe it will work," I said. "I have not your Excellency's faith in savage honour. I doubt if they will receive a flag of truce, and even if they do I am certain they will not allow us to carry their reply to General Wolfe."

He looked annoyed. "Are you afraid?" he demanded. "You may refuse the duty if you wish."

I smiled grimly. "Your Excellency," I said, "you asked for my opinion as to the probabilities of success for your mission. As for myself, my one object is to get to Saint Francis in any way that I may!"

He looked relieved. "Good!" he said. "And you gentlemen?"

"You may count on me, your Excellency," said Kennedy.

"And upon me, sir," Hamilton nodded.

Amherst nodded his satisfaction.

"Excellent!" he said. "How soon can you leave?"

Since he looked at me I took it upon myself to answer.

"We had best go at night, your Excellency," I replied, "to avoid the enemy patrols upon the lake. I am ready to start at once."

The general smiled. "You are impatient!" he exclaimed. He turned to the other two. "What do you say, gentlemen?" he asked.

"It seems as good a time as any, your Excellency," said Kennedy.

Hamilton nodded.

Amherst looked pleased. He stood up.

"Very well, gentlemen," he said, "so be it. You will start at dusk. That will give you some hours to get ready. I will see that a patrol goes along to escort you as far as the head of Missisquoi Bay. After that you will be on your own. You understand what you are to do?"

We all nodded in turn.

"Good!" he said. "Captain Kennedy, if you will present yourself here in two hours I will have the despatches prepared as well as your message to the Indians and presents for their chiefs."

He shook hands with each of us then.

"Good-bye," he said, "and good luck."

2

So far as outward appearances went it was nothing more than a routine scout that gathered at the lake shore that night at the hour of dusk, when the light is not yet far enough gone for lanthorns, nor yet strong enough to see plainly without straining. At my insistence Kennedy and Hamilton had laid aside their scarlet coats and buff breeches for the less conspicuous and more serviceable green buckskin jerkins and leggings of the Rangers. Lieutenant Tute and Ensign Wilson had been told off, with a detachment of some twenty men, to see us well on our way; and our own party consisted of the two Englishmen and myself, Captain Jacob, the Stockbridge Indian, and two braves of his company. Major Rogers accompanied me as far as the landing place.

"You know the way?" he said, as we came down upon the narrow strip of sandy beach where the boats were drawn up.

"It was in my mind to go east," I said, "from the head of Missisquoi Bay to Memphremagog, and thence north—"

He cut me short with an impatient gesture.

"God's blood," he said, "don't do that! 'Twill get you there right enough, but 'tis God's own hell of a long way 'round! Here."

He searched round for a twig, then hunkered down upon the beach and began swiftly tracing a rough map in the wet sand.

"This is the end of the lake," he said, as he worked. "Here is the Saint Lawrence. Here is the Saint Francis." He drew a wavy line southeastward from the Saint Lawrence. "Here is the Richelieu flowing down from Champlain, and here is the Yamaska, flowing down into the Saint Lawrence between the Richelieu and the Saint Francis." He looked up to see that I followed him. I nodded. "Missisquoi Bay jigs out here at the end of the lake like a great pocket," he went on.

"I'm all right so far," I said. "I've been to the head of Missisquoi."

"Good!" he said. "Then go to the head of Missisquoi. You'll leave your boats there. Better sink 'em. Fill 'em up with stones and sink 'em. They keep a pretty close eye on those waters for fear we'll slip around behind 'em."

He looked up again.

"Go on," I said. "How do I go from there?"

"From the head of the bay bear north and a hair east," he said. "You'll find it rough going, but you'll make it all right. In about a day you'll strike the Yamaska, if you travel fast. Follow the Yamaska two days, and then strike off northeast. You'll hit the Saint Francis somewhere above the town, not far. You'll probably have to make a raft to get across, but once you're over you'll find it clear sailing on down by the Indian path."

He stood up and scratched out the map with his toe.

"You have it?" he said.

I nodded. "North by east to the Yamaska," I said, "then down the Yamaska two days, then northeast to the Saint Francis. How will I know the Yamaska?"

"It's a big stream," he said. "It flows west and then north. You'll know it."

"All right," I said. "I guess I can find it."

I handed my pack to one of the Indians in the boat and shook hands with Rogers.

"Good luck," he said.

I stepped into the boat, and we pushed off. A moment later I looked back at the camp: row upon row of tents, silhouetted in the glow of the campfires, with long columns of ghostly grey smoke rising above them in the twilight. Rogers' figure still bulked upon the sand at the landing, watching us as we pulled away. I waved.

" 'Twill be a long time before I see him again," I thought.

I did not know how long it was to be!

The other boats had drawn ahead a little. I turned to the men and bade them row hard until they caught up.

We were five days reaching the end of Missisquoi Bay, rowing by night and lying up through the day for fear of the enemy patrols that were plentiful upon the lake, alert and nervous lest we come down upon them by surprise.

At that, it was fast going, for I was not of a mood to brook delay. On the third night Tute left us with ten of our escort to carry out his instructions and scout along the west shore towards Isle aux Noix. The rest of us bore to the east of Grand Isle and entered the mouth of Missisquoi.

At the head of the bay Ensign Wilson offered to look after our boats for us, as he was to leave us there with the remaining men of the escort and scout towards Saint John. I told him to sink the boats, after filling them with stones to weight them down, and showed him the exact spot in which to do it. I did not know when we might be returning this way, and I did not mean to be without transport if it came to that. We should need them in a hurry. This done, we picked up our packs and swung off north and east through the swampy woods.

It took us four days—not two as Rogers had predicted—to reach the Yamaska. Rogers might have been able to do it in two days. I believe I could have made it in three, but my companions, who were unused to this sort of thing, made hard work of it.

Indeed, I could scarcely blame them. For mile after mile the country was one vast tangled spruce bog, through which we had bodily to force our way, as often as not in water up to our knees. We were fortunate if we found a dry spot to lay our heads at night, and had it been a wet season, or any other time of the year than August, I believe we should not have found that. No sooner had we crossed the low height of land on the evening of the second day, leaving one morass behind, than we plunged down into another still vaster bog that seemed to stretch away endlessly to the north.

But this was only a part of our hardships. Add to this the myriad swarms of black flies and mosquitoes that danced incessantly about our heads, buzzing, biting, getting in ears, eyes, nostrils, even finding their way into our food and being eaten; add the fact that the constant soaking softened the skin of hands and feet and rotted the threads of leggings and moccasins, and some picture of the discomforts of that journey will be imagined. Indeed, they were more than discomforts. For one of us at least they were actual dangers. I have heard it said that the bite of black flies is poison to some, and that when one of these comes among them they will feed upon his blood in preference to that of all others. I have laughed at the theory, but I will not laugh again. Never have I seen a man so tortured by the pests as was Lieutenant Hamilton. Never do I want to see another. His face, his hands, his neck, his wrists, even his legs, where they crept in through the binding of his leggings, were bitten and swollen to twice their normal size. In fact so puffed up were his cheeks and eyelids that on the third day of it he was unable to see at all, and I found it necessary to delegate one of the Indians to guide him by the hand. Yet be it said for him, never once did I hear him complain save jokingly of what must have been the most exquisite torture.

Captain Kennedy was somewhat better off, for they did not seem so much to enjoy the taste of him. And, as for myself, I was comparatively immune, having long since been bitten by all the flies in the north woods, and so become an old story to them!

It was late on the afternoon of the fourth day when we came at last to the Yamaska, and I promptly crossed it and sought higher ground on the far side. We found what was at least dry earth, some two miles beyond, though the dense spruce growth continued as impenetrable as before. At least we were grateful for solid ground beneath our feet. We turned northward and followed the course of the river, as nearly as we could judge, at a distance of about two miles.

It had taken us four days to come a distance that Rogers had said could be done in two. Now our pace was somewhat mended. Nevertheless I allowed three more days for following down the river. After that we swung away northeastward once more, in somewhat better going; and on the ninth day after leaving Missisquoi Bay, a little after midday, we came to the bank of the Saint Francis.

Rogers had said it would be a big river, and he was not wrong in that. But he had not added that it would be swift. I saw that we could not hope to cross it where we were, and turned downstream, following the bank in hope of finding dead water farther down. About three miles below we came to a comparatively still stretch, where we halted while I sent one of the Indians on down with the thought to see if the village might be near. He returned about midafternoon with the report that he had gone two leagues without sighting the town. Thereupon I decided that it would be best to cross and follow down the Indian path, and we all fell to work to make two rafts stout enough to carry us all across.

This proved no very difficult matter, for there was an abundance of dead timber standing close along the bank. By evening the rafts were ready, and I determined that we should cross at once and camp upon the far side, in order to be ready to push on immediately in the morning. Accordingly we loaded our baggage and ourselves upon the clumsy craft—Captain Jacob and one of the Indians with Captain Kennedy upon the one raft, and myself with Hamilton, whose condition was by now somewhat improved, and the third Indian upon the other—and pushed off.

The rafts were unwieldy. And the current, for all its sleek smoothness, was strong. So that we were put to some considerable effort to push our way across it. We were in midstream, and I was giving my undivided attention to the work of poling, when I heard the Indian on our raft give a grunt of surprise. Looking up I followed the direction of his gaze, and saw that a solitary Indian, armed with a long musket, had come out upon the bank and stood watching us.

I promptly made the sign of peace and called to him in French that we come under a flag of truce with messages from the White Father in London for his chief. But he gave no sign of understanding; only standing there staring stolidly. My shout had aroused Kennedy, and now he too saw the Indian. He hailed me.

"You told him who we were?" he asked.

"Yes," I replied. "I don't know if he heard me."

"What'll we do?" he shouted.

"Nothing," I told him. "Keep on to shore. Don't make any sudden moves. There will be others in the brush. If you've a white handkerchief, tie it on the end of your pole."

He laughed. "After these last few days," he called, "I haven't anything white about me!"

Hamilton began rummaging in his pack and presently produced a white nightshirt which he handed over to me with a sheepish grin on his puffed features.

"I didn't know," he said, "I thought I might need it."

"Well, it's going to come in handy now," I told him, and tied it to my pole.

At sight of it a half-dozen more Indians came out of the brush along the top of the bank and joined the first at the water's edge. They watched in silence as we approached, without giving the least sign of their intentions, until the first raft bumped upon the stones along the shore. Then several more came out upon the bank above, until I counted some fifteen of them. I knew that they must be from Saint Francis, yet I felt no misgivings. Whatever their business, it was not war. They were not painted for that. I suspected we had stumbled upon a hunting party.

My raft was the first to touch, and I leapt ashore, still carrying my pole with its nightshirt flag.

"Who is chief among you?" I demanded of the nearest.

There was a slight stir at one end and a squat, thickset brave with the mouth and eyes of a half-breed stepped forward.

"Me chief," he said. "Who you?"

I told him. By this time the others had come ashore and gathered about me. I could see that our Stockbridge Indians were ill at ease, and it was equally apparent that the Saint Francis braves held them in slight respect. The man to whom I had spoken gave no sign of interest. Instead he looked at our packs, then bent down suddenly and picked one up and opened it.

"Here!" I said. "Never mind that. We come under a flag of truce with messages for your chief. Take us to him."

He made no sign that he heard me, and I reached out my hand for the pack. He slapped my hand away sharply, and nodded to one of his companions. In the next instant I felt myself seized from behind and thrown among the rocks that lined the shore.

I realized instantly that there was no use in struggling. I lay quiet, while two of the Indians caught my arms behind me and bound my wrists together, Captain Kennedy they served likewise, but Lieutenant Hamilton, who was so foolish as to fight back, they laid unconscious on the shore with a blow from a musket barrel. One of our Indians, who turned to run, they shot down in cold blood, and the other had his throat slit and was scalped, all seemingly in a single gesture. Captain Jacob wisely saw the futility of resistance or of any attempt to escape, and submitted with stoic dignity to being bound.

"See here!" I cried, when they had jerked me to my feet. "You can't do this. We are under the protection of a flag of truce. Your chief will be angry. General Montcalm will be furious."

"Tell them where we come from," suggested Kennedy.

"Much they care," I replied.

Hamilton moaned, and showed signs of coming round. They dragged him to his feet.

While this was going on, their leader had paid as little attention to us as if we had been but a buzzing flock of bothersome mosquitoes. Now he gestured up the bank and gave guttural orders that we be taken up.

At once we were hustled off, each escorted by a pair of Indians, while the rest brought up in the rear with our packs. Some twenty yards back from the top of the bank we came upon the Indian path, running parallel to the river, and perhaps two hundred yards along this brought us to their camp.

I needed no second glance to see that my first guess as to their identity was correct. Three whole deer, gutted and washed, hung from a stout limb on the edge of the camp. The carcasses of three more were done up in their hides as packs and hung in the fork of a tree. In the centre a tiny smokeless fire of hardwood twigs burned in its ashes; and various bits of equipment, a filthy shirt, a greasy blanket, a pair of worn moccasins, half a dozen small packs, lay scattered about carelessly.

My companions and I were bound to trees for safe keeping, and our packs flung upon the ground and broken open. It was growing dark. Their leader poked at the ashes of the fire and threw some twigs on after shifting a small iron kettle. Three of the Indians had found a bottle of rum in Captain Kennedy's pack and fell to quarrelling over who should have the first drink, until the half-breed came and snatched it from them and sucked an enormous swallow. After that it passed from hand to hand until it was empty. I was glad there was no more.

In the meantime, after taking his pull at the bottle, the breed had fallen to examining the contents of our packs. Some of the trinkets, a compass, a watch, a hatchet, a knife, seemed to interest him. But on the whole he appeared little pleased with what he found. When he had finished with the packs he came and searched us, one by one. My pouch, which I had made myself, seemed to please him, and he took it, as he did also Lieutenant Hamilton's wig. On Captain Kennedy he found the oiled-silk pouch containing the letter which Amherst had given him. At first he made as if to toss it in the fire, but then a second thought appeared to occur to him. He turned the packet over several times, eyeing it curiously, and at last pocketed it.

"D'ye think he can read?" Kennedy whispered to me when he had gone back towards the fire.

"Not he!" I replied.

"Those letters would convince him if he could," he said.

"At least he knows they're important," I said. "He'll turn them over to his chief."

Kennedy groaned. "The despatches to Wolfe are there too," he said.

"You fool!" I whispered. "You should have destroyed 'em and taken a chance on giving the message verbally."

He rolled his eyes towards me.

"Too late now," he said. "Damn 'em! They needn't have made these ropes so tight. They've stopped circulation in my arms."

I made no reply to that. My own arms were numb.

Presently the Indians lifted the pot off the fire and squatting about it in a circle ate. When they had finished several of them came and untied us, leading us over to the fire and making motions to us to sit.

"At least they mean to keep us alive until they reach Saint Francis," I said.

The others rubbed their wrists and said nothing. The half-breed gave us each a piece of bark and motioned towards the kettle.

"Eat," he said.

I dipped my hand in the pot and found that it contained a greasy stew, half venison, half rabbit. Hamilton made a disgusted face.

"I can't eat that!" he exclaimed.

"It may be your last full meal," I told him.

He dipped in then and ate with evident distaste. When we had done we were led back to our trees and trussed up once more.

I number that night among the most miserable I have ever spent. For a time I would try to ease my bonds by standing, bearing my weight upon my feet, first one and then the other, then presently I would doze and my weight would fall gradually upon my arms and the thongs that held them, and I would awake to find my whole back throbbing with pain. Then I would try to shift my position a little to ease the pressure, and repeat the whole thing again.

At last, however, the dawn came, and with it the Indians returned to life. They made a hasty meal from the remnants of the stew, after which one of their number set off down the trail at a dogtrot. The rest skinned out the three deer and cut up the carcasses, which they packed in the hides. After that they broke camp in leisurely fashion, piling by far the greatest weight of their baggage upon us. When this was done they placed us in the middle of the line, and set off down the trail in the direction of Saint Francis.

I do not know how many leagues that day's march was. Probably it was not above four or five at the most, though to me it seemed like forty. My arms, still bound behind my back, were swollen so that the thongs bit deep into them, and from my shoulders to my hands I seemed to have lost all feeling save a kind of dead prickly numbness. If one of us stumbled beneath the weight of his load our captors would gather behind and beat him with sticks until he had gained his feet once more and started on.

However much we may have lightened their burdens for them, one thing is certain, we did not increase their speed. It was mid-afternoon before we reached the village.

We heard it first as we approached through the woods in the yammering, yapping, howling, barking of a thousand dogs. Then all at once we burst into a clearing beside the river, and the town unrolled before us, a double row of log and bark huts, sprawling up a high bank parallel to the stream, each facing upon a sort of wide street, filthy beyond description, that ran down the centre. At the north end of the village, where the bank was lower and there was a strip of sandy shingle, some thirty or more canoes were drawn up. Before each lodge stood a long pole from which dangled anywhere from six to fifty bloody scalps, some fresh, some covered with flies and dried. In the centre of the town, at the high point of the bank, was the inevitable mission church, built of logs, the solidest building of the lot, and with a rough steeple upon which stood a rough cross. In front of this building was gathered a handful of older Indians, dignified despite their dirt. And in the centre of the group stood a tall cadaverous-looking man with the thin ascetic face and deep-set eyes of a fanatic. On his head he wore the great flat, shovel-shaped hat of a French priest; and a long black cassock clothed his bony frame. Even at that distance I knew that here must be the infamous Père Roubaud, who in New England, next to that of Rale and Le Loutre, was best known and most fervently hated of all Frenchmen for the way in which he had set his savage charges upon our defenceless frontiers.

As we swung into the clearing a great crowd of women and children and dogs and old men surged down the hill to meet us, clustering about us, pelting us with sticks and stones and mud and filth; spitting upon us, tripping us, screaming curses at us; while the dogs snarled and snapped at our heels, until at last our captors were obliged to force a way through for us to the group before the chapel. As we approached this group, however, our tormentors fell back, and we were left for the moment in peace.

The half-breed who was spokesman for our captors thrust his way forward and spoke rapidly to the eldest of the men gathered there, a chief so old and wrinkled that he might have been the great Passaconaway himself. Though he spoke in the Abenaki tongue, of which I have some smattering, it was so rapidly and with such a slurring accent that I could not follow him. The old man listened to his recital for some moments, then gestured him to silence and spoke a brief command.

We were relieved of our packs then, and these, our own as well as those of our captors, were carried inside the chapel. When this had been done the old man reached out a hand to the half-breed. Without further words the latter reached sullenly into his pouch and produced the oiled-silk packet of letters which he had taken from Kennedy. This the old chief took in silence and handed to Roubaud. The priest quickly broke the seal and, one by one, began to peruse the letters within.

"Look here, Father," burst out Kennedy. "You're a white man. You understand these things. We came here under a flag of truce with an offer of peace to these Indians. They can't treat us this way!"

Roubaud looked up from the letter he was reading and fixed the captain with his great deep-set eyes.

"You say you come under a flag of truce," he said in perfect English, "yet you bear letters to General Wolfe. How can you explain that?"

"My orders," said Kennedy stiffly, "were to treat with the Indians for peace. I was to carry their answer to General Wolfe, and those letters are instructions to him to act accordingly."

Roubaud shook his head.

"They say many other things besides," he said.

He turned to the old chief and spoke in the Indian tongue, more clearly and slowly than had the half-breed, so that I was able to understand him.

"These writings," he said, "should be sent to the governor, and at least one of the prisoners should be sent to Quebec, that he may be questioned by General Montcalm. The others should go to the governor in Montreal. See that they are lodged safely until we can send them, and the governor will see you well rewarded for your trouble."

Once again the old chief gave swift orders, and we were unceremoniously bustled away for safe keeping. For a moment I dared to hope that we were all to be kept together, but I was not long in realizing my mistake. Scarce had we left the chapel when one of our captors drew me aside and led me to a low bark hut, scarce larger than a smokehouse, into which he thrust me without ceremony. Following after me, stooping for the low entrance, he thrust me down upon the hard-packed earthen floor and bound my ankles tightly together. After that he stepped outside and affixed a brush mat across the doorway, leaving me in total, stifling darkness. I could hear the mat creak and give as he squatted down outside and rested his back against it.

Not until that moment had I full opportunity to lie back and survey my plight. I had accomplished a part of my object. I had come to Saint Francis. But much good might it do me—a bound and helpless prisoner! Was Purity here? I asked myself. I had seen no sign of her, though I had looked as we were dragged through the one long street. Or was she gone? Had she ever been here? Or if she were here now what could I do for her in my present plight? All my fine efforts were thus, it seemed, to be brought to naught; and presently I myself would be carried away to Montreal or Quebec. After that, who was to care what became of the child? A fine great help had I been, I thought, for all my grand ideas and determination!

With that thought, and the realization of my own helplessness to do anything at all, I wept bitter tears of rage and chagrin. And presently, because I was exhausted, I fell asleep.

I do not know how long I slept; but when I awoke it was suddenly and with a start. In the pitchy blackness of the hut I could not tell if it were day or night outside, though I guessed the latter, for there was a damp chill to the air that had not been there before, and on the other side of the mat door I could hear my guard snoring heavily. At first I thought it was this that had aroused me, and I was about to shift my aching bones into a slightly more comfortable position when a faint scraping sound at the back of the hut came to my ears. For a moment I thought it must be a hedgehog, gnawing at the bark, or a dog scraping himself a nest against the wall of the building. But then a faint clink of metal upon stone told me that the sound was made by human hands.

My first thought was that some fledgling brave had determined upon this way to secure a scalp; my second, that one of my companions, possibly Captain Jacob, had made good his escape and was now come to rescue me. But then I remembered how tightly those others were bound, and my first idea returned to me with redoubled force.

How long I lay and listened to that gentle scraping, I could not say. For a few moments it would continue. Then there would be what seemed an almost interminable silence. Then it would begin again. In those hours—for, however long it may have been, it seemed hours to me—I went through all the horrors of a lifetime. I felt like a child who walks a narrow pathway in the darkness, ever fearful of the horrid monster that he knows rides at his shoulder, ready to pounce at the first sign of light ahead. If only I could know the source of the sound, if only I could understand the reason for it, I told myself, I might be able to bear with it. It was not knowing what caused it, what it meant, that was so unbearable. I broke out in a cold sweat, but something sealed my lips—whether fear or hope, I could not at this moment say—and I did not cry out to my guard.

Little by little the sound grew louder, clearer, until it seemed to fill the entire hut, and I felt certain the guard must hear. But instead he snored serenely on. At last there came an uproarious grating, crackling, smashing sound as a section of the bark wall was torn away, and a wave of cool air swept across the floor and past my face. It seemed to me the whole village must be roused by such a clatter; and so it must also have seemed to the unknown on the far side of the wall, for after that there was a long silence which was finally broken by a great, long, whooping snore from the guard.

After that I heard different sounds. The scraping ceased, and presently I heard the faint scratch of bark catching upon clothing as it passed. An instant later there was someone in the room with me. I could feel the presence, though in the pitch blackness I could see nothing. Presently I heard a faint sound of breathing, and the rustle of a body being dragged across the ground. Cold sweat came out upon me once more, and trickled down my back between my shoulder blades. Then all at once fingers touched my leg, and I jumped. A hand found my face in the dark and rested against my lips. A voice whispered.

"Sh-h! Jamie?"

"Purity!" I gasped, forgetting in my amazement to be quiet.

"Sh-h!" she repeated.

Her fingers fumbled with the thongs that bound me. I heard the blade of a knife snick among them, and felt them suddenly go loose. I sat up and rubbed my wrists.

"Child," I whispered, "how come you here?"

"They brought me here," she replied. "I saw them bring you in. Oh, Jamie, I was so happy to see you alive, I didn't care if you were a prisoner! I've been so worried for you, Jamie!"

"You worried for me!" I said. "My dear, you don't know what worry is! McClary made the camp, and told us what had happened."

We were talking now with our lips against each other's ear lest we rouse the guard. I took her in my arms and drew her to me.

"Oh, 'tis good to find you safe!" I said.

"Do you think I do not feel the same for you?" she asked. "There was none here to tell me what had become of you."

I kissed her then, and told her as quickly as I could all that had happened: how the trial had gone, how Dorcas had been shot— here she clung to me and whispered, "She did not deserve that!" —how Hubert had made good his escape.

When I had finished she sat silent for a moment.

"Oh, Jamie," she said at length, "I am glad 'tis over!"

"But is it?" I said. "We are still prisoners here."

That reminded me that she had not answered my first question.

"How did you come here," I said, "to this hut? Do they keep no watch on you?"

I felt rather than saw her shake her head.

"They do not keep close watch on women captives," she replied. "Perhaps they think they cannot escape. There are many of us here, and mostly we are allowed the freedom of the camp. They make us help their own women with the work and keep us in their own lodges with their own families. I have been in Titigaw's lodge. Tonight they had a great feast to celebrate your capture and prove their loyalty to the French. I waited until they were all asleep after their drinking. Then I stole this knife and came to you."

I began to laugh softly.

"What is it?" she asked.

"I have just thought," I said, "how funny it is! I come to rescue you, and you rescue me!"

She clung to me. "I knew you would come if you were alive," she said.

"You have heard nothing of my cousin?" I said.

Again I felt her shake her head.

"Titigaw brought me straight here," she replied. "Aside from the priest, Roubaud, I have seen no white man since that day."

"He will come for you," I said. "Mark my words!"

"He will not find us," she said, then broke into an abrupt exclamation. "Jamie!"

I was suddenly aware that I could see her faintly in the gloom. She was pointing towards the back of the shack. Following her direction I saw that it was growing lighter outside. I could make out the jagged outlines of the hole she had torn in the bark of the back wall.

"It is almost dawn," she whispered. "We must go at once!"

I nodded. "What about the others?" I asked.

"They are scattered, I don't know where," she replied. "We cannot hope to rescue them without arousing the village."

She was right, and I agreed, albeit with reluctance. There seemed something wrong in my going free while they remained behind. She must have sensed what was in my mind, for she whispered reassuringly:

"They are to be taken to Montreal," she said, "where they may be exchanged. You were to be taken to Quebec."

Before I could answer she placed her hand upon my lips.

"Sh-h!" she said.

We both listened, holding our breath. Outside the guard gave a stertorous gasping snore.

"It is all right," she said. "Come on. Can you pass through that hole?"

"Yes," I said, and squeezed her hand.

She gave me an answering pressure.

"Try not to rouse the dogs," she said. "Keep close behind me."

We crept out then through the hole at the back, and for once I thanked God that I was no larger than I was. Once outside, she led me along behind the row of cabins, behind the chapel, to the landing place where the canoes were drawn up. I drew close to her there and whispered in her ear.

"We had best try to get to Wolfe at Quebec," I said.

She nodded. By now it was grey dawn, and I could see her plainly. I chose the smallest of the canoes and laid my hand upon it.

"Do you punch holes in as many canoes as you can," I said, "while I get this one into the water."

I lifted the craft carefully on its side and removed the paddles that were in it, that they might not clatter. After that I slid it gently into the stream. While I did so she went along the line with her knife slashing at the upturned bottoms of the larger canoes. She had got perhaps halfway down the line when she stumbled upon a pole that some Indian had carelessly thrown down. The pole thumped against a canoe, which rolled over on its side with a clatter of paddles.

On the hill above a dog barked once. Another answered, and within an instant bedlam broke loose. Every beast in the village, I believe, began snarling, yapping, baying, yelping until it seemed that everyone within miles must be aroused. I saw an Indian thrust his head out the door of one of the lodges. At sight of me he shouted something I could not catch above the barking of the dogs and ducked back.

"Quick!" I shouted to Purity.

There was no longer any need for silence. Only speed would serve us now.

She ran to me lightly, and I lifted her bodily and swung her into the bow. In a single movement I pushed the craft off and slipped onto the stern thwart. As I did so the Indian reappeared at the door of the lodge and threw up a musket. A puff of smoke bloomed at the muzzle. There was a ponderous booming thump, and the ball whizzed past my head, to throw up a fountain of water far beyond us, and then go bouncing off across the surface, whacking into the bank upon the far side. I seized my paddle and dipped the blade deep.

"Paddle!" I cried, and threw all the strength of my back into it. Purity followed my example, and an instant later we swept beyond the range of gunfire. When I glanced back, however, the village had come alive. A stream of pursuers was pouring down the bank to the landing, and already two canoes were swinging away from the shore. On the downstream side of the village I could see others setting off down the trail, evidently with the intent to follow us afoot and prevent a landing.

There are rapids in the Saint Francis below the town, long stretches of white roaring water, where the black rocks jut up through the current like jagged fangs ready to rip the bottom of any frail craft that comes within reach. For four miles the river runs swift and dangerous, before it sweeps about a sharp bend and reaches the dead water that extends back from its mouth at the Saint Lawrence.

In August the water is low, and the rapids just so much more threatening, for the rocks are nearer the surface and more difficult to avoid. In ordinary circumstances I should not have dared to run such a chute, but now we had no choice. We could not land. We could not turn back. Only by running had we any chance of escape. And so we ran the rapids. Pitching, bouncing, tossing through the angry whitecaps, helpless, almost, as a cork in a tempest or a blown leaf in the autumn wind. Again and again I wrenched the frail canoe aside barely in time to avoid some jagged boulder. Once a snag scraped the full length of her keel, but as luck would have it the skin remained unbroken. A dozen times water sloshed in over the gunwales, until I was kneeling in a puddle inches deep, and the canoe became hard to handle with its weight.

I called to Purity that if we did not come through soon we were lost, for if we shipped much more water I could not continue to control the craft. She pointed ahead quickly with her paddle.

"We are coming to the dead water," she shouted above the roar of the rapids. "I can bail there while you paddle."

I looked ahead and saw the last long swirl, where the water swept about a great rock at the bend. Just inside it was the still tip of the dead water.

"Hang on!" I shouted. "We'll run for it!"

I worked the canoe across the current, through the boiling thick of it, and headed down into the dead water. We swept down along the face of the great rock at tremendous speed, slid into the dead water, and round the tip of the rock—to come suddenly between two long canoes, working upstream upon the other side.

I avoided collision with the first canoe by the merest hair's breadth, and our momentum swept us on beyond in a semicircle to come up broadside with the second, our gunwales touching. Busy as I was with our canoe I had not time to look at the occupants of the other craft, beyond noting from the corner of my eye that they wore the white blanket coats of French militia. Of their faces I saw nothing until I heard Purity cry out. Then, as our canoe scraped down the length of the other, I looked up to find myself come suddenly face to face with my cousin Hubert!

He must have seen and recognized me an instant before I did him, for he had already raised his paddle above his head, and held it poised, like a club, to strike. I had not time to parry his blow, yet I acted instinctively. I flung up my arm and twisted sideways. But I was not quick enough. For a brief instant I could see the murderous hatred in his eyes. Then the blade of his paddle flashed and descended sharply upon my arm. I felt the bone snap sickeningly. In the next moment his paddle caught me just above the ear. Lights danced before my eyes. I could feel the canoe turning under me. And then suddenly everything went black.

3

How long I was unconscious from the blow Hubert had dealt me, I do not know. It could not have been long, for when I opened my eyes at last I was being dragged out upon the bank. Someone in Hubert's canoe, it appeared, had had the presence of mind to grasp me by the hair of the head as I swept past, while the other canoe had come about and picked up Purity, who had been dipped in the river at the same time.

There was a good deal of controversy over something, all of them babbling at once, and it was some minutes before my head cleared enough to realize that they were talking about what should be done with us. Not that I cared greatly, for I was sick at heart at this sudden reversal of our fortunes.

A young French officer of colony marines, a lad scarce out of his teens, appeared to be in command of the detachment, and it was to him that Hubert addressed himself most vehemently.

"I tell you the man is a dangerous spy," he was saying, "an officer of the notorious Rogers. You will do well, lieutenant, to despatch him with no further ceremony."

The young officer looked at me uncertainly.

"But, m'sieur," he said, "that is most irregular. If he is what you say, he should be carried to Quebec."

"Irregular be damned!" Hubert stormed. "I tell you the fellow's slippery as an eel. He'll be sure to give you the slip, lieutenant, unless you follow my advice."

It was at this point I spoke for myself. I cared little what might happen to me, but the thought of Purity moved me to protest. I did not know what I could do now to save her; but it was apparent that something must be done, and that quickly.

"Can you think of naught but spies, Hubert?" I demanded weakly. "M'sieur, this man is my cousin who bears a deadly grudge against me! The truth of the matter is that I came to Saint Francis under a flag of truce, as you may prove for yourself if you will take the trouble to consult with Father Roubaud."

The young officer turned quickly at the sound of my voice. He had not known that I regained consciousness. He made a gesture to two of his men.

"Seize that man and bind him!" he commanded.

I was grasped roughly from behind and my arms brought behind my back and tied. I could feel the bones in my broken arm grate together, and a stab of white-hot pain ran up into my shoulder and down my side. I had to clench my teeth tightly upon my lip to keep from crying out, and for an instant I thought that I must slip back once more into unconsciousness, so weak and dizzy was I.

It passed, however, and I could see that the young fellow was impressed with what I had said, though he meant to take no chances. It was a faint hope, yet I clung to it. To be brought up before Roubaud of course meant prison, possibly death, for me; but I dared to hope that if it were done I might somehow, some way, be able to arrange a higher ransom for Purity than Hubert could pay, and in this way save her at least.

Hubert snorted. "Quel menteur!" he exclaimed. "You see, lieutenant? I told you he was a slippery one. He comes back from unconsciousness with his story ready-made!"

The officer shrugged helplessly.

It was at this moment that the first canoe of the pursuit burst around the projecting point of rock, and a second and a third were close behind. I groaned inwardly. The Indians, I knew, would be enraged at the trick we had played them. Unless a miracle happened it seemed likely that Hubert would shortly have his wish. They saw our little group upon the bank, and straightway turned and paddled towards us.

As the prow of the first canoe grated on the shore a tall hawk-nosed warrior leapt from it and ran up the bank, knife in hand. The others crowded up behind him. At sight of me he turned and would have reached for me; but the young officer proved his mettle. He barked a sharp command at his militiamen, and several of the white-clad soldiers moved between me and the Indian, barring his way with their muskets. The fellow looked at the officer angrily.

"This man is my prisoner," the officer said. "I will not surrender him without proof of prior capture."

I could hear other canoes grate upon the bar below, and saw the band of Indians swell in numbers. For a moment I feared they might turn ugly and overpower the Frenchmen; but all at once there was a stir among them and, black-robed and hatless, Father Roubaud stepped forth.

The effect of his presence on the Indians was immediately evident. They became at once respectful, less menacing.

"Back!" he said to them.

They fell back a pace or two docilely. He turned to the young officer.

"Your presence here at this time is fortuitous, lieutenant," he said.

He went on in staccato French to explain what had happened the day before while the officer listened respectfully.

"This man," he concluded, "was to go to Quebec today under my escort. He has but hastened his journey."

The young officer smiled.

"Yes, Father," he said. "I will be pleased to give you an escort." Roubaud turned to me. "It was a foolish attempt," he said.

"I did my best," I replied as defiantly as I might in my position.

For an instant there was a gleam in his eyes that was almost admiration. Then he shrugged and turned away.

"The girl," he said, "belongs to Thomas Titigaw. She will go back with him."

"No, Father!" I cried. "Please!"

He looked at me curiously; but before I could speak Hubert stepped forward.

"Your pardon, Father," he said. "The girl is my captive. It was by my arrangement she was carried off. I was but now on my way to get her."

Roubaud raked him with a contemptuous glance and turned away.

"I know nothing of that," he said. "You will have to treat with Titigaw."

He spoke sharply to the Indians in Abenaki, and an immense brave stepped forward.

"The Englishman says the girl is his," Roubaud said.

I looked at the Indian curiously. From where I lay upon the ground he seemed to tower above the trees. Full six feet six in height, I judged him to be, and broad in proportion. His scalp was shaven, after the fashion of warriors, and but for a broken nose and eyes too close together he might almost have been called handsome. So this was Titigaw! I tried to remember him as he had appeared paddling up the Connecticut with Stark in his canoe, returning from the raid upon the Asquamchumauke in which little Dan Stinson had been killed. But I could not. Those dark figures in the moonlight, bending to their paddles, all seemed alike to me now.

As I watched he spoke rapidly in the Abenaki tongue to Roubaud. When he had finished the priest turned to Hubert.

"He says the girl is his," he said. "If you want her you must pay for her."

"I will pay more than he!" I cried sharply.

Roubaud looked at me quickly and smiled, thin-lipped without showing his teeth.

"Be still!" he said. "How can you pay?"

"I have money at home in Portsmouth," I said. "I will give a writing for it and stay in Canada, a hostage for its payment."

The priest spoke briefly to the Indian, and the latter looked at me curiously. Hubert gave me a sardonic glance and pulled a heavy purse from his pocket and weighed it in his hand, making the coins within chink against one another.

"A beaver's pelt in the lodge is worth two in the forest," he said.

Titigaw hesitated an instant and then stretched out his hand for the purse. He opened it and counted out the contents into his hand. For a moment he stood looking at the gold in his palm.

Then he grunted in satisfaction, poured back the money and slipped the purse into his pouch. Roubaud shrugged.

"So be it," he said. He turned to the officer. "Let this man be placed in the canoe," he said. "We will start at once for Quebec."

I will not go into the details of our journey to Quebec. Disheartened as I was, I was also filled with anxiety lest I was to be parted from Purity then and there. None too gently, at the lieutenant's command, I felt myself lifted and dumped into one of the canoes, where I lay upon my throbbing arm, suffering the most exquisite torture. I felt sick and dizzy with pain, but I managed to keep my senses long enough to see Purity handed into the other canoe, whereupon I promptly signified my relief by fainting once again.

We were four days reaching Quebec, by dint of steady paddling, and in all that time my left arm, which was the broken one, was not once unbound from its painful position, my right arm only being freed at infrequent intervals that I might feed myself, and thereafter being promptly trussed up once more. Neither was any move made to set my arm, though it became swollen thrice its normal size and was discoloured horribly. The pain of it, as may be imagined was excruciating, and I fear that a good half the time I was out of my senses with it. By the time we came to land at Cap Rouge, above the city, I was both weak and dizzy with the agony, and my head buzzed with fever.

As I have said, we landed well up-river from the town, and were hurried overland, across the heights that lie to westward. At the Saint Louis Gate I had the pain of seeing Purity separated from our party and led into the city under the escort of three soldiers, who had orders to carry her to Hubert's quarters and hold her there. Momentarily she was safe, for Hubert came with the rest of us to Montcalm's headquarters in Beauport. But once he was free of that duty, I knew, she could hope for no mercy at his hands.

It was late when we came to the general's house in Beauport; but the great man had not yet finished his supper, and we were kept cooling our heels in an antechamber for the better part of an hour, while I blew hot and cold with a fever, dizzy with the pain of my arm.

At last, however, we were summoned into Montcalm's presence.

He held audience in his dining room, still seated at the table with all the officers of his staff about him, and though he was my enemy I saw at once that he was a gentleman and a person to be respected. His officers were a handsome group in their white coats trimmed in gold. Among them I recognized, from descriptions I had heard, the Chevalier de Levis and Colonel de Bougainville, who were his right and left hands, according to rumour. There were other officers present, but the one among them who took my eye immediately upon entering was a jaunty little man scarce larger than myself in the uniform of a captain, with the cross of a Chevalier of the Order of Saint Louis dangling upon his chest from a ribband about his neck. Something in his appearance was vaguely familiar to me; and it appeared that I aroused an equal interest in him, for he stared at me curiously with an expression of startled surprise.

Montcalm turned to us after a moment, having first finished a conversation with the Chevalier de Levis who sat at his right, and bent sharp inquiring eyes upon me.

"What's this?" he asked.

Father Roubaud stepped forward and rapidly told of my coming to Saint Francis with a peace offer from Amherst to the Indians. He added that I had evidently also been carrying despatches for Wolfe, whose army then lay at Point Levi, across the river, and upon the Island of Orléans. It was at his instance, he said, that I had been brought to Quebec for questioning.

The general frowned. "If he came under a flag of truce," he asked, "why did you not send him back?"

"It was the message for Wolfe decided me," replied the priest. "I thought it best to bring him here. Perhaps he can tell you Amherst's intentions."

Montcalm nodded. "I see," he said.

He turned and looked at me.

"It seems he was none too gently handled," he said.

Roubaud told him of my escape and subsequent recapture, pointing to Hubert as the one responsible for that. The general ignored Hubert and looked at me.

"What is your name?" he demanded.

"James Ferguson, your Excellency," I told him, "captain in Major Rogers' Rangers."

The officer who had looked so familiar to me upon my entry gave a sharp exclamation, and half rose from his seat. The general silenced him with a slight gesture.

"So!" said Montcalm. "Any relation to—" He nodded, or rather jerked his head, in Hubert's direction.

"I take shame to admit it, your Excellency," I said bitterly. "That is my cousin."

I must have swayed then, for as I have said I was dizzy with the pain of my arm. Instantly the general was on his feet.

"Are you wounded?" he asked, looking at me narrowly.

"It is my arm, your Excellency," I replied, and turned so that he could see the tight cords that had bitten into my swollen flesh.

"*Sang Dieu!*" he cried angrily. "Are you swine that you torture the man so? Johnstone, cut those ropes free and take him into the anteroom. De Bougainville, find Doctor Malreux and have that arm attended to. There will be time enough for questions when that is done!"

He turned furiously upon Hubert and Father Roubaud and loosed a blistering tirade upon them for their cruelty and inhumanity, while the officer whom he called Johnstone, the same who had appeared so familiar to me, led me from the room.

I knew the man then. He was that same James Johnstone who had brought word of Prince Charles's landing to my father's house at Kintulloch, and who had later served through the rising as Lord George Murray's aide de camp. Surprised as I was to see him, I was not astounded, for many of those who had served the Prince had taken service with the French. I dared to hope that in him I might find a friend, and not without reason.

He was as gentle as might be in cutting away my bonds; but for all that the pain of it was such that I went giddy and light-headed and had to be brought round again with a glass of brandy. I found myself seated in an armchair in the anteroom, with Johnstone bending over me. I looked up at him and smiled.

"We meet again!" I said.

"Aye!" he replied, a little grimly. "Your father?"

"Dead," I told him, "at Culloden."

He nodded. "He was among those we never heard of more," he said.

"And for good reason," I replied bitterly, thinking of the part my cousin had played in his death.

He did not question me further on that matter, but looked at me curiously.

"And now you fight for the King that murdered him?" he said.

I shook my head. "I fight for no King," I told him, "but rather for the Province of New Hampshire, where I have made my home. I fight to rid her and her neighbours of a cruel and desperate enemy, who will give us no peace until we have driven them out."

He smiled a little at that.

"We will get nowhere with that argument," he said. "I have noticed," he went on presently, "that there is little love lost between your provincial soldiery and the regulars."

"Is it not the same here?" I retorted.

"Aye," he said with a wry smile as he set himself to cut away my sleeve where it hung in tatters about my arm, so that the doctor would have a free hand to work when he came. "It is the same everywhere," he went on speaking as he worked, "rivalry in the high places as well as the low. You do not know the tension that exists between our general, yonder, and the governor de Vaudreuil, or the intendant, Bigot. Your cousin is a protégé of Bigot's. We of the army will have little to do with him."

At his words a sudden inspiration struck me.

"Look you, Mr. Johnstone," I said, "I have no need to inquire if you are a gentleman. Your general Montcalm appears to be one as well."

He looked at me with an amused smile.

"There never was a grander!" he exclaimed.

"Then perhaps between you," I said, "you would be pleased to help a lady who stands in sore need of aid?"

He stopped his snipping and cutting and sat back on his heels eyeing me curiously.

"What is this?" he asked.

As rapidly as I could I told him about Purity, and how she came to be carried off at Hubert's instigation. I left nothing out, and in the end begged him to use his influence with the general to see that she was placed out of harm's way, beyond reach of Hubert.

"I do not ask you to return her," I said, "for all that she was kidnapped in a most high-handed way, not at all in accordance with the rules of war, but only that she be placed in some spot where she will be safe. Let her be protected against this man who is both her enemy and mine, and when this war is over I will see that she gets safely home again."

He listened to me in silence, watching me curiously the while. When I had finished he nodded speculatively.

" 'Twould be a grand thing," he said, "to diddle yon villain Ferguson of his rotten revenge!"

" 'Twould be a fine thing," I cried, "a good thing! And one that would earn you my everlasting gratitude."

He grinned up at me.

"I will speak with the general," was all he would say.

I was about to plead with him further, but at that instant the door opened and De Bougainville entered, followed by a stocky man in a white coat. This I took to be the doctor, and, indeed, I later learned that he was Montcalm's own personal physician. Over their shoulders as they entered I could see, in the hallway, the figures of Hubert and Father Roubaud.

The doctor came over to me without a word, and lifted my arm, his lips puckering in a soundless whistle. The movement made me suddenly sick and giddy. I heard the doctor say something sharply to De Bougainville; felt the latter grasp my upper arm; then felt a sudden wrench upon the lower arm that made me cry out in agony. Then quite abruptly a wave of darkness swept over, and I sank once more into unconsciousness.

⟨[1 When I opened my eyes once more I could not, for the moment remember what had happened. I was lying upon a bunk made of rough planks in a room that was not above eight feet square. The walls of the room were of stone, as was the floor. Opposite the bunk was a heavy, ironbound door with a narrow grille set in it; and above my head a beam of yellow sunlight streamed through a narrow opening in the thick wall, casting a shadow pattern of stout bars upon the opposite wall. Wherever they had put me, they meant to take no chances upon my escaping.

When I tried to move my arm I found I could not, and I looked down to see that it was neatly dressed and strapped to a board which, in turn, was bound across my chest. I remembered then the general's physician and all that had occurred at the house in Beauport.

I swung my feet off the bunk and sat up, looking about me curiously, though there was little to see beyond what I have already described. A jug of water had been placed beside the bunk, and I took a long drink from it. Then, feeling my strength returning, I stood up and began to explore.

I gave my first attention to the ironbound door. Grasping the grille, I shook it, only to find it securely bolted on the outside. I peered out through the bars, and found myself looking into a long empty corridor. So deserted did it seem that I wondered for a moment if they might not have put me in there and then forgotten about me.

By standing on the bunk I found I might look out the barred window through which the sun was shining. The opening was narrow, and the wall in which it was set was deep, so that my outlook was limited. But by grasping the bars with my good hand and pulling myself up on tiptoe I could bring a large enough field within my vision to gain some idea of where I was.

Overhead was a patch of bright blue sky, and far below the broad waters of the Saint Lawrence sparkled in the sunlight. Between these, and directly opposite me, was the high wooded bank of the south shore, with here and there a patch of leaves, already touched by an early frost, standing out, a brilliant splash of colour, against the green of the hillside. A little to the right I could see a British column, at this distance a mere string of red dots, picking its way laboriously down the slope; and farther to the west I could see, by laying my head against the casement and peering past the corner, an English frigate with the Union Jack flapping at her staff, lying at anchor in the river. Between the ship and the shore a dozen boats plied busily, going shoreward empty, and returning packed with scarlet coats. In the opposite direction I could make out the English batteries on Point Levi, and as I watched a great ball of white smoke blossomed from one of these; and seconds later I heard the dull boom of the cannon, followed almost immediately by the crash of the shell, falling somewhere below and to the left, out of the range of my vision. Though I knew but little of the plan of the town, I guessed that I was confined either in the citadel or in the Fort Saint Louis.

For some time I stood and watched the desultory bombardment that went on almost continuously from Point Levi, considering the irony of my position; to be in plain sight of Wolfe's troops and yet as helpless as a newborn babe to reach them. At last, growing weary, I lay down upon the bunk and gave myself up to speculation as to the possibilities of escape, and whether Wolfe might take the city.

I must have lain there for several hours, for the sun had moved so that the shadow of the bars now lay to the right of the doorway instead of to the left, when all at once I was aroused by the sound of sliding bolts. An instant later the ponderous door swung open and the Chevalier de Johnstone entered, followed by two soldiers of one of the regular French regiments.

"Well," he said by way of greeting, "how do you feel now?"

"As well as might be expected in the circumstances," I told him glumly.

He laughed and said that with the care I had received that should be pretty well.

"I have news for you," he added, "that should be pleasant hearing."

I sat up sharply.

"She is safe?" I asked.

He nodded. "For the moment," he replied, "you need not fear for your young lady. I spoke to the general concerning her, and he was pleased to order that she be placed in the care of the Ursuline sisters at the Hôpital Général."

I was conscious of a great wave of relief.

"I have no words to thank you," I said unsteadily.

He brushed my thanks aside.

"It is nothing," he said, "I would not be glad to do in any case."

"I'll warrant my cousin was furious," I said.

He chuckled. "Major Ferguson did seem somewhat put out," he grinned. Then abruptly he sobered. "I must warn you, however, in all fairness, that your cousin appears to have the ear of the intendant, who bears no love for our general—the rivalry of the civilian and the military branches of the government, you understand. Bigot, the intendant, is extremely powerful here, and if he chooses to issue an order for her release it will supersede that of Montcalm."

"You think he will?"

He shrugged. "Who can tell?" he replied. "It depends largely upon your cousin's influence."

I beat upon my knee with my clenched fist.

"If it is to be done," I said, "he will find means to do it, or I do not know him! Is there nothing more you can do to save her?"

He looked doubtful.

"If there is," he said, "I do not know of it."

Then, seeing how worried I was, he came and laid his hand upon my shoulder.

"I would not fear too much for her," he said. "The intendant is a busy man. It will take your cousin some days, possibly even weeks, to reach him. In the meantime I will see what we can do."

I thanked him fervidly.

"The general has asked that you be brought to him," he said. "If you are ready we will go."

I stood up. "I am ready," I said.

We went out then by what seemed an endless maze of corridors, all deserted and echoing to our footsteps, past rows and rows of grilled and barred doorways. At length we came to the guardroom and passed out into a sunlit courtyard. Johnstone dropped back beside me, and the two guards fell behind a respectful distance. We turned and walked along beneath a high wall.

"This is the citadel," said Johnstone. "We keep only a few of the most important prisoners here. The rest are kept in the general prison near the Palace Gate. The general's headquarters in town are in the Fort Saint Louis. That is where we are going now."

"So I am an important prisoner?" I said.

He shrugged. "That remains to be seen," he replied.

We came at last to the grim walls of the great fort and passed through the low-arched gateway, crossed the parade, and entered the commandant's house. On the outer walls I could hear the thud of cannon, as the French batteries answered the fire of the British across the river. Johnstone led the way to a small anteroom, where he left me in the care of my two guards. A moment later he reappeared and beckoned to me. I followed him, and was ushered into a larger room where I found General Montcalm by a window talking to Doctor Malreux. As we entered the general turned with a smile.

"So!" he said. "You look better, captain. And how is the arm?"

"It feels much better, thank you, your Excellency," I said.

He nodded to the doctor, and the latter came forward and examined the dressing. He appeared satisfied and nodded to Montcalm.

"I think he will have no further trouble, your Excellency," he said.

The general dismissed him with a nod. When he was gone Montcalm turned to me.

"So now," he said, "we may get down to business."

With that he began to question me closely as to the strength and disposition of General Amherst's forces, and as to that gentleman's plans for the rest of the season. At first I refused to make any answer whatsoever to his catechizing. But he bade me consider the young lady he had sent to the Ursulines, and asked me if I would care to see her returned to Hubert.

"Your Excellency," I replied, "is not one to make such use of an innocent and defenceless woman."

He smiled grimly. "Ah, but, m'sieur," he said, "I am French, and you have doubtless been told how wicked we French are. We stop at nothing to gain our ends."

"That is what I have been told," I replied dryly. "Nevertheless I shall continue to judge for myself. I still have faith in your Excellency's honour."

He shrugged and looked grim, but I could see that he was pleased. At the same time I made up my mind that if he wished to play at bluff it was a game for two. I would meet him on his own ground.

"Very well, your Excellency," I said, "since you force me! General Amherst is at Crown Point with an army of thirty-five thousand—"

He laughed at that.

"I know General Amherst's strength does not exceed eleven thousand," he said.

"That was so when we took Ticonderoga, your Excellency," I said, keeping my face as serious as I might; "but the fall of that fortress has so heartened the colonies that reinforcements have been pouring in daily."

He looked at me unbelievingly, but said nothing.

"The sawmill at Ticonderoga has been repaired," I went on, "and already two sloops are nearly finished. Two more are on the ways and will be finished before the middle of September. A half a dozen gundalows have been built, and the schooner from Lake George has been hauled over to the inlet, launched, and armed. She carries fifteen eighteen-pounders, and two twenty-fours."

I knew this fleet, imaginary as it was, to outnumber by far the French forces on the lake.

"By the first of September," I went on—it was then the thirtieth of August—"General Amherst plans to move against Isle aux Noix. The Rangers have been recruited, and their strength increased to three thousand. These men, all seasoned woodsmen and frontier fighters, as your Excellency well knows, will serve to cut Monsieur de Bourlamaque's communications with Montreal and Quebec. At the same time five thousand Indians will fall upon Saint John and burn it to the ground. Monsieur de Bourlamaque can hardly hope to hold out longer than the first of October. After that General Amherst will move against Montreal. In this he will be joined by Brigadier Gage, who will come down the Saint Lawrence from the lakes with an additional handful of some ten thousand men. Your Excellency has probably heard that Fort Niagara has fallen?"

Montcalm nodded. "I have heard," he said sombrely.

Some of my surprise must have shown in my face, for this last had been entirely a shot in the dark. At the time of my departure from Crown Point word had not yet arrived of this development of our western campaign. Seeing my expression, the general laughed.

"You see, m'sieur," he said, "I am better informed than you. All this that you tell me would indeed be very terrifying, if true. Unfortunately for you, it is not. General Amherst cannot possibly be ready to advance before October. By that time De Bourlamaque will be fully prepared for him. No, my friend, Montreal is safe for this year at least. And with luck, we may say, for ever."

I shrugged. "Your Excellency seems to have small need for me," I said.

He laughed again. "I had hoped we might learn something we did not already know," he said. "I see it was a vain hope."

He turned to Johnstone.

"You will see that our gentleman is made as comfortable as possible under the circumstances," he said.

Then he swung to me.

"If you will give me your parole, captain," he said, "I shall be pleased to grant you the freedom of the town within the limits of the wall."

I hesitated. I could do Purity little good if I were cooped up inside the city. Indeed, it seemed I could help her but little in any event. At the same time I had always been against giving parole on principle.

"Your Excellency," I said, "my comrades in arms are at this moment engaged in their various duties. Some of those duties are mine, and I feel that I should return to them as quickly as I may. I feel it only just, in consideration of your kindness to me, to warn you that I shall let no opportunity to escape go by."

He smiled sardonically.

"One admires courage and fidelity even in one's enemies," he said. "You are frank, sir. I shall endeavour to be equally frank. We shall make it our duty to see that no such opportunity arises."

He turned again to Johnstone.

"You will lodge the captain with the other prisoners of his rank," he said, and nodded to indicate that the interview was over.

Outside, Johnstone once more led the way, not back to the citadel this time but down into the town and across in the direction of the Palace Gate, where we came presently beneath the grim grey walls of the great prison. Entering, he led me to the guardroom, where a captain of colony marines rose to meet us.

"Another prisoner, Captain La Fourche," said Johnstone. "See that he is placed with the officers."

He gave the other my name and rank, and La Fourche wrote them down in a great book. When he had done Johnstone turned to me.

"I would like to stay and talk of times gone by," he said. "But so long as this war continues I have other duties to attend."

He offered his hand, and I took it.

"Good luck," he said. "I will try to see you again if I can. If you have need of anything send word to me by one of your guards, and I will see what I can do."

With that he nodded, turned, and went out. I thought then that here was a friend worth having, and hoped that I might see more of him. But in that I was doomed to disappointment, I was not destined to see either the Chevalier de Johnstone or General Montcalm again.

Captain La Fourche turned me over to another pair of guards, and I was led again through an interminable warren of corridors, up steps, around corners, and down again. At last we came to a long passageway at the end of which sat a wizened old Frenchman in a dirty white coat. In front of him we halted, and one of my guards thrust a paper at him. He stood up, lifting his lanthorn high, for it was dark here, and thrust his face close against the paper.

"So, captain of Rangers?" he said, and spat.

He took a great bunch of keys from his belt and, lowering his lanthorn, led the way down the corridor. In front of a door he finally stopped, and I heard the creak of his key in the lock. The door swung back, and a breath of foul air gushed out at me. The old man jerked his head at the opening. I hesitated, and one of the guards gave me a push with the butt of his musket that propelled me through the door. Behind me the door slammed shut again, and I heard the key grate as the lock turned.

I found myself in a great long room, low-ceilinged and lighted only by a single tiny barred window high at the far end. Along one side ran a low platform perhaps six feet wide and as many inches high. On this I could make out, in the dim light, the forms of a number of men lying. At the far end, in the corner, was a high-built privy, open and perched at the top of three stone steps like an altar, the only sanitary arrangement the room contained. Even in the gloom I could see that it was slippery and foul with offal.

But it was the men in the room that caught and held my attention. As I entered they surged towards the door; there must have been close on two hundred of them, though in that dismal gloom I could make out the faces only of those in the front rank, and these but dimly.

As I stood wondering which way to turn, someone called, "Who are ye?"

"What's your regiment?" said another.

"How is it outside?" said a third.

"Who's winning?"

"What's your name?"

"James Ferguson," I said, conquering a wave of nausea at the foul stench of the place. "Captain in Rogers' Rangers."

"Another stinking provincial!" said a disgusted voice in the rear.

"Shut up, you bastard," someone said.

There came the sound a smacking impact of knuckles on flesh, and a scuffling broke out about halfway down the room. No one seemed to pay any attention.

"Is Rogers with Wolfe?" someone asked.

"I came over from Crown Point," I said.

"Crown Point!" said another voice. "Is Crown Point fallen?"

"Aye," I said, "and Ticonderoga. Amherst took 'em three weeks since."

"Ye hear that, lads?" said the first voice. "Crown Point's fallen! We'll be out o' here before winter!"

There was a thin burst of cheering. At the door a guard rattled his bayonet on the grille.

"Silence!" he shouted.

"Boo!" someone jeered.

Immediately the crowd set up a great booing and wailing and catcalling.

It was at this point a man of medium height and stocky build came forward. At first I took him to be an older man, for he was heavily bearded; yet when he spoke his voice was young, and, peering at him closely in the dim light, I saw that he was about my own age.

"I'm Scott," he said, "Captain Scott of Lascelles'. Your servant, sir."

He bowed. I nodded.

"My pleasure, captain," I said. "Have you been here long?"

"Almost two months," he replied. "I'm an old-timer, though there are a few who've been here longer. Step down, sir, and join our company."

I moved down with him then into the room, and he took me by the arm and steered me through the throng. He made a broad gesture about the room at the howling mob.

"All officers and gentlemen once," he said, "but it doesn't take long in a place like this for a man to sink to the level of an animal. It takes a French prison to bring out what's really in a man."

I made no answer, and he led me down the room to a point under the window where three or four others sat upon the platform against the wall. He introduced me to each in turn.

"Major Carleton, of Kennedy's," he said; "Lieutenant Gordon, of Fraser's; Captain Sears, of Goreham's Rangers; Lieutenant Harrison, of the Royal Americans."

I shook hands with each in turn, and they moved over, making room for me to sit down.

They were all eager for news and pressed me to talk freely. I told them all I could of what had happened, of the fall of Ticonderoga and Crown Point and Niagara, and of the preparations going forward towards the completion of the campaign. They were disappointed that Wolfe appeared no closer to taking Quebec than he was, and they pressed me politely to tell my own story. I told them how I had come to Saint Francis, and they were indignant at such a violation of a flag of truce. But Major Carleton shook his head.

" 'Twas the letters to Wolfe," he said. "You shouldn't have had 'em, captain."

"I know," I said. "I didn't know Kennedy was carrying them until we were taken, and then it was too late. I thought Amherst would give him verbal messages."

The major shook his head again.

"The best of men will do the most remarkably foolish things at times," he said.

Someone plucked at my sleeve, and I looked up to see a slightly built, shifty-eyed fellow standing nervously at my elbow.

"Cap'n Ferguson, sir?" he said fawningly. "I'm Clark, Ensign Clark o' the Louisbourg Grenadiers. Your servant, sir. You wouldn't happen to have a shilling on you now, would you, sir?"

"Why?" I said, somewhat taken aback, and at the same time sharp, for the fellow's obsequiousness was a little too flagrant for my stomach.

"Why," he said, "if you did and you had any little odd jobs you'd like attended to, like gettin' extry rations, or maybe the loan of a blanket, I'd be glad to see to it for you, sir."

My companions had fallen silent, and were looking away.

"That's very kind of you, Mr. Clark," I said, "but I think not, thank you."

He looked at the others and licked his lips. For a moment he appeared to hesitate; then he spoke again hurriedly.

"You might be a married man, sir," he said. "If there's any other little services—if you feel the need of anything—o' course I couldn't get the real thing, but I might arrange a substitute."

He winked. I turned away, sick and disgusted at the fellow's implication. Scott looked up wearily.

"You damned he-whoring little pimp!" he said in flat tones. "Get out!"

The fellow made a pretence of injured dignity.

"I was speaking to Captain Ferguson," he said.

"God damn you, get out!" roared Scott.

The fellow moved away hastily out of reach.

Scott looked up at me.

"That's what I meant," he said. "There's fellows here would sell their souls and worse for the feel of a bit of money! Officers and gentlemen, somebody must have thought them, once!"

I made no reply. I was still too shocked for speech. Scott leaned forward and tapped me on the knee.

"I'll give you a word of advice," he said. "That fellow puts me in mind of it. Chances of escape are few here, but once in a while they happen. If you get a chance, if you make any such plans, keep them to yourself. If you learn anything or see anything don't speak of it to anyone. To anyone, you understand?"

He looked about at the others. They nodded soberly in agreement.

"No matter how much you trust them," he said. "Keep your mouth shut."

"I see," I said. "I'll remember, thank you, captain."

He nodded. "You may never need it," he said, "but I thought I'd tell you."

The light outside the window was fading, and the room was gloomier than ever when there came a rattle of cans from outside the door. Instantly there was a surging rush in that direction. Scott grasped my arm.

"Come," he said. "Get in line. We eat."

I realized suddenly that I was famished. I had not eaten since my arrival in the city the day before. There was a moment's confusion, and then the line began to form back from the door. I found myself wedged between Scott and Lieutenant Gordon.

The line moved slowly. When my turn came round, a hand thrust a chunk of bread perhaps eight inches long and a pan of greasy, evil-smelling soup through the grille. I took it and followed Scott back to our place beneath the window.

"It isn't much," said Major Carleton, looking up as we approached, "but it's all you'll get. The same thing every day, except when you exercise."

"Exercise?" I said as I sat down.

Scott nodded. "They exercise us in relays," he said, "about a third at a time on the parapet; so that your turn comes round about once in three days. They pass out soup out there, too, so you get fed twice that day. Save some of your bread for breakfast."

Despite my hunger I found I could stomach no more than half the soup in my pan.

"Give it to me," said Gordon, when he saw that I did not want the rest.

I gave it to him, and he divided it with the others. Presently the rattle at the door was repeated and Scott gathered up our pans and took them up.

"Your turn tomorrow," he said as he returned. "We take turn and turn about."

"Fair enough," I said.

It was the third day of my imprisonment before my name was called for exercise. We were led out to a space upon the parapet, perhaps a hundred yards long and twenty wide, where the grim wall of the prison towered overhead upon our left hand, while on the right, beyond a breast-high rampart, the walls dropped sheer into a narrow cobbled street some seventy feet below. At either end of this space a number of guards lolled idly, while others marched slowly along the rampart.

It was a grey drizzly day, but the air tasted sweet and fresh to my lungs after the foulness of the long cell, and I breathed deeply of it. My new-found friends had all been called the day before, and as I knew none of the others in my group closely I walked by myself along the rampart, my good arm thrust behind my back, my bad one in its sling, my head down against the misting rain, my eyes upon the ground.

I had walked thus perhaps a third of the way when I became aware of someone pacing along beside me, and I looked up to see the fellow Clark.

"What do you want?" I demanded. "Go away."

"I don't mean no harm, sir," he whined. "I won't mention that other again, on my honour, sir."

"I don't care," I said, "go away."

But he was persistent.

"Don't send me away without thinkin', sir," he said. "There's other things I can get you. Little things. I have ways. A bit o' tobacco, now, or maybe something fit to eat."

I did not want to listen to him nor have him polluting the same air I breathed. A guard was strolling past us at the moment, and because I did not want to look at Clark I turned my head and stared at him.

In the next instant I stopped dead in my tracks, stricken suddenly dumb with amazement. The guard who strolled by so leisurely was tall and spare and heavily bearded, and there was a fresh scar that closed one eye. But for all the scar and the beard and the unfamiliar uniform I knew him! The man was Jed Stiles!

For an instant our eyes met, and then he passed on without the least sign of recognition, though I knew he must have seen me. Clark stopped because I did, and stared at me.

"What's the matter?" he said. "Crimey! You look as if you'd seen a ghost!"

"I—" I began, and then thought suddenly of Scott's words of warning. "It's nothing," I said. "I just felt a bit weak for a moment."

Clark shrugged and shook his head.

"Jesus!" he exclaimed. "It does get some of 'em bein' in here. I've seen 'em go crazy quicker than that!"

He snapped his fingers.

I paid him no heed, but began my pacing again, and he fell in beside me, babbling on of what he could do for me.

But I no longer paid him any heed. Indeed, I think I scarcely heard two words he said, for my mind was in a turmoil. It was Jed Stiles I had seen, I was sure of that. Yet how could it be? Stiles was dead these three years since, or at least I thought he was. But he couldn't be if he was here. And this was either Jed or someone enough like him to be his twin. If it was he, how came he here? What had happened? Had he taken the opportunity of our scout to desert? That was not like him. Yet here was the evidence of my eyes: Jed Stiles in the uniform of French colony marines!

We were come near the end of the enclosure by then, and all at once there came the rattling of cans from the other end. Clark turned.

"God!" he said. "It's soup."

He went a few steps and stopped, looking back at me.

"Come on," he said. "Ain't you coming?"

I shook my head. "I'm not hungry for that stuff," I said.

He looked at me strangely.

"Crazy!" he said. "You may not be hungry, but I am. I'm always hungry."

And with that he turned and ran off towards the line that was forming rapidly. I turned away and leaned my good arm upon the rampart. There were no guards near, and this pleased me. I wanted space and a moment to think.

I had stood thus, thinking, pondering this new situation, for no more than a brief moment, when I felt myself suddenly seized roughly from behind and flung down upon the stones that paved the enclosure. As I rolled over upon my back I looked up to see Stiles towering over me.

"*Garde!*" he was bellowing.

"Jed!" I exclaimed.

"Shut up!" he hissed sharply and shouted again, "*Garde!*"

Several of the guards came running towards us followed by the serjeant in charge of the detail.

"*Qu'est-ce qu'il y a?*" demanded the serjeant, shouldering his way through the others. "What goes on here?"

"*Celui-là,*" said Stiles pointing at me with his musket. "He was planning the escape."

"Escape!" exclaimed the serjeant, looking at him as if he doubted his sanity.

Stiles made a swooping gesture over the rampart.

"He was about to jump," he said.

The serjeant looked over at the street far below.

"It would have been complete," he said.

He turned to me.

"*Hein!*" he said. "A melancholic, eh?"

"A dose of solitary would give him better regard for the company of his fellows," said Stiles.

The serjeant looked at him.

"Solitary, eh?" he said. "That's good. 'Twould serve him well. Eight days!"

Stiles nodded. The serjeant jabbed a finger at him.

"You," he said, "take him away. Report it to Captain La Fourche."

Stiles shouldered his musket sharply and grasped my good arm. The serjeant looked about.

"Wait!" he exclaimed. "If the fellow's crazy it may need two of you. Tremblay, here! Go along with Perrier!"

A dull-looking youth detached himself from the group and fell in upon the other side of me. A moment later they marched me away before the silent staring ranks of my fellow prisoners.

Once we were within the corridors, I pulled my arm free of Stiles' grip.

"Jed, for God's sake!" I said.

"Be quiet!" he snapped.

"*Qu'est-ce qu'il dit?*" said Tremblay.

"*Il est fou!*" said Stiles. "Looney as a louse!"

" 'Tis the young ones get that way," Tremblay said, evidently satisfied.

We marched along in silence, I wondering bitterly what it was all about. This was a new Stiles to me, one I had never suspected. Even now I wondered if I had not been mistaken.

We came into the guard room where Captain La Fourche sat. He looked at my curiously.

"This is a crazy one, *mon capitaine*," my captor reported. "He was about to jump off the parapet. Serjeant Beaujeu recommends eight days solitary to teach him appreciation of his fellows' company."

La Fourche wrote laboriously in his book, repeating the words as he wrote. "Captain Ferguson, *huit jours, seul, le cafard*." He looked at me sadly.

"It comes to all of them soon or late," he said, "but with you it is sooner than most. You will get over it alone."

He gestured to Stiles to take me out, but the latter hesitated.

"*Mon capitaine*," he said, "this one is violent. He should have guards at his door so if he should seek to do himself a violence down there—"

He left the sentence unfinished. La Fourche considered, and then nodded.

"What is your name?" he said. "Perrier? You have a good head on you, Perrier. If this war lasts long enough you will be a corporal. You will take the duty."

Stiles saluted. "As the captain orders," he said.

"Tremblay will relieve you," La Fourche added.

The dull Tremblay looked sad and bewildered, but said nothing.

They led me out and turned down the corridor. Presently we began to descend, down and down until I lost count of the flights of stone steps. At length we came to a dark corridor that seemed to me to be in the very bowels of the earth. Stiles stopped before a door and opened it. In the light of the lanthorn Tremblay had picked up I saw that within was a tiny cell, scarce five feet square, and devoid of any ventilation save by the narrow grille in the door. I hung back, and Stiles gave me a hearty shove that sent me

sprawling inside. Behind me the door slammed and I heard the
bolts shoot into place. Filled with blind unreasoning fury I turned
back and grasped the bars of the grille.

"Don't say your uncle Perrier doesn't know how to work a good
thing," I heard Stiles say to Tremblay. "Run along now, my lad,
you'll have the night watch."

I heard the other start to protest.

"What?" said Stiles. "You don't want it? Here I play a fine game
and land you a soft berth, with nothing to do but sit here four
hours at a time and all the rest off, and you tell me you don't
want it! Is that gratitude? What an animal! You'll take it whether
you want it or not, my lad. Go on now, and see you're back here
by eight when the guard changes! Report to the guardroom as
you go."

I heard Tremblay's steps die away down the corridor.

"You must be having a fine time!" I said through the grille.

"Don't be a fool!" said Stiles. "How else could I get to talk
to you?"

"You don't mean you did all this to me, just to talk to me?"
I said bitterly.

"What else?" he replied.

"How did you come here?" I said. "Did you desert?"

It was more an accusation than a question. He was silent for a
moment. When he spoke his voice was reproachful.

"That isn't like you, lad," he said. "You're bitter. What's
turned you?"

"A man who's seen everyone he ever trusted turn against him
has a right to be bitter!" I said, feeling mighty sorry for myself.

He was silent a long time.

"I haven't turned against you," he said then. "I couldn't do
anything for you with all that crowd around up there. Down here
there may just be a chance."

"To escape, you mean?" I said. My heart thumped.

"That's it," he replied.

"You haven't told me how you got here," I said.

"Haven't I?" he said. "It was simple. When we separated out
there near Crown Point the Indians got between me and Lake
George and cut me off. I saw there was nothing for it. If I surrendered to them I'd lose my scalp. If I gave myself up to the
French I'd land in prison maybe for ever. Nobody was going to

exchange for the like o' me. I just went in to Crown Point and made out like I'd deserted. Told 'em I was French and my name was Perrier, and that Rogers had forced me to serve with him. First chance I had, I said, I'd come over to them. They asked me if I'd serve with 'em."

"And you took it?" I said contemptuously.

"I'd rather to be a live Frenchman than a dead Englishman," he said. "An' 'twas better'n being where you are now. What difference does it make what army you fight in? They're all the same. One's as bad as another. I was afraid for a while I'd meet someone that'd know me, but I've been lucky that way, and it might be lucky for you too, before we get done. I served two years at Louisbourg, and then they brought me back here."

There was a good deal of homely truth in what he said, and I was forced to admit it.

"I guessed you'd see it that way," he said, "when you'd time to cool off a mite. The way I figured, whichever side I fit on wouldn't make much difference which way the war'd go, and my hide's a sight more precious to me as it is than it'd be to the British if I was dead. I figured if they ever made me serve at Ticonderoga I'd watch my chance and slip out back to where I belonged first chance I got; but it never fell out that way."

"I misjudged you, Jed," I said. "Will you forgive me?"

"Shucks!" he exclaimed. "That wasn't nothing. It was just natural. Tell me about yourself. Where's Toby, and how's Purity and all?"

"Toby's dead," I said.

"What?" he cried. "Old Toby dead?"

I nodded miserably. "Dead," I said, "and all through my doing. He was the best friend a man ever had."

"Easy, lad," he said. "None of us live for ever. You must not blame yourself for the fortunes of war."

"Damn the fortunes of war!" I cried.

"Aye, lad," he said glumly. "Amen to that."

I told him then all that had happened since his disappearance. When I spoke of Hubert's villainy he clicked his tongue severely.

"Tchk! Tchk!" he said. "I gorry! I never liked that lad. I always thought he was a bad un!"

He listened to me after that with only occasional curses and mutterings. When I had done he was silent for a moment.

"The girl's here in Quebec now, you say?" he asked.

He sounded old then, and worried, and I scarcely blamed him.

"At the Hôpital Général, last I heard," I said, "in care of the the sisters."

"Thanks to you, lad," he said. "She'll be safe there for a while."

"Aye!" I said bitterly. "Thanks to me in more ways than one!"

"You must not blame yourself, lad," he said. "She loves you. She always has, ever since she was a bit of a brat in your mother's house."

"The more fool I for getting her in such a mess," I told him.

He did not answer me, and I knew he was thinking.

"I could go straight and shoot him," he said.

"No," I said. "He's too smart to be caught that way. And besides, they'd get you."

"What we need is help," he said.

"Aye," I said once more, "help! Here's the whole British army scarce a stone's throw away, yet they might be in India for all the good they do us!"

"That's it!" he said sharply.

"What?" I demanded.

"Why, the British," he said. "I know my way around here. A small flying party might be able to make it with me to show 'em the way. Look here, my lad, I'll get you out of this, and we'll go to Wolfe and ask him to help. If he won't do it, will you give me your word you'll help me alone?"

"Give you my word!" I exclaimed. "Why, man! With you or without you, help or no, there's nothing I want more than to see her safe! Give me the chance, and I'll give my life for that!"

He was silent for a long moment; when he spoke his voice was strained and husky.

"What was that again, lad?" he said. "I didn't quite get you."

"There's nothing in this world I want more than to see her safe out of harm's way," I said, "and I'll give my life for that!"

He chuckled in the darkness of the corridor.

"Man! Man!" he said. "If only you'd felt that way ten years ago we'd have none of this trouble!"

"I know," I said bitterly. "I was a blind fool, Jed."

I heard the creak of the bolts as he slid them. In the next moment he was inside and his hand was on my shoulder.

"We'll save her now, lad," he said. "We must! 'Twas your love she wanted—the only thing she ever really wanted. We can't let her lose it now."

"We won't!" I told him.

The only means I had of telling how long I was in that cell was what Stiles told me as he came on guard each day, and from that I knew my stay to total six days. Each day I greeted him with more impatience.

"When do I get out of here?" I demanded.

"We're not ready yet," he said. "You wait till I give the word."

Each day he brought me something towards the final dash; now an officer's boots, now breeches, now a coat, a hat, a sword, a pistol, until I stood at last completely arrayed, a full-fledged lieutenant of French marines as far as the world might see.

I hid these articles carefully beneath the straw that was my pallet and spent my nights shooing the rats away from them. At last the day came when Stiles brought me a razor, a cake of soap, and a small mirror.

"This is it!" he said. "By God, I'm getting light-fingered. I even lifted a watch for you."

He pulled an enormous turnip from beneath his coat.

" 'Tis the serjeant's," he said. "He was fit to choke when he found 'twas gone!"

I put it into my pocket.

"Here," he said. "Shave off those whiskers, but leave a mustache. 'Twill be some manner of disguise if you meet anyone that knows you."

By the light of a candle he had brought me I shaved, using the water from my drinking jug to raise a lather. And while I shaved he outlined his plan.

"Beauport's the watchword," he said. "Can you remember it?"

"Beauport," I said. "That's easy."

"Good," he said. "Tonight, then, at ten. La Fourche will be off and Lieutenant Ferrand will be on. Do you know him?"

I shook my head.

"You shouldn't meet him anyway," he said. "At ten he'll be making his rounds of inspection in the east wing. When you're ready to go, and not before, call in Tremblay; tell him your jug's empty, anything, but get him in. As he enters hit him, and don't be afraid of breaking his skull. You can't do it; I've tried before now!"

He paused to see if I followed him. I nodded.

"Tie him up," he said. He went on to give me explicit directions on how to get out. "The guardroom will be your big problem, but if Ferrand is not there you should have no trouble. Walk right through as if it was your business to be there, and no one'll stop you. When you get outside turn towards the Palace Gate. I'll be watching for you in the street. At ten now, mind!"

I spent the rest of that day in a dither of excitement. At last the guard was changed, and I dressed myself in the darkness. Tremblay always brought a lanthorn with him, and by its ray, streaming in feebly through the grille, I kept track of the time. At quarter to ten I called to him.

"My water jug is empty," I said. "That oaf Perrier did not fill it for me."

"Go thirsty then," he said.

"Man!" I said. "I am dying of thirst. You would not deny me one little drink, would you?"

I clinked two coins together.

"I will give you a gold louis if you will fill it for me," I said.

That got him. I heard the bolts slip in their sockets and stood to one side, gripping the pistol Stiles had brought me by the barrel.

Tremblay was a tall man, and he had to stoop to come through the low doorway. As his head came past the frame I let him have it with all my strength, as simply as that. Without a sound he fell forward on his face.

I had some difficulty dragging him inside with only one arm. He was so limp that for a moment I thought I had killed him, but when I placed my hand over his heart I could feel its pulse beating strongly. I lost no time trussing him up and then gagging him with a strip of my old jerkin. When I had done he had his eyes open.

"I will leave the door ajar and the lanthorn lighted so they will find you," I told him. "Be a good fellow and make no disturbance."

He rolled his eyes; but I had no fear of him then, for I had done my work well.

It was five minutes to ten when I stepped out the door of my cell and turned down the corridor. I had feared I might get lost in that maze of passageways, but I had taken good pains to memorize Stiles' directions. Now left. Now right. Ahead a file of soldiers crossed by an intersecting passage. I waited until their footsteps died away, and then went on.

The guardroom was well lighted, and so bright that my eyes, accustomed to utter darkness save for the feeble glow of an occasional candle or lanthorn, were almost blinded. I hesitated a moment before entering. A corporal sat in the chair I had seen La Fourche occupy before. My heart pounded as I stepped inside. The corporal bounded to his feet, and my heart bounced into my throat. I almost cried out in fear, but the man merely snapped to attention and saluted. I returned the salute and went on through. In the street outside I turned to the left.

I had not gone fifty paces before I became conscious of someone walking beside me. I cast a hurried glance that way and breathed heavily with relief when I saw that it was Stiles, in full marching equipment. He slipped a hand under his coat and produced an official-looking pouch.

"De Johnstone'll swear when he sees that's gone," he said. "I was passing his quarters and saw it lying on his table. You're carrying despatches for Colonel de Bougainville. Don't forget the password."

I nodded. We marched on without a break in our pace. There were people on the streets, but none of them spared us a second glance.

At the Palace Gate a serjeant stepped out of the guardroom and barred the way.

"I'm sorry, *mon lieutenant,*" he said, "but no one passes out tonight. Those are my orders."

"I carry despatches to Colonel de Bougainville," I said as steadily as I could.

He hesitated. "Fool!" I cried. "Let me pass."

"The password, *mon lieutenant?*" he said.

"Beauport!" I snapped.

He stood aside. We passed out the gate and turned left along the walls. I was free. It did not seem possible, yet it was so. I drew great gulping breaths of fresh clean air into my lungs and almost laughed aloud for sheer joy. Stiles plucked my arm.

"Come this way," he said.

We angled away from the wall and struck up the hill to the plain that lies behind the city on the west. Across this we went almost to the edge where the land drops away practically sheer to the river's edge far below. In the stream, far out, I could see the riding lights of the British fleet at anchor. Stiles gripped my arm and pointed to a little cluster of tents huddled black at the edge of the plain.

"There's a road there," he said. "It goes down to the river at a cove called Anse au Foulon. At the top there's a guard, but it's not a strong one. A hundred men, no more."

He left his pack and musket beneath a bush.

"We can't use those where we're going," he said.

I followed his example and left my coat and sword and pistol there also. After that he led the way over the brink of the cliff. The drop was not quite sheer, though it was near enough to it for me. Far below I could see the sheen of the water, black in the starlight, and here and there the glow of a sentry's fire. The air was sharp and frosty.

There were holds for hand and foot here and there, and for a whole man it was not difficult climbing, even in the dark. But I was handicapped by my bad arm. Stiles helped me, however, and we got along slowly but surely.

Some fifty feet down he stopped and began to edge along upstream towards the roadway, where it dipped down from the camp on the plain. It took us a deal of scrambling, but in the end we came to it, and from there down to the water's edge was easy.

When we came to the river Stiles sat down behind a bush and began to strip.

"Here's where we swim," he whispered.

I followed his example until I stood stark naked. Once a sentry passed by upon his rounds, and we lay shivering beneath our bush until he had passed. When he was gone we crept forward and slipped into the water.

As we stepped in Stiles came close to my side and pointed out a cluster of lights riding directly opposite us. He put his lips close to my ear.

"The *Centurion*," he whispered, "Admiral Holmes' flagship."

I nodded, understanding that if we became separated or if anything happened to one of us we were to head for that ship. Without further words we plunged in.

I had forgotten that water could be so cold or the tide so strong. The current was running strongly upstream and we had to fight it every minute to keep from being carried wide of our mark. Once we heard the muffled chunk of oars and lay still while a patrol boat passed almost over our heads. With my arm strapped to its board I swam awkwardly to say the least, and the time came once when I thought I should never reach the ship. But Stiles held me up until I was rested, and we went on until at last we felt the solid planking beneath our hands. I hailed then, "Ahoy, the ship!"

A head popped over the rail above, followed by another with an arm attached, holding a lanthorn aloft. The first head brought up an arm holding a musket and pointed it down at us. In the lanthorn's glow I could make out the outline of a grenadier's cap.

"Oo's there?" demanded a voice.

"Escaped prisoners from Quebec," I gasped. "Heave us a line."

"Yus?" said the voice. " 'Ow do I know it?"

"For God's sake," I cried desperately, "heave us a line before we drown!"

A new head popped over the rail and a voice of authority ordered a line dropped. In an instant it came snaking over the side. Stiles grasped it and made one end fast about my waist, after which he swarmed up hand over hand. Presently the line came taut, and I was hauled up. There was a little group at the rail including one officer, whom I took to be the officer of the watch, the man who had ordered the line dropped. There was a lanthorn on the deck, and another hung under the break of the high poop casting a ruddy glow over the scene.

The officer stared at us curiously.

"Come, come," he demanded. "What's your story?"

As rapidly as I could for the chattering of my teeth in the chill September air I told him of our escape.

He looked at me suspiciously.

"You mean to say you came down over that cliff in the dark?" he said.

I nodded. He looked at Stiles, swarthy and bearded.

"This man looks like a Frenchman to me," he said.

I opened my mouth to explain that Stiles was no Frenchman but as good an Englishman as he, when the door to the poop cabin opened and a group of officers came out. One whom I noted particularly, seemed to be the centre of the group: a short, bandy-legged little man, with an enormous sharp nose like a sparrow's beak and a pale face that showed for a brief instant in the light streaming from the cabin. The tall man in naval uniform behind him, I guessed, was Admiral Holmes.

At sight of our little group by the rail—a half-dozen soldiers, an officer, and two naked men—they turned and came towards us curiously. The group about us fell back, all except the officer who had been questioning us. He stood forward and held up his lanthorn so they could see us.

"What's this?" said the bandy-legged little man, and at the sound of his voice I started, for there was a ring about it that, once heard, could never be forgotten. I peered at him, trying to remember where I had seen him.

"They say they're escaped prisoners from Quebec, sir," said the officer. "Just came over the side. One of 'em's a Frenchman by the look of him."

As the group of officers came forward into the brighter light of the upheld lanthorn I gave a gasp of recognition, for the little man was the same who had rescued me from the terrible Captain Ball, that night long since at the Bridge of Cally in the Gorge of Erricht.

"Major Wolfe!" I exclaimed, for I had not noticed the epaulettes he wore upon his shoulders, and I did not for the moment connect his name with that of the commander of the expedition.

The other officers stiffened expectantly, as if they thought he might blast me from the deck, but instead he gave me a tight smile and peered at me curiously. There could be no mistake, I saw. Those sharp eyes, that lank red hair, that absurd nose, never combined twice in one man under heaven! By the pallor of his face I could see that he was a sick man.

"What makes you say that?" he demanded curiously.

"Your pardon, your Excellency," I said, for by then I had seen my mistake. "It was as a major I saw you last. You'll not remember me, sir; the lad you rescued on the Erricht near Blairgowrie one night in the 'Forty-five. It never occurred to me that you were the General Wolfe in command here."

He took the lanthorn and held it high as he advanced towards me, examining my face by its light.

"God bless my soul!" he exclaimed suddenly. "I remember now, the lad who led Captain Ball such a sorry chase!"

"The same, your Excellency," I replied.

"What do you here?" he demanded, and looked around him at his officers, and then back at me, standing in all my nakedness in a pool of water.

I told him as rapidly as possible of our escape and our subsequent adventures. All at once he stopped me, a peculiar light in his eyes.

"You say you came down that cliff tonight?" he demanded.

"Yes, your Excellency," I replied.

"Do you think you could find your way back?" he asked.

"I believe so, sir," I said, "and I am certain that Mr. Stiles could."

Instantly he was all action.

"Mr. Jervis," he bawled, "fetch cloaks for these gentlemen and see that they are brought into the admiral's cabin."

He rubbed his hands together gleefully.

"By Heaven!" he exclaimed. "Just when all seems blackest new hope appears!"

2

The cabin was at least out of the wind, but I was not warmed, nor did my teeth stop their chattering, until I had a stout coat upon my back and a glass or two of brandy in my belly. In the meantime the general settled himself in an easy-chair, while the others disposed themselves about the cabin, or excused themselves to attend upon other duties. Wolfe watched me throughout with a spot of hectic colour on either cheek accentuating his pallor. It was easy to see that he was in but ill health. Indeed, I learned later that his surgeon had only by the greatest effort pulled him back, so to speak, from the very jaws of death and set him upon his feet, that he might make one last attempt to break down the enemy's resistance. For four days the greater part of the army had been on board the fleet, which had been sailing up and down the river between the city and Cap Rouge, searching for a suitable place to land them. But either the enemy had appeared in too strong force at the available spots, or the heights along the shore had been judged unscalable; and until our arrival on board it had seemed that even this last forlorn hope must be abandoned, and the army decamp for home with the city untaken.

For the present, however, General Wolfe gave me no hint of this. As I dressed myself in the clothes which Captain Jervis produced for me he kept up a running fire of conversational questions, by which means he drew from me most of what had happened to me since that day in the 'Forty-five when he had so befriended me. For the most part he exhibited no more than a polite interest, but when he learned that I was an officer in Rogers' Rangers he pricked up his ears.

"So?" he said. "You are one of the famous Rogers' men. I understand the major has built up a highly efficient organization, considering his material."

I was amused. It was plain the general had no high opinion of provincials as soldiers.

"We like to think so, your Excellency," I said, "though I make no doubt the Captain Goreham's corps is equally good."

He made an impatient gesture.

"Oh," he said, "Captain Goreham does well enough. One cannot expect too much of these provincials. My own experience with them is that they are independent, insubordinate, dirty, and none too courageous in the face of fire. Set them to skulking in the woods like red Indians, and they do well enough. But for a massed attack or a prolonged siege, give me regular troops every time."

"If you will pardon my boldness," I replied, "I think your Excellency is unfair. I will not deny the regulars' superiority in such mass affairs as can be fought according to the rules of war. But you must remember that by far the greater part of our fighting both in the York Province and in the west has been with an enemy who can only be met with his own skulking tactics. Another point which your Excellency has overlooked is that but few of our provincials are professionals. Rather they are untrained men, farmers, sailors, carpenters, small tradesmen, who have volunteered of their own free will to serve in a cause in which they believe. They cannot be made into steady, well drilled, efficient soldiers overnight. Their lack of discipline, the dirtiness of their camps, their hesitancy in the face of concentrated fire, may all be laid to inexperience. Moreover they have no wish to make a career of soldiering. They want only to get the war over with and return to their homes. Give them the proper training and send them out as bush fighters and light infantry, and I'll warrant you'll not find their superiors anywhere. The Rangers and the Royal Americans prove the point."

He shrugged indifferently.

"There may be much in what you say," he said.

"Moreover," I continued, warmed to my subject, "they are learning rapidly. Five years of war have taught them much, and when the time comes to fight again, I'll warrant you'll find the situation changed."

He smiled. "You argue the point well," he said. "But this does not get us to the case in hand. You say there is a pathway up yonder cliff?"

I nodded. "There is, your Excellency," I said.

"How is it guarded?" he demanded.

"Apparently by a very small force," I replied, "but Mr. Stiles can tell you more of the forces behind the city than I."

He turned upon Stiles then, who appeared very uncomfortable to be thus in the limelight, and questioned him closely as to the strength of the enemy in and about the city. When he had done he turned to me.

"You can vouch for the accuracy of this?" he said.

"You may depend upon anything Stiles tells you, your Excellency," I replied.

He stood up then, rubbing his small hands together in satisfaction.

"Good!" he exclaimed. "You will hold yourself in readiness to lead the way. We will make an attempt at the earliest possible moment. Tomorrow night, if the weather permits."

He dismissed us with a nod.

"Mr. Jervis," he said, "you will find these men quarters on board where they may be instantly at hand if we need them."

As we followed Jervis from the cabin Stiles gave me a sidelong glance.

"Crimers!" he said, once we were on deck again. "You came near giving him what for about the provincials! Why didn't you tell me you knew him?"

"I didn't know it myself," I replied, "until I saw him!"

That was on the night of the seventh of September. Our troubles, I dared to hope, were at last over, but on the eighth it set in to rain, a cold, penetrating drizzle, and, lest the troops' powder be wet, the attack was postponed.

For four days it rained intermittently, while we sat on board and gnawed our fingernails with impatience and anxiety. In the meantime the troops were held in readiness on board the ships, and the fleet moved up and down the stream with the tide, in order to confuse the French who, under De Bougainville, shifted from point to point along the heights to keep abreast of our movements. On the ninth we moved up to Pointe aux Trembles, far upstream. On the tenth we came to anchor off Sillery. On the eleventh we lay off Cap Rouge. On the twelfth we were back in our original position, and the rain stopped.

On that day a deserter coming off from the enemy brought word that Bougainville had found his men so exhausted by the incessant marching and countermarching which our tactics had forced him to that he had camped at Cap Rouge to allow them to rest. Moreover, he said, that night some provision boats would attempt to slip down to the city. This was welcome news, for it was thought that with the provision boats expected we might have a better chance to land undetected.

It came on a dark night, though clear. The stars were out, but there was no moon; and a sharp cold wind blew downstream. An air of tense expectancy hung over the fleet, and I for one was so filled with anticipation that I could not eat. We were advised to lie down and try to catch some sleep. But this I could not do, for I was well aware of the import of what we were about to attempt. Instead I prowled about on deck with Stiles at my side, awaiting the signal, two lanthorns at the masthead of the flagship, to embark.

Midnight came and went, and still the signal did not come. About two hours later I felt the tide slack off, and saw the line of ships begin to swing with the ebb. A midshipman came picking his way across the deck to where Stiles and I stood leaning upon the bulwark staring at the shore.

"Captain Ferguson?" he said.

I nodded. "The general is asking for you in the admiral's cabin sir," said the lad.

I turned and, with Stiles at my heels, made my way aft. The

general was pacing the cabin. He turned upon us sharply when we entered.

"Are you ready?" he asked.

I nodded. "Yes, your Excellency," I said.

"You understand the success of this venture depends upon you?" he said.

"We understand, your Excellency," I replied. "You may depend upon us."

He looked at my arm, which was still in its sling.

"You'll find that in the way, I'm afraid," he said.

He turned to Stiles.

"I've arranged for you to take the lead," he said. "We have a hundred volunteers from Howe's and Fraser's. They will open the attack upon the camp at the head of the path. The light infantry and the Highlanders will follow close behind."

He looked at me.

"You will lead the way for the light infantry and Highlanders," he said.

I saluted. "Very good, your Excellency," I said.

"You are ready now?" he asked.

"At any time," I told him.

He turned to Jervis, who was standing by.

"Very well, Jervis," he said, "you may raise the signal."

When we came on deck once more I was surprised to find the men already going quietly over the side into the boats below. The general walked with us to the rail and saw us down. In the boat someone pointed to a thwart forward, and we stumbled thither over feet, muskets, legs, and oars, and settled down upon it. A moment later Colonel Fraser came over, followed closely by Colonel Howe of the light infantry, a brother to the Lord Howe who had died before Ticonderoga.

As they took their places in the stern Wolfe's head appeared above.

"Ready?" he called softly.

"Ready, your Excellency," replied Howe.

"Remember," said Wolfe, "when you reach the top hold your ground until reinforcements arrive. We need no more than a foothold on the plain. The main body will start to advance at the first sound of firing from above."

With a nod of his head he drew back. The sailors cast off, and an instant later we were away, leaving the black hulk of the ship, slipping down the tide, pulling for the dark loom of the shore below.

We rode in hushed silence, listening only to the slap and chuckle of the water at the boat's strakes. Presently the black shadow of the shore loomed ahead. Simultaneously came the sharp bark of a challenge.

"*Qui vive?*"

I have never been known as a swift thinker beyond the ordinary, but on this occasion I must have been inspired by my responsibility. Wolfe and all the army were depending upon the information that Stiles and I had brought. If aught went wrong it must reflect on us. Hence, perhaps I thought more clearly than usual, and a reply was ready upon my tongue.

"France!" I called softly.

"*A quel régiment?*" came the demand.

"De la Reine!" I replied, knowing that some of that regiment were with Bougainville at Cap Rouge.

Apparently satisfied, the man fell silent, but as we swung in towards the landing place a second sentry ran down to the water's edge and challenged again.

"*Ne faites pas de bruit!*" I called. "*Ce sont les vivres!*"

We were not disturbed again, and passed on a little below the point, and there swung in to shore a little farther down. The men landed quietly. Other boats followed us in. I heard Fraser send off parties east and west along the shore to silence the sentries, "with as little noise as possible." Presently the word went among the men, "Volunteers."

Those who had offered themselves for the first ascent came forward. Colonel Howe inspected them. This done, he turned to Stiles.

"Ready?" he asked.

Stiles nodded.

"Off you go," said Howe.

Stiles saluted and turned away in the darkness. Captain Glazer, in command of the volunteers, followed him. Presently we could hear the light scrape of boots above us, as the volunteers scrambled upward. Colonel Howe turned to me.

"How long do you think it will take them to reach the top," he asked.

"Ten minutes at the most," I replied.

"Good," he said. He turned to Colonel Fraser. "Are your men all ashore, colonel?"

Colonel Fraser said they were.

"Have them ready to follow Mr. Ferguson," said Howe, "when he gives the word."

"They are ready," said Fraser.

I listened. The sound of footsteps had died away above. Out on the river I could hear the chunk of oars in the water.

"Now!" I said.

I found the beginning of the path and started up. Behind me I could hear the creak of equipment, an occasional clink as metal touched metal, the heavy breathing of the climbing men.

We were halfway up when a rattle of musketry broke out above us. I quickened my pace. As we came over the edge of the ascent I saw that Stiles and his volunteers had driven a wedge through the camp, and the French had already fled. We had a dozen casualties, but the force on guard must have been less than Stiles' estimate. Behind me the light infantry and the Highlanders poured over the crest and deployed across the level ground through the camp. Howe and Fraser came up, and suddenly I realized that it was growing light.

To westward, up the river, a cannon thumped, followed by another and another. Howe turned to Stiles.

"What's that?" he said.

"There's a battery at Samos," said Stiles, "about a mile up. They must have seen the boats."

"We'll take that," said Howe. He turned to Fraser. "Hold the position," he said.

The light infantry formed quickly and moved off under Stiles' guidance. Presently we heard the sound of fighting to westward. Looking down over the brink of the cliff, I could see the boats below coming in to shore and the waterside already acrawl with scarlet coats. I became aware of Colonel Fraser standing beside me.

"Ye're not armed, mon," he said.

I held up my bad arm.

"I can't do much fighting with this," I said.

"No matter," said he. "Ye should ha' means o' defence."

He looked about and took a shortsword from one of the Frenchmen we had taken prisoner. This he strapped to my back, the hilt

protruding above my shoulder after the manner in which a High-
lander carries his claymore. When he had done this he thrust a
pistol at me. I took it and stuck it in my waistband, resting my
left hand against its butt.

"Now ye've the means o' defendin' yersel'," he said, "if need
be."

I thanked him, and he turned away. Other troops began to pour
up onto the plain from the path's head. After a little Stiles came
back along the edge of the plain, looking for me. When he found
me his face lighted, and he came over.

"The battery's silenced—Howe's gone on to take Sillery," he
said. "How about it?"

"Wait," I said. "We'll find an opportunity."

I knew he was anxious to get to the General Hospital, which lay
outside the walls of the town on the Côte Sainte Geneviève beside
the river Saint Charles; but I felt that there was no need to hurry,
and if we waited we might have the covering support of our own
troops.

Our own men were coming faster now, many of them having
abandoned the path and taken to climbing the slope by whatever
means presented. They kept pouring over the edge, a dozen here,
a single man there, a whole company at another point, and forming upon the plain beyond. Presently Wolfe appeared with his
staff. He was jubilant, and turned away at once to direct the disposition of the troops. Stiles and I sat forgotten, watching, our duty
done.

What followed is history. At six o'clock a battalion of French
regulars appeared on the plain between us and the city, but were
driven off by sheer weight of numbers. After this, our lines formed
rapidly, General Wolfe taking the centre, with Brigadiers Murray and Monckton on the right and Brigadier Townshend on the
left facing the wooded slope which led down onto the flats of the
Saint Charles. Colonel Burton, with a part of Webb's and the
Forty-eighth was stationed as a reserve upon a wooded knoll a little distance in the rear. It was to this point that I led Stiles, over
his vehement protests.

"Nonsense!" I said when he insisted that we should seek out
places in the front line. "I was in the van at Ticonderoga under
Abercrombie, and I have no wish to repeat the experience. We

have no place with any of these troops, and no one can blame us if we keep in the rear. Besides, we will be able to see what is happening."

In this last at least my guess was correct. We could not have asked a finer position from which to watch the fighting. At about ten the French appeared in great numbers opposite our position, between our lines and the city. From where we stood, upon the knoll with Colonel Burton, they looked like so many white ants swarming upon the high ground, and we could almost feel the shock of surprise that ran through them at the sight of our lines drawn up and ready. Even at that distance I could make out the figure of Montcalm upon a horse, riding up and down before them, rallying them to the attack.

The onslaught was not long in coming. Under Montcalm's urging they formed swiftly and advanced in several columns to within some forty yards of our front—before either side fired. But then, all at once, a dense smoke hid the entire field from our view. The thunderous crash of the first volley came back to us an instant later, followed by a steady crackle of sustained fire; but of what had happened, whether our line had held or the French broken through, we could see nothing.

Then almost as suddenly as it had appeared, the wind lifted the smoke and sent it drifting out across the river to southward, and to our delight we saw that the French ranks had broken and were streaming back towards the city. Everywhere upon the slight rising ground we could see white and scarlet dots mingled, fighting. And the scattered pop and crackle of musketry still carried back to us. But the sight that caught and held our eyes was that of the white columns eddying back against the walls, and there breaking to stream off to the left in the direction of the Saint Charles.

"By God," said someone close beside me, "they run! See how they run!"

Stiles pulled at my sleeve and pointed. Following the direction I saw that Brigadier Townshend's line had straightened out and now extended part way down the slope towards the Saint Charles flats, though in the heavy brush which provided cover for the enemy they seemed to be making difficult going of it. At the same instant I saw a runner dash up to Colonel Burton.

"General Wolfe's compliments, sir," I heard him say. "You are

to take your men down on the slope to support Brigadier Townshend, and attempt to get across the flats to cut off the enemy's retreat across the Saint Charles."

I plucked Stiles by the sleeve.

"Here we go," I said.

He looked about and nodded. Already the first companies were
swinging away to the left towards the steep, brush-covered slopes
that led down onto the flats. Stiles and I fell in behind them. As
we went I threw one last look in the direction of the main battle.
Our men seemed to be meeting some resistance on their right,
where the ground was patchy and spotted with brush; but in the
centre they were still going forward over the crest of the slight rise
and were approaching the suburbs that extend out from the Saint
John and Saint Louis gates. After that I saw no more of the battle
that went on upon the plains.

Instead I turned my attention to what was before us. Across our
line of march lay the road from Sainte Foy. Beyond this, and parallel to it, ran the brushy slopes, steep and densely thicketed, all the
way to Saint Roch at the mouth of the Saint Charles. Beyond this,
again, at the foot of the slope lay the flats, with the great grey bulk
of the Hôpital Général looming at a bend in the river. To the
right of the Hospital lay more flats, and then the suburb of Saint
Roch, from which last the road which ran between the city and
Beauport stretched to the head of the bridge across the Saint
Charles. There we could see the first of the routed French already
streaming down from the heights towards the bridge.

It was a sight to urge us forward, but it was soon apparent that
we were not to reach the flats unhindered. We were not yet across
the Sainte Foy road when the bushes at the edge of the declivity
began to spout flame and smoke. Overhead I heard the hiss and
whisper of bullets. At the head of the column a number of men
stumbled and fell. Hoarse commands rang above the distant roar
of battle, and the column deployed and moved forward in line
abreast. As I ran beside Stiles I stooped and took up a musket
from a fallen man. When I tried to use it, however, I found I
could not manage its weight with my bad arm. I could load, however, and this I did, passing the musket on to Stiles, taking his for
reloading while he fired, and then repeated the movement. In this
way we formed a team that worked rapidly and with efficiency,
and soon found its imitators.

We soon discovered the thick brush of the slopes to be alive with French colony troops, who put up a stubborn resistance, falling back only slowly, a step at a time, and taking a heavy toll among us as they went. Our men fought doggedly, however, and little by little pressed them back onto the Côte Sainte Geneviève. There we found the Highlanders of Fraser's already come in upon our right and attempting to dislodge the Canadians mainly with the broadsword, in which they were receiving severe punishment. With the weight of our fire to support them, though, matters went forward with more despatch; and presently the last of the enemy broke from the patchy brush and fled precipitately down the slope and onto the flats with us at their heels.

I will not pretend to know exactly how long it took us thus to fight our way from the knoll behind the lines to the flats below; but when we came out at the foot of the slope I looked up and was surprised to see that the sun was already well over in the west. Of what had been taking place on the plains above I knew nothing; but I could see the French still pouring out of Saint Roch towards the bridge. At a point midway between the village and the river they had thrown up a breastwork and were putting up a stubborn resistance covering the road. All at once I became aware of the fact that we had passed the bend in the Saint Charles, and that the great bulk of the Hôpital Général now lay upon our left and behind our lines. At the same time Stiles plucked at my sleeve.

"Come on!" he said.

I turned and followed him, running behind the fighting towards the high wall that surrounded the building. He went straight to a stout door set in the wall.

"The main gate," he said as we came up, "is on the other side, but this will do as well."

He beat a thunderous tattoo upon the door with the butt of his musket.

"Pray God she is still here!" I said under my breath.

We waited then for some moments, restless with impatience, until with an oath Stiles thundered at the door once more; an instant later we heard the patter of feet upon a stone walk beyond. A grille in the door flicked open and I saw the coifed face of a nun beyond.

"Why do you come here?" she demanded. "There are none here but women and children and wounded."

"Sister," I said, "we do not come in search of soldiers, but rather for an English girl who was brought here some two weeks since at General Montcalm's orders."

She seemed to hesitate.

"In the name of God, sister," I cried, "say if she is still here. This man is her father, and there will be another who has perhaps come in search of her, who means her no good."

I have heard all manner of calumny spoken against these papist nuns, that they have no heart, that they are immoral women, that within their cloisters they practise strange rites. But this I have always held to be but the ranting of fanatics against them. I know now that they are as kind and human as any. Perhaps she caught the urgency in my voice. Perhaps it was because I said Stiles was her father. She hesitated no longer. I heard her fumbling with the bolts upon the other side.

"There is a man but now come for her in a boat," she said, "with an order from the intendant. Perhaps if you hurry you can catch them."

The door swung wide, and we burst in past her.

"That way!" she called, pointing.

We found ourselves in a broad, well tended garden upon which the grey bulk of the Hospital fronted. At the far end, in the direction the nun indicated, we could see that the garden turned and ran along the end of the building towards the river. Without further words we turned and raced in that direction.

It took us no longer to run the length of the building and turn into the pathway leading down to the river than it does to tell it. There was a hedgerow there that shut off our view for a moment, but as we burst through this we saw a sight that brought us up short.

A boat had been pulled up on the little sandy shingle that ran along the river's edge. Standing at the bow of this and holding it was a French regular, and beside it, kicking, biting, struggling furiously to break free from Hubert and a second soldier, who between them were trying to put her in, was Purity.

The sound of our feet must have come to them suddenly, for they all looked round quickly, as if surprised. Then Purity gave a little half-choking cry and wrenched free and came running towards us. At the same instant I saw the guard at the bow of the boat reach for his musket and cried out.

Behind me Stiles' musket cracked, and I saw the guard pitch slowly forward and roll off the bow onto the wet sand. At the same time I saw the second guard raise his musket and aim at Stiles. I whipped out the pistol Colonel Fraser had given me, and levelled it. We must have pulled the trigger at the same instant, for the two reports rang out as one. Behind me I heard Stiles grunt. Simultaneously the second guard dropped his gun and clapped his hands to his stomach. Fascinated, I watched him bend slowly in the middle and fall forward on his face.

All of this happened so swiftly and in so short a space of time that it is difficult to keep to the order in which they fell. It was Purity's scream that snapped my attention back to the realization that it was not yet finished. I turned swiftly to see that Hubert had overtaken her, and now held her, with his left arm about her middle, as a shield, while with his right he levelled a pistol at me.

Once again I saw that hateful, mocking smile upon his lips as I tossed aside my now useless pistol and fumbled for the short-sword at my shoulder blade.

"Think quickly, cousin!" he mocked. "Which is it to be? I might shoot you, and take the girl for my own needs. Or I might shoot her and leave you to mourn!"

As he spoke he moved backwards a pace or two towards the boat. I drew my sword and started forward furiously, but he turned the pistol against Purity's side, and I saw his thumb upon the lock.

"Stop!" he said. "Stay where you are! What I have done once, I may do again."

Behind me I could hear Stiles breathing heavily, but there was no time to look at him. Back at the outer gate I heard muskets pounding. If I could but delay him for a moment, we might yet win out. But he was careful to keep a good distance between us. I moved a slow step forward. He flourished the pistol, and retreated a step.

"You hesitate?" he jeered. "Why do you wait? The lady needs your help, Jamie, but—"

It was at this point that Purity herself saved the day.

Bending down she buried her teeth in the wrist that held her.

"Ah—ow!" yelped Hubert ridiculously.

For the briefest fraction of a second the muzzle of the pistol wavered while he turned his attention to this new attack, and in that instant I leapt. With shoulder low I flung myself upon him, at the same time with arm and elbow thrusting Purity clear of his grasp. As I struck I tried to wrench myself sideways to avoid the muzzle of the pistol, but I was not quick enough. There was a great crash almost in my ear, and a flash of fire, and a cloud of white powder smoke filled the air around us. At the same instant I felt as though some great hand had struck my side, lifting me off my feet and flinging me down upon the grass beside the path. As I fell I saw the flicker of red coats running beyond the hedgerow.

"Run, child!" I cried. "Run!"

But Purity did not hear me, or if she did she did not heed the advice. Instead she came from where my blow had sent her spinning and dropped on her knees beside me. Hubert stood before us, hesitating, the empty, smoking pistol still in his hand. I raised myself upon my elbow and pointed my sword at him.

"It is my turn now," I said.

His eyes darted to the hedgerow, and I knew that he too had seen those scarlet coats beyond. Then he looked down at us, and for an instant I believed he would risk a sword thrust to take Purity from me. Had he so chosen to do, I knew I had not the strength to beat him off. Already I felt weak and dizzy, and the sound of running feet upon the path came to me as from a great distance.

But he too must have heard those feet, for suddenly he tossed his pistol down in front of me and made a mocking leg.

"You win this once, cousin; but"—here he dropped his eyes to the hole in my side from which the blood was pumping out to stain my leg and breeches crimson—"I doubt you'll live to enjoy the victory."

And with that he turned away, striding jauntily to the tiny beach, where he pushed the boat out and stepped in. Settling himself upon the thwart, he waved a mocking hand in our direction and began to row. From the grass on the other side of the path I heard a gasping breath, and turning my head slowly, laboriously, for every movement now took a great effort, I saw Stiles rise up on one knee, blood streaming down the side of his face, and level his reloaded musket.

"Let—" I began.

The musket cracked.

I looked back at the river. Hubert had stopped rowing. He was standing up, and his hands were at his throat, low down. I could see the blood flow from between his fingers. As I watched, his body turned slowly until his face was away from us. Then, suddenly, his knees gave way and he fell against the gunnel. The little boat rocked violently, and as if in a dream I saw him pitch over, head-first, and disappear beneath the water.

3

I must have fainted then, for I remember no more until I awoke in a room, all white, upon a great bed, with Purity sitting by my side. When she saw my eyes were open she leaned over me.

"Oh, Jamie!" she said. "I thought you would never wake again!"

I smiled weakly.

"But I have, you see," I told her. "What is this place?"

"The Hôpital Général," she told me. "The French have fled, and Quebec has fallen, two days since."

"Two days since?" I exclaimed, surprised. "What day is this?"

She laughed. "The twentieth," she told me. "You have been eight days waking!"

"Eight days!" I said, falling back among my pillows. "'Tis a wonder they have not buried me!"

"They would have," she said, "but I would not let them."

I laughed, and then grew thoughtful.

"And Quebec is ours!" I said. "This will be a great feather in Wolfe's cap."

She did not speak at once, and I looked at her inquiringly.

"General Wolfe died in the attack," she said. "So did Montcalm."

"Both!" I cried.

She nodded. Somehow I felt that I had lost two good friends.

"They were good men both," I said. "The world will stand the loser for their passing."

There came a knock at the door, and Stiles came in, his bushy beard shaven, his head in a bandage, and a new red coat upon his back.

"Oho!" he exclaimed at sight of me. "So you've decided to stop playing dead and be a man again instead of a leaden dummy for the women to cry their eyes out over?"

"Father!" cried Purity severely.

He grinned and patted her shoulder.

"I'll warrant he knew it all the time," he said, "and was but fooling you."

She turned away from him, and he laughed.

"Well, I've news," he said.

Purity looked back at him.

"What have you learned?" she asked.

"The colonel says there'll be a packet for Boston within the week, if you think we can move him," he said. "It's like to be our last chance this year."

I looked at Purity and saw that she was doubtful.

"Don't wait on my account," I said. "If they won't let me go now, I can join you in Portsmouth."

She turned upon me. "And leave you here alone?" she demanded. "I should think not!"

I reached out an arm stiffly and took her hand in mine.

"Dear child!" I said.

Stiles looked restless. "Has she told you Quebec's ours?" he asked.

"Aye," I replied, "and all the rest of it. What news of Hubert though? Is he dead?"

He looked away.

"He's dead," he said flatly. "They didn't find his body, but he's dead. The man couldn't live with a bullet where I put that one!"

"He's alive," I said. "He's alive somewhere, you mark my words. If they didn't find his body it's because he's alive. He's too slippery not to be."

"I tell you he's dead," said Stiles.

I shook my head. It was Purity who settled the argument.

"What difference does it make?" she asked. "He'll not bother us again. If he's dead he's dead; and if he's alive at least we know he can do us no harm now."

Stiles nodded. "That's so," he said.

Purity turned to him. "Go along," she said, "and find the doctor. He'll want to know Jamie's awake at last."

Stiles winked at me heavily and went out. When he had gone Purity came to kneel beside my bed and took my face in her hands.

"Oh, Jamie," she said, "I have been so afraid these eight days since!"

"Poor child!" I said. "Did it mean so much to you then?"

She nodded, and I could see tears in her eyes.

"It meant everything to me," she said.

I made no answer but only reached out and touched her cheek softly.

She put her head upon my chest then and sobbed. I put my good arm about her shoulders and drew her to me.

"There, child," I said, "there is no need to cry. Kiss me."

"B-but I am so happy," she choked, smiling.

And with that she leaned down and pressed her lips to mine.

If the Boston packet had left in the next week—or even the next —I fear we should have had to spend our winter in Quebec, for I was in no condition to be moved. When at last she finally did sail, however, I was so far recovered that I could be carried on board on a stretcher. By the time we reached Boston I was able to sit up for a little on deck each day. And by the time we came at last to Portsmouth I was able to hobble about with the aid of a cane and my wife. We went at once to the old house on the hill, and I sent away to Albany to have James Hubert sent on to us; for I meant to bring him up as my own child since there was no one else to look out for him.

We found Portsmouth still in a great turmoil of excitement over Major Rogers' destruction of Saint Francis, and as one of his men, even though I had missed the expedition, I was well received by everyone. The major himself came to see me when he visited Portsmouth towards Christmas time.

"General Amherst thought it was on account of Kennedy," he said when I greeted him at the door. "But I told the men it was on account of you we went out to Saint Francis. It made 'em feel better about it."

He punched me in the ribs, and laughed. Purity came into the hallway and stood smiling as he bowed low over her hand.

"I declare, ma'am," he said, "I'm glad to see him getting some sense at last. I always said if there was one girl fit to marry in the Province 'twas yourself. If he hadn't asked you I'd 'a' done it myself."

"Much good would it have done you," I laughed. "She wouldn't have had you. No one would have you."

"A lot you know of it, mister!" he said. "Why, there isn't a maid in New England wouldn't be mine for the asking right now. I'm the Great Rogers!"

The way he laughed when he said it took the conceit out of it.

"I may fool you yet," he added, with a wink.

At the end of his visit, he turned to me.

"Well, lad," he said, "we've still work to do in Canada next summer, and then there's the west to look after. But I suppose you'll be wanting to settle down and toast your toes by the fireside, now, eh?"

"If it's all the same to you, major," I replied. " 'Tis what I hoped for."

"It's not all the same to me," he said. "Not by a long shot. But I guess we can arrange it."

He said good night then, and left us. When he had gone Purity turned to me and put her arms about my neck.

"That's the way it will always be, isn't it, Jamie?" she said.

I kissed her.

"That's the way," I said. "I'll never leave you, and you'll never leave me—not ever!"

THE END